A KINGDOM OF EXILES

Book 1 of the Outcast Series

S. B. NOVA

CONTENTS

Also by S. B. NOVA   v
Exclusive Content   ix
Map   xi

Prologue: Mother   1
1. The Blacksmith's Daughter   7
2. The Evil Stepmother   18
3. Changeling   31
4. The Trial   38
5. The Cage   58
6. The Crossing   72
7. The Winged Fiends   88
8. Embrace   98
9. The Ogre and the Warrior   117
10. Allies, Friends, Enemies   139
11. A Rough Start   160
12. The Grind   178
13. Endure   196
14. Chosen   219
15. Hunted   242
16. The Past   252
17. The Eerie   272
18. The Witch   297
19. Following Breadcrumbs   324
20. By the Lake   341
21. Hazel   351
22. The Monster in the Woods   381
23. The Thief   390
24. Begin!   406
25. Tea and Whiskey   433
26. A Quest Beginning   444
27. The Heart of the Forest   460
28. Because of You   482

29. Flying, Falling   503
30. The Bond   530
31. The Bloody Battle   543
32. Unmasked   560

   Author's Note   581
   ALSO AVAILABLE BY NOVA   583
   Acknowledgments   585

ALSO BY S. B. NOVA

THE SOUTHERN FIRE SERIES

Draken

Skyla's Diaries

THE OUTCAST SERIES

A Kingdom of Exiles

For Dawn,
Sister, friend, superfan. I'll never stop being grateful that through a dream, we found our way back to each another.

And to all those who dream of the impossible. This is for you.

EXCLUSIVE CONTENT

Never miss any bookish news!

Want to be the first to learn about Nova's new releases? And get newsletter only bonus content for free? Sign up to Nova's newsletter at sbnova.com.

Aurora Court

Mysaya

Lumen

Crescent
'Witch'
Court

Luna
Canyons

The Sighing
Plains

The Crossing

Aldar Kingdom

Tunnock

Undover
Capital

Ewa Lake

Barsul Mountains

Barsul Pass

Azar Forest

Kastella

Attia Forest

Alexandria

Wisinder Cliffs

Solar Court

Riverlands
Court

Nola Swamps

Maggie One-Eye's
Cabin

Sapor Village

Kasi Camp

The Gauntlet

Estari Lake

Pÿha Holy Tower

PROLOGUE: MOTHER

They won't tell you fairy tales
of how girls can be dangerous and still win.
They will only tell you stories
where girls are sweet and kind
and reject all sin.
I guess to them
it's a terrifying thought,
a red riding hood
who knew exactly
what she was doing
when she invited the wild in.
~ Nikita Gill ~

RAIN CLUNG to the earthen floor of the forest as a light mist and white petals from the Mourning Roses scattered the edges of the grave. My eyes fixed to the willow casket where Mama's body now lived. Heavy grunts filled the air as several men from the village lowered her slowly into the ground. She was being laid to rest beneath the ancient elder tree

—it was our place. Then the keening and whispered prayers started around me. I was six years old.

Papa had explained it: death meant leaving and never coming back. But Mama had been the brightest of all flames, nothing could keep her from returning, so I didn't cry as the casket hit the bottom of that deep dark hole.

Papa squeezed my hand. I looked up to see tear tracks marking his face. My heart twisted. He never cried. Yet here he was, his hand shaking as my mother's best friend, Viola, sobbed as she threw dirt atop Mama's grave.

Didn't they understand? Didn't they know she was coming back?

Papa crouched so that his watery eyes were level with mine.

"It's time to go, Poppet. Mama's resting now."

He tucked a strand of loose black hair behind my ear. Only a few days ago, Mama had named a new color after it: raven's wing.

I shook my head and bit my lip. "I don't want to leave her alone."

Papa grimaced and swept me up into his arms—his broad chest shuddering as he carried me away—leaving Mama in the barren, cold earth alone. My gaze closed on the grave and a raging beast awoke in my chest, clawing and fighting its way to the surface. I let out a strangled scream and beat against Papa's shoulders with tiny fists. But he wouldn't turn. He wouldn't go back. I had no other choice—I'd have to return and free her tonight.

When Papa slept, I'd come back for her.

I WAITED, impatient for the shadows to fall and the distant light of the stars to flicker to life. A bright, full moon shimmered above, one that would help illuminate the path through the trees. So, when I finally crept downstairs and out the front door I didn't bother taking a lantern, knowing it would only draw the dark things that prowled the night. I did wrap up warm in knitted gloves, a scarf, and a hat. That was the first thing I learned out here in the remote parts of the Gauntlet—the winter could freeze me solid if I wasn't careful.

As soon as I was out in the open, I ran into the forest and that deadly cold. My breath came rushing out in large puffs of steam, my chest seized with icy air, but I didn't slow down. Mama had been alone for too long.

The canopy thickened enough that the moon's glow dimmed to a sullen light and I stumbled, scraping my knees against the gnarled roots. I bit down on my lip to stop a sob breaking free and pushed myself up. I had to keep moving.

The grave site wasn't far. Papa had broken with village tradition and laid Mama in her favorite hollow instead of the local boneyard.

There. I spotted the ancient tree where Mama was buried; it had been blown free of snow and now lay bare and black. I'd know it anywhere. Skidding to a halt, I craned my head left and right. The hole wasn't there. Instead, there was just a mound of freshly turned dirt.

I plunged toward it, clawing at the frigid ground. I made little progress, but I kept going until my cheeks were glazed over with frozen tears and my voice cracked with sob after sob. "Give her back," I wailed. "Give her back!"

I wept and pleaded and beat at the hard earth until I was numb and only stopped when I couldn't hold my head up; my cheek found the unforgiving ground. If the old gods and the earth didn't want to give her back, I'd stay until they realized I needed her more than they.

A fresh snowfall whirred lazily overhead and kissed my face.

No sound pitched the air.

The whole sorry world seemed dead and still, and I didn't fight when it faded from view.

I awoke to the sound of someone shouting my name. My eyes opened and dislodged the remnants of a snowmelt. A buttery shaft of sunlight had filled the hollow, warming me a little.

"Serena!"

I tried to cry out, but it came out as a hoarse whisper. "Papa?"

I coughed. My lungs were on fire and my head pounded. Before I could riddle out what was wrong, I sank back into darkness.

Raised voices snapped me from the dreamworld.

I blinked and realized I was back in my bedroom. The door was open a crack, enough to hear the conversation happening downstairs.

"What are you trying to tell me?"

Papa sounded furious. He never got like that.

"She has a wicked fever—she may not make it. If you'd just let me bleed her ..."

It was Dr. Fagan. I recognized his voice from when he passed out sweeties to the other children in town. Mama hated him and called him more of a butcher than a doctor.

"You're not touching her," Papa hissed. "My wife didn't approve of your methods, and neither do I."

A loud, reedy sniff answered. "If your wife had listened to my advice, she might be alive and not tormenting that poor girl with her spirit."

"Get out of my house before I do something I regret," Papa demanded.

I tried to climb out of bed to continue eavesdropping, but my body wouldn't respond to my commands. I was still in the fever's grip and too weak to even raise my slender arms.

Dr. Fagan continued, "Let me bring someone who honors the old gods to the grave. He could drive out the evil spirits that linger."

A hot flush of anger flooded me. Mama was no evil spirit.

"If you won't walk out, I'll throw you out."

I shivered when I recognized that warning tone. Papa never used it on me, reserving it only for men in the village who'd leered at Mama or tried to cheat him at the forge.

The front door slammed shut causing the glass in my window to rattle something fierce.

I shut my eyes when I heard heavy footsteps on the stairs. The creaking of a door, a shuffling sound, and then a cool cloth bathing my forehead. I tried to be strong, but failed to stop a pitifully weak groan from escaping.

"It's just you and me now, Beansprout. Mama's gone for good, and you freezing to death won't bring her back, do you hear me?" Papa's voice broke on the last word.

Shame and grief churned; my chest ached so badly I thought I'd burst.

"You must live, Sprout ... for me."

I couldn't hold it in anymore. Two shuddering gasps, then the tears rolled.

made every Yuletide. My mouth watered, and I jogged the rest of the way.

I came upon the village border—a spiked wooden fence acting as flimsy fortification. There was a gate of sorts, but it was rarely barred. The village was too far north to interest pillagers or highwaymen, and our greatest danger came from the predators of the forest: roaming wolf packs, a stray bear, and of course, the fae, and if the tales were true, there was no wall high enough or barricade strong enough that could keep those winged devils out.

As I passed through the open gate, the frost-glaze underfoot transformed into mud, squelching up the sides of my boots. I strode on through the village, and seeing Father's forge on the right, I veered left. My father wasn't there yet, but Gus, his apprentice, would be.

Father had hired Gus in my fourteenth year. At first glance, we'd appeared to be two sides of the same coin—all elbows and angles. But whereas I could eat for days, he came to us malnourished. Father took pity on him. So did I.

For months afterward, I'd visit him in the forge. Far too often he'd come in with an ugly bruise and his temper would turn evil; I'd have to stay away. Things only got worse after his own father died. Whenever I saw him then, his gaze, laced with violence, latched on to mine and his fists clenched as if he wanted to strangle me. Viola told me he carried a poison in him, that he needed to dull the edge of his pain like a knife needing a whetstone.

My aversion to Gus didn't go unnoticed. I felt my stepmother's eyes watching, calculating. Given her hatred for me, her sudden sly hints about advantageous marriages made me assume she'd heard the women gossiping about Gus's growing notoriety—seducing girls with marital promises, and when their reputation lay in tatters, tossing them aside.

Those rumors were why I'd altered my appearance. At sixteen, he'd stared too long at my long hair so I'd cut it short. Then, his eyes roamed down to my budding breasts. Baggy dresses were my answer.

Today, I'd gotten lucky: Gus wasn't in sight. The muted sounds of a hammer striking metal assured me he was in the back of the forge. I relaxed as I was greeted by a painted white door, with framed glass windows misted over from the heat brewing inside.

Viola and John's cottage was small—just a few rooms added onto the side of the bakery—but it felt like home. I knocked and gave my shoes a swift tap on the mat while I waited. A moment later, the door swung open. Viola's round face, crinkling blue eyes, and wiry gray hair welcomed me. She quickly waved me into a combined living and dining space, of which I knew every inch. The ceiling was supported by dark beams, hung heavy with sweet and mallow-scented bushels of herbs. Faded rugs covered the floor, and the paneled cherry-wood walls gleamed as the winter sun poured in. A fire already crackled and roared in the hearth, and a bottle-green couch and armchair had been artfully arranged beside it. The door on the right led to the bakery, but it was the large breakfast table in the center of the room that held my attention. Breathing in deeply, I savored the smells of cake and the fresh pot of tea waiting on a checkered tablecloth.

"Boots off, young lady," Viola demanded, scowling down at the mud I was tracking in.

Kicking them off and placing them by the door, my stare locked onto the table again. I failed to hide a look of piggish delight, and Viola chuckled. "Darling, I've never known someone so in love with food."

"Sorry," I said, flinching.

She didn't need to add the part about me not having the curves to show for it. Elain had exhausted that topic. Anger sparked in Viola's eyes as if she'd guessed my thoughts—nothing, or no one, but Elain ever caused her to lose her temper like that.

Snapping shut the door, she waved a hand at the table. "Go, sit and eat."

Settling in one of the wicker chairs, trying not to gobble up everything in sight, I waited for Viola to sit and pour the tea. Then I couldn't restrain myself any longer. I groaned, *actually groaned*, as the first crumb touched my lips. Blushing, I angled my head into what I hoped was an apologetic look.

Viola laughed. "Don't be silly. It's your birthday. If there was ever a time when you're allowed to indulge, it's now. Besides, you know John loves it when people appreciate his food."

At the mention of his name, John appeared in the doorway that joined the bakery to the house. I got a heavenly whiff of that warm deliciousness before he shut the door and held his arms out for me. I straightened, a muffin clenched between my teeth, and gave him a quick hug. As I broke away and sat to resume my feast, John clapped a hand on my shoulder. "So good to see you enjoying my baking."

"How could I not?" I mumbled through a mouthful.

John flashed me a quick wink. "Viola, d'you want to give it to her now?" he asked, turning to his wife. "Or should I?"

My attention piqued. I set the muffin aside and took a sip of tea to wash it down before asking, "Give me what?"

Viola's blue eyes sparkled. Bustling over to the mantelpiece, she picked up a small silver box and placed it in front of me with a faint smile.

My brow wrinkled. "You shouldn't have gotten me anything. I don't want you spending your money."

"I didn't," Viola breathed. "It's an heirloom of your mother's family. She gifted it in her will with instructions to pass it on to you—when the time was right."

My frown deepened. As far as I knew, my mother had no other family. "Why didn't she leave it to my father?"

Viola's expression flickered. "We don't know, darling."

I paused. "Why didn't you pass it on when I came of age?"

Sixteen marked the rite of passage into adulthood. Not eighteen.

"I wanted to; I knew how much it'd mean to you," Viola said, an apology welling behind her eyes. "But your mother never specified the age I was to give it to you. And I thought Elain might steal it once she discovered where it had come from."

I blinked. Viola knew exactly how cruel my stepmother could be.

"Then, you should keep it." I pushed the box back across the table. Each word quieter than the last, I added, "Until I'm free of her—if I ever am."

I gulped down the raw emotion clawing at my throat and stared at the table, unable to meet their stares. The only way to be free was to marry, and since the village boys had largely shunned me, it seemed like a remote possibility.

Viola sat and cupped my chin; my eyes had nowhere to go but to meet with hers. I knew that look—pity. "Open your present, Serena."

John took the seat to my left and when I didn't move, he pushed the box under my nose. His mouth tugged upward. "Choppers, choppers," he urged. "I've got a bakery to run."

A tremor claimed my hand as I reached out and unhinged the clasp. Inside was a delicate silver chain joined by sculpted leaves and flowers with a pale blue gem dangling from the center link, and when I held it up to the light, something moved within. A droplet.

"There's water inside this gemstone." My hands lowered as I asked Viola, "Do you know why it's there?"

Viola smiled weakly. "No. The only instructions left in your mother's will were that the necklace must go to you and that it'd protect you in times of great danger."

"Danger," I echoed and put the chain back in the box, suddenly wary. "Is this about those kids who've gone missing? Is that why you're handing it over now?"

Everyone in the village had heard about the disappearances. They'd started over three months ago with twelve-year-old Annie Tanner, and every month since then a child had just up and vanished.

"Those kids were all younger than me. They weren't even of age—"

Viola exchanged a furtive look with John. She was scared. They both were. "We know," she said heavily. "But to the fae, you are still a child. I don't know what age those immortal fiends mark the end of childhood, but it won't be eighteen."

All of Tunnock's inhabitants knew the fae were taking them. The tales the village bard had spun were clear—long ago we'd welcomed the fae into our lands and paid the price. After years of peace, they'd turned on us and thrown collars around our necks. In a desperate move, the royal line of Undover ordered our High Priests to call down the gods and throw a lock on the bridge between our realms, exiling the fae to the lands in the north. In the fae's absence, the southern lands grew fat and rich. That was until the Undover line fell into ruin as son murdered father and brother slaughtered brother to seize the crown. The High Priests used the corruption as an excuse to steal away to their towers among the stars, banning all others from practicing magic and taking their knowledge with them. For centuries, remote villages like ours had been left defenseless. Yet we'd endured, scratching out a living from the earth, forever in the shadow of the monsters across the bridge. Now, every person living above the Estari Lake had heard the rumors—the fae had returned. Rumors of sightings and disappearances stretched back ten years. Until now, our village had remained unscathed, but no longer ...

Viola continued. "I don't know how a necklace is meant to help, but I'll feel better with you wearing it."

I closed the box. Thinking of my stepmother, I shook my head lightly. "She'll notice if I wear something like this." I faced Viola to see her sad eyes fixed on me. "I'll have to find somewhere to hide it before I can take it home with me."

She wavered, then nodded once. "Even with the necklace, I doubt you'd be safe until those ruthless sprites are driven from our lands—your father knows it too. That's why he's signed up to be part of the watch tonight, along with John," she said, disapproval marking her face.

I stilled. The watch had been reinstated by the elders the minute Annie vanished. But with wild animals roaming the forest, not to mention the risk involved in meeting an actual fae, it wasn't surprising that few villagers wanted the job. So far, my father and John hadn't served because their work sucked up every spare minute. No one had complained since the village couldn't afford to lose a blacksmith or a baker.

"*Ach!*" John scowled and waved her concern away. "Don't scold me, Vi. I'm not a child. This is important. We can't let the fae bastards take our children—our future."

"They're not our children, John." Viola had steel in her voice, but I detected the quiet sadness underneath.

"No lass, they're not ours," John said gruffly. "But Serena is as good as."

I glowed at that remark.

Viola's anger seemed to vanish with a sigh. "I know ... I'm just worried."

I looked to John. "D'you think you'll be in danger tonight?"

"I might've handled more bread than weapons, but I can look after myself. So can your father. He's as strong as a bull, that one." He braced his hands on the table and stretched up. "Besides, it's two weeks until the full moon, and that's when the fae have been most active. We're not expecting trouble tonight."

He gave me a pat on the back before moving to give his wife a swift kiss on the cheek. "Got to get back to work, but I don't want either of my girls worrying."

A warning and a plea.

Viola mumbled something noncommittal. I opened my mouth and then closed it. I wanted to beg him not to go, but it wasn't my place so I said nothing as he walked back into the bakery. No matter the reassurances he'd given, a rising panic turned my mouth dry and set my heart moving apace. Against fae warriors, they'd be helpless.

JOHN'S REVELATION put a serious dampener on my birthday tea. I spent most of the time afterward watching the clock and pretending to read books while Viola bustled around. I waited until Father would've dismissed Gus for the afternoon and then struck out for his forge determined to make him reconsider signing up.

Due to his obligation to the watch he had to finish early, so I kept up a steady stream of desperate pleas the entire walk home. I didn't let up all through dinner, thanks to Elain's unusual silence.

"Why now? You said there'll be more of you going tomorrow—can't you go then? The watch can wait for one night. It's my birthday ..."

"I won't say no again, Ena." My mother's nickname for me, and a punch to the stomach every time I heard it. "I'll be fine," he said, his face softening at my fear. "By the smith's fire, even Gus has volunteered for tonight's watch. I can't let him wander the woods alone."

"He won't be alone—"

"Ena." He cut me off with a little growl. "I've already told you. Only five of them signed up for tonight and they need at least six to patrol the forest." Again, his features thawed at my open mouth and pleading eyes. "My place is with them. Both as a man of this village ... and as a father," he finished quietly—soberly.

I stilled as his warm eyes met mine. That familiar steady stare wore me down. We both had iron wills, but he so rarely showed affection nowadays. Perhaps, he knew that. Maybe this was his way of showing he still cared.

Father's eyes flitted to my open palms on the table as if he wanted to reach out, but he didn't. Instead, he turned to Elain and said, "Now, where's that delicious blueberry tart I can smell? I'm ravenous."

Or maybe, he'd just wanted to stop me nagging.

Elain simpered and sat on his lap, practically purring.

Feeling embittered, I slipped off to my room upstairs. The door shut behind me and I fell against it, closing my eyes and breathing heavily. I forced calm into my veins and with one great effort, straightened and looked around my sanctuary. It was all I had: this small room with its single bed pushed up into the corner, the chest of drawers that doubled as a bedside table, and a few shelves where I placed my most prized possessions. I'd stacked these with the books my mother had taught me to read by; a bow and a quiver of arrows, which remained the only weapon my father had let me train with; and most importantly, several shells from my mother, which she'd claimed to have picked off the beach. Every night since she gave them to me and whenever I closed my eyes I saw the ocean—a breathing, living beast that roared at me to join and swim and play among its waves.

I pushed myself away from the door and walked over to sit on my quilted bedspread. The light was failing, so I lit a candle on the bedside table and waited.

Twenty minutes later and with a stiff back, I watched through my window as my father left the house. His hood was up and his lantern guided the way as he strode to the tree line. He stopped and turned in the growing velvety dark. My throat bobbed when he raised a hand in farewell. For once, I knew it was for me. Not Elain. I lifted my arm and forced myself to give him a little wave. It came out as more of nervous twitch but he seemed to appreciate it, because he waved back before wheeling around and disappearing into the shadows.

I stayed awake, staring out the window until all I could see was my face and the candle flame reflected in the glass. I scowled and stuck my tongue out at those angular cheekbones, pale skin, and the smudges of violet under my eyes that darkened as the night deepened.

Hours later, my eyelids drooping and the candle sputtering and dying beside me, I breathed onto the windowpanes, making little clouds of mist and idly drawing shapes in their wake. While tracing a star and a crescent moon, I saw it. A lantern in the distance. I jumped and ran for the door. Racing down the stairs, taking two at a time, I clattered into the living space. Cursing at the dark, I felt my way to the door. I knew this cottage inside out, so it didn't take long before I was feeling for the iron handle. Wrenching the door open, a light blinded me. My father cursed and lowered his lantern. But when I dared another peek, blinking between the fingers of my outstretched hand, a shape came into view. Too short and wide to be my father.

"Who's there?" I asked warily.

"Serena," replied a familiar voice.

"John? Where's Father?"

"I'm so sorry, Serena." His voice stumbled.

"What's going on?" Elain appeared from my father's room—or should I say "their" room. Wrapping a robe around herself, she scowled into the light. "Hal? Is that you?"

"No, it's John Baker. I came ... I came to tell you both that Halvard's gone—he's dead. Gus dragged his body back from the forest on his own. I took him to Martha; she thinks it was a heart attack. Dr. Fagan insisted on seeing him as well, and he's agreed on the cause."

The world tilted; the ground slipped out from under my feet. Just before darkness claimed me, I heard someone scream.

THERE WAS a soft slide accompanied by the grind and grunts of men lowering the casket. That coffin contained my father. The sounds of people weeping freely beside me, the keening laments and the smells of the damp graveyard dirt—I tasted bile as I realized why this felt so familiar.

I didn't cry.

The grief and despair didn't burn and twist and shred the way it had with my mother. I didn't know what that meant about me—more importantly, I didn't *want* to know.

The funeral blurred past while I continued to be absent in spirit.

Then, a hand appeared on each of my shoulders. Viola and John stood, flanking me. They muttered something, and I felt myself being steered away.

≈

THEY SOON HAD me bundled into their cottage. Viola marched me over to the couch and swaddled me in blankets until I could scarcely move. Not that I had any intention of doing so.

After they'd tried and failed to get me to speak, they whispered to each other in the corner of the kitchen.

"John, she's in shock. She has to stay. I'd sooner die than let that *woman* near her."

"Vi—we can't keep Elain from her forever. Serena might be of age, but she's still her daughter by law. You know she won't let this go."

"I don't care," she hissed. "She's not going back. Mark my words, there's a sickness in that woman, and if the will doesn't name Serena as his heir, there's no telling what she might do—"

John cut across her. "Vi, don't say such things."

I felt their eyes on me then. But I'd barely registered their words, preferring to disappear into the bleak landscape that was my mind.

Minutes later, or perhaps hours, someone pushed a mug of tea into my hands. I held it there with no intention to drink it, not even feeling the warmth. Nothing felt real, my body least of all. My mind detached and played with the idea it wasn't me, Serena, sitting on their couch, but a corpse instead. Staying as still as possible, I held my breath and watched the flames dance in the hearth, willing its heat to bring me back to life. There was only ice coating my bones, and even in this baker's cottage with a fire blazing, it wouldn't melt.

CHAPTER 2
THE EVIL STEPMOTHER

I spent every moment curled up on John and Viola's sofa in the week that followed. The only exception occurred on the sixth day when the reading of the will took place. John accompanied me to the Village Hall; Viola stayed behind. I didn't ask why, but I suspected she was afraid of what she might say if my father had left everything to my stepmother.

Baird, the Chief Elder, ushered us into his office in the back of the Hall. Elain was already there waiting and didn't even bother to look up as we entered. Then, my father's last wishes were read out to us.

The cabin had been left for Elain and me to share until I got married, at which time the house would transfer to my husband. The forge was to be divided between me, Elain, and Gus who would manage the business.

My stepmother struggled to conceal her fury, and even risked provoking Baird by insisting she read the will for herself. I seized the opportunity to slip out with John and make it back to the bakery without her following. Once we'd caught Viola up, she was more stunned than anyone. It seemed we'd both sold my father short. He'd not only secured an income for me through the forge, but a house and a dowry. My prospects of making a good match had increased tenfold overnight. Despite a touch of relief that I wasn't suddenly a pauper, I knew in my heart that nothing good could come of provoking Elain. The next morning, my stepmother turned up on the doorstep.

"She can't stay here for the rest of her life. She's my daughter!" Elain yelled at Viola, as she blocked the doorway.

"Why do you even want her back, Elain?" Viola asked, crossing her arms, refusing to budge.

I watched the scene unfold with an odd mixture of dread and premonition. Somehow, this felt inevitable.

Elain pushed past Viola, leaving her fumbling for balance, and stormed over to my spot by the fire. "Enough of this moping," she sneered, her brown eyes crinkling with disgust. "We have a house to run. I can't do it alone."

Maybe it was the aching *emptiness* inside my gut, or perhaps I'd just had enough, because I snapped, "I'm not going anywhere with you. Chop your own damn wood."

I didn't have time to react. She bent down and slapped me across the face. My cheek stung, and Viola roared loud enough for John to come racing in from the side door. Flour stained his hands—he'd been baking. "Vi ... what's going on?" he stammered, his gaze flitting between the three of us.

Slamming the front door behind her, Viola marched over to Elain, hair askew, wide-eyed, and pointing a damning finger. "This *bitch* hit our girl!"

Elain let out a sharp bark, "She's not yours."

John turned to Elain, the end of his squashed nose reddening. "She's every bit ours, just as we're hers. And if you ever hit her again, I'll get you exiled from this village," he said, his chest swelling with emotion.

I thought that might be the end of it. John had more standing and power and she knew it, but it seemed losing my father had caused her to forget herself. Elain was unmasked. "You wouldn't dare," she drawled. Facing me, she continued. "We're meant to live together. That was Hal's wish." Her eyes shuttered as if the idea pained her. "If you don't come back with me, I'll go before the elders. Nowhere in his will did it say you could leave me alone with the upkeep of the cabin. Carry on this way, and I'll see you disinherited."

"You hideous old toad!" Viola shouted, her eyes bulging.

Elain had played her hand, and by the feline smugness lighting up her face, she knew she'd won. Elain peered down her nose at me. "Tell me, Serena, who do you think the council of elders will side with? A girl too lazy to help out around the house or a grieving widow?"

"Get out," Viola snarled at her back.

"No, it's okay. I'll go," I said, resigned. "I'll only end up causing trouble for you both."

John looked crestfallen and Viola's face went slack. "You haven't. You won't."

"Don't worry on our account, girl—we're tougher than we look," John said, placing a reassuring arm on his wife's shoulder.

Elain snorted.

"Get out of my house." John took a step toward her, and for the first time it gave Elain pause. "Fine. I'll wait outside." She glared down at me. "Five minutes, or I go to the elders and lodge a complaint."

She left in a rush, perhaps more concerned by John's thunderous expression than she let on.

As soon as she'd closed the front door, Viola confronted me. "You can't go with that woman."

I sighed and rose from the couch, letting the blankets that had covered me fall. "It's no good. Those aren't idle threats, and you two can't care for me forever."

"Nonsense! You can stay here for as long as you like." Viola puffed up, tears in her eyes.

"And depend on you for everything? I'm not a child, and I don't want your lives ruined by this—"

"That wouldn't happen—"

"Maybe, maybe not. I can't take that risk."

Before my courage could fail, I hugged Viola and then it was John's turn. I whispered into his ear, "If you don't hear from me in a week, come check on me."

I pulled back, and although grim-faced, he nodded. Relief enveloped me—he'd understood that I couldn't ask Viola. If she knew how worried I was, she'd never let me leave. I said goodbye, squared my shoulders, and walked out.

I just hoped John wouldn't need to come to the cabin, and that my fears about what Elain might do now were unfounded.

~

"GET UP!" Elain shouted while pounding on my bedroom door.

There was no need. I'd been awake for hours, staring at the ceiling, letting the apathy wash me away into a stupor.

I'd arrived back home almost a week ago, and the second I'd stepped through the door, Elain had thrust a long list of chores under my nose. There was everything from weeding the vegetable patch to re-painting the house. Since I no longer had to make peace for Father's sake, I'd resolved to fight back.

When I'd asked what household duties she'd be performing, she'd shrugged and told me as the elder, she wasn't expected to work as hard. I quickly earned myself another slap, arguing that she was only twelve years older than me. She must've seen my hands curling, itching to return the favor, because she'd grinned like a cat that got the mouse and threatened to go to the elders with tales of lazy stepchildren. Warning me not to play games I didn't understand, she'd set me to scrubbing floors. With sweat pouring down my face, I tried to think of a way out of my predicament. I considered just leaving, but I couldn't rely on the elders to side with me. The village council amounted to five men and only one woman. And as someone with gangly limbs, sharp awkward lines, and the grace of a boar, I couldn't hope to replicate the way Elain's soft golden hair, ample cleavage, and doe eyes influenced men's hearts.

So now, every day began by wondering what fresh hell she'd conjured up for the day.

Today it was chopping wood until she'd decided we had enough. By mid-afternoon, my hands had blistered and bled in spots. Losing patience, unable to bear the pain, I walked back into the house, rummaged around for some cheese, and poured myself a glass of water.

I leaned against the kitchen counter and savored the peace and quiet —Elain had gone into the village for market day.

Scanning the ground floor of the cabin, grief pressed in on me. Beneath me were dark floorboards that creaked constantly, and opposite was the hearth. A staircase and a rickety dining table took pride of place in the middle of the room. And as you entered from the front, an L-shaped kitchen lay to the right. Nothing fancy—just a few cupboards, a stone sink, and a woodstove tucked up against the wall. The bones of the room were still there. It even smelled of the same pine residue, and yet... everything was different.

Once upon a time, my mother's rocking chair had sat beside the fireplace, while the potted herbs she'd tended dotted every surface. Now, thirteen years later, my father's winter coat, his boots of reindeer hide, and the warm, acrid smell of his piped tobacco had also gone.

Breathing became difficult and my knees almost gave way. To distract myself, I went looking for a salve to soothe my hands. I found a tin in a kitchen cupboard and rubbed the salve's waxy substance into my sore palms before tossing it back in the drawer.

I stole back upstairs and sat, reaching under the bed sheets for my father's jumper, the only piece of him I'd been able to salvage. Elain wasn't just at the market to buy food and find "a few luxuries," as she called it. She was selling his possessions and hadn't bothered to tell me. Gus had arrived with the wagon this morning. I saw them piling his belongings into the back, and I'd run downstairs to snag the first thing I could find.

Now, I put his jumper to my face and breathed in smoke and pine—his scent. The smell of the forge and the forest he loved to roam in. Despite my attempts to forestall it, a small whimper escaped me. It quickly turned into a sob.

My stepmother's voice cracked like a whip. "Where are you? Why aren't you outside chopping wood?"

I flinched. Rushing to stash the jumper under the mattress, I looked out the window to check on Gus. He was already driving the horse back to the village. A small comfort.

Wiping my eyes and sucking in a steadying breath, I walked to the door and down the stairs as slowly as I dared. She was waiting for me on the bottom step. "What were you doing up there?" Elain asked, her nostrils flaring as if to sniff out a lie.

"Tidying my room. I've already chopped enough wood to last a month."

"Good," Elain said, baring her teeth. "You can go foraging then; we need more mushrooms for the pie this evening. Be back by five."

Not quite ready to submit to this latest demand, I dared a question. "How was Gus able to help you? Shouldn't he be working at Father's forge?"

"It's his forge now," she snapped. "His and mine."

"Father left it to the three of us," I replied coldly.

"Of course," Elain said, a sickly, sweet smile stretching across her face. She moved into the kitchen and grabbed a wicker basket from a cabinet. "Collect the mushrooms in this, and don't get lost—we wouldn't want the fae catching you, now would we?"

She stretched out her hand, dangling the basket in front of me with a simpering smirk. My palm twitched. I didn't say a word. I just marched over, snapped that damned basket from her, and practically sprinted out the door.

Angling left, I strode along the beaten trail into the forest and savored the cool breeze kissing my face, the earthy smells, and the freedom from the cabin's toxicity. Ancestors help me, I couldn't bear much more of this—I'd go mad.

But to be free of Elain I had to marry, and that course of action was fraught with its own particular dangers. I had the house to act as a dowry. One that might tempt the men in the village to overlook certain facts, like my distinctively unfeminine hair, or that I'd received an education—Viola had been my teacher since the age of thirteen. Any boy who feigned an interest in me now would only be interested in one thing. Did I want to marry a fortune hunter? What if I traded in one cruel master for another? I needed someone kind, and strong enough to stand up to Elain, but that person did not exist. There were few young men in the village, and even fewer who weren't spoken for. That only left the prospect of traveling to another village, but the second I left, Elain would have an excuse to claim the house for herself.

Frustrated, feeling defeated, I came upon a spot rife with mushrooms and spent the next hour collecting them, contemplating my predicament. With my hands covered in dirt and smelling strongly of fungi, I peered up at the sky and marked the sun's position through the dappled canopy. My heart sank: it was time to start back home. I retraced my steps, my mind whirling and plotting.

I arrived at the cottage to find the two chimneys puffing out smoke and the lanterns' flames glowing through the glass. On a deep, shuddering inhale, I opened the door and walked through. I could only stare at my stepmother. She'd started dinner.

"You're cooking?" I said, barely believing my eyes.

She hadn't so much as lifted a pan since my father died.

"Yes, well, you've been working so hard, I figured you could use a treat!"

Elain hummed merrily to herself while rolling out pastry. The hairs on the back of my neck bristled. Something was very, *very* wrong. Entering the lair of the wolf, I closed the door and placed the wicker basket on the dining table.

I watched her. "You're in a good mood ..."

"Yes, I am. It can happen, Beanpole," Elain scoffed.

I felt like saying "since when," but instead asked, "D'you need any help?"

"No—you go upstairs and relax. I'll call when it's done."

I didn't move for a whole minute. Shock seemed to have frozen my core.

Move.

I climbed the stairs to my bedroom, only to pace up and down the length of the small space while a voice inside screamed to jump out the window and run to the bakery. Elain had never spoken to me with kindness, at least not when my father was absent. This nicer version of my stepmother had me on edge, waiting for the final drum beat to sound, and for the monster to rear her ugly head. Was it all a game? Another mode of torture to add to her collection?

Still, nothing had happened ... yet. If I ran, I'd have no excuse other than my stepmother was being too nice. That didn't stop my skin from crawling when Elain called me down.

Breathe, I reminded myself.

As I stepped off the staircase I spotted dinner on the table in the form of a pie, some bread and butter, and a pitcher of water. Suddenly, the threat she'd made years ago to poison my food came rushing back.

Something clicked, and my instincts roared, *Don't eat it!* Gods help me, I sat down anyway.

"I hope you like it." Elain smiled at me.

That, there, felt like enough to confirm my suspicions. I could still run, but then what? I stalled for time by cutting the pie on my plate into smaller and smaller pieces. Finally, Elain took a bite from the pile of ham and mushrooms heaped high on her plate. Nothing happened.

But maybe she'd just poisoned my portion rather than the whole pie. Yes, that made more sense. I hadn't seen her dish it out, after all.

"Is there something wrong with my cooking?" Elain asked, waving her fork at my plate.

"No—the pie's delicious. Thank you."

"Really?" She cocked an eyebrow. "By now, you've usually cleaned your plate and are asking for a second helping."

I forced a breathy laugh as my cheeks burned. She was right. I had to act and think fast. An idea formed as I surveyed the table.

Grabbing two linen napkins, I placed them over my lap. As the meal progressed, whenever Elain looked away I slipped more pie onto a napkin. To stop her getting suspicious, I occasionally forced a forkful into my mouth, praying the poison wasn't strong enough to kill me there and then. And when an opportunity arose, I brought the other napkin to my lips and deposited the food inside it. I didn't touch the bread or butter.

Halfway through the pie, I was wondering if I'd missed out on a perfectly good meal for nothing. Then, Elain poured me a glass of water from a jug and my instincts rang out in alarm again. I pretended to take tiny sips and waited for my moment.

My stepmother carried her plate to the kitchen. In one smooth movement, I tipped the water into the pie dish in the center of the table. I followed that up with the food collected in the napkins. Hands trembling, I tried to disguise the mushy heap by lifting leftover piecrust over the top. I snatched my glass, tipped it toward my mouth and waited. She turned back around, and I lowered the glass as if I'd just downed the liquid.

"No second helping?" she asked, frowning as she walked over to pick up my plate.

"My stomach's acting up." I rubbed my belly for effect.

Elain smiled coldly and went to stack my plate in the sink. "Too bad. We need to talk."

My stomach lurched.

She spun back around and moved to the table to hover behind the chair opposite. "About the forge."

"The forge?" I echoed, surprised.

"Yes." Elain grimaced. Sliding into her chair, she clasped her hands. "Gus has the power to make things very difficult for us. He's alone now, doing the work of two men, and he never had Halvard's talent. We need to make him happy ... keep him on our side; otherwise, he could let the forge fall into ruin and us along with it. Or even swindle us and keep the profits for himself," she snarled, wearing an ugly look.

"If he does either, we can go to the elders—"

"Don't be so stupid!" she barked. "He's a man and the only one in the village trained as a blacksmith. The village needs him far more than it needs either of us."

"What do you suggest then?" I tried to steady my hands and ignore the yawning chasm threatening to open beneath my feet.

"Nothing drastic," she said too breezily. "I've asked him round to talk tonight. I want to persuade him that it's in his best interests not to cheat us. We must use our feminine charms ..."

My heart was racing now. What in the rutting hell was she on about? She'd spent years telling me I couldn't charm a carrot, let alone a man. What changed?

A sickening prospect occurred. But surely, *surely*, not even she could be that bold. Elain knew I had a little protection in Viola and John, and if they caught wind she'd forced me to whore myself, they'd bring down the wrath of the whole village upon hers and Gus's heads.

"Nay, child, there's no need to look so scared." Elain smirked, clearly enjoying my fear. "I only want to get on his good side. And it's time you learned that as women, we have no power other than what men give us. No matter what the will says, we must use whatever advantages we have."

Her eyes lingered on my face, tracing my features. Whatever she saw there made her grimace and my chest constrict, as her silent insult found its mark. Glancing away, she leaned back and added, "You must trust me on this—give him company after a hard day's work, add in a few compliments, and he'll be eating out of our hands."

I nodded once. As my panic cranked up another notch, I decided for a direct approach. She might let her mask slip, giving me time to glimpse her true intentions. "You don't want me to marry him, do you?"

Elain let out a harsh croak and faced me. "He wouldn't marry you, even if that's what I desired. You might have a proper dowry now, but he's a blacksmith. He has his pick of girls in the village."

Some pathetic, vain part of me burned at that. I chewed on my lip, longing to spit out a curse or throw back an insult. Maybe I would have, if it weren't for the knock. I jumped a bit, and Elain rose to answer the door, but not before I spotted something in her eyes that made me reach across the table and slip the bread knife up my sleeve. It'd be blunt, but better something than nothing.

An icy blast blew through our cabin, and my lungs tightened.

"Get in out of that cold—you look frozen." Elain brushed the fresh snowfall from Gus's shoulders as he stepped inside without a word. The door clicked shut; it sounded like a death knell. The cabin returned to its former warmth, but the chill didn't leave my bones.

I stilled as his gray eyes found me. My whole body clenched, waiting for something to happen. But he walked to the woodstove and without looking at me said, "You're looking well, Serena."

I mumbled my thanks, but my stepmother's glare was enough for me to add, "How's the forge?"

"Same as always," he said, a brittle snap entering his voice. He held his hands closer to the stove and rubbed them together. "Elain, how about a glass of something warm?"

"Of course, sit down," she said, waving to the table.

He prowled over, choosing the chair next to mine. I strived to suppress a shudder and failed.

"Serena!" Elain barked. "Get a glass of wine for our guest."

"That's Father's—"

"Don't make me ask again," she hissed through gritted teeth. "And while you're at it, bring the bottle through."

I deflated under the weight of her glare and stood to walk over to a

door to my left. I went through into the pantry and found the wine rack
—one of my father's few indulgences. The labels of his favorite vintages
stared back at me, and I ground my teeth. *Bitch.* The only reason she
hadn't sold his liquor was that she loved it too much.

After picking the cheapest wine possible, I seized the opportunity to
slip the knife from my sleeve into the pocket of my dress. I stalked back
into the living room, fighting the urge to fling the bottle at them. I
grabbed a glass from a cupboard and filled it halfway while Elain
gossiped about the villagers—one of her pastimes.

There was no choice; I had to sit down next to Gus again. I set the
bottle on the table and pushed the glass toward him. He made an odd
grunting noise I supposed meant thank you. I tried to hide my revulsion
as he snatched the glass, then the bottle, and gorged on Father's liquor.

For five long minutes he let my stepmother have free rein, spinning
tales and talking nonsense. Still, I kept my eyes trained on her the whole
time. Anything to avoid Gus's roaming eyes.

Once he'd finished the whole damned bottle, I moved quickly and
offered to wash his glass. He handed it over without a word. I grabbed
the pie dish at the same time and made a great show of looking busy at
the sink.

Elain turned to the topic of the forge, and Gus became more
animated. I let their words flit in one ear and out the other, losing myself
to the slow, meditative task of scrubbing. It was because of this I failed to
notice the conversation slow to a trickle. I was watching fresh snow fall
outside the window when something in its reflection caught my eye.
Elain paused outside the door to her bedroom; her eyes locked onto
mine, her expression was hard and unyielding, her smile twisted and
triumphant.

Heart in mouth, I whirled as she shut the door and Gus stalked
closer. I grew rooted, frozen to the earth, trapped.

Run, run, run, run, run.

I'd seen it in Elain's expression—Gus would ruin me. She'd set this
up. In one fell swoop, she hoped to break my spirit and destroy my reputation, ensuring no man would ever marry me. Afterward, she'd likely
offer me a choice—give up my inheritance, or stay and be at the mercy of
them both.

A potent, undiluted fear rushed in, poisoning my veins, paralyzing me. Angry, hopeless tears stung my eyes as Gus's hot breath found my neck. My mind flitted from thought to thought as a stone would skip across a pond. I sought distraction. I looked to the hearth—the one my mother taught me to read by—then to the table where I'd last spoken to Father.

This was my first kiss. That was all I could think as Gus's mouth found mine. His grasping tongue forced its way into my mouth. He tasted like sour wine; it made me gag.

Gus drew back at the sound. He regarded me for a moment and with a twitch of his lips, his greedy eyes drifted down. My body screamed in protest as rough hands found my breasts, tugging and pinching hard enough to bruise. "I always knew they were in there somewhere." A soft laugh passed his lips. "I guess Elain's little tonic must've worked. You're much more docile than I'd imagined you'd be. I've got to say I'm disappointed—it's so much more fun breaking in a wild horse."

His words oozed into my ears, striking cord after cord. I'd been right. My stepmother had tried to drug me, and my father had been the one to let these monsters into our lives. He hadn't believed me. He hadn't seen. Then he'd gone and died, and left me to be a doe among wolves. But I'd seen through her, enough to not drink or eat her poison. I'd saved myself. I wasn't paralyzed—I could fight back.

Gus grabbed my crotch. A chain I hadn't known existed unfurled itself inside of me, awaking and unleashing a bloodthirsty and vicious animal. The *possession* in that touch made me bite down on the tongue that had forced its way into my mouth again. I tasted blood.

Good.

I loosened a snarl and pulled out the knife from my pocket, slashing out. Gus staggered away: the knife had done nothing. I threw it to distract him and grabbed a soapy pan from the sink. There was no hesitation. I ran at him, swinging wildly. He swerved and moved in close, those muscled arms reaching out to stop me.

If he wanted a rutting wild horse, I'd give him one. I brought my knee screaming up between his legs and landed a savage blow.

He collapsed to his knees. At the precise moment, he screamed,

"Bitch," I brought the pan down on his head. He slumped to the floor, a dead weight.

Elain appeared, screeching, "You stupid girl!" She ran over to check his pulse. A quick, relieved sigh told me he'd survived. "Thank the mother," she murmured and turned to glower up at me. "What were you thinking? You could've killed him!"

With fury singing in my veins, I pointed the frying pan at her like a sword. "If either of you ever come near me again, I will *end* you, d'you hear me?"

Her eyes widened in shock and satisfaction flooded me, but when her mouth curved into a sneer, I'd had enough. Pan still in hand, I went to the door and stepped out into the swirling white.

Shit. A sharp wind whipped through the night, carrying eddies of snow that had already stuck to the ground and lined the path to the village. It was freezing, and I didn't have a cloak. There was no going back. I'd just have to sprint and hope the cold didn't find me.

Taking the right path, letting my long legs work for me, I ran hard and didn't look back.

Elain had won. I'd failed to play her game. The elders wouldn't believe me, but that didn't mean I had to go quietly. I'd been silent for too long. *Enough.* My father's wishes no longer mattered. I'd kept the peace for him. Always for him. That lingering respect died in my veins the instant Gus had touched me. I couldn't honor Father's memory when I couldn't forgive him. Not just for bringing them into our lives, but for not seeing that the cabin hadn't been a home in years. The only home I recognized was the one I ran to.

CHAPTER 3
CHANGELING

I ran until my leg muscles screamed and my heart felt fit to explode. The starry tapestry and the pale face of the moon were the only lights guiding my way. With sweat slipping down my back and staining my dress, and my body shaking, I staggered to a halt and dry-heaved on the side of the path. Thankfully, there wasn't anything in my stomach, so the retching soon ended. Checking that no one had followed me, I threw the pan into the forest and set off again, redoubling my efforts and arriving at the village like a whirlwind gone mad.

Nearly there. Heart in mouth, I continued along the mud-clotted path until I spotted candlelight in their window, the only sign that Viola might still be up. John would be in bed—the life of a baker demanded early nights.

Not wanting to terrify her, I allowed myself a few seconds to nurse the stitch in my side and compose myself. I doubled over, sucked deep breaths into shuddering lungs, and used my sleeve to wipe the sweat from my face.

One last stumbling run and I was knocking at their door. I tucked my hands under my armpits, trying to manage the shivering. I knew it wasn't the cold causing my body to react that way, not after sprinting for fifteen minutes straight. The door opened, Viola took one look at me and I burst into tears.

~

AFTER VIOLA CALMED me down enough to hear what had happened, she went upstairs to wake John. Once they'd joined me in the kitchen, all of us nursing steaming mugs of hot chocolate, John was all for going straight to Baird. He looked ready to fling his coat on and drag me there.

I disagreed. "I don't think the elders would appreciate us banging on their doors in the middle of the night. Let's at least wait until morning."

Viola looked distant, but John nodded. "I'll take you at first light."

"I'll go get sheets for the couch," Viola said quietly before exiting the room.

Swallowing the lump in my throat, I met John's knowing stare. "She feels like she's failed you. That's why she's ..." He slumped back in his chair, unable to finish his sentence.

"She hasn't," I said hoarsely. "She couldn't."

My voice sounded hollow, even to me. I tried to summon the fierceness I'd felt earlier in the night, but the creature that had slipped its leash now slept. The sharp edge of my panic had dimmed, leaving behind a black pit of nothingness eating away my insides.

Something of this must've shown on my face, because a quaver entered John's voice when he said, "Serena—can I do anything?"

Not wanting to cause him more worry than was necessary, I scraped back the chair and stood. "I'll be fine. I just need sleep."

Not stopping to check whether he'd bought my flimsy lie, I padded over to the couch and sat in front of a dying fire.

Now standing, his heavy eyelids drooping, John asked, "Do you need anything before I go up?"

"No, thank you. Sorry about waking you."

He made a disbelieving noise and mumbled, "Don't be silly. We're always here for you, Serena."

Words failed me.

John stayed, suspended in the doorway to the bakery until Viola came bustling back in and said, "John, you go on up to bed now. I'm staying here with Serena."

"There's no need." A feeble protest on my part.

Viola silenced me with a look, and John simply nodded as if he'd expected nothing less. Swooping down, he kissed his wife on the cheek. "G'night."

When the door shut behind him, Viola placed a pillow and several thick woolen blankets next to me in a pile. She straightened, only for her brows to knit together as her eyes met mine. "I think given everything that's happened tonight, you should wear this."

She stepped toward the mantelpiece, opened the silver box, and plucked out my mother's necklace. Twisting back around, she extended her arm, offering it to me. When I didn't take it, her arm lowered. "Serena, you can't let bullies dictate your life. This is your birthright. Take it." Pushing her hand out again, she said, "If not for yourself, then do it for me. I'll sleep better knowing you have its protection."

My tongue felt heavy as I formed the words. "How could it protect me?"

"Because it was your mother's."

Annoyed at this noncommittal answer, I took it anyway and fastened it around my neck, hiding it under the fabric of my rough homespun dress. The gem encasing the droplet of water felt surprisingly heavy and warm against my chest.

"I'll be right here," Viola said, slumping back into her favorite chair by the fire. Laying a blanket over her lap and picking up her knitting, she continued. "I'm not going anywhere, so try to sleep, okay?"

I mumbled my thanks and grabbed the pillow and a blanket. Curling up on the couch, dreading the nightmares to come, I watched Viola's hands dance and listened to the soft clacking of her needles. The night passed in stretches of fractured sleep as thoughts and nightmares blurred together. Certain images and feelings kept resurfacing, forcing me to taste bile at the back of my throat as I recalled the violent lust in Gus's movements and the triumph on Elain's face.

Hovering on the edge of sleep again, a knocking noise made me vault off the couch. My whole body quivered, readying to fight or flee.

Through the foggy glass-paned door I saw only the faintest hint of pink in the sky. Dawn hadn't yet arrived. The only light in the room came from the dying fire and the odd stubby candle. It wasn't enough to make out the figure knocking to come in.

Viola was at my side instantly, steadying me. "It's all right, you're safe with us," she cooed. "I want you to go get John for me."

"No need." John appeared at the side door, already dressed in a flour-covered apron. "I was just putting the first loaves in."

"John? Viola?" a voice sounded from outside. "Are you there? It's Timothy."

My heart slammed up against my chest. "They've already gotten to them."

"We can't be sure if this is about last night," John said quietly.

A breathy note entered Viola's voice as she said, "Oh, I think we can —that's Baird's grandson knocking on our door." Her face taut, she turned to me. "Serena, if you want to run, if you think you won't get a fair hearing, then we'll hide you and send Timothy away."

I shook my head. "You can't shelter me forever."

John, who'd been silent during Viola's rushed speech, stepped forward with stiff shoulders and a straight back. "No, but we can smuggle you out, and I can get you money—enough to start over in a new village."

My mouth popped open. "The elders would ruin you—"

"Serena, don't think for one second we wouldn't risk that and more for you," Viola said, her eyes darting to the door as another knock echoed through the house.

A pause. The offer hung thick in the air, and I felt a fork in the road. Two choices, two paths, and two very different fates awaited me. Neither choice felt good, and other than a vague sense of wrongness that dogged me when I thought about running, it felt like a stab in the dark. Is this what it was to be an adult then? Gods, it sucked.

I vacillated, twisting my hands together. "You're the only family I've got left." A flimsy, inarticulate way of describing how much they meant to me.

John moved to Viola's side and wrapped an arm around her waist in support. "That won't change, whatever you do."

Viola winced as another knock sounded. "Darling, it's all right. Go into the bakery," she whispered, gesturing to her right.

I sighed. "No, you were right last night." I met her confused expression, and continued. "I've let bullies run my life for too long. Please, open the door—Timothy must be freezing."

Viola and John exchanged furtive looks.

"Are you sure, Serena?" he asked.

I gave a nod. John stared at me, his mouth a hard line. Respect glimmered true and bright in his eyes. My heart swelled.

John patted Viola once on the shoulder and walked to the door to throw it open.

I glimpsed seventeen-year-old Timothy hopping from foot to foot, rubbing his hands together for warmth. He was already taller than John, with messy brown hair and tanned skin from working the fields. "John!" He sounded relieved. "Sorry for disturbing you, but my grandfather asked me to come to see if Serena was here."

"What do you want with her?"

That brutal command for information made Timothy mumble, "Is she here?"

John stepped aside. Timothy's eyes found mine. "Serena." A tone of surprise. "I—I didn't think," he stuttered. "My grandfather, well, I mean to say—the elders sent me to bring you to the Village Hall."

"Is this about Gus and Elain?" I questioned, preparing myself for the worst.

He nodded sheepishly. "They've accused you of something …"

"Of what?" Viola barked, stepping in front of me as if she could protect me from the answer.

My instincts told me that whatever was making Timothy avert Viola's glower like that—it was worse than I could've imagined.

"They say you're a changeling. Elain's convinced that *you're* the reason the children are disappearing."

Sharp, cold shock ran through me.

The myths and tales surrounding changelings were infamous. The songs and stories we heard from cradle to grave all spoke of human women being tricked or forced into conceiving fae progenies. Their full-blooded sires never claimed them, and so the demi-fae lived as outcasts. These children of two worlds, abandoned by fae society, had no choice but to grow up among humans, hiding their identities. This isolation and rejection drove the changelings mad. Turning them wicked, bloodthirsty, and endlessly hungry. And if humans discovered there was one living among them, the punishment was often death.

My heart raced.

Viola stumbled back a step as if the words had assaulted her. "That's madness," she gasped, a hand over her chest.

Timothy squirmed. "There's support for the idea. Some villagers seem convinced."

"What? Why?" John asked, his face now roughly the color of sour milk.

Timothy's tongue flicked over his lower lip. "The thing is, Serena's always been a little, well, she's always looked ..." he trailed off.

Pathetic.

A raging tempest swelled and swept me along in its wake. My voice shook, but not with fear. "I know I'm odd, Timothy. You can say it."

"Rats and flies," John ejected, using his favorite curse. "You're not odd, Serena, and even if you were, that doesn't make you a changeling."

Timothy towered over John, and yet he still lowered his head when subjected to his glare. He mumbled, "It's just, everyone knows changelings eat a lot."

My gut twisted.

"And Elain pointed out ... well, you're always here at the bakery. The girls in the village say it's unnatural for someone to eat so much and to never gain weight."

"Of course," Viola blurted out, crossing her arms. "Why wouldn't the elders listen to the testimony of a bunch of silly, jealous girls? That makes perfect sense!"

John murmured something pacifying, but I barely noticed. Again, this proved another masterful move by Elain. I was the perfect scapegoat for a frightened, grieving village. And with my father gone, there was no one with enough influence to protect me. I was easy prey.

A flash of searing heat flared at my throat, and my hand flew to the gem.

"Serena?" Timothy shot me a little pleading look. "They want to keep you in the holding room in the Hall until ..."

"Until the trial?" I finished, glaring at him.

At least he had the decency to look embarrassed.

"Over my dead body," Viola snarled. A tiger in disguise.

Timothy gaped at her while John looked to me. I saw the offer behind his gaze. He would follow my lead: my decision. There was only one path to take. I had to protect them even if it meant facing the wolves to do it.

"I'll go," I said to Timothy who sighed, relieved.

"*No.*" Viola spun to stare at me, ashen-faced. "This isn't right. You don't deserve this."

I managed a small shrug. "Maybe not, but if people got what they deserved, Father would still be alive and Gus and Elain would be the ones in the ground."

Timothy's eyebrows shot up to his hairline. I ignored him and spoke to John and Viola. "I promise you both, I'm not going down easily. I'll tell the elders what happened. They won't believe me, but the story will stick. Enough to make life difficult for them. And when more children go missing after ... whatever they do with me, people might finally see Elain and Gus for the monsters they are."

My adoptive family stood staring at each other. It was John who broke the silence. "We would've been proud to call you our daughter, Serena Smith."

I forced out thickly, "I hoped I would've deserved parents like you."

I went to walk past Viola, but her arm shot out to stop me. Pulling me into a rough hug, she whispered in my ear, "We'll be at the trial. You won't be alone."

She broke away and turned with me to look at Timothy. "Tell your grandfather we'll see him in the Village Hall at noon."

He quailed under her stare, dipping his head. In a breathy voice, he said, "Yes, Ma'am."

I stalked straight past John and Timothy with my head held high. My eyes stung when they met with the chill dawn air, and I tried not to think about hours spent locked away in the Village Hall. Timothy moved to my side and after a sneaky sidelong glance, as if worried I might bolt, he set off, leading the way. I didn't hear the door close behind me; I knew John and Viola would watch until I disappeared.

CHAPTER 4
THE TRIAL

The Hall was centered in the heart of the village, standing as a bedrock of law and order and a witness to the rituals that made up the lifeblood of its citizens: everything from weddings and funerals, to indoor markets.

Inside, it held a large rectangular room that led to a warren of smaller ones in the back. Composed of wood, its structure was supported by pillars marked with hundreds of ancient carvings. Rows of polished oak benches split the room in two, providing an aisle, and ended in an altar or high table, depending on the occasion. Of course, today they'd have to drag out the high table to seat the members of the council.

Through the small mullioned windows in my holding cell, I watched the sun climb to its zenith. I'd been locked away all morning, sitting on a cold, hard floor, terrified and starved. Timothy finally appeared to lead me to the main Hall, where he placed me in the center of the aisle in front of the six current members that made up the village's voice. John and Viola sat behind me on the right side of the aisle while Gus and Elain took the left. I felt a brief stab of relief that there weren't more people around to witness my shaming. For by now, there'd be no one who hadn't heard what was happening; many villagers were likely eagerly awaiting the news outside the doors.

I willed my pulse to steady as Baird, the Chief Elder, caught my eye. He was easily the oldest person in the village: eyes sunken, white hair wispy, and skin hanging from him like leathery hide. My attempt at bravery shattered, and I almost vomited at his feet when he rose, *slowly*, from the table, speaking in a rich baritone, so at odds with his tired appearance. "Thank you, Timothy." He dismissed his grandson from my side with a wave.

Timothy strode over to stand in what looked like his usual position, behind the council, tucked away in a corner where he could observe. Baird must be grooming his heir. Lucky him, I thought bitterly.

My legs threatened to buckle as Baird called out my name. "Serena Smith, you stand accused of being a changeling, and therefore, are in part responsible for abducting three children from this village. How do you answer these charges?"

My chin riding high, I spoke the words I'd practiced for hours. "Innocent. I'm not a changeling, and I would never kidnap a child. These accusations are false, made by two people who want to cover up their own crimes by destroying my credibility."

Hushed conversations and titters spread among the elders. I looked to each of them in turn and held their gaze, willing them to see the truth in my eyes. Baird sat in the middle. To his right sat a farmer by the name of Duncan. Then, there was Nathan—father to Annie Tanner, one of the missing children—and Dr. Fagan, the local surgeon. On Baird's left sat Castiel, our only mason. Next to him was Gertie, the only woman on the council.

Baird continued. "Your accusers are here. Now that you have declared your innocence, we will hear their claim that you are, in fact, a changeling, otherwise known as a demi-fae. I concede the floor to Elain and Gus to air their grievances and put forth evidence supporting their claims."

The rustle of skirts. A shiver spider-walked down my back, and I knew Elain had arisen first. I refused to look back as she began. "Thank you, Chief Baird."

Disgust crept under my skin. She spoke with just the right amount of tentativeness, but she couldn't hide the slight quaver or the breathiness. Not from me; I knew her too well. My stepmother was excited. After all, humiliating me while also being the center of attention—this was Elain's dream.

My hands curled into fists at the thought.

"Over the years," she continued, "I've tried to do my duty as both wife and mother. I believe I've fulfilled my duty to Halvard—gods protect him."

A pause, to remind them she was grieving the loss of a husband. Nathan and the farmer, Duncan, offered her commiserating looks. The former had lost his daughter, and the latter his wife in childbirth. No surprises there, but I took heart that the others looked unaffected. Maybe this wouldn't be a total sham of a trial.

Elain hit her stride. "Yet today it pains me to come before you and speak out against my stepdaughter, Serena, for it means I've failed as a mother."

I almost laughed out loud.

"But the abductions have forced my hand. I can no longer ignore her ... oddities. I'm ashamed that I haven't spoken out sooner, but gods help me, I'd grown to love the child."

I couldn't help it—a weak rasping chuckle escaped.

Elain paused. I sensed her eyes boring into me, her anger raining down like blows to my head. The elders gave me a few disapproving looks, and I stared down at my clasped hands in a submissive gesture. I couldn't afford to earn their ill will.

"Please, continue Elain. Although, it might be wise to speed things up a little," Baird said, his white eyebrows knitting. "Why don't you tell us what led you to believe that Serena is a changeling?"

"Yes, Chief," Elain said, stiltedly. This time it was nerves, not excitement making her sound breathy. I hid a smile.

"It was small things at first. A bottomless appetite, her awkwardness, her foul temper, and of course that puberty never seemed to find the girl."

I cringed, fighting to hide the stiffening of my shoulders and the battle raging inside. My impulse to turn around and fly at her—fists swinging, spitting and clawing—almost got the better of me. Despite this, there remained a tiny separate part of me that marveled at her skills in deceit. She was lying with the truth, which was what made this so much more excruciating.

"At first, I dismissed the signs. I put them down to the child's loss, and that she'd grown up without a woman in the house."

Rage roiled in my gut. That evil *hag* actually had the stones to bring my mother into this.

"But over the past few months, I spotted an odd pattern in her behavior. Whenever a child vanished, Serena went missing for hours at a time. She'd skip her chores and then come back from the forest, irritable and disoriented. When Annie vanished ..." Elain wavered masterfully.

My mouth popped open. She was baiting Nathan Tanner with news of his beloved daughter, using his grief as a weapon.

Nathan shifted and leaned forward. "Go on."

My heart sank. Nathan still looked like the loss was eating him alive. Those purple blemishes under his eyes showed he wasn't sleeping. The hunched posture, the haunted, hungry gleam in his eyes—it all stank of desperation. He wanted someone to blame for his daughter's disappearance, and I would be the sacrificial lamb.

The noose tightened about my neck.

"Well, on that day ..." Elain paused again.

A dull throbbing started up behind my eyes. The hesitancy and sadness in her voice was perfect. She would play them like a lute. Truthfully, if I hadn't known they were lies, I'd have believed her too.

"Yes," Nathan urged.

"Serena arrived back from the forest speaking in tongues. When she came to her senses, I explained what had happened ... She grew evasive and called me a liar."

Elain gave another dramatic pause. I almost sighed, exasperated by the theatrics.

"After that she shut me out, but my concerns didn't go away. I kept on asking where she'd been and what she remembered, but the only answer I ever got was that she'd been hunting. Yet, I remember that day clearly enough: she wasn't carrying her bow."

"Did it not occur to you to tell us about her then?" Nathan snapped.

I couldn't bear to look behind me, but in my mind's eye, I saw Elain acting cowed, imploring him to take pity on her with her big doe eyes. *Ugh.*

"Of course," she murmured. "But Halvard convinced me not to. He said it was a touch of the brain fever, and that she'd suffered from it ever since her mother had passed on."

"This is crazy!"

I whirled around as Viola exploded up out of her chair.

"Please, *listen.*" Viola looked up at the elders, hands clasped, beseeching them. "I've known Serena from the day she came into this world and have seen her almost every day since then. She's never once exhibited anything close to madness—"

"Enough," Baird ordered with a short bark. "You will get your moment to speak, but for now, John, I look to you to restrain your wife."

Viola bristled, but John placed a calming hand on hers. Gently, he pulled her down and Viola sat with a huff.

Baird added, almost lazily, "Elain … continue."

I turned back to the elders, unable to stomach facing my stepmother as she spun her web of lies.

"Well, you see—" Elain stuttered. "I trusted my husband's word. So, to my ever-lasting shame, I let the matter go. I'm so sorry, Nathan," she ended with a little sob.

Pretty, poisonous lies—her voice was even shaking. I tried to smother my panic and push away bleating thoughts. The last thing I needed was to have a breakdown when accused of madness. Perhaps, I *should* forgive my father for being taken in by this she-demon. This game came to her as easily as breathing; her words carried both weight and conviction.

"What's made you come forward now and go against Halvard's wishes?" Baird interrogated.

The sound of a throat clearing from behind me cut through the hall like a knife through butter. I'd know that phlegmy sound anywhere—it was Gus. What fresh misery was this?

Gus drawled, "I convinced her to come forward. After Halvard died, Elain wanted to keep protecting her, but last night Serena attacked me, unprovoked. Elain was a witness. If someone would inspect my head, you'll see a nasty gash from the blow. She used a frying pan," he finished, his voice deepening: a sure sign that he felt real anger over what I'd done to him.

A savage urge welled up; I wanted to turn around and laugh in his face.

There were more accusatory glances in my direction. Baird, in particular, fixed me with a hard stare and scanned my face, frowning.

Don't believe them, I silently begged.

Baird's thin mouth puckered in disapproval. Fear and frustration almost made me bow my head, but my instincts screamed not to look down; I couldn't afford to look guilty. My spine stiffened in response.

"Timothy, go check Gus's head," Baird said gruffly.

Timothy appeared from the shadows and marched over to Gus. I didn't bother to turn and look because I knew the result.

"There is a wound," he informed the elders.

The heaviness in his voice offered little comfort as I appeared that much closer to being found guilty. Would it even matter what I said now?

A touch of heat kissed my throat. The droplet at the end of the necklace was burning, and a soft, strange voice entered my mind.

Don't give up.

As quickly as it had come the heat vanished, the voice along with it. Alarm flooded me, and it took all my strength and stubbornness not to let it show.

Had Elain's words somehow been foresight? Was I going mad? The only other alternative was that the necklace contained magic, but that seemed even less likely than a blip of insanity. For either my mother had unwittingly handed down a magical item, or she'd known and done it anyway. The High Priests had declared magic blasphemy long ago and forbidden its use throughout the Gauntlet. Now, any human practicing witchcraft got burned at the stake or drowned. Would my mother have risked subjecting me to that? All to pass on jewelry supposedly gifted with protection? Surely not.

"Can you think of no reason she might attack you?" Baird asked, his voice snapping me back to my present.

"No." The lie slipped off his adder's tongue so rutting easily. "I was visiting their cottage, at Elain's invitation, as she wanted us to discuss the running of the forge. Serena grew more erratic as the night wore on.

Eventually, she insisted on leaving the cabin after dark ... It was like she was possessed."

Noticing the elders' uneasy shuffling, my mood darkened further.

"She seemed determined to leave, but wouldn't tell us why," Gus continued flatly. "After what happened to her father ... I would never have forgiven myself if the wolves or the fae had found her. So I tried to stop her. That's when she attacked me and ran out into the forest. Once I'd regained consciousness, Elain confessed that this behavior was nothing new, and that she suspected Serena of being a changeling. Of course, Elain doesn't believe she's involved in the disappearances directly. She thinks the fae are using magic to addle her mind."

He wavered, letting the doubt in his voice speak for him. Now every member of the council was staring, eyes heavy with accusation. Honestly, he could've taught Elain a thing or two.

"Now I can't say if that's true or not, but it's just as likely that she's made a deal with the fae. Maybe, she's even trading innocent lives for a chance to live among her kind."

Hysteria nudged at my insides. I clamped down hard on my lips: bursting out laughing now would be tantamount to death.

"Even *if* she's innocent," he added in a quiet hiss. "Her presence alone could draw these fae to the village. We've all heard the tales that they can sense their own. But if we send her away or give her to them, the fae might leave our children alone."

Despair wrapped around me like a cloak, choking the air from my lungs and encasing my body in ice. Viola cursed under her breath, and the council just looked dumbstruck.

John suddenly stood and turned to glower at Gus. "Correct me if I'm wrong, Gus, but by saying that Serena is a changeling, you're suggesting that she's the product of an infidelity. You are accusing her mother, Sarah Smith, of fornication with a fae? Something of which you have absolutely no evidence."

"I certainly don't mean to smear Sarah's reputation."

Such a smooth response. A mad urge to claw his eyes out struck me —he'd been doing nothing but ruining women for years. But I hadn't fought harder to make Father see his true nature because I'd been too proud to listen to gossip. Shame coated my tongue like bile.

Gus went on. "Only the fae are notorious for tricking and forcing women into the act." No hesitation. No backing down. "We all know that Sarah was odd, too. She scorned the company of the other women in the village and didn't come to feast days. I imagine she was so damaged by the experience—"

"That's enough, Gus," Baird interjected. "I believe you've reached your point. Sarah Smith is not on trial here—if there is any truth to your suspicions, it lies buried with her. Even *if* she was guilty of infidelity, I would see that her memory went untarnished. For even the wisest of us can fall prey to those pointy-toothed devils."

Distaste was clear in Baird's voice, and relief sparked within me. Gus had gone too far and sounded too eager. Elain's acting skills aside, the elders weren't all fools, and the Chief was as sharp as a razor.

Baird said, "Serena, you're accused of being a demi-fae—a changeling—and for assaulting Gus. You may now speak in your defense."

I felt a pull around my midriff, a desperate urge to look back to John and Viola for strength. But realizing this would just look like guilt, I pushed back against the weight in my chest and stared down the council. "I swear by all the gods in the light court, I am *not* a changeling. I know people think I'm odd, but that proves nothing."

Baird's heavy brows nudged together. "Then, how d'you explain these absences on the days the children went missing?"

"Elain is lying," I said firmly.

"Why would she do that?" Nathan demanded through flinty eyes.

I spoke directly to Baird. "Because she hates me. She has always hated me. Since the day she came into our family, she has taunted and threatened and hit me. When I was younger, I tried to tell my father what she was like, and she told me she'd poison my meals if I didn't stop."

Castiel and Gertie exchanged shocked looks, but the rest of them merely frowned.

Baird peered down his beak of a nose. "Do you have any evidence? Any witnesses to these events?"

A heaviness settled on my shoulders. Elain had been so careful to appear the dutiful and loving mother in public. The sound of rustling had me turning; Viola was standing. "A week after Halvard's funeral, Elain came to our house. She barged through the door, uninvited, and when Serena refused to leave with her, she slapped her across the face."

Elain made a furious noise and snapped, "I would've hardly called that a slap."

"So, you don't deny that you hit her?" Gertie retorted.

I tried to hide my smile. Elain had made a mistake. Finally.

She let out a sound that reminded me of a toad being stepped on. "I was grief-stricken; I wasn't thinking straight."

"Hardly an answer," Gertie argued, her aged features hardening.

John rose from the bench and the tension etched a little higher.

"You have something to add, John?" Baird asked gravely.

"I was also there when Elain Smith promised to lie to the council of elders, to force Serena to go with her. She said she'd report her for not helping around the house and get her disinherited."

I could almost see the wheels spinning in the elders' minds. John was, after all, a respected member of the community, and more importantly, a man. His word meant something.

After a moment of silence, Baird's heavy gaze turned on Elain. He used a high, cold voice to say, "What say you to these charges? Did you promise to *lie* to the council of elders?"

"Never." She said it with such conviction, I almost screamed in frustration. "But Hal left the house to both of us. He wanted us to share responsibility for the running of it, and knowing him, he did it so we would always have each other." Elain's voice had become sad. Stars, how did she do it? Lie, and lie again, and keep them all straight in her head. "That day, when I visited Serena, she was still so withdrawn. She looked like death itself. And Viola and John, although good people, have never raised a child."

I twisted to see the devastation alight in both my surrogate parents' eyes. In that moment, I wanted to tear Elain's heart out with my bare hands.

Elain droned on. "I've learned that sometimes you have to push them. So, I begged her to come home. When that didn't work, I said she was leaving me in an impossible situation, and that I'd have to go to the elders for advice. If I made it sound like I was threatening her, then that is my shame to bear. I thought it'd be better for her to come home rather than waste away, even if it was painful to face the memory of him." She wavered, letting out a small sob.

"Why would John lie to us?" Gertie said coldly.

"Isn't it obvious?" Nathan interjected, sounding sad. "They love Serena like a daughter—they're not thinking straight."

Gertie and Castiel voiced their disapproval at his interruption. Baird silenced them with a wave of his hand.

"That's enough," he said, his deep voice putting an end to their bickering. "John is an honorable man. I do not believe he would lie outright. However, Gus remains the only witness without a strong, personal attachment to Serena, and therefore, a motive to lie." His steely eyes settled on me. "Can you give me any reason to doubt his word?"

A lump formed in my throat at the prospect of reliving last night. But if I were to have any chance of surviving this, they needed to see Gus for the cold-blooded predator he was. "He lied to save himself. Last night ..." The hairs on the back of my neck prickled. I gulped in a breath and continued. "Elain surprised me by making dinner. She's hardly said two kind words to me my entire life, and yet suddenly she was making me food and trying to be nice. Something felt off, and I remembered what she'd told me when I was younger—"

"About poisoning you?" Gertie said abruptly.

Encouraged that she hadn't thought my suspicions farfetched, I nodded and added, "It was just a feeling, but it was strong enough that I didn't eat or drink anything she served. I hid the food in napkins and pretended to drink."

Gertie snorted and mumbled her approval. "Smart girl."

Baird cleared his throat. A clear warning that silenced her.

I continued to summarize the events that followed as best as I could. Once I'd revealed Elain's plan to drug me with sedatives and Gus's assault, there was only one thing left to admit. "So I panicked and hit him with the pan, but if I hadn't defended myself, he would've kept going."

That's when the room exploded with noise. Elain and Gus shouted, "Lies! Slander!"

Viola yelled at them in my defense, and John tried to placate her in hushed tones. The rest of the council—Dr. Fagan, Nathan, and Duncan —didn't bother lowering their voices as they talked among themselves. A few words drifted over the din: "Fantasies," "No proof," "Liar," which made any hope in me wither and die. Gertie and Castiel were too quiet to make out as they put their heads together to whisper.

Only Baird remained silent. He stared at me, his face inscrutable. Finally, I couldn't stand it anymore and shouted, "Please, listen! It's not just me—lots of girls in the village know about Gus's reputation. Ask them."

"We don't have time to interview every girl in the village," Dr. Fagan snapped.

"No, we do not," Baird said in a way that was both firm and pacifying. "What happened after you attacked him?" he asked me.

"She ran out into the forest, probably to meet with her fae brethren," Gus cut in viciously.

Violet pushed out a snort of contempt. "For that to be true, you'd have to accuse us of being fae, because she didn't run into the forest. She came straight to the bakery."

Baird's head whipped to them. "What time did she arrive?"

"Around eight in the evening," Viola answered.

"What sort of state was she in?" Baird asked.

"Bad," John added angrily. "She was sobbing when I came downstairs, but after Vi calmed her down, she told us what happened—"

Baird interrupted. "And does her account from last night match the one she just gave?"

"In every way," John confirmed.

A curt nod. "I see." Something final locked into place behind his eyes. He'd decided. I prayed to the courts—light, dark, and moon—that he'd come down on my side.

The other council members weren't so difficult to read. Gertie and Castiel seemed inclined to believe me, but the rest still looked upon on me with doubt and suspicion clouding their eyes. They voted according to a majority, with Baird having the final say. If I could sway just one of them, it might be enough to go free. I gnashed down on my lip, weighing the risks. Making a quick decision, I put in, "Can I speak?"

Baird said nothing, only nodded.

"If you send me into exile, or … kill me," Viola's whimper almost broke me, but there was no choice but to persevere, "Elain inherits my father's house. She won't have to share it with a girl she hates, or have to leave like she would if I'd found a husband. And like Gus, she'll get to keep my profits from the forge. They both have motives to lie."

"Very well." Baird sighed heavily. "The council will deliberate on both the alleged assault and the claims against you—"

"Wait!" Gus exclaimed. A hint of something had my head turning back toward his seat. The gleam on his brow stank of nerves, but there was a curious curve of his lip that had my stomach twisting.

"What is it, Gus?" asked Gertie, her voice prickly.

"I have a witness who says she saw Serena meeting with a fae."

Shock crackled through the air and the elders, who'd been rising from their seats, slumped back down, stunned.

I couldn't stand much more of this.

Baird's next words came out as a soft growl. "I find it very odd that you haven't called this witness *before* now."

Gus groveled. "I apologize. She only confessed this morning after she'd heard the rumors about the trial. She's terrified of Serena—we didn't want to push her to testify if it was unnecessary."

"Unnecessary?" Baird echoed; that one word carried a quiet question and a reproach.

I glanced over. Elain was squirming, Gus was sweating. But Baird said nothing; he only continued to dissect them with his hard stare.

Nathan snapped out, "Well, who is this witness?"

"Rebecca Price."

"What are we waiting for?" Nathan demanded, both fists hitting the table. "Go fetch the girl. I, for one, want to hear her testimony."

I watched Elain scramble toward the back of the Hall. A loud creak resonated as the heavy oak door opened, and a wave of sound crashed over me. My assumptions had been right, then—there were people gathered outside the doors, waiting to hear the verdict. A steady rise and fall of inane chatter reached my ears. There were a few concerned whispers, but the majority seemed excited.

A sickness churned in my gut. Did they want to see me burn?

The noise died as the door closed, and a petrified sixteen-year-old appeared. Rebecca's plain face looked bloodless, and her soft brown hair was falling into disarray as Elain hurried her up the aisle.

"Thank you, Elain, but I believe the girl can probably walk by herself," Gertie said, her weathered skin wrinkling with anger.

Baird nodded wryly. "Indeed."

Elain murmured something in Rebecca's ear and gave her a little push toward the elders. Baird pursed his lips at the movement, but kept quiet as Rebecca approached, hands clasped and head angled away so that when she passed by me, she avoided eye contact. She didn't stop walking until she was in front of the high table, a few paces ahead of me.

"Rebecca Price." Baird peered down with clasped hands and a grim mouth. "Gus and Elain have told us you witnessed Serena Smith meeting with a fae. Is this true?"

In a squeaky voice, she replied, "Yes, Chief Elder. Last month—the night Henry Baddock went missing—I was gathering logs from the wood pile outside our house. Then I saw a light coming from the woods ... it called to me."

"That's when you saw her?" Dr. Fagan asked, a little too eager.

"Yes." Blinking fast, she continued in one breath to say, "I don't know how long I followed, but when the light dimmed, I heard voices—"

"Was it a fae?" Dr. Fagan asked, the light of conspiracy in his eyes.

A pious fool. A zealot and a mystic. The surgeon had that reputation.

Rebecca nodded fervently. "Just one. She was talking with Serena," she said damningly. "I couldn't hear what they were saying, though."

"Are you sure it was Serena you saw that night?" Baird pressed.

"Yes."

"Even though the light had dimmed?" Nothing got past Gertie.

Rebecca stumbled over her words as she said, "Yes. The moon was bright—"

"If that was the night Henry went missing, then the moon would've been full," Nathan intervened.

Gertie wasn't deterred. "What did the fae look like?"

I prayed her interrogation was a sign of skepticism, and that she at least recognized the rehearsed nature of Rebecca's testimony. Gertie had a fierce reputation as a cranky old woman, but if she helped me, I'd love her forever.

"Beautiful," Rebecca mumbled. "Much more beautiful than a human. She had golden wings. Oh! And the pointy teeth."

Unable to contain myself any longer, I interrupted. "So, you were close enough to see this fae's teeth, but not to hear what was being said?"

Gertie snorted. The others, however, didn't look impressed.

"Yes," Rebecca's said in a very small voice.

I persisted despite Nathan's glare. "You knew about Henry going missing, so why didn't you tell your father or the council about what you'd seen?"

Rebecca squeaked, and for a split second her eyes darted to Elain and Gus.

But Baird caught everything. He leaned forward and barked, "Rebecca! Has someone told you to say these things? Has anyone threatened you? Because if they have, we can protect you. You wouldn't be punished for your testimony today. But if we discover that you've lied to us later, the consequences will be severe."

"Speak the truth, child," Gertie said roughly.

Rebecca whimpered and wrung her hands together.

"Please," I murmured to her back, "whatever they've said or promised to do, don't help them destroy me."

Rebecca burst into noisy tears, crying, "I was an idiot for following the light—I see that now. It was like I was under a spell, and I said nothing ... because ... I ..." she trailed off, making loud *uh-hu-uh-hu* noises.

Elain ran forward, put her arm around her, and dragged her in close. Quite a show.

"There, hush now. Please, forgive her." Elain looked up to the elders, a pleading note entering her voice. "Rebecca's terrified of Serena. That's why she hasn't said anything before now."

Rebecca wiped her eyes while hiccuping. "Yes ... that was why."

Viola huffed something under her breath that sounded remarkably like, "How convenient."

I squeezed my eyes shut. This had to be a nightmare. It had to be.

"Very well," Baird said with an exasperated sigh. "Thank you, Rebecca."

Baird instructed Timothy to take Rebecca to one of the back rooms so she could recover her damned poise.

I opened my eyes to see Timothy ushering her out. My gaze traveled to the elders, and knowledge gripped my heart, rendering it still and cold. The council would find me guilty.

Baird stood, sounding plain tired as he said, "The council must deliberate. We shall retreat to our chambers. You are all confined to this room until we come back with a verdict."

He led the others one by one into an adjoining room. Once gone, John and Viola rushed forward and I got pulled into a three-person hug.

"Everything will be all right," Viola said, rubbing my back.

The tremble in her voice betrayed her true thoughts.

"No. It won't," I whispered.

They both pulled away. Viola could barely look at me. John moved to block my sight of Gus and Elain. "Don't despair," he began, clapping a hand on my shoulder. "Baird's a good man. And call me naïve, but I don't believe they can find you guilty on such flimsy evidence. A blind man could see that Rebecca had been coerced."

They were empty words, and we both knew it. Fear twisted me up, and another spark heated my throat. My hand flew to the gem. I whispered, "Viola, I thought I felt something earlier, and it just happened again—my mother's necklace was burning. That can't be normal, can it? D'you think—" I didn't dare utter the word "magic," with Gus and Elain in the same room, so I went with, "Is this the protective power you were talking about? Is it sensing I'm in danger?"

Eyes clouded with worry turned to confusion. "Your mother never warned me about anything like that. Don't think about it for now."

She reached up and brushed my hair away from my face. A soothing gesture that made my eyes prickle. Gulping down the emotion that threatened to strangle me, I choked, "If they find me guilty ..."

"Shh, it'll be fine." Viola drew me into an even tighter hug than before, and John put his arms around both of us. We stayed like that, frozen in a bubble, ignoring the odd rumbling coming from Elain and Gus, until a door creaked open. We broke apart and looked up to see the elders filing back into the Hall.

I thought they'd move back to their seats, but they came to rest in front of the long oak table instead.

"Serena Smith," Baird started gravely, and my heart slammed into my lungs, forcing the air out in a shaky exhale.

"We've weighed the evidence against you and in the matter of the assault, we've reserved judgment. Despite your confession, we cannot find you guilty when you're claiming self-defense. As it's a matter of your word against Elain's and Gus's, we're dropping the matter for now."

"What?" Gus hissed. "I could've been killed! I want to see some punishment!"

All he got was a scowl from Baird. "This is our judgment, and you will respect it if you wish to remain in this village."

A disgruntled mumbling followed.

Baird faced me again. "However, we have an eyewitness claiming to have seen you in fae company. Rebecca gains nothing by speaking out against you, and while some among the council remain skeptical of the girl's reliability ..." His nostrils flared a touch. "There was a vote, and the majority have found you guilty of consorting with the fae, and of being a changeling. The sentence for this is often execution—"

My knees almost gave way.

"But I do not believe this to be the answer, and the council agrees."

I breathed again.

"It would accomplish nothing in the long term. So, we will place you in a wagon cell and drive you into the woods. You will stay there for three days; we hope that if you are a changeling, they will sense you and see that you can't help them anymore. If the past is anything to go by, tonight they will seek to take another child, but instead take you, or at least take our treatment of you as a warning to stay away. With any luck they will move on, leaving the children of this village in peace."

I gaped. Disbelief and panic rippled through my body. "I'll die," I said stiltedly, struggling to remain upright. "The cold will kill me before any fae can."

Baird sighed through his nose. As if irritated. "You'll have blankets, provisions, and a bucket to last you the three days."

A *bucket?*

Viola's chin rose an inch. "What happens after three days?" she asked, her voice smoldering with repressed anger.

"We haven't been able to agree," Baird replied in an annoyingly calm voice. "But while the council have voted guilty, we are not murderers. If you are still in the cage after three days, we will bring you back to face judgment."

Gus scoffed, "You've all gone soft."

A small furrow appeared on the Chief's wizened brow, but his gaze did not move from my own. "However, I must warn you, Serena, that given the mood in the village, exile may be the only judgment left to us."

The tattered ruins of my life caught fire. My stomach roiled in horror at the thought of my fate: locked in a cage for three days, and *if* I was lucky enough to avoid attracting the fae, I faced separation from the only family I had left.

I'd crawl and beg to avoid that fate. "Please, have mercy! I know some of you don't agree with this." Gertie's lips tightened, confirming my theories. "I'm no changeling. You're throwing me out into the woods to die! And why? Just because I'm an orphan with no father or husband to protect me, you'd throw me to the wolves in the place of another? This is a sacrifice, not justice!"

Nathan bent over a little and hissed, "Be grateful that we're dragging you into the woods and not to your execution, changeling."

I recoiled. No surprises who'd voted against me, then.

"Hear, hear!" Gus cried. "What of the families of the lost children? Don't they deserve justice?"

Baird shot a sharp look in his direction. "Silence."

No one breathed. The Chief turned to Nathan and said in a low rumble, "I make allowances for you because you are in pain. But you will not go around riling up the villagers, do you hear me? I won't have a mob on my hands."

Nathan appeared mutinous. Castiel's cool, even voice rang out. "If Serena is a changeling, what do you think would happen if we executed her? The fae may not welcome half-breeds, but executing one of their own is something they might find hard to ignore. They could slaughter us, or gods forbid, take all the children."

Nathan's mouth shut tight at this, his face a picture of resignation.

"Serena Smith," Baird called.

Recognizing it as a summons, I clenched my fists and let the pain from my biting nails take the edge off my mounting hysteria.

"Castiel and I will drive you into the heart of the woods."

Trembling, I breathed, "Now?"

"Yes, for your own safety if nothing else."

"Safety," Viola echoed bitterly.

Gertie explained. "The families of the abducted children may let their grief get the better of them," she said, angling her body toward Nathan.

Baird nodded once. "Indeed. As long as you are here, you will be in danger. Now, say your goodbyes."

He stepped out of the line of elders with Castiel beside him. They waited for me.

I turned and hugged first John, then Viola who whispered in my ear. "You're stronger than you know. You *will* survive, d'you hear me?"

There was nothing more to say. I glanced between them, trying to paint their images into my memory. "Take care of each other."

I got two very strained smiles in answer.

From the corner of my eye, I noticed Castiel inch closer, so I forced myself to pull away from them.

Gertie snorted and snapped from behind me, "Elain, as you are so fond of reminding us, Serena is your daughter—have you nothing to say to her?"

"Of course, I'm terrified of what might happen to her, but the lies she's told today are hard to forgive."

Gertie's voice held only contempt. "You betray yourself. I realize now that you've never felt any affection for your stepdaughter. There you sit, content to watch her be exiled without so much as a teary farewell, when her true mother stands beside her."

I watched as Elain struggled and failed to hold her apologetic, simpering demeanor. Brown eyes met mine, and that angelic face hardened. Eager to put distance between us, I spun and nodded at Castiel to show the way. Viola let out a strangled noise, and tears filled my vision, but I didn't look back.

Baird joined Castiel in leading me toward the warren of back rooms.

I kept my spine straight and shoulders stiff as I followed. It took all my strength to stop from flinging abuse or falling to my knees and begging them to reconsider. What would be the point?

Castiel held the door open for me while Baird disappeared around the corner. Anger washed through me: nice to know he still observed the niceties while sending a girl off to her doom.

I entered a narrow hallway with dark paneling, and the sounds of Viola's muffled sobs vanished as the door closed behind me.

Castiel pointed to the far end of the corridor. "That's the way out."

Baird had gone through. Castiel was obviously staying behind to guard me. I almost laughed. There was nowhere to run to.

We came out into a side alley where a prison wagon and two heavy horses waited. Gods, when had they set this up? Had they decided on the verdict before the trial even started?

The cage was made of dark iron bars, with a flat roof. I breathed a little easier. Snow and rainfall were common this time of the year, and a roof would limit my exposure to the elements.

"I believe Timothy should've gotten you everything you need," Baird said while grabbing the horses' reins and jumping into the driving seat of the wagon.

Should have. My rage trembled and blew out, leaving behind a cold, sick feeling.

Castiel drew out a key from his smock and walked to the back of the wagon. He opened the door to my prison.

Numb, going through the motions, I stepped up into what would be my home for the next few days. I flinched as the key turned, locking me in. The cell hadn't been made with tall people in mind. Wanting to avoid the inevitable crick in my neck, I sat down and did a quick inventory: a pile of moth-eaten furs, a bundle of woolen blankets, food packets wrapped in brown paper, twelve skins of water, and, of course, the afore-mentioned bucket. I shot it a reproachful stare.

Were they really expecting me to squat in that? *Bastards.* Old, senile bastards.

I watched through the bars as Castiel went to jump up next to Baird.

"Walk on!" Baird commanded.

With a snap and a flick of his wrists, he swished the reins down onto the horses' flanks. The wagon creaked forward.

That jerking movement had the angry, sad, hopeless tears I'd been suppressing rolling down my cheeks, staining them with salt. I curled up into the blankets, hiding from the people who, despite knowing me their whole lives, had just condemned me to being trapped in a stinking cage in the heart of the forest under a full moon. I probably wouldn't even last the night. Because if the fae didn't get me, the cold, or the spirits rumored to roam the forest might. My morbid imagination raced forward to three days from now. Someone from the village would come to check on me, but there would be nothing but clean-picked bones, or a frozen corpse. The council had lied: no matter what the charges, this wasn't punishment or exile. I was the bait on the end of a stick—a nice juicy pound of flesh. To the villagers convinced of my guilt, it must've been a blessing. Spare the innocent children by offering the orphaned oddity instead.

The only question left was if the fae found me ... what would they do?

CHAPTER 5
THE CAGE

It turned out that traveling through a forest in a prison wagon was slow, bone-jarringly uncomfortable and *tedious*. The sun peeking through the canopy marked an hour passed with nothing to do but listen to pine needles cracking under wheels, and heavy snorting from horses. Every jolt of the wagon resulted in me being thrown bodily about the cage. Grabbing ahold of the bars and bracing my feet against the floor were the only things that stopped me from being smashed to bits against the hard iron. Yet the resulting sickness was unavoidable, and for the first time, I found myself grateful that my stomach lay empty. The thought of sitting in my own vomit for days without reprieve sent a shiver down my spine.

I veered between wanting to reason with Baird and Castiel and screaming myself hoarse, but the will to do either had left me. I decided against begging. It hadn't worked during the trial; why would it be any different out in the forest? And deep down, I didn't want to give them the satisfaction. This streak of stubbornness had gotten me through years with Elain, so maybe it would see me through this too.

Mindlessness swept in as we went deeper into the forest. I watched the pattern of trees shift, and instead of young pines and silver-barked saplings, there stood ancient oaks and proud, tall firs.

The wagon finally slowed and shuddered to a stop. A splinter of panic cleaved through my senses as Baird jumped down and Castiel unhitched the horses. He didn't say a word; he only moved to lead the bay Shires back to Tunnock. But Baird stopped and faced me. "We'll be back in three days."

There were so many things I could have said. It was my chance to plead for mercy. All I said was, "If I don't make it, can you tell them to get on with their lives?" I hoped Baird knew who I meant. Saying their names might just break me. "Just make sure they know I love them."

"I will." He nodded, perfectly grave. "Good luck, Serena."

He left, hobbling down the track made wider by the wagon. As the forest swallowed sight of the two men, my pride died enough for me to whisper so that only the wind could hear me say, "Come back."

I SAT ROOTED to the floor for over an hour, watching the path, willing them to return. When nothing happened, pain pulled me from numbness and plunged me into survival mode. For my lack of movement had caused a brittle stiffness to settle into my limbs, accompanied by a bone-deep cold.

I took stock of my surroundings: spring still hadn't bloomed in this part of the forest. The minute the sun dipped below the horizon, the temperature would plummet further.

My father had drilled how to survive the cold into me long ago. The basics being eat and drink and if you can't move, conserve warmth. Given the dimensions of the cell, proper exercise was out of the question. That didn't stop me from doing light stretching to warm up. Extending my legs to the length of the cage, I flexed.

Point toes, retract. Point toes, retract.

After a few more sets, I moved on to massaging my arms and legs, encouraging blood flow. The tension locking my muscles eased a little, but it wouldn't be enough to save me when darkness fell.

Fuel was next on my list. I grabbed one of the brown packages containing food and tore into it to find dried oats and nuts. Grimacing, I wolfed down handfuls, not stopping to taste them. It wasn't filling, but I thought only of rationing my supplies, so I moved on to the water. I picked up a bottle and took two sips. Just enough to quench my thirst.

A few minutes passed as I gathered every available blanket and fur, and arranged them to make a nest of warmth. During this rummage, my numb fingertips came upon a pair of mismatched mittens and a red scarf. I thought of Timothy and smiled. A small act of kindness, and he'd never know how much it meant to me.

I slipped the gloves and scarf on and snuggled into the furs to prepare for a night spent in the freezing cold.

Time slipped into a stream of drip, drip, drip. Sleep proved elusive as the light dimmed. I sighed heavily. Winter still held sway, which meant it was probably only six AN, or After Noon. I had a long night ahead of me. Of course, if I'd been home, I'd have been eating right about now.

My belly rumbled as if in protest. Food plagued my thoughts until twilight passed and night descended. Not wanting to rip into another food parcel, I scrambled for something to occupy my mind with. That soon failed, and boredom set in.

The more I dwelt on my situation, the more absurd it seemed. My impatience ticked up a notch, and when a series of howls echoed through the forest, I came to a decision. Burn the elders—I refused to be their rutting bait.

I threw off the furs and fumbled in the dark for the bars. I pushed against them, testing for any weakness. My father had probably built this cage, so I doubted I'd find any. Still, I had to try.

The iron didn't yield to my efforts. But I was a blacksmith's daughter —I knew my best bet lay with the lock. Lying down on the floor of the cell, I put an arm out on either side. I held onto the bars and kicked out. All the blows were intended to bust the lock.

Ten minutes passed and not only were my legs trembling, but my brain felt like it had shaken loose of its skull. I took a breather, resolving to get back to it as soon as my limbs had stopped twitching.

Snap.

Adrenaline flooded my system and my muscles clenched in alarm. I sat up, ears straining, waiting. Another snap filled the air. It sounded like tree branches cracking under foot. The moon was a perfect sphere, hanging low in the sky. It cast an eerie glow over the woodland floor, but not enough to illuminate what, or who, was out there.

My pulse pounded in time to my whispered words: "It's just an animal. It's just an animal."

There was that snap again.

A light blinked in the distance. It moved toward me through the trees, growing brighter every second.

My mouth went dry. I was too deep into the forest for anyone to hear me scream.

"There you are." A chill scuttled down my spine.

Fear set my pulse screaming; its heavy, frantic beat rang in my ears. I shrank to the back of the cage.

Gus's face came into view with the help of a lantern. "Did you think I wouldn't find you? Even a blind man could spot this wagon's tracks." He slunk over, dissecting me with a look. As if he were a wolf sure of a slaughter.

Words failed me as the lantern danced within touching distance of the cell.

Fight. Don't cower like a frightened rabbit. The voice came from inside, and yet it retained such a *separateness*, that I knew they weren't my thoughts.

With no time to puzzle out this riddle, I braced myself. "Congratulations," I mocked; his eyes narrowed to slits. My courage roaring to the surface, I added, "But the only good thing about being locked in this cage is that you can't get in here with me."

"Aren't you forgetting something?" he murmured, and my blood ran cold. "I helped your father build this thing."

His onyx hair and thin face pitched into shadow as he held the lantern aloft, using it to illuminate the lock. An unmistakable jingle followed. My heart did a feeble flip-flop of dread as he raised a bronze key.

"This cage is Halvard's design; we still have the mold in the forge." His eyes lit up with his characteristic taunting style, intermingled with fury. But with Gus, his rage never presented like passion. There was nothing inflamed behind it, only a detached, steely wrath that came from nowhere. Somehow, he'd always felt more dangerous because of it.

The scrape of the key's metal against the lock had my nerve endings on fire. "Did you know we have orders for two more of these cages? It's been a nightmare trying to keep up with the work; I often wonder whether it was worth helping Elain kill Hal."

My emotions broke, sending my thoughts scattering. A lie. It had to be.

Easy now. Think. Once he opened this cage, I'd be at his mercy. He needed me unbalanced; the only thing that could save me was a strategy: a plan. It'd be harder to escape if my heart pulled focus.

A half-baked idea formed just in time. The lock clicked, and I lurched forward, crashing into him. Gus dropped the lantern and staggered. I was too light, and he recovered faster than I could run. An arm snapped out and grabbed me by the waist. Having caught me in his snare, he spun me around to face him.

I screamed and struggled so rutting hard, but he wouldn't be denied again. He squeezed me in a death vise, constricting my chest until I gasped for air. Leaning in, his breath kissed my cheek. His voice laced with violence, he said, "I've learned my lesson, Serena. I won't underestimate you again."

I wanted to retch.

Thrashing harder now, I aimed for his groin. He wrestled me to the forest floor. I tried biting the arms that pinned me to the frost-glossed ground—it did nothing but make him spit out a laugh.

He grappled for the hem of my dress and I kicked out viciously. He batted my leg away and walloped me in the stomach. Agony crippled me. My eyes watered, but I didn't scream. There wasn't time. He'd dealt me a blow, but he'd also loosened his grip. His first mistake.

Before he could stop me, my fingertips had found the dropped lantern. Swinging it upward, I smashed it into the side of his face. The lantern shattered, and the light extinguished. His resulting scream pierced the air, echoing through the skeletons of the winter-bare trees. I writhed and wriggled out of reach, scrambling off into the dark as he clung to his bleeding face. The strength of the moon's light saved me from running headlong into trees, but it didn't stop the roots and branches underfoot from tripping me. Through a mixture of stumbling, flying, and falling, I put distance between me and the stream of curses Gus screeched at my back.

Fear made me fast, but not fast enough.

A hand snaked out and caught me.

Exhausted, I whipped around and flung out a wild punch. Before I could connect, an arm blocked mine. Gods, the *strength* of those arms.

"There's no need for that."

My body stilled: it wasn't Gus. It was much, much worse. A fae man. The storm-gray wings gave it away, as did the second set of lethal-looking canines retracting back into his gums. He wore a mixture of green and brown leathers, lined with fur and cloth. The daggers at his hip and the bow and quiver at his back promised violence.

Stunned into submission by golden peach skin, delicate features, and his liquid, dark eyes, my mind failed to register his tentative smile. Having grown up with half-starved farmers and loggers, it was difficult not to compare. Even with boys like Timothy, it was different. Very different. Their good looks came from a certain ruggedness, whereas this stranger exuded something else entirely. The legends of the fae didn't do them justice.

He let my punching arm go. I swayed, and the man's—the *fae's*—arm darted out to steady me.

That touch was a spark, waking me up. I'd allowed him to distract me. I swallowed hard. He was danger and death. This was what they did: seduce, beguile, manipulate.

"Where did you ..."

I couldn't even finish my damned sentence. I was in so much trouble. He moved, his hand settling on my lower back. What was he going to do? Would he hurt me? He didn't look terrifying.

"Come on—I'll take you somewhere safe."

His arm slid to my wrist, gently leading me away. Now reeling from shock and the death of my adrenaline, I forgot to fight him.

It took a minute to orient myself. Finally, snapping back to my senses, I pulled away and blurted out, "Are you working with Gus?"

"Gus?" A curious tone: a question.

"You're taking me back in the direction of the cage. The man I was running from, you're not helping him?"

The stranger's head cocked to one side with polite incredulity. "I've never worked with a human, but if I did, it wouldn't be a rapist."

"If you don't know him, how d'you know about what he ... tried to do?"

"Your cries drew me. If I'd had any doubts of his intentions, your scent would've told me everything I needed to know."

I let out a strangled noise. "Scent?"

"You're terrified," he said, gesturing up and down my body. "But you don't have to fear me. I don't rape or abuse women. I'm a hunter, not a monster."

"A hunter?" I said stiltedly. "What exactly do you hunt?"

The silence stretching between us filled in the blanks. My body started to shake. "Oh, stars, you're the one snatching the children."

The fae's delicate brows met, creating a small frown. "Yes, but like I said, there's no need to fear me. I've always stuck to taking the runaways and outcasts, like you."

My heart slammed into my chest. "What do you do with them?" My voice dropped to a whisper. "What will you do with me?"

"Take you to our realm."

I lost my mind. Like a frightened deer bolting, I spun and ran. I didn't make it three feet before he'd caught me. I struggled, dug my heels in, but only succeeded in almost tearing my arm from its socket. It had no effect on the fae; I may as well have been fighting stone.

The fae twisted me around, scooped me into his arms, and set off running. He didn't so much as blink when I beat my fists against his chest. Boiling with panic and fear, I zeroed in on his face, poking at his eyes and pulling his hair.

Next moment, my finger was between his teeth. And I made an unpleasant discovery: he didn't even need his second set of canines. His first set were perfectly sharp.

"Enough," he said, his voice muffled by my finger still jammed between his teeth. He hadn't even broken stride. "I don't want to hurt you."

"How can you say that?" I asked, incredulous. "You're kidnapping me."

He had the audacity to look only mildly sheepish. "If I release you, do you promise to stop attacking me?"

"Do I have a choice?" Silence. I sighed, irritated. "Fine."

He released my finger. Before I could think better of my promise, he said, "Maybe you'll trust me when I tell you that Gus had already set out after you when I arrived; I stopped him catching up to you."

Another surprise. If he was telling the truth, then he'd saved me. Something niggled at me though. "What d'you mean you stopped Gus? Where is he? Are you taking him to your realm, too?"

"Filth like that?" His features scrunched up in disgust. "Never."

The fae halted and set me down. "My hunting companion might've considered him for our armies, but it'd go against my nature to let him cross. Fae males protect. It's our first instinct, even before fighting and hunting."

"Male," I sounded out, rolling the strangeness around on my tongue. "Not 'man'?"

"We're not men." His jaw clenched, but the line of his mouth was soft. "And you don't have to worry about him hurting you again."

The fae pointed to the ground. I turned—we'd arrived back at the cage.

I blinked rapidly, taking in the scene. There was Gus, his ribcage on display, his internal organs splattered across the grass, his mouth frozen in a silent scream.

Such silence filled my head. Then, the smell hit. A kettle spitting out steam sounded in my head. A wave of wailing, terrified, throat-tearing screams started up.

I wasn't aware it was me howling until the dark-haired fae moved to block my view. He was pulling me away, shaking me.

Suddenly, there was another fae by his side. This one was female.

Slap.

My voice splintered, and a roaring began in my ears. Disoriented, my hand went to rub my stinging cheek.

"Hunter, you chose this one, seriously?" the female snapped. "She seems touched."

The male fae, named Hunter, shrugged his shoulders and said, "She's in shock. It'll pass."

I could only gape in horror. Gus was lying not six paces away, split open from throat to groin, disemboweled, and this monster was shrugging it off.

The female *tsk*ed, looking exasperated by her companion. "Your weakness for damsels in distress will ruin you one of these days."

She was tall with ebony skin and gray wings that were more bat-like and even deadlier-looking than the male's. Her skin was ageless, but the severe set of her mouth and confident jut of her jaw aged her. Her clothes and weapons were identical to Hunter's. The entirety looked like a uniform.

Her hand shot out, grabbing my chin in its steely grip. I jerked away, but her fingers clutched short strands of my hair. A fierce *yank* had my head falling back. With the other hand, she fixed my chin in place. The female gripped hard enough to bruise. It seemed the tales told in the village were true: the fae were stronger than us. That didn't stop me from biting down when she went to peel my lips from my teeth. The female huffed a laugh. "Girl, you can cooperate, or I can snap your neck. Which would you prefer?"

The instinct to survive ran too deep, and my pride guttered. I stilled and said nothing. I wouldn't struggle, but I refused to answer her. She held me there, and like a farmer surveying livestock, checked my hair and teeth. And then she leaned in. Wincing, I angled away, afraid she might bite, but she just took a quick sniff and released me.

"No lice or disease, but she stinks of fear and grief and brittle anger. I don't care about the first two, but an angry slave is a dangerous slave."

My bowels turned watery. *Slave.*

"She's got fire in her. That's not a bad thing," Hunter corrected, assuaging her damning claims. "We could take her to Diana's training camps."

"Don't be stupid," Kesha scorned. "She's got no muscles. She wouldn't last a day, let alone make it as a foot soldier."

Hunter stepped in closer. I flinched but didn't move away. What would be the point?

But he didn't touch me. He only leaned in long enough to take a deep sniff of my neck. He backed off, and if I hadn't known better, I would've said he looked almost apologetic.

Hunter faced the female. "There *is* fire in her blood. Better to sell her to Diana's armies as a foot soldier, where she can channel it. She wouldn't do well in the other training camps or as a domestic."

The female tilted her head, scanning me, weighing, appraising. "I don't smell a male on her, and given her age, she's probably unseeded. The brothels would pay extra for that."

Unseeded. Vexation and disgust choked me.

"Kesha," Hunter growled.

The female who Hunter had called Kesha rolled her eyes and crossed her arms. "Fine, but she's your responsibility. And when the training camps don't take her because she's a weakling, just remember— I warned you." She snarled and turned with an enviable grace.

As she quickened, Hunter lifted me into his arms and followed in her footsteps. Unflagging in his sprint, we traveled through the forest like an errant breeze. Movements assured, he never made a misstep or stumbled in the dark. If I hadn't known they were fae before, it would've been all too obvious now.

Despite being trapped in the embrace of a killer and a slaver, the fear from earlier in the night faded. I hated to admit it, but being out of the cage and warm in the fae's arms felt like an improvement. I might've even been thankful for the rescue if not for the little fact they planned on selling me. And while Gus's mutilated body would haunt my nightmares, I wasn't sorry he was dead. Some dark animal instinct whispered that he wouldn't have stopped at violating me—I doubted I would've seen the dawn if not for Hunter.

At least with the fae, there would be time to escape. They certainly seemed invested in keeping me alive, even if only to profit from my sale. Although, just why they needed human soldiers eluded me. As did how I'd slip away with two fae watching my every move.

A stranger's voice echoed, *That's not the right question.*

My body clenched in unease. The words echoed as if from a distance. I couldn't be sure, but the voice sounded feminine, if unfamiliar. *Who is that?*

The question you need to ask is where would you go?

What are you talking about? Who are you? How are we speaking like this?

This time there were no answers. Repeating the words to myself, understanding dawned. Whoever—or whatever—had spoken, had seen what I hadn't. There'd be no going back to the village. After what I'd confessed to the elders about Gus, they'd never believe I hadn't helped slaughter him. I wouldn't even get exile, not that that was so appealing: cast out to live in some foreign place, my only choices of livelihood being back-breaking labor, or selling my body. No, the punishment for murder was the same as witchcraft: death by fire.

Where did that leave me then? Hopeless. That's where.

Embrace what is before you.

What does that mean?

Again, silence. I loosened a breath. Hunter must've noticed my agitation because he asked, "What's wrong?"

"Would 'everything' be a good answer?"

He didn't speak, nor did he look at me. The only sign he'd heard was a faint crease between his eyebrows.

Annoyed by this—forgetting he could rip my throat out with his teeth—I glared up at him. "Sorry, is it somehow difficult to understand that a person might not want to see a mutilated corpse and then be kidnapped into slavery?"

"No," he murmured. "But take my advice. I might like your spirit, human, but others in my realm—Kesha, for instance—won't be as tolerant. You should try to embrace this new life. I can't promise it'll be easy, but it might be better than you think." Lowering his voice, he added in a whisper, "Better than being locked in a cage."

I opened my mouth to argue, then closed it.

That word: *embrace.* Embrace a life as a slave? As a soldier? Had that been what the voice meant? I waited for a confirmation that never came. Frustrated and confused, I swore to stop listening to cryptic truths from an unknowable source and trust my instincts instead. They'd kept me alive so far, and right now they told me to watch, learn, and ask questions. Given that Hunter had admitted to liking me, it couldn't hurt to make an ally. So I tempered my voice and said, "Don't call me 'human.'"

The moon's glow showed the angles of his face softening as he smiled. "What should I call you then?"

"Serena."

"A beautiful name."

I didn't stop to wonder at that. Too many questions filled my head. "Where are we going?" I dared to ask.

"North, to the crossing and the divide between our realms. I've heard the humans refer to it as, 'the bridge.'"

Hoping for a timeline to come up with some sort of plan, I asked, "How long until we get there?"

"Two days, maybe. Our hunt's over with for the month, so we'll set out at first light."

So soon. My curiosity got the best of me. "Why first light? Why not straight away?"

His lip curled at that. "Fae need rest, too."

Tucking that information away, my attention turned to the apex of his wings. Every human in the Gauntlet knew the fae realm lay north. Viola's maps and history books had contrasting views—some depicted an impassable bridge as far as the eye could see, extending out to sea, and others spoke of a door in the woods or a giant rainbow connecting the lands. The histories agreed upon one thing: the bridge lay weeks away from the northern settlements.

"How are we getting there so fast? Are you flying us?"

He let out a low, gentle laugh. "No. We can only carry one human at a time, and we've taken too many to fly to the crossing."

My stomach dropped at that, and Hunter dipped his head slightly, as if expecting more questions. "How then?" I didn't bother elaborating.

"The humans in the Gauntlet have forgotten much about us, but the land remembers. There are old fae roads that are still open to us. We'll take those."

I almost snorted. Evasive much? Still, I picked up the scraps he'd given me and turned them over in my mind. When I'd gleaned what I could, I went to ask another question. "You say we've forgotten things about you, but the legends got some things right, didn't they? Like the fact you're stronger than us."

His lip twitched up expectantly. "What else do the tales say?"

"That you can hear a pin drop in the next room, and see in the dark, as well as any beast. Your teeth ... your teeth can tear the throats from your victims."

"Fascinating," he said, his voice quivering with suppressed laughter.

"I want to know what else you can do."

"Maybe another time."

I tested how far I could push him by asking, "Why not now?"

"Because we're close to camp."

Hunter slowed, and a makeshift base appeared. Kesha had vanished, but there were three sleeping humans curled up next to a campfire. Two appeared to be young boys, and the third, a woman, looked to be in her late twenties. Two chestnut horses grazed nearby.

Hunter gently lowered me to the ground.

I rounded on him. Struggling to keep my voice even, I said, "I'm guessing you didn't find them locked up in the woods by villagers."

A muscle tweaked in his cheek. "No."

That line between needing an ally and wanting to kill him blurred. "You seem ... nice. Why would you steal children from the people who love them most?"

He frowned and pointed to the smaller of the two boys. "An orphan."

I looked down at the sandy-blond hair peeking through the blankets and felt a stab of pity.

"Runaway." Hunter motioned to the larger boy on my left. "Judging by the bruises on him, he had good reason to flee."

The runaway had brown hair and a dirty face. Pity found me again.

"And what about her?" I asked, looking to the black haired, honey skinned woman sleeping across from me.

"She was accused of witchcraft and sentenced to death."

I considered Hunter's words. As far as I knew, the children taken from Tunnock hadn't been abused. But who knew what went on behind closed doors? No one had ever seen through Elain's loving façade.

"You said you only took outcasts. Are there other fae kidnapping humans?"

"Yes ... And there aren't many of us who try to only take the unwanted."

My breath caught. "What about Kesha?" I asked, guarded.

Hunter's wings stirred at his back. "She goes along with it because it's less dangerous to take outcasts. Fewer people come looking." He tilted his head, considering. "And since human mobs wielding pitchforks and kitchen knives pose little threat to us, it's better all-round if we try to avoid a slaughter."

I winced. "How thoughtful."

The sarcasm in my voice wasn't lost on him. He looked confused, almost sad, but before he could form the words, Kesha interrupted us.

"Hunter!" She appeared carrying more wood. Dumping it next to the fire, she glared in our direction. "Enough chatter."

A flicker of something ghosted into Hunter's eyes. I thought it might've been hesitation, but then he dragged out a small vial of liquid from within his brown overcoat.

"Drink it," he said, passing me the crystal vial.

Eyeing it with suspicion, I asked, "What is it?"

"It'll send you to sleep—like them," he said, nodding to the slumped bodies around the fire.

"I don't want—"

"And we don't care what you want," Kesha barked.

Hunter scowled at Kesha. "Just drink it, Serena," he added quietly.

"Take it, or we'll force it down your throat," Kesha snapped. "Is that what you want?" She came to stand in front of me, hands on her hips.

"It's for the best," Hunter breathed.

I peered down at the clear liquid, hesitating long enough for Kesha to lose patience. Before I could lift a hand to defend myself, she'd lurched forward to force my mouth open and pinch my nose. Caught in a grip like steel, pain streamed out of my eyes in the form of tears. Liquid coated my tongue, and Kesha clamped my jaw shut, ensuring I didn't spit it out. I choked and retched, but it was too late.

I slipped into a nightmare: trapped in a winged cage with the bloodied mess that had been Gus, and outside was Elain, rattling at the bars, laughing at me.

The dream shifted, and the trial was happening all over again, except this time Elain and Gus were gloating about having murdered my father. Instead of punishing them, the council laughed and laughed.

Then there were ravens everywhere, surrounding me, never touching; forming a protective circle.

CHAPTER 6
THE CROSSING

The smell of bergamot, peppermint, and salt clawed up my nose. Jerking awake, my eyes fluttered open to find night had become day. I was flat on my back, covered by a wolf pelt.

Hunter was by my side. He tucked a small bag into an inner pocket of his overcoat, saying, "Sorry, you weren't waking up. I had to use smelling salts."

My mind, still fuzzy from the sleeping potion, grappled for a sense of time and space. "Have we crossed over?"

My tongue felt thick and heavy in my mouth.

"No."

A whoosh of relief.

"You need sustenance," Hunter said, placing a flask against my lips.

Parched and unable to refuse, I opened my cracked lips and managed a few mouthfuls. The rest of the water dribbled down my chin. I started to choke; Hunter rolled me over onto my side.

"Easy," he murmured, patting my back.

I coughed in to the dirt and reached back to snatch the flask from Hunter's hands. I took more sips, hoping it would ease the retching. When the convulsions subsided, I peered up at Hunter. "Please don't tell me you're putting me under again?"

He slipped his hand to the back of my head, cradling it, and then pulled me up to sitting. Letting his hand drop, kneeling in front of me, he replied, "I have to do it again. We haven't reached the divide yet. I woke you because we can't let you get dehydrated, and I thought you might need to relieve yourself."

I fidgeted. "Oh."

"Kesha will take you somewhere you can have privacy. We know these things are important to humans."

I hadn't noticed where the female was before now, but at the mention of her name I peered around for signs of her presence. She was to my left, tending a black pot in the middle of a lit fire. The other prisoners were sleeping, and the horses still grazed.

After a quick scan of the area, I realized we'd moved on since last night. The trees were now abloom in bud and stem, and the frost underfoot had given way to spring grass.

I frowned, perplexed. If my schooling had been right, the climate should be colder, more inhospitable the farther north we went. Tunnock still slumbered in winter's grip. Yet wherever we were, the bitter snap in the air had melted into mildness. Did this anomaly have something to do with the old fae roads Hunter had mentioned? Had we somehow bypassed the northern wastes?

The tantalizing smells drifting from the pot that Kesha stirred reached me, driving all thoughts of this mystery from my mind. When had my last full meal been? Not the bag of nuts or the pie.

Sniffing hopefully, my stomach groaned in protest.

"Kesha—" Hunter began.

"Yes, all right," she grumbled and let the ladle drop. "Come on then. I don't want to be clearing up your piss."

Kesha stalked over and pulled me to my feet. I wobbled dangerously, like a newborn finding its footing, and only managed a few steps before she lost patience. She dragged me a short distance, and as soon as we were out of Hunter's sight, she shoved me into the dirt.

"Be quick about it."

Gritting my teeth, refusing to feel embarrassed, I pulled up my skirt. At least she had the decency to turn around. After I'd finished, Kesha hauled me back to where the pot lay over the fire. Hunter transferred ladlefuls of hot stew into a wooden bowl and handed it over without a word. I went to sit on my wolf pelt and brought the watery stew to my lips. I slurped my way through it, savoring the taste, trying to postpone when they put me under again.

My mind hatched and played out different escape plans. All died a swift death after reaching the same obstacle; if we were on fae roads, in their territory, what would happen to a human traveling alone? How could I hope to navigate them?

You can't.

My spirits plummeted as the voice put an end to my hoping.

You could just help me instead of killing off all my ideas.

I already did.

Telling me to accept slavery isn't helpful!

No answer. Fine. Just rutting fantastic.

Hunter ducked down beside me and gave me a tentative smile. "Not hungry?" he asked staring at my half-empty bowl.

"Yes." I clutched the stew tighter.

His smile curved up into a grin, and he dipped his head. That made me think of Timothy who I'd always had a soft spot for. Not romantically; I saw him as the younger sibling I'd always wanted. Something of his sweetness lived in Hunter ... Yet they'd both aided in ruining my life.

"Are you okay?" Concern wove into his frown lines. "You look ... Are you in physical pain?"

"No, why would I be?" I took another tentative slurp of the stew.

"We can't carry you all, so we use the horses. I thought you might be feeling the effects."

My eyes darted to the animals. "You put us on their backs? How d'you even keep us on?"

Kesha marched over. "We slump you on their backs with the supplies and hope they don't bolt." Looking down at us, her mouth hardened into a thin line. "Finish that stew. It's time for you to go to sleep."

"Can't I stay awake just a little longer?" I directed my question to Hunter but Kesha answered.

"You should relish the chance to rest. Training to be a soldier grunt isn't easy, even in Diana's camps." Kesha's lip curled, and for the first time, I sensed her contempt wasn't meant for me.

"The drug is only for today and tomorrow," Hunter said mildly.

That was what worried me. Freedom was looking less and less likely.

"Eat up," Kesha growled.

I flinched and decided nothing would be gained from not finishing it. Once I'd drained the bowl, Kesha swapped it for more sedatives. Not wanting to go through another repeat of last night, I downed the vial and threw it aside.

~

THE NEXT DAY started out as a repeat of the previous. Hunter woke me up and Kesha accompanied me into the woods to relieve myself. The decision to use this moment to risk running had formed during sleep. As if my dreams had chosen for me.

I waited until she'd turned her back to me but I didn't get two steps before she'd pounced. She carried me back to their camp and smashed my body to the ground, knocking the air from my lungs.

It was a miracle I didn't wet myself.

My second attempt at freedom was even more desperate: I refused to drink the sedative.

"Fine." Kesha shrugged. "Hunter, hold her head back."

He didn't hesitate. I tried pleading with him anyway. "Please, don't do this. Let me go."

No response. He just held my head steady and pinched my nose. I could tell he was trying to be gentle, but I didn't care. I glared into his eyes and damned him. "You'll burn in the dark court for this."

He was silent, but Kesha snarled, "You know nothing, human."

She pried my mouth open, poured the poison in and held it closed, waiting for me to swallow. All the while Hunter kept his hand over my nose. I struggled, but it was hopeless. It was over. The next time I woke, I'd be parted from John and Viola.

Permanently.

With that knowledge a sob choked me, and the sedative slipped down my throat, burning as it went.

~

"Serena. We've crossed."

It took a whole minute for those words to sink in. My eyes remained closed—it was easier to pretend it was a nightmare that way. I had no clue what to expect once I opened them. There were no maps of the fae lands in the Gauntlet. The history books said they'd all burned when our peoples divided. I knew one thing; it should be impossible to move freely between our realms. The fae had somehow managed it, but I'd never heard of a human returning from their fabled kingdom. No descriptions of the place existed. Curiosity struck, but I remained stubborn and fixed the image of John and Viola in my mind's eye instead.

Kesha was at my side, nudging me with her foot. "Get up!"

"Serena?" Hunter called softly.

I hesitated. The minute my eyes saw their world it would be real: me, parted from my surrogate family by a bridge no human knew how to cross.

"I know you're awake," Kesha growled in warning.

My resistance crumbled—I wasn't about to push her. Sitting up, my eyes opening, I swiveled left and right and drank it in.

A path of flattened grass trailed behind, marking our passage through what was another wooded area. I breathed in its scent, sweet and earthbound with a hint of sharpness that cut through and made me feel *awake*. The temperature was pleasant, if a bit cool. Not winter, then. Autumn colors painted the forest: gold and ruby with a spattering of emerald and silver bark, but that telltale whisper of decay was absent. It looked like autumn and felt like spring.

Pine cones, fallen leaves, and sparse groupings of spotted toadstools, foxgloves, sorrel, clovers, and lavender covered the ground. Thanks to Viola's tireless attempts to give me a broad education, I knew what was edible and what was poisonous. It seemed my lessons wouldn't be a total waste ... if I ever got free.

I squinted upward, noting the sun's high position in the sky. Midday, or close to it, which meant the bridge couldn't be far. Even without food or water in my possession, I might survive the crossing.

You'd have to find it first, the voice reminded in a whisper.

Hope died. Grief burrowed into my chest, crippling me. I'd known the truth for days but hadn't wanted to admit it. Now, there was no getting away from it. I'd had my roots torn from under me, and fate had handed me a permanent exile. Even if I found a way back to John and Viola, I'd only land them in an impossible situation. Hide me and risk punishment, or leave with me and lose everything they'd worked for. That sudden awareness moved something inside me. A barrier crumbled; acceptance lay on the other side. Tunnock was no longer home.

Not realizing I'd closed my eyes amidst this inner turmoil, I opened them again and blinked. Tiny golden firelights floated above me, and weaving in among them were creatures with faces and bodies too small to make out individual features. Their wings, however, were gloriously visible and akin to butterflies, a few carried bright bursts of blue, others pale yellows, and some appeared so opaque they looked like spots of light dancing in the breeze.

My mouth popped open in surprise.

"What are they?" I wondered aloud.

At the sound of my voice, the creatures and balls of light scattered. When Hunter and Kesha didn't react, I looked over to find them rousing the other humans in our company.

The first to wake was the woman. I stared as she sat up, squinting in the brightness. I inched closer to her as Kesha and Hunter moved to wake the two boys. "Are you all right?" I muttered under my breath.

She frowned in my direction and nodded once. "Are you?"

I shrugged.

"What's your name?" She had a soft lilt to her voice that instantly made me feel at ease.

"Serena Smith. What about you—what's your name?"

I peeked over at the two fae, feeling jumpy. Hunter hadn't confirmed whether their hearing was better than humans, but given their other advantages, it seemed likely. If they had heard, they didn't acknowledge it.

"Isabel." Her troubled gaze slid to the boys. "We should try to help them ... adjust."

I didn't have time to agree before the smallest of them was sitting up, wiping away sleep. Kesha left his side to mutter something to Hunter, and with their backs to us, I sidled over to him.

In a gentle tenor, I introduced myself. "I'm Serena. What's

your name?"

He viciously gnawed on his lower lip. He was terrified.

"It's okay, we're human. No wings, see?" I twisted, showing him my back.

His eyes scanned and when satisfied, he leaned forward with wide eyes. "I'm Brandon."

He retreated quickly and his eyes snapped to Kesha and Hunter, tracking every movement as they continued their hushed conversation. The sight sprung a well in my chest. Emotion poured out. He looked like a boy waiting to be hit. My sorrow sighed and tipped over into pity.

I glanced toward Isabel to check how the other boy was coping. They were whispering, but I caught his name anyway: Billy.

"Are we definitely in the fae lands?" Billy piped up. "It doesn't look that different."

He spoke directly to the fae and showed no fear. My hero.

Kesha met his interruption with a scowl, but Hunter replied, "Yes, we're in fae lands, but seeing as this is your new home, maybe you'd like to call it by its proper name—Aldar?"

His lip twitched into a tiny smile. Stars, he was *trying*. I wanted to hate him for it, but somehow, I failed miserably.

Billy, however, continued as irreverent as ever. "This isn't my home." He stopped to consider. "Why would I call it Aldar?"

His curiosity had won out. Mine piqued when Hunter's straight brows knotted together. "Have the humans forgotten the name of our kingdom too?"

No one in the Gauntlet knew the name of their kingdom—that knowledge was long gone. When Billy didn't answer, Hunter peered between Isabel, who looked lost in thought, and Brandon, who flinched underneath his scrutiny, before finally locking eyes with me.

Still. Hesitant. Maybe, a glimmer of pain and remorse.

The memory of last night and what I'd said lay between us. With one gesture, I could widen the gap or heal the rift.

An awkward mix of emotions battled to the surface: savage triumph at having gotten under his skin, intermingled with twinges of unease for having cursed him.

He had saved my life. Sort of ... And accepting exile didn't mean I wanted to become a slave. Understanding this land and how it worked seemed essential to my survival and eventual freedom. Therefore, I still needed that ally. Decision made, I didn't turn from him. I let my features visibly soften.

Relief, quick and bright, flared into his eyes. He even dared a little smile. I tried to return the favor, but it came out as more of a grimace. It seemed deciding to forgive someone and feeling it in my heart were two very different things.

Hunter didn't seem to notice my hesitation; his smile born of uncertainty now looked relaxed and easy.

"Where've the horses gone?" Billy suddenly demanded, staring around.

Shock tugged at me. I hadn't even noticed the silent beasts' absence.

Kesha bared her teeth. "We ate them."

Brandon gasped. But Billy crossed his arms and glowered. "No, you didn't. I can tell when someone's lying."

Isabel and I exchanged worried looks. There was bravery, and then there was this.

Yet despite his attitude, Kesha restrained herself and Hunter replied, "Useful talent." His eyes sparkling with hidden mirth, he went on. "You are quite right. We left them in the human realm."

Billy gave an assured little nod and declared, "I'm hungry."

"Why don't you hunt something for lunch then?" Kesha said, a little too quiet for my liking.

A child—a boy not even in the grips of puberty—stared down the vicious hunter of humans and folded his arms. "I don't need to."

"Oh, and why's that?" Kesha rolled out in a deadly purr.

"You've got wings," he said, jabbing his finger damningly. A tad redundant, considering how her wings extended from the top of her head to her tailbone.

Cool amusement drifted across Kesha's face: the look of a cat playing with a mouse.

A laugh bubbled up in me like fizzy wine and hysteria threatened. Clenching my jaw and pressing my lips tight were the only things saving me.

Hunter's nostrils flared delicately, and for a second, the whites of his eyes showed. Gods, what had he smelled? Tension hung heavy and thick in the air, but before the storm could break, he dove into a rucksack that lay on the ground. He pulled out an apple and threw it toward Billy. Not stopping there, he threw one to each of us.

"Eat quickly," he said, intending the words for everyone but directing them at me. "We have a long road ahead."

Isabel twirled the apple in her palm, thoughtful. "You told me you were taking me to other witches, but you never said where, exactly."

Her question implied, she didn't stray from being polite, causal, and non-threatening. Masterfully done. Not even Kesha could take offense.

"I'm taking you to the Witch Court," she answered begrudgingly. "Although its true name is the Crescent. The Wild Hunt has agreed not to sell your kind to the markets, so we deal directly with the clans."

The most words I'd heard her use. And *Wild Hunt? Clans?* Stars, there was a lot to learn about this realm.

"What are they going to do with me?" Isabel asked quietly.

"No idea. It's not our job to know," Kesha shot back.

Brandon shuffled closer. I wrapped an arm around him and tucked him in close.

"What about me?" Billy asked stoutly.

After a nervous sidelong glance at Kesha, Hunter picked up the conversation. "We're taking you and Brandon to the markets in the Solar Court. The military might buy you—they're always looking for new recruits. Or if the nobility takes a liking to you, they'll take you on as part of their household."

"Hunter, enough." Kesha grabbed one of two huge packs and shouldered it. "We need to cover good ground before nightfall, and I'm done conversing with these bags of meat."

My hand twitched, itching to punch her square in that jutting jaw of hers.

"I don't want to be sold," Billy said. No fear. Just grim words.

My heart broke for him. He'd seen too much already. An old soul trapped in a child's body.

Hunter's lip turned down. From pity? Or irritation? "You'll have a better quality of life than if we'd left you to starve and beg on the streets."

Contempt swept in. Was this how he justified it? Did he think if he took outcasts it made it all okay? That he was a hero?

My hands clenched. *Fool.* Stupid, naïve fool.

Billy's thoughts seemed to match my own; his chin lifted a touch and his eyes tapered. "I would've been free."

Isabel's gaze touched mine. I read the unspoken words: *This boy is too smart for his own good.*

"Free." Kesha sneered. "To do what? Die from hunger in some shit-stained town while the humans do their best to ignore you? Interesting idea of freedom you've got. Now, eat your apple." A low, dangerous tone.

Billy tilted his head to one side, considering. After the tense standoff, he condescended to take a bite.

A sigh of relief left my lips. I started in on my own apple. Praying this wouldn't be our only meal for the day, I devoured it in four big bites. Once water went around us humans, we were ordered to march.

An hour went by. The woods and path underfoot didn't change much, apart from the odd new smell or burst of color. I kept watch for the return of the golden lights and tiny winged creatures, but there was no sign of them.

Hunger soon clawed the insides of my belly. Blisters formed and erupted inside my boots, causing me to gnaw on my lip in agony every few steps. I grew too hot for the mittens and scarf, but I couldn't bear to toss them aside. I carried them for a time, until Hunter dropped back and took them from me without a word. But even without them, sweat clung to me in my plain, rough dress. I did the math—four days without a bath or a change of clothes. The stink would quickly become eye-watering. With the fae sensitivity to smell, I wondered how they could bear to be so close. Although in Kesha's case, I welcomed causing her discomfort.

Things continued to deteriorate, moving in snail-time. When the light softened to an afternoon glow, cramps disabled me to the point where I was leaning on Isabel, hopping along the path. But my discomfort was nothing compared to Brandon's and Billy's. As the sun waned, starvation and exhaustion made Brandon miserable enough to complain to Hunter. Not Kesha though: never her.

Not long after that, Billy made two escape attempts. I hadn't seen the fae move like that in daylight, and it quickly become clear why they didn't bind our hands or shackle us. Their wings meant that he only had to run as far as the trees before he was caught. On Billy's second attempt, Kesha lost her temper.

"ENOUGH!" She caught him by the arm and flew back to the path to drop him at our feet. Addressing all of us, she snarled, "Clearly, we've let you believe you might escape. But you are human." She stabbed her finger down at Billy. Making a fist, she brought it to her chest and beat it once. "We are fae. If you test us again, you'll find out why we're the apex predators in this group."

She bared her teeth. Brandon squeaked in terror but Billy didn't flinch, not even when her canines grew and sharpened.

"Kesha," Hunter called from farther up the path.

There, a warning. But he didn't stop her when she pulled Billy up and bit down on his shoulder. He cried out in agony and my blood boiled.

Isabel and I moved at the same time. "He's just a boy!" she cried out.

Kesha growled in her throat. "Quiet."

We stopped. And didn't so much as breathe when she glared down at Billy. "Try running again and I'll break your arm."

After that, there was no more complaining. All Isabel and I could do was help the boys when they stumbled, uttering words of encouragement. I felt empty, saying the same platitudes over and over again.

"Don't worry."

"We'll be fine."

"This'll be over soon."

Lies. I'd no idea how long it would take. I couldn't imagine surviving a week at this pace, or gods forbid, more. But we had to keep moving, so I went on lying.

We came to a stop as the sun dipped low in the sky, casting a lilac and rose-colored tint over the woods.

"We need to hunt before we can make more stew. Until then, get some rest. Do whatever you need to do," Hunter told us, winking in my direction.

Kesha scowled at him as if his cheerful manner was offensive.

I needed to pee desperately, but the thought of spending more time with Kesha made me swallow my embarrassment and ask Hunter to accompany me instead. "It's okay. You can go alone if you like. Just stay within easy reach. These woods aren't as safe as they look."

My jaw slackened. He was that confident? My question got answered, not by him, but Kesha. "Remember, our hearing is acute and we can take to the skies before you can blink. Don't be stupid."

I'd guessed right about their heightened senses then. Too uncomfortable to care, I sprinted for a clump of bushes that looked dense enough to hide me. It wasn't until I hitched my skirts that I noticed Isabel had followed me. Sensing an opportunity to communicate without the fae seeing us, I squatted down and wrote in the dirt.

Use magic?

It had to be short, to the point, and a message easily rubbed out if Kesha or Hunter checked on us. I just hoped she'd understand.

Maybe she'd had the same idea about talking because she didn't wait for me to finish before crouching down next to me.

She read my message. One breath and then a shake of the head. No.

My heart sank, and she made an apologetic face. But Isabel wasn't done. She pointed toward the fae, clasped her hands in the prayer position, and rested her head against them.

Sleeping, I mouthed.

She nodded and then wrote in the loose earth, *Steal weapons?*

My mouth tugged to one side. Mere seconds to choose and everything to lose if I got it wrong. Weighing the odds, I balanced the probability of success against the much more likely possibility they'd wake and Kesha would break all our bones, one by one. I didn't need the stranger's voice to *tsk* in my head to know it'd never work.

I looked to Isabel and mouthed, no. She gave me a grim smile in response, as if she'd known it'd been a bad plan and only needed a second opinion.

Once we'd relieved ourselves, we walked back to camp, and I went to sit next to Brandon, while Isabel settled near Billy. Without discussing it, we'd somehow agreed that we'd guard them. We couldn't stop Kesha from hurting them, but the instinct remained.

Currently, Kesha was sitting cross-legged, eating a foreign kind of pastry roll. It became difficult not to stare outright and drool. I'd noticed both fae had eaten several pieces for themselves throughout the day.

"Do all fae like sweet things?" I asked Hunter.

His eyes lit up, and his mouth parted.

"Hunter!" Kesha snapped from her position on the ground. "Don't tell her anything about us. She can learn what she needs, once she's delivered to her new owners."

My temper flared. "I'm a person. I can't be owned."

Isabel shot me a wild look. I didn't care: Kesha had touched a nerve. Too many people in my life had tried to own me.

For the first time, a ghost of a smile touched Kesha's lips. "Live for a couple more decades, and you'll see that is incredibly naïve." She wiped crumbs of pastry from her mouth and added darkly, "Now, we've still got miles to cover over the next few days. So, unless you want me to pull your tongue out by the root, quit whining."

Emboldened by my outburst, Isabel murmured, "How long until we get there?" Her eyes flitted between the boys.

Kesha continued to eat her pastry and ignore the question.

I swore I heard Hunter sigh in exasperation. "It takes about a week to travel to the market," he said. "Once we've sold the boys, Kesha and I will split up and take you and Serena your separate ways. We'll be carrying you, so that journey won't take as long."

"Carrying us," Isabel wondered aloud. "You mean you're flying us there?"

My mouth swung open and stayed like that.

"Of course. It'll be quicker and more comfortable for everyone."

"Can't you fly on ahead with one boy and then come back for the other? That would be just as quick." She didn't need to add, *and better for them.* Her real reason was obvious from the way she peered over at Billy's and Brandon's ashen faces.

He wore a bemused expression. "We need to stay together. It's too dangerous to separate."

As if that should be obvious. The fae couldn't be all powerful, then. Their strength must have limits. Interesting.

"There are outlaws and outcasts hiding in these woods. Some among them wouldn't be able to resist capturing you."

That made me ask, "Why? What do they want with us?"

Kesha growled low in her throat. Having finished her pastry, she shifted and pulled out a whetstone from an inner pocket. Then she unsheathed one of the knives at her hip and started to sharpen.

Everyone went silent, eyes glued to the dagger.

Hunter broke the hush. "It depends. They might want recruits, or if it's just money they're after, they'd sell you on the black market."

I smothered the urge to scan the woods for invisible threats and instead, shifted nearer Brandon.

"Lazy, dishonest, *faithless*," Kesha muttered while her dagger sparked against the whetstone.

"The Wild Hunt's the only pack that can travel between the realms," Hunter continued mildly, the cool head to Kesha's raging temper. "No one else has permission, so some fae choose to hang around the border and attack those returning from the Gauntlet to make a quick profit."

The odd words and turns of phrases tumbled around in my mind. *Pack. Permission*, granted by who?

"Leeches," Kesha cursed.

I traded another silent exchange with Isabel. Neither of us mourned that their jobs would be made harder, but still ... Viola loved to say, "Better the demon you know, than the fae you don't", whenever she'd play cards with village gossips. It didn't quite work now, considering both our enemies were fae, but Hunter wasn't so bad. It could always be worse. Gus and Elain had taught me that.

"Anyway," Hunter deviated, "maybe you should all try to nap. Dinner will still be a bit of a wait."

Groans of agreement had Hunter unpacking the hides and blankets we'd slept on. Once I'd climbed onto the wolf pelt again, I looked down at my boots. My blisters had blisters, but if I took them off now, I might never get them back on.

I loosened a breath and lay down. It was too much effort anyway.

Moments before I passed out, Hunter threw a blanket over me and whispered, "I'll wake you in a few hours so you can eat."

I mumbled something and had just enough time to wonder at his confusing blend of kindness and cruelty before drifting away.

He was true to his word. But my body felt too heavy with exhaustion to move once he'd woken me. Then Hunter was there, putting one arm under my neck, pushing me into a seated position. "Come on, you need this."

I opened my eyes and took in a twinkling blanket of velvety blackness stretching out overhead, a blazing fire in the center of our camp, and a bowl being shoved under my nose. My stomach clenched painfully, and I thanked him before thinking better of it.

Hunter flashed me a bright smile and placed it in my waiting hands. I raised the bowl to my lips, sipping greedily.

"Don't get attached," Kesha scolded from behind us. "She's not a pet; she's an object we're selling."

Hunter rolled his eyes at me. I almost giggled.

I checked myself. Monster or not, he was a kidnapper: a murderer.

Hunter straightened and went to fill another bowl to offer a still-napping Isabel.

It promised to be a cold night despite the spring warmth that had blessed the day. I basked in the taste of the meaty stew, rolling it around on my tongue. It was bland but hot, and therefore, delicious. I watched on as Billy, Brandon, and Isabel received their own dishes.

"This again," Billy grumbled.

"Be glad we're feeding you at all," Kesha said, poking at the fire with a stick.

I bit my tongue.

If what Hunter had told us proved true, I'd be parting ways with Kesha soon. Another week was nothing—I'd put up with Elain for years.

Done with the stew, I set the bowl aside. I had every reason to believe tomorrow would be more of the same, so I didn't want to waste a single second not sleeping. Lying down, I let the crackling fire and soft whispers of the others act as a lullaby. It was on the verge of a sleep-induced haze that I noticed the whispers taking on a more clipped pitch.

Some embedded instinct, now sensitive to all manner of horrors, made me force my eyelids open. Hunter was standing, staring out into the forest. Kesha did the same while *slowly* stringing her bow.

Isabel, still awake, stared hard at the two fae. I waved my hand up and down violently and caught her eye. She shrugged: she didn't know what was going on. Thankfully, Billy and Brandon hadn't noticed anything and appeared to be sleeping, having inhaled their food within seconds.

"What ..."

Kesha cut off Isabel, hissing at her.

I pushed myself up onto my knees.

Hunter ran to me, leaning in to whisper, "Wake Brandon up, but keep him quiet. We have company."

He pulled back to stare down at me, awaiting my response. I nodded to show I'd understood, and then he left to tell Isabel.

I moved closer to Brandon's side and bent down to shake him, ever so gently. Eyes fluttering, he mumbled, "What ..."

I clapped my hand over his mouth and breathed into his ear, "It's Serena. You need to be quiet. Hunter says we're being watched."

Brandon's arms instantly reached out and tightened around me. I pulled him up into a hug and stroked his hair, as much for his comfort as for mine. I had vague memories of my mother doing the same thing—I still dreamed about it.

My gaze darted to Isabel and then to Billy, who was wide awake, looking solemn. The gap between us bothered me—something told me we'd be safer together.

I said into Brandon's ear, "Should we move closer to Isabel and Billy?"

He nodded his head against my shoulder. So, with him still clinging to me, we shuffled around the flickering fire. Isabel and Billy watched us with grim faces. As we moved into touching distance, Isabel reached for my hand and Billy pulled Brandon closer. I wasn't sure if we did it intentionally, but we ended up huddling together, making a cocoon around Brandon.

Hoots filled the air. Hunter took a protective stance in front of us. Warnings about roaming fae packs rang in my ears.

Kesha hissed, but this time to Hunter. A signal.

She raised her bow skyward. Her eyes must've seen something in the gloom, because she released one.

A mocking laugh answered back. And all hell broke loose.

CHAPTER 7
THE WINGED FIENDS

A moment to wonder, a second of confusion, then red and blue fireballs sailed into view.

Hunter twisted to us. "Get down!" he cried.

Kesha moved like a whirlwind, stringing arrow after arrow. But nothing could stop the missiles from landing. Our tiny, insignificant huddle of four humans caved inward as the balls of heat and flame exploded on impact. Heat seared my cheek. Isabel and I tried to shield the boys as they clung to us.

Someone screamed. Isabel gripped my sweaty palm tighter.

I waited for the pain that was sure to follow ... only it didn't.

The chaos trickled in all around us. Left in the wake of the projectiles were smoking patches of scorched earth. These were centered to the right of me. They'd aimed for Kesha and blown her backward. Now, Hunter crowed in challenge. A series of howls answered back.

From out of the forest flew half a dozen masked fae, dressed in brown leathers, their masks resembling creatures of the sky and wood.

Hunter went for his bow. Stringing it, he unleashed himself. His aim was deadly. He'd pierced two sets of wings and sent the masked fae tumbling before their archers could even nock.

Then their bows answered back and arrows rained down. Hunter darted this way and that, dancing, playing with his enemy. None of the arrows found their target. All overshot or buried themselves in the ground in front of him.

The masked fae hovered. A whistle sounded. Hunter paused and looked to me with a fear that was plain and savage in its intensity.

A second whistle sounded and several things happened at once. The four fae still aloft split up. Three dove toward us, while the fourth fae stayed behind. His wings beating in place, he drew something bright and glistening from within his leathers. He threw it, and Hunter wavered just long enough to see it unravel in mid-air, spinning, spreading out into a giant silver net.

With one last agonizing look in my direction he unfurled his wings, speeding along the ground to Kesha. Once she was in his arms he flew, disappearing into the night. Abandoning us to the mercy of strange fae.

"He's leaving us," Brandon squeaked.

"Good riddance," Billy spat.

Harsh laughter rippled off the three fae who'd landed and surrounded our group, trapping us in place.

The male who'd thrown the net touched down. "Now that's my kind of human."

The fire behind us illuminated his face mask, which was fashioned in the likeliness of a hawk. He was tall and thin, with silver hair. I didn't dare move as he whistled again—I half-expected another net to appear and be thrown over our heads. Instead, lights twinkled into existence and lit up the gloom. My first thought was glowworms, but as they moved closer, their bobbing golden forms grew familiar. Like bees to honey, this swarm focused in on the net-thrower, dancing over his head as he bent over to pick up a thread of the net. With a graceful flick of the wrist, he twirled the silver mesh back into a ball and tucked it into an inner pocket.

He whistled low and directed the swarm over to the two injured fae lying at the edge of the forest. The firelights obeyed. They flew over to bathe the wounded males in an eerie glow as they struggled to get up. I couldn't see any arrows sticking out of them, but their wings were slick with blood, and their faces had become bone-white.

The hawk turned to our group and barked out commands. "Stag, take Badger and Wolf back. Bear, Fox, keep a watch out. Those wily bastards are still out there."

One of the fae guarding us leaped forward, lifted the one with the Wolf mask, and retreated into the forest's depths. Meanwhile, the one named Badger, who could just about stand, limped along behind them, struggling to keep up. And just like that, three of their group had gone. Since we hadn't broken free of even two fae, the remaining three may as well have numbered a hundred.

The net-thrower prowled over to us and bowed deeply. "Apologies. We haven't formally introduced ourselves. I am Hawk."

He waved to the others, signaling them to add, "I'm Bear," and then, "Fox."

They bowed one after the other, fists clenched over their hearts. Their names suited them: Bear had shaggy black hair and was large and hairy, whereas Fox was slight and had a mane of red hair.

"Please stand," Hawk said. "You need not cower in the dirt anymore. The Winged Fiends have liberated you."

Fae dressed up as woodland creatures bowing before us, lights glowing above us ... The whole thing had a distinct dream-like quality, as opposed to the nightmare it'd been only moments ago. Rattled and dazed, I stood. Isabel still held my hand while Brandon pawed at my other arm. I clasped his wrist and faced Hawk.

"Liberating us?" Isabel said by my side. There was already a hopeful lilt in her voice.

"Correct, Milady," Hawk answered with another solemn bow. "Your freedom awaits. We will take the two boys into our charge, but you women may go wherever you wish. Although, if you'll permit me, I'd recommend waiting for your two captors to find you again, as twisted and evil as they may be. This is no place for humans to be without fae protectors."

Something cracked. Anger built and built until I was a tower of smoldering rage. "How is that liberating us?" Close to shouting, I went on. "You're taking two children against their will and leaving the women to be recaptured!"

"Milady," Hawk said with an audible gasp. He actually had the balls to look offended.

"We're giving you a chance at freedom," he continued, gesturing lazily up the forest path. "It is up to you whether you run. As for the boys, we'd never take them against their will. Unlike the rest of our brethren, we cannot abide slavery. However, I would make them an offer they can't refuse. Unless ... you would stop them from listening to a simple request?"

I ground my teeth. Why, you *slippery, slimy—*

Hawk eyed Billy and Brandon. The former was regarding him with a thoughtful expression, and the latter flinched and leaned against me.

"You both seem like fine fellows, and I hate to be the bearer of bad news, but honor compels me to be honest, and if you *don't* come with us, you'll have to brave the markets, where they'll throw you to the mercy of a private buyer. Most of which treat their humans like shit at the bottom of their shoes, and that's the best-case scenario."

I wanted to intervene, but what if he was right? How could I deny them a chance to escape a life in chains?

"If you're picked and thrown into the Solar Court army, you'll be likely dead in a month. Now, let's say for a moment you do survive ... then your fate will be to die on the battlefield in service to that fae-witch, Morgan."

Bear and Fox hissed their displeasure. Apparently, the name was a familiar one.

"What's the alternative?" Billy demanded.

Hawk smiled at his stern features and folded his arms. "Come with us; make the forest your home." He motioned to the trees. "We have a few humans who live among us. They provide honest labor in exchange for our protection."

"How's that different from being a slave in the other place?" Billy challenged.

I fought back a smile.

Bear's laugh sounded like falling rocks. "He's got you there."

Hawk just smiled. "Because, unlike the fae you'd find in the courts, you won't call us masters, and you are free to leave us. Although, many don't choose that option. For what better adventure could there be than sleeping in the treetops with a blanket of stars above you? For that is true freedom, don't you agree boys?"

The wink that followed almost made me pull Brandon behind me. I'd seen his kind in my village. Every week, during market day, there would be the odd bawdy salesperson selling miracle cures, or claiming to see the future. They spun lies into wicked webs and waited for their prey to trap themselves.

I looked down at the two boys. Billy was frowning, but Brandon had stopped fidgeting. He even looked a little wistful.

"Why can't Serena and Isabel come with us?" Billy pushed. "They're good people—they wouldn't be a burden."

My chest warmed.

The one called Bear crouched and met Billy's glower head-on. "I'm sure they are," he said in a gruff voice. "But we can't take every human we come across, and we have too many women as it is. We don't have the room, or the food to feed them."

"Then let us come with you tonight, and we'll go our separate ways tomorrow," Isabel reasoned.

Bear straightened and fell silent. It wasn't his choice it seemed.

"Sorry," Hawk said in a hard voice. This sounded like the real male behind the mask, not the charming, gallant one he'd pretended to be. "We have to leave you. There's less chance they'll track us if we do. Fox, grab anything of value and let's go."

Fox went straight for Hunter's and Kesha's rucksacks to rifle through their contents. Next, I heard a cheery jangle and spotted him pocketing two coin purses.

"You don't care about our freedom." I squeezed Brandon's hand tighter. "You just want to rob us."

"My dear," Hawk began in mock outrage. "If I was as heartless as you make me sound, I'd cut your throats just to spite those wingless cowards."

He'd tried to hide it, but real anger simmered there. Interesting.

Brandon fidgeted. Worried Hawk's words were appealing to him, I added, "And if the boys went with you, what's stopping you from selling them on the black market?"

He inched closer. It was so deliberate, so careful, I knew it was a threat. All I could see were the eye sockets of Hawk's mask as he said, "I'd sooner starve myself and my people before I sold them on to someone who saw them as nothing but a set of body parts or holes to abuse."

His irises were the color of his hair: the silver of steel. Yet somehow, they were aflame.

"Stop it—you'll scare them!" Isabel hissed.

Hawk didn't acknowledge her. He kept his focus pinned on me. I didn't look away. "If you can't take my word, use your head. Why didn't I shoot the male down?"

"You missed."

Fox snorted loudly, and his flaming red locks swung wildly as he tossed his head in a clear sign of contempt. I ignored him.

Hawk continued in a low, lethal whisper. "Our archers are better than most. The first few times we had these raids, we rained death down upon them, but not before the Wild Hunt had used the humans they were transporting as shields. Even we weren't quick enough to stop them from dying."

I suppressed a shiver as a cloud passed over Hawk's eyes, smothering the fire that had been burning within.

Hawk took a step back and peered down at his fingernails. He pulled free a dagger from his belt and picked at the dirt beneath his nail beds. Another skin, another mask to slip into: boredom, irreverence. "We may not be willing to risk our necks to save you women from slavery. But every second we spare a member of the Wild Hunt is a second we're endangering everything we hold dear."

"Don't expect gratitude," Isabel breathed out in a fierce exhale.

Bear growled, making Brandon flinch.

"Enough." Hawk gave the order quietly, but it still caused a hush to descend. His head cocked. "We need to go. I can hear those two wingless nightmares preparing another attack. So, what'll it be, boys?" he asked, peering down at Brandon and Billy. "Come with us, or stay and roll the dice with your new masters?"

He was a master manipulator. Maybe he should wear the Fox mask. A moment of silence followed. Hawk sheathed his dagger and turned away, and that was all it took.

"Wait!" Billy took a step toward him.

Isabel grabbed at his mockery of a coat. It was the poorest of cloth, dirty, frayed, and coming apart at the seams. "You can't trust them," she whispered to him. "They're fae."

Hawk barked a laugh while Fox and Bear gave appreciative chuckles.

"I know," Billy admitted with a mournful shrug. "But I can't trust the other two either."

"Well said," Hawk crowed.

Billy cut a sharp look in his direction. "Did you really mean it? Would I be free to leave if I wanted?"

Hawk gave a curt nod. "You would—but to be clear, if you hope to go back, you won't achieve it. Only the Hunt know how to cross the bridge between realms, and trust me, others have tried. The more ruthless among us have even tried hunting the hunters, risking Morgan's ire, just to force them to show us how to do it. So unless you can do what the rest of faekind has failed to do, there's no hope in it."

Whoever Morgan was, he didn't elaborate, and I refused to admit more ignorance for him to poke fun at. I waited to hear Billy's thoughts on this, hoping he'd ask the questions I was too proud to. "Even if it were possible, you wouldn't want a human to go back, would you? You wouldn't want fae secrets coming out," he said, wearing his trademark scowl.

Fox gave an appreciative snort, although the Bear remained stoic.

Hawk's upper lip curled. "You're a smart fellow. You'll be a fine addition to our company. If that's what you want?"

A light, questioning tone. As if he didn't already know the answer.

Billy nodded, seemingly resigned to his fate. "I've got nothing to lose."

For the first time, I heard a note of grief. My heart ached for him. It'd become too easy to forget he was only a child.

Billy walked forward and joined Bear's left-hand side. Brandon shifted beside me again, causing me to pull him in closer.

"Excellent." Hawk stroked his chin. "Well, now we've filled our purses and we've bagged a recruit, I'd call that raid a successful one. Don't you agree, lads?"

Fox crowed, but Bear grumbled, "Let's go. I need a draft of ale and a fire to rest my wings by."

"You shall have it, my friend!"

Hawk clapped Bear on the back and turned to the forest. "Farewell," he said without a backward glance.

Fox bowed once more in our direction. Bear picked Billy up in his arms and prepared his brown wings for flight. Before the company could take to the skies, Brandon wrenched himself from my grasp and ran forward. "Wait, take me!"

Hawk whirled and spread his wings outward. They looked like Hunter's and Kesha's in they were bat-like, only his wings were an ungodly obsidian. But Brandon didn't even slow—he just held out his arms expectantly.

Hawk flashed him a fatherly smile and reached down, swooping him up into an embrace.

Isabel moaned, and I went to clasp her hand in solidarity.

"Take care of them," I murmured. I wanted to warn, to threaten, but they'd be empty words.

Isabel added, "I'm not much of a witch, but hurt them, and you'll wake up on fire."

That took care of that then.

Hawk didn't look remotely ruffled. "I'd expect nothing less. Good luck!"

He beat his wings, and Bear and Fox followed his example. The gusts of wind they created blasted cold air against my face and nearly blew out the flames dancing behind us.

The firelights returned to the forest, and we watched until the Winged Fiends disappeared into the shadow of the night.

Isabel cursed. "What now?"

My eyes locked onto the rough forest track we'd been following. "We should run."

She dropped my hand and stared longingly at the path. Turning her head with a sad shake, she added, "We can't just run off into the dark with no supplies."

Galvanized, I ran over to the plundered satchels and rifled through one. "These still have food in them—the Fiends only took the coin. It might not last long, but shouldn't we try?"

Isabel clasped her hands, twisting them. A second of doubt was a moment too long.

"I wouldn't do that if I were you," sounded Kesha's voice from above.

She was floating above with Hunter at her side, their wing-beats silent. As soon as their feet touched the ground, I straightened.

Kesha snorted in my direction. "There's no point trying to hide it."

I lifted my chin. "I wasn't."

"It's better that you didn't run," Hunter replied quietly. "We'd have to hunt you, and ..."

"My predatory instincts can get the best of me," Kesha added with a smirk.

Monster.

"Now they have the boys, we should split up," Hunter said pointedly.

"All hail, Freyta!" Kesha sounded genuinely pleased for once. "Finally, there'll be an end to this mindless drudge."

I peered over at Isabel, and her expression matched my own: despair.

Kesha continued, clearly eager. "We should head out now, then. We don't want to give any more roaming packs a chance to steal these two as well."

She never once looked at us. Hunter grunted in approval, and Kesha went to pick up her satchel. She peered inside and made a low growl in her throat. "The gold's gone—no surprise there."

A steady stream of curses flowed from her mouth as she attached her quiver and bow to her pack. She slung the whole thing over her shoulder so it seated nicely between her wing joints, and then lifted Isabel to prepare for their flight. Meanwhile, Hunter donned the other rucksack, kicked dirt over the fire, and before I could protest, had hooked an arm under my knees, braced my back and pulled me up, pinning me against his chest.

"Wait!" Isabel interjected. "Will the boys be okay?"

Kesha's lip curled. "No idea. Either way, it's not our problem anymore. They made their choice."

Isabel's mouth formed an angry line. Who could blame her?

"I'll see you at the rendezvous point next week," Kesha told Hunter.

"See you then."

Isabel's eyes bored into mine. She was saying goodbye. "If you're ever in the Crescent, come find me."

Kesha shot upward into the sky. I'd no idea where the Crescent was, but I shouted at their retreating forms, "Good luck! It was nice meeting you ..." I trailed off lamely.

I watched Isabel get swallowed by the night and a great weight pressed down on my chest again. I should be used to loss and loneliness by now, but I can't say I welcomed those feelings as they settled in like two unwelcome houseguests.

"Good job we're leaving. Shouting into the wind is enough to bring all the packs in the area running straight for us," Hunter remarked.

He didn't seem remotely upset; he was smirking.

Not in the mood, I muttered, "I'm pleased I amuse you."

My mood took a sharp turn toward fear as Hunter unveiled his storm-gray wings and took to the sky.

I gasped as my stomach dropped sharply and the ground melted away. The force of the wind breaking against my face made my eyes water. I shut them and leaned into Hunter's chest, soaking in the warmth from his layers of leather and cloth. He sped up, and I couldn't stop from groaning, "I feel sick."

"You'll get used to it," Hunter said with laughter in his voice.

"Doubtful."

I yelped as we got caught in an updraft, and Hunter's soft laugh tickled my ear as we climbed higher and higher. He was *enjoying* this. Ass.

CHAPTER 8
EMBRACE

My dizziness was over as soon as it began. We leveled out, so I dared to open my eyes and peek down. There was nothing but liquid dark—no glowing lights from villages or towns, no more firelights, just shadows darker than the rest. My guess would've been trees. I tried to use my other senses, but there was only the flap, flap, flap of wings and the air pressure rattling against my ears. After a few steadying inhales, the cold bit down deep and made my lungs feel like they were being impaled by shards of glass. Coughing, I gasped out, "If flying's always this uncomfortable, I'm not jealous of your lot one bit." I meant it.

Hunter let out a little laugh. "Look up."

I did. My breathing eased, and a knot loosened somewhere around my midriff, making way for wonder and exhilaration. The night sky was *alive*; the moon, full and resplendent and cloaked in its usual robe of silver; countless stars burned strong and bright in their usual iced white light, but unlike back home, there were also whole constellations painted pink, yellow, and pale blue. A heady feeling of desire surged; I wanted to reach out and touch them. Color and movement and light in perfect harmony—that's what this was.

How did that work? Were our lands so different? Or was this fae magic: some form of low trickery? It didn't feel that way. Instead, it struck me that I'd been looking through a clouded lens my whole life. That thought disturbed me, and a splinter of shame and embarrassment crept in. The world was so much bigger, grander, more *magical* than anything I'd imagined from my tiny cabin in the woods.

"Do you like it?"

"It's indescribable." It really was.

My eyes dropped to see a smile radiating there. My inhale broke apart—he forgot so easily. But I couldn't forget. I couldn't let my guard down. He'd fled from the Winged Fiends, leaving us to fend for ourselves. Not to mention helping to shove that sleeping potion down my throat.

His smile smoothed out into an earnest expression. "You can relax now. You're safe with me."

It was as if he'd reached into my head and plucked out the exact words I needed to hear most. *And* the ones guaranteed to antagonize me. My grip around his neck grew tighter, and my spine stiffened. "Oh?"

"Truly." Hunter stared and stared and didn't blink once as if willing me to see into his soul.

A flicker of heat warmed my throat, and with it my repressed thoughts came tumbling out. "Then why fly away when Hawk appeared? Are we so worthless that you'd abandon us? Now, Billy and Brandon are gone, and who knows if the Fiends will honor their word!"

"I didn't! You aren't! That's not what that was." Frustration was there, and maybe even something close to bewildered panic.

"Explain?" I wanted to give him a chance, if only to make the idea of turning him into an ally easier to bear.

"Serena, what is it you want from me? Did you want me to get captured and tortured?" A *tone*. Demanding. I thought there was something else, too; a hint of neediness, or exasperation. It was hard to tell.

"No, but you were doing fine until he got the net out ..."

"Those nets have lightning currents running through them."

I gaped up at him. That was possible? Stars, I knew nothing. And Billy and Brandon would soon live among fae like that.

"How?" My voice sounded faint and childlike.

"Magic," he uttered. "Not all witch clans wage war and worship the gods all day. Some are actually useful." The celestial light from above revealed his eyes searching my face, seeking my reaction. "Those nets are thanks to the crafting witches, but their weapons and allegiances are hard won because they're often crucial in times of war. That's why it's so disturbing to see an outlaw like Hawk with one." A crease appeared between his brows, and his hands tightened against my body.

His casual mention of wartime stopped me short. There hadn't been a war in the Gauntlet ... well, since we'd fought and ousted the fae, allegedly. Sure, there'd been a couple of peasant uprisings here and there, but *war*?

My silence didn't go unnoticed by Hunter. "I'm sorry for leaving you, Serena," he whispered my name. "Please, believe me that if it had just been about being outnumbered, I would've risked it. But when I saw that net ... I just panicked." He gave a rather violent flap of his wings. "I had a choice: I could grab Kesha or you. And the Hunt's despised in these parts. They would've killed her. Maybe even tortured her for information."

My attention piqued at this.

"Look, even if they'd taken you as well, you were too valuable to kill. We would've tracked you—*I* would've tracked you down."

His rising agitation made me brace my hand against his chest. Just a reflex, but it made Hunter's whole body tense; thankfully, his wings never faltered.

I pulled away instantly. I'd no desire for him to get the wrong idea.

"What was that for?" He sounded like he had a head cold.

"You were rambling. I wanted you to slow down for a second."

"Oh." Disappointment.

I squirmed at the words forming themselves on my tongue. "Hunter ... I don't blame you for choosing Kesha over me. We hardly know each other, and she's one of your own."

The vibrant night sky showed me his mouth pop open to protest or agree. I'd never know, because I continued. "I guess now that you've explained about the net, I understand why you ran."

He let out a heavy sigh, weighted with relief, but I wasn't finished. "And you seem nice—well, nice enough for a fae."

He chuckled at that.

"It's why I was so angry when you helped Kesha pour those sedatives down my throat."

His next wingbeat was off and we dropped a few feet. On pure instinct, I flung my free arm up and out to wrap around his neck.

"Sorry, sorry," Hunter babbled.

I said nothing. Shock kept my arms locked in place. That is, until he reached back and gently tugged my hand away. "It's okay, I just lost control—"

"Well, don't!"

He looked down at me. His lip twitched. Maybe it was the shock, but when he tipped over into laughter, I went with him.

The shadow living in my heart, the nightmare I was still living through, faded. Just for a moment.

Then, the laughter disappeared and a painful silence stretched ...

I cracked first. "You seem ... you are better than this. You have compassion. So, why do it?" I wanted—*needed* a serious answer; nothing else would suffice. "You have to know it's wrong? It doesn't matter if we're outcasts. If we don't come here voluntarily ..."

I hated manipulation, but I needed to tap into those protective instincts of his. So I went for the jugular. "How does that make you any different from men like Gus? He violated my sense of safety, my freedom, my body."

A low growl reverberated in his chest and throat. It was working. A whoosh of guilt. I continued anyway. "Don't be like him," I added, in a begging tone for good measure. "I know a human can't return to the Gauntlet by themselves, but you said it yourself, the Winged Fiends too; the Wild Hunt is the only pack who can cross."

A plan formed in the back of my mind. I didn't have an end game; I couldn't return to Viola and John, but wasn't life—any kind of life in the Gauntlet better than enslavement and probable death here? At least life in the human realm would make sense to me.

Hunter rushed out, "I know what you're about to ask of me, but even if I turned around, it would achieve nothing. The bridge isn't something I can cross on a whim. The only way to do it is by going through certain channels that keep us from going rogue and doing exactly what you're suggesting. I know you heard what Hawk said—about how some outlaws have tried to capture us. That's an understatement. Don't let their pretty speeches fool you: they're brutal when it comes to getting what they want. And yet, they never got it. Not because we couldn't break ..." He trailed off, either from sadness or uncertainty. I couldn't tell.

I tried to finish his thought. "You didn't break because ..." My mind whirled, fitting his words into a scenario that made sense. Fearing a worse punishment didn't quite feel right.

They've been bound to silence. Spelled. Either that, or they're just ignorant of the process.

The feminine voice sounded clearer. As her words sunk in, my mouth dropped. "Is something stopping you from saying? Or d'you not know how you're crossing over to the Gauntlet?"

Hunter's smooth flight rhythm was interrupted by a burst of speed. My gut roiled. When he slowed again, I groaned, "Unless, you want me to be sick, don't do that again."

He dipped his head to me and stared. "Sorry. You just surprised me."

I thought it was much more likely I'd made him nervous, but I didn't challenge him on it.

"Look ... I can't talk about this anymore." His stare took on a dazzling intensity. "D'you understand?"

I nodded mindlessly, too frustrated and miserable to find the words.

Hunter continued. "I'm sure you'll want to bite my head off for saying it, but I *really* don't get why you'd want to go back—"

"I wasn't planning on going home. They'd never believe I hadn't killed Gus, or at least helped you do it. If they caught me," I paused to gulp and wet my now bone-dry mouth. "I'd burn." The stark truth made me want to scream and cry and rage.

"Why would they think you'd help us? Or murder someone, for that matter?" Hunter asked softly, thoughtfully.

I had no answer for him.

He interpreted this as guilt. "Whatever your crimes were, they cease to matter. Our lands don't recognize human laws, you can tell me—"

I flushed hot. "I'm not a criminal!"

"If you're innocent, why did they put you in that cage?"

Sly ass. He certainly knew how to interrogate. The silence stretched between us. Expectant. Waiting. "Serena, please. Tell me."

I didn't want his pity, but the plea in his voice broke me. Maybe a part of me needed to say it. Viola always said confessing eased the soul.

I told him as much as I could stomach. My father's death, Elain's cruelty, Gus's first assault. I sketched out the basics from the trial and my imprisonment in the cage, not wanting to linger. Finally, I moved on to what Gus had tried to do, and what he'd confessed. That he'd helped my stepmother kill my father. I hadn't said it out loud before—I'd dismissed it as a lie. But after telling him everything in one go like that, it became painfully obvious: there was nothing they weren't capable of.

That truth ... it was too much to bear. Elain, my tormentor, had made me into an orphan. And I hadn't tried harder to make my father see her for what she was. Why hadn't I tried harder? *Why?* The answer came swift, shredding every leash and tether on my grief. I'd felt that if I kept pushing him, he'd choose her. Believe her over me. And if I'd been braver, louder ... maybe he'd still be alive. My every emotion came screaming, roaring to the surface.

Something must've shown in my scent, because Hunter gripped me a little tighter. "Serena?" A note of panic.

I couldn't answer him. I couldn't think. His body was too hot; too close. The air burned and clawed at my throat. Tears sprung beneath my lashes. One, two, and then the memory of his coffin being lowered into the dirt like my mother, years before, shattered me so thoroughly that angry, guilty sobs exploded out and cleaved the night. It was too much, too overwhelming: I collapsed into myself. With my body trembling, I clawed at my hair, pulling at it, wanting this to be over. I'd drown in this —I *wanted* to drown in it.

Hunter went into a nosedive.

My grief-stricken bones cried out in fear. And instinct took over. I reached out, clinging to him and burying my face into his neck, not caring how close it made us. We free-fell for longer than I could stand. When he did snap his wings out, the resulting jolt sent me into a coughing fit. Sick with adrenaline, I was now a hiccuping, sobbing, retching mess.

Hunter landed in the forest and nestled in among a tree's gnarled roots. His bag, his wings, and his quiver and bow now pressed into his back, but he didn't dump me on the floor or strike me in the way Kesha had. He kept me in his arms. "I know." His voice heavy, he repeated, "I know."

I believed him. Hunter had felt *this*—a sadness so intense it made me want to rip my way out of my body to escape the weight of it. And just like that, I was too tired to rage at the world. My head slumped against his chest and my body went limp, occasionally wracked with another hiccup. The tears still flowed whenever the memories forced their way back over the wall in my mind—the wall that eventually blotted out the emotions, letting blessed numbness take over.

We didn't move or speak for a long time. We just sat huddled together in the dark. If only John and Viola could see me now ... What would they think? Would they judge me—hate me—for not loathing a fae? For seeking comfort? Something told me ... no. Not if they'd gone through what I had in the last few days.

"I'm sorry," I finally croaked out.

"You have nothing to be sorry for. I shouldn't have pushed you to tell me those things." He sounded so sad. "All the same, I'm glad you did. I can sleep easier knowing when I knocked Gus out cold and left Kesha to finish him off, it couldn't have happened to a more deserving human."

"You—you weren't the one," I started, wonderingly. "Kesha did that to him, not you?"

"If I was going to kill him, I'd have snapped his neck."

Another piece of him settled into place.

"I never said thank you," I breathed.

His chin dipped a little, waiting.

"You saved my life that night."

"You're welcome." His voice grew hoarse as he added, "I know that to humans we're the monsters, but I have to be honest—your kind don't seem much better."

"They're not," I admitted, thinking of home.

"But it doesn't stop you wanting to leave." He was hesitant, questioning. Before I could say anything, he continued with deliberate slowness. "After everything you've gone through, wouldn't you be happier here in the long run?"

Gods, talk about twisting my words. I wriggled out of his grip and he let me. Vaulting upward, I strode a few paces away before turning to stare down at him. "Can't you see what you're doing?"

Nothing. I couldn't even see his face in the dark. Only the vague outline of a body. I directed my words and anger at that. "You're trying to justify your actions. You keep doing this! Pretending it's fine to kidnap someone by making this about how terrible things were in the Gauntlet. And this probably won't matter to you, but it wasn't all bad for me. I had people who loved me. Two people who took me in as their own." I wobbled, but surged on. "If I'd stayed, I might've seen them again. When you took me and force-fed me a sleeping potion, you stole that from me. You took the last shred of hope: the only good thing I had left."

Hunter sighed heavily. The rustle and crack of undergrowth made me squint. What was he doing? I tracked his outline as he moved out of the tree's shadow.

"What are—"

"Building a fire. It's Aldar springtime but the nights are still cold, and without my warmth, you'll begin to feel it in just that dress of yours."

My stomach dropped. "After all that, you're just making a fire?"

He didn't respond. Maybe I'd been wrong about him having a shred of decency. He was right about one thing. Now I didn't have his body heat to rely on, the night air was starting to chap. I rubbed my arms and jogged on the spot to keep the blood flowing.

A fire sparked to life in front of my eyes. I stopped moving and stepped closer, breathing in the smoky scent.

Hunter shoved a fragment of flint back in his pack, which now lay next to him along with his quiver and bow. Then, he set to feeding the fire, poking it fiercely with a stray stick. Surprisingly, he looked thoughtful rather than angry, which I supposed was a small blessing.

He jerked his chin at the pack. "Your scarf, gloves, and the wolf pelt are in there."

A nod. I didn't bother to say anything; it seemed my words had no effect on him. So I stepped around the fire, bent over, and donned the red scarf and mittens. The wolf pelt came out next. I spread it out next to him and as close to the fire as I dared before I sat down. Crossing my legs, I watched the amber and ruby flames dance, reveling in the heat that soaked and bathed my body.

I felt him watching me. "Serena ..." Oh, gods. "I can't give them back to you."

Soft, contemplative.

I sighed and met his gaze. "I realize that."

A crinkle formed between his brows, and he broke our staring contest to consider the flames as they moved like ripples in a pond. The silence went on for a minute or so before he spoke. "But I swear to you, the next time I'm called to the human realm, I'll let the people you love know you're safe."

My heart leaped painfully. "You can't just walk into a human village and knock on a door." Although, it was difficult to stop hope from gaining a grip on me.

"I'll find a way." He shrugged, so casual. "A note on the doorstep, or something similar. I don't have a paper or quill, but if you let me know what to say ..."

It wasn't ideal, but it was better than nothing. I nodded.

Hunter bowed his head. His shoulders drooped. He looked relieved and that easily, my frustration returned.

"Hunter, this doesn't wash out the bad or make up for what you're doing. You're still selling me: denying me the freedom to choose what happens next."

His wings shifted and spread out as if restless or agitated. "What is it you want from me? To leave you here?" He waved at the darkened forest. "Leave you to be defenseless in a realm that you know nothing about?"

"It sounds better than being sold like a calf for the slaughterhouse!"

He made a disgusted noise in the back of his throat. "You're speaking from anger, not reason. Whatever you think of me, I'm not heartless. I chose Diana's training camps because it was the best place for you."

I shook my head, despairing. "You chose. What you think is best. I'm not an object, Hunter. I'm not your property. You don't get to just decide —or at least you shouldn't." I gritted my teeth. "Stars, you haven't even told me anything about this place. You say it's the best place, but look at me." My voice went up an octave as I swept a hand down my body in one smooth move. "How can I be a soldier? You heard Kesha. I've got no muscles. I'm skin on bone!"

"Serena," Hunter began lightly, leaning in. "Training camps can be harsh, even brutal." My stomach churned. "But if you can see it through, you'd gain the skills to defend yourself, and something tells me you crave that more than anything: not to be at the mercy of others. Or am I wrong?"

I remained silent. Of course he wasn't wrong, but I wasn't telling him that the most secret and desperate desire of my heart was to be free—to never be at the whims of bullies and savages again.

He might've guessed though, because he was wearing a sad look, as if he understood that desire. How could he? He was fae.

"Look, if the choice means that much to you, I won't drag you anywhere kicking and screaming."

I blinked. "What changed your mind?"

"You did," he said as if he already regretted his decision. Hunter rubbed a hand through his short hair while gnawing at his lip. "But I don't doubt you'll end up agreeing with me."

I resisted the urge to roll my eyes. I didn't want to irritate him. Not if he was willing to give me a choice ... but what choices were those, exactly?

I bit my lip, seeking the right way to persuade him to tell me. "Kesha didn't want us knowing anything, but you're not her." He raised his eyebrows at that. I didn't want to slow: I went on. "You've already told me a lot of things you shouldn't. And I appreciate that, but I need more. I need you to tell me more about this realm; otherwise, I'm groping round in the dark for the right decision."

Hunter frowned. My heart thumped painfully.

"I'll ... do my best."

A sputter of relief.

"Let me think things over. There's so much I could tell you, but we haven't got years." He moved into a kneeling position and plunged into his rucksack. "And you should eat. You haven't since ..." He didn't bother finishing. The Winged Fiends' attack already felt like a lifetime ago. "It's also cold. You're human—you should wrap up."

He handed over a sticky bun in the shape of a ring and then threw a thick woolen blanket around my shoulders. I pressed my lips together. The movement felt protective, *nurturing*. My body tensed; the idea was so foreign to me, almost awkward. I angled my body away, needing some distance.

Hunter noticed. I could see a question form on his lips, so I quickly explained. "Sorry. It's just if you'd told me a week ago that a male fae would be taking care of me, a human ..." I shook my head. It was too strange for words.

"Ah." His lip quirked upward. "Well, it's a new experience for me too."

I didn't know what to make of that. So I took a huge bite out of the sticky bun and delighted in the rush of sweetness on my tongue. I almost choked when Hunter sprang up like a tightly wound coil.

"What are you doing?" I whipped my head left and right. Was there another fae pack about to attack?

But he wasn't stringing his bow. Instead, he grabbed a stick off the ground and drew in the earth beside the fire. "I'm giving you a very abridged geography lesson." A thoughtful frown creased his brow as he drew the Gauntlet to the south, a vast landscape above it and a bridge joining them.

I squashed the rest of the bun in my mouth and watched as he traced lines into the dirt, intrigued.

"There's your village," he said, marking the forest floor with his stick.

I moved in for a closer look at his crude map. "I didn't realize that Tunnock was so close to the divide," I said while licking the sugar glaze off my fingers.

Ignoring my observation, he went on. "Right now, we're in what the fae call Hollen, or the in-between. Above us are the four courts of the fae. To the far east is the Riverlands Court, ruled by Queen Diana. That's where I'd planned on taking you." He tapped a section of the map with his stick before moving on. "In the center, at the very heart of Aldar is Solar, and to the far west is the Crescent Court. That's witch territory, and where Kesha has taken Isabel."

I nodded vaguely. "What's the land at the top called?"

"Aurora."

"What can you tell me about the courts? Which are the friendliest to humans?"

"The Riverlands is the most tolerant."

I bit my lip. "What's wrong with the others?"

I looked up in time to see him toss the stick and his wings droop.

"Hunter ... I need to know these things."

I got a slow, careful nod in response. "Solar, Aurora, and to a lesser extent, the Crescent, are ruled by a fae-witch named Morgan. The Wild Hunt work for her."

He froze. Everything about his body screamed that this wasn't something he was happy about. Interesting.

Hunter seemed to have stalled, as if he'd thought better of telling me more. I scrambled up to stand next to him and *quickly* gave his hand a jostle. He shifted ever so slightly, staring down at where my hand had been. It gave me a twinge of unease, but I'd needed to keep him talking. "Go on."

Something loosened in his core, and the ice he'd been encased in melted.

"Morgan conquered three out of the four courts barely eighteen years ago. One after the other." Such glum tones. Again, interesting. "She created the Wild Hunt with the sole purpose of tracking down the former queen of Solar. Sefra was meant to be powerful—one of the few who could stand up to Morgan—but she fled her own court to avoid a confrontation. That should give you a feeling for how feared the witch is."

Hunter looked miserable when he added, "Morgan eventually declared her dead, and ten years after her conquests, she did the impossible. She found a way for the Hunt to cross the divide and bring back humans. She opened up slave markets in Solar and Aurora. So do you see, now, why I don't want you near those lands? She's the one responsible for the disappearances—for the enslavement of your kind."

I frowned. It felt like he was shifting the blame. "Weren't you going to send Brandon and Billy to the Solar Court?"

Hunter looked uneasy. "There was no choice. You must be over sixteen to train in one of Diana's camps in the Riverlands, and they didn't have magic. There was no other place for them."

I bit down on the tirade I wished to hurl his way. "Why does your boss hate humans so much?"

Hunter flinched but answered in a steady voice. "Her official reason for hunting them is that we needed numbers, and you produce quicker than us."

I tried to keep my voice even as I asked, "Why would she need the numbers if she's conquered most of Aldar already?"

He sighed. "There are neighboring fae kingdoms across the seas to the east. She thinks further conflict with them is inevitable. Ever since she's been in power, she's been pushing for humans to drive up our numbers and fill out the ranks, either as servants or foot soldiers. Anything to keep an invading host at bay."

An icy tingle ran the length of my spine. "How would humans even work in your armies? What good would we be against a horde of fae?"

He shifted, casting a sidelong glance my way. "Most fights between fae happen in the air, but humans can be used to pick off our enemies that fall to the ground. Or if our enemy also has human soldiers, then those two armies would face one another on the battlefield. How many humans each side has can often be the deciding factor in a war: it's how the Aldarian fae were driven from our homeland," he added sadly. "We had raw power on our side, but in the end, we were overwhelmed by the opposing human army and their vast numbers."

I was lost again. "Your homeland?"

Hunter blinked. Then added, "Sorry—I forgot who I was speaking to. The Aldarian fae used to live in those kingdoms to the east with our brethren, but there were endless conflicts and wars, so we fled." The line of his jaw tightened.

Absorbing his words, I struggled to align them with my mortal knowledge. I'd no reason to believe Hunter would lie, but if humans had once ruled these lands alone, no one in the Gauntlet had known about it. No history book or scholar had even suggested it.

A terrifying idea interrupted this string of thought and caused me to blurt out, "So, these other fae—that you used to live among and that you fled from—if they attacked Aldar, do you have enough humans and fae to defeat them?"

Hunter regarded me. "Honestly, I don't know. Because despite the efforts of the Hunt, there still aren't that many humans in Aldar, and most of them are witches living in the Crescent. Morgan holds the High Witch position in their lands, but the clans' support is based on conditions. One of which is that Morgan doesn't take slaves from the Crescent, so she can't compel them to fight if the time came."

"And there's no way you could take me there? To be with Isabel?"

"The witch clans won't shelter you unless you've got magic in your blood. Do you think there's any chance you might?" He scanned me doubtfully.

"No." My stomach dropped in disappointment. "I'd know, wouldn't I?"

"Not necessarily. Give me your hand." Hunter held out his palm, expectant.

I didn't move. "Why?"

His hand lowered. "If you've got magic in your blood, I'll be able to taste it."

"You want to drink my blood?" I tried to hide my disgust but failed, apparently.

Hunter's mouth thinned and turned down in disapproval. "If your magic's particularly weak, then you might not be aware you have any. This is the only way I can be sure."

That made sense, kind of. I peered down at my hand and stalled for time. "Would they still take me if my magic was weak?"

"Yes." No hesitation.

Wielding magic sounded more appealing than becoming a soldier. Could I trust Hunter to do this? Did I have a choice?

"Take it." I held my palm flat out.

His canines grew, and my stomach turned. There was a tenderness in the way he enveloped my hand with his and brought my palm up to his lips. He stopped just before he bit down and eyed me. I nodded, and he sunk his teeth into the fleshy pad under my thumb.

A shudder of disgust and a flinch of pain ran through me as his tongue lapped up my heart's blood. Suddenly he stilled, his nostrils flared, and his back stiffened. He unstuck his teeth and released my palm. I couldn't read his expression.

"What is it?" I pressed down on the pinprick wounds in my palm to stop the blood flow.

"I don't sense magic." Disappointment thudded into my gut. "But you taste unusual. There's a heat to your blood, and it's saltier than—" Hunter's eyes bulged and he grabbed for his throat.

"What's wrong?" I bleated, unnerved.

He retched, wheeling away from the fire to stick his fingers in his mouth. I rushed to his side just as vomit splashed to the ground. I crinkled my nose, trying to stop the sour stench from filling my nostrils.

"Water," he cried out, still clutching his throat.

I scrambled over to his satchel and rummaged around for a water bottle. Grabbing one, I hurried over to shove it under his nose. He snatched it, straightened, and took two deep swigs. Once he'd finished, he coughed to clear his throat a couple of times and wiped his mouth on his sleeve.

"What was that?" I asked shakily. "I know I haven't washed in a while, but it couldn't have been that bad."

He wet his lips again. "It wasn't the smell—it was the taste of salt and iron." He shuddered and put the cap back on the flask. "I've never known a human to carry so much in their blood it could make a fae sick."

I turned over what he'd let slip. The fae had a weakness, then. Salt and iron could be my new best friends in a world that saw my kind as *things*. "Do the fae often taste humans?"

Hunter moved, chucking the skin on top of the rucksack. Turning to me, he said, "Biting's one way we subdue our prey or establish dominance over others. It's also used on faelings if they act out."

I wrinkled my nose. "That's barbaric."

Hunter shrugged. "Our lives are long. Harsh words and pain fade, but our scars leave us with a permanent reminder, once our memories fail."

I blinked. That way of thinking was so alien, so ancient, and yet it made sense. When their minds failed to recall centuries-worth of memories, their bodies could act as maps to anchor them to their past.

I looked down and traced the puncture marks with my finger. He was right—the pain was already fading.

I caught Hunter watching me. "So, no magic then?"

With a small shake of his head, my stomach seemed to fall away. Where did that leave me? The Crescent was out of bounds. Aurora and Solar were run by someone who saw my kind as fodder for an army. A truth settled into my bones. Only one place left, but I wasn't ready to give in completely. "If you took me to the Riverlands, would you drop me off in a village?"

Hunter moved over to my wolf pelt and dropped to the floor like a stone. Folding his arms over his long legs, he stared into the flames. "I can't do that," he whispered. "You wouldn't last a week."

No explanation. I flopped down next to him. "Why?"

His throat bobbed visibly. "I can't show up with no money or record from your trade. There are those in the Hunt, Kesha among them, who already think I'm soft. They wouldn't take my word for it if I told them you died or escaped. They'd send out other trackers, and when they found you, they'd kill you."

I sat in mute horror. My future unraveled in front of me. I supposed I should be used to that by now—a lifetime of no options. But before I could accept my fate, I needed something from Hunter. "You never answered my question from earlier."

Hunter looked at me, bothered and bewildered.

"So do it now, Hunter. Why would you ever be part of this? Prove I can trust your judgment ... please."

He broke eye contact. Air rushed out of him, leaving wisps of white mist behind. "My story won't justify anything."

"I told you mine." I pulled my blanket tighter around me and waited.

It took him a while. "I had nothing growing up," he started.

That immediately gave me pause. Somehow, I'd never imagined any of the fae being poor.

"I had to hunt to stay alive, and eventually it became second nature. Working for Morgan, joining the pack: it seemed like a good fit." He rolled his shoulders. "I didn't think about what we'd be doing. Not really."

That wasn't an excuse, I thought. "And now?"

"I think about it all the time."

"So, why not leave?"

"Once you're in, it's for life," he said, looking drawn. A lengthy pause followed this revelation in which his face inexplicably hardened into granite lines. "Look, I've been to the Gauntlet. I've seen the poverty and desperation. But in Aldar, my story is rare. There aren't many who go to bed at night hungry. And while there are occasional cruelties, the slaves don't starve. If they get sick, their owners make sure they're healed. It's not perfect, but from what I've seen, it's still a better kind of life."

His mouth set in a thin line again. Ever obstinate. Always making excuses.

I didn't know what to say. At least his story made me understand him a little better.

"Serena?"

"Mm."

"Can you ..."

Holy fire—he looked so vulnerable that I almost reached out to comfort him.

"Can you forgive me?"

Well, damn. My mouth curved into a half-smile.

Hunter responded with his own hesitant grin. "What?"

"This must be another first: a fae asking a human's forgiveness."

His smile faltered. I sighed. "Hunter, if you think I will ever condone what you're doing, you're wrong."

His posture and face turned brittle and sad.

Something shifted inside me, enough to admit, "But today you gave me a choice. Not much of one, but I won't forget that. I know it was a risk."

Hunter didn't respond, he just clasped his hands and frowned, thoughtful. "So, what is your choice? Your decision?"

A chill entered my voice. "I suppose you can take me to the Riverlands—to one of Diana's camps. Although, I still don't see how it's going to work. I'm no soldier."

He moved his hand to rest over mine, and I stared down in a kind of detached shock, watching the shadow and flame from the fire move over them.

"I doubt this means much, but I wish things were different. You deserve better." My eyes found his. He was smiling, but he looked sad. Resigned. "If I can do anything ..."

"Except give me my freedom, you mean?"

He looked crushed. *Damn.*

He'd drugged me, kidnapped me, and was about to sell me, but I felt *sorry* for him? Madness. A sly voice that belonged wholly to me slipped in through my confusion. *Ah, but he also saved you*, it sang in mocking tones.

I bottled that voice and pulled my hand away. We were silent for a long time. Finally, I couldn't take it anymore. Whatever he'd done or was about to do, ripping him into even smaller shreds would achieve nothing. "Just promise me you'll deliver that message to John and Viola."

He'd been watching the flames; now he was watching me. "Of course. Anything."

I gave him a tiny nod. "Tell them ... thank you. That I'll never forget what they did for me. They took a lonely, broken girl and threw her a lifeline. And tell them I'm safe ..." My throat tightened with the lie. I went on in a hoarse voice. "Tell them not to look for me, and that I won't be coming back. That I love them. And goodbye."

Blinking fast, I tried and failed to stop the tears from falling. Hunter's hand twitched as if he wanted to reach out to comfort me again. That thought provoked a twinge of unease and made me quickly brush salty drops from both cheeks.

"They'll hear every word," he vowed.

I bit my lip, nodding. An errant breeze had me smelling myself; it wasn't pleasant. With a rueful look down at my spoiled dress, I asked, "D'you think you could find me a stream to bathe in tomorrow?"

A whisper of a chuckle. I looked up—he was fighting back a laugh.

"It's your fault I stink."

He burst out giggling. I tipped my head, contemplating. There was something so childlike in him. It almost hurt to remind myself of what he was. A slaver.

He sobered up quickly, though, enough to say, "Of course, I'll take you somewhere to wash. But right now, we should try to sleep. We still have a journey ahead of us, and today has been ..."

"A nightmare?" I offered.

He gave me a wan smile. Not giving him an opportunity to agree, I lay down and spread the blanket over my body; I wouldn't be warm, but neither would I freeze. Still, that didn't seem good enough for Hunter. Before I could protest, he'd lain down behind me and extended his wing over us.

"What d'you think you're doing?" I peeked over my shoulder, incredulous.

"Body heat," he replied.

Such an air of innocence. *Pfft.*

The light from the fire disappeared as his leathery wing went over us, cocooning us. I was about to bat it away when Hunter said, "Sleep now."

His breath tickled my hair. I frowned and decided that since I couldn't force him to move, it might be better to just suffer. He wasn't touching me—not exactly. And I was so very, very tired. He hummed low, his body sending vibrations into my back. Somehow, his hums soothed away the jagged edges and the horror of the last few hours, enough for me to relax and drift away.

CHAPTER 9
THE OGRE AND THE WARRIOR

We were up at dawn, quenching the fire and filling our bellies with food and water. True to his promise, we lingered long enough to find a stream for me to wash. It didn't stop the dress from smelling, but at least my face and hands were now clean.

With a pounding heart, I held my arms out for Hunter. He shot into the sky with the brilliance and speed of a shooting star, but I was too exhausted to feel the thrill. It didn't help that the rustle of his wings, mixed with the warmth from his body, created a powerful soporific effect. Then, I was dozing.

Two days of mind-numbing travel followed. Hunter became shifty and evasive if I brought up anything remotely interesting. Like details about Morgan or the fae. Instead, he bombarded me with questions about my life in the Gauntlet. On the third day, with the sun high in the sky, I stirred in Hunter's arms. I'd been drifting in and out of sleep all morning. Now, my eyes opened and slid past his face to the blue, blue sky behind, and to his wings. They still made me gasp. Spread open in their full glory, the sun lit up the delicate skin, illuminating the fragile bones and tapestry of vital veins.

I stared, open-mouthed. And before I could think better of it, said, "They really are incredible."

He beamed sweetly. Confusion seated itself in my heart. Something had shifted over the past few days: we weren't enemies any more, but what had we become instead?

I needed a moment to think clearly. Yet there was no chance of putting physical distance between us; avoiding eye contact it was. I let my gaze wander below, and my stomach rolled as Aldar spread itself beneath us.

It was a new landscape. The forest had splintered to become a patchwork of ruby and gold threads that ran through rolling hills and rippling grasses, banking rivers and streams. No sign of any buildings or anything close to a training camp, but the sheer amount of water ribbons making up the countryside led me to guess. "This is the Riverlands, isn't it?"

I felt the muscles in Hunter's arms grow taut. "We're not far from the training camp."

My gut jumped. "You've already decided which one to take me to?" I fixed him with a frown. "I thought you wanted me to have choices."

"I thought we'd built trust." He sounded exasperated, maybe even annoyed. "Kasi is the one of the best, if not *the* best training camp in the Riverlands Court. They don't separate fae recruits from the humans, and more importantly, they treat them fairly."

That didn't stop my panic from climbing. I needed information, fast. "What happens when we get there?"

"I'll take you to Bert." Hunter suddenly swerved right. The delicate gray membrane stretched wide, and his wings caught a breeze wrapped up in brininess and the taste of salt. He vaulted forward and rode the wind.

I closed my eyes against the sickening jolt and shouted over the howling air currents. "Who's he?"

"Bert runs the day-to-day operations of Kasi," Hunter yelled. "It'll be better if we see him first. He's one of the few with direct access to Hilda; otherwise, we'd be waiting for hours."

"Hilda?"

The wind lessened, enough for Hunter to reply evenly. "She's in charge. One of her jobs is to assess all new recruits. Once she's seen you, you won't have much contact with her."

Assess. As in a test? Breathing became difficult.

"You didn't say anything about an assessment." The words sounded hamstrung with nerves, even to my ears.

"It's nothing," he assured. "Hilda rarely turns anyone away. She likes to give everyone a fair chance."

"But she turns people away sometimes." My tongue flicked out to wet my lips. "What happens if I fail—will you take me to another camp?"

A nod and a promise. "I won't give up."

It didn't stop me from shifting through various scenarios, each more hideous and grueling than the last. What would she expect? Someone strong, fit, quick; remotely competent? I'd be sure to disappoint on all accounts. The only weapon I'd had practice with was the bow.

"What will I be doing in the training?" Confidence at a low ebb, I had to add, "If they let me stay."

"The exact training routine isn't known to outsiders, but I can tell you that Kasi's dedicated to training recruits to the rank of Iko." Before I could ask, he clarified. "Iko means 'foot soldier' in Kaeli, so I imagine you'll undergo weapons training, and endurance-building exercises."

"Kaeli?" I questioned.

"The ancient fae tongue."

Ah. There was so much—too much—to learn about this new land. This new life.

We settled into silence again. The sun blushed pink with the afternoon light, and I passed the time soaking in the scenery. That was until a shimmering blue line glinted underneath the columns, orbs, and spires of cloud. It filled the horizon and wrapped around the entire right-hand side of the land. I stiffened, and my heart skipped a beat. "What is that?"

"What d'you mean?" he said, bemused. "It's the Eastern Seas."

Excitement exploded inside of me. I fought the impulse to lurch forward, but the stretch of water called to me with its siren song. That restless, churning mass of cobalt-blue and white flurries.

Hunter gripped me tighter. "Are you okay? You look like you're about to leap out into thin air."

"I've never seen the sea." Too many emotions claimed me at once, reducing my speech to a murmur. "My mother ... she promised we'd see it together."

"If it means that much to you, we could make a detour."

I whipped my head around and stared. He'd meant it, every word.

A rolling wave of gratitude flooded me. "Thank you ..." I couldn't finish the sentence.

I'd had few aspirations in my life. The only two constants were being free of Elain, and to see the sea. The first had been granted, and he was offering the second as if it were nothing. The temptation was almost overwhelming, but something stopped me. I searched my heart, trying to riddle it out.

Then, it came to me. I didn't want to live without an unrequited wish and risk the emptiness that might follow. That realization filled me with horror, cutting deep. Had I truly lived in such a hopeless place that I'd never dared to dream a bit bigger?

"I don't want to go," I found myself saying. "It feels wrong to see it without her." Truth or lie? I wasn't sure.

"Of course. You must miss her very much."

"Mm." I lapsed into quiet, keeping my thoughts and memories to myself.

Underneath, the world blurred past and shifted. Hunter soon banked left and shot straight, leaving behind that thin, blue smudge: that dream of mine.

Not wanting to regret my decision, I didn't look back over Hunter's shoulder. Instead, I focused on observing and creating a map in my head of what would become my new surroundings. I wasn't a soldier yet, but that didn't mean I couldn't act like one.

I noted the rushing streams flowing down the land, cutting the colored meadows and valleys into segments, and the purple-topped mountains that rose on my left. Eventually, a thin silver blur showed itself on the horizon with forest sitting on either side, and as we got closer, it morphed into a great, snaking river. And there, just beyond, individual matchstick-sized buildings.

I didn't have to ask, but I did need to hear the answer.

"That's it, isn't it?" I looked back at Hunter.

Just a nod and a grimace. As if I wasn't nervous enough.

"You're sure?" I croaked.

"Positive. I can see the guards on duty."

"Really?" I squinted. My mortal eyesight picked up the buildings, but they were blurry at best. I clucked my tongue, annoyed. "Is your kind better at everything?"

"No. Humans beat us in the act of love," Hunter replied.

That was unexpected. I stared, dumbstruck for a moment, before a whisper of a chuckle made its way out of me. "I wouldn't have guessed. Not with all your physical advantages."

I blushed. It wasn't made better when Hunter let out a soft laugh. "I didn't mean sex."

My face was on fire. "Oh."

"I meant to love another and express it." He frowned, his earth-brown eyes crinkling. "Your lives may be shorter, but you love more fiercely because of it. It's said the fae were like that a long, long time ago —slaves to our emotions, perhaps more so than humans."

I tried and failed to swallow that insult with good grace. "What changed?"

Hunter went on. "We evolved. We had to if we wanted to survive. Fae find it difficult to conceive," he explained, "so we couldn't allow ourselves to be ruled by passion, waging a war every other week. I don't know when or how, but the ancient fae say our society adapted, becoming more refined: more rigid. Colder."

"So, is it possible for a fae to be friends with a human?" The words spilled out before I could clamp down and shove them in a dark hole where they belonged.

Hunter stared straight ahead, fixated on Kasi. "I wouldn't know. I've never had any, and certainly no human ones."

His voice was a murmur. And maybe it was that, or the sad eyes that made me say, "You could use some practice, then. Why don't we try being friends?"

I cringed at my pathetic attempt to forge a connection, but at least he didn't laugh in my face. But he did blink *slowly*, and then he peered down at me.

"You'd want to be? With me... After what I did to you?" His words carried such hesitancy and hopefulness.

Things felt too serious, too overwhelming. "Only if you don't mind being friends with an emotional human."

My lip twitched. I needed him to smile with me.

Thankfully, Hunter beamed and his eyes shone. "I'd like that."

"Good." His eyes flitted behind me, and my stomach did a funny turn. "We're here, aren't we?"

A nod set my pulse racing. Hunter circled in for a landing. I looked down and there it was: Kasi Camp. A palisade of dark oak made up the outer walls, which stood roughly twenty feet high. Two watch towers and a walkway held the guards on patrol. Inside the walls, mismatched wood and stone structures had been built of varying sizes, each one connected to a path. The landmarks included a small lake with still midnight waters. Above this was a large circular ring of sand, with a stable crowning it and two buildings adjacent. A stone structure with stacks of weapons out front rested on the left, while on the right lay an arena with no roof, and rows of ascending benches inside.

A call came from a watchtower. "Hunter! Is that you?"

My eyes tracked a dusky-skinned fae with pine-green wings who rose to meet us.

"Elias." Hunter nodded in acknowledgement. "I've brought you another recruit."

The male scanned my face and body. A line formed between his brows, and his mouth thinned in silent disappointment. Withering under the scrutiny, fighting to hold his gaze, I waited for his judgment.

"You're a bit late with this one." His mouth dipped as he added, "The other recruits are halfway through the training cycle."

My breath seized in my chest. What would that mean for me?

"Hilda's taken on people late before," Hunter pointed out.

"True." Elias scanned me again as if seeking some hidden potential —a reason for why I was here.

I stared him down, the whole while not breathing.

"Very well. Bert's in the usual place."

I breathed again.

Elias didn't stop to say goodbye before gliding back to his post. And with a few flaps of Hunter's wings, we passed over the wall and began the descent.

All too aware of the fae's sensitive hearing, I leaned in to whisper, "Are you still sure this is the right place? If the others are halfway through, how am I going to catch up? I hardly have any muscles as it is."

"Hilda's an honorable warrior; she values courage and a willing heart. She won't turn you away because you don't look the part. Just show her respect, do what she asks, and you'll be fine."

Something in me refused to believe it would be that easy.

Hunter's landing was smooth, his feet grazing the trampled path and his wings collapsing in at the joint. He set me down but kept his hand at my lower back while I adjusted to solid ground again. I shook out my legs and took a deep breath. Then another, which was then expelled in a sharp gasp when a green-skinned ogre stepped out in front of me.

The ogre—Bert—grunted at the sound. "What's this? Another recruit?"

Behind beady yellow eyes, I thought I spotted signs of a sharp intelligence, weighing and assessing us. Something I never would've believed from an ogre. The stories from the Gauntlet painted them as huge, bloodthirsty brutes, but this ogre wasn't much taller than me. And his violent nature was cast into serious doubt by the striped apron he wore, bearing the words, "Proud to be Green."

He pulled out a pair of spectacles from the front pocket of his apron and placed them on the end of his squashed nose. Definitely not a mindless animal, then.

Taking a step toward me, his nose went up in the air to sniff. "Scrawny, but tough. She's also in desperate need of a bath." My face burned with shame. "You found 'er in the human realm."

It wasn't a question, but Hunter answered anyway. "I found her in the Gauntlet a few days ago. She'd been locked in a cage and left to die."

A lump rose in my throat.

"What she do?" Bert grumbled.

"The humans suspected she was a changeling."

Hunter sounded guttural, even savage, but whatever emotions I'd heard in his voice hadn't reached his face. His favorite mask was still in play—mild and detached.

"Changeling, indeed," Bert snorted. "Human stupidity never ceases to amaze me." He stomped his feet a couple of times as if to show his anger. "Come along, youngling," he said softly, almost affectionately. "You'll wait in me rooms while I fetch Hildy." He ushered me toward a one-story stone cottage built next to the outer wall. It had just two mullioned windows, an eggshell-blue door, and a chimney that puffed out green smoke. The ogre didn't wait before loping away on his bare, stumpy feet.

Hunter's hand moved to my elbow. From the outside, it must've looked like he was escorting me, but the gentleness in his touch told me it was to comfort me. While following the ogre, Hunter whispered, "Now you've met Bert: I'm guessing he's different from what you were expecting?"

I flashed him a crooked smile. No, not what I'd expected at all. We arrived at the cottage to find the ogre holding the door open for us. "In yah get. Sit anywhere you'd like."

He pointed with one of four sausage-like fingers. I walked over the threshold to find a box-like room. A chipped sink and one lone cupboard adorned the right wall, a large, cushy chair and an open fire covered the left. Two doors on the far wall, straw mats on the floor, and a circular table with two chairs set in the middle made up the rest of the room. However, it escaped the label "plain" due to several fussy decorations. Colorful throws, cheery curtains, and heaps and heaps of woolen cushions dotted the room. And given the huge needles and balls of multicolored yarn sprawled everywhere, I supposed he did his own knitting, too.

The ogre didn't bother to say goodbye or shut the door. He clomped away with his long arms swinging by his sides. Hunter, however, did close the door and the cottage instantly warmed thanks to the green flames licking up the chimney breast. I couldn't resist moving closer to this blaze, for hours of flight and wind burn had damn near frozen every bare inch of skin. Hunter motioned to the armchair next to me and said, "You may as well sit."

A tempting offer. Especially given that the anxiety surging through my every vein and muscle was causing my legs to weaken beneath me. I settled into its velvety folds. "I hope Bert doesn't notice his chair suddenly smelling," I said, staring down at the brown woolen eyesore that was my dress.

"They'll give you a uniform. It's standard practice in a place like this."

I couldn't help replying. "If Hilda will even take me."

Hunter didn't respond. Great. As if I wasn't feeling shitty enough already. As the silence stretched into minutes, my anxieties pressed down hard on my chest, suffocating me.

I cracked. "If she says no—if they all say no, can I stay with you?"

Hunter's loamy eyes softened, and his mouth went down at the sides. That told me everything I needed to know.

"I won't abandon you—friend," was his only response.

A tiny smile touched his lips, and the weight in my chest lightened. I opened my mouth—to say what, I had no idea. And I never found out, because Bert chose that moment to reappear. This time in the company of a formidable-looking female. Her height meant she had to duck as she walked in, and her broad shoulders and tawny wings seemed to fill the room. She looked the part of a true warrior, even though she carried no visible weapons.

I vaulted out of the chair and wavered, nervously waiting.

"Hunter." It was a short acknowledgement with little feeling. "This is the recruit?" She didn't wait for an answer before she was barking at me in a gravelly voice. "Name?"

Not intimidating at all, I thought wryly. "Serena ... Serena Smith."

"Mm." She frowned at me. My instincts told me to keep silent and still.

"Bert told me your people threw you in a cage?" she rasped as her wings twitched.

"Yes, they did," I said immediately. This fae didn't seem all that patient.

"You had no family to speak up for you?"

Her blue-eyed stare was piercing, and it seemed to bore right through me. Was this an interrogation?

"No. My parents are dead. And my friends ... couldn't help."

"Do you *want* to be here?"

Something about the hard line of her mouth made me pause and turn to Hunter. But that was the wrong thing to do, as she suddenly snapped, "Let me clear, I've no interest in breaking in another unwilling human. We're not training horses here, you know?" Hilda directed her ire solely at Hunter, who refused to meet her ominous glare. "I take the slaves you bring because I need to fill my quota, but I've done that. I've no interest in filling the Wild Hunt's pockets any more than needs be."

Well, that was unexpected. I waited for Hunter to say something, only he didn't. Bert was frowning, and Hilda seemed a second away from marching out. I could say nothing, but if their dislike of slavery was anything to go by, this definitely seemed like the best place for me.

"Hunter gave me a choice; I'm here of my own free will now."

Hilda's eyebrows shot toward her hairline. She turned to Hunter, her eyes narrowing. "Is this true?"

A muscle feathered in his cheek, but he met her gaze again and nodded.

Bert cackled beside Hilda. "I'm guessing Kesha doesn't know that. Where is she, anyway?"

I saw a pulse go in Hunter's jaw. "The Winged Fiends attacked us on the road. We split up after that. She's taking a witch we brought over to the Crescent."

"Very well." Hilda scowled and turned to me again. "Why d'you want to be here then?" she demanded.

The answer rolled off my tongue. Better to be honest. "Hunter said you don't discriminate against humans."

"Did he now?" Hilda frowned.

Oh, gods. Had he got it wrong?

"Well, I suppose you'd both better follow me."

Hilda didn't wait. She strode out the door. Hunter went after her, but I hung back a little.

"Don't let 'er intimidate you." Bert pulled out a pipe from his apron pocket and bit the end. "Still, it's probably best not to keep her waiting, either," he suggested with a wave of his hand.

That got me moving. Lingering just a moment more to thank him, I went to leave. I spotted Hunter and wheeled right, hurrying down the beaten track. There didn't seem many humans or fae around, apart from the odd guard walking or flying along the wall. A stroke of luck; I'd no desire to be the object of people's curiosity.

I caught up with Hunter, but Hilda had stridden ahead, somehow managing to put a distance between them. The path had too many bends and odd clumps of trees to see the intended destination. "D'you know where we're going?" I asked Hunter.

"The training pit. It's where she takes all new recruits. Sometimes she'll shove a sword in their hand or make them use a bow. Other times it's laps."

My gut did a sickening twisting motion. "I haven't touched a sword in years." Father had never liked me touching the weapons in his forge. Then, Gus had come along and I'd barely set foot in there. "And I'm not brilliant with a bow."

"There's no need to panic. She just wants a baseline of your physical abilities."

He nudged me with his elbow and tried to get a smile out of me. But one glance down at my spindly arms made my confidence plummet even further.

The path straightened and opened out to the arena. Hilda went left here, and followed the fencing that encircled a giant sandpit. She spun and waved us over. Not a patient woman, at all.

We sped up. As we approached, she told me, "I'm going to the armory. I want to see you with a sword in hand. In the meantime, you're to run laps around the training field. Every time you complete one, do ten lunges on each leg. Keep going until I say otherwise." She finished by slapping a heavy hand on the fencing.

A large village—my village—could've fit inside the training ring's boundaries. My lower lip almost trembled and my leg muscles locked up. What if she refused to stop me? Would I have to keep running laps until I collapsed? Was this Hilda's way of showing me that I didn't deserve to stay?

"Well, get on with it," Hilda barked.

I tore off my mismatched mittens and scarf, tossed them at Hunter, and moved.

I veered left and ran clockwise, sticking close to the fence and pacing myself. Hilda was already ahead of me, disappearing into a stone building. The weapon racks along the wall confirmed my suspicions. It was the armory. As a blacksmith's daughter, I could identify a few of the weapon types on display: broadswords, longbows, falchions, crossbows, and winged spears. Others, however, were so foreign and beyond what my father could've created, they blew me away. I suddenly felt that loss again like a punch to the gut; my father would've been brimming over with excitement to see such an arsenal.

I followed the curve of the ring, leaving the building behind, and focusing on the task. My vision blurred and my body slipped into a familiar and comforting rhythm. I wasn't a stranger to this: I'd often gone running along the forest tracks in my village. Something about the relentless grind and meditative state had always helped wring Elain's poisonous words from my mind.

My feet pounded the sandy grass, and with each movement there was an accompanying inhale and exhale. Just *breathe*.

Coming upon the end of the lap, I noticed Hunter had moved. He was now standing outside the armory with Hilda and a male fae who had dull-blue wings and nut-brown, leathery skin. I dropped into the lunge position, keeping a count in my head while seizing the moment to stare at them. Thankfully, they weren't watching me. Hilda and Hunter talked between themselves, while the strange male sat on a stool beside the racks, polishing a sword. I was ogling him now. I'd heard about the fae's supposed immortality from songs and tales growing up, but I'd never thought to see an old one. Yet, with those slow, careful movements, the male moved and looked like the elderly in my village. He must be *ancient*. Upon finishing the lunges, I set off again.

Seven laps later, I was suffering. My leg muscles burned, and shooting pains racked the length of my spine, but I kept going. Two more sets of lunges and circuits dried up any hope of getting through this test. Every damned inch of me was slick with stinking sweat underneath my dress, and I thought I might pass out from the smell alone.

After crawling to the end of my tenth lap, Hilda called out, "Recruit! Cease action."

My chest shuddered with exhaustion and relief.

"Come join us."

I walked over. Hunter wore a sneaky smile, but Hilda tapped her foot and crossed her arms. Yet, the gods themselves couldn't have convinced me to run. Knees trembling, thighs cramping, I came to rest in front of them.

"Colt, if you will?" Hilda didn't take her eyes off me, but at her behest, the ancient male rose from his stool with a creak and a groan. "This is our armorer. He'll be examining you."

He lumbered over with the newly polished sword and when barely a foot separated us, he stopped and peered at me through heavy eyes. Without warning, he grabbed my left arm in his non-sword hand and examined my palms, ran a finger over my joints, and moved up to feel my nonexistent bicep.

I couldn't riddle out what he was testing for; his face betrayed nothing.

He switched to the other arm and repeated the process. I was sure his thumbs would leave bruises, but I gritted my teeth and waited it out. Finally he let go, only to shove a sword into my right hand.

He stepped back and raised his hand. "Up!"

I used both hands and lifted the thin, straight blade. It wasn't quite a longsword, but it was *heavy*. Hilda and Colt moved farther back, but Hunter joined me at my side.

"One arm!" Colt growled to my right.

My jaw clenched. Damn it.

I peeled my left hand from the cross hilt and the sword dropped an inch or two.

"Keep the sword level," he snarled.

Sweat beaded on my top lip with the effort of holding it aloft. As the pain worsened I gritted my teeth, bottling a scream. My body betrayed me anyway, and my arm muscles convulsed. Tremors shook me.

"She's not awful," Colt grumbled. "Tall, thin, fit for action, but if she can't hold a sword without quaking, then her endurance isn't where it needs to be."

Hilda grunted in agreement and my cheeks became a firestorm.

"Endurance takes time to build," Hunter added in my defense.

"She hasn't got it," Hilda murmured. "The others already have a month of training under their wings."

At least she didn't seem pleased at my failure. Maybe there was still a chance.

"It'd be different if she was starting with the others. She wouldn't be at such a disadvantage, then."

As if to prove her point, my arm quivered again and almost buckled. I didn't need to look at Hunter to know he was disappointed. His silence was everything.

But I wasn't ready to give up. Not bothering to waste energy on words, my eyesight narrowed to the eye of a needle as I glared at the steel and waged war on the sword.

Focus. Keep your arm straight. Don't drop it.

I sang those words like a mantra.

Somebody—maybe Hunter—droned on in the background. But I didn't take it in. Instead, I shifted my weight and slid my left foot behind me. It didn't stop the fiery ache in my bicep, but it kept me from collapsing. I clenched my stomach muscles and focused on drawing deep breaths in between clenched teeth. Despair sunk in when my arm cramped.

Seconds from dropping it, my necklace flared and heated my skin. A surge of new strength flooded my muscles, my back straightened, and the trembling subsided.

I came out of my silent war with the sword and glared in Colt's direction. They were all staring at me now.

He nodded once. "You're stubborn—I'll give you that."

I recognized it as a release, a silent command. My arm lowered. I gasped as the blood surged into starved, throbbing muscles, and the full force of the pain hit—I had to gulp down a mouthful of bile.

"You'll do," Hilda declared.

Colt snatched the sword from me and vanished into the depths of the armory.

"I can stay?" I asked, dazed.

"Yes." Hilda frowned. "But you must work twice as hard to catch up: remember that."

My newfound wave of relief flattened.

"Pick up your money from Bert," Hilda said to Hunter, her mouth twisting to the side. "Serena, go with him and ask for Liora Verona. She's one of Bert's favorites and one of the few humans in your training cycle. She'll tell you how it all works and show you to your barracks. I'm putting you in Wilder's class—luckily for you, he has a spot open."

I nodded and thanked her.

Hilda dismissed the words with a careless shrug and a wave of the hand as if to say it was nothing. "You should know that the recruits will go through an elimination phase in one month's time. And we can't offer second chances. Neither will the other camps take you on if you fail, so don't fail."

My gut roiled in horror at the thought.

Hunter shifted. I noticed a bob at his throat. "No second chances?"

"No." Hilda's mouth fixed into a hard line. "New policy." And with that, she gave me a cursory nod and took to the skies at a run. With a few flaps of her wings, she was up and gone.

I rounded on Hunter and said in one fearful breath, "You didn't mention an elimination, and you *swore* to take me to another camp if I didn't make it. Now that's not an option?"

The lines in his forehead deepened. "You heard her, Serena, it's a new rule. I didn't know things had changed. And as far as the elimination goes, all the camps run tests during training, but I don't know the exact set-up. No outsider does."

Half-truths. I opened my mouth to say so, but Hunter continued. "If it doesn't work out ..." His eyes flooded with intent. "I'll still come back for you. Bert can always get a message to me if needs be."

"You told me there's nowhere else to go, other than the markets." I cringed at the thought of being sold at auction like cattle.

"We'll figure something out."

There was a jolt around my midriff, and any response withered and died on my tongue.

"Come on. I'll wait with you until you meet this Liora, but after that I should be going." He twisted toward the ogre's cottage and reached out as if to take me by the wrist.

I angled out of reach. His jaw worked furiously and the lines around his eyes tightened. I'd no wish to hurt him, but soon he'd leave me to fend for myself. I needed to prepare, to rebuild my defenses.

His arm fell back to his side and he set off without touching me. "Back to Bert's, then." His voice had an awful false cheeriness to it.

I kept stride with him, and we lapsed into silence. It hung heavy in the air, splitting us into our separate worlds again. A mix of emotions roared through me. In the space of a week my world had been torn from me—literally. Hunter was a big part of why, and yet without him, I'd soon be alone, adrift in a sea of strangeness. More than that ... I hadn't told him—hadn't wanted to be that vulnerable—but he was my only friend, too. Maybe I'd even miss his company. A strange thought indeed.

Loud, raucous noises interrupted my brooding and appeared to be coming from one of the bigger buildings nearby. It had double doors, three stone chimneys, and windows that had steamed up, preventing me from seeing inside.

I jerked my chin to the left. "What's that building?"

"The food hall," Hunter said, distant; not like his usual self.

Now he'd mentioned it, I could've sworn the air carried the whiff of baking bread and sweet things. My stomach rumbled in appreciation. I hadn't eaten since breakfast. In another heartbeat, the smells gave rise to something else: homesickness, spawned from memories of John's bakery.

My heart ached fiercely. I didn't breathe again until the food hall lay behind us. Bert's cottage came up on the left, and I spotted the doors, wide open in welcome.

We arrived in the doorway to find Bert knitting and puffing on his foul-smelling pipe. Without looking up, and with the pipe clenched in his teeth, he said, "You made it then?"

"Mm." I couldn't muster up anything more articulate.

"Hilda said you'd direct us to a recruit named Liora? She's meant to show Serena around." Hunter stepped inside and I went after him.

"Aye." Bert counted stitches, and added, "I sent for 'er the moment you left. She's already in the supply closet getting you some new togs."

Huh. "How did you know I'd be allowed to stay?"

Bert peered over his knitting needles and gave me a very crooked grin. "I have a gift for sniffing out the rotten eggs, and you're no stinker."

Oddly proud, I responded, "Thanks, Bert."

"Did Hildy tell you which instructor you'd be working with?"

"Err ..."

"Wilder," Hunter answered for me.

Bert nodded. "Well, tell Liora so she can take you to the right barracks."

"We're okay to wait here?" Hunter asked.

Bert grunted. I took that as a yes.

From the corner of my eye, I noticed Hunter shift his weight and run a hand up the back of his hair as if uncomfortable. Something clicked, and I said, "Hilda also said you could pay him for bringing me here."

Hunter threw me an apologetic look.

Bert sighed and threw down the blanket he'd been knitting. Mumbling to himself, he stood and reached into his apron's pocket to draw out a set of keys. He stomped over to the cupboard in the right-hand corner, slotted the key in, and opened a drawer. A jangling of coins followed.

Bert turned and banged the drawer closed with his hip. Arms swinging, he walked over and handed Hunter a pouch of money. "That should be everything. Over there's a red book." He jabbed his sausage-thumb at the table behind him. "Sign yer name and amount received." Bert lumbered back to his armchair.

Hunter quickly tucked the money into some inner pocket of his leathers and strode over to the table to put pen to paper. His shoulders knotted and hunched up. Not for the first time, I wondered what was going on inside his head.

Someone called out behind me, distracting me. "Merry meet!"

It was a musical voice with soft notes underneath. I turned to see a girl about my age with masses of flaming, springy strawberry curls. She was shorter than me, but had curves for days. A swift stab of envy pierced my gut, but it melted as soon as her green eyes lit up with a smile. As she moved toward me, a warm breeze rushed in, one that set my skin tingling in recognition. It smelled of grass, roses, and something sweet, like sugar-spun strawberries.

Spring meets winter, whispered the disembodied voice.

I blinked. *What the rutting rats does that mean?*

There was no answer, and I wondered ... Maybe this wasn't some strange, unknowable protective magic after all. Maybe I'd just gone mad from the trauma.

The red-headed girl stopped in front of me and held up a leather satchel. A swirling floral tattoo decorated her left hand. I'd seen nothing like it before. Sure, girls in Tunnock had sometimes worn makeup, but tattoos? Never. "You must be Serena. Bert told me you'd need supplies."

"Apparently," I mumbled.

Liora's heart-shaped face shone with another swift grin. "Well, I've signed out everything you'll need, including two sets of our oh-so-stylish uniform."

She gestured down to her body. She wore thick black leggings tucked into heavy-duty boots, a long-sleeved top, and a thin black jacket.

"How did you know my sizing?" I asked.

"Bert said you were tall and thin, and there aren't many sizes to choose from," she said brightly. "I've also brought along a few different boots to try. We'll use Bert's back room so you can change."

"Oh, will ye now?" Bert grunted.

I looked over to see his eyelids drooping. My instincts told me we'd interrupted his afternoon nap. The sound of shuffling wings snapped my attention back to Hunter, who'd moved next to my shoulder.

"This is Hunter." I motioned to him.

"Ah." The warmth in Liora's voice dipped. "You're from the Wild Hunt?"

Hunter didn't get to answer, because Bert chose that moment to grumble, "Liora, get a move on. I'd like my house back sometime today."

"Of course, Bertie." Her voice overflowing with mirth, she added, "This way, Serena."

She led me through one of the back doors. I walked through to find a jumble of assorted junk; a brass bed frame in the corner; piles of books on the floor; and several trunks splayed open to reveal stubs of candles, jam jars, and countless sweet wrappers that were lovingly grouped together according to color.

I was speechless.

Liora's laugh was like a river rushing to the sea, spirited and musical. "I'm guessing you don't know much about ogres?"

I shook my head slowly, mouth slightly agape.

"They're consummate hoarders," she said with a broad grin. "Bert even has books stacked in his bathtub."

I couldn't help but smile. "I wasn't even aware ogres had baths."

"Ha! Well, I haven't met many, but Bert's one in a million. Anyway, d'you want to change out of that dress? If you leave it, I can come back later and pop it in the laundry."

"I wouldn't bother." I touched the layer of wool gingerly. "Just burn it. Nothing's getting rid of these stains."

My face burned in shame, but there was no judgment in her voice when Liora said, "Sure, if that's what you want."

Desperate to hide my creeping blush, I ducked and went to open the satchel she'd brought for me. Liora talked while I peered inside. "I've packed everything recruits receive on arrival. Towels, soap, a jar of paste for your teeth, medical kit, a water flask, and your uniform. Plus, a spare set of everything, some gloves, and a cloak. Also, try not to lose any of your clothing. If you do, the punishment is *horrendous*."

Alarmed, my eyes found hers. "Why? What is it?"

Images of torture devices ran through my head.

"Kitchen duty." She grimaced.

I loosened a breath, a note of hysteria lingering. That was nothing.

"I also packed undergarments. Sorry if you wanted to do that yourself."

"It's fine." And still, I flushed deeper.

I dragged out the clothes that resembled Liora's, along with three pairs of boots. I straightened, but I hesitated before lifting up my skirts. Liora instantly turned her back, giving me privacy.

I breathed a sigh of relief. No one had seen me naked since I was a babe, and I didn't want to start now. Although, things were obviously different for women here. They wore pants and trained alongside men for the battlefield. I wouldn't have the luxury of being squeamish about such things. I'd have to adapt.

Not today though. I'd start tomorrow.

The soiled dress came up over my head, and my skin sang when released from the heavy, stinking wool. I chucked it into the corner of the room, glad to be rid of it. My tattered boots, shift, and undergarments followed. I was divesting myself of every thread of my old life. Still, it became painfully obvious as I stepped into new black pants and a bandage-like bra that a change of clothes wouldn't help with the thin layer of grime coating my skin.

"D'you think it'd be possible to clean up somewhere soon? I haven't had a proper wash in ... well, it's been a while."

My face burned as I pulled on the leggings.

Liora murmured, "Of course. I daresay you haven't had much oppor-tunity; the Hunt isn't famous for its kindness."

Pity, and maybe even disgust, rang out in her voice. I wondered if Hunter could hear her. Probably. I didn't see the point in contradicting her for his sake, not when she was right.

The socks came next, and then the v-necked top and the jacket which had a scrap of cloth with my name hastily stitched inside. "These name tags—are they so we don't lose anything?"

"Yup." Liora's head bobbed, and I felt another low twist in my gut as her shining strawberry locks bounced along. "Without the tags, we'd get nothing back from the laundry."

"You can turn around now."

She spun just as I tried shoving my feet into a pair of ill-fitting boots. I kicked them off and went for a larger size. They fitted well enough, so I tied the laces and straightened back up.

Liora gave me a swift nod of approval. "We'll leave the dress and the shoes. Bert won't mind. I'll take you to the baths now, and then we can go to the food hall. We'll probably be late, but I'll figure something out. You shouldn't go to bed hungry in a place like this."

My stomach cramped—gods, I was *starving*.

"Plus, my brother's been dying to meet you. Unless you don't want me to introduce you?"

A concerned pause. Instinct told me she wouldn't mind if I refused.

I played for time. "Why would he want to meet me?"

"He's a shameless flirt and a busybody." She tossed her head in mock despair. "He was with me when Bert showed up in our barracks. He helped me put these things together for you." She quickly added, "Except for the underwear, obviously."

She held back a smile as if unsure how I'd react. I'd be damned if I'd go back to being that girl that made others so uneasy, so I flashed her a grin and felt relieved to get one in return.

Liora moved around me to the door. "Best not keep the Wild Hunt waiting." There was that disapproval again.

I shouldered the satchel which was mercifully lighter now it'd been deprived of three sets of boots. Liora swung the door open to find Hunter lurking outside.

"You didn't go far, I see," she said, amusement alive in her voice.

She stepped around him and went to check on Bert who, by the loud snores coming from his armchair, had finally gotten his nap time.

"You've got everything," said Hunter, stepping in close.

It wasn't really a question, which made me think he was stalling. I gave him a nod and a strained smile.

"I'm going to take Serena to the bathhouse and the food hall now," Liora said, over by the door. Her attention flicked between us, coming to rest on Hunter. "If you need to eat—"

"No." Hunter's eyes hadn't left my face. "I don't like to fly on a full stomach. Before I go—Serena, can I talk to you outside?"

Taken aback, I mumbled, "Sure," and followed him out into a dawning twilit sky.

Liora snapped Bert's door closed behind us, but kept a distance, waiting patiently as Hunter drew me away from the cottage.

"I wanted to give you something," he said, turning to face me.

"What is it?"

He spread his wings out and brought them in close, blocking us from view.

"Take this." He opened his palm and shoved two gold coins into my hand. "I'm sorry it's not more. If I thought I could've gotten away with it, I'd have given you the whole damned amount."

I took a second to put it together. "If this is the money you got for me, I don't want it."

I tried pushing the coins back but he was too fast. He clamped my fingers down, making it a fist, and held it against his chest.

"Please, just take them—for me."

I wrenched my hand out of his grip. "Why are you doing this? D'you offer a cut to all the humans you've taken?" My voice broke with emotion.

Hunter's expression grew uneasy. "It's different with you, Serena."

"Why?" A demand.

"Because you offered me friendship, despite everything I'd done. This is the least I can do. Please."

He was close to desperation: this was about assuaging his guilt. On that thought alone, I wanted to toss the gold at his feet, but the day may come when I'd need it. Relenting, I shoved the coins deep inside my bag.

His smile had faded when I peered back up at him. "I've still got your scarf and gloves."

He jostled the pack on his shoulders, drawing my eye. "Keep them. You never seem to get cold, but maybe you'll make another human friend who will."

I let my mouth curl just a little.

He smiled, and the shy hesitation battered against my resistance. I almost pulled him into a hug, but the most stubborn parts of me couldn't forget what he was leaving to do.

"It's time."

"Right." I nodded, feeling awkward.

What exactly did you say to someone who'd just sold you?

Hunter cleared his throat. As if nervous. He croaked, "We'll see each other again—I can promise you that."

I met his gaze. "You'll remember your other promise?" His forehead crinkled. "To get my message to Viola and John. D'you need me to repeat it?"

"I haven't forgotten a single word. Goodbye." He nodded and curled his fist over his chest.

He stepped back. The world yawned open around us; without the privacy of his wings, I felt exposed and conscious of Liora's stare. So when his wings beat and he shot upward, I whispered the words, "Goodbye, friend," instead of shouting them.

He rotated mid-flight and looked down. Treading air, he held up a hand in farewell. I flashed him a smile. Fae hearing really was better than human.

CHAPTER 10
ALLIES, FRIENDS, ENEMIES

Hunter was a speck among the burgeoning stars when Liora wandered over to my side. "I never thought I'd see a member of the Hunt become attached to a human."

It seemed Hunter's wings hadn't hidden us that well after all, but she'd spoken gently, thoughtfully. If she judged me, it wasn't obvious. I considered lying or laughing it off, but something told me this girl would see right through it. So I was honest. "I didn't expect to stop hating him."

Liora cast her eyes skyward. "I imagine it's been a nightmare trying to figure out what to think, or how to feel."

I huffed an awkward laugh. "You've no idea."

"Come on." She hooked up with my arm. "I'll take you to the bath-house. Everyone should still be at dinner now, so you'll get some privacy."

She led me up the path, back toward the arena. My mind racing ahead, I couldn't help asking, "Do the men and women have separate baths?"

Liora let out a trilling laugh. "I wish."

My gut did a nervous dance. Somehow, Liora sensed my anxiety because she added, "It's not as bad as it sounds. We're not separated by gender, but the fae don't bathe with us. Most recruits are fae, so it means we only have to share the bathhouse with eight others."

I supposed that wasn't *so* terrible. "How many recruits are there overall?"

"Well, there were twenty-nine, but now you're here, thirty," she said, steering me right.

Many, many questions stormed through my head, but it seemed they'd have to wait. Liora stopped in front of a black-boarded building. "Baths are in there. Take your rucksack; you can use the towels I gave you. I'll wait out here and stand guard."

I frowned. "You'd do that?"

"Of course," Liora jostled my arm before releasing it. "Although, be as quick as you can. The kitchen staff don't like latecomers."

I promised to be fast, and went through to find two large, steaming pools. The interior was basic—no decoration or embellishments—but the water was *deliciously* hot. Using the soap from my pack, I rubbed and scrubbed at my hair and body until the horror and grime of the last few days slid away. I toweled my body but not my hair. Too hungry to care, I ran my fingers through it and put my uniform back on. I lingered only to pack the towels and soap, and then slipped outside.

Liora turned to me with raised brows. "I didn't expect you to be *that* quick."

I shrugged. "I haven't eaten since this morning."

With a knowing nod, she jerked her chin right. "Food hall's two buildings up."

We walked in line beside each other, and as we neared the hall, I noticed the cacophony from earlier had disappeared.

Liora pulled the handle of the heavy door, which opened with an almighty creak, and she ushered me in. I went through to be greeted by a blast of warm air filled with mouthwatering smells. My eyes were immediately drawn to a massive stone fireplace on the left, which stood out among the dark wood panels. The heart of the space was dominated by six long tables positioned in rows throughout the room, with a smaller table at the far end. Unlike the others, this high table was horizontal and manned by a young woman with a ladle in her hand, standing guard over several black pots. There were only two fae and one other human nearby, and they were all seated at the benches, eating quietly.

Liora sighed. "Thank the sisters, they're still serving."

My sentiments exactly.

Liora walked up the room. I trailed after her but dipped my head as soon as the stragglers shot me hostile stares.

As we neared the serving table, Liora chirped to the blonde-haired server, "Hi Patti."

"'Lo," she muttered. "Who's 'at?" Patti pointed the ladle at me. She looked ready to spear me with the end of it.

"This is Serena. She's new."

"Bah! Never. It's too late in the season," she said and continued to glare at me.

Liora ignored her and turned to me. "What d'you want, Serena? I recommend the pie."

She nodded toward the exposed middle pot on display. There were five in total. To my surprise, they were iron and had small, glowing stones set beneath them. I guessed this must be to keep the food heated, although we had no such innovations back in Tunnock. The pie brought back sickening memories from the cabin, so I mumbled, "I think I'd prefer the casserole."

"Great. Patti, would you mind serving?" Liora was polite, but there was a touch of something else—irritation, maybe?

The freckled girl snorted and grabbed a bowl from the stack piled high on the table. She scooped out a ladleful of casserole, dumped it unceremoniously into the bowl, chucked in a fork, and slid it over to me.

"Oh, come on, don't be stingy," Liora needled and pushed the bowl back to the scowling blonde.

Patti shrugged. "Rules is rules."

A strong desire to hit her over the head with her own ladle seized me.

"Oh? That's not what you told Cai last weekend ..."

My mouth tweaked up at the side. Liora had kept her voice light and airy but since Patti's cheeks were now glowing pink, I wagered there was a threat hidden in there somewhere.

"Fine," she grumbled and heaped two more ladlefuls in.

I made sure to thank her. I didn't want enemies in this place, least of all ones who served me food. Patti grunted but looked less sour. Pleased, I took my bowl and walked with Liora over to one of the empty benches. As I dropped my bag to the floor and sat, she slipped in next to me and murmured, "Don't mind Patti. She's just sour because our mentor put her on kitchen duty."

"It's fine." It really was because my thoughts happened to be elsewhere. Should I ask about the pots? "Liora," I said, faking a casual attitude, "is it true that the fae hate iron and salt?"

Afraid to look at her, I stared down at my plate.

If she guessed at my motives, she didn't show it. "Well, it'll poison them if they ingest enough. Or if it enters their blood through salt-tipped or iron weapons, then their accelerated healing can't kick in, and they're easier to kill. Why d'you ask?"

My pulse fluttered. Accelerated healing? Another advantage they had over humans then. Still, at least they had *some* weaknesses. And I had a means of defense. "Just curious," I said, brushing off her question.

Not able to wait any longer, I tucked into my beef casserole. It was achingly good. After my first few eager forkfuls, Liora groaned.

"What is it?" I asked, looking up from my plate.

Liora was staring toward the double doors. "Remember I told you about my brother? Well, he's spotted us. I can only apologize."

Twisting around, I saw a golden-haired human moving toward us. He came to rest on my left, sitting so that his back rested against the table. In a mellow voice, he said, "I'm Cai, Liora's brother. You must be the new girl."

I blinked but resisted the urge to do so again. His toothy smile stretched from ear to ear and plainly invited mischief. Up close, the similarities between the siblings were obvious: green eyes, sun-kissed skin, a cupid-bow mouth, and a hand tattoo, though Cai's looked more tribal in nature. And where Liora had flaming hair, Cai's was a lion's mane of light blond. He was also tall and lanky, which became even more apparent as he stretched his long legs out from the bench.

His confidence was disarming in the extreme. I realized my mouth was hanging open, so I snapped it shut. "Nice to meet you."

Liora clucked her tongue. "I forbid you to flirt with her, Cai. You have enough female problems as it is. Patti's still waiting for you to take her to the lake again."

Cai frowned. Although, it looked more like a playful pout in certain lights. "Last time I checked Li, you couldn't forbid me to do anything."

"Fine," Liora said airily. "Don't blame me when our food gets poisoned."

Cai flashed his teeth. "Sure thing."

My stomach cried out for more food, so I took another forkful.

"Ignore my sister," Cai coaxed. "I'm not really a flirt."

Liora snorted loudly.

Cai raised his voice and added, "But a recruit coming in to training this far in is hard to ignore." He moved to straddle the bench and face me. As if to shift to a more serious tone. This impression was tempered by his relaxed manner; producing a bread roll from his jacket pocket, he took a huge bite, and his speech became muffled by his chewing. "I wouldn't mind making an ally out of you."

He waggled his eyebrows at me. It was so ridiculous, I almost choked on my mouthful of carrots and beef.

"That is, if you'll tell us all about how you came to be with us mid-season." Cai flashed me another toothy grin.

I stiffened, but Liora said, "Ignore him." She leaned forward and glared past me. Thankfully, she directed her ire at her brother. "She doesn't have to tell us anything."

"No offense intended," he drawled as he raised his hands in surrender. "You know me, sis. I love solving mysteries."

She wrinkled her nose. "Ugh. You're just like Patti, looking for any old bit of gossip to sink your teeth into."

Cai mock-grimaced. "Tad harsh, Li. Besides, I'm sure Serena forgives my prying, don't you?"

He shot me another dazzling smile. My eyes narrowed. "Does that usually work?"

Liora chuckled appreciatively. "Guess your charms won't work this time, dear brother." She stood and addressed me. "I'm going to get us some water. Don't let him bully you in the meantime."

Liora threw him a warning glance, but as soon as she was out of earshot, Cai tossed the half-eaten bread roll on the table and stooped down, leaning in. "Sorry," he said softly. "I'm being a nosy ass, but I can tell my sister likes you."

He peered over my shoulder. I followed his gaze to Liora. He seemed worried for her. Perhaps this interrogation had more to it than a search for idle gossip.

Cai continued. "We really could use an ally."

I turned back to him.

"The fae recruits think it's beneath them to be friendly with humans, and the humans don't like us because we're from the Crescent."

That got me thinking. Did that mean they were witches?

"I thought since you're from the Gauntlet and have come in so late, you wouldn't mind as much." Despite his words, he didn't sound that convinced. "The question was a way to feel you out—see if we could trust you."

"Are you asking to be allies, or for me to answer questions?"

Cai let out a gruff laugh. "Can't it be both?"

"You should know that I'm useless. I barely passed Hilda's test."

Cai shrugged as if to say it didn't matter. "It was the same with Li. I'd still rather have you on our side. What d'you say?"

I was about to reply when Liora showed up. She set two glasses and a water jug on the table and sat down. "Well, that took longer than I expected," she mumbled, pouring. "Patti refused to get me any glasses from the back."

"Seems you persuaded her." Cai jerked his chin to the glass she was sipping from.

"I told her you'd be pissed if she was mean to your sister," she said breezily.

Cai let out a low whistle. "Brutal. I didn't know you had it in you, Li."

Liora smirked and took a swig.

I finished my plate, poured myself a glass of water, and pondered Cai's offer. I was taking sips as an idea formed. "I was thinking; to satisfy Cai's nosiness and my own, maybe we could make a deal?"

"I'm intrigued," Cai said, cocking an eyebrow and grinning broadly.

Liora shuffled and moved to straddle the bench. "Go on."

I put the glass down. "Hilda said you'd tell me about how this place works, but I don't think that'll be enough. I need someone to watch my back." Liora gave me a grim smile, confirming my worst suspicions. My stomach jumped a little. "And if you want an ally too, then we need trust. So, how about an answer for an answer? We can keep that going until all our nosiness has dried up."

Cai made an appreciative snorting sound and Liora smiled. "You underestimated her, Cai. She's as good as you are at wheedling information out of people."

I surveyed her, concerned the question had annoyed her. But if anything, she seemed glad. "I knew my brother would pry the minute I was gone. I'm just glad you're getting your own back."

"Li, your lack of faith in my self-control astounds me," Cai said, feigning sadness.

Liora didn't grace him with a response. She answered me. "You've got yourself a deal, but it might be an idea to have that conversation with more privacy than we do now." She shot a meaningful look at the one remaining fae left in the hall and then at Patti.

"Should we go somewhere else?" I lifted my legs over the bench and faced away from the table.

"No—that's not what I meant. Cai?" Liora pinned her brother with a knowing look.

I waited for an explanation but I didn't get one. Cai closed his eyes and muttered something. Next, a shimmering breeze blew past me, causing my skin to hum in delight.

I lifted a brow at Liora.

"Sound barrier," she said. "No one outside the three of us will hear anything we say."

"I've had to use it every blasted day, thanks to being around so many earwigging fae," Cai said, his voice huskier than before.

He'd used *magic*.

My village, like most of the Gauntlet, had feared witches. But not Viola, John, or me. I'd always wondered whether their only crime was simply being too different. Too odd. They were the anomalies, the outliers of society, and their whole lives had to be conducted in a state of isolation, forever doomed to hide the very core of their being. All to escape a brutal end atop a pyre. The fear that must haunt them day after day ... In my mind it forged a common thread; something linking me to their kind. Meeting Isabel had only strengthened that idea.

"So ... are you both witches?"

A shadow passed over their faces.

"Yes, but Cai's the one with the magic." Liora kept her voice neutral, but pain blazed bright and true in her eyes. Before I could ask more, she said, "Now that we're cloaked, what d'you want to know first?"

I ran through about a dozen different questions before settling on two. "What's the training day like? And Hilda mentioned an elimination period—what does that involve?"

Cai blew a low whistle.

Liora began. "We train every day in our packs. There's a bell that sounds at 7:30. They give us an hour for breakfast, then the bell goes again at 8:30. That's the signal for us to meet in the training field."

"The one next to the arena and armory?"

She gave me a quick nod.

"How long do we train for?" I waited for the hammer blow to fall.

"We don't stop until noon. We get a half an hour for lunch, and then it's straight back at it until 6AN."

I blanched. *Gods.*

"And," Cai rolled the word, extending it. "How painful that is depends on your instructor. Ours—Goldwyn, is amazing. Have you found out who you're assigned to yet?"

"I'm in Wilder's class."

"Ah." Cai stilled.

"What?"

Cai met my eyes. "His pack's got a reputation."

When he didn't say more, I looked to Liora. She went on smoothly, "There's nothing wrong with Wilder. He's not cruel like Dimitri."

"But ...?"

"His recruits aren't very nice."

Cai *tsked* and continued. "Don't coddle her, Li. His class has by far the best collection of fighters, but they also happen to be the biggest bag of dicks."

Liora did an impatient sigh. "It's not that bad. Adrianna and Frazer are all right. They just don't like talking to anyone."

Cai huffed a laugh. "Frazer hasn't said a word since he got here, and he's wingless, which in their world usually means dishonored. Then there's Tysion, Cole, and Dustin." Cai continued relentlessly. "They're nasty little shits, so watch out for them."

My bowels turned watery. "Will they hurt me?"

"Honestly?" Cai's back went ramrod straight. "I'm not sure."

Liora must've sensed my mounting dread, because she said, "If they bother you, tell us. Cai's one of the better fighters here, much to his delight."

Her lip curved, but she also rolled her eyes. I sensed she did that a lot when it came to her brother.

"You're right—it does delight me," Cai smirked. But when he faced me, his green eyes crinkled with genuine concern. "Avoid your barracks and stick with us. We'll protect you as much as we can."

I tried to smile but given his wince, I guessed I'd failed spectacularly. Needing a distraction, I followed up with, "So, what about the eliminations?"

Liora groaned and Cai laughed softly. "It's the cloud we're all living under," he said. "In about a month they're giving us seven trials. If we pass, we qualify as soldiers. If we don't ..." He rolled his shoulders, loosening them.

My pulse quickened. "We get thrown out," I finished.

Cai's face hardened while Liora nodded somberly.

And they were already half-way through their training. Stars, what did that mean for me? Hunter had promised to come back, but where could he take me? The slave markets? No, that could not—would not—happen. "What are the trials?"

"They won't tell us." Liora rested her elbow on the table, sighing.

Cai's shoulders tightened. "We can guess though, and the most popular theory is we'll have to fight one another." He grimaced. "That's why so many of the recruits aren't bothering with allies—there's too much paranoia they'll get stabbed in the back."

Doubt gnawed at me. I hadn't considered that there would be good reasons not to befriend them. "But you want to risk being mine?"

"Yes," Liora said without hesitation.

Cai gave me a lazy half-smile, and said, "Now that we've answered some of your questions, maybe you'd answer ours? Like, how did the Hunt capture you? And why they didn't take you to the markets? I find it hard to believe your handler wasn't aware we were midway through the training cycle."

That stopped me cold. Had Hunter known and brought me, hoping Hilda would take pity on me? He was definitely pig-headed enough.

Liora interrupted my thoughts. "We don't need to talk about this stuff, Serena. We can be allies either way."

Allies, but not friends, I thought. And if I was honest with myself, there was a part of me that wanted to share my past with them. Maybe, then, I wouldn't become lost amidst this new life. Some things I welcomed losing, like recollections of Elain and Gus, but did I really want John and Viola to become a distant memory?

While Cai had said nothing to contradict her, he didn't look convinced by his sister's optimism. I opened my mouth, hoping very much I wouldn't come to regret this decision. "I'll tell you." I fixed my eyes on the hall floor, unable to look at either of them. "Although, you might change your mind about being allies once you've heard. The story's long and horrible, but short version: my stepmother was ..." I searched for kinder words, but there were none. "An evil bitch."

With that, I outlined the events that had put me in the cage, and what had happened directly afterward. The Winged Fiends, losing Brandon and Billy, and then Isabel. After I confessed that Hunter had been rescuer and kidnapper, slaver and friend, Liora was slack-jawed and Cai wore a frown. I ended by telling them that he'd given me a choice—a crappy one, but a choice nonetheless.

Liora sucked in a rattling breath. "The rest of the Hunt wouldn't have liked that. They've killed their own for less."

My stomach jumped. Damn. I'd known it'd been dangerous, but *execution*? And now, that's four people I'd told. I'd have to be more careful.

"If you don't mind me asking one more thing," Cai began, "why come here? You don't seem all that confident that soldiering is for you."

Face aflame, I kept my eyes lowered. "I'm not, but he told me about Solar and Aurora, and it sounded rutting awful. And I couldn't go to the Crescent because he tasted my blood for magic and there wasn't any."

Cai dragged a hand through his messy hair. "That makes sense, I guess."

Liora cut in. "I guess it's our turn to repay your honesty."

"Li." A warning tone. Cai bent forward so he could stare at his sister.

"She took a risk, we should too." Liora seemed to steady herself with a breath and began. "We come from the Crescent, from one of the clans within the healing coven."

A pause. I glanced between the two. Cai's expression had grown stormy, and Liora's eyes tightened as if she was in pain.

What hornet's nest had I stumbled into with these two?

Liora persevered. "We had to leave our clan. My father insisted on it."

Cai exuded a huff of air that warped into a bitter chuckle.

"I told you that we're both witches, but Cai's the only one with any active power. That's anything beyond simple potion-brewing."

I was already drowning in a sea of my own ignorance. There were *types* of magic?

An undertone of deep, deep sorrow sounded in Liora's voice as she said, "But that wasn't always the case. Eight months ago my raw magic, my gifts, were bound. I can't access them, but the instincts are still there."

She looked sick. I didn't know what to make of it—I hadn't known binding magic was even possible.

I had to ask. "Why were you bound?"

Cai chuckled tartly. "She was becoming so powerful that we couldn't hide her magic anymore. And if we'd gone on as normal, word of her abilities would've spread, and witch-trackers would've been sent after her."

My eyes widened. Peeking at Liora from under my eyelashes, I saw zero pride or pleasure at his claims. Just sadness and maybe a pulse of anger.

Liora took up the story. "If it had just been me, I would've risked it, but our father grew worried I'd draw attention to our family—our whole clan—because of it."

"Draw attention from whom?" I asked Liora with jittery softness.

"There's a fae-witch called Morgan—"

A memory sparked. "Hunter told me about her."

Liora blinked, surprised, and Cai forced out a joyless laugh. "You know he works for her, right?"

I gave a nod. "He didn't seem to like her very much."

Cai was the one to say, "Don't say that to anyone you don't trust."

I rubbed the nape of my neck, trying to will my stomach to settle. Surviving here suddenly seemed like an impossible task.

Liora went on. "Anyway, Morgan likes to collect other powerful witches for her court. Kind of like glorified puppets." A twitch found her lip. "If I'd stayed, she would've come to *recruit* me. And often, the families of the people taken, mysteriously disappear. So our father insisted on a binding and banished us, to stop our clan asking questions."

That irritated and stirred a memory from my time with Hunter. "I thought she wasn't allowed to take anyone from the Crescent." I feared the worst for Isabel.

Cai snorted derisively.

Liora continued, sadder than before. "She gets around the clans by insisting they don't become slaves, but honored *guests* of her court."

"The clans are cowards," Cai ground out.

Wide-eyed, I asked, "Why come here though?"

Cai didn't seem to want to meet my eyes, but Liora loosened a shuddering breath and said, "Well, the truth is, the binding has a cost. After the banishment, I got headaches. Nightmares. Then, one night something snapped its leash, and I woke with a beast clawing at my insides. Cai found me tearing my hair out—"

Cai interrupted. "Our useless father forgot to tell us there might be side effects."

His eyes turned dark, haunted, and I felt a current of warm air rush past. The hairs on the back of my neck stood up and my arms prickled.

Liora tensed. "Rein it in, Cai."

The wind died but Cai said nothing; he only stared ahead.

I guessed I'd just witnessed magic, but their tale had me in its grips now, so I ignored it and turned to Liora to ask, "You seem fine though ... Are you still sick?"

She went on in a strained voice. "Yes and no. Cai took me to a distant relative—someone we trusted. She told us my magic couldn't be contained. Not completely. The only thing that would stop it ripping me apart or driving me mad was physical exertion. Life as a soldier guarantees that."

Her passion resonated through her words and her body emanated energy, but her eyes, gaunt and lined, told a different story.

I had to know. "Can you get your magic back? Are you trying?"

Liora gave me a wan smile. "It's possible, but it's more complicated than the binding itself. Few witches would attempt it. And there'd be no point. Not with Morgan."

She seemed to want to say more, but Cai cut in. "I hope we've proved you can trust us?" His words had a sharp edge to them; he wanted reassurance.

"I won't betray you."

"Good." An odd grin appeared on Cai's face. "Would you agree to be spelled so you can't repeat anything we've told you?"

Spelled. There was a price then.

Liora groaned as if embarrassed.

Cai's eyes burrowed into mine. He reached out his hand, offering it to me. "Please. It'll help me sleep at night. And without this, we're vulnerable."

I studied his hand for a heartbeat. It was another test. One which if I refused, would shatter the fragile trust we'd built. "What'll happen to me?"

"You won't be able to tell anyone what we've told you, not without our permission."

I offered him my hand and nodded consent. He sagged in relief and interlocked his fingers with mine.

"Repeat after me." His grip tightened. "I'll never speak of, or betray the secrets Liora and Cai have shared with me today."

I repeated the words, careful not to stumble over the phrasing. My palm flashed hot then cold. He untangled from me, and I stared down at my tingling hand, flexing it gently. Nothing had changed.

Our trio fell silent until I dared to say, "So, are we allies now?"

Liora corrected me. "Friends."

A heady feeling of relief and joy—a bubble of giddiness—erupted in my chest and rose fast and strong. I broke out into an ear-wide smile.

"*Hem, hem.*"

Cai's muting spell must only work one way because the sound of banging had me looking over to the top table. Patti was packing away the cookware and oh-so-subtly clearing her throat. Amidst our talking, I hadn't realized the food hall had emptied.

"That's our cue." Liora gave me a swift grin and stood. "Curfew shouldn't be for another hour, but they don't like you wandering."

I rolled up off the bench. "Where to now?"

"I'll take you to your barracks." Liora waited while I donned the rucksack again, and then she led the way to the exit.

"I'll walk with you until we get to our quarters." Cai opened the door for us.

We exited into the open night air. There were crystal-like lanterns, hanging from the buildings and dotting the path, illuminating our way.

"One sec," Cai said. He raised his tattooed hand, and I *felt* magic tug at me like a current in a stream. I assumed he'd just broken the sound-proofing spell because he loosened an extremely loud whistle. As if to call something forth.

Familiar lights appeared from every direction, flying toward us and filling my sight. They gathered above, making a tight unit. A few of the tiny wonders fell around our ears like golden rain, and one broke free to bob in front of my nose, leaving behind patterns and a glowing trail in its wake.

In awe, I said, "The Winged Fiends used these when they attacked."

"Firelights." Cai named them with an impish grin. "They're found all over Aldar. No idea how they work, but give them a whistle and a thought, and if they're close enough to hear, they'll come."

He strode ahead onto the path. Liora and I walked in his footsteps and the firelights followed.

Liora pointed out two buildings on the right. A supply closet, the fae baths, and then she motioned to a long building, divided into sections— the Barracks. Wilder's pack, she told me, was at the very top.

My body stiffened at the thought of the fae awaiting me there. "D'you know if … if any of the fae in my pack have magic?"

Cai looked back and frowned at me, but Liora murmured, "Why d'you ask?"

"Well, it's bad enough that they're fae, but if they can use magic against me ..."

"As far as we know there aren't any other witches among the recruits, but even if they had any affinity with magic, it wouldn't do them any good in the training ring. Magic's forbidden during sparring."

There was no relief. They were fae; it didn't give me an edge.

Cai snorted. "Shame. I'd love to use magic to knock Tysion on his ass."

"The fae in my pack?"

He came to a stop. "He's the worst. Where he leads, Dustin and Cole follow. A little gang of horrors." My shoulders inched up to my ears. "Anyway, this is me." He motioned to a section of the barracks. "So I'll say goodnight."

Liora huffed. "Let me guess, you're off to put a bet on whether Serena makes it through."

My heart flipped. "Is that true?"

"I don't know what you're talking about," he said, feigning innocence. "But if I did place a bet, it'd be that she made it. After all, with us as friends, how could she possibly go wrong?"

He winked at me, spun on his heel, and slipped into a long, lazy stride.

Liora watched her brother for a few seconds. She glanced over at me and added, "He's not always such an ass—promise."

A chuckle whispered out of me. "I've known worse."

"I hope you feel the same way in a month."

I said nothing. I doubted I'd last the week.

Liora might have sensed my mood because she didn't push for conversation. She just nudged me onward.

Heart in my mouth, we approached the door to my barracks. A tiny carving of a bat greeted me. We came to a stop.

Liora must've noticed me staring at the door because she explained. "The bat's your pack emblem."

How fitting. An ugly night-dwelling creature with zero charisma.

"What's your pack symbol?"

"A white tiger."

I groaned inwardly. Yes, of course, Cai and Liora with their bright smiles and red and gold hair. A noble, majestic creature was fitting.

Liora grasped my hand, squeezing. "Ready?"

I nodded to say yes, while the rest of me screamed no. She let go of my hand to open the door and wave me through. Light spilled out from crystal lanterns hanging from the boarded walls. The only furniture, six single beds, ran in a row down the left side. At the end of the room was an open doorway that led to a toilet and sink. It was cheerless and exposed. There also happened to be a person—a wingless fae—lounging on one of the single beds in the middle.

"Frazer." Liora spoke loudly.

I thought I detected a note of hesitation, but she strode toward him confidently enough. Deciding not to just cower in the background, I went to join her at the foot of his bed. He was stretched out, glancing over the top of a book. His eyes pulled me in—dark, dark blue, like a midnight storm—flickered first to Liora in mild irritation, and then settled on me. His thick, straight brows drew together to make a scowling expression.

My gut tumbled.

His pale nostrils flared delicately, and my stomach hollowed out. Maybe, he *smelled* the fear on me ... He continued to frown, as if I presented a puzzle he couldn't solve.

"This is Serena," Liora said. "She'll be joining your pack."

Frazer put the book aside and stood. His movements screamed predator—the hunched shoulders, the feline tilt of the head. I took a step back. Then another. He didn't need to speak to communicate his confusion.

Why, his eyes seemed to say.

Even without the wings, I wouldn't have mistaken him for human. He wasn't like Hunter, all smooth planes and perfect angles. Where Hunter's looks reassured and drew you in—Frazer's beauty did the opposite. It was close to terrifying. A cold mask, hard-edged and hollow cheeked.

Nightmare made flesh. Another bat.

And yet ... The way his shoulder-length black hair lined the sides of his face, it made me think he used it like I had when my hair had been long: to hide, to become a shadow in the corner of the room.

With a sharp jolt to my midriff, the rest of his features clicked into place. He might've been my male fae counterpart, even though his expression made him seem like a haunted man.

Liora was speaking. Her voice snapped me from my gawking. "The Wild Hunt brought Serena here."

She'd obviously read the question in Frazer's silence, too.

Liora quickly scanned the room before meeting Frazer's scowl again. "I don't suppose you'd look out for her? When Cai and I can't."

My face heated. Frazer ran an eye over me and tilted his head as if to say, *Why would I do that?*

Liora seemed to interpret it the same way because she replied, "You don't abuse other recruits, even though you're the best fighter here."

I thought I caught a hint of a smile, but it must've been the shadows clinging to his face because when I looked again, he was still scowling.

"So," Liora went on calmly, "I'm going to take a leap and say you're not like those bastards you share a roof with."

Frazer's eyes narrowed. This could seriously backfire.

"All you'd have to do is step in if they target her."

The backs of my ears were burning at this point. I almost heard his thoughts as he held my gaze for a heartbeat. *Not my problem.*

"I can make it worth your while," Liora needled. "I do the odd favor for Bert, and he's generous with his money."

I felt a stab of gratitude but my pride—my stupid, gods-damned pride—got in the way. "Don't. I'll be okay."

Her eyes darted to mine. The tucking of her mouth told me that I most certainly would not be okay.

Liora looked to Frazer again with her hands now braced on her hips. "Well?"

If she'd glared at me like that, I would've recoiled. A flare of heat from my necklace seemed to serve as a warning sign. Liora might be bound, but there was *something* emanating from her. A low purr, a rumble, as if a beast had stirred.

But it didn't rattle Frazer. With a shake of his head, hopes of an ally within my pack vanished. He lay down on his bed and disappeared behind his book. Liora stood defiant, waiting. After a tense minute, she made a disgusted noise in the back of her throat and spun on her heel.

I followed her to a bed in the far-left corner. It was the only one that didn't have someone's belongings scattered on or underneath it. I dumped my pack at the bottom of the bed.

"Thanks for trying with him," I breathed, sneaking a peek at Frazer.

She didn't bother to whisper when she said, "Sorry it didn't work. But that's the fae for you. They don't make friends easy."

She let slip a smile. We both knew Frazer could hear.

"It's what makes Hunter's reaction to you so surprising." Liora inched closer to me.

I folded my arms and stared down at my boots, troubled. There was a dark corner of my mind that took pride in winning a friendship, even if said fae in question happened to be a slaver.

"So..." She dropped to a whisper. "Should I let you settle in, or d'you want me to stick around?"

I saw it for the offer it was. Liora would stay to face the others with me. But she couldn't hold my hand the entire time, as much as the weak, cowardly part of me might want her to.

I put on a brave smile. "Thanks for offering to stay, but I'll be okay if I can sleep."

I almost changed my mind when Liora nodded.

"Don't forget, first bell means go to the hall. We'll see you there —7:30."

I gulped and said, "Got it."

Without warning, Liora pulled me into a swift hug. She whispered in my ear, "We'll wait ten minutes, and if you're not in the hall, we'll come looking for you."

My courage sputtered like a flame flying in the face of the wind.

Liora broke away and shot me a bracing smile in parting. "See you soon." She pivoted on her heel and walked out, throwing Frazer a cold, steely look on the way.

If he noticed, he didn't react. I watched him for a full minute, daring him to meet my gaze. Other than when he turned the page, he was impossibly still—a statue.

Admitting defeat, I sat on the bed and ransacked my satchel. The barracks weren't exactly cold, but who knew what the night would bring. Layers seemed the best way to go. My spare jacket went on while my boots came off and got packed away, just in case someone thought it'd be a good idea to steal from me. After slipping on a second pair of socks and burying my rucksack under the covers, I climbed into bed beside it, hugging it in close to my body. It didn't take long for me to heat up. I took nothing off, though: each layer felt like armor, although I couldn't say why.

I closed my eyelids, and the darkness beneath my lashes was comforting; certainly better than a blank, foreign wall.

My mind drifted, first to John and Viola. How were they coping? How long would it take for Hunter to give them my message?

Somewhere in between sleep and consciousness, my thoughts went to my mother. The smell of lavender and orange; the soft, smooth timbre of her voice; the feel of her fingers braiding my hair.

Another image interrupted this chain of dream and memory: the sight of gray wings in flight ...

～

"Oi!"

Hands ripped away my sheets. My heart slammed into my chest; adrenaline flooded my system. I flung my arms in front of me, instinctively shielding my body.

"Who gave a meat bag permission to sleep here?"

I could only babble, "I'm Serena—I'm part of your pack."

The male above me snorted. "Who says?"

He had the same light almond skin and high cheekbones as Hunter, only his mouth was a cruel slash, not softened by kindness. Adding in his shorn black hair and pitch-dark wings, he looked like a minion of Death.

A second uniformed fae appeared at his shoulder. Then another, until a solid wall of muscle surrounded me. And with three males standing side by side, it didn't take long to riddle out who they were— Tysion, Cole, and Dustin. These bullies were what I'd grown up believing the fae to be. A nightmarish image that I'd accepted to be true, until Hunter. Fear lashed against my insides. As it poured into my veins, their nostrils widened.

Shit.

Don't show it. Stand. Now.

The strange female voice shook loose the paralyzing fear. Pushing myself off the bed, I almost came nose to nose with the inky-winged fae. He tried and failed to stare down his nose at me. I was suddenly thanking every star in the heavens that I was tall. Elain could go screw herself.

"Hilda says so." My chin rose an inch. "I've just started training late, that's all." I cringed inside. Great idea—remind them they've got the advantage. As if they needed another.

"Is that right? Well, where are our manners—I'm Tysion," said the servant of Death. "This is Cole." He slapped the brutish fae next to him, who was tanned and easily the largest of the three with great hulking arms and a thick neck. Onyx hair hung to the nape of his neck, and a dark shadow covered his jaw.

The voice whispered, *He's the muscle.*

Tysion then waved a casual hand toward the red-headed fae. "That's Dustin on the end."

He was the tallest one, with a head of copper, wine, and flaming strands, and amber wings to match. Something about his hollow gray eyes had that voice whispering to me again. *He's the knife in your back. The poison in your cup. Don't underestimate him.*

I said nothing, and as the silence lengthened, the redhead's face cracked into a spider's smile. And I was the fly caught in his web.

Have courage.

"Nice to meet you." My reply came out in clipped tones. "Can you return my sheets?" I gestured to Tysion's hand.

"Don't think so," Cole growled.

"Why not?"

I gulped as a second pair of canines inched past Cole's gums. "Because you're human," he said with a snide curl of the lip.

My palms itched to clap slowly, but a sliver of self-preservation held me in check.

Tysion patted his lackey's arm. "It wouldn't be wise to antagonize him. Cole's not very good at controlling his urges."

"I wasn't trying to annoy him. I'd like to go back to sleep—"

A sudden smack almost knocked me off my feet. My head spun, reeling as a metallic saltiness coated my tongue. Blood.

"You were warned," Tysion said with cold amusement.

Stand strong, my dear.

Annoyed at the voice's useless advice, my fists clenched into little balls of fury.

You're not helping.

Forcing myself to face the fae again, I clamped down on the urge to wince and cower at Cole's murderous stare. Dustin snickered; I shot him a glare.

"Act as saucy as you want," Tysion mocked. "You'll soon see that Kasi is no place for humans, especially females. A twig like you won't last long before getting snapped in two."

Cole cut in with a growl. "This is our pack, and we're not letting some uppity bitch shame us. That's our bed from now on." He thrust a meaty finger behind me. "Your place is on the floor."

My reply was short and swift and reckless. "You don't need another bed."

I didn't see the second blow coming. My ears rang, and I got another mouthful of salt.

"It's none of your business why we need it." Tysion got right up in my face. "You'll sleep on the floor, or we'll do worse than slap you."

A reckless rage gripped me. *Enough.* I bared my teeth at Tysion. "You think you're the first of my tormentors? You're not even the worst. And the last person who targeted me died with his chest cleaved open and his insides shredded to ribbons."

I infused it with as much venom as possible. Dustin and Tysion seemed to hesitate, but nothing could reason with Cole.

The third hit landed. A sharp, searing pain rent my head in two. I doubled over, falling to my knees with a bone-jarring thud. On the edge of a blackout, pain erupted in my side. Iron filled my nostrils, and oblivion claimed me.

CHAPTER 11
A ROUGH START

Stirring in darkness, my muted groan became a whimper of panic. Had they blinded me? Squinting, it took a moment but my sight adjusted enough to spot the low flicker of the lanterns. My hearing identified the muffled sounds of sleeping bodies. A sigh rushed out of me.

I sat up gingerly, assessing the damage. A burning pain lashed my entire right side. Hoping the ribs were just bruised, my hand traveled to my jaw, the source of another throbbing ache. Tracing the tender swelling, I winced and bit my lip.

Shifting onto all fours, I crawled, *slowly*, toward the shadowy outline of my bed. I groped and almost cried with relief when I found my satchel. Unfastening the top, I rifled around inside. Amazingly, there didn't seem to be anything missing. Not wanting to take any chances, I pulled out the boots and stuck my feet inside—I needed to be ready for anything.

Using the bed for support, I climbed onto the edge and sat, thinking. I could risk sleeping on the mattress and hoped they wouldn't be bothered come morning. It didn't take long to dismiss that idea. Gus and Elain had taught me the nature of bullies—there'd be no end to this.

There was nothing for it. I'd sleep on the floor, at least for tonight. Let them think they'd won and figure out what to do later. I'd need Cai and

Liora's help, pride be damned. Then, there was my instructor, Wilder. But if they'd marked my face, they must be confident of escaping punishment. No hope there.

I yawned, and my mind collapsed under the weight of exhaustion. Looking down, I shivered just thinking about sleeping on the floor. Some stupid, defiant part of me made me snatch the sheets and wafer-thin pillow. The trio of terror obviously thought fear would be enough to stop me from taking them.

Lowering myself, I dragged my rucksack down off the bed and retreated to the only place in the room that felt remotely safe—under my bed, dust bunnies and all.

After a minute or so, the dull ache and sharp pains had tears prickling the corners of my eyes. I concentrated on easing my breathing. In through the nose, out through the mouth. Again, and again.

My eyelids grew heavy.

~

SOMEONE WAS SHAKING ME. My eyes shot open. I expected to see Tysion and his minions, but it wasn't them.

A female's face stared back at me. A finger to her lips, she ushered me out from under the bed. I gritted my teeth against the pain in my side and slid into the open. The female stood, offering me a hand. I grabbed it and heaved myself up. She gestured toward the exit and tugged my hand a little.

Wary, I scanned the room for half a heartbeat, searching for why the fae might've woken me. The alarm hadn't sounded; every bed was occupied, all except one. And there was only one female in my pack—this must be Adrianna.

She tugged again. No closer to an answer, I decided to go with it for now. I nodded and followed in her footsteps while my gaze swept over the sleeping forms of the other fae. My heart nearly burst from my chest when a pair of eyes met mine. The lanterns shed enough light to reveal Frazer, staring. He did nothing. I breathed again.

Once we'd reached the exit, Adrianna inched the door open and waved me through. I stepped out to a royal blue sky with a thin hazing of indigo.

A click behind made me turn around. Adrianna closed the short distance between us and whistled softly. I waited for their arrival. Sure enough, the firelights appeared and lit the female and the darkness up with their fiery glow.

"D'you know who I am?"

I nodded, still suspicious. "Adrianna."

She leveled me with her eyes. No hint of a smile. A tilt of the head, assessing.

Ancestors help me.

We were the same height, but unlike me, she wasn't gangly. Her long limbs were strong and sure. An athletic build gave her enough curves to cut a striking figure in her uniform. A thick, black braid snaked down between graceful navy wings that were scaled. They caught me by surprise as they were so unlike the leathery hide I'd become accustomed to. Almost lizard-like. Her skin was bronze and her eyes a crushing azure blue. But it was the row of rings piercing her ears and the delicate silver tattoos marking her forehead and collarbone that held my attention. In short, this ridiculously elegant female embodied everything it was to be fae. So, what in the stars could she possibly want with me?

I got my answer in the next heartbeat.

"And you're, Serena." My name rolled off her tongue. Her voice was velvety, with hints of an accent. "Today, I'm going to stick a wing out and help you, but you only get one day. After that, you're on your own."

I studied her posture; her stiff back and the tightness of her face. She seemed uncomfortable as if she might be doing this against her better judgment. "How will you help me?"

"I'm one of the best fighters here."

I didn't doubt it.

"And it's a small thing, but I'll show you my morning routine." She shifted and looked to the sky. "It might be too much for a human." My guard went up at that. "Because the only way you'll survive here is by training harder and longer than everyone else, even when injured." Her eyes went to my ribs, like she knew the pain that dwelt there. "And when others rest, that's when you pick up a weapon." She maintained a detached air—one that made me wonder why she was bothering with me in the first place.

She sighed softly through her nose. "And I suppose I'll get Tysion and the other two to leave you alone."

"You can do that?"

Adrianna cocked an eyebrow. Uh-oh.

"It'd be my pleasure. I've been looking for a reason to smash their wings into the dirt." And with a cruel smile, she added, "I got them to leave your shit alone, didn't I?"

"My ..." Something clicked into place. "You stopped them from stealing my stuff—how?"

I was in awe.

A shrug, as if it were nothing. "There's more than one way to skin a korgan."

I blinked. *Korgan?*

"I'll keep them off your back, but that's it." Adrianna put her hands on her hips. "Don't come crying to me every time you stub your toe, got it?"

I didn't stop to think. I nodded sharply.

"Good. Follow me."

She whirled and headed left. I had to take two steps for every one of Adrianna's, despite our legs being the same length. And the pain in my side meant every breath lashed against my lungs like a burning whip. I bit down on the discomfort and didn't complain or ask where we were going. Adrianna didn't seem the type to invite questions or excuses.

But as we veered off the path, I almost came to a halt. The only thing ahead seemed to be the lake. She might have noticed my hesitation because she said, "We're going out there to jog around the lakeshore and then swim."

I sped up. "Won't we freeze?"

It wasn't Gauntlet-cold, but there was still a coolness to the air.

"I won't—you might."

Rutting hell.

Adrianna nodded to the lake. "There's a platform that I swim to, but it's in the center of the lake. Your ribs are bruised, so when the pain gets too much, turn back."

"What's too much?"

"After you've vomited and before you've passed out."

I felt myself shrink. "What about our clothes? How do we get them dry in time for training?"

Adrianna gave me a sideways look that I recognized from my days in Tunnock. It was the what's-wrong-with-you face.

"We don't keep our clothes on," she said, bemused. "That's why we run around the lake first—to get our body temperatures to climb. Hopefully, you'll avoid catching the sneezes that way."

Dread sluiced through my veins as I caught another glimpse of the deathly black mass of chilly water. Nerves fired sparks into my gut. I'd loved swimming in the rivers and shallow pools of Tunnock, but they looked like mere puddles compared to this.

Adrianna came to a stop lakeside and turned my way. "I will only say this once because I don't want you moaning—you've got very little muscle."

As if I didn't know.

"Running and swimming should build your endurance and strength without putting too much strain on your body. You want to tone and condition it, not break it. Remember that. Also, the cold will teach you how to control stress responses, but there's another obvious advantage."

"Mm."

"You won't lose time bathing in the barrack baths."

No wonder this girl—female—was one of the best if she never even slowed to wash herself. I prayed she didn't believe food was an inconvenience, too.

"Let's go."

She set off running. I wept on the inside.

For five minutes I tried to keep up and failed. For the following twenty, I blanked out. My focus narrowed to keeping my body working, one foot in front of the other, sucking air into ragged lungs, and wiping burning sweat from my eyes.

Finally—*finally,* I saw Adrianna stop up ahead. I was wheezing, my side screaming, as I reached her and collapsed to my knees. My starving lungs drank in the air like nectar. Dry retching came next. Thank the stars my stomach was empty.

"You sound like you're dying." Adrianna held out a hand.

"I think I am."

She pulled me up and straight into a walk. My muscles were jelly.

Leading me close to the water's edge, Adrianna released me and started to strip. My face burned as she bared her breasts; I looked away, embarrassed.

"Do you like females?"

A blunt but innocent question.

Surprised, my gaze went to hers. She stood without a stitch on, and yet she owned every inch of it. I didn't have a frame of reference other than myself, but I felt like a pale, slack-jawed mortal looking upon a bronze goddess. It hurt to compare. Safe to say, Adrianna was bringing out my insecure side.

"Your blood's heated," she said by way of explanation.

"Oh ... it's not for that reason."

Her head tilted, so I added, "Humans in the Gauntlet aren't used to seeing anyone naked, not until they're married."

Adrianna freed a husky cackle. "Humans always were slow."

I wasn't sure whether to feel offended or amused.

Her face slipped back into its distant, aloof mask, while her posture betrayed idle boredom. "I'm going in. Follow when you're ready."

I watched as she silently glided out into the lake and swam for the landing platform. Her strokes were smooth, fast, powerful—nothing I could match.

With fumbling fingers, I shed layer after layer until only my undergarments and socks remained. Spotting a hollowed-out tree trunk and stepping gingerly to avoid the sharper stones, I placed everything into the stump in case a wandering fae decided to play a joke. Pausing only to quickly whip my underthings off, I made my way to the water's edge.

When the water reached my belly, the pain in my side turned to agony. If I didn't move now, I never would. Plunging in headfirst, my muscles screamed in protest, and as I broke the surface, the cold bit deep into my lungs, squeezing. My breath came in jolting gasps, and my neck burned with icy fire. Kicking out desperately, I did the butterfly stroke. But my panting became so violent, I took on water, gulping and choking.

"On your back, now," I heard Adrianna shout.

I flipped. The ache in my ribs and jaw eased a touch. And my next inhale didn't almost drown me. I kept a slow pace; the movement, and watching the star-freckled sky turn to budding dawn diverted me. Time ceased. Then, Adrianna was there, swimming by my side, making it look too easy. A little part of me hated her for it.

"You're done."

Surprised, I went onto my front and peered at the platform. It wasn't that far. Caught between iron will and the cowardly part that wanted to curl into a ball, I exhaled, "I could go further—I'm getting used to it."

"Because your body's acclimatizing, but it's sapping your energy reserves. You'll cramp soon, and you've still got hours of exercise ahead."

I wanted to cry.

"Turn around, now." It wasn't a request.

Back on the lakeside and shivering violently, I wobbled to the tree trunk. Adrianna had come ashore with me and while I pulled clothes on, she got changed in silence. My limbs were leaden and shaking, but I still angled my body and kept my back to her. With only my boots to go, Adrianna moved closer and asked, "Are you ashamed of your body?" No filter. A blunt demand.

Too tired for lies, I pushed my feet in boots and then faced her. I told the truth, horrible as it might have been. "Yes."

She gave me a curt nod. "If I'm the first female you've seen naked, how do you know what's normal?"

"Humans find other ways to tell you what's normal. Back in the Gauntlet ... there were people who thought I looked so weird, they exiled me as a changeling."

Adrianna peered at me. "Why? What's wrong with you?"

Somehow her candidness didn't bother me. The fact she even asked made opening-up easier and the past seem more distant.

I detached slightly as the words poured out. "My stepmother said I looked like a boy." I ran a hand through my short, wet hair. "And called me hopeless because men didn't find that sort of thing attractive."

Adrianna cocked her head, eyeballing my body. "You don't look like a boy, and besides, males don't find one thing attractive. Some like curvy and petite, others like slender and tall." She jerked her head at me. "Haven't you considered it's a good thing to be the way you are? For one thing, you don't have to lug these ..." She grabbed her breasts and jiggled them. "... around with you during your training."

I couldn't help it. I laughed freely.

A bell clanged in the distance. Adrianna's head turned toward the noise, her face settling into a grim frown. Playtime was over. "Enough self-pity. We're going to the food hall. Sit near the fire. Choose foods that give you the most energy, not ones that fill you. You don't want to be throwing it up in front of the instructors. We've already got too many recruits doing that on a daily basis."

A joke? I couldn't tell with her.

Adrianna blew a whistle and the fireflies dispersed. The sun now lit our way. She walked off into a loping stride.

I scrambled after her, my mind wandering, dreaming of the hot meal and fire that awaited. My clothes had stuck to me with the damp, and the crisp morning air caused shivers to rack my body.

We hit the smooth paving stones of Kasi's pathway, and I lifted my nose to draw in the smell, so like John's bakery, deep into my lungs. There, a sour tint of bread rising, and that warm loveliness, melting down the throat, signaling cake being laid out to cool.

Despite the stiffness seizing my limbs, I kept up with Adrianna this time, and as we stepped into the hall, my stomach rumbled in appreciation. No one was serving at the top table, but it didn't stop me flying up the aisle to grab a bowl.

The giant cauldrons from yesterday had gone, replaced by platters of hot and cold breakfast foods. I stayed clear of anything leafy and green and went straight for high energy. Oatmeal piled high with honey and sugar, a mouthwatering plate filled with donuts, cupcakes, and bear claws. The finishing touch, a glass of milk. Adrianna served herself fruits and various sweet buns beside me.

Engrossed in the food, I didn't notice Cai and Liora's arrival until a familiar voice sounded out, "Save us, will there be any food left once you're done?"

I swiveled to find Cai's toothy grin and Liora's gentle smile, which both vanished the second they saw my face.

"Mother moon!"

"What did they *do* to you?" Liora gawked.

My hand fluttered to my jaw. "They weren't happy I'd joined the team."

Liora's mouth hung open in horror. Cai, on the other hand, looked murderous. "They won't get away with this."

I tried for nonchalant. "Something tells me they've gotten away with much worse."

Neither said anything, but Liora's face became a picture of pity, and Cai simply stared at my jaw, scowling.

Adrianna moved to my side and made no sign of welcome. "Are you joining me?" Hands full, she jerked her chin to the bench nearest the fire.

Cai cut in, "*Of course,* we'll join you."

He flashed his teeth in a taunting grin, but Adrianna was more than a match for him. She surveyed him for half a second and marched to the bench, dismissing him as easily as she might a speck of dust.

Cai's throat bobbed. I might've called him intimidated. He caught me staring and bent to whisper, "You have some explaining to do."

He pulled away with a smile. I gave him one in return—the kind that promised answers. I left them to fill their own plates and went to join Adrianna.

Close to drooling, I tucked into my food. But after Cai and Liora slid in opposite with a collection of fruit and cereals, it became impossible not to be distracted from my gorging by Cai's relentless staring. Except, it wasn't me he was studying. Adrianna, of course, carried on wolfing down her breakfast without so much a look in his direction.

Liora's eyes soon found mine. She was the first to break the silence. "At least you won't have to live with what those bastards did to you." She nudged her brother while spooning fruit into her mouth.

Cai broke from his watchful vigil to turn to me. "Shit—sorry. I wasn't thinking." He reached into his jacket pocket and pulled out a tin. "This is a salve. It'll bring down the swelling and ease the pain. We might be banned from using magic during sparring, but healing cuts and scrapes isn't against the rules."

He winked. Adrianna stopped eating to cut an icy glare in his direction. Maybe she thought bruised ribs and a swollen jaw made you a better soldier. Maybe this proved I'd fail—that I was a coward—but I took the salve with a nod of thanks and rubbed it on the affected areas. The pain eased as the sharp pine and lavender scent stung my nostrils, and the sharp twinge accompanying my every gods-damned breath faded.

I let my relief and surprise shine through. "That's amazing."

I handed the tin back to Cai. He pocketed it, his expression becoming somber. "What d'you want me—us," he twisted a wrist toward Liora, "to do here, Serena? We could try threatening those fae bastards."

Adrianna huffed in contempt.

"Yes?" Cai said lightly, raising an eyebrow.

She bared her teeth. I jumped in. "Adrianna's offered to warn Tysion and the other two off."

Liora had switched to eating cereal; her spoon paused on the way to her mouth. "Looks like we didn't need Frazer after all."

She gave me a quirky smile, one that spoke of a quiet, dry amusement.

"And Adrianna's offered to show me her training regime. She thought it might help."

"How nice," Liora added.

The sarcasm in her voice was very subtle. Adrianna didn't seem to notice, either that or she simply didn't care.

Silence fell. Liora had finished her meal, so she spent her time pushing food in front of Cai, who'd barely touched anything. He seemed far too interested in sneaking looks at Adrianna every other minute. I could almost hear him say, *Come on. Notice me. Speak to me, damn you!*

I was washing down oatmeal with a gulp of water when a pinprick of heat blossomed between my shoulder blades. I rolled them, ignoring it, but the pressure kept building. Massaging my neck and back, I caught sight of Liora staring past my shoulder, an image of irritation and wariness.

I swiveled on the bench, and a pair of night-blue eyes met mine. Frazer had sat at the table closest to the far wall. The hall had slowly filled since we'd arrived, but there were still ample spots available. A hunch told me he'd chosen the one farthest from us for a reason.

His gaze left mine and lowered to his plate. His black hair fell forward, covering his face. I felt a hook grapple in my chest and tug. That strange pull made me want to go sit with him. What was *wrong* with me? He didn't want company, that much was obvious from his actions.

"D'you like him?"

Of course, it'd been Adrianna speaking. She must've seen me staring.

A tingling sensation traveled along my bones. I recognized its unique song from yesterday: magic. My focus shifted to Cai.

"I figured you wouldn't want the male listening in," he explained.

Gods, no.

"What did you do?" Adrianna asked.

Folding his arms, he said, "It's a spell protecting us from nosy fae."

Cai's trademark grin, noticeably absent, was replaced by a highly resentful look. I guessed it had nothing to do with me and everything to do with Adrianna ignoring him. Something told me he wasn't used to rejection from beautiful women—females.

Adrianna popped fruit in her mouth and stared him down. A worthy adversary.

I caught Liora's eye. We both looked away at the same time, close to laughter. That disappeared pretty damned quick when Adrianna added, "So, are you interested in him?" Her back grew rigid. "You should know wingless fae are often dangerous. Just some friendly advice—take it or leave it."

"It's not like that." I shook my head slowly. "He's just ..."

Strange. Terrifying. An enigma.

"I think he's fascinating, even if he has the manners of a hag," Liora said, coming to my rescue.

Adrianna frowned. "He's wingless and silent, and that's attractive to you?"

I wasn't rising to that bait.

Liora's chin went up a fraction. "He's not my type. But I wouldn't say no to allying with him."

Adrianna *harrumph*ed softly. "I wouldn't get your hopes up. The last time someone tried to cosy up to him, he snapped at them—literally."

Liora just shrugged and took a sip of water, but Cai continued. "Oh, I don't know." He smirked at me. "Our Serena might be able to convince him. She's obviously got a talent for befriending solitary fae."

"What does that mean?" Adrianna asked, her voice cutting through me like a honed blade.

"Nothing." Cai scooped a handful of raisins and ate them in one go.

His attempt to mimic her uninterested behavior didn't go unnoticed. Adrianna let out a sigh from her nose, part exasperation, part amusement. Maybe he was wearing her down.

"So," Cai said, chewing slowly, "since you've shed the whole loner angle ..." I could've sworn a growl ripped free from Adrianna, but Cai went on as if he hadn't heard. "And as we're Serena's allies too, maybe you'd like to extend that courtesy to us?"

Liora tensed.

Adrianna crossed her arms. "We're not allies." Her face perfectly composed, she added, "I said I'd show her what she needed to do to survive—one-time deal. After that, she's on her own. I don't believe in coddling. I'm only stepping in now to prevent Tysion from ripping her to bits."

My shoulders slumped, and my breakfast churned in my stomach.

Cai's attention remained rooted to Adrianna. "Don't pretend that helping her isn't in your best interests."

"What?" I rasped out.

Liora went completely still, staring at the table.

Cai began stiffly. "A lot of recruits think one of the trials will be to test the packs as a whole. Maybe, she wants you strong enough so that you won't be the weak link, but not skilled enough to be a threat."

Rutting hell. It was an ugly idea, but it made sense. I watched Adrianna, waiting for her reaction.

There was a glimmer of an icy rage brewing and then, nothing. Her features smoothed and she slipped back into the cold-blooded, haughty skin. Angling her head with a kind of casual grace that was both dismissive and amused, she flashed her teeth at him, like she was a predator seizing up her prey. Like she was about to eat him alive.

"Think what you want." Every note tinged with ice, she said, "If Serena doesn't want my help, she can stay here while I head to the training grounds early."

She braced her arms on the table, readying to stand, when Liora cut in. "No one at this table is a threat to you. That won't change any time soon, so why treat us as rivals when we're stronger together?"

Unlike her brother, there wasn't a trace of arrogance or hostility, just cool reasoning. It seemed to resonate with Adrianna because she hesitated. "What could you offer as allies?"

I guessed it would take hard reasoning, not a chance at friendship, to convince her.

"Cai's powerful. He's a witch, and while we don't have official rankings, everyone knows he's at the top," Liora said, arguing her case.

Adrianna didn't blink. "What about you?"

"I'm a decent fighter." With a shrug and a curl of the lip, she went on. "And I have a talent for reading people."

Adrianna turned her attention to me. I tried not to wither under the scrutiny of those sky-blues. She didn't even bother to ask. It was obvious —I had nothing. She'd found me battered and sleeping under a bed. If that didn't say useless, I didn't know what would.

"Has my darling sister convinced you then?"

Cai looked ready to explode as his cheeks and ears reddened.

Adrianna cocked an eyebrow imperiously. "I'll think about it." She stood and barked, "Serena, I always train in the sandpit before anyone else. Are you coming?"

"Oh ... yes," I muttered.

"Excellent idea." Cai rose from his chair.

Liora groaned audibly, and Adrianna didn't say a word. She swept out the room without a second glance.

I shared a brief look of anguish with Liora before our trio followed, clearing the hall and turning right onto the path together.

"Is it really necessary to keep goading her?" Liora whispered to Cai. "Not every woman in the world will find you attractive, you know?"

"No idea what you're talking about," he said without looking at her.

He suddenly sped up to walk at Adrianna's side.

Liora muttered a curse under her breath. "No subtlety."

My mouth twitched at that. "Well done, by the way. She refused to even consider being my ally."

Liora shot me a half-smile. "I doubt it worked. And you underestimate yourself—if anyone can change her mind, it'll be you."

I clamped down on the impulse to snort aloud, not wanting to shatter her illusions. There were enough people seeing me as incompetent, including myself. I didn't need that from Liora too.

We reached the training grounds to find it deserted. Adrianna pulled a locket from her jacket pocket and opened it. I saw liquid silver form the numbers 8:02BN beneath a crystal face. She put the watch back and said, "It won't be that long before the bell goes, and I like to do warm-up exercises before then. So, first, we're sprinting from one side of the pit to the other two times. If you feel like you need to vomit, don't."

Ugh. More running. "Right."

Adrianna gave me a warning look, like she expected me to complain; as if I would give her more excuses to doubt me.

"Ready?" Adrianna asked, her attention fixed on me.

"Yes."

Adrianna veered left and aimed for the fence. Cai was already jogging over to join her. She'd placed her hand on the fence but didn't move. She appeared to be waiting for us. Gods, how did she keep going like this every day?

Pride and training, the voice answered. Indeed.

Liora gave me a commiserating look. My pulse ratcheted up another notch as we went to lay our hands next to theirs. As soon as Adrianna bounded forward, we sprang after her and ran two laps. Cai won, much to Adrianna's annoyance. But the real surprise was that I came in a close third. I needed to work on my endurance, though. My breath was shallow and rapid, and my chest ached with every savage pound. At least the effect of Cai's salve wasn't wearing off. The pain from my side and jaw had all but gone.

Adrianna stepped away from the fence. "Follow my example."

She'd directed the order at me, but Cai and Liora snapped to attention. With her back facing us, we imitated her movements. We moved through lunges to push-ups to squats.

I invented very colorful curses for her as my limbs shook. But I didn't stop. Elain had been right to call me willful. She'd meant it as an insult. That it'd made me cold and remote, like a star in a winter's sky. But right now, it was the only thing keeping me going.

Finally, *mercifully,* Adrianna turned to me. "That's enough. You need a breather before Wilder shows up and starts the real training."

Was I crying? I put a hand to my face—no, just sweat. I wiped my face on my jacket sleeve, brushed the sand from my hands, and collapsed against the fence. Liora and Cai slumped down next to me.

Adrianna refused to slow down and walked over to the five weapon racks pressed against the fence. She picked up a sword and shifted through different positions. It was exhausting just watching her. Liora's head slumped onto my shoulder. And as the smell of roses tickled my nose, a smile touched my lips. Maybe this was friendship then: having someone to lean on when the world has beaten you senseless.

For the next ten minutes, we three watched Adrianna dance with a sword in hand.

"Where does she get the energy from?" Liora asked in a scratchy voice.

"Sheer will," Cai replied with a crooked grin.

I kept my mouth shut.

The clang of the bell sounded, and we pushed ourselves off the ground while Adrianna returned her practice sword to the rack. Anxiety and fear sluiced through my veins. I guessed the real training was about to begin. What happened next didn't soothe my nerves. Five fae flew into the pit: two females and three males. Each looked fierce and every bit the warrior. They carried several weapons apiece. They were all clad in layered pieces of the same black-silver fabric and leather, with knee-length boots to match. But their coloring varied, as did size, for only two of the males were large or muscular.

"They're the instructors," Liora explained needlessly.

She pointed to the tallest female. "That's ours—Goldwyn."

"And by far the nicest," Cai added.

She also was painfully beautiful with short gold hair, and a willowy frame supporting yellow wings.

Cai thumped me lightly on the arm. "We should go meet her. We'll see you at lunch."

My heart skipped into a nervous beat. He winked and moved off with Liora, who gave me a quick, reassuring smile over her shoulder. "See you at lunch."

My throat got stuck, so I gave her a nod.

Adrianna sidled next to me and jerked her chin at the tallest fae male. "That's Wilder," she whispered.

At that, he turned and looked our way as if he'd heard from halfway across the ring. He started forward, looking every bit the powerhouse, with a small sword and a long dagger resting on his hips. My pulse leaped and swept through my body, carrying a low buzzing: a humming.

He stopped not two feet in front of us. I cursed fae senses, hoping he wouldn't hear or gods forbid *smell* my body reacting. "I thought you didn't like training with other people, Adrianna?"

His voice rumbled, deep and rough. The sound prickled my skin, setting a fire in my belly. Alarmed, I scrambled for control.

"Just a one-off." Adrianna gave a casual shrug.

"You must be my new recruit?" The weight of his gaze settled on me and roamed from head to toe. As if he saw every weakness, every flaw.

"I'm your instructor, Wilder."

I needed to say something. He was waiting, but my blood was boiling in my veins. I'd forgotten my own name.

His tied-back hair, a caramel gold, matched his tanned skin. His eyes were a forest green. The matching scars marring both stubbled cheeks, the muscles and broad shoulders, marked him out as a true Warrior and stalker of battlefields. Next to this male the others looked like boys at play, and it was doing funny things to my insides.

"Sere—" Before Adrianna could finish, I blurted out, "That's my name. Serena."

My cheeks flamed. This was beyond visceral. Like being punched in the gut, fifty times over. What in the darkest court was *wrong* with me?

His lip twitched. For one glorious moment, I thought he was about to smile.

No such luck.

"Well, Serena ..." he rolled the "r."

I wondered what that tongue could do to me ... *Damn.* Snap out of it!

"I hope you've realized I can't hold the others back because of your late arrival. I'll be training this pack at the same level and pace as before. You must do your best to keep up."

"Of course," I bleated. I may as well have been a sheep.

"I haven't finished," he growled softly.

My knees knocked together. It was getting harder and harder to look him in the eye.

"Hilda and I have agreed that I should give you extra lessons. You're to come back to the ring every evening, 8AN sharp—understood?"

I didn't know if it was excitement or dread that settled into my belly. All I could do was nod in agreement.

"It won't be easy," Wilder said with a grim turn of his mouth. "Even fae find our training demanding, and you have the disadvantage of coming into this in poor shape, with only a month to go before trials start."

Something crumpled in my chest. *Poor shape.* Those words would stay with me for a while.

Wilder continued. "You're here because Hilda liked your spirit. Now, you must prove worthy of the challenge. The other recruits are on their way." He cocked his head as if listening. "Serena, follow Adrianna's example—she knows the strengthening drills by heart. No point waiting for the rest of the pack."

"Which one is it today, Master?"

It was the first time I'd heard her sound remotely humble.

"Level two—four sets. Move onto grappling exercises after that and pair with Serena. I'd like you to continue in your role as a mentor."

I dared to peek at Adrianna; if she was annoyed, she didn't show it. She just stalked off to a space closer to the middle. Wilder grabbed my arm before I could follow. "I don't expect you to keep up, but that's not an excuse to slack off. D'you hear me?"

I didn't trust myself to speak. I nodded instead.

His eyes flitted to my jaw. "I'll keep you paired with Adrianna from now on." He stepped in closer, lowering his voice, which I suspected had something to do with the recruits now strolling through the gate. "Don't expect her to like it. She's used to partnering with me. I'm only doing it because your bruise tells me I can't risk putting you with anyone else."

"Frazer's okay." I didn't know why I felt the need to defend him. "And Adrianna's training shouldn't suffer. Put me with whoever."

I raised my chin a jot. I'd spoken with fire, but my insides were ice.

Wilder gave me an appraising look. "Adrianna can partner with

Frazer tomorrow. You'll be with me. We'll take it in turns." He released his grip on my arm and continued. "Be aware, my other students call me Master, but you're not fae and therefore, not bound by our rules. You may call me Teacher, or Wilder, if you wish."

Was it a test?

He jerked his chin to where Adrianna was waiting. "Go."

The command was unfeeling and absolute. As if he was used to complete obedience. A spark of defiance flared as memories of Elain ordering me about like a dog flooded my consciousness. But then, the sight of those twin scars quickly snuffed out my rebellious streak.

"Yes ... Wilder."

His eyes flashed. Amusement or contempt, I couldn't tell.

I jogged over to Adrianna, who was moving through a series of poses. They looked fiendishly complicated and exhausting.

It'd be a miracle if I survived until lunch.

CHAPTER 12
THE GRIND

My first day at Kasi set the pattern that ordered the weeks that followed, with two notable exceptions. Adrianna kept her promises, which meant Tysion, Cole, and Dustin didn't touch me: yes, there were endless sneers and insults, but nothing I couldn't handle. I wasn't so thrilled when her other vow held true; Adrianna refused to seek me outside the ring. The only sign of that initial kindness was she never failed to wake me before the bell sounded. After that, she always went her own way. Her refusal to talk with us had even beaten Cai into submission.

Thankfully, Cai and Liora more than made up for her absence. They'd meet me every morning without fail, and join me for our own pre-ring regime. Ironically, these moments outside the training pits with Cai and Liora were my only solace from the relentless grind and my consistent failure to improve. Listening to their stories about their lives prior to the camp, hearing them joking, and talking—I'd never talked so much in my entire life. Although, I remained silent when it came to the necklace and the disembodied voice. I didn't want them thinking the worst. It was probably stupid. They were witches; they might've been able to riddle out its mysteries. Yet ever since that first day it had gone cold and silent, despite the questions I'd hurled its way in the dark hours of the night. I was beginning to suspect the magic that sustained it had died. I preferred that idea to the alternative of the voice being nothing more than a temporary blip of madness, a way to comfort myself during the horror of exile.

Yet despite that companionship, once the fourth week rolled around, I was on the edge of a meltdown. Then, during an evening meal mid-week, I snapped. I'd wolfed down my meal and was procrastinating heading to my training session with Wilder, when Cai asked for the salt. I grabbed for the shaker ... and failed to lift it. My muscles were dead weights.

Such a little thing. But it cleaved my iron will apart and shattered my self-control into a million pieces. I covered my face with my hands, struggling to stifle wheezing sobs. A familiar rush went over my skin. Sound barrier.

"Mother have mercy, what's wrong with you?" Cai dropped his fork next to the pile of potatoes he was consuming to stare at me, wide-eyed.

"Serena?" Liora placed her hand on my back.

A shrug and then it came pouring out. "I'm waking *up* exhausted. I'm torturing my body every rutting minute. Wilder won't step up my training until I've mastered the basics. The trial's three days from now—how much more can I do?" A wobble of hysteria echoed in my voice.

A relentless stream of encouragement followed. That meant Cai employed bad jokes and waggling eyebrows, while Liora used unfailing compassion. The heaviness and anxiety eased, and when I'd stopped wheezing, Cai leaned in conspiratorially. Uh-oh. "This'll cheer you up," he began. "I've heard some *fascinating* rumors about a certain male we all know."

He winked and my throat bobbed. I hadn't told either of them about my feelings for Wilder. It was just too pathetic and totally absurd, especially when he kicked my ass every gods-damned day. I braced myself, willing my face to show only bland curiosity. "Who?"

"Frazer. Apparently, he's not just faking this whole strong-but-silent type to get the females winging his way." He rushed on, his eyes bright. "People are saying he used to be a Sami."

I blew out a shaky breath. Wrong fae. And thanks to my friends' unceasing efforts to educate me, I recognized the word. Sami was *the* elite rank in the fae army tiers.

Liora tutted loudly. "Is this bloated bit of gossip from the same fool who told you one of the trials would involve battling lions with our bare hands?"

I let out a watery chuckle. That had to have been one of my favorite theories. Cai definitely had a touch of the theatrical.

"Might've been—and we still don't know that the lion story isn't true," he added, as breezy as they come.

Liora rolled her eyes skyway. "Oh *please.* It's as likely as the one you told us about fighting our instructors one on one."

I was scheduled to do just that. And the last time I'd been late, Wilder had ordered me to do fifty push-ups. I'd almost vomited at his feet after thirty. Not wanting another repeat of that humiliation, I slipped out from behind the bench. "I've gotta go."

Cai said goodbye, Liora wished me good luck, and they went back to arguing about the trials. I stepped out into the night, whistled for light, and headed back to the ring at a run with a powerful surge of dread snapping at my heels.

～

WILDER HAD me locked in a hold. I'd tried throwing my weight back, dislodging him, scratching him. All in vain. Stars, at this point I'd settle for making him sweat a little.

He was showing me how to combat an attack from behind, but I'd been in his grapple hold for so long, I was convinced he simply enjoyed the sight of me squirming. Every ounce of cunning and rage, every single maneuver I'd used, he'd matched.

No matter how hard I trained, I couldn't shift stone. Compared to Wilder's strength, I was a kitten. Worse—a bug. An insect he could squash. I might be quick and agile, but a fae could run me down within moments, thanks to their wings. Maybe it made me childish, but it stuck in the throat. It was so rutting *unfair.*

"Get your chin down, Serena."

"I'm trying," I gasped out.

"Try harder."

I clenched my fists. Gods. I wanted to hit him, badly.

With one giant, raging push, my chin dipped low enough that the pressure on my throat eased.

"Good. Now—"

I seized the moment and brought my foot up, aiming to stamp on his. He'd moved his leg back before I could blink.

"This is hopeless." I went limp.

Wilder's erupted canines grazed my neck. While I struggled to lean as far away as possible from those cold points, he growled, "Are you going to make me discipline you as I would a fae?"

A moment of pure recklessness, spurred on by exhaustion and despair, made me snarl, "Go ahead. I've known worse."

His second growl reverberated into my back, hitting my ribs. "You don't know what you're talking about. You're barely past childhood."

A hot blush burned my skin. Wilder didn't look a day past thirty, yet given his skill, it wasn't difficult to believe he was *old*. I must seem like an infant to him. A child, indeed. I felt like a fool for failing to control my body whenever he was near.

"Serena," he barked, "are you listening to me? If you're willing to give up, then Kasi isn't the place for you."

His arms shifted into a cage, a prison, sucking away my will. I waited for a burst of defiance but it never came. I searched, groped, for a flicker —a desire to fight and be free—but there was just a pit filled with shadow and ash.

Suddenly, the necklace was burning and burning. Searing at my flesh. A heartbeat away from screaming and tearing it from my throat, the stranger's voice that was somehow part of me and separate arrived.

You don't get to quit. Fight him tooth and nail and wing. You can't measure suffering in years. He's wrong. Now, prove it.

That's when the anger came. A sweeping tide of flame, a storm of perfect clarity. He'd done nothing but criticize and refuse to acknowledge fae advantages since our training had begun. I paid no mind that he was probably ancient, or my teacher, or that to him I'd always be a stupid little girl. She—the voice—was right. He'd presumed I hadn't suffered, because I was young.

My temper reached boiling. I wanted to *hurt* him.

Stop raging. Start thinking, she hissed inside my head.

How? He's fae.

Learn to play by their rules. Go for their weak spot.

The heat at my throat rose to unbearable levels. Strength surged, coating my bones and suffusing my veins. Angling my head, I bit down on his wrist. I didn't hold back. It wasn't enough to draw blood but Wilder still snarled and his grip slipped an inch.

Good, I thought savagely.

I slammed my foot down again, using my left side—my weaker side to surprise him. At the same time, I tucked my chin in farther and rammed my elbow into his solar plexus, throwing my weight behind it. All three maneuvers worked. His grip slipped another inch. Twisting, ducking under his right arm, hugging into his body, I slipped out from his grasp.

I did the only thing I could to stay in control: I went for his wings. His magnificent green, leathery wings. It was a dirty trick—unforgivable, really—but the fire at my throat sang to my blood. *Don't back down. Don't back down.*

Somehow he saw the attack coming. His wings burst out, spreading wide.

One of them clipped me on the jaw; I didn't even flinch.

I aimed for the joints, grasped ahold with both hands, and tugged back viciously. Wilder roared, thrashing madly, fighting my grip. Two seconds from being thrown wide, I swung a ruthless knee up into the small of his back.

Wilder grunted, but somehow the bastard was still standing. An image flashed into my mind's eye. Anticipating his next action, I moved just in time. He catapulted himself backward. I swung around his body, one hand clinging to a wing, and threw myself onto his front.

Sure, it only worked because he was off balance, but he went down, giving me the split second I needed to jam my knees up into his chest and regain a stranglehold on his wings.

He let out a mewling sound. Something told me it was an act to get me to falter. "Concede."

A growl ripped through him. It was nearly strong enough to dislodge my knees.

Do it, she said without mercy.

I didn't stop to think. I gave his wings a savage tug.

"You have made your point," he muttered.

"Say it," I barked.

"Wicked thing," he said. I could've sworn his voice took on a softer, more seductive timbre.

Another trick, she whispered to me.

That voice had taken ahold. I accepted her observation without question. Digging my nails—claws—into his wings, I scraped across the thin membrane. He was fae. He'd survive. All the same, he let out a small gasp.

"Say it," I warned.

"I concede." His voice sounded dark, ominous.

I slowly released my grip on his wings. Of course, he couldn't just let it be. The second my stranglehold weakened, he jolted up into a seated position and pinned my arms to my sides. My legs now dislodged from his chest, I was astride him as he moved in close, so that we were nose to nose. I barely heard him above the beating of my heart as he snarled in my face. "That was very, *very* stupid. Attacking fae wings like that can drive us out of our minds—enough to kill first and ask questions later ... And to make me submit—that's just cruel."

He sounded as serious as usual, but his eyes were dancing, and there was a definite sulky pout to his lips. A hysteria tinged laugh erupted out of me. He unleashed a vicious growl.

Rolling my eyes and clucking my tongue seemed like a mighty tempting response. He didn't get it. But who would correct him? Who would be that stupid?

You would. A warm chuckle sounded.

Ah. True.

My chin lifted. "I don't care. You've been exploiting your advantages this whole time. I needed to do *something*."

Strong hands released my arms and clinched my waist. His eyes lowered to my hips—to that point of contact. A thrill rushed through my blood, pooling in my core. I hadn't thought—hadn't considered that I was on top of him, straddling him. I couldn't help it. The *wanting* punched a hole through my gut.

His gaze met mine; the firelights illuminated his dilating pupils. "I know," he said, his voice evoking images of silken sheets and entangled limbs. "That's why I won't kill you."

"How generous," I sniped.

His eyes turned cold and his canines punched out. "Since you seem determined to act the savage, I *should* punish you like a fae."

My throat undulated in fear, and maybe something else. His eyes went there.

Oh, shit.

I fought to bring my forearms in front of my chest to keep him from striking. He swatted my resistance away as if it were nothing—a cobweb —and cupped the back of my neck, crushing me against his body. Not an inch of space separated us. I cried out in rage as his teeth bit down on the oh-so-sensitive flesh at the nape of my neck. It was shallow, but it still rutting hurt.

"Bastard," I hissed.

His chuckle skittered over my bones.

I ought to have felt pissed. I did ...

I should push him away, and I was—feebly.

But there were other emotions, other things, to consider. The warmth of his body soaking into my skin, the fire licking my insides, the gentle stroke of his tongue, as if to ease the sting.

The pressure at my neck suddenly soothed and became something else entirely—a feather, a moth-like pressure. "There's a thunderstorm in your blood," he mouthed. Breathless, maybe even in awe.

The words whispered against my skin. An unleashing. I relaxed, molded into his body, and rested my head against his. I yearned for his touch—for *more*. His body tensed and hardened beneath me.

The grip on my neck and back vanished. I waited for him to push me away, but instead, he ran a gentle sweep of his fingertips up my spine. I could've drowned in relief; died from it.

I was flying high. I made a bold decision and moved my arms up his back, intending to reciprocate.

That triggered something; he bucked and threw me from him. I landed a few feet away, winded, but not injured. I propped myself up and saw him scrambling, standing, clutching his stomach. The firelights showed him double over and heave his guts up.

I stood, motionless. Should I go to him? Try to explain? Apologize?

Once he'd regained control over his stomach, he stared up at me, sweat beading his forehead. "What's happening to me?" Wilder choked out.

I took a step forward. Then another. He didn't move. "I'm sorry—it's my blood. Someone told me it's supposed to have more salt and iron in it than normal, but ..."

Lust made me forget? I chose not to add that part.

Wilder wiped his mouth with his sleeve, removing any sign of blood. Bracing his hands on his knees, he uncoiled. His back ramrod straight, he looked at me differently: suspiciously. The gap between us seemed to get a bit wider; colder.

"You've seen this reaction before?"

I decided on the truth. "One of the fae who captured me, he bit me. I wanted to go to the Crescent, and it was the only way to test—"

Wilder was nodding. "Your blood," he finished.

"Your reaction was much slower though. He vomited straight after he tasted it. It's why I forgot," I babbled.

He frowned and broke eye contact. I felt a pang of something. Desire, loss—I had no idea. "I've never tasted anything like it. The salt and iron were just suddenly *there*, burning a hole in my gullet," he said low and soft.

I bit my lip. "My blood didn't taste like that right away though, did it?"

I tried to make it sound like an innocent question, like his answer meant nothing. Wilder wasn't fooled. He stared into my eyes—into me— and the strength of that look made me want to dip my head. I fought the impulse.

"No, it did not," he said, ice woven into every word. "Serena ..."

Oh, there was that tone again. I'd heard it during training a hundred times over. A warning, a scolding. Ugh. He took a deep sniff as if to clear his nostrils of my scent, and said, "You must not mistake my bite as a claim."

Stars, how did he always get under my skin?

"I didn't. Because I don't know what that means."

Mimicking his coolness, I folded my arms and dropped a hip.

Again, a warning look. "You know exactly what it means," he said, rotating his shoulders and grimacing. "I'm old enough to be your ancestor, and while age gaps don't usually matter for fae couplings, it does when one of them is human. I'm also your instructor—"

Enough. I was done. *Done.* "Don't you think I know that?"

Wilder firmed his jaw.

"But what just happened ..." I almost choked on the words, on what it cost me to say them. "It wasn't nothing."

"You are a human," he said, louder than necessary. "And you clearly know nothing about fae." My chest splintered. "When we bite, we can lose ourselves. That's all that happened here tonight—overwhelmed senses on my part, and a naïve crush on yours."

That hollowed me out. "Go fuck yourself, Wilder."

I went to turn; he caught me by the arm, gripping hard enough to leave a bruise. He tugged me toward him, his teeth extended. Only he didn't bite this time. He just got up in my face, snarling. Big baby.

"You've no idea how dangerous it is for a human to talk to a fae like that. We've broken bones for less. If you can't control yourself, you'll be punished."

Pure, uncomplicated rage shook me. A fire built at my throat again. I savored it, embraced it, and then released the strength it poured into me. I shoved, hard. Somehow it worked and he staggered, releasing me. Not done yet, I went nose to nose with him and gave my best fae impression, baring my teeth and growling low in the throat. "Don't threaten me. I might be just a *lowly* human to you." I could've sworn he flinched for a second. "But if you break any part of my body, then so help me—"

"Yes," he said, uncurling a wolfish smile. "What are you going to do? I'm no fool. That sort of mad attack won't work again."

My gut screamed to back down, but something was pushing me. Huffing a laugh, I said, "I'm not stupid. I won't go for your wings again, but fae have other weaknesses: salt and iron, for instance."

I let the threat hang in the air. He looked close to ripping my head off, but instead he breathed, "Did you just threaten to poison me?"

Stars, did he sound impressed?

I'd actually been thinking of using an iron weapon to fight him, to even the odds, not to poison him. The very idea filled me with shame. After what Elain had tried to do to me, how could I? What was happening to me? He was still staring. I could back down, apologize. But my damned pride got in the way. It kept my spine stiff, unyielding. So I let a shrug roll over my shoulders. Oh, so casual. "You threatened me first."

He replied with a soft, reluctant laugh. "You really are a perfect little savage."

I shifted, gulping. That hit hard, even if he'd made it sound like a compliment.

Don't let him get to you, dear, said the singsong voice.

I blinked at the odd comfort that bestowed.

He took a step back, inclining his head. We were back to cool detachment, then. "If you'd listened properly, you would've realized I wasn't threatening. I was warning you what another fae might do." He flared his wings slightly. "For your own safety, you need to keep a civil tongue in your head. As for what just happened, I am first and foremost your instructor." He emphasized that last part. "You will go back to adopting a respectful attitude and treating me as nothing more or less than your elder and trainer. This," he gestured up and down my body, "blood rage must stop tonight."

"Blood rage?"

"The fury—the anger in your heart. You need to tuck it away for when the time's right and you can use it to survive."

A part of me felt shame for my actions. And as I knew close to nothing about the necklace, the fire, or the strength it'd given me tonight, it was an easy promise to make. "Fine."

"Good," Wilder said bluntly. "See you tomorrow."

Wilder spread his wings and shot into the sky.

I stalked to the barracks, wiping the blood from my neck with a sleeve. On reflection, I realized he'd asked the impossible. I could wash away the evidence of what'd happened, but *I* couldn't pretend he meant nothing. There was no going back. Not for me.

~

IN THE DAYS leading up to the first trial, Wilder resumed his pre-bite behavior. So basically, the hard-ass teacher who pushed and pushed and never said anything nice. However, there was one tiny improvement. He had less reason to criticize, because I'd started to improve. It wasn't enough to make me a real threat, but it stopped my limbs shaking after every exercise. Wilder even introduced me to more advanced forms of combat, but as the instructors gathered side by side to announce the trial to the class, those achievements felt wholly pathetic. I was still outmatched.

The mentors: Cecile, Goldwyn, Wilder, Dimitri, and Mikael had waited until the end of the training day. Everyone was on edge—cruel, cunning bastards.

Dimitri stepped forward. My hand flew to my throat, a reflex. He was the slenderest of the male instructors. All tanned skin, dark features, and hooded eyes. He was also a brutal taskmaster. I felt a comforting trickle of heat warm the skin at my throat.

"RECRUITS!" Dimitri's sharp voice boomed. "Today marks the end of regular training. Tomorrow, the trial phase begins."

Excited whispers and moans of terror followed this statement.

"Silence!" Dimitri's voice cracked like a whip.

Every recruit hushed and faced him, waiting ... except for me. I couldn't stop looking at Wilder. If regular training was over, then today would mark the end of our private lessons. My gut knotted at the thought.

Dimitri continued, eyeballing the crowd with a menacing expression. "Tomorrow, you are to report to the gateway behind the stables." He drew himself up to his full height, relishing a lengthy pause before he went on. "You have an hour for breakfast. We begin at 8:30BN. The trial in question will test your individual levels of endurance and resilience. Your pack's performance will mean nothing." I breathed a sigh of relief. "All you have to do is outlast the other recruits. The first two to give up of their own accord, pass out, or show signs they need urgent medical attention will be the first to go. This is non-negotiable."

Dimitri let that sink in as he browsed the crowd with a satisfied smirk.

Cai angled his head toward me and to Liora who was next to me. "Don't break anything then," he whispered.

Stars ...

"This is a message to the fae in our group."

My head whipped back around to the sound of Wilder's voice.

"We've decided on a new rule. One that has each fae wearing a weighted bag. This trial is about pushing each of you to your limits, and given our advantages over the humans, this is the only fair way to assess you as a group. Flight will also be strictly prohibited during the first trial."

Furious whispers broke out among some of the fae. But I, I was beaming at him.

"Quiet!" Dimitri yelled, his tawny skin flushing. "Despite this new *development*, the human recruits should be aware we will not be enforcing this new rule again, so don't get used to the special treatment. And you won't be able to cheat and use magic either," he said, glaring at Cai.

"Yes, Dimitri," Goldwyn said in an amused voice. "I think we've all grasped your point."

Wilder quickly added, "Just remember if any of you, fae or human, try to sabotage another recruit, you'll be immediately disqualified."

"Dismissed." Goldwyn clapped her hands.

Dimitri threw her a filthy look, clearly miffed he'd been denied a chance to bellow out more dire warnings. Most of the recruits dispersed but a few grouped off to talk to one another. Cai, Liora, and I included.

A familiar tingle in the air was preceded by Cai saying, "I can't believe it. An endurance test—how boring. When I place a bet on facing a man-eating lion, I expect to get a man-eating lion."

I humored him with a shallow chuckle and Liora smiled weakly.

Cai seemed to sense our lackluster enthusiasm. "We'll be fine," he said in a braced whisper. "You two know that, right?"

I shared a look with Liora. She seemed as nervous as I was. Nothing was certain.

"Li, your energy levels are already above average thanks to the binding," Cai reasoned. He turned to me. "You won't give up. You're far too stubborn."

I blew out a wobbly laugh and scanned his face. Not a hint of doubt.

"Serena, I think Wilder wants to speak with you," Liora muttered from the corner of her mouth.

He'd stayed in the center of the sandpit; the other instructors had taken to the skies. Wilder caught my eye and gestured for me to join his side.

"We'll see you in the food hall." Liora took Cai's arm and pulled him into a swift retreat.

I walked to where Wilder was standing. "What—"

He held up a hand, silencing me. "Recruits," he shouted at the stragglers. "Leave the gossiping for the food hall or your barracks. Go, now!"

The few remaining members of my class left at a run. Wilder slid his eyes to me. "I needed to check you still know to come to our sessions."

I blinked. "Training's finished—"

"Yes," he drawled. "Scheduled lessons have finished, but there's still a month's worth of training to catch up on. How d'you expect to hold your own if you don't continue with an evening training regime?"

"I'm sure Cai and Liora—"

He stilled. "You'd rather learn from them?"

I was on dangerous ground. "No, I just didn't think you'd want to continue, what with me being such a pain in the ass and all."

Surprise shone in his eyes, and he gave me a rare smile. That had become our customary farewell since the biting incident. He called me a pain in the ass, and I thanked him. It seemed to defuse some of the tension and aggression spawned during our fighting.

But the smile faded all too fast. "We're going to keep training because you need the practice."

I winced as my confidence plunged. "An extra two hours of training won't save me tomorrow."

Wilder's wings rustled at his back. As if uncomfortable. "No. It won't."

The blood turned to ice in my veins. Not what I needed to hear. Especially from him. "Maybe we should spare my battered body and give up now, then."

I tried for a laugh—it came out sounding weak. I hated the self-pity in my voice. The lack of belief. There was nothing left to say, so I turned to leave.

"Serena Smith." Wilder's tone was pure dominance; it stopped me in my tracks. "You are not a coward, so don't act like one. Turn around and face me."

My stupid, traitorous, good-for-nothing body obeyed him.

His eyes were cold but intense. "Listen to me, Kovaysi."

My mind stuttered over the last word. I wanted to ask what it meant, but the way he stepped closer urged me to hold my tongue. "I don't think you'll withdraw." His back went rigid as he added, "But neither will the others. The humans are too desperate, and the fae too proud. The recruits who've failed in the past did so because they suffered injury or collapse. The instructors don't like pulling people out, but we don't have a choice if they can't continue. So, while you might not give up ..."

His head angled as if looking for the right words. I provided them. "My body might have different ideas?" I broke eye contact as despair squeezed my heart.

"Look at me, Kovaysi," he said in a whisper.

I kept on staring at the stables to my right. "What does that mean?"

"Make it through all seven trials, and I'll tell you."

My gaze shifted to his and my breathing hitched a little. "You think that's possible?"

"If I didn't believe it, I wouldn't insist on keeping up your training." His eyes tightened with an emotion I couldn't place as he said, "And I wouldn't have fought so hard for the fae to carry weighted bags."

"Why would you do that?" A careful question.

He shrugged, as if to say, it was nothing. "It's never sat well with me that the fae have advantages in the trials. But there's always been opposition to making things fairer." His nostrils flared. "To tell the truth, I gave up. You reminded me that it was still something worth fighting for."

Emotion swelled inside my chest. "Thanks."

A tiny curve of his lip had my insides melting. *Damn* him.

The grim warrior returned; his hands locked behind his body in a soldier's stance. "Now, I'll be generous and let you have the night off. Although, you should know exhaustion won't be your biggest battle tomorrow. It will be dehydration. We do not allow recruits to use their canteens, so drink plenty of water beforehand."

"What if the trial lasts for hours? Drinking lots of water might backfire pretty quick."

Wilder cocked an eyebrow. "Then act as a warrior on the battlefield would—piss yourself and hope no one notices."

A nerve induced giggle rushed out of me.

Wilder folded his arms. "You think I'm joking?"

I clamped down on the laughter itching to burst forth. "No. It's okay, I get it. Pissing yourself is preferable to fainting from thirst."

Wilder's eyes widened in surprise. "Well, good."

"Any other tips?" A sincere plea. I needed all the help I could get.

A piercing gaze held mine. As if he sought answers. "First, I need to ask you a question about the night we came to blows."

We. I hadn't been the one to draw blood.

He closed the distance until we were sharing breath. His furtive looks made me believe this had everything to do with avoiding eavesdropping fae, and nothing to do with wanting to be closer to me. "I've been going over that night in my head, and the truth is you shouldn't have been able to shove or pin me. Few fae can claim to have done what you did, and certainly no humans."

Surely his pride wasn't so injured that he couldn't accept a human had got one over on him?

His brows lowered, his expression darkened. "I need you to tell me if you've been keeping anything back during training. Maybe a secret."

I regarded him with growing alarm. "What are you talking about? You've seen me fight."

"Exactly." He fixed me with a hard stare. "I've memorized your movements, and the way you fought that night was something I haven't seen before. It shouldn't have been possible."

I swallowed the panic surging to the surface. He was just guessing. "You said it yourself. I played dirty."

He shook his head and exhaled a strained sigh. Obviously frustrated. "Serena, if there is something ... it's nothing you need to hide. At least not in this realm."

Huh. "What are you talking about?"

Wilder's eyes shuttered. "I didn't taste magic in your blood, that's true. But ..." He rubbed the back of his neck and huffed, irritated. "I must've missed something, because it's the only thing that makes sense."

"Is it? Or is this about the fact I'm human?" I tried to honor his rules on that respectful *tone*. It wasn't easy.

His brows knitted together. "Serena, if you have magic, I *want* you to use it."

"How? We're not allowed to use magic during sparring or the trials."

"That's not true," he corrected. "We're allowing magic in some of the trials, and as for the rest of it," he gestured behind him to the sandpit, "you can't use offensive magic, but what you did that night—it was like you used the magic on yourself. That's not against the rules."

"Oh." I tucked that bit of information away. A flicker of fear and maybe a smudge of relief uncurled in my chest. If he thought magic was the only explanation, then the voice and the necklace might not be a spell of madness. I wanted to tell him; I wanted answers. But what if he betrayed me? Took the necklace away?

"You must know that whatever you say will stay between us ... you can trust me to be discreet," Wilder muttered.

I squirmed. Just like Liora—able to see into me. Of course there was always the option of a half-truth. In a whisper, I recounted my experiences with the stranger's voice, leaving out the necklace.

If he was shocked, he didn't show it. "You think she gave you the strength to fight me?"

I nodded once.

He looked lost in thought as he added, "Do you know where this voice is coming from?"

"It's difficult to tell." Truth or lie, I wasn't sure.

"If you don't think the magic and the strength comes from you, then there should be a conduit." His mouth turned down. "When you first heard this voice, did you start wearing anything? Were you given something?"

My mouth popped open a touch. Gods.

A knowing smile stretched across his face. "There is something, then."

It's all right, Serena. Trust your instincts.

My muscles contracted but something loosened in my core. I decided then and there to stop calling her just a voice. If this was magic—if this was *real*—she couldn't be nameless.

She hummed as if content with my choice. For one mad moment I considered Viola, but it felt wrong. I went with Auntie. It was what the youth in my village would often call female elders. I'd never used it with Viola—she'd told me it was too formal—but it seemed fitting for this ghost inside my mind. The humming grew louder. She sounded pleased.

"Are you going to tell me, or ..." Wilder trailed off.

For once, he looked less than sure of himself.

Decision made, I reached up to my throat and pulled the necklace out from under my jacket. Caressing the droplet, hiding it from outside view, I said, "I think it's been coming from this. It's been giving off odd bursts of heat, and the voice only appeared after I started wearing it."

His hand went to my neck and stopped, hovering. His eyes found mine and silently asked permission. I gave a nod. He picked up the hollow bead and stared and stared. "Who gave it to you?"

"Viola, a friend from my village." Grief twisted in my gut, but I was used to that by now. I'd always miss John and Viola. "But she just passed it on. It belonged to my mother's family, originally."

No point adding in the rest. Too many painful memories.

Wilder looked intent on asking another question, but I must've imagined it. "Well, I can't sense anything, but I'm glad you told me."

"Oh?"

"The trials are tough. It's good to know you've got something watching over you." He released the necklace and stepped away. The sudden loss of his heat and scent was like being plunged headfirst into ice water. And a desire to keep him close tugged at me. I drew a ragged breath, clearing my nostrils of musk and sweat and earthy pine.

"Remember what I said about the water. And tomorrow, line your stomach but don't overdo it. Now, go." He inclined his head toward the gate. "Be with your friends."

He turned, his wings flaring. And I stupidly blurted out, "You could join us."

Wilder pivoted slowly back around. Seeing the deep creases marking his face, I backtracked. "Never mind. I get it—no socializing with the underlings."

I walked away before he could spot the flush burning my cheeks. I'd made it halfway to the gate when I thought I heard him say, "Thanks anyway."

I wasn't sure what to make of it.

CHAPTER 13
ENDURE

The next morning Cai, Liora, and I left the food hall to head to the outskirts of camp. We'd found the hall packed with pre-trial nerves. Recruits had either hunched up to whisper to one another, or they'd sat staring into nothingness as their food went cold. Not a welcoming sight.

Now, we hit the dirt path and Cai took the lead with his loping stride. "Good day for it," he observed, staring up at the bright sky. "Not too cold, not too hot."

Liora mumbled in vague agreement.

My sugary breakfast and accompanying glassfuls of water churned in my gut. We'd heard from the other recruits that an obstacle course had gone up overnight. There were other rumors, even more troubling. "D'you think they've really built a wall of fire?"

Liora's sun-touched, freckled face had faded to a parchment-white. "We're about to find out."

"We'll be fine," Cai said bracingly. "Apart from maybe pissing ourselves. I'm already regretting taking Wilder's advice."

I attempted a weak smile. He wasn't wrong. I almost regretted repeating his words about staying hydrated. I'd also made sure to tell Adrianna. She hadn't bothered to thank me.

After passing through the training ring, we skirted around the stables and got our first glimpse of the gate. The double doors were flung open to reveal a vast expanse of meadow with forest beyond. Cai stumbled, coming to a halt. Liora let out a little gasp as we settled at his side.

A section of the grassland had been transformed into a looping obstacle course. There were four wooden barriers which consisted of two thirty-foot ladders, a planked wall, and twin airborne platforms with lines of rope suspended between them. The wall of fire rumor proved true, and the next obstacle was a tightrope suspended over a water trench. How thoughtful. A chuckle edged with pulse-pounding fear burst from me. "At least if we're set on fire, it won't be for long."

Cai squared his shoulders. "We'll be fine. Come on."

We moved through the gate and joined the growing crowd of recruits. As the full glory of the course hit me, I almost kneeled and wept. Flour sacks and cut logs also lay nearby, no doubt another form of torture.

Cai rose onto his tiptoes to scan the crowd. "No sign of the instructors."

"So, how long do you think you'll last, Stick?"

Tysion's voice compelled me to wheel around. "Do me a favor, will you?" he said, emanating smugness. "Hold out until someone else quits. I placed a bet that you'd be the second."

I arranged my features into an unfeeling mask. "How nice. I didn't know you believed in me that much."

"Oh, I don't. I can make more money if you're the second to drop out, because nearly every recruit thinks you'll be the first." He flashed his teeth in amusement, and added, "Courts, I saw Cai with Hamish only yesterday. Why don't we ask him what bet he placed?"

The bottom dropped out of my stomach.

Cai snarled, "You bastard. I'd sooner cut off my own arm than bet against a friend. Not that I'd expect you or your dim-witted grunts to understand that."

Cole and Dustin instantly flew to Tysion's side, cracking their knuckles and staring daggers. A few heads swiveled toward us but only in passing. No one cared much about some spat between recruits. It happened too often. Frazer, however, wasn't among that group. As our eyes met, a crease etched between his thick, straight brows. The most concern he'd shown, well, ever.

"Why not insult us again and see what happens?" Dustin's eyes guttered with shadow.

Cai looked ready to start throwing punches. Liora gripped his arm tightly. "We haven't got time for this. Come on." She grasped my hand and pulled us both away.

Tysion called after us. "By the way, *Liora*, you're one of the favorites to fail too."

Liora flinched but she was quick to hide the self-doubt.

Cai muttered, "Evil bastard."

My sentiments exactly. I broke free from Liora to turn and flip them a filthy gesture. It felt good for all of one second, then their sneers and cruel smiles made me feel like losing my breakfast. I'd pay for that later.

We came to rest near to the obstacle field, and Cai let off steam by griping about Tysion. He was struck silent as the bell tolled. A jolt in my stomach caused my necklace to warm. *Get ready*, whispered Auntie.

The five instructors landed in the meadow, not ten feet from us. My heart leaped seeing Wilder, but his gaze never met mine. They wore the usual black and silver uniform; something about that comforted me.

"Recruits, forward! I don't feel like shouting for the human herd," Dimitri barked.

Ugh.

Once we were standing in a close-knit semi-circle, Wilder said, "Find the rest of your pack and join them—now."

Recruits moved and traded places. My eyes traveled to Frazer as if pulled by an invisible thread. It helped that his inky hair and lack of wings stood out from a crowd. I whispered to Cai and Liora, "See you on the other side." We exchanged tight smiles and went our separate ways.

Coming to rest beside Frazer, he gave me a brief up and down scan before going back to ignoring my existence. I wasn't sure why his blatant dismissal bothered me. Surprisingly, Adrianna came to us and even deigned to give me a little nod of acknowledgement. Next, I searched for the horrible trio that made up the rest of our pack—the Bats. They came into view as the crowd thinned and merged into groups. The three fae met us with curled lips and stony masks.

Irritation clawed my insides. "We should go to them," I told Frazer and Adrianna. "We'll be waiting forever, otherwise."

Adrianna frowned but nodded in agreement, and Frazer just blinked. Gods, why did I get the dysfunctional pack? Leading the way over to the fae, I positioned myself next to Dustin, leaving a sizable gap between us.

Thankfully they didn't get time to insult me because Wilder bellowed out, "You'll be starting on the obstacle course with your pack, but you don't have to end it with them. Just remember, this isn't a race to see how many laps you can do."

Dimitri cut in smoothly, "So, don't bother trying to impress us."

"I think what Dimitri means to say is pace yourself," Goldwyn called out with an impish smile. She gestured to the obstacle course behind her and put in, "There won't be any breaks until one of you has left. Once that happens, we'll be moving on to the next phase of the trial."

Next *phase*. There was more than one? My legs weakened.

"Mikael, d'you want to start?" Wilder asked.

Silently, Mikael ushered his six recruits to one of the ladders.

"All the fae, remember to pick up your weighted bags before the start of the course," Wilder shouted into the crowd. "You'll find them at the foot of the first obstacle."

Goldwyn let out a laugh. "I'm sure they haven't forgotten, poor bastards."

Dimitri glared at her. "Goldwyn's White Tigers can go second."

Goldwyn threw him a taunting smile.

My anxiety intensified as I watched Cai and Liora line up with their pack. The Ghost Cats led by Cecile were next, and then Dimitri's Boars. Our group came last, filing in behind the other packs in front of the ladder. I positioned myself next to Wilder, not daring to look at him.

"Recruits," Mikael barked from next to the ladder, "if one of you wishes to quit, go directly to your instructor." He turned to his own pack. "Snakes—you will begin in one, two, three!"

I couldn't bear to watch. The other packs were called forward one by one, until finally it was our turn.

Wilder addressed our group. "I want you three to go first." He pointed to Tysion, Cole, and Dustin and continued. "The rest of you, wait for them to clear the first few rungs. Understood?"

I nodded distantly.

"You three—go." Wilder jerked his chin at the ladder.

Tysion and his two minions moved off. After they'd cleared four planks, Adrianna and Frazer grew impatient and went to pick up their weighted bags.

That was my cue. My pulse now galloping through my veins, I marched over to the ladder. Adrianna was already climbing, but I hesitated. It was only for a moment, but it was enough to notice Frazer mirroring my movements.

I blinked, puzzled. What did he have to worry about?

I put my foot on the bottom plank and reached for the rung above. Compared to the four fae above me who now neared the top, I was painfully slow. Yet Frazer stayed beside me. I'd no idea why; he was more than capable of outpacing me.

Apart from a heart-stopping moment when I reached the top and had to transfer to the other side, I didn't have any issues. Thank the gods, I didn't mind heights that much.

My feet soon touched solid earth. I breathed a little easier and moved off—I didn't bother running.

The next obstacle loomed large. The wall. There was no rope; I'd need to jump and pull myself over, which was an action that required upper body strength. Something my thin arms refused to offer.

I tried anyway, clinging on for a moment, but it was no good. My arms shook, and my hands were slick with sweat. I dropped back down, and suddenly Auntie was there, in my head. *Legs are stronger than arms —use them.*

That means, what?

She tsked loudly. *You've got long legs. As soon as they're within reach of the top, bring your knees up and hook one over. Pull yourself up that way.*

Frazer was now moving over the top, and yet to my eyes he still seemed to be going slow for a fae. Must be a strategy, I reasoned.

Not stopping to think, I did a running jump and my freakishly long legs got me over the wall. I dropped down to the other side; Frazer was still nearby, walking at a snail's pace. The next obstacle was another ladder. I made short work of it this time, but what awaited me next filled me with dread.

The course made a loop and on the other side, the fire wall. Breathing shallow, I walked forward slowly.

You're going to do this fast, d'you hear me?

I swallowed the lump rising in my throat.

Pull your jacket up to cover your mouth and take the fire wall at a run.

The flames weren't high, but they covered a good stretch of the ground in front of me. Five feet, maybe more.

I did as Auntie suggested and braced myself.

Go now!

Run, run, run. Jump.

I slammed up against a wall of heat; acrid smoke stung my nostrils. I landed and kept running a few steps, adrenaline spiking my blood. Once I'd come to my senses, I stopped. I wasn't on fire and neither was Frazer, who'd gone a second before me. Breathing a little easier, I came to the tightrope that stretched over a deep trench of mud and water. Of course, Frazer had practically skipped over the rutting thing. Staring at the water, part of me wanted to bypass the drama and just swim across.

It'll be cold, Auntie warned.

I kneeled, dipped a hand in and hissed through my teeth. Near freezing. Damn. I blew out a heavy sigh and straightened. "Screw it," I muttered to myself and walked onto the tightrope.

There were a few gut-wrenching wobbles, but I didn't fall in. A minor miracle.

Ah, the next obstacle: two taut lines of rope suspended between two platforms. The design made it plain that one must cross from one stage to the other, all the while dangling from a rope, suspended over a drop. My arms drained of strength just looking at it.

I climbed a spiraling staircase to reach the top of an enclosed landing platform. Frazer was there, idling. What the rutting hell was he doing?

He's waiting for you.

I blinked. *What?*

Auntie was silent. Was he going to try to take me out of the running? I kept a careful distance and gave him a sidelong glance. He was just standing, staring straight ahead.

A riddle and a headache.

I turned my attention to the opposite platform and the gap between.

I sucked in a sharp breath. It wasn't the ten-foot drop that bothered me so much as the shards of glass scattered on the ground.

"Crap," I whispered to myself.

Frazer coughed beside me. I faced him warily.

He reached for one of the ropes above us. Grasping ahold, he brought his legs up and hooked them over. Shooting me a pointed look, he pulled himself across, his bag weighting him down.

He was helping me. Gods, this was confusing.

He's smarter than he looks, sang Auntie.

No time to reply, not with the sounds of recruits snapping at our heels. It was tiring making my way over to the adjacent platform but mercifully doable. Frazer was waiting for me on the other end. I lowered myself to the planked floor and before he could move off, I flagged him down to mouth, "thank you." He shrugged it off, but he also didn't leave my side.

We moved down another staircase, hit the ground, and the first obstacle loomed large again. My second circuit had a nasty surprise—the mentors chucked smoking projectiles at us. Of freaking course, I got caught up in a cloud of it going across the tightrope. I slipped and toppled over into freezing water and crawled out caked in mud. The next few loops were even more miserable, and I fell into the trench three more times. At least I hadn't caught fire ...

When Goldwyn called out to the recruits to stop and join the mentors, I thought I might cry. There was no way to know how long I'd been out there, but hours didn't seem a stretch. Frazer was at my side as I limped over to the first ladder. I still had no idea why he'd chosen to stick close, but I was infinitely glad he had.

Once every sweat-stained, mud-speckled recruit had assembled near the grim-looking mentors, Dimitri boomed out, "The next phase will not begin immediately."

My heart leaped.

"Because we're still not done with the first," he ended.

I almost collapsed right then and there.

"Since no one has quit ... or died ..." The cold drawl in his voice spoke of nothing but regret at that fact. "We've decided we must be going easy on you."

I swayed and almost reached for Frazer to steady me.

"First, you'll need a partner. Choose wisely. You don't want a weakling by your side." Dimitri eyeballed a few of the human recruits, including me.

My cheeks flushed. Cai would pick Liora. There was nothing for it. I turned to Frazer and held out my palm. If his language was silent, I'd have to learn to speak it.

Frazer looked down at my hand, frowning. When his eyes lifted to mine they seemed to say, *Why should I?*

I lifted my chin and stared into him. *We're outcasts; we should stick together.*

His eyes widened as if he understood me. A pause, and then a tiny nod. He took my hand in his but not before shooting me a look that plainly said, *I better not regret this.*

Together, we turned to the mentors, waiting for further instruction. Like magnets, Wilder locked eyes with me. His gaze traveled to Frazer and finally, to rest on our clasped hands. Surprise, and maybe a rumble of something darker crossed his face. His expression set to stone, then left to scan the crowd. In the same heartbeat I resented him for his detachment and hated myself for wanting to inspire envy in him, stars help me.

Frazer made an amused chuffing noise somewhere between a growl, a cough and a sneeze. My eyes found his. I felt a jolt around my midriff and a *tug*. Instantly, I felt exposed and unsettled but also clear. Like I'd sailed through darkness and weathered countless storms only to see a guiding light from the cliffs. Except, my light came in the guise of a haughty brow and a deadpan stare.

Don't look at me like that. I can't help it if I find your drama amusing.

I blinked. His words had felt closer that time, more intimate. As if I'd heard them spoken.

Goldwyn cried out, "The first task you'll be carrying out with your partners will be to toss a flour sack back and forth. No rests. We will be watching." Somehow, she'd managed to make that sound like a threat *and* a joke.

The class surged toward the bags. I was about to follow when Frazer squeezed my elbow, stopping me.

Stay—I'll get it.

He broke away and my stomach flipped over. He hadn't even looked at me. This wasn't just guessing at his silence anymore. Enough was enough. There was only one person—thing—that could give me answers.

What the rutting rats is going on? Am I really hearing his thoughts?

Something like that, said Auntie, clearly amused. *If I'm right, he should be able to hear you too. Visualize a connection—a thread or bond, linking you —and then try to communicate with him. But be careful. If he thinks you're invading his mind, he might attack you.*

Before I had time to ask more, Frazer took a position opposite me and threw me a small sack of flour.

This was crazy. Utterly mad. As we flung the bag back and forth, I followed Auntie's advice and imagined a thin gold thread connecting us. Partially out of curiosity, but also to distract myself from the pain riding my body.

I started by whispering down the bond, *Hello? Frazer?*

And I glared at him, thinking it couldn't hurt to have the facial expression to match. Frazer's face creased into a frown and he fumbled a catch.

Sweat slid down my brow. *Hello? I think I can hear your thoughts ...*

His nostrils flared and his eyes narrowed. *I shouldn't be able to hear you or vice versa. I've been trained against mind readers. My shields are up.*

I could almost feel the aggression roll off him, the springs tightening in his body as he prepared to pounce. Fearing he was about to tear me in half, I rambled, *I'm no mind reader. I'm not even a witch. I thought maybe you were.*

A grumble of some half-forgotten laughter traveled through the thread as he threw the flour sack back to me. *Definitely not.*

Are you sure?

I didn't want this to be about me.

I'm a grown fae. If I possessed such a gift, it would've manifested itself before now, especially since I haven't spoken to anyone in years, he projected. *Although, I often imagine myself to be.*

Something clicked. *And were you doing that a few moments ago, when you told me to stay while you got the flour?*

A pause.

I suppose I wanted you to understand me, yes. But no one's ever actually heard me before. They shouldn't be able to. The magic to fuel this must come from you.

The necklace? Putting that aside for a moment, I had to ask him. *Can you speak ... or—*

I choose not to.

But, why?

If I'd wanted to explain myself to strangers, I wouldn't have a problem talking to people, would I?

Snarky ass.

I heard that, his mental voice snapped like a whip.

Shit. *Great, so now you can hear things that I don't want you to?*

There were several excruciatingly embarrassing thoughts that I didn't want shared, most of them involving a certain muscled fae.

Frazer's shoulder rolled. *It's not like I'm trying. Your thoughts just blasted through that time.*

Disturbing.

So, why help me on the obstacle course? You've refused to before now. I was desperate for a reason, not least because I wanted to ignore the searing heat building in my arms.

He tossed the flour toward me with more force. *Your guess is as good as mine.*

Catching it, I added, *That's not an answer.*

It's the only answer you're going to get.

Imagining the gold thread again, I inched along it until I reached something that felt distinctively different. Something that was solid and distant and sad, like the hush of midnight, or a still pool.

You won't be able to read his mind like that. You shouldn't even try. His thoughts are his to share, Auntie chastised.

Feeling guilty and churlish, I replied, *He did it to me first.*

No, he didn't. Think of your connection as two mirrors reflecting each other's chosen thoughts. When you want to understand each other, you can. Just like a normal conversation.

But he heard me even when I wasn't trying to speak with him.

That's because you're an open channel. An undisciplined mind. Frazer's been taught to guard his thoughts and emotions ... Although, while you can't ransack his mind at will, his mental barriers won't keep you out. You could speak to him and he wouldn't be able to stop you, unless you get far enough away from each other. Then, the connection would break.

If I'm so open, doesn't that mean he can hear us?

I'm shielding our conversation from him, and I'll hide any thoughts you have about the necklace. As for the rest, you'll need to learn mental discipline. Start building your own wall.

One small problem: I'd no sense of how to do that.

Why can't you hide all my thoughts?

No answer.

Dimitri yelled for us to quit the flour exercise. Frazer dropped the bag like a stone.

"I think we'll move on to another gut-wrenching exercise. This isn't testing you enough," Dimitri shouted.

As if on cue, Patti from Cai and Liora's pack vomited and her knees buckled. Goldwyn was immediately at her side, holding her limp body.

Dimitri actually grinned—a viper's smile. "So, have we our first quitter then?"

"Give her a chance," Cecile called quietly.

Dimitri glared at the female, his expression murderous.

Silence fell over the recruits as Goldwyn muttered something to Patti. She wasn't exactly the friendliest recruit, but she was like me. A human in a fae world. I wanted her to get back up. To survive this with me.

Can you hear what they're saying? I asked Frazer.

No. They're whispering.

Fae hearing had its limits then.

We didn't have to wait long for a verdict. Goldwyn nodded sadly to Cecile, who was the smallest of the mentors. If the rumors were true, she was also Goldwyn's partner. Cecile turned to the recruits to confirm. "Patti from the White Tigers is now the first recruit to fail this course."

Whispers spread through the recruits like lightning, many of them tinged with relief. I couldn't blame them. Not really.

Cecile carried on. "We can now enter the next phase. This will involve you heading out into the forest as a pack." She gestured to the hills. "You'll follow a trail led by your mentor. After the first pass, they'll leave you to run a loop. No stops again. Not until someone quits." She'd spoken softly, but somehow her words carried.

I bit my lip. I'd never been outside the confines of the camp—it hadn't seemed safe for a human. Now, along with the rest of the class, my head lifted to survey the area. Before us was a stretch of sweet-smelling grass, dusted with weeds and wildflowers alike, and undulating in a gentle breeze. The meadow's dominance continued until the terrain steepened into hillsides thick with forest. In the west, a fast-flowing river surged down from this highland, marking a clear boundary line between the prairie and the labyrinth of trees. The task ahead was starting to look impossible. Again.

Goldwyn rose with Patti in her arms. The girl had her eyes closed— maybe from shame, maybe from having passed out.

Dimitri added in a high, cold voice, "Since Goldwyn's pack has lost a recruit, she'll be the first to lead her recruits into the forest."

"Of course." Goldwyn inclined her head toward Dimitri. It looked more like an insult than anything. "But I need to take Patti to the infirmary and notify Bert. I guess you'll have to wait for me to return." With a sweet, *sweet* smile, she yelled, "Recruits, take a breather."

There were a few strangled cheers, but most of the trainees just collapsed to the ground like dead weights. Goldwyn flew off, and suddenly Frazer was at my side, speaking through our bond: our twin mirrors. *You should sit down.*

I'm not sure I'd get back up.

Tears threatened. I whirled away to put a little distance between us. He didn't follow, but there was a tentative touch at the edge of my thoughts. Almost as if he was patting my back, showing comfort the only way he knew how. I wasn't sure what to make of it.

I folded my arms and considered what was in front of me. A steep hillside and a forest. All I had to do was keep walking to pass. Yet my frozen, filthy, exhausted husk of a body screamed one simple truth at me: I wasn't going to survive this much longer. I was being held together by fraying stitches. Panic played its faithful tune.

Frazer tugged at our bond. *Hold onto this then.*

I turned to find him staring. That was the second time he'd sensed something I hadn't wanted to share. *So apparently, I've got no mental discipline but you do. Can't you tune me out?*

Frazer must've sensed the snap of irritation in my thoughts because his face clouded over.

I didn't ask for this. Besides, I can't hear everything. At least, I don't think I can. You might just be losing focus when your emotions are particularly intense.

Auntie had said very much the same thing.

How did you learn to shield? Could you teach me?

He stiffened. For a moment, I thought he wouldn't reply, but then he was saying in a dry wit, *I had an annoyingly persistent teacher who made me practice. A lot. But our connection—being able to hear and talk to you despite having my shields up—is something I've never encountered. I've no notion of how to control it. I don't even know if visualizing a mental barrier would work with you. You seem very ... expressive.*

I felt a shiver of unease. I'd just have to build that wall. I imagined black stone encircling my mind.

Keep practicing.

I sent a rippling snarl his way and got a whisper of a laughter for my trouble. It was hollow and rasping, as if his voice had forgotten how. Gods, what had made him choose to live like that? Losing his wings?

My musings were cut short by the return of Goldwyn. The mentors called for us to follow them, and we trudged past the obstacle course to come to rest in the middle of the grassland. If I hadn't been half out of my mind with fatigue and pain, I might've appreciated the space and beauty.

Once the recruits had gathered, the instructors spoke among themselves until Goldwyn broke away and spoke. "I want my pack behind me, ready to set off at my command."

I spotted Cai and Liora going to join her, and sent out a prayer to the light court for them to make it through.

Wilder waved us over. "Bats, we're going next. Gather up."

I limped over and settled alongside Wilder. Almost instantly, he barked out a one-word command: "Stay," and whirled away. He left us and muttered something to Goldwyn. She gave him a quick flash of her bright teeth in response. Something dark and vicious woke in my chest and roared at her.

I blinked. Maybe Wilder had been right—I was a savage. Berating myself, I strived to soothe the beast. It wasn't easy: Goldwyn's perfect fae features taunted me. My hands curled into fists, and my nails itched to become claws.

A rumble of distant laughter echoed down the thread connecting me to Frazer. Protecting my thoughts behind a wall of black stone failed spectacularly. He saw right through me. *You should rethink your affections, Matea. Humans often find us cold because we're known to withhold affection for years until we're sure of someone. It's one of the reasons relations between our two peoples is so fraught with difficulty.*

What happens when you are sure?

Depends on the fae. We'll either shut you out or grip you tight and never let you go.

My heart stuttered.

You need to keep a clear head. Think of nothing but survival.

As if I didn't already know that? I strived to harden my nonexistent defenses against him.

Goldwyn cried to her recruits, "Move out!"

I watched their progress. They veered left, heading toward the river and the trees. We waited maybe five minutes, perhaps more.

Wilder called our pack forward as the White Tigers reached the forest. "Stick together, but don't feel like you're glued at the hip." It was his only advice before he led us onto the loop at a swift pace.

I dropped to the back, letting my pack overtake me. Frazer went in front of me but stayed within easy reach.

After a few minutes, the constant knee-jarring rhythm caused a spider-webbing of pain to wrack my legs. A muscle cramped in my back. Thirst had become a problem—I'd have sold my soul for a drop of water. Then there was the warm liquid filling my boots.

I was white-knuckling it, barely holding it together. Every muscle pushed beyond normal limits and with no end in sight. Frazer tugged on the thread connecting us, but it wasn't enough. I felt myself slow. Stumbling along, rather than jogging.

Don't give up, Auntie encouraged.

A familiar flare at my neck had a trickle of strength flowing into my tight muscles, soothing away enough soreness to keep me going. My vision cleared a little, and my head lifted a fraction higher.

I can't keep doing that, warned Auntie.

I wanted to interrogate her, to ask why and how, but there was no energy left in me. No curiosity. So instead, I projected, *Thanks, but y'know one day I'll need you to explain what you're doing, and who you are.*

I'm using magic.

My mood darkened. That much was obvious now, and she knew it.

A picture of an old woman in an armchair swam into view. She had a lined face, long, long white hair, and she smiled as if pleased with what my imagination had conjured. *As for the rest, one day I will tell you. But not today, my love.*

What about my connection with Frazer? Are you going to tell me how you're helping us communicate? Or, hell, I'd settle for why. The necklace is meant to protect me. How does talking to him do that?

Silence. Ugh. Fine.

I banished the image and used the momentary respite from exhaustion to speed up and flank Frazer. *How are you coping?*

Probably not much better than you, he huffed.

Really?

They gave us the weights for a reason, remember?

Interesting. I'd presumed their endurance and strength reached godlike levels, but that couldn't be true.

Our pace slackened. "All right," Wilder yelled into the wind, "we're about to cross the Cutlass River. If you refuse, it'll count as a voluntarily drop out."

It looked fast-flowing; I prayed it wasn't deep as well. Wilder came to rest beside a muddy riverbank. I shuddered to a halt.

"If you slip, let the current take you and don't fight. If you want to avoid crossing again, aim for the opposite shore. Walk until you reach the track." Wilder pointed to a spot directly across from where we stood. "Cole, you can go first."

Wilder jerked his chin at the river. A command. To his credit, the male didn't hesitate.

"Dustin, you next."

The slender male used speed to his advantage. Tysion was next, with Adrianna and Frazer following in his footsteps. Standing alone with Wilder, I itched to say something, to spar with him verbally as we'd done in our sessions. But right now he wasn't the same fae. That vein of cold kindness and the hint of dark humor was gone. In its place was the hard mask of the Warrior.

Ask if you can drink the river water, said Auntie.

I could've sworn she sounded ... playful.

Screw it. "Can we drink from the river?"

He didn't look at me. "I won't stop you."

Frazer and Adrianna, who were halfway across the Cutlass, immediately bent over and cupped water into their hands. I cracked a smile.

Wilder caught my eye. "Your turn."

I waded in. At least my morning regime had done one good thing: cold water no longer cut through me the way it had on that first day. A quarter of the way across, the river up to my thighs, I stopped to suck down handfuls of water. Thirst sated, I splashed the sweat from my face.

I straightened to find Wilder standing next to me. He wouldn't look at me, but neither was he moving. Adrianna and Frazer were already on the other side of the bank, walking into the forest. There was no one else in sight now as the humped riverbank shielded us from view. My body instantly heated. *Damn.* I dipped my head and moved on, stepping carefully.

Wilder muttered, "You're doing well."

Startled, I blurted out, "I've nearly collapsed a hundred times."

"But you haven't," he said stoically. "And you won't. Just don't slow after you complete the first circuit."

In a small voice, I said, "I don't think I can keep this pace up for hours."

Wilder continued wading slowly, whispering from the corner of his mouth. "That's how recruits fail. They use our absence as an excuse to slow, and the second that happens, their adrenaline dies. In the past, we've had recruits stop and fall asleep. It only takes a moment. You need someone to keep an eye on you. Frazer's been sticking close to you —use him."

He didn't wait for a reply. Wilder pushed on ahead. Climbing onto the pebbled shore, he jogged down the winding path. I did my best to keep up, but upon hitting dry land again my soaked leggings and water-filled boots caused my discomfort to escalate. I pushed out a heavy sigh, imagining my exhaustion going with it, and followed the vein of a forest trail that forced unwelcome memories of home. The path to John and Viola's was very much the same. As was the one to my mother's coffin, and the one to the boneyard where my father rested. Not next to my mother, Elain had made sure of that. Now I'd never stand before them again. I'd never see John and Viola again. The wave of grief rolled in and swamped me.

Don't stop, don't stop, don't stop.

You stop, you fail.

Wilder had disappeared along the twisting road, but it was a glimpse of Frazer limping along that saved me. *Are you okay?*

I could feel the exhaustion echo down the bond as I reached him. A stupid question, then.

Surviving, he projected. *Just waiting for you to catch up.*

I felt like snorting in disbelief, but instead I relayed Wilder's words.

There was a flicker of amusement, but also something else—something strained. *What crappy advice. I think I'd prefer to just mangle Tysion so this nightmare can end now.*

A rasping chuckle floated out of me.

Frazer picked up the pace anyway, and I stayed by his side. We ran into Adrianna first, and without a word we fell into formation. Wilder came next and eventually the whole pack was reunited and moving along the path together. Noticing that the stiff and slow movements of the fae reflected my own, I felt a vicious stab of satisfaction. The extra weight really had evened out the odds.

Of course, as the path grew steeper, I was suffering just as much as anyone. The water sloshing around in my boots and the damp clothes rubbing against my skin saturated my thoughts. A constant irritant.

Finally, we came to a stone plateau—a viewing platform—where the trees thinned, grass grew underfoot, and the camp laid itself at our feet. Wilder stopped and turned to face us. "I'm leaving you now."

"Thought that was at the end ... Master," Cole grunted.

"Technically, yes," Wilder said stonily. "But this is the last leg of the loop. It's all downhill from here until Kasi, and it's easier when recruits run it at their own pace. It'll get your blood pumping, and the exhilaration should help you push through to the second circuit."

"How do we know when someone quits, Master?" Tysion drawled.

"They'll tell you when you near the camp and you're about to start a new circuit," Wilder replied. "Now, we're doing this staggered, so who wants to go first?"

"I'll do it," Adrianna piped up.

Wilder nodded. "Good. You're free to go."

She set off at a sprint; something told me it was for Wilder's benefit. I tried not to think ugly thoughts and failed. Dustin was next and the others followed one by one until it was just Frazer and me. Then, as he disappeared around a bend in the forest, I felt him tug on the bond as if to get my attention.

I won't go fast. Let me know when you get close.

I will, I told him.

Wilder cleared his throat. "I'm taking a different route to the bottom of the loop." He sounded strained, worried even. "The instructors have a few ... helpers watching our recruits' movements. Remember what I said: don't stop to rest and ..." his eyes bored into mine, "don't be tempted to sabotage the others, because we'll find out."

My mouth set hard with irritation. "You can't seriously think I'd do that—"

His lips hardly moved as he muttered, "No, but others might."

With that he sped off, becoming a blur on the path behind me.

What in the burning courts had that been? A warning?

Shaking my head clear, I ran in the opposite direction. The path became a gentle slope downhill; I increased my speed. My gait was jerky, but the trodden grass path was soft and smooth. The wind whipped past and exhilaration flooded my core, strengthening my legs.

As I joined Frazer's side, a wild laugh broke loose.

His thoughts nudged mine. *Want to go faster?*

I bared my teeth at him in wicked amusement. Together, we bolted forward and stayed in sync. Pulse singing in my veins, a zephyr cooling my cheeks, I felt unbound. *Free.*

A fierce, cawing laugh from beside me, from Frazer, made my face crack in two with a smile. That died the moment Tysion appeared on the track ahead. Frazer shifted to my right, grasped my hand, and tugged me off the path. We didn't go far, but we kept a healthy distance from the male. Frazer didn't let go until we'd passed him by. The second we had, we broke apart, and by unspoken agreement, didn't bother to return to the track. I barely noticed overtaking Cole, who was also running along the designated trail. We doubled our speed again, and the loop flew by. Minutes, maybe seconds, passed. We couldn't see the path anymore.

Frazer vented his feelings with another feral laugh and did a flip off a fallen log.

Show-off.

His response down the bond was a flash of unbridled joy. Then the next emotion flinging its way toward me was panic. Frazer whirled and sprinted straight for me.

What's wrong? I slowed. Fear squashed the joy right out of me.

Dustin's tracking us.

I stopped. *Why?*

Don't know. We passed him a minute ago.

Frazer made it to my side just as Dustin appeared from behind. His cheeks were flushed as red as the hair atop his head. He prowled toward us, his back hunched, his nostrils flaring. Instinct kicked in, flooding more adrenaline into my system. A prey response.

Dustin sniffed the air, drinking in my fear. But Wilder had given me something—a way to threaten him. Had he known?

"They'll kick you out if you try to sabotage another recruit."

"Who's going to tell them? You? They'd never believe a human over a fae, and as for that monstrosity—"

Frazer's growl vibrated in the back of his throat.

Dustin responded with a huff of contempt.

"Cai was right about you," I said.

That got his eyes narrowing. Good.

"You're a dim-witted troll if you think the instructors don't have the loop covered with fae. They'll see, they'll know—"

The words died on my lips as Dustin flashed his teeth.

"If there were any strange fae close by, I'd smell and hear them, you dumb bitch," he mocked.

My heart tumbled and sank.

Dustin stepped closer. "Surely you haven't got yourself another body-guard? First Adrianna *and* now this wingless worm."

Frazer didn't move. A cold calm emanated from him. His body language screamed of confidence with his head tilted, almost bemused-like, and his arms hanging loose at his sides.

Dustin must've noticed too because his eyes fixed on my fae protec-tor, the actual threat. "Something tells me this one's only interested in an easy lay. He won't actually lift a finger to stop me from doing what's necessary." His eyes sparked and his back arched. "Because if I knock you out—one blow, no mark—this hell ends. And you're just the bitch who fell asleep."

I wanted to pound Dustin's teeth down his throat, but I knew the words were meant for Frazer. All to convince him I wasn't worth the trou-ble. Concerned they might be working I tried to sense Frazer's inten-tions. Either he projected his thoughts or his barriers were down because it was all there: a swirling vortex of black, pitiless wrath. A storm of bloody rage.

I turned to Dustin, smiling.

He pounced. Frazer's body blurred.

They crashed into each other, the force knocking me back. I scram-bled away from them as they tumbled through the air. One, two ... four seconds later, Frazer had Dustin pinned and he bit into his throat. Worry knotted in my stomach as he shook his head, like a wolf snapping the neck of its prey.

Frazer?

He growled. I hesitated. Would he turn on me in this state?

He won't hurt you, Auntie told me. Again, cryptically. Nevertheless, I took courage from it.

"Frazer. Enough. Cole and Tysion will pass by soon. We've got to go. Dustin's got the message. Haven't you?" I demanded.

Silence. Frazer snarled and bit down harder.

"Yes! I've got the fucking message," Dustin blurted out. "She's *your* bitch. I won't touch her."

Really? That's what he thought?

Frazer sheathed his canines and hissed in warning before releasing him and backing off. Dustin rose, pressing a hand down on the bite to staunch the bleeding.

"You'll regret this," he said with a haughty curl of his lip. "You both will."

A throb of maddened rage pulsed on the other end of the thread. Something told me that this was actually part of Frazer—something constantly seething under the surface, ready to spring forth and devour the world.

It didn't frighten me. Worryingly, it felt—tasted—familiar.

I went to tap Frazer's elbow. Just a light touch to bring him back to the moment. "Let's go."

"This isn't over," Dustin snarled with fresh venom. "All I have to do is show Wilder this bite—"

A hot line of anger sliced through me. "You do that, and let's see who he believes. Just remember, *I'm* not the one he despises." A bluff.

Dustin expelled a harsh laugh. "You think a renowned warrior would believe a human over a fae? What did you do, open your legs for him?"

That hit a nerve. "There's a fae standing right in front of you."

"Him?" Dustin spat at Frazer's feet. "He's a mute. What's he gonna do? Mime? Act out what happened? He's a joke."

"All he has to do is nod to confirm my story. So, *please*, go crying to the instructors. It'd make my day if you got kicked out."

I turned my back. The ultimate sign of trust that Frazer would protect it.

I ran toward the path and he joined my side a moment later. *That was reckless. Don't insult a fae by showing them your back if I'm not there.*

My lips pressed together in an effort to quell the wry laughter and stay quiet. As if he was in any position to give advice. Given he'd been inches from snapping someone's neck only moments ago.

The thrill from our sprint had gone, and with its death the ache in my limbs returned in full force. We jogged along in an exhausted silence until the trees thinned, giving way to open grassland and a clear vista of the valley below. We came to a natural stop as the path ahead descended abruptly, sloping all the way down the hillside back toward camp.

Frazer grasped my arm. He was squinting.

"What is it?" I asked aloud.

A bob of his chin. I tracked his gaze toward a small group congregating near the start of the loop. I was too far away to see individuals, but excitement exploded inside of me anyway. I peeked up at Frazer, hardly daring to believe it. His tiny half-smile had me blinking back tears. "We made it?" I croaked.

He gave a nod to confirm.

Overwhelmed, I cried out and pulled him into a hug. He stiffened so much it was like embracing a statue, but I was too busy sobbing on his shoulder to let go. That is until he deigned to pat me on the head. A clear signal that my time was up.

"Sorry." I pulled away, wiping my eyes on my sleeve. "I just didn't think I'd make it."

He gave me a tight smile. *I know, but it's still best if people don't see affection like that.* His mental voice was a whisper.

I didn't question his logic. It'd be easy for people to get the wrong idea. Damn, I didn't understand our connection either. Only that it felt natural and pure. A mutual understanding. Although, I also got the sense he just wasn't very comfortable being touched. I'd have to respect that. To remember.

Once at the bottom of the slope, we walked the last leg of the loop together. Frazer slunk off at the same time as two people broke away from the main crowd to envelop me in a hug. Smothered in red and gold hair, my friends' relieved laughter rang in my ears.

"Thank the moon!" Liora broke away. "We didn't know what had happened ..."

Cai pulled back. "A ranger flew in and pulled Goldwyn aside. Then she announced the trial was over, just like that." He clicked his fingers.

"Rangers?" I questioned.

Liora answered by drawing my attention to Goldwyn and a strange male deep in conversation. A gray hood covered the male's face, but he was armed to the teeth and his wings were feathered—something I'd never seen before.

Cai was the one to answer. "Apparently, our instructors *forgot* to mention they had a group of Sami warriors watching us."

I blinked. Wilder had warned me there'd be "helpers" monitoring us, but the *Sami*? They were a different breed of warrior, able to kill in three blows and move undetected even among the fae. Yet they hadn't stopped Dustin's attempt to sabotage me. Helpers, indeed.

Cai added, "Anyway, we should go eat while we have the chance. Goldwyn's asked us to come back in an hour."

Oh, gods.

"It's nothing to worry about," Liora said quickly, reading my dismay. "They're just going to tell us what the next trial is."

"Oh." I wouldn't call that nothing.

Cai slipped his arm into the crook of my elbow. "While we're walking, you should tell us why Frazer's suddenly taken an interest in you."

He nudged me toward Kasi, and Liora fell in beside us.

I shrugged it off. "We understand each other, that's all." There was time for explanations later. After food.

Liora looked curious, and Cai grinned, dimpling.

"Fascinating," he said.

"Mm."

He didn't push for clarification. Although, it was clearly killing him not to. As we moved through the gate that marked the boundary of Kasi, Cai said in a rare moment of humility, "I can't believe I made it."

I nodded numbly.

"One down, six to go," Liora murmured.

Rutting fantastic.

CHAPTER 14
CHOSEN

Cai, Liora, and I crowed in delight at the sight of the feast awaiting us in the food hall. Not many recruits were back, so we had the run of the place. And while eating and drinking our fill within a soundproof bubble, we shared stories from the loop. Cai and Liora went first. Largely uneventful. And then it was my turn.

I started by telling them about Dustin. After they'd finished cursing the male into oblivion, Frazer's involvement and his willingness to protect me only led to more questions. I confessed to the mental connection we'd forged, but left out Auntie's explanation. I hoped that as witches they might have their own answers. They seemed more baffled than anything.

Cai rubbed his chin stubble, frowning. "Mind reading is a rare gift. He really denied having the ability?"

I nodded.

"Maybe he was lying," Liora wondered.

"I don't think so," I murmured.

Cai pressed on. "But for him to say his mental shields were up—that *must* be a lie, or ..."

A note of uncertainty struck my ears. I could guess why.

"I didn't lie." Steel entered my voice. Then I relented. It seemed wrong to keep it hidden any longer. "But ..."

"There's a 'but'?" Cai cocked an eyebrow.

Liora shushed him.

I gave her a smile of thanks and braced myself to tell them about the necklace and the voice. Once I'd finished, Cai rushed out in one breath, "*Holyshitamazing.*"

Liora passed a hand over her face with a rasping chuckle. "What he said."

"I've never heard of a magical object acting like that. Burning courts ... And your connection with Frazer. For him to hear and talk to you from behind his mental barriers ..." Cai shook his head. "Unheard of."

I tried to summon the courage to ask questions, but all I managed was a breathless, "Oh."

"A witch from the crafting clan might know more about the necklace," Liora added, frowning down at the table. "But for it to do all the things you're saying, to lend you its strength *and* talk to you; to make it possible for you and Frazer to communicate—those aren't the actions of a mindless protection charm. Whatever, or whoever—"

"Auntie," I cut in. "That's what I call her."

Cai smothered a laugh. A prickly heat flushed my cheeks.

Liora continued. "Well, this Auntie sounds sentient."

"Could I have a look at it?" Cai held out his palm expectantly.

My hand flew to the droplet; a protective instinct I didn't understand.

"You wouldn't have to take it off," he said, gentler than usual. "I just want to hold it."

Liora explained, "He wants to see if he can sense anything."

I tried to speak, but my mouth had dried and reduced me to a knotty silence. I had allowed Wilder to touch the droplet. This should be no different. I did a quick scan of the hall to check if there were any eyes on us. There were more people now. The hall had steadily filled during my story, however, the recruits that had returned were either falling asleep where they sat, or too busy consuming vast quantities of food and drink to bother with us. I tugged the necklace from out of my jacket and gave him the go-ahead. Cai palmed the droplet and closed his eyes. I'd no idea what he was doing, but he held it for a while.

Finally, he let it fall back against my skin. "She wouldn't answer me."

I could've sworn he was pouting. Laughter sounded in my head. And it didn't come from me.

He wanted to talk to you.

I know, Auntie replied, clearly amused.

"You said your mother passed it to you in her will?" Cai asked, staring at the necklace until I hid it back underneath my jacket.

"Mm." I didn't like talking about my mother. It opened too many doors in my mind—doors that needed to remain closed.

"Was she a witch, Serena?" Liora asked oh-so-gently.

"I didn't think so," I whispered back.

"I sense another 'but' coming." Cai's upper lip twitched in jest.

A listless chuckle rolled out of me. "She kept secrets from me. From my father. She wasn't meant to have any family, but this is an heirloom. A magical heirloom meant to protect me. And she knew that. She must've known it had magic." My heart bled at the idea. "Perhaps she was a witch. The people in my village liked to gossip about how she wasn't normal; that she was unusual. I figured that was just because she didn't always do things their way. Because she pushed against tradition."

Doubts circled like a wake of vultures, eager to pick me and my memories apart.

Cai smiled broadly. "Well, she sounds like my kind of woman."

"You don't think ..." Liora stopped and gnawed at her lip.

She wanted to say something. Whatever it was, a hollow pit in my gut told me that I wouldn't want to hear it.

Liora finished her thought by saying, "The voice ... could it somehow be your mother's?"

The world grew hazy, and I spun at the possibility. At the idea. But that swell of hope flattened the minute Auntie whispered sadly, *Darling*—

"I know," I said aloud, cutting her off.

I didn't need to hear. It would just hurt more.

My throat stuck with swallowed tears as my eyes found Liora's. "I can still remember my mother's voice ... It's not her."

I could feel the emotion swelling, threatening to spill over. Thankfully, the sound of a bell spared me from more questions and guesswork.

"That's the signal," Liora said, sighing. "How long d'you think they'll give us before the next trial?"

Cai stood and a whisper, a cold kiss, brushed over my skin. He'd released the sound barrier. "Well, as long as it's not right now, I'll deal."

I wish I had his confidence. My stomach churned as we joined the crowd half-walking, half-stumbling, back to the loop. There were plenty of drawn faces, limps, and mud-splattered clothing. A few sported bandaged limbs and nasty-looking burns. It seemed I'd gotten off easy.

Our pace slowed to a crawl after passing the obstacle course. Ahead were a dozen recruits who'd waited for the announcement rather than go eat. Adrianna and Frazer were among them. Meanwhile, the instructors were grouped up, whispering to one another—of what, I wondered.

Before I could stare too long at a certain long-limbed, broad shouldered fae, I turned my attention to Frazer.

Where did you disappear to? I projected down our thread.

I was around, Frazer shot back.

If you don't want to tell me, you could just say so.

Silence.

A girl belonging to Cecile's pack ran over to Cai. "Thank the courts! You made it," she trilled, her elfin face erupting into a smile.

"Annie." Cai acknowledged her in a warm voice. "Have you no confidence in me?"

She practically melted on the spot. Gods, I hoped that wasn't what I looked like with Wilder.

He slung an arm over her shoulders and steered her away, but not before giving us a wink over his shoulder. Liora clucked her tongue. "Why in a witch's warts did I get stuck with such an insufferable flirt for a brother?"

"Just good luck, I guess." I linked arms with her.

A whispered hush descended, and our heads turned toward the instructors. They were breaking apart and moving to face us.

"We need a count," Dimitri said with his typical scowl.

Goldwyn rolled with it, adding, "Thanks for volunteering."

Dimitri snapped his teeth at her. She answered with a smile. Damn, how did she restrain herself?

Dimitri's hands locked behind his back as he regarded us. "I want every recruit standing in a line, now!"

Liora and I positioned ourselves on the far left. Dimitri started counting heads. I was peering up the line, trying to riddle out which recruit had failed, when Liora tugged on my jacket. "Someone's watching you," she breathed.

I blinked. "Who?"

She gave me a feline smile, satisfied and smug. "Guess."

Her gaze shifted to rest on the instructors. One look for myself told me she'd meant Wilder. He *was* staring.

A twitch of his lip and then he was gone, his eyes roaming. I wasn't sure what to think. Liora must've seen my confusion because she whispered, "He's happy you made it."

I almost denied it, but this was Liora, not Cai. I'd never told her about my feelings for Wilder, but she'd seen anyway.

"How long?" she whispered. There was no trace of her smirk now, only curious eyes staring up at me.

It was obvious what she meant. With too many earwigging fae around to give a proper answer, I whispered, "A while."

A nod, as if to say she'd known the whole time.

Dimitri finished counting and walked over to the rest of the mentors, nodding.

Wilder shouted, "Now that we have you all here, we can announce that the second recruit to fail the loop was Dustin Rover."

My heart slammed into my ribcage. And Wilder's eyes found mine. "He was caught sabotaging another recruit." He looked elsewhere and called out, "The next trial begins in three days and will depend upon your ability to work in a team."

He allowed a few seconds of excited whispers—just enough time for Dimitri to cut in. "But, you won't be staying in your old packs." Obviously relishing the shock wave he'd unleashed, he said, "Each mentor will now pick a leader to head up a new group. All except for Wilder. The rules of the first trial mean that since his recruit failed last, he cannot pick a leader. In plain speech, he'll be left with the ones that don't get picked. The weaklings. And only five, at that."

His words hit me like a smattering of stones. Blow after blow. To leave Tysion and Cole behind would be a relief, but Frazer? Adrianna?

Mercifully, Goldwyn interrupted. "To be clear, due to numbers and as a punishment for the recruits we lost, Wilder's pack and my own are to face the upcoming trials with five members, as opposed to the six on Cecile's, Dimitri's, and Mikael's teams. In three days from now, these new packs will be sent on a quest that begins with us giving you a map. On the back will be written an object that we expect you to retrieve. You'll have nine days, and you won't complete the trial until a member of your pack hands the item over to your instructor. If a group fails to retrieve their quest object ..."

A pause followed, which Dimitri filled. "The whole pack will be kicked out."

I stopped breathing. The *whole* pack.

Goldwyn's wings rustled in annoyance. "Yes. I think we should move on with choosing the leaders."

Dimitri snorted derisively.

"One moment."

Goldwyn's head whipped to her right. Cecile, like Mikael, rarely spoke, so she was easy to overlook. Especially as she was short and petite, with snowy-white wings and hair that seemed destined to fade into the background. Ghost Cat, indeed. Something told me that made her more—not less—dangerous.

"Shouldn't we tell them what happens if more than one group fails?"

"Of course, Ceecee." Goldwyn gave her a warm smile that spoke of a much deeper intimacy. Her eyes swept up and down the line of recruits. "If more than one pack is unsuccessful, you'll fight it out in the ring. Winner stays, loser goes home."

Murmurs met this announcement, and a heavy doom settled on my shoulders. My fate felt decided. No one would pick me. I'd be in the reject pack—the one most likely to fail.

Auntie *tsk*ed loudly. *Don't count yourself out so soon. Or are you secretly hoping no one picks you?*

Why would I do that?

I'm in your head, child. I see the way you look at your instructor.

My cheeks boiled.

"Now, let's get on with the selection," Goldwyn said airily. "I'll be kicking us off. I choose Caiden Verona to be the leader of the White Tigers."

Cai detached himself from the line and went to stand next to Goldwyn. He caught Liora and I smiling at him and winked in our direction.

"I choose Tysion Kato," Dimitri declared.

The burly male fae strutted over to his new instructor and something sank in my chest.

"Myla Peron will be the leader of the Ghost Cats," Cecile said smoothly.

I silently cheered as the first female was chosen. Myla also happened to be one of the nicer fae in Kasi, and easily the most vibrant with braided blue hair and vibrant pink wings.

"I pick Moso Yumi," Mikael said in his usual deep timbre.

Moso mirrored his instructor in appearance; muscly with ebony skin and black wings.

"Now that we've chosen," Dimitri drawled, "we leave it up to the leaders to pick the first recruit. But we expect that each of you choose wisely because your second will choose the third member of your pack. Just as the third will pick the fourth and so on and so forth. We do it like this so no recruit can turn around and blame us for your poor decision-making—"

"Yes," Goldwyn snapped, beating her yellow wings in a show of impatience. "Let's not drag this out. Cai, you can pick first, but remember our pack's only allowed five recruits, so make it good."

I glanced sideways at Liora to find her tense, worried. She wasn't the best of the best, but surely family would mean more—

"Li."

My face split into a grin. He didn't even bother with her full name. Why would he? Everyone knew who he meant. Dimitri proved this by making a disgusted noise. "No surprises there, then."

A powerful urge hit me. I *really* wanted to bite the courts out of that wingless worm.

Liora wasn't moving, so I gave her a small push at the base of her spine. "Go on."

She stumbled forward; she looked almost embarrassed. Goldwyn smiled as Liora came to rest by her brother. "Good choice."

Dimitri stared at Goldwyn in open contempt. "Tysion, I trust you'll make your decision based on merit rather than familial ties."

"Of course," Tysion drawled. "I pick Cole Vysan."

My insides froze over as his familiar bulk moved to join Dimitri. The thought of those two together sent my stomach spinning.

Tysion's eyes met mine. His face said it all. *We're coming for you, bitch.*

Did he know what had happened with Dustin? Would Cole risk picking a weaker recruit just so he could torment me? My panic mounted as Cole's black glower turned to me as the last of the seconds were chosen. I had to fight an impulse to make a run for it.

"Serena Smith."

I blinked. Cole hadn't spoken.

"Serena," Liora called out softly.

My head turned to find my friends smiling at me. Liora had her palm extended, beckoning me. A glorious, wonderful rush of relief passed through me.

Dimitri snorted again. It didn't stop me from going to hug her. Cai put his arms around our shoulders and stood, beaming out at the class.

He's a cocky bastard, isn't he? Auntie mused.

I let a smile slip past my defenses. But soon it'd be time for me to choose the fourth member of our team, and I had to pick a great warrior to make it up to them. They'd chosen me out of friendship. I wouldn't let them suffer because of it.

Auntie sighed. *You already know who to pick. Follow your heart.*

Something clicked. Ugh. Obviously.

When Goldwyn gave me the go-ahead, I waited just long enough to say, *Surprise,* through our bond.

"Frazer."

I looked to Goldwyn, and she gave me a quirky smile and admitted, "I don't know his second name either."

My head shifted back to the recruits lined up in front. No one seemed surprised I'd called his name. He was arguably the best. I guessed the only reason he hadn't been chosen yet was because he was wingless and mute.

He broke formation and strode over, showing no emotion. And yet, I knew better. There'd been no thought—his shields, his mental discipline, were too strong for that. Still, I thought I detected a dull throb of gratitude from his end. Maybe he wasn't so good at hiding his emotions either. Or perhaps our connection was simply too intimate, too raw, for him to hide behind those thick, dark walls forever.

Happy? I projected as he positioned himself on my left.

Ecstatic. Faint amusement sang through our thread.

You know you'll have to choose an amazing recruit to make up for me.

A frown. *Did you have someone in mind?*

I swept the crowd. And my gaze stumbled over Adrianna. Why in the stars hadn't she been picked?

Frazer must've sensed my confusion because his voice trickled in. *She's got a reputation for being difficult.*

I almost laughed. *You get the irony of you saying that, right? And I picked you.*

It's different with us, yatävä.

I never found out why because Goldwyn cut in, announcing it was Frazer's turn. He marched into the crowd. I held my breath.

He stopped, extending his hand. Adrianna frowned at his open palm as if considering his offer. She nodded once, strode past him, and settled next to me.

Frazer turned positively lethal. Furious she'd taken his position, he walked back over to us, anger billowing through our bond like a gale force wind. I felt him struggle with a mad desire to bite and show dominance. I didn't understand those urges, or why it was important to him. But they were both my picks—I felt responsible.

Frazer came within reach. I held out my hand for Frazer. *No bloodshed.*

His mouth curved, and he allowed me to pull him into the space between Cai and I. I didn't bother seeking Adrianna's reaction. This clash of wills hadn't exactly filled me with confidence for the days to come.

The selection process came to a close, and three humans and two fae remained. Wilder gestured to them with a graceful flick of his wrist. As he gathered his new pack to him, there was a vicious twist in my heart.

The one sour note in all this—I'd lost the opportunity to talk and train with him during the day.

"Each pack is to meet in this spot at 9BN in three days, and bring your own supplies," Dimitri yelled over the recruit's heads. "We won't be outfitting you with a list, so use your common sense, as difficult as that is for some of you."

Goldwyn whirled to us—her pack. "White Tigers, follow me."

I didn't allow myself to look back at Wilder. Goldwyn was my instructor now. There'd never been a chance for anything real between us anyway.

Goldwyn led us to the empty food hall. She stood at the head of a table and gestured for us to sit. Cai and Liora took up positions to my right, and Frazer and Adrianna moved to sit on the opposite bench.

"This is the only time you've got to ask questions, so make them good," Goldwyn said while staring at Cai.

Adrianna got there first. "What supplies are we allowed to take with us?"

I cringed, hoping it wouldn't bother Cai—our leader—that she'd taken charge. Choosing her had been my idea. But one look told me that Adrianna could've bashed him on the head and declared herself queen of the world, and Cai still wouldn't have minded.

Goldwyn regarded Adrianna with a cool openness. "The kitchen will give your pack set food and water rations. And you'll need to go to the supply closet and sign out sleeping bags. Then, visit Colt at the armory. Fair warning, you'll only be allowed one weapon each and they won't be blunted like in practice." Her focus shifted to Cai. "If you want my advice, have your fae carrying bows. You and your sister should take blades."

When she didn't go on to say anything about me, I stared down at the table, my face burning in shame.

"And what about Serena?" Liora asked. As if Goldwyn had simply made a mistake in forgetting me.

She cackled. "Well, apparently she can get a Sabu Warrior to submit with nothing but her claws and a growl, so she clearly doesn't need a weapon."

My head lifted. Meeting gold-flecked eyes, the amusement in them melted my reservations. Wilder must've told her what had happened between us. And ... what had she said—Sabu Warrior? Cai and Liora's lessons came to mind. The Sabu class was reserved for the leaders of the fae armies.

Leader—well, that explained a lot. Sadness cleaved my heart in two as I realized this only put him farther out of reach.

"Serena, does Goldwyn know something we don't?" Cai cocked an eyebrow.

"It's not important," I deflected. "And I'll take a sword—if that's okay?"

I'd been more familiar with the bow on arrival, but I'd since grown partial to the long, thin blades the fae called Utemä.

"Of course." Goldwyn's eyes danced. "But you needn't be so modest. If I'd pinned Wilder, I'd be crowing it from the rooftops. Very few fae—let alone humans—can claim to have done the same."

The shock on their faces was almost bordering on insulting. Liora regained her composure first. "Well, I'm glad she never said anything; otherwise, I might not have gotten a chance to pick her."

Cai snorted and banged the table jubilantly. "Their loss is our gain."

Embarrassed, I spotted an opportunity to change the subject and clarify something. "Goldwyn, d'you know what happens with my evening training sessions? Wilder told me yesterday that we'd be continuing them, but seen as how he's not my instructor anymore ..."

I prayed no one sensed the emotion behind the question.

Just me. Frazer's voice floated down the thread.

I threw a curse back at him.

"Wilder knew what might happen today," Goldwyn began. "He obviously wanted to train you regardless, and I don't have a problem with it. Obviously, you'll get tonight off. But tomorrow, report to the training ground as usual."

Liora asked, "Where do we sleep? Our old barracks, or ..."

Goldwyn shook her head. "No, take the Bats barracks. I'm sure Tysion and Cole won't mind moving." A hint of mischief glinted. "Cai, Liora, transfer your stuff over this evening. That should give me time to talk to Wilder about it."

Cai asked one last question: could he use magic during the quest?

Goldwyn told him yes and excused herself, wishing us luck. I watched her go. A pulse of knee-quaking relief ran through me. The prospect of seeing Wilder tomorrow excited me more than it should have. Nothing could happen between us, so why couldn't I let it go? Why couldn't I turn these feelings off?

It doesn't work like that, dear, Auntie said with a touch of sorrow.

No shit.

∽

AFTER GOLDWYN LEFT, our pack started a conversation we'd have on repeat over the next two days. Two long, tedious days.

How much food should we bring?

What might the quest object be?

What should we do if we got separated?

These questions, among others, were debated so thoroughly, it seemed inevitable we'd drive one another crazy. Only we didn't. Adrianna would occasionally push against Cai's decisions, but he never came across as threatened. Damn, he enjoyed it. Clearly Goldwyn hadn't just chosen Cai because of his physical prowess. He was a leader, born and bred.

Whereas I was useless, with no strategical or geographical knowledge that could be helpful. During our daily meetings I acted as an interpreter for Frazer, who very quickly proved himself the more experienced warrior. And after a few probing questions from Adrianna, she accepted the bizarre nature of our connection under the guise it must be a latent magical gift. I didn't tell her about the necklace. Not when Frazer didn't even know about it. Of course, he deserved to know, but fear held me back. Liora and Cai seemed convinced it was powerful—dangerous, even —enough to be coveted. What if Frazer resented being dragged into that? That alone made me hesitate, but there was also his refusal to share anything about himself. It created a wall—a barrier between us— despite us being intimately connected every heartbeat. Because while his mind remained his own, our bond was more than shared thoughts, that much had become clear. Even when our minds weren't connecting, our more intense emotions seeped through the strings that were now so tightly woven that I wondered if we'd ever untangle. That didn't scare me nearly as much as the glimpses of the darkness, the grief that defied words, existing in the depths of his soul. And I was powerless to help so long as he acted like an animal afraid to show its underbelly to the world.

It wasn't until the evening before we were due to leave that the effect of being shut out and sidelined as Frazer's mouthpiece caught up to me.

"Serena," Wilder barked, disarming me for the tenth time that session. "What in Zola's fire is wrong with you? Usually you'd be dancing around too much; now you're as stiff as a plank of wood."

My sparring sword dropped to my side, hanging limply.

"Is it the new pack? Are you unhappy?"

I must have been miserable if the concern marking Wilder's face couldn't lift my spirits. "It's nothing, really."

With a twist of his wrist, he sheathed the blunt sword he'd been swinging. "Say what you need to."

"How can I?" The words stuck in my throat. I swallowed hard. "You're my instructor. You're not here for me to complain to."

"Ex-instructor," Wilder corrected.

It was an effort not to smile. "Still, you can't blame me for being guarded."

"Skies above," he rasped out. "If this is you guarded, I'd hate to think what you're like normally."

Shame and rage heated my blood, blotching my skin. I let the sword drop to the floor.

His eyes flitted to where the blade lay. "Serena Smith," he growled, his gaze pinning me. "You are never to treat a weapon like that again, d'you hear me? Pick it up."

I didn't move. A haze of blue mist was descending over my mind. And a faint warning hiss sounded. Water was boiling somewhere.

Careful child.

"Serena?" Wilder showed me his palms. "Just tell me what's wrong. I want to help." He took a step toward me.

There, obvious concern.

I blinked. And the anger caved inward, leaving behind nothing but a black pit of insecurity and doubt. I shook my head clear, releasing the fog that clouded my mind.

Wilder ducked to grab the hilt of my sparring sword. He slipped it back into the sheath at my hip. We were so close—I fought the impulse to move into his scent. His eyes found mine.

"Ex-instructor," I breathed.

I didn't know what made me say it, but the creases around his eyes softened and his hand moved. Barely an inch, but it was the difference between him touching the hilt and my fingertips.

I was stuck, frozen. *Think. Do something!*

Any daring plans to seduce him died when his gaze moved to where the droplet lay.

"May I?" He motioned with his hand.

I gave a nod and his fingers brushed my neckline, along the chain. The slightest touch—a graze. But it still set my nerve endings alight, drying my mouth out. Wilder dipped below my jacket and held the droplet for a heartbeat, and then his eyes fluttered upward.

"Is this what burns away the shyness and insecurity?" he mused.

My breathing hitched and my heart was going so fast; so very, very fast. It wasn't just the lust though. It was the discomfort of having my failings repeated back to me.

"I wish they hadn't chosen me," I blurted out.

Eyes widening, he tucked the droplet back under my top and his hand fell from my neck.

"I love them. I mean, I love Cai and Liora and Frazer. And although she ignored me for weeks, I liked Adrianna the moment she offered to help me on that first day."

"And yet ..." Wilder prompted.

"I see *their* worth."

Wilder's jaw clenched; his mouth set with silent disapproval. "But not your own."

A nod. "Liora chose me because we're friends. Now, I'm in a pack with two of the best fae warriors here, and two witches—"

"Liora isn't powerful though. I've never scented magic on her," he reflected, frowning.

Not true, of course, but Cai's spell prohibited me from saying much in her defense. "It doesn't matter. She's the center, the heart."

"And what are you, Serena?" Wilder said lightly, searching my face.

"That's what I'm saying—I don't contribute anything."

I couldn't hold his gaze. My eyes dropped to the mean-looking daggers at his hips.

"Perhaps," he began slowly, "you should try seeing your own worth before you go putting everyone else on a pedestal."

Those words cut deep. "What makes you think if I look, I'll find anything?"

An attempt at a self-deprecating joke. A total sham, it was met with silence.

Peeking up at him from under my lashes, the brightness in his eyes told me he'd seen through me. "There's everything to find, but you need to learn to see it; otherwise, no matter how many times your friends praise you, or how many lovers show you affection ..." Green eyes fluttered to my lip. I forgot my own name. "... you'll never believe them. And all the compliments in the world won't mean a damned thing."

I hated myself for needing to hear his approval. He sighed and took a step back. I almost reached out to stop him. "If it makes you feel any better, Kovaysi, I speak from personal experience."

I gaped. "What have you got to feel insecure about?"

He blinked; he actually seemed thrown by the question. "I'm a grown male. I have the scars of dozens of battles. And ..." he stumbled, his exhale coming out in a whooshing sound. "Never mind."

"Don't stop."

He fixed me with a hard stare. "I used to be a Sabu—"

I nodded.

"You knew that?"

"Goldwyn," I said by way of an explanation.

He snorted. "Of course. Well, once I had that honor, and now look at me, training foot soldiers in a court on its last legs."

A raw, bleak smile.

I shifted, rolling to my other hip. "A court on its last legs?"

Wilder tilted his head. "I'll answer that question when you've finished these trials and I'm not bound by my position as a mentor."

Closing the gap he'd created, I dared to try for a husky, sultry voice. "You said it yourself, you're not my teacher anymore."

He had the worst possible reaction—he burst out laughing. I flinched, preparing to flee, but he stopped me by bringing his hands to the sides of my face. Trailing his fingers through my hair, he reached around to cup the back of my head and leaned in, whispering, "How can you be bold as the sun one moment, and quiet and shy as the new moon the next?"

An open smile dazzled me. He tipped my head forward and our brows touched, setting a fire in my gut. I shut my eyes, every sense narrowing to the spot connecting us.

"Nimän telo, Tästien Valo."

I opened my mouth to ask what he'd said when a high, cruel voice interrupted. "What's this?"

I jumped back. I couldn't have looked guiltier if I'd tried.

Dimitri continued. "Is the infamous fae of stone cracking? Surely your taste in females doesn't extend to scrawny humans barely capable of holding a sword?"

I clamped down on the tirade of abuse threatening to spill from my treacherous mouth. Not that I thought telling him he was as likable as dog shit would really wound him.

"Dimitri." Wilder bowed his head a touch. Adopting a pleasant, brisk tone, he added, "Out for a nighttime stroll?"

A shake of his head but it was slow, careful. "I'm on my way to see Hilda."

"Of course," Wilder remarked. "I might see you there. Goldwyn and I have to meet with her later on tonight."

"I hadn't planned on keeping her that long, although maybe we'll have more to discuss tonight." He smirked at me, eyes roaming, judging. "A human, Wilder—really?"

"What can I say? We all have our favorite pupils, don't we?"

That comment hit its mark. Dimitri's face paled and tightened; I couldn't imagine what it meant. "And that's all this is." His hand waved between us.

The floating firelights illuminated Wilder's blank expression. "We've done nothing to be ashamed of."

A faint, taunting smile marked Dimitri's face as he replied, "Glad to hear it." He took a step toward us. A clear threat. "Because if you *were* doing something, I'd feel obligated to tell certain ... interested parties that you've been sullying yourself with human filth."

Wilder raised his brows a touch. "I'm surprised at you, Dimitri. I thought your strongest objection would be that she's my student," he said lightly. An act, playing casual.

Dimitri angled his head. A sneer playing around his mouth, he said, "As you well know, whatever you did would be nothing compared to how Goldwyn acted before Cecile, or the amount of recruits Mikael goes through."

Wow. Interesting.

"It seems that I am the only one with any propriety left," Dimitri sniffed.

Auntie cackled. *Pfft! He just can't find any poor, innocent soul willing to let him stick it where he wants.*

A bubble of hysterical laugher popped. I saved myself at the last minute by turning it into an explosive cough.

Dimitri scrunched his face in disgust. "I'd have that one checked if I were you. She appears to be in the grips of a disease."

Wilder pulled me under his wing. "I'll take her to the healer right away."

"And just some friendly advice—"

I choked back a laughing snort.

"Stop these cozy training sessions," Dimitri finished.

"Serena has a month of training to catch up on," Wilder reminded him—*politely.*

"That task should now fall to Goldwyn. Of course, the situation might have been overlooked if your *interest* in this human wasn't so apparent. But you don't want to be accused of favoritism, do you?"

Wilder tensed beside me. "I'll discuss the matter with Goldwyn, but I believe you might be right."

I screamed internally.

"Is there anything else, Dimitri? We wouldn't want to delay you from meeting Hilda." A shallow smile.

Dimitri bared his teeth and gave a mocking bow. "Your concern is touching, *Wilder*."

He shot into the sky without a goodbye. I turned to Wilder, ready to fight him on the training sessions, when he pressed a finger to his lip. He gazed upward, searching the navy-blue sky, listening for something outside my mortal hearing.

Then he was moving, pulling me toward the stables. Stalking across the pit, I prepared myself for the worst.

We entered the stables, and the sweet smell of hay and the whinnies of horses greeted us. The firelights that accompanied our sparring had traveled with us. They illuminated Wilder as he twisted to face me. He didn't make eye contact—he was too busy scanning every inch of the stable block.

"Are we alone?" I dared to ask.

A pause, and then a curt nod.

"Are you in trouble? Are we?"

"No, not yet."

"You're being evasive."

Wilder grimaced. I spotted his hands clenching, then unclenching. "He was right, you know."

"About what?" I felt a scythe swish over my head.

"Over the years, the mentors have taken lovers from among the students."

My blood chilled. "Are you with someone at the moment? Is that what you're trying to tell me?"

My voice trembled. And I didn't care. It wasn't in me to pretend the answer didn't matter.

"No. I'm saying the complete opposite," Wilder said flatly. "I've never sought out a recruit's company. I'm not free to act on such desires, Serena."

An awkward silence, in which heat and tension built in the air between us, crackled like lightning. "Are you telling me you're married?"

He actually smiled at that. Smiled, when I was breaking and bleeding from the inside. "It's nothing like that."

He didn't elaborate, and my patience snapped. "Why did you bring me in here?"

"To apologize."

"For?" I pushed out.

He continued smoothly, not missing a beat. "If I hadn't shown you affection, we could've continued on with our training. I'll hate myself for that in days to come."

My heart plummeted down, down, *down.*

He continued. "I wanted to see your progress. You've been one of my more ... surprising students." His mouth quirked to the side, creasing his scars. "One second I've got you figured, and the next your whole body shifts, your fighting style changes, and you're showing flashes of brilliance rare in humans *and* fae. I wanted to see you use the moves I taught you to show everyone, especially the fae, what you're capable of."

I had to push down the impulse to run over and throw my arms around him. Either that, or hit him—I couldn't decide which.

Bitterness and panic were clawing at my throat. "We can still see each other outside of classes."

"And what reason would we have to see each other?"

He kept his tone light; I shrank inside. "Do we need a reason?" I breathed.

Courage, Auntie whispered.

Before he could answer, I took a deep breath to combat my racing heart and went on. "I'm not suggesting that we become ... intimate, but there's something here, isn't there?"

Raw emotion thundered through my veins. There was no looking him in the eye. I took to staring at a nearby stallion, praying, pleading. He was moving, drawing me in close and wrapping me into a hug. His broad chest expanded against mine. "There are so many reasons for us to never see each other again; you can't even imagine half of them. I almost envy your ignorance."

My pride bridled at that. "I don't know how to walk away. To pretend. Help me understand," I whispered against his chest.

He pulled away to give me an appraising look. "Number one, official fae and human couplings are outlawed. We can take you as lovers, but a fae cannot marry or produce faelings with humans. Offspring—demi-fae —are denied the rights any full-blooded fae can expect in society. That's if they're not killed outright at birth."

"I don't want to do any of those things," I blurted out. "At least not yet, anyway."

Wilder huffed and closed his eyes, grimacing. "I don't blame you, but that alone should tell you how many fae in Aldar view our kinds mixing."

"I don't care what people think," I said, defiant.

"It's not just that you're human," he croaked out. "Even if you only wanted a friendship—"

"That would be enough." A lie.

His nostrils flared, not once but twice. "We both know that's not true."

Rutting fae senses.

"Can you know my mind just by smelling me?" I sounded harsh, distant.

And yet, really, I was just a hot, weeping mess inside.

Choosing to ignore me, he continued. "Serena, you don't understand —Dimitri has it in his head that we're something more now. That puts you in danger. And the only way I can get you out is by ceasing contact with you."

"What danger?"

Wilder's scars tightened. "There are things about my past that I'm not ready to share with you. All I can say is that if we continue down this road, there'd be some very powerful fae taking an interest in you. If they suspected for even a moment that I had any real feeling for you, they'd use you to get to me. And I can't have that on my conscience."

"Are you talking about Dimitri?" I grasped for answers.

"It's not just him," he replied.

Damn him.

"I know that you don't want to let this go." His stare pinned me in place. "But you must—for both our sakes."

I opened and shut my mouth. A mindless fish. That's what I'd become. What could I say? How did I fight something I didn't understand?

"Serena." A warning tone.

I winced.

"From now on, we can't talk to each other. The less contact we have, the better it'll be for you."

I stepped back, wrapping my arms around my body. As if they alone could stop me from unraveling. "Right."

Turn around and don't look back, Auntie said, iron in her voice.

I nodded distantly. "Bye, then."

His eyes flashed with something. It didn't matter what—not anymore. "Good luck with the rest of the trials," he said. Cold. And so sure of himself.

My heart hurt. Actually *hurt.* I'd heard the expression broken-hearted, but I hadn't known, hadn't guessed, that it could feel like this.

I left the stables and arrived back in my barracks with no memory of walking there. I briefly scanned the empty room. They must still be eating. Good.

I sank to the floor and didn't get back up.

~

My mother.

My father.

John and Viola.

Wilder.

Each loss painful, soul-shredding, in different ways.

A wretched grief. A cold numbness. A burning anger. Now this.

They really were adding up.

Oh, sure. Wilder wasn't family. He'd never promised me anything. He'd never *claimed* me. We owed each other nothing.

And he hadn't died. I hadn't known him for years. An impenetrable barrier hadn't separated us forever. Somehow, inexplicably, I still felt the loss as keenly, as sharply. It felt wrong somehow, for this grief to rival true loss, that it could be akin to a death.

When would it end?

Was this my fate?

A memory floated to the surface. A few years ago, after my first blood had arrived, I'd run to Viola in a state of panic. After calming me and gleaning that my father had neglected my education in this area too,

Viola filled in the blanks about the change and about sex. From that day onward she'd made my ears bleed with dire warnings about falling for the wrong boys. She'd said most young girls had shitty taste, and that was why it was better to wait to pursue the right one.

It seemed I hadn't listened. Gods, I missed her.

Liora found me there later, still slumped against the wall. She sat next to me and slipped her fingers through mine. I didn't need much provocation to spill my guts. There were no tears, but my voice sounded breathless, disjointed, even to my ears. I felt numb throughout, like I was floating. Still, I retained enough presence to realize this was shock. I was in shock.

Liora didn't interrupt, she didn't judge. No surprises there; kindness always came easily to her. When I finished rambling, she said, "He sounds scared. He cares for you."

I stayed silent. Hope felt more like a curse.

"I'd no idea you felt like that." Liora squeezed my hand tighter.

Lifting my head from its slumped position, facing her, I frowned. "I thought you'd guessed."

Confusion, then her eyes lit up. "Oh, I knew about your feelings for him. But what you said about thinking you were an outsider. Like you were useless to the pack. I didn't know you felt that so deeply. You don't even believe you're good enough for Wilder."

That wasn't a question. It was a statement, and it rutting hurt.

"Maybe I didn't see it because we have the same problem." Liora tried to smile, but her eyes stayed sad.

I went to form a question, but she was already explaining, "I've felt worthless. Like a burden, for a long time. And in case you missed it, the only reason I got picked was because my brother took pity on me. That's all he's ever done—protect me. And in return, I got us exiled from our clan."

Her words were hollow, and the tattered pieces of my heart bled a little more. "But in your case, I didn't choose you just because we're friends, although that was part of it," Liora admitted. "But ever since we met, you've defied every expectation. A captor who made friends with her jailor, a girl with no obvious magical gift able to give another a voice, and now, someone who can melt the heart of a battle-hardened fae. By my broom, you've even earned Adrianna's respect."

I let out a weak chuckle. Not possible.

"She criticizes you a lot less than the rest of us," Liora said, laughter in her voice. "I think for her that means she likes you. Now," she braced her palms on her thighs, "I want you off this freezing floor. The rest of the pack's in the food hall. They sent me to see if you'd finished training. Adrianna wants to go over things for tomorrow. Again." She let out a little sigh.

"We've discussed everything twenty times over. What's the point?" I asked, half-exasperated, half-amused.

"My guess is that she secretly likes spending time with us."

Her waggling eyebrows and dimpling grin reminded me so much of her brother that a belly laugh shook me. It felt good.

Liora rolled off the floor in one movement. "Not that I'm complaining."

I pushed myself off the wall and stood, facing her. Liora looked odd, contemplative, and I dared to ask, "D'you … find her attractive?"

Her eyebrows rose.

Oh dear. Maybe I'd overstepped—Liora hadn't told me she liked women, but Cai had dropped enough hints for me to guess the truth. In the Gauntlet, same-sex relations weren't outlawed, but it wasn't seen as normal; it remained a taboo. Viola's common-sense views had informed my own opinions. And enough memories remained of my mother's compassion that I wanted her to know she could trust me, if it needed to remain a secret. Although, I doubted the Riverlands could be that strict about such things. Not if Goldwyn and Cecile's relationship was anything to go by.

Her voice was soft. "I think one Verona in love with her is enough to be getting on with, don't you think?"

I broke into relieved laughter. "Maybe."

Liora walked me out. She'd worked a miracle; I didn't think about Wilder for the rest of the night.

Well, maybe just a little …

CHAPTER 15
HUNTED

The second trial began with the packs waiting outside the wall of Kasi. No obstacle course in sight. Just a cloudy sky, windswept meadows, and forest pines. I waited in between Frazer and Liora who, like me, were as tight as bowstrings and frozen still from the tension. Cai and Adrianna, on the other hand, strived to look bored and failed. There were three new additions to my uniform; a black fur cloak, a rucksack, and a sword.

The instructors lined up in front of us once again. I kept my eyes fixed on Goldwyn and the map she held in her hands. Wilder couldn't exist for me anymore.

Don't look, don't look, don't look.

"Right. No long boring speeches this time," Goldwyn announced, clapping her hands together.

Dimitri scowled. Ha.

Goldwyn continued, oblivious. "Each instructor has a map to give to their pack. On the back is written a quest item. And fair warning: there is one group among you that'll be given the task of capturing a recruit of their own choosing from a competing pack. They'll be hunting the hunters. However, at no point is this group permitted to use weapons and endanger life or sabotage the *packs'* mission. And to be clear, if a recruit is taken, they won't be kicked out. As long as their team members complete their quest."

Holy courts.

Wilder cut in. "We've circled the general area you can expect to find your pack's item. We've been generous with you—don't waste it."

"Also, don't feel the need to come back too soon. We like having the place to ourselves," Goldwyn added to a spattering of appreciative laughter.

Dimitri interrupted, scowling. "Let's get on with it then."

"Excellent idea," Goldwyn said with a brazen smile.

The mentors broke formation and went to hand a map to their pack leader. Goldwyn gave ours to Cai and backed off quickly. "Good luck."

Her yellow wings spread out and *whoosh,* she soared upward. The rest of the instructors followed.

A burst of frenzied activity came next. Three packs instantly scattered, flying or running, if human, for the nearby hillsides. As for us, Cai passed Liora the map and stepped in front of her. Adrianna nocked an arrow. With sudden violence, Frazer grabbed my arm, whirled me behind him, and sunk low, growling. All this happened in the space of a breath. Reeling, I peered around Frazer. Tysion's pack, comprising Cole and four other deadly looking fae were moving, prowling. As if they wanted to cut off escape routes. As if they wanted to trap us. It wasn't hard to guess which quest they'd been given—capture a hostage. And they'd chosen our pack. Big surprise.

Mocking laughter filled the air. Tysion. "Don't worry. We won't take your two weaklings yet. Where would be the fun in that?"

"Don't even think about hunting us. Not unless you want me to rip you to shreds." Cai's voice was guttural, vicious. At odds with his character.

Stay behind me, Matea. Frazer's mental voice sounded cold enough to fill my belly with ice.

Tysion sneered. "Your threats are empty, Caiden. You know it; I know it. Your pack knows it. All you've got are two decent warriors, a redhead who can just about wield a sword, and a stick who's as useful as a drunk whore."

Frazer snarled and pushed me back another step.

Tysion's black eyes focused in on me, narrowing into slits. "You're very protective of the girl, Frazer. Tell me, what was it like to rut a human?"

He gave me a serpentine smile. Frazer only growled deeper.

"You seem to have forgotten about me," Cai said, composed.

Cole chuckled dimly. Tysion dismissed him with a snort and a head shake. "Take your sword away and any fae here could crush you with their little toe."

"Doubtful." Cai's voice had deepened, now hoarse and husky.

Their pack stilled while their leader's expression hardened. "Some dirty witch's trick won't save you," Tysion retorted.

"Sure about that, are you?" No laughter. No mockery. Only wrath. A very different Cai. Bringing his inked hand up and baring his palm, he conjured a groaning, howling wind behind him. A pause and silence.

He flicked his wrist. A whirlwind broke out and barreled across the meadow, ripping their wings open, sending their pack careening backward. Before they could recover, Cai turned to us, snapping out orders. "Adrianna, take my sister. Fly into the forest. Frazer, can you run with Serena?"

A blunt nod.

"Good."

"What about you?" Adrianna asked while lifting Liora into her arms.

"I'll find you—just go."

"Cai ..." Liora moaned softly.

"No arguments."

Adrianna didn't hesitate. Extending her wings, she sprang into the steely sky. Heaving me into his arms, Frazer sprinted for the shelter of the trees. His long legs ate up the meadowsweet grass while I watched Cai over his shoulder.

Is he running? Frazer projected.

Yes, but he's not as fast as you.

He huffed. *Obviously. Are the others in pursuit?*

No, they're still looking kind of stunned.

Good.

I felt a blast of relief shudder along our bond. Surprise claimed me. *You're scared of them?*

No. But they can fly; I can't, which means I'll always be at a disadvantage.

The temptation to ask about his wings was almost too much.

Now's not the time child, Auntie reminded.

That much was obvious. He'd never tell me anyway. *How far until we reach cover?*

I'm sorry, should I put you down and you can carry me?

Ho, ho. Definitely grumpy. *No, I was just worried. Cai's flagging and I think ...*

I squinted, hard.

What is it? Frazer asked.

I think Tysion's pack are moving; maybe getting up. D'you think Cai can blast them back again?

Depends how powerful he is. Magic's not without limits. Frazer put on a quick burst of speed that put us within touching distance of the tree line. *Can you still see them? Have they taken to the skies yet?*

No. What'll happen when they do?

The hunt begins.

We entered the forest; the thick canopy dimmed the morning light to eventide. Frazer whizzed past trees, crunching down on pine needles and whipping up leaves in his wake. Cai was nowhere to be seen.

"We have to go back. Leave me—"

My leader gave me a command.

"So?" I glared.

He snorted through his nose. *Give it up. There is absolutely no scenario that has me abandoning you for him. You'd be as helpless as a newborn against six fae.*

That ended my objection. I hated him for pointing it out. Even if he was right.

Frazer sniffed at the air. *Liora and Adrianna are close.*

Where? I was desperate for any sign of our fractured pack.

Soon.

I almost snapped my teeth at him. Gods, I'd been spending too much time around fae.

A minute more and Liora appeared in a clearing. Seeing us, she hurried over with windswept strawberry locks and wide eyes. No sign of Adrianna.

"Where is he—where's Cai?" Liora demanded, her gaze flitting between us.

Frazer came to a halt and set me down.

I answered. "The last time I saw him he was heading for the forest."

Liora's throat bobbed.

Tell her that he's probably taking a longer route to throw them off and divide their forces, Frazer projected.

I blinked. *How can you know that?*

He stared me down. Right. Whatever.

I relayed what he'd said. Liora spun away, her eyelids fluttering. I glimpsed tears and forced myself to go place a hand on her back. Shame and guilt writhed in my gut. "Can I do anything?" I asked, feeling helpless.

She shook her head and hastily dashed the tears from her cheeks.

I whispered into her ear, "Where's Adi?"

Liora stepped away and turned to face me. She nodded up to the tree canopy. "Acting as a lookout." Her expression smoothed as she looked to Frazer. "You should sit. Catch your breath. Serena and I can keep watch."

By now the bond had made me finely tuned to his mood. One look was all it took. "He'll want to keep watch."

Liora gave a nod as if she'd guessed as much. "Then we should look at the map. I don't even know which task we got given."

"Where is it?"

Liora dragged the now tattered parchment from her jacket pocket. And Frazer faced out toward the forest, his head cocked, listening.

Liora turned the map over.

"What do we have to get?" I questioned tentatively.

She was silent, unblinking. I moved next to her, gripping my Utemä sword.

"A lock of hair from a swamp witch," I read aloud.

Frazer circled the clearing as Liora unfroze and blew out a shaky sigh. She pocketed the map once again. "I don't know much about the witches in this area, but I doubt they'll give us the hair willingly. They might think we want to curse them." She shot me a look laced with anxiety. "And now, we've got those jackals hunting us."

"We'll find a way."

Damn. Did I believe that?

Liora's eyes churned with sorrow and the flames of anger. "If I hadn't been weakened, I could've stopped them, Serena. Cai shouldn't have to play the protector every gods-damned time," she whispered, breathless. She must have been close to losing it if she was willing to hint at her binding with two earwigging fae nearby.

Feeling weak, needing to contribute, wanting to protect: they were all running threads in my life. And it sucked. "I get it ..."

Liora nodded distantly. "I know."

"It wasn't your fault what happened back there." My hands grew clammy thinking about Cai. "We'll find a way, Li. We won't be the weak ones forever."

"We can hope," she said under her breath.

That small sound punched a giant hole through my chest.

A familiar rustling and a gentle thud announced Adrianna had landed in the clearing. With a snap she tucked her wings in. "Neither of you are weak, and you might be strong if you'd stop hiding behind males and developed your own gifts."

Well, *damn.*

My eyes naturally darted to Liora, expecting her to look confused. She was sharp-eyed if anything. "What gifts?"

Adrianna folded her arms, challenging us. "Well, for one thing, Serena can hear a fae's thoughts." She stared me down. "I might not have questioned you about it, but I'm not stupid. The power to forge the connection between you and Frazer must be immense. Other witches blessed by air—blessed with skills to connect via thoughts—train for years to sustain what apparently comes naturally to you."

I had trouble swallowing as Adrianna's frown deepened. "There's also the mystery of how you pinned one of the greatest battle commanders in fae history."

Greatest. Holy hell.

Adrianna looked bemused as she added, "When we've sparred, I've seen potential. You'd make a decent soldier."

High praise, indeed.

Sarcasm's no substitute for wit, my dear, Auntie sung to me.

"But ... Wilder?" Adrianna's voice hitched an octave higher. "He's something else. You didn't just beat him; you made him submit. Now, I haven't sensed you using magic, but there must be something—some great potential or ability you keep hidden."

My cheeks reddened as Auntie and the necklace came to mind.

"So, why aren't you pushing yourself? Using that potential?"

Weighing her posture, her *tone*, I guessed she was demanding an explanation.

"I'm not sure how helpful this is, Adi," Liora argued. "My brother's out there somewhere. We should be thinking about what to do next, not giving lectures."

Adrianna's back went up. "You're the ones complaining you don't want to be weak. This is how: use what you've got."

Liora's eyes grew tight at the corners. A storm was brewing. "What's your suggestion for me? What do I have? Because I train just as much as you—"

"You're a witch," Adrianna said bluntly, her nostrils flaring as if smelling it on her. "Why didn't you use whatever magic you had to help Cai back there? Even if you aren't as powerful as he is—"

"You can shut up now." Liora was so very, very quiet. She went rigid, hair crackling with static. The surrounding air shifted, churning out heat waves, and the nape of my neck prickled. Frazer materialized at my side. I felt his protective instincts kick in—he must have sensed it too. A caged predator rattling at its bars. A dragon eager to shed the guise of a lamb.

When she spoke, it wasn't quite all Liora. "I'm not using them, because I can't access them."

Adrianna guessed. "You're a bound witch?"

Only curiosity, no fear. I had to admire her courage as she stared down the beast.

"Yes," Liora hissed. "Not that it's any of your business."

"No, it certainly isn't." Cai's voice carried through the clearing.

Liora's wrath broke apart and scattered. She spun and ran to her brother, choking back sobs. She threw her arms around his neck. He rubbed her back and shot over her shoulder, "It didn't take long for things to fall apart without me."

I laughed, the sound bleak and strained.

"We didn't hear you ..." Adrianna began. Alarmed, alert, and scanning the area.

"No, you wouldn't have."

"Magic?" I asked.

A nod to confirm. "I muffled the sounds of my movements and then stayed behind to blow away our scents. Tysion and his pack of worms are currently winging it in the opposite direction." He took his sister's hand and pulled her toward us until we stood in a circle. "I don't know how long it'll fool them for though, so whatever conversation I just interrupted, we should move on."

Cai sounded glib, but I sensed the razor-edge embedded—he was pissed.

Adrianna calmly went on. "Maybe it makes me a bitch for saying it, but if it helps Serena and Liora, I'm prepared to say what no one else will."

"And what's that?" Cai asked, his voice rough.

Adrianna looked to me. "Over the past three days, all you've done is act as a mouthpiece for a male fae—a fae who hasn't returned the favor by helping you train. Even though he's clearly the best recruit," she said through slightly clenched teeth. "And now he's decided to act as your official guard dog."

Frazer's teeth snapped down. Oh, gods.

Adrianna continued, purposefully oblivious. "Liora, you've got the diplomacy and communication skills of a leader. But from what I've seen, you always refer to your brother when a big decision needs to be made. I don't know why; frankly, I don't care—"

"Then why are you still talking?" Cai snapped.

I gaped.

I guessed that potential love match might be at an end.

Adrianna's chin rose. "Because if they want what they say they want, they need to step up."

"What would you have us do?" Liora's words were distant.

"Whatever it takes."

"Excellent," Cai began dryly. "So now we've all received a good tongue-lashing, can we get on with the trial?"

"Fine," Adrianna said, her eyes like chips of ice.

Liora was giving Adrianna a calculated look. "I'll think about what you've said because there is truth to it. But at some point, you should turn that perceptive gaze on yourself and ask why you weren't a leader's first pick when you're a first-class fighter."

Adrianna looked dumbstruck.

I tried to smother a wink of smugness.

Liora handed the scrap of parchment over to Cai. "We have to get a lock of hair from a swamp witch."

Cai stared down at the map, and muttered, "Shit."

"The closest witches to us hail from the Nola swamps," Adrianna said, slipping back behind the haughty mask. "We should go there. We won't need the map."

"You've had dealings with them before?" Cai cocked an eyebrow.

Adrianna loosened her wings. "Something like that. It lies northeast. We can be there in four days."

He nodded, his shoulders stiffening. "Best get started then. Since you've got the wings, you can fly overhead and scout the terrain. Just stay in sight so we can follow."

Adrianna pressed her lips together but didn't object, surprisingly. Spreading her scaled blue wings, she shot upward. I could just about spy her floating form through the pine boughs.

Liora regarded me wearily. "I hate to admit this, but Adrianna was right about something else."

"Oh?"

"We've been ignoring the connection between you both." She motioned between Frazer and me. "It's a mystery, which going forward could be problematic—even dangerous. Or it could help you both."

She gave my necklace a furtive look. Just long enough for me to guess her meaning. My breathing turned shallow. Auntie sensed my panic. *Perhaps it is time you told him?*

A chasm opened before me. Fear crawled, writhing in my belly. What if he rejected me? What if he turned away from me, too?

"Serena?" Liora sounded cautious.

Her call snapped me out of my internal conflict. "Mm?"

"Maybe it's time."

My blood chilled, recognizing Auntie's words being echoed through her. "Time for what?"

Liora opened her mouth but looked lost. Cai picked up the conversation by infusing each word with meaning. "To start exploring its limitations."

I knew he meant the necklace.

Frazer shifted. As if uncomfortable. *What's he talking about?*

"How do I do that?" I asked Cai.

Serena? Frazer's mental voice was insistent.

My temper flared. "Frazer, just give me a damned minute."

Stars, he did not like that. For one unbearable moment we glared at each other. His will bent first and he looked away, jaw pulsing, hands clenching.

Cai regarded us carefully. "A good place to start would be figuring out if what you share with Frazer is unique, or whether you can communicate with others in the same way."

"How?"

"Ask."

It was obvious again he meant talking to the necklace—to Auntie. It wouldn't do any good. She never answered my interrogations.

Anger quivered in our thread, throbbing, insistent. Frazer had guessed Cai knew something he didn't. That I was hiding something. And Frazer hated it. I didn't blame him.

Cai looked up toward the canopy and beyond. "Anyway, we should go. Adrianna's probably getting pissed we're taking so long. I'll take point."

He turned and walked into the forest, leading us, trusting us to fall in line. Liora hesitated, glancing between Frazer and me. Then, hand on hilt, she went after Cai. Frazer stepped back and gestured for me to go next. His face was stone.

Shit. I could tell him now, but ...

We will talk about this.

He just stared. Unconvinced. I moved off without another word.

CHAPTER 16
THE PAST

Time slunk by. Although, in the eternal twilit forest it was impossible to say how much. It felt like hours. We didn't slacken our pace once, and apart from the odd call from Adrianna to adjust our direction, no one talked. My mood steadily declined as I spent much of that time trying to pry answers from Auntie, who gave me nothing. Just the odd reassurance that she'd tell me everything—one day. I tried to bypass her and talk to Liora, mind to mind. A headache was my only reward.

My patience eventually broke. Whatever magic the necklace contained, I couldn't control it any more than the changing weather. A damned shame, because the airless forest had grown heavy with the cloying scents of sharp pine and damp earth. Warm droplets began to rain down, and the dry, splintering crack of thunder sounded, making me pull my cloak's hood up and glance skyward. Adrianna was just a blur; she seemed fine. Perhaps it was cooler up there, above the suffocating weight of the canopy. Envy flooded me. What must it be like to have that kind of freedom? To leave everything behind, even if just for a moment.

It's glorious.

The bitterness rolling through Frazer's words made my skin itch. I slowed, and he barged past. Never a good sign.

Frazer?

Don't, was his only reply.

I watched his retreating back, feeling for echoes, whispers, in the bond. It was the only way to know what was going on with him: the only way to read him if his thoughts were closed to me. An aching loneliness sounded back. A distant, dark place, like his soul had turned the shade of nightmares.

I walked fast and caught up to him. Flanking his side, grasping for his arm, I said, "You're angry and you want answers, but you won't tell me a single thing about your past. I don't even know your second name. How is that fair? I've shared things with you—"

His arm went wide, breaking my grip. *And most of those things I sensed through this connection first.* He waved between us. *Who knows if you'd have shared them willingly. And as for my past, that is mine to share if and when I feel like it. But you're hiding things that affect us both, so what makes you think you've got the right to hear my story?*

His eyes were bleeding wrath. Bracing myself, I moved my hand to his. Frazer pulled away and tried to storm off again. I blocked his path and showed him my palms. His deadlier set of canines erupted.

A growl ripped loose from his throat. A vicious warning.

To push this now, when we were vulnerable, was lunacy. But I couldn't take the deafening silence. I couldn't take being shut out. Not anymore. "I know I should've told you." I gestured up and down his body. "But this darkness—whatever this is. It's eating you up. Talking might help."

What would you know? What d'you know about anything? You're a child.

My chest hollowed out.

Adrianna landed beside us, shaking her scaled wings free of the rain. "Get away from him, Serena. He's not himself."

"What's wrong?"

Liora had obviously doubled back. But I didn't listen; I didn't move. Frazer was in deep, deep pain. Shadows haunted his eyes, and his chest fluttered with shallow breath.

Cai appeared. "Serena, leave him."

The demand—the order—in his voice set my teeth on edge.

Adrianna began, "You can't push him to be ready. If he doesn't want to let you in—"

"You want to let me in though, don't you? A part of you does." I was speaking only to Frazer.

You know nothing. He snapped his teeth at me and hunched down, threateningly.

"Serena!" Liora called out, alarmed.

"He won't hurt me." A certainty.

Adrianna cautioned, "Really? Because anger and aggression are coming off him in waves right now. I can smell it."

"Enough." A clear command because it was *my* choice. "You wanted me to explore this supposed power." My eyes darted first to Cai, then Liora, and finally to Adrianna. "But *she* won't let me connect to anyone else. There's only him." My gaze settled back on to Frazer. "Only you."

Another clap of thunder boomed out overhead. And Frazer looked ready to attack or flee. I couldn't tell which.

"What d'you mean by 'she'?" Adrianna sounded intrigued.

I ignored her and added, "I don't want any of you interfering."

Now, I focused all my attention on to Frazer; instinct made me pull on our bond. A fierce, sharp tug to hold him. Then, I hurled my whole self toward that dark, glittering shield like a wave cresting the shore.

Frazer's face went slack. He threw a hand in front of his face, hissing, *If you try to ... What are you doing?*

His arm lowered; a confused expression appeared as I flooded the outside of those high, high walls, letting my memories, my essence, rise around him and shine ...

My mother holding me, brushing her fingers through my hair.

Father sweeping me into his arms—his strong, bear-like arms—keeping me safe from a storm outside.

Weeping at my mother's grave.

Viola knitting me a scarf, her hands blurring as she brought the needles clacking up and down.

Elain screaming. Slapping me hard.

John teaching me to bake a cake.

Smelling the pages of a book Viola had just bought me.

The memories came unbidden now. A tempest with no rudder. *My story*—a collection of thoughts and feelings flowing out of a well so vast, I feared drowning us both.

Gus's hot, sticky tongue. The sickening possession in his eyes.

Elain's insults. Her joy when she thought she'd ruined me.

I wanted to turn away and hunker down into some distant corner of my mind. I was trusting Frazer with everything—maybe too much. But the thread sang to me his awe and rage and sadness as he processed my memories. So I hung on, and let go.

The torrent went even quicker.

Gus's ribcage lying split open on the frost-bitten earth.

Hunter helping to force a sleeping potion down my throat. Hunter's wing sheltering me.

My doubts, my fears of coming to Kasi.

Fighting with Wilder. The resulting desire uncurling itself in my belly like some sleeping, half-starved beast.

The necklace came next. Then, Auntie's voice.

Shock radiated from Frazer. My recollections of him came next. His eyes watching me from afar, me questioning whether he was lonely or looking for a weakness to exploit. The strange pull I'd felt toward him. And finally, the stream of consciousness slowed to a trickle. As if we'd neared the bottom of the well.

The last piece of me poured out: my fear that he might reject me—that he might resent our connection. Also, the hope and comfort it'd brought as it offered a point of light in a long history of loneliness and loss. A star in a dark sky.

I felt drained, but clear. *You see? I've been on the outside looking in my whole life. And living in a fae kingdom didn't change that. Meeting Cai and Liora didn't change that. You—us, connecting like this—did. You make me feel like I belong. Except when you push me away.*

He wasn't just surprised; he was amazed.

I've shown you everything. I didn't hold back. And I don't expect you to do the same. I know that whatever's on the other end of this thread might make my nightmares look like rainbows and sunbeams in comparison. But show me something, Frazer, because continuing to live in this silence isn't the answer.

How is showing you my nightmares going to help me? Tell me, Serena—how?

I blinked back tears. We hadn't known each other long. I could turn away—ignore the thread. It would hurt less. But if I left him to this silence, to rot behind that wall, I felt sure he'd go mad. Or become so twisted that he wouldn't be worth saving.

I think it'd help if you shared whatever it is you're carrying. I can bear the weight. But, I can't force you to do anything. Show me, don't show me, it's your choice. I'll love you, whatever you decide.

I hadn't planned on saying it—the only man I'd uttered those words to was my father. And that had gotten harder and harder to say over the years.

Frazer couldn't have looked more stunned if I'd shot him through the heart. The thread trembled with fear, suspicion, even horror, at my declaration. But finally, there it was—a glimmer of a joy so pure, it sent a crack running through the shield. *Why?*

It was clear what he meant. Why he needed me to explain. *I know that our bond only got forged a few days ago, but from the moment we met, I've felt connected to you. And to be honest, it's just easy to love you.*

His unease urged me to clarify. *I don't mean romantic love. You're ... you're like my brother, Frazer. I'm sorry if that upsets you, but—*

My thoughts broke apart as images swamped me and enormous, feathered, indigo wings burst into my mind's eye.

I *was* Frazer, standing atop a black cliff with the sun warming my wings. Peering below, seeing a churning sea with its white-capped breakers, and breathing in the deep notes of salt and brine. Giddy excitement and terror coated my tongue, but I knew in my bones—in the most primal parts of myself—I was ready.

I took a running leap. Leaving my stomach behind, I nosedived toward the rocks and the waves smashing up against them. Fear churned in my gut and then, relief: ecstasy as my wings burst open. I beat them furiously. For a few heartbeats my core failed to support me; the muscles in my shoulders cramped and my wings felt like they might rip from my back. I leveled out just in time for an updraft to take me and toss me around as easily as a bit of fluff. Eventually, I found the rhythm. Gliding in and out of clouds, chasing curtains of rain, brushing over waves, letting salt spray hit my face. This was freedom—this was *everything*. The parts of my mind still belonging to me ached to experience it for myself.

Sorrow slammed into me. Unending, relentless. The squalling sea and open sky vanished, replaced by a room. One of cold white stone, grand columns, gossamer and silk fabric, and a balcony that looked out onto three lakes. The water was so still, so pure and pristine, it reflected the mountains and star-spangled darkness above. A perfect portrait.

The parts that remained mine gasped in awe.

"Have you nothing to say in your defense, Frazer?"

It was a deep, imperious voice that spoke of centuries of wisdom and boredom. A huge male moved to stand in front of me—of us. A crown, decorated with a black star and a glittering silver tail, sat atop his inky hair. It served to highlight his snow-feathered wings, bloodless skin, and silvery-gray eyes. A lightning strike. A winter storm. That's what this male was.

Frazer's recognition shone through, telling me this was the former—and now very dead—King of Aurora, Linus Johana.

"No," I said as Frazer.

The corner of my mind that belonged to Serena ached at hearing his voice for the first time.

"Then, you leave me with no choice."

Linus made a small gesture and two male fae appeared at my side while six watched my back. They were strangers—that was a mercy, at least. But each had come armed to the hilt, and one held a wicked-looking fae scimitar. A curved blade that had dread pooling in the pit of my stomach.

I tucked my wings in closer to my body. "Why are you doing this?" My voice came out trembling—I hated myself for it.

"Why do you think?" he asked, as cold as the ice encasing his court. "Because if I don't, *she* will, and she'll make your pain eternal."

"Then fight her." A growl slipped past my restraint. I muzzled myself —this was still my king. I had to remember that.

"Morgan's too powerful. She has an army of magic-wielders behind her," Linus said in clipped tones. "There's nothing to be gained from fighting when we can work *with* her and save fae lives."

"You can't work with her! She's mad! She killed Dain—"

"Enough, Frazer," Linus bit down, his eyes lighting with anger and a warning.

He nodded to the two unfeeling blocks of stone at my side. The males drove me to the floor, pinning my arms to each side. I stayed focused on the king—my king. "Punish me, but let me stay. I want to serve."

"If you stay, she'll insist on your execution."

Linus—a male who'd given me a position, a home—now stared down like I was *nothing*, a nobody. "Or worse, imprison you and use your life as a stick to beat my son and heir over the head with. Our court cannot afford for Lynx to get distracted."

"Where is he?" I couldn't even say his name.

"The Lionheart is safe. I sent him south to the border. He's acting as an escort to Morgan's court. They will be here within the week."

"What will you tell him? About what you did." Undiluted resentment was dripping from my tongue, clouding my vision.

Linus's eyes slid away. I recognized it for the merciless gesture that it was. "The truth. That you sabotaged the mission. You betrayed us. That I had to send you into exile before Morgan could destroy you."

"He'll come after me. He'll want to hear it from *me*."

It wasn't a threat. We both knew Lynx's people had named him well. The Lionheart didn't abandon his soldiers, especially those he called friends.

"Perhaps." Linus's head tilted in cold contemplation. "But if you care for him at all, you'll go into exile willingly and never darken our court again."

Choking on a rising tide of terror, I forced out, "Why don't you just kill me?"

A shrug. "Lynx would never forgive me. This'll be better in the long run. Do it."

Linus jerked his chin at the fae with the blade and swiveled on his heel, showing his back to me. He was walking away. He didn't even have the guts to carry out the sentence himself.

A powerful hate gripped my heart, twisting it. Poisoned words slipped out. "They were right. Your people were right to call you the Ironhearted King."

Linus halted. Motionless and rigid, he didn't look back as he breathed, "Goodbye, Frazer Novak."

My king made it to the balcony opposite and fled to the skies. *Coward.*

The fae on my right grasped the curved blade in both hands while the other held me fast. Honor and dignity forgotten, I started to struggle. More fae rushed forward from the back. They held me down, pulled my wings out wide.

Pissing myself, screaming, begging, crying—none of it stopped a scimitar from coming up. Then down. My wings. My beautiful wings fell away, and heart-stopping pain rushed in, sweeping away everything. Darkness came, consuming me. I welcomed it with open arms.

I, Serena, awoke on a rolled-out sleeping bag near a roaring fire. My rucksack lay beside me and night had closed in. The rain and thunder had passed. I sat up and touched my arms, legs, and face. I had to make sure it was me—only me. The human—the girl from Tunnock with no wings—who'd never known the King of Aurora.

Liora moved to my side and braced a palm against my back. "Thank the light! Are you okay?"

At the same time, Cai was saying, "What happened?"

I studied the glade. Adrianna was gone but Cai and Liora were kneeling on bedrolls either side of me. Frazer was sitting opposite on a dead tree stump, treating his arrows. The flames of the fire flickered between us, casting phantom shadows across his face.

Aren't you going to look at me?

His hands trembled; he wouldn't meet my eyes.

"Serena?" Liora breathed.

"I'm fine."

"Aren't you going to give us more than that?" Cai asked, his voice strained with exhaustion. "You make us all shit ourselves with fright and—"

"I showed him my memories. All of them."

Liora muttered something like, "Moons above," and Cai pressed his lips together. "That was ... reckless." He seemed to be biting his tongue—quite literally. My instincts told me he'd wanted to say something a lot more damning.

"Did it help?" Liora asked, studying Frazer. Doubt was written all over her face.

What could I say?

Frazer stopped fussing with the arrow fletching to peer at me from under sooty lashes.

"Here we were thinking you were having a seizure," Adrianna said as she came in to land.

"Mother have mercy—why do I even bother?" Cai stressed. "You're meant to be keeping watch!"

Her shoulders rolled into a careless shrug. "I'd hear someone before I saw them in this light. And my hearing works just fine down here." She snapped her wings into place and kneeled in between Liora and Frazer.

"Why agree to go up there then?" Liora asked, staring at her.

"I prefer to be alone."

Cai huffed a half-laugh. And Adrianna pretended she didn't hear. She raised her hands to the fire to warm them.

"Why did you all think I was having a seizure?"

I turned to the kindest set of eyes, the safest bet for a simple answer. Liora. "Both of you went into a kind of trance," she said, sounding spooked. "We couldn't get you to respond, and then you started screaming."

"You sounded like you were being murdered," Adrianna said bluntly. "And Frazer just stood there looking like he'd been force-fed poison while these two clucked over you like hens." She shot Cai and Liora a *look*.

Gods, what had happened between them?

Adrianna continued. "So, I did the only thing I could think of and knocked you out before you had a fit or tore your voice." A note of defensiveness.

"Good."

Adrianna blinked.

"It was the right thing to do," I told her. "And I'm sorry. I didn't know that would happen. But it was worth it. I'm glad it happened."

I stared at Frazer, willing him to believe me. His eyes had become fixed on the blazing fire while his body remained still, lifeless. *I survived—you survived it, and we're together. We're whole.*

Frazer's burning glower met mine. "How can you say that?" he rasped aloud.

Liora gasped, Cai cursed, and Adrianna croaked out a harsh laugh. "Guess he wasn't mute after all," she drawled.

Frazer didn't respond. He just glared at me, unblinking.

I braced myself and said, "Whatever happened back then ... It doesn't have to ruin the rest of your life."

His face was bleak. "You don't know what I did to deserve the sentence."

Cai, Liora, and Adrianna stiffened as their attention piqued.

"It doesn't matter." I didn't care why Linus had done it. He'd hurt Frazer in the worst way possible. I was *glad* his king was nothing but dust and bone. "Whatever you did, you've paid for it a million times over."

Adrianna scowled over at Frazer. "Well, Serena might not need to know what you've done, but if you are a criminal, we deserve to know."

Protectiveness roiled in my veins, firing my words. "No—you don't."

Frazer's next words were so quiet, they were barely audible over the crackling of the flames. "I'm an exile from the fallen court—from Aurora. The king shredded my wings because I refused to work for Morgan."

Well, that answered some of my questions.

Cai's and Liora's wide eyes and open mouths said everything.

Adrianna's reaction was the most extreme. Color drained from her face, leaving behind a gaunt mask. "When?" A sharp rasp.

"Eighteen years ago—about a month before King Linus was killed and Prince Lynx was taken."

Frazer sounded like he'd been reduced to smoke and ash. My heart bled.

"Taken." Adrianna flared to life again. "A nice word for it. Turned traitor might be more accurate."

"What happened wasn't his fault," Frazer growled. "Lynx would've killed himself before becoming puppet to that evil bitch. Morgan must've done something to him, bewitched him—"

"I don't care," Adrianna hissed, her face twisting. "He has oceans of fae and sprite blood on his hands. It was because of his strength that she was so successful."

Blinding rage drummed down our thread. An urge to bite and maim. I shot up and over the fire in a vain attempt to restrain him. The impulse died as quickly as it'd been born; I found him cradling his head in his hands. I kneeled and put my palm flat on his knee. It was all I had to offer—a comforting touch.

I was fumbling in the dark. There was so much I didn't understand about this realm. "Why was he so important?" I asked faintly.

I directed the question toward Frazer. A heaviness that spoke of years of anguish echoed in every word of his reply. "Lynx is gifted with the old magic." Noticing the confusion in my eyes, he clarified. "Aldarian fae were known for light magic but over the centuries, the gifts became rare. But Lynx—his power was ... vast, undiluted. And somehow Morgan turned him. I wasn't there to protect him. The lives lost, the bloodshed, it's all on me."

"Don't try to scrub him clean." Adrianna's nose wrinkled in plain disgust.

Something snapped in me. "Don't speak to him like that!"

Frazer's hands dropped, revealing his haggard eyes with the light of the fire. "Matea," he said softly. A call to back off. Straightening his back a touch, he looked to Cai. "Can you shield our conversation?"

Cai gave a little nod. The air shimmered.

Frazer freed a breath, easing into his explanation. "My king wanted to ally with Morgan, but it came with a price. A heavy one. For one of the demands she made in the treaty was for the famed Sami Warriors of our court to kill her enemies for her, which meant murdering anyone brave enough to stand up to her. I was put in charge of that mission."

Adrianna's low growl pierced the air.

The little whistle of appreciation came from Cai. "I guess the rumors were true for once. Why would you ever train as a foot soldier? Surely becoming an Iko's beneath you?"

Frazer's reply was gruff. "I wasn't a Sami Warrior. Not really. I trained with them, but I remained part of the king's personal guard. But when he put me in charge—"

"You couldn't do it," I guessed.

The sorrow in his eyes made my chest crumple. "I knew those fae. They were loyal, but to become Morgan's assassins would've ripped them apart. I took them outside the city walls and gave them a choice. Disappear or submit to Morgan's wishes."

Adrianna's back straightened. "The Aurorian Samite were massacred along with the rest of the court ..."

Frazer shook his head.

"Holy hell," Cai gaped. "They're still out there?"

Frazer continued, sounding grim. "Yes. And because of my act of defiance, I heard the witch's fury was something to behold. That it made her deaf to every treaty, every plea, and the negotiations fell apart." He looked as sick as I felt. "My king was imprisoned, publicly humiliated, and finally, executed. The whole court followed him into the grave and my friend's soul was obliterated. All because of what I'd done. Because I was so rutting sure that Morgan lied when she told King Linus that he could keep his court and his crown. But Morgan allied with the River-lands not long after, and she's kept her word to Diana—she's never invaded." His shoulders slumped. Utter defeat and years of guilt—this was what they did.

Gods. He could've worked for—been enslaved to—that *demon* witch. I shook my head clear of those thoughts and said, "You're taking too much on."

The look he gave me made my throat stick. As if I could never understand.

"Serena's right," Liora put in softly. "That burden isn't yours alone to carry. There were a lot of people responsible for the fall."

Cai made a noise of agreement. "Besides, the could'a, would'a, should'a helps no one. If you ask me, you showed mercy and saved a shit-ton of people the day you let those warriors go."

Adrianna couldn't look any of us in the eye; she was so quiet when she spoke. "And don't make the mistake of thinking Morgan didn't destroy the Riverlands. Our kingdom—what we once were—is ashes. Our court made the biggest mistake of all. And our Queen didn't fight when the whole damned Solar Court begged us to. Instead, Diana forsook Queen Sefra and signed a beggar's alliance with Morgan, giving into all her demands. By the seven seas, we may as well have gotten on our knees and sucked her tits." Disgust infused her voice again.

Frazer frowned, nodding as if accepting she might have a point.

"But everyone knows Queen Diana hates Morgan." Liora's breathlessness made me stare at her.

Adrianna snorted. "Of course she does, but then who doesn't? She's a hellish bitch."

Cai cut in. "Then there's still hope, while the Riverlands is fighting—"

"Haven't you been listening?" Adrianna asked, annoyed. "We're not fighting. We're beggared and broken by Morgan's *taxes*."

"What about the Riverland's armies?" Liora sputtered.

Why in stars did she seem so panicked? It wasn't just her, either. Cai was white-knuckling it, staring into the fire.

"What of them?" Adrianna asked, scowling.

"They answer to Diana. She's been increasing recruit intakes for over a year, building her military."

"Li ..." Cai's whisper rang with a warning.

Adrianna watched them both carefully. "So, that's why you're at Kasi?" she asked, her eyes narrowing. "I wondered why two witches would travel from the Crescent to become foot soldiers for the Riverlands."

My eyes fixed on Liora. Her expression was riddled with grief and shock. "I thought you left because you were—"

Cai's spell prevented me from speaking another word; it choked me off.

Liora's features flickered with unease. She turned and whispered to her brother, "Undo it. Undo the spell. Serena's more than earned our trust, and Frazer's willing to share secrets that, in the wrong hands, could mean death. We should return the favor."

I shared a look with Cai. There was a heartbeat of hesitancy that I hoped had everything to do with Liora's safety and nothing to do with me. Then his lips moved, his eyes fluttered, and something loosened in my chest as the release of my oath to never speak of their secrets broke.

"Anyone want to tell me what that was all about?" Adrianna lifted a haughty eyebrow. She was fooling no one. Curiosity burned deep in her eyes.

She wasn't the only one with questions; Frazer's thoughts interrupted my own. *Serena? Anything you've neglected to tell me?*

Due to the tight grip of the spell, my friends' secrets were the one thing I'd been unable to reveal, even in shared memories. But it wasn't to him that I answered. My attention was solely for Liora.

"You said you were exiled from the Crescent because your father feared Morgan. Because she might come after you ..." I tried not to sound too accusing.

"That's right," Cai answered for Liora. A little too defensive.

I bristled; my spine locked.

"Maybe that's why you left, but it's not why you came to Kasi, is it?" Adrianna pressed. "You believed the rumors those fools spread about Diana leading us against Morgan when the time is right."

Adrianna didn't look smug, just sad. Liora dropped all pretense at this point. Her voice grew louder, more insistent. "If Diana wasn't planning anything, why recruit more soldiers? Why did she break her rule about training human slaves?"

Interesting.

Liora seemed so desperate that a smidgen of sympathy entered Adrianna's voice. "Because Morgan *persuaded* our queen it was the right course of action."

Liora deflated, shoulders caving inward. But Cai didn't seem ready to give in. "How d'you know this?"

Adrianna met his challenging tone. "I have friends in the Riverlands Court."

I could almost taste the argument brewing.

"The rumors must've started somehow—"

Adrianna cut him off. "There are some who believe Morgan started those rumors to flush out rebels. Besides, don't you think that if you two heard those rumors on the other side of Aldar, that Morgan's court wouldn't know about them too? If there was ever a shred of truth to them, the fae bitch would've gathered her forces against Diana a long time ago."

I couldn't bear the weighted looks Cai and Liora shared. They reeked of despair. "Did you come here to join a rebellion?"

Liora was the first to nod. "I'm sorry we didn't tell you. I wanted to."

"It's my fault. I told her not to," Cai confessed. "I didn't want you dragged into our problems—we've got enough on with the trials."

I nodded. It was an effort not to seem hurt.

"We should've told you," Liora muttered, staring up at the canopy with tears in her eyes. "You also deserve to know that my motives for wanting to be part of a rebellion aren't selfless. I want Morgan gone, but it's more than that. I *need* her gone. The binding's starting to take its toll."

Fear choked me. Breathing became difficult. "I thought you told me the side effects were manageable with exercise."

"That's what we were told," Cai answered, as if all the emotion had drained from him. "But when it comes to Liora ..." A pause and a sigh. "We think her power might be too raw, too wild to be contained forever."

Liora's tears had dried up. She was diminished, wraith-like and staring into the flames at the center of our circle. "I've been getting weaker for a while now. The exercise calmed the beast, but lately ... It looks like it'd rather die and take me with it than remain caged."

"You speak as if it were a living thing," Frazer breathed.

A nod. "It is, in the way all magic is alive," said Liora

A pregnant pause. No one seemed to know what to say or do. Liora was dying; her magic was ripping her apart from the inside. That couldn't happen. We had to free her. But what would become of her with Morgan ruling these lands? Captured to be a slave? A trophy?

No. That. Could. Not. Happen. "So, if the rebellion's a dead end, how can we defeat Morgan?"

Adrianna exhaled a sharp laugh.

My fists became balls, and fire burned at my throat. *My* fire. Heat rippled through my nerves like lightning, setting my heart pounding. "I was being serious."

Adrianna just shook her head, smiling. Liora and Cai looked at me with something resembling pity. Only Frazer became wary—tense. The droplet at my throat lit up, glowing. I looked down and that's when I saw it: an ember encased in water. A spark that had, until now, remained hidden. I seemed to drift above my body and a stiff breeze was born, tickling the nape of my neck.

"Serena," Frazer called, tugging on the bond.

He reeled me in as though I were a fish caught on a line. Blue-silver eyes found mine, calming me, drowning me in water. Fire quenched, a rush of tiredness followed.

"Care to explain what that was?" Adrianna stared at me, her back ramrod straight.

"Not now," Frazer replied for me.

Adrianna's jaw ticked, but she said nothing.

Cai served up a distraction. "Morgan might not have light magic like Lynx, but she's still the most powerful fae-witch in, well ... ever." Burning with the dark court's fire, his eyes held mine. "A witch who's breached the human realm and leashed a fae like the Dark Prince—"

Frazer made a sound of disapproval. "Don't call him that."

Cai didn't break stride. "The point is we'd need a legion to bring her down."

"We'd need more than that," Adrianna huffed ruefully.

I shot her a cutting glance. "I wasn't suggesting we take her on single-handedly."

"Good. Because we wouldn't survive long if we did," Adrianna replied.

Not bothering to respond, I turned to Liora. "But she isn't invincible. Hunter told me that she was worried about neighboring fae realms. You might find sanctuary there?"

Cai looked to Liora. "We've considered fleeing to Asitar or Mokara, but the crossing ..."

"Can be fatal," Liora finished, her eyes creasing with worry.

"It's suicidal," Adrianna cut in. "What d'you know of our eastern brethren?" Her focus snapped to me, her mouth a hard line.

I scrabbled to remember all that Hunter had revealed. Slowly, his words trickled to the forefront of my mind. "Only that it used to be your homeland, but there was a conflict with the other fae, so you fled and came here. And Morgan thinks war might be coming."

Frazer shifted a bit while Adrianna tensed and said, "All true, except the last part. Morgan might say war is imminent, but we only have her word for it."

"Oh?" I voiced carefully.

Frazer quickly, quietly informed me, "The Aldarian fae and the Eastern Alliance signed a truce after three hundred years of war. Both sides suffered untold losses. We were broke, bleeding, and tired, so our people agreed to exile on conditions." The line of his jaw tightened.

Adrianna pushed out a dry huff of laughter.

Frazer quirked his head. "The treaty stopped foreign fae setting foot on our soil, but we *could* travel to their lands. It made trade complicated, but possible—"

"That was before Morgan's reign of paranoia and authoritarianism." Adrianna spoke passionately. "She banned all trade and crossings to those countries." Her voice tempered as she looked to Liora. "Even if you could get past the triggers and the border force, once you got to Asitar or Mokara, then what? There's not a human alive who isn't in a collar."

Liora's eyes traveled to Cai, who was staring—frowning—at Adrianna. He didn't look convinced. "All we're left with is rumors now, partially inspired by Morgan's ravings. Things might've changed."

Liora was the one to add, "But they might not have. I won't risk you being thrown in chains, Cai."

"And I won't stand aside and watch you die," he fired back.

Liora's expression crumpled as her brother's expression turned ferocious.

No one spoke.

The only sounds now were the hissing, cracking of the fire and Adrianna pulling out an apple from her bag. This spurned Frazer to reach into his pack beside him. *You should eat something too. You were out cold when everyone else had their evening rations.*

Fine, but I'm not eating your food.

Frazer didn't listen and pulled out a few thick slices of wrapped fruit loaf. When I didn't take the wrappings, he sighed through his nose. *You can give me some of your food tomorrow if you think it's necessary.*

I do.

He gave me a little smile. *Deal.*

I scarfed down the loaf slices in three mouthfuls, but it didn't take the edge off my hunger. Frazer simply handed me more of his rations. I cursed myself as a greedy, selfish wretch but took the pouch of dried fruit anyway.

Adrianna tossed an apple core over her shoulder and peered over at me. "You said a male named Hunter told you about the other fae realms?"

I nodded at her.

"There aren't any recruits by that name," she said, her mouth puckering slightly.

"It was a male from the Hunt. The one who captured her." Liora was smiling at me.

"River and sky protect us," Adrianna muttered, her eyes rolling. "What is it with you? You seem to induce every male fae you meet to fawn over you."

A croaking laugh burst out of me. "Hardly."

"I hope that barb wasn't directed at me," Frazer snarled.

"You, in particular," Adrianna said, giving him a twisted smile.

Frazer's hackles lifted and shook with a grumpy growl.

Hardly concealing the exasperation in my voice, I retorted, "Adi, Frazer's like my brother." Her eyebrows knotted together. "As for Hunter, I've thought about it since, and I think he was nice to me because he wanted —maybe needed—a human to ease his guilt."

It wasn't a lie. Sadly.

Liora caught my eye. "I think it was more than that," she said gently.

Adrianna clucked her tongue. "First, a member of the twisted Wild Hunt and then a legendary fae Warrior."

My mouth dried. "What are you talking about?"

Adrianna didn't blink. "I've seen the way you stare at each other."

My cheeks burned.

Cai cocked an all-too-amused eyebrow in my direction. Questioning. Liora hadn't told him then.

Frazer tossed his head to the velvety pitch sky and said, "Maybe we should get some sleep."

Cai grinned wide. "Nice distraction."

Frazer flashed his teeth in answer.

I sighed and tucked the pouch of fruit back in Frazer's pack. "I'm not sure I could sleep."

"Then don't," Adrianna said evenly. "Act as our lookout. The southern parts of the Riverlands is home to fewer dangers than the north, but we have to remain vigilant. Especially with Tysion's pack on the hunt." She jerked her chin into the forest and then looked back to me. "We'll take it in turns to keep watch. You'll need *some* sleep. We've got a long march ahead tomorrow, and maybe you've all forgotten amidst talk of starting rebellions and conquering queens, but we still need to finish these damned trials."

Cai motioned to his sister haphazardly. "And what, I'm just supposed to ignore what's happening to my little sister?"

I thought I spotted Liora's eyes shining just a touch too bright. She looked crushed.

Adrianna pulled a bedroll from her pack. Shaking it out, she continued. "Well, you could go and take your chances elsewhere, but the way I see it, your best chance for helping your sister is right here with us."

"Why d'you say that?" Liora stared at Adrianna as if she already suspected the answer.

Adrianna moved to sit on her sleeping bag. She crossed her legs and said, "Any warrior fae knows that a pack that sticks together is the stronger for it."

"What are you saying?" Cai said with a delighted, playful expression.

"I've already said it—we trust in our pack, we guard each other's backs. And maybe, somewhere along the way we'll be able to help one another. But to do that, we need to complete this trial. We need to survive tomorrow and whatever else they throw at us."

"You'll help us? You'll stand with us when the time comes?" Cai asked. As if he were desperate to know.

Adrianna cut him a blazing gaze. "I'm part of this pack, aren't I?"

"Yes," he admitted. "But we've all been banished from our homelands or are running from something. All of us, except you. That doesn't make us the best allies or the best company to keep. So why ally with us? What d'you get out of this?"

I felt sure that Adrianna would punch his teeth down his throat, but she just considered him for a moment. "Unlike everyone else here, I'm not ready to bear my heart." Her voice was unyielding. "If you want to work with me, you have to accept that. Now, I really am going to sleep. Serena, you can wake me in a few hours for the next shift."

"No, wake me," Frazer said. "I'll take her shift."

My eyes flashed to him. *What—*

His thoughts were echoing before I could finish mine. *You might feel awake now, but you're still mentally exhausted after sharing your memories. You need to rest.*

I was about to protest but I got interrupted by Adrianna. "Fine. You wake me then." She tucked her wings in tighter, lay down, and turned away from us. Cai didn't stop staring at her back for a good long while.

CHAPTER 17
THE EERIE

I woke suddenly, violently, to find Frazer suspended over me, his hand clamped over my mouth. *Don't struggle.*

What's wrong?

Frazer pulled me up to a sitting position. The fire still blazed, and dawn hadn't broken. *Something's not right. I'm going to wake Adrianna—you do the same for Cai and Liora.*

Wait. I went to grab his hand. *Tell me.*

He gave me a look. One that confirmed my worst fears. *I can smell something.*

A spider-tingle pricked my spine. *What?*

An eerie might be close.

I'd no idea what that was, but it definitely didn't sound good.

I'll be back. He moved away, barely disturbing the surrounding air. I watched as he bent over and shook Adrianna. She was wide awake and standing in moments. Their lips moved, but I heard nothing. Not even a whisper.

My throat bobbed. Turning first to Liora, a touch was all it took for her to stir. I doubled over, whispering in her ear, "Frazer thinks something's wrong."

Alarm swept across her face, and her eyes went straight to her brother sleeping on the other side of me. I shuffled over and repeated the same warning in his ear. He instantly rolled into a sitting position. His gaze swept the clearing, coming to rest on Adrianna and Frazer who still talked outside the range of human hearing. Cai looked to me for information, demanding it.

"Frazer thinks he smelled an eerie," I breathed.

Cai's nostrils flared, and he leaned in close. "What did you say?" he asked in a violent whisper.

"An eerie."

Cai jumped up, his arm sweeping the air in front of him. A sound barrier erupted. Adrianna and Frazer stopped and stared.

"Is it really an eerie?" he hissed.

Frazer gave a nod.

Liora's mouth popped open in a soundless gasp of horror. "That's what's out there? Aren't they meant to be impossible to kill?"

Adrianna answered. "Everything can be killed."

She was too still, too quiet: Adrianna was terrified.

Liora clambered up. I followed her. Cai waved a hand wildly. "What the fuck are we doing? We need to be running."

Adrianna raised her head higher. Her eyes flashed dangerously. "The eerie's got our scents. We can't go charging off into the night. We need a plan."

Cai cut in. "I'll move our scents away—"

"That won't work," Adrianna vetoed. "Eeries are air incarnate; you can't trick them like that."

My knees knocked together. "What happens if it catches us?"

Liora and Cai exchanged a dark look. And Frazer blurred, stuffing his bedroll into his rucksack, shouldering it, and moving to my side to do the same for me. Since he'd been acting as a lookout, he hadn't removed his bow or quiver. Cai and Liora immediately copied his example and started packing, strapping their swords to their sides.

Not exactly reassuring.

Only Adrianna answered my plea for information. "Eeries suck the air from the lungs of their prey. What they do afterwards, you're better off not knowing."

My heart sputtered. The fear permeating the air seeped into my very bones—the necklace began to burn. "So, what do we do?"

Frazer was fastening my Utemä onto my hip while Adrianna replied, "We can't run forever, and our weapons won't work against it. We need to keep it at bay long enough to trap it." She stared out into the shadow of the forest, fists on hips. Something told me she placed them there to hide her trembling hands.

"How?" Cai asked, standing with his bag now secure on his back.

"It's not keen on fire," Adrianna's eyes shifted to her own belongings. She moved and in two blinks had her rucksack, quiver and bow nestled between her wings.

A bloom of light flared into existence. Cai had stuck a fallen branch into the fire. Adrianna pointed and scowled at the makeshift torch. "That little pig sticker won't do anything but annoy it."

"I'm a witch and air-blessed," Cai retorted, raising his tattooed hand to his chest. "I'll blow the flames into a fury."

I was the only one to see doubt fill Liora's eyes.

"The fire will only keep it from killing us quick," Frazer said as he strapped my rucksack onto my back. I didn't even bother to fight him. "Only earth can neutralize an air sprite. A sealed well or cave would work."

Liora's face had drained of all color, but her voice was steady. "Adi, you know the terrain. Can we get to either of those things in time?"

"There aren't any mountains for miles," Adrianna rushed. "But we're close to a fae village—"

A howling, groaning wind cut her off. Frazer grabbed the back of my neck and forced me to the ground. He kept my head pressed into the dirt, hovering over me, shielding my body. I tried to move, to see something, but his grip was too tight.

"Adrianna, take my sister. *Go!*" Cai roared.

The sound of wings stirring told me Adrianna had taken flight.

Liora screeched, "*Let me down!*"

The murmur of wingbeats continued. From Liora came a throat-tearing scream. "*Cai!*"

Her desperation spurned me to fight Frazer. "Let me up."

"No." His voice wobbled slightly.

"Frazer," I spat through gritted teeth. "This isn't your choice."

A moment of hesitation. He relaxed his grip and pulled me up, but he angled his body in front of mine. The eerie was floating not ten paces away. I muffled a scream.

The eerie had lodged itself into a meat suit—a faeling female. Just a child. Empty, rotting pits, which used to contain eyes, stared back. A blood splattered smock hung loose over gray skin that had withered and sagged. Shards of bone jutted out at awkward angles. Nothing remained of her wings except the joints, visible above her shoulders. Like the broken spokes of a wheel. And pitch-black hair fanned out behind her, rippling in invisible wind currents.

My bowels turned watery as the eerie forced the faeling's broken wrist into a wave. Pulling on her strings like a doll. The grating sounds of bones crunching against one another made me double over and vomit.

I quickly wiped my hand on the back of my mouth, straightened, and stared at Cai. He held his torch aloft, swiping it back and forth. The flames burned higher, directed by a dancing zephyr that he was summoning and sustaining. His face was contorted; sweat beaded on his brow. He couldn't keep this up for long.

We were nothing more than prey now. Mice to a hawk.

The eerie forced its shell into a manic grin. "Pretty little things—want to play?"

That was no faeling voice, but a grating rasp.

Frazer hissed. "Leave now, gutless demon."

A snickering, high-pitched sound answered back. The stench of its rotting flesh wafted toward me. Clamping a hand over my mouth, I desperately fought the urge to dry retch.

"Leave now, and we'll let you live," Frazer said, his eyes shifting between the creature and Cai.

"Let me live?" It giggled, delighted.

"Fluff and flies. Such lovely lies.

That's all you've got before you die."

The eerie sang, conducting with its mangled arms.

My mind was in chaos. We had to get to Cai. We had to run.

The eerie twisted in a breeze of its own making to stare at me. "I like you best." It sucked in a rattling breath through jagged teeth and riven lungs.

"*You smell like spice and everything nice,*
Like snowflakes and frozen lakes."

Frazer's voice was a violent calm. A storm in a glass jar. "Touch her, and I *obliterate* you."

It gnashed together its blackened teeth. "Not nice to make threats. I'll kill you last. You can watch while your kindred's soul is flayed and gutted from her body. I *like* wearing pretty girls. This one's almost spent." It waved expansively toward the faeling skin with a perverse pout.

Frazer stepped back, taking me with him. A cold, feral snicker slipped from the eerie's shriveled lips. It jerked to the side, rushing at us, but Cai sent flames skyrocketing into its face. The eerie was blown back a few paces, hissing and screeching and cursing. But it didn't leave; it wouldn't run.

Cai made a half-retching, half-groaning noise that stopped my heart. Exhaustion was close at hand, and without his magic, we'd be defenseless.

A familiar sound compelled me to look skyward. Adrianna appeared from the shadow of the trees. Liora wasn't with her.

Good. Somebody should live to see the morning.

"Spineless wretch. You're nothing but bloated air," Adrianna sang down to it, taunting it. "Why not pick a real challenge? A warrior fae with strength in her bones and power in her veins. Come on—let's dance you and I."

She soared through the canopy and disappeared. It made an ungodly howl and sped after her, taking the bait.

Cai instantly collapsed to his knees. Frazer went to grab the burning branch he still clutched. I swooped down in front of Cai, clutching his burning face in between my hands. A quick assessment: hair plastered to his face, body drenched in sweat, eyes rolling into the back of his head.

Slap him, Auntie cried.

"Forgive me," I breathed, and hit him hard across the cheek.

He jerked, his eyes focusing.

"Stay awake—we need you."

He slurred his words, but his gaze didn't blur. "I'm ready."

I doubted it. His whole damned body trembled under my touch.

Frazer moved to my side. "Serena, take the torch. I'll carry Cai."

No argument from me. I gingerly grasped the burning branch while Frazer heaved Cai into his arms.

Run, Serena, Auntie whispered, frantic.

My legs were moving before my mind caught on. "Come on! Adi can't out-fly it forever."

"Where are you going?" Frazer came after me.

My gut had driven me right. "No idea, but we can't stay there."

I plunged into the forest, holding the torch aloft, skipping over gnarled roots and jagged stones. And I started to think ... Frazer wouldn't need the light. He'd be better off without me—last longer. Maybe long enough to trap the rutting thing.

"Don't even think about it," he growled from behind me.

"You can find a populated area faster without me. You can see in the dark—"

"No."

I felt his will steel itself. An unyielding force. He wouldn't listen.

"Can you smell anything? Hear any people? Any settlements near-by?" I asked frantically.

There's nothing. I knew he couldn't stomach saying the words aloud.

Keep moving. Auntie's mental voice carried a strangled, panicked sound.

A sob shook loose, choking me. The fear was so violent it seeped into every pore, consuming my body and mind.

I did not want to die. Not here. Not now.

A second, or maybe minutes passed by and we—I—didn't slow. Even though Frazer heard and smelled nothing except the forest. Even though we were lost, running aimlessly.

Serena. Our bond went rigid. *I hear it. The eerie's circling back to us.*

Terror and bile coated my tongue. I spun around, holding the torch aloft. Frazer came to a halt just in front of me.

"Put me down," Cai ordered.

Frazer frowned but set him back on his feet.

"You two need to run on ahead," Cai said doubling over, bracing his hands on his thighs. "I'll hold it off. Just trap the bastard."

A pleading note entered my voice. "Cai, come with us."

He straightened and leveled me with a hard stare. "We're out of options. Go. Tell Liora that it was my choice ... And not to hate me too much."

Frazer ground out, "It'll kill you."

"Better me than all of us." Cai shrugged it off.

Brave, stupid man.

Frazer tilted his head. I knew the signs. "What d'you hear?"

"Adrianna's shouting—" He broke off and gave Cai a *look*. It was pitying, and my belly clenched in dread.

Cai just nodded. "Go."

Frazer grabbed my arm. I struggled, but it was too late. A whooshing sound splintered the air. Adrianna's voice reached us. "*Run!*"

A breeze touched my back. Adrianna landed, and Frazer didn't have time to drag me anywhere.

A whirlwind tossed Adrianna and Frazer aside like leaves. Cai pushed out his inked hand, but he was too late and too tired. He crumpled to the forest floor. I was left standing, frozen, with the torchlight extinguished. The dead faeling materialized in front of me. Invisible claws sliced into my arms. I dropped the branch and my will deserted me as my eyes met that decayed, stinking flesh. A cold sweat broke out, coating me.

Not real, not real, not real.

It leaned in and a breath snaked around the shell of my ear as it whispered, "Mm. I'll be nice and warm wearing your meat."

The surge of panic was so violent, it sparked me into action. My legs were still free. I kicked out, but hit nothing. The eerie had abandoned its shell. All that had survived—rotting skin and splintered bone—clattered to the floor.

My body exploded in agony. My knees would've buckled if not for the *thing* currently slithering inside. It clawed at my insides, gaining control, setting my skin on fire, and boiling my blood. Something hot and wet tickled my upper lip and earlobes. Blood, maybe.

I heard hissing in my ears: it was laughing at my agony.

An icy grip seized my lungs, squeezing, constricting. It would lock me away to suffocate inside my own body.

Auntie whispered, *It's time, child.*

Time to die?

My eyes popped. White sparks obliterated my vision, leaving me blind to my pack. And there it was. Frazer's screams tore a hole through my heart like nothing else could.

Serena. I'm keeping the eerie out of your mind, but I can't stop it suffocating you. I have limited strength, but you can kill the eerie. There's an ember, a spark in your necklace. It's magic: your magic. I've been slowly gifting it back to you, granting you strength, but I can't use it myself. To kill the eerie, you'll need all of it.

My mind skipped over my initial shock and hunkered down, delving into primal, animal instinct. Survival was all that mattered.

What are you waiting for?

Sadness and fear emanated from Auntie. *Gifting it back to you now— all at once ... it'll have consequences.*

Do it.

My throat burned and burned and burned.

A roaring began in my ears, and pain moved like lightning, hitting every nerve. It consumed me. I prayed for death. That's when I saw what was passing through me. A golden liquid fire flecked with silver stars pumped through my blood, cleansing it, driving out the oily second skin of the eerie. The iron grip on my lungs vanished. I sucked in mighty gasps: glorious, beautiful air. A metallic scent filled my nostrils, singeing them. Oblivion.

AIR BRUSHED AGAINST MY CHEEKS.

Finally. A sigh of relief.

Auntie?

I opened my mouth to speak, but my tongue felt blistered and swollen. Like burning smoke and sand.

Take it easy, she whispered.

What is that?

A fog clouded my thoughts, but something about the constant breeze beating against my cheeks had bile rising from my stomach.

Is it the eerie?

Adrenaline spiked my heart so forcibly that despite bone-aching exhaustion, my eyelids fluttered open and my muscles seized, expecting a fight. As my vision adjusted to the light, it wasn't the eerie that filtered in. Adrianna floated above me, eyes crinkled in a wide smile. We were flying.

"Thank the rivers," she mumbled. "Cai told me you'd come back to us, but I wasn't sure I believed him."

Nothing she said sunk in. I wet my lips and forced out, "What's going on? Where's my bag ... sword?"

The effort to say anything triggered a caustic stinging at the back of my throat and brought tears to my eyes.

"Cai can explain once we land. And Frazer's been carrying your stuff for you."

My stomach dropped an inch as her wings angled into a soft glide toward the forest beneath.

"You should know you've been out cold for two days. The eerie's dead. You killed it."

She sounded odd. Was it awe or fear inflecting her voice? How did I kill that thing? Auntie's words trickled in. Magic—*my* magic. Not hers. It was contained, and now it's released? Now it was inside of me?

Consequences.

That word reverberated through my bones, shaking my core. She told me there'd be repercussions for doing it then, and in that way.

Questions circled, getting jumbled in the fuzziness. *Whenwhathow?*

I shuddered.

"It'll be all right," Adrianna said soothingly.

I peered up at her from under my lashes. "Things must be bad for you to be so soft with me."

I'd meant it as a joke, but Adrianna cringed.

"Sorry." My voice was paper-thin, barely more than a whisper.

"Don't be. I deserved it."

She didn't elaborate. I didn't ask. Sleep called, a warm hum lulling me back into its embrace. The whisper of leaves against wings and the musty scent of pine filled my senses. I pinched myself and propped my hot eyelids open.

Adrianna's landing rattled my bones. I hissed through my teeth. Viola's pain remedies now seemed like a light-blessed gift.

"She's awake."

"She is?" Liora choked.

"Thank the sisters," Cai said, sounding hoarse.

I craned my neck and saw them dash forward to encircle me. Frazer held back, looking positively wraith-like. As if he'd been swallowed by his own grief.

What's wrong?

No answer.

"How are you feeling?" Liora asked.

"Alive," I croaked. What else was there to say?

Cai followed up. "There are things you need to know."

Fear pumped through my veins, making me cagey, alert. "Like what?"

Adrianna cut in. "I've told her about the eerie, and that she's been out a while—"

Cai held up his hand. "That's not what I was going to say." He peered down at me. "Serena, after you passed out, I had to make a decision. We could've had Adrianna take you back and risk failing."

Nausea, fierce and grim, struck me. "You didn't do that though, right?"

Liora shook her head, causing her red curls to catch the sun. "No, but only because as soon as we'd done some basic tests, it was obvious you weren't hurt; you were suffering from a burn-out—"

"Not 'we.' Liora figured out what was wrong," Cai said, glancing at his sister. A mixture of pride and awe settled over his features. He looked to me again and said, "The body often goes into a hibernating state if it uses too much magic. It's a common problem among young witches, but I hadn't thought to look for it in you." His head cocked to the side at this.

I almost sighed. My body and mind felt close to collapse, but I knew we'd have to have *that* conversation soon. No way could I kill an eerie and not explain how.

Liora went on. "Now that you're awake, your body will catch up with itself. You'll need to drink a lot."

"And piss," Cai said with a smirk.

Liora rolled her eyes. And Adrianna said, "I'll take her."

Before I could protest, she'd skimmed across the ground with the help of her wings and bounded a healthy distance from the others.

I bristled. "I wanted to talk to Frazer."

Adrianna just shrugged. "Well, maybe you can get something out of him. We haven't been able to. He's retreated into his self-absorbed silence again."

It would've been easy to see only the irritation in her words. But there was something else. Something wholly un-Adrianna. "You're worried about him?"

She blinked. Damn. What had I missed these past two days?

Adrianna's azure eyes regarded me. Calculating. But I didn't see someone unfeeling. Not this time. It felt more like she was weighing how and what she should say.

She began slowly. "When that *thing* came for you, Cai had already collapsed, and Liora was stashed away up a tree, despite serious attempts to scratch my eyes out." A faint curl of the lip, which vanished the moment she added, "But Frazer and I had to watch while it choked the life from you. We couldn't move. And his screams ..." Her eyes closed; she looked pained. "You should try talking to him."

An echo from the attack rang inside me. I remembered his fear. Not for himself, but for me. Heart in mouth, I replied, "I will."

She gave me a curt nod. "So, d'you need help to piss, or—"

"No!" That loud rasp had my throat aching.

Adrianna's eyes danced in cool amusement, and she lowered me without a word.

I wobbled, but my legs didn't give way. Choosing a tree, I hid behind its thick trunk and lowered my leggings. Cai had been right. My body did need to catch up; I was behind that tree for a while. When done, I hobbled out toward Adrianna. My body stiff and aching, I didn't resist as she lifted me and flew back. The others now sat, resting up against a dead log with packs and weapons beside them. Liora and Cai smiled the second they saw me. Frazer, however, didn't move. When his eyes traveled to mine, it was a slow, tired movement.

A blank stare.

My throat got stuck. I tapped Adrianna's shoulder. She didn't need me to explain. Walking over to the dead log, she set me down in between Frazer and Liora, and then sat opposite us, stretching out her legs.

I let my head fall onto Frazer's shoulder. *We're alive.*

The reply echoed. As if from a distance. *Barely.*

I didn't have an answer. He was right.

I couldn't get to you. I couldn't move. It was a whisper, one filled with guilt and fear.

I nodded against his shoulder.

Your mind's been closed to me while you slept. I couldn't reach you.

My heart ached something fierce. He'd been left alone again—left in silence. I reached out and entwined our arms. There weren't words.

"Serena." Liora offered me a flask. "You need water."

Frazer shifted. Gently, he untangled his arm from mine. "Take it slow. Just sips for now." He sounded as bad as me. Nothing but hoarse whispers and grating rasps. At least he was speaking.

Thanking Liora, I reached out and tipped the canteen to my parched lips. It hurt to swallow, but the water's touch soon turned soothing, and a terrible thirst gripped hold. But instead of gulping it down greedily, I did as Frazer suggested. I sipped and sipped until I'd drained the flask dry. Cai was there in an instant, dropping down in front of me and handing me his bottle. I didn't hesitate. Passing Liora back her canteen, I took Cai's and repeated the process. After that second flask's-worth, my tongue no longer felt so swollen, and I breathed a little easier.

I set the canteen aside and found Cai staring at it, lost in thought. I could sense something coming. He looked up, his bright gaze fixing on me. "Serena," he began with a *tone.*

Oh, rats.

To my surprise, it wasn't a demand to explain myself that came next. "I owe you an apology." A bleak statement. "I should've held it off—"

"Stop." I raised a hand in front of me. "You don't owe me anything. The eerie ..." A slow, measured breath. "No one could have done more. No one messed up."

I directed that last bit at Frazer as well as Cai. It didn't seem to make much of a difference. They both still looked haggard and a touch nauseous.

"I could've done more," Liora retorted.

For the first time since touching down, I saw the rage there, boiling away underneath a calm visage. Adrianna stiffened. Uh-oh. Liora didn't level a glare in her direction, but in her brother's. That was new.

Cai spoke through gritted teeth. "Li, we've been through this. Bound or not, you couldn't have defeated the eerie."

"I guess we'll never know." Liora's eyes turned glacial.

It made my spine prickle with unease. Liora had never told me exactly what form her magic had taken. Oh, I'd known she'd been a healing prodigy in her clan, but there was something more. I felt sure. Something darker and infinitely more savage. Yet Cai hadn't believed it would've been enough against the eerie? What did that say about me, then?

"We need to move past this." Adrianna brought her legs in, crossing them. Her shoulders slumped as her eyes met mine. "Serena's awake, and we're alive. You know I have to ask you about that, right? How that's even possible?"

It seemed an explanation couldn't wait a few hours. And nobody was stepping in to give me more time. My pulse grew erratic, and my mouth dried out.

Come along. You'll feel better once you've told them.

Auntie was right, of course. But ... everything was about to change. Rubbing my face a few times, I leaned against Frazer, taking comfort and strength from him. From his warmth and sturdiness.

I started. "I need to tell you something first. Something the others already know."

Plucking the droplet from out of my jacket, I let it dangle for Adrianna to see. She tilted her head, her nostrils widening as she beheld it. A tingle of magic rippled through the air. I recognized our trusty sound barrier.

In a hoarse voice, I summarized the magic it seemed to possess and my connection with Auntie. Adrianna stayed quiet throughout. With the fear of stopping in case I couldn't start again, I filled in the blanks from the eerie attack and relayed Auntie's words.

A stunned silence followed. Stretching on and on.

Liora broke it. "I suppose we know why Hunter never sensed any magic in you. Because it wasn't actually *in* you at the time."

She wore a frown. Contemplating. They all carried similar expressions. Relief found me: they weren't turning away.

"And Wilder," Frazer remarked.

Everyone else looked confused. My cheeks flushed. Frazer had seen Wilder gagging on my blood amidst the other memories, but no one else knew.

Adrianna suddenly snorted and guessed. "He's tasted you too."

My throat closed up on me. I gave her a sharp nod to confirm. Liora and Cai looked like they were trying not to smile, but Adrianna was openly smirking.

Embarrassment heated my body. I changed the subject quickly. "What I can't figure out is how my magic got into the necklace."

Adrianna cut in. "Actually, I'd say that's the least confusing thing about all this."

Adrianna, ever the bearer of good news.

Cai fired two words at her. "How so?"

Adopting her go-to brisk attitude, she replied, "Isn't the Gauntlet anti-witch, anti-magic, anti-anything they don't understand?"

"I suppose," I replied, frowning.

Adrianna nodded. "Well, it sounds to me like your mother wanted to spare you from that."

"Interesting theory," Cai admitted.

I resigned myself to the unavoidable. "That would have made my mother a witch." A disturbing thought.

"Would that be so bad?" Liora quirked her head.

I breathed in deep. There was a faint whiff of stale sweat and dirt, but beneath that was Frazer: cedar, snow and citrus. I latched onto the scents as if they alone could keep me afloat in a restless sea. "I don't know what it is because I can't ask her to explain herself."

Frazer's head turned so that his nose became buried in my hair. The only comfort he could give me. Words wouldn't bring her back.

Adrianna looked odd. Almost sympathetic. "It's completely possible that your mother found someone else to transfer your magic. Either way, whoever did this to you would've been incredibly powerful."

My head rose, dislodging Frazer, and I looked over to Cai and Liora for confirmation.

Liora noticed first and nodded. "I wouldn't have thought it possible to hide your magic without binding you."

Her words and their meaning battered against me. "I'm sorry, Li."

We both knew what that knowledge would've been worth to her. Liora's eyes shone a little brighter. "Don't be. It gives me hope."

I blinked and bit my lip. *Auntie, is there a way for her to replicate what was done to me?*

The answer was slow in coming. *I don't believe it's the answer Liora is looking for, no.*

What does that mean?

Silence.

My jaw tightened painfully. *You've got to be joking! This is her life we're talking about!*

There is another way, another path for Liora. What happened to you is not something she could imitate.

My heart sank. I didn't dare look Liora in the eye and steal that hope. Auntie was just wrong—she had to be.

Adrianna sniffed in my direction. "I still can't smell any magic on you, though."

"Maybe in time you will," Cai suggested, his brow furrowed.

"There's something else," Adrianna said, staring at me.

I tried not to sigh. What now?

Adrianna continued. "If you're capable of killing an eerie, your magic must be powerful too. Which means if Morgan gets one whiff of you—"

Frazer cut her off with a snarl. His hackles had risen at the mention of our invisible enemy. "You think those are the consequences the voice spoke of?"

He wasn't looking at me, but at Adrianna. I felt a swift stab of annoyance.

"Perhaps." Adrianna rubbed her forehead, smoothing out the silver tattoos and wrinkles etched there.

No one said anything for a while. I was left to stew on the idea of being snatched by a fae for the second time. A morbid tapestry of images flashed into my mind.

Auntie cut in to these nightmares. *Focus on the trials ahead. Don't worry about Morgan finding you. Not yet, anyway.*

I didn't bother replying. I was too mad. Through clenched teeth, I told my pack what she'd said. It was met by a dead silence.

A moment passed. Then another. Finally, Adrianna spoke. "Just one fae's opinion, but this Auntie sounds like a teasing prick."

A fevered laugh spilled out of me. The others forced a few smiles, but they were clearly too disturbed to find it that funny.

Once I'd settled down, Liora said, "You should eat."

Frazer immediately sorted through the pack at his side. My pack. He brought out a bun, still in its linen wrappings. "Take this."

It was one of my favorites. Doughy, sugary deliciousness with a hidden pocket of honey at its center. My mouth watered at the prospect, and I tore into it eagerly. A bit stale, but oh-so-good.

Cai scanned the canopy above. "We should make camp here," he said, his gaze settling on Adrianna. "There's probably only a couple of hours of daylight left."

Adrianna scowled, unconvinced. "Shouldn't we—"

"We're staying." His expression turned flinty.

Adrianna's lips pressed together in an obvious but valiant effort not to snap back at our leader.

"Don't give me that look," Cai countered. "We're all exhausted, especially you. How could you not be, flying with a passenger all this time?"

Her expression darkened. "Don't coddle me."

"Wouldn't dream of it," he replied, as breezy as could be. "Can you take Liora and scout the area for a water source? We might not get another chance tomorrow."

I could almost sense Adrianna's pride chomping on her restraint. Control won out in the end. She stood, pulled her flask from her pack, and unfurled her wings.

With that concession, Cai straightened and stretched his legs. He held out his arm, offering it to his sister. Liora stumbled up and grabbed the two drained flasks from the forest floor.

"Can you take ours with you?" Frazer dug into his own pack and mine, bringing out our half-empty bottles.

Liora shouldered two using the flasks' straps. Then, she took ours with a nod and shot me a small smile. Adrianna picked her up, and they soared up and away.

"I'm going to collect some firewood," Cai briefed. "Will you two be okay staying behind?"

I nodded. Cai loped off and a comfortable silence fell. I finished the sugary bun and licked my fingers clean.

I felt Frazer's eyes touch on me every now and again. The thread shimmering between us told me the rest. I needed to distract him from his lingering guilt and fear for me. "I don't suppose you lot came up with a plan for how we take a lock of hair from a witch?"

"Why bother? Our plans don't work anyway."

The dark circles under his eyes told me the rest.

I gulped. The memory surfaced of that *thing* crawling underneath my skin. Not wanting him to feel it in the bond, I locked it away. And my chest grew tight, constricting with blood-ice terror.

My efforts to hide my fear from him amounted to nothing. Frazer grabbed my chin, forcing my eyes to his. "You got out. Thanks to this."

His strong fingers released my face and lowered to brush against the droplet. He held onto it for a few seconds—long enough for his eyes to widen and his nostrils to flare. He blinked and dropped it as if it had burned him.

"Did she ..."

A curt nod. He looked away, his body tensing. Whatever Auntie had said, had caused him to turn jumpy. On edge.

Frazer didn't seem willing to say more. I didn't push. Falling back against his shoulder, I said, "I'm sorry."

"What have you got to be sorry for?" A sound of disbelief.

I almost smiled. "It's not my fault, I know that. But if things had been reversed back there ..." I suppressed a shudder. "And I'd had to watch the eerie do that to you, part of me would've hated you for it. Hated you for making me so scared; for making me care so much. Maybe it's not the same for you, but if it is, I'm sorry for putting you through that."

It was stupid and irrational, but it didn't stop it from being true.

He was pressing his nose into my hair again, sighing. "I could never hate you, not really. But ..."

Ah, the "but."

"When I saw you ... dying, it was ... I never thought I'd feel fear like that again. But you've given me so much of yourself, all your memories—

all of you. It's been like absorbing a whole other person. So when that eerie crushed the air from your lungs, it felt like my heart stopped. Like it would stop the second yours did."

The world tilted, went askew. I dared to utter, "That's a bad thing, right?"

He shifted, dislodging me. I had to look him in the eyes or be branded a coward.

"No," he began softly. "But you have to understand the magnitude of what you did, Matea. You gave me your whole life in an instant. You placed a level of trust in me that—" He stopped, his face gaunt.

My heart felt too big for my chest. I spooled myself back in. And failed. Frazer being in pain was the opposite of what I'd wanted.

"You've bonded us, Serena."

A glitch of panic grew wings in my chest. "What kind of bond?"

Frazer barked a laugh. "Don't worry. I haven't developed romantic feelings for you. I'm aware your heart belongs to Wilder, or at least your lusty loins do."

"Lusty loins ..." I echoed.

Frazer and I burst out cackling. His laugh a low rattling purr, while mine killed my throat, but felt so good.

Frazer stopped first, his smile turning tight. That sobered me up quick. "Go on."

"Fae bonds aren't the same as human ones. They're more intense. And it's precisely because of our resistance to friendships that when one develops, we cherish and protect them above all else."

He lapsed into silence. I felt like clucking my tongue but didn't. Whatever he was trying to say, must be difficult for a reason. "Frazer?" It was the only prompt and sign of impatience I gave.

Frazer seemed flustered as he ran his fingers through his raven hair, leaving it messed at the back. The image caused a dull ache to flare in my chest. This must've been what he looked like after flying. "When you told me that you considered me to be like your brother, did you mean it?"

"Of course."

He nodded, distant.

"Is something wrong?" My defenses slammed up.

His brow creased in thought. "There are three kinds of fae bond. Mating, kin, and guardian. And for a fae, whenever those connections are there, we strengthen them through a process called myena, which is an oath. We don't take them lightly. In fact, I've only felt the inclination to say the words once before."

I took a wild guess. "Lynx?"

His eyes deadened. Anguish sung through them, making my heart squeeze.

"Which bond did you share?" I wondered.

A curve of his lip. "We weren't mates, if that's what you're implying. In the beginning, I wanted to be sworn to him as a champion and guardian of his court, but our friendship grew and turned into something else. We couldn't officially become kin though. A prince and the offspring of a soldier isn't an equal match. I had nothing to offer then, and I have even less now."

Hesitant, lost eyes ... Oh, stars. "Frazer ..." I stopped to reel myself in again. "You have everything to offer."

"You'll do it?" His voice sounded strained, disbelieving.

I nodded and smiled.

Frazer smiled back freely.

"What d'you need me to do?"

"Mirror my actions. I'll tell you when." He reached for the Utemä propped beside him, unsheathed it and dragged its smooth edge across his palm.

I winced as the blood welled. He raised his palm in front of me. "I need to place my hand on your forehead—is that okay?"

A nod. He put his hand there, marking me. He pulled away, slicing his other palm with the Utemä. This time he didn't raise it to my forehead; he clasped my hand.

"Serena Smith," he began gravely. "From this heartbeat until my last, I share your blood and bone, joy and grief. No words or acts could make me turn from you. You are my pack, my kin, my home."

My vision blurred. I pushed against the weight settling on my chest.

"Ovet perheen nyx, ihuseti jai aina," he recited.

I'd no idea what he'd said, but the sincerity emanating from him was enough for a tear to fall.

He grasped my wrist. "May I?"

I gave a quick nod and resisted the temptation to look away as he cradled my palm and drew the sword across quickly. A sharp pain, then a dull ache followed.

Frazer branded himself with my blood and let go of that hand only to prick my other palm. Setting the sword atop his lap, encircling our hands, he said, "Repeat after me. Frazer Novak ..."

I repeated the vow he'd made to me and even got through the fae tongue without faltering. That is until I reached "aina," and a scorching heat broiled me. Clawing at my necklace, my fingers grasped the droplet. There was no heat. The burning was coming from within. As if my very ribs had become branded with the oath.

Frazer's eyes flared wide, and he clutched at his own chest, choking a little.

The pain slipped enough for me to round on him. "You didn't tell me that would happen."

"That's because I didn't know," he panted, his hand falling to his side. "If I had, I would've warned you. Sorry."

Rubbing my chest, I took a breath and said, "Fine, but let's not do that again for a while."

A slow but pure smile radiated from him. "We won't need to. We're officially kin—siska."

He sheathed and set the Utemä aside, and then gathered his sleeve in his palm and rubbed the blood from my forehead, and then his. Once done, I voiced, "Siska?"

"It means sister," he answered. "Although, I'll only call you that in private and through our bond."

I braced myself against the dead log behind me. "How come?"

"Well, there's no fae law against making the kin bond with a human ..." There was a flicker of fear in his voice. It was obvious what was coming.

"But?" I waited for the blow to fall.

"We still shouldn't go shouting about the fact we've done it."

"Why?" Impatience snapped at my heels.

Frazer shrugged, but I sensed his discomfort though the thread.

"Some fae hate humans on principle. If they found out that a fae bound himself to one, they might want to make an example."

I let my expression grow dark. "You tell me this now?"

He gestured between us and said, "The bond is here whether we make it official or not. And the kin bond has its advantages. They say that kin can sense each other across great distances. That we'll be able to find each other. Always."

He studied my chest as if that's where he imagined the link connecting us lay.

The magnitude of what we'd done hit me then. Because all it took for our connection to vanish was getting too far apart. This kin bond might've just fixed that and bound us even tighter.

I bit my lip in angst. Had we done the right thing? I waited for Auntie to say something, but there was only silence. Shadows and doubt gathered in my mind. Fortunately, my rumbling stomach provided the perfect distraction.

"You haven't eaten enough." Frazer twisted in his seated position and handed my pack over, placing it on my lap.

I undid the clasp and rummaged. I brooded long and hard and after finishing my eighth oat biscuit, Adrianna landed in front of us, her bottle slung over her shoulder. Liora rolled out of her arms with four skins and handed our two flasks back to us.

"Where's Cai?" Liora dipped down, packing away the other two bottles.

"Collecting firewood," I said.

Adrianna snapped her wings in and sniffed the air. "Why do I smell blood?"

Her eyes narrowed, her lips set into a harsh line; the cowardly part of me won and relinquished the explanation to Frazer. Once he was done, Liora slumped to the forest floor nearby. "I didn't even think kinship between a fae and human was possible." She was still, dumbstruck.

The color leeched from Adrianna's bronze skin, but her eyes burned with the fires of the dark court. I couldn't help feeling relieved when she directed her ire toward Frazer. "Are you mad? You made a kin bond with a human?"

Frazer glared. "You don't choose the bond. You know that." A tad defensive.

Adrianna shook her head as if trying to rid herself of a buzzing gnat. Taking another delicate sniff, she said, "You realize, of course, that you've merged your scents. She'll smell less human. Other fae might be curious as to why."

Frazer's features tightened. "I've also made her harder to track."

"True," Adrianna conceded. "But I don't think her admirer will be thrilled once he smells you all over her."

I couldn't stop a blush from blooming.

"Admirer?" Cai's voice hummed with interest behind us. "Who are we discussing?"

I twisted around to see that Cai had brought back a heap of kindling, which he unceremoniously dropped in the middle of what would be our camp for the evening.

"We were talking about Wilder," Adrianna answered, sitting down opposite us.

"Of course." Cai winked at me.

Liora made a noise of impatience.

Adrianna continued, a steely thread beneath the lilting accent. "And the fact that Serena and Frazer have just made an irreversible blood vow declaring themselves kin."

Cai swore, loudly—viciously. "We weren't even gone an hour."

My reply was tart. "I guess that was all it took."

A ghost of a playful smile. "Clearly."

After another ten minutes, during which Adrianna made more barbed comments and Cai built a fire, the shock of what we'd done lessened. Enough for Liora to say she should've seen it coming. And for Cai to become interested in developing his own special bond.

"I don't suppose you'd fancy sharing a bond with me, would you?" he asked Adrianna, who suddenly choked on the rations she was eating. "Sounds like it'd make all the other females wild with curiosity. You'd be doing me a big favor."

He waggled his eyebrows. Adrianna laughed, albeit reluctantly.

Amazing. Obviously not immune to his charms after all.

This thread in the conversation piqued my curiosity. I had to ask.

"Adrianna, is it true they've banned fae and human couplings in all of Aldar?"

She put aside her packet of dried fruit and faced me fully. "Taking a human as a lover isn't, but a true union is. It's always been a divisive issue because many believe being with humans thins our blood. But in the end, it was Morgan and her fanatics who got the law changed."

My eyes flitted to Cai. Then back to Adrianna. I shouldn't meddle. And yet ... "Even with witches?"

Liora was the one to answer, quietly. "Being a witch gives a human some status in Aldar, but not enough to let us love who we want."

Those last words rang in my ears.

Cai was crouching down, throwing a few sticks on the blazing fire as he carried on. "When Morgan seized power, the fae and human couplings in the Crescent vanished in the middle of the night."

I gulped.

Frazer growled. "Morgan might want humans in our lands, but only to see them in chains, serving us, while we act like their fucking fae overlords."

Cai snorted with laughter. Liora's face twisted with disgust as she bit down on an apple.

"It's just as bad in the Riverlands," Adrianna said baldly. "Diana agreed to adopt the same stupid law in the *negotiations*." She pinned me with a look. "But, it isn't uncommon for a human to invite a fae to bed, especially if the male—or female happens to be ... exceptional. It's just safer to be discreet." A sharp tone. Still, her expression had a softness to it. Maybe pity?

I looked away, swallowing hard. "You think it's an infatuation?"

"It was for me."

My eyes snapped to hers. "You and Wilder?" Almost immediately, an unwelcome pang of *possessiveness* unfurled in my stomach. A fierce and jealous need to claim him had come surging from nowhere—my rational mind was losing the fight.

Adrianna laughed. A soft, self-conscious sound. "There was never anything between us. Nothing I didn't invent in my own head. He put me straight after I invited him to spend the night with me."

"Moons, that was bold," Cai said. No judgment. More like awe.

Liora muttered something about sparing her from the male species. Adrianna simply shrugged it off. "More like stupid."

I took a breath. "Let me guess, he gave you a line about how you'd be in danger if you were together?"

I'd tried for a light tone but ended up with sour.

Adrianna's brows nudged together. "No, he said he wasn't interested. And if I didn't stop pursuing him, he'd have me thrown out."

"Oh."

A powerful swoop of surprise claimed me.

Adrianna only angled her head. "He told you that you'd be in danger?"

For Cai and Adrianna's sakes, I gave a quick recap of what he'd said the last time we'd spoken. The story complete, Cai let out a low whistle. "Sounds like Wilder's got secrets. No wonder all the females are crazy for him."

He wore a little frown and a pout. Liora and I exchanged smiles.

"He could've been lying to you, to spare your feelings," Adrianna dropped into conversation. "He does get a lot of attention from the female *and* the male recruits. Hard to ignore a beautiful, scarred male who reeks of power."

How true.

Adrianna began, "Still, he didn't speak to you as if you meant nothing to him." I could've kissed her. "He's better at hiding it than most, but he *is* different with you. Just because he's never batted an eyelash at anyone else, doesn't mean he abstains. Why not give seducing him a go? Show him what he's missing." She gave me a crooked grin.

Liora laughed, delighted, whereas Cai stared. A man falling head over heels—that's what it looked like, anyway.

"He seemed convinced that Dimitri would use our connection against him," I said.

Adrianna inclined her head causing her glossy braid to swing free. She regarded me carefully. "Well, as long as you don't get pregnant or marry, Dimitri can't do shit. At least not publicly. He might be a traitor and Morgan's bitch, but if taking a human lover was illegal, he'd have to arrest half the fae in Aldar."

Traitor? Interesting.

"How d'you know he's Morgan's bitch?" Frazer probed.

"I've lived in the Riverlands Court my whole life. Dimitri's loyalties are well-known in those circles," she said flippantly.

Frazer glanced sidelong at me. "Then she should be even more careful. Traitors are capable of anything."

Adrianna just frowned.

Cai's eyes flitted to Liora. "Either way, we should keep an eye on him. For all our sakes."

A general murmur of consent.

I don't want you going anywhere in Kasi alone. Not anymore. Understood?

I met Frazer's intense glare. It was tempting to snap back. To insist that he could shove his orders. But he was in my head, my heart, my blood; I knew his protective nature hadn't sprung from nothing.

Still, there had to be boundaries. There had to be a gods-damned line somewhere. Of course, he saw straight through me.

Draw a line some other day. This isn't the time. You've just had magic fired into your veins. We already have too many unanswered questions about that and other things. You're vulnerable ...

His thoughts broke and scattered on the last word. My heart went out to him. I nodded, caving. *Then we stick together... briska?*

Frazer smiled at my pathetic attempt to speak Kaeli. *Brother is brata. Brata.*

His lip twitched. He bowed his head. *Siska.*

CHAPTER 18
THE WITCH

We woke to a cold and cheerless breakfast of berries and nuts, followed by a long slog in the gloom. With every passing mile I noted the pines thinning, replaced by red maples, and oaks spattered with furry lichen. The air grew thick, stale, and heavy with moisture. Moving was akin to swimming through honey.

The afternoon rolled around, and a report from Adrianna told us we'd be arriving soon. After hours of walking on blisters, it was a gift. The forest floor started to slope downhill; I focused on navigating the ferns, loose stones, and slick moss underfoot. Not even a whisper of a breeze stirred the leaves in the trees, and yet the rich scents of muddied water and decaying vegetation hit me anyway, smothering me.

Frazer grasped the top of my arm, yanking me back. "Careful."

I blinked stupidly. The swamp had arrived, silent and unseen. The earth gave way suddenly, revealing an overgrown tawny, copper swampland marked by climbing plants, purple waterlilies, and gnarled trees that rose from the water, standing proud like pillars. Like watchful guardians.

A lumpy and rather narrow path started to the right of me, cutting and snaking through the swamp. Our way forward. A sense of foreboding crept in as I failed to trace the track's direction—its destination was hidden due to wisps of smoke curling off the water, extending toward us like phantom fingers outstretched.

"Well, I've seen worse places and lived to tell the tale," Frazer said in dry amusement.

Ever optimistic.

Cai strode to the swamp's edge, peering out, hand on hilt, assessing. He turned to us and said, "Well, I'd still rather face whatever's out there than battle another eerie."

My stomach lurched, recalling the feeling as the eerie slid under my skin, taking possession. Frazer angled his body toward mine as he sensed my discomfort. It wasn't a hug, but then that wasn't his style. I took comfort from it all the same.

With a flap and a thud, Adrianna landed next to us. Cai's hands slackened at his sides as he regarded her. "This is your court. Any advice before we head out there?"

Adrianna's shoulders arched and rolled as she flexed her wings. As if loosening them from some deep seated tension locked in her body. "The witches here aren't like those in the Crescent. They're loners. They don't form clans or pool their magic, which makes them suspicious of outsiders. But they still need to make a living, and certain *individuals* sell their magic," she said, sounding brittle. "They also ward their doors, so we can't sneak in. Our best bet might be to visit a witch who has regular customers from outside the swamp. There's a fae-witch who lives nearby. She might let some of us inside."

Not much reassurance there.

Cai obviously thought the same as me. "Will she, or won't she?"

A pause and a frown. Adrianna began, "She's a strong, solitary fae-witch, living out in the swamps. She'll be cautious. Especially of strange witches or a wingless fae. Maybe if I go in alone—"

Cai interrupted. "Not a chance."

He sounded absolute, unyielding. Like a General issuing orders to a soldier. Adrianna's features darkened. She opened her mouth, no doubt intent on an angry retort. Liora shut that down quickly. "What's this witch's name?"

Something distant and sharp sparked in Adrianna's eyes. "They call her Maggie OneEye."

"Maggie OneEye?" Liora breathed, as she looked to her brother. "We've heard about her in the Crescent."

Adrianna's hand fluttered up to grip her bow handle tightly. "What do they say about her?"

Cai's words reflected awe. "That she's blessed with the sight. They say she even predicted Morgan's accession."

Adrianna huffed. A poor attempt at nonchalance. "Yes, she predicted it, not that it did much good. I only mention her because other than divining our deaths as a punishment, she can't do much if we need to use force."

A harsh laugh passed Cai's lips. "And divining our deaths isn't enough of a deterrent for you?"

Adrianna clucked her tongue. "I just meant she can't send people flying with a wave of their hand, like you."

A coy smirk was his response. "You noticed."

His expression invited verbal sparring, but Adrianna didn't bat an eyelash. "If you want to choose another target—"

Cai shook his head. "We just need to decide on an approach. If she's a seer, then the best way to get inside is to ask for a reading. As for stealing her hair, I'd prefer to avoid a fight, and I don't want to barter, either. Not when some witches would sooner ask for a finger in payment than a bag of silver."

I flinched at that.

"That leaves deceit," Frazer voiced quietly.

Cai nodded once. And eyeballed Adrianna. "If I can make an odorless sleeping powder to knock her on her ass, d'you think you could get close enough to dose her?"

Adrianna's expression tightened. "Yes."

The thought of her going in alone bothered me more than it should. She was more than capable.

In the next heartbeat, Cai slipped his rucksack from his shoulders, brought out a small red journal from the bottom, and opened it. His eyes scanning, his finger following a line of text, he said, "I think I've got the basic ingredients."

Cai kneeled next to his bag, placed the journal face down, and pulled out linen pouches filled with herbs, and a wooden mortar and pestle.

"Why bring that stuff with you?" Frazer asked, frowning down at him.

Crushing a few pinches of a yellow herb, he replied, "Habit."

Liora clarified. "A witch gets taught from an early age to carry supplies."

"Will it be strong enough to drop a witch?" Frazer asked.

Cai became too busy mixing ingredients and muttering to himself to answer. Liora was left to assure us it would, but her eyes shifted to Adrianna as she said it. I knew then that Liora was just as concerned about her meeting with Maggie alone as I was.

An idea formed; I made Adrianna a quiet offer. "I'll go in with you. I'm not fae, and if you can't sense any magic on me, then neither will she."

Frazer's canines punched down. "Absolutely not," he said, his voice deepening in alarm.

My brows vaulted to my hairline. "This isn't your decision—"

He snapped, "I disagree."

I flinched. Damn, what was wrong with him?

Adrianna cut in, amusement coloring her voice. "Welcome to the world of fae males."

Frazer shot her a sharp look. "Serena's my kin, *and* she has powerful magic. I don't think it's unreasonable to not want her near a seer who for all we know is sympathetic to that bitch's cause."

Adrianna bristled. "Her magic isn't traceable. And she's already used it to kill an *eerie*."

Frazer retorted, "You heard how she did it. It was a fluke. She hasn't learned to control it yet."

Stubborn mule.

I gave Liora a beseeching look. She got the hint. "Cai can mask our scents easily enough, so we'll follow and stay close in case anything goes wrong."

I spoke. "You should be able to sense if something goes wrong ... Right?"

That had Frazer grumbling low, but his teeth receded into his gums.

A win.

The conversation stalled, and I seized the opportunity to take a gulp of water. Despite what I'd said, my mouth had dried out at the prospect of meeting and lying to a one-eyed witch.

I was just putting my flask back into my bag when Cai covered his nose with the top of his jacket, transferred the finished powder into a linen pouch, and pulled the strings tight. He packed his equipment away, stood, and placed the pouch in Adrianna's waiting palm. "All you'll need is a pinch. Blow it in her face, but don't inhale any yourself."

Adrianna pocketed the powder. Her eyes lifted, and she stared out into the swamp. "Maggie's is the first cabin we'll come to. There's an old goat willow not too far from the house—it'd make a good place to hold up and listen in," she said with a tiny dip of her chin toward Frazer.

He angled his head away, causing dark silky hair to fall into his eyes.
Stop being sour, I muttered down the thread.

Silence. Grumpy silence.

"Let's get on with it then," Cai suggested.

Adrianna pursed her lips and freed a piercing whistle. We waited.

Firelights appeared along the path, twinkling, lighting the way. They bobbed, dancing as if eager for us to join them.

Adrianna led the way. I slipped in behind her as the trail was only wide enough for one of us to walk along it at a time. We fell into a line, our pace slow.

The hazy burn of the lights above prevented us from being blinded, but the gray-lined fog still impaired human and fae vision alike. Enough that the ominous dark waters, cobweb-strewn trees, and ripples in the water had my scalp tingling and my imagination whirring, wondering what could spring from such gloom.

It took a few minutes, perhaps more, before we spotted the goat willow and just beyond, a house. Although, a log cabin on stilts would've been a more apt description. Moss, lichen, and hanging vines mottled the outside, giving it a speckled green and brown appearance. For a moment, it looked as if the roof was aflame; it was nothing but a swarm of firelights that had settled there. Mesmerizing: as a breeze stirred them, the soft fluttering of their shapes resembled waves breaking against a lakeshore.

We came to rest by the ancient gnarled willow with its soft, cotton-like catkins hanging low enough that they brushed against my cheeks, tickling. Our path had widened and split, so there was now enough space for us to group up. Adrianna signaled for the others to stay put, then beckoned me forward. The left path would take us straight up to the witch's doorstep, while the right continued on into the swamp.

Frazer's eyes met mine for a pulse. I whispered goodbye through our thread, but it was met by chilly silence. Fine. If he wanted to act like a sulky brat, then so be it.

Adrianna and I walked side by side up to the house. She gripped my elbow and leaned in a little. "If you're okay with it, I'll tell Maggie that you're the one seeking the reading."

My brow furrowed as I whispered back. "Any reason?"

"Maggie knows what I think of her profession. Will you do it?"

An anxious thrill shocked the hairs on my arms, but I still nodded.

Adrianna's breath tickled my ear again. "We'll ask for a general reading for you, but if she questions you, stick to the truth as much as you can. Lying under pressure is harder than you'd think. Just know that if I can't dose her before the start ... Be prepared to hear things you might not want to."

My body grew taut. A jumble of nerves. "I'm not expecting her to predict me a happy ending." I was so quiet.

There was no judgment or pity in Adrianna's expression. Just grim understanding.

We reached the end of the path and took our first step onto a wraparound porch. It was littered with dried herbs, ribbons, poppets, and something that on closer inspection looked like dangling chicken feet.

I tried to swallow my fear and disgust. And failed.

Adrianna raised her hand to knock. The door swung open, revealing what could only be Maggie OneEye. I'd expected an old crone with yellowing teeth and wild gray hair. In reality, we stood before a female that looked about thirty in human years, with a carefully painted face and braided hair that fell to her waist. One eye was a rich amber, the other a bright silver. Her wings were scaled like Adrianna's. And a pale, ice blue.

"Maggie OneEye," Adrianna began stiffly. "I've come to ask you to give my friend a reading."

I willed calm into my veins as the witch's silver eye settled on me, and the gold eye continued to stare at Adrianna. She nodded, satisfied. "Good. I was starting to think you'd be late. I can't tell you how much tardiness irritates me."

Maggie flashed her teeth. It could've been a smile or a threat. Either way, it made my heart stumble.

Adrianna stilled. "You were expecting us?"

Her tone was light, but I thought I detected real worry.

Maggie's gold eye widened, while her silver one narrowed. The effect was disorienting. "You know of my abilities, and yet you doubt me. You always were hard-headed—no appreciation for subtlety. By the sisters, you would've made a terrible witch. Now, get in. I don't want to be standing on the doorstep all day." She moved aside and ushered us in.

Adrianna peered over her shoulder to me. Her expression screamed, *careful*. She spun back around and went to step over the threshold.

Maggie threw out an arm, blocking her. "You know the rules: leave your weapons outside. That means you too, young lady," she said peering at me.

Young lady? She sounded like Viola. A pissed off version, anyway.

Adrianna didn't hesitate. She laid her bow and quiver up against the outside wall.

I unbuckled the Utemä from my belt and propped it next to the bow and quiver, then looked up to see strange but beautiful symbols adorning the threshold. They looked innocent—merely decorative, but I doubted that very much. My chest seized as I stepped through into an herb- and smoke-scented space. Nothing happened. Freeing a held breath, I took in the area before me.

The room's bones were a smooth gray wood, and its furnishings included two bookshelves that groaned under the weight of candles, crystals, and mighty tomes. Right in the center was a small, rectangular table with six chairs crammed around it, and a beaten-up velvet stool that rested by a brick hearth. Maggie closed the door behind me, flooding the space with the heat from the roaring fire. My taut and knotted muscles eased into that heavenly warmth. The same muscles that still ached from my encounter with the eerie and the day's march here.

Maggie waved a hand at the back of the door. "Hang your cloaks and bags up."

Adrianna gave me a look. My own reservations were reflected there. I wanted this over as soon as possible, but we had to play our parts. We shrugged off our bags and cloaks. As we hung them, Maggie spun left. "I'll make us a pot of herbal tea. Maiden knows we'll need it."

She cackled once and set to filling a kettle, drawing the water by pumping a black handle above a large stone sink. Maggie's kitchen wasn't much more than that. A few cupboards, and jar upon jar of herbs and spooky fluids scattered on counter tops.

With the kettle filled, Maggie set it on the side and dug out a tea chest. She was searching for her strainer when Adrianna reached into her jacket pocket for the powder.

My pulse jumped. One wrong move ...

Maggie swiveled toward us in one graceful step. "Your powder won't work—"

Adrianna blurred; the sedative suffused the air as a shimmering ruby-gold dust. Pulling my sleeve over my mouth, I waited for it to take effect. It never did.

Maggie sneezed. Her fingers casually brushed the powder from her hair. "That was bracing."

Totally unfazed, the witch grabbed the kettle and stalked across the room to place it on a stand in the open fire. She stoked the flames with a poker, her wings tucked in behind her. She seemed completely at ease.

Faced with the failure of our plan, the ground beneath me felt like it was shifting—a sheet of ice weeping and cracking—and I found myself frozen. What the rutting hell did we do now? My instincts reared, and I sought the thread linking me to Frazer. Except there was nothing. An emptiness swooped in, hitching my breath.

Auntie was there, saying, *Don't panic. Her wards are putting a dampener on your connection. That's all.*

That's all? *Was she serious?*

The total lack of him caused a lurching sensation around my midriff. Like I'd missed a step and stumbled down a flight of stairs.

"Serena, go," Adrianna growled, moving in front of me.

I almost did.

Maggie straightened and brandished the poker at us, saying, "You have nothing to fear from me. And neither do your friends waiting outside. It might be best if you invited them in out of the fog. The swamp isn't the best place for them to be after the sun sets." She placed the fire iron aside and patted her long navy robes down, showering more dust over the floor. And I just stared. *How?* Had her gift really warned her of our arrival? I supposed that was the only thing it could be.

My back prickled.

Maggie's brows slashed together as she glanced behind me. "I'd open that door if I were you."

"Serena!" A distant call. It was Frazer, panicking.

Now Liora. "Serena? Adi?"

Adrianna moved toward the door, but I got there first.

I pulled on the handle and only just managed to move aside as Frazer burst in, his breathing frantic, his eyes wild. They fixed on me and he stilled. I sensed a mighty surge of relief and then a glittering rage on the other end of the thread, now that it had re-awakened. His quivering body promised destruction and violence as his focus shifted to Maggie.

Liora rushed through the entrance next and rambled, "Are you both okay? Frazer said he couldn't sense you."

I nodded numbly.

"We're fine," Adrianna said.

Cai was the last in. He slammed the door behind him and said in mock cheer, "Sorry, did we interrupt? You must be Maggie." He gave her a cocky smile. "I'm Cai. That's Liora," he waved toward his sister, "and the fae growling at you is called Frazer."

"Nice to meet you," Maggie said. All calm and a tad amused. "And there really is no need for the hostilities. I'd just finished suggesting that they invited you in, when Frazer obviously noticed his kin bond with Serena had been smothered by my warding."

"How do you know she's my kin?" Frazer asked menacingly.

Maggie pointed to her silver eye, clearly irritated. "This isn't for show."

Frazer didn't seem inclined to relax, so I went to squeeze the top of his arm. Just a touch to calm him. Haunted eyes flitted to me. *I couldn't feel you ... I reached out. There was nothing there.*

Those words wrapped a fist around my heart and squeezed.

That's the second time this week. His eyes shuttered; he couldn't even finish his thought. It was obvious what he'd meant. He'd thought my life had been at risk again.

I'm sorry ...

As long as you're safe, that's all that matters. Frazer sniffed the air. "You used the powder?"

A not-so-subtle change in subject.

"It didn't work," Cai said. It wasn't a question; his attention had locked onto Maggie's robes and the shimmering remnants of the ruby-gold dust that clung there.

Adrianna lifted an eyebrow. "You could say that."

Liora was the one to ask the one-eyed witch, "D'you know why we're here?"

Maggie regarded her for a moment before looking to Adrianna. "I don't need my sight for that. Your mother—makena—has told me you're training at Kasi."

"What else did *she* tell you?" Adrianna retorted. That stress in her voice spoke volumes.

"Why is it so difficult for you to forgive her flaws, little Ana?" Maggie sighed.

Adrianna stood a little taller. A steel blade, rigid and unapologetic. "Because I find some flaws more difficult to accept than others."

Maggie just stared. "Am I right to assume you're in the middle of a trial?"

Adrianna gave her a little nod.

"What is it you want from me?"

Adrianna reminded me of a tower of ice. "A lock of your hair."

Maggie didn't look surprised. "I see. Well, you may have it, but only if you do something for me in return."

Adrianna folded her arms and dropped a hip as if that could defuse the tension. "Can't you consider it a favor to my mother?"

Maggie didn't blink. She looked to the whistling kettle, dismissing Adrianna entirely. My mouth turned to sand as the witch puttered around. I watched, nerves firing adrenaline, as she used a towel to cover her hand and grab the pot handle. No one moved as she went to set it on the table in the center of the room along with six mugs, a caddy, a teapot, and a strainer.

As she was preparing and pouring, she finally gave an answer. "A lock of my hair in the wrong hands could do untold damage. I won't give it lightly—not for just any favor. But, what I propose for payment is simple." She stemmed the flow of tea into the last cup with a flourish. "I want to read the cards and the bones for you in return."

Adrianna's shoulders tightened. "Why in the seven seas would you want to read my fortune?"

A haughty eyebrow rose in challenge. "Who said anything about reading yours?" Maggie's silver eye settled on me.

My stomach churned. Adrianna looked back at me startled and asked, "Why Serena's?"

Maggie's reply was to fix Cai, Liora, and Frazer with hard stares and say, "First, you three need to take your weapons and put them outside my door. That's the rule in this house. Then, we're all going to sit and help ourselves to some tea."

Liora was the only one to obey immediately. Cai and Frazer shared a dark look, speaking of their shared alarm before following her outside.

Maggie sat at the head of the table, clasping her hands together, waiting. Once the others had returned and hung up their cloaks and bags, she gestured to the chairs and said, "Sit. I won't bite."

Adrianna inched toward the table. "No, but you might've poisoned the tea."

Maggie took a very deliberate sip from her cup. She grimaced—the tea must've been scalding. "I've no reason to harm you."

I chose the chair opposite the witch. Frazer and Cai slipped in on my left, while Adrianna planted herself on Maggie's left and Liora joined her side.

Adrianna and Frazer bent over and sniffed delicately at the fumes rising from the cups, presumably checking for poison. The witch pursed her lips but said nothing.

I didn't touch the tea. I was more interested in getting some answers. "So, why would you trade reading my future for your hair?"

Now both of the witch's eyes fixed on me. I resisted the temptation to flinch, to show fear. I crossed my arms and braced them on the table. Leaning into her.

That got her saying, "Because eighteen years ago, I saw us meeting. Usually, my visions are fragmented, but this one came in as clear as glass. I saw Adrianna trying to dose me with the powder, and then heard myself offering you a reading in exchange for my hair." She blew on her tea, thoughtful. And took a little sip. "I tried to see more—to riddle it out —but nothing worked ..." She clucked her tongue and set her cup down to glare at us. "I really haven't poisoned that tea, you know. It's just rude not to drink it."

Stunned and flustered, I raised the cup to my lips and breathed in chamomile. Frazer caught me drinking and scowled. But when I didn't keel over, he consented to take a tiny sip of his own drink. The others did the same, probably just to be polite.

"You were saying?" I prompted, putting my cup down.

Maggie drummed her fingernails against the table. "Well, not every vision of mine comes to pass. I forgot about it in the end. Although, seeing Adrianna for the first time certainly gave me pause. But still nothing happened. That is, until a week ago ..." She watched me carefully as she added, "I saw you battling an eerie. Killing it. A feat even more impressive now I've met you and can't detect magic in your veins."

I willed my face into a neutral expression. A blank portrait.

Maggie studied every inch of my face, her concentration almost feral in its intensity. "Your outline's all fogged up." She pinched the bridge of her nose and continued. "You're gonna be an ache between the ears. I can feel it."

Irritation built in my chest, demanding to be let out. "Why bother with a reading then?"

Maggie's hand dropped back to the table, and she peered at me from under a scowling brow. "You can't ignore the visions, child."

Child. Condescending hag, I thought viciously.

"Do we have a deal? What say you, Serena?" Maggie spoke my name softly. Almost reverently.

I took another sip of sweet tea to buy myself time. She might see me failing the trials ... Ancestors help me, she might predict my death. No one should have that hanging over them. But running through the options, this seemed the best way. The only way to avoid potential bloodshed or becoming the victim of an ungodly curse.

"Fine." I took a gulp of chamomile, seeking to steady my nerves.

Maggie bolted upright and marched into a back room beside the kitchen.

Liora inclined her head to me, whispering, "Are you sure?"

I wanted to say no, of course not. I shrugged instead and sought Adrianna's advice across the table. "Will she keep her word?"

Adrianna's nostrils flared. "Yes."

She sounded annoyed by the fact. They had a history, obviously. Something she hadn't been willing to share. I chose to ignore it. "Then, yes. I'm sure."

All around the table were jittery expressions and tense body language. Definitely not reassuring. Anxiety got the best of me, sending my foot into a toe-tapping rhythm beneath the table. Something stalked and clawed at my insides, wanting to run away. But it felt too late to back out now. Maggie was rejoining us from the back room, muttering to herself. She carried a few items. One, a bundle of herbs wrapped in a silver ribbon that got thrown in the fire. Then, she set to laying the table with a black mirror, a card deck, and a velvet bag containing what appeared to be small bones.

Maggie was still talking to herself—I couldn't understand a word.

All at once, the flames crackling in the hearth flashed purple. I flinched and watched as it became an inferno, licking the sides of the chimney, belching out pungent smells. Wood chips, rosemary, and cinnamon saturated the air.

Maggie settled back into her backless chair opposite me. The mumbling stopped, but her silver eye began to twitch. The amber one drifted. Staring into nothingness. "Give me your name: your full name," she rasped. As if the words she'd spoken had taken a toll.

A hot, sick twist in my stomach followed. "Serena Smith."

Sweat beaded on Maggie's upper lip. "Smith doesn't sound right. D'you go by any other names?"

The cabin's walls, the fumes from the fire—the very air—seemed to close in. Trapping me. "I'm a Smith. That's my family name."

Maggie gave me a bland smile and waited.

Something itched beneath my skin. A flush of heat followed. I could taste burning. Whatever was inside—my magic—it was getting restless.

Frazer's hand twitched atop the table. As if he wanted to reach out and grab mine. My eyes shifted to his, and he looked toward the door. *You don't have to do this. She can't possibly take on all of us.*

He meant it, too. That swell of anxiety—the itch … It settled as his presence anchored and sheltered me. Like a shadow in the midday sun, he stopped me from igniting; from being swept away by my own magic.

He gave me courage.

My eyes went to Maggie's. "I don't know what you're looking for exactly, but my mother used to call me Ena. And recently, I've been called Kovaysi, Matea and … siska."

A whisper of pleasure at the word played through our bond.

Maggie hummed, satisfied. "That's more like it—Fierce One, Sweet One, and sister. One day, you'll go by many more names, but for now, those will have to do."

Wilder had called me fierce. A vain, pathetic part of me wished it'd been Beautiful One.

Maggie shuffled the silver-backed cards. We all followed her every move, transfixed. Liora reached out and clasped my hand. I was grateful.

The tarot went face down on the table. The pattern, a six card semi-circle above a cross. Maggie picked up the shard of black mirror in her right hand, and her silver eye stared into it while the amber eye remained locked onto the spread.

The witch sighed heavily, leaning in, studying the cards while biting her lip. "This cross anchors me in your past." She traced the line of the four cards and moved up to the crescent spread to say, "And this shows me your present trajectory. I'll leave scattering the bones until last."

Finding my throat like burning sand, I drained my cup of chamomile dry. Maggie didn't seem to breathe as she flipped the cards over one by one. "The Reaper, the Tower, the Six of Swords, and the World," Maggie reeled off without looking up from the cross. "Death has brought you great sadness. You've known the loss of both parents. And yet, one recent death has also brought you release." She tapped the Tower with a sharp nail.

Gus? His mangled body floated into my mind's eye. I tried to shove it away, but it stayed there, branded on the inside of my eyelids.

Maggie nodded as if she saw the nightmares. "Whoever he was, shed no tears for him. He was rotten. If he hadn't been stopped, he would've carved you up and slit your throat for good measure."

I felt a sudden, unexpected rush of gratitude for Hunter. It was one thing thinking he'd saved my life but quite another to *know* he had.

Maggie held the black glass in one hand while using the other to bring a cup to her lips. She downed the rest of the tea. Only once she'd placed it down did she continue in a quiet, rasping voice. "Mm... The World and the Six tells me that the journey you made from the Gauntlet to Aldar is permanent." My heart slammed into my ribs as she touched the World card. Maggie must be powerful—how else would she know I'd originated from the Gauntlet?

"If you ever go back, it'll be because the divide is no longer what it is now."

Adrianna couldn't contain herself, exclaiming, "What in the burning rivers does that mean? You can't ever be more specific, can you?"

Maggie silenced Adrianna with a look and a snap of her teeth. Her attention then fixed on me, adding, "Your life in the human realm has died. You must focus on what's in front of you."

A hole smoldered in my gut—anger and grief mixing. I'd known that. Sort of. It still hurt, *deeply*, to think that John and Viola were now part of my past.

With deft fingers, Maggie flipped over the cards in the crescent spread. There lay the Queen of Wands, the High Priestess, the Mage, the Ace of Cups, the Ace of Wands, and the Wheel.

The witch was frowning, nibbling her lip, rubbing her eyes. She dropped the mirror to pour herself another cup of tea and wipe the sweat from her brow.

A whole rutting minute passed. My impatience and stomach-cramping anxiety ticked upward. Adrianna's and Cai's glaring and fidgeting didn't help, either. The rest of us stayed motionless. Frazer and Liora were like me—prone to turning to stone when the truly wicked nerves kicked in.

Maggie simply drank her tea, staring at the spread.

Finally, she set the drained cup aside and reached for the bones.

The tether on my anger snapped. "After all that, you're not going to explain the cards?"

Maggie refused to answer. She closed her eyes, picked up the bone pouch, and croaked, "Autta mina oh vilsa, ole soka ja olet vilsa. Naytä mien Serena tulavasus."

Her eyes flew open; this time they were both pale silver. Liora let go of my hand in shock. Cai and Adrianna tilted back, wincing. Frazer looked ready to pounce.

Maggie was oblivious. She scattered the tiny bleached bones over the cards and blinked. Her amber eye reappeared, and she stared down at the cards with it, while her silver eye resumed its vigil at the mirror.

Maggie suddenly sucked in a sharp breath and shuddered.

My palms went slick with sweat.

"What's going on?" Frazer demanded.

Maggie didn't speak. So Adrianna snapped, "Drop the theatrics. Now. Or I swear by Indrina, I won't stop at a lock of hair. I'll shave your whole damned head."

The witch smiled faintly. "I don't doubt it."

But my attention got snagged on someone else: Liora was gaping down at the table. At the bones.

I dared to ask her, "Can you read it?"

Liora eyeballed me. "A little," she said breathlessly.

Cai finished her thought. "Enough to see it's a powerful reading."

Rutting hell.

Frazer poured more tea and slid it toward me. Maybe he sensed my nerves fraying. Still, I doubted a cup of chamomile could help me now.

Maggie wet her lips with a nervous flick of her tongue. "The crescent spread and the bones combine to tell me that there's a woman—a female —tied to your future. It is *essential* that you find her."

"Who is she?" Frazer asked intensely. He looked at the reading as if he was about to rip it to shreds. As if it was a threat. "Where do we find her?"

"I'd need to scry to find her location. But as for who she is—"

Her voice broke.

I offered her my cup, and she took it with a nod. After a few gulps, she set it aside and cleared her throat. "She's the one who can give you answers. There's something you carry ... An object of great power."

I almost reached for my necklace, but stayed my hand at the last second.

Maggie's silver eye snapped to the mirror. Whatever she saw made her jab her finger toward my throat with such force, Frazer growled savagely.

The witch ignored him. "Whatever that is, you must present it to the Priestess. She'll recognize you if you wear it. Don't wait: seek her out as soon as possible."

Squalling, chaotic emotions swelled within me. Terror and confusion and panic. "What about the trials? Should I leave Kasi?"

Adrianna cut in. "You can't just run away. Deserters are tracked and—"

Maggie silenced her with an open palm. Both her eyes shifted to me. "There are two quests in front of you. The first lies in finishing the trials. The second will be to find this Priestess. These paths walk side by side and weave together. You cannot do one without the other."

Something about that made a cold shiver touch my back, forcing my spine to go ramrod straight. "What happens if I can't do both?"

A part of me knew, but I had to hear the words.

Maggie's expression softened. "If you fail, you die. That thing around your neck: whatever it's done, will end up killing you."

Frazer lurched forward. He was at my throat, fumbling for the chain.

"*Stop!*" Maggie banged the table, causing the bones to jump.

I stopped breathing and Frazer froze. As did everyone else.

Maggie's jaw and shoulders were too tense; a vein bulged in her neck. "Taking it off won't stop what's happening to her, and it won't save her: quite the opposite. I think it's been protecting her."

Frazer slowly sat back down. My hand splayed across my chest, guarding the droplet underneath. I was speaking before I could stop myself. "It has. It protected me when the eerie showed up. There was this voice ..." I didn't want to share more, but this was my chance for answers. Something Auntie had refused to give me. "It told me that there was magic inside. My magic. Then that *thing* appeared, and it gifted it back, but ..."

Maggie was nodding, her silver eye rolling. "There will be consequences. It's given you something ... pure. The purest of all magic."

Cai sucked in a rattling breath. Adrianna's knuckles whitened as her hands curled, and Frazer and Liora became petrified blocks of stone.

"What's that—"

"That isn't possible," Frazer uttered. He didn't blink as he stared down Maggie. "No human has *ever* been gifted with light magic. It's too raw, too volatile."

Maggie didn't flinch, even when his stare intensified.

Light magic ... *Light* magic?

Any attempt to remain calm shattered, and hysteria rode my voice. "What will happen to me?"

No one looked capable of speech. No one except Maggie. "The second that magic entered your system, you should've combusted from the inside out."

The world tipped. A fall was imminent.

"But you didn't. You survived." Maggie set down the mirror to brush the beading sweat from her brow. Both eyes rested on me as she continued. "Still, even if your body can somehow bear it for now, the magic in your veins will kill you. Eventually. Because you can't access it, and if you can't channel your power, it'll build up and rip you apart from the inside out."

Fuck, fuck, fuck. I tried to reel myself in. But it proved impossible.

"So, it's like she's been bound?" Liora breathed.

My heart stumbled at the sight of my best friend's face, grief and panic etched in every line.

"Not quite," Maggie replied wearily. "I don't fully understand what's blocking her magic. But Serena is a unique case ... I've never come across another witch who's had their magic returned to them after they were stripped."

That didn't sound pleasant.

Maggie looked to Cai and Liora. "You're both witches. Didn't you guess?"

They looked sick. Like they'd just watched someone flayed alive.

Cai rushed out on an exhale, "Stripping a witch of their magic is so rarely done, so extreme. I didn't even know it was possible for any of the magic to be kept. I thought it was just gone, lost to the ether."

"Can someone please tell me—"

Liora explained. "Stripping a witch is like cutting the wings from a fae."

The bond grew taut. I detected a tremor and yearned to take Frazer's hand. But his hooded eyes carried a warning. He didn't want to be touched.

Liora turned to Maggie. Anger ringing in her voice, she asked, "Who would do that to her?"

Maggie's steadfast but exhausted gaze settled on me. "The Priestess. The odd thing is the reading shows her as a protector—a guardian. I don't believe that her goal was to part Serena from her magic forever; otherwise, she wouldn't have preserved it. As for why she'd strip her magic—your magic—only she can answer that question. You must find her; she's the only one who can help you."

A pulse pounded between my eyes. A lightning web of thoughts, all tangled and knotted, took hold.

None of it made sense. None of it …

There was no memory. There was nothing that could explain this. Had my father known? Had my mother? Surely, she must have to pass on the necklace, to warn me of its protective qualities. How had this Priestess and my mother even met? Somewhere in Tunnock? That brought up another issue. Eyeballing Maggie, I said, "My mother gifted me this after she died. It comes from the Gauntlet." I flashed the droplet above my jacket for a moment before hiding it again. "You know that's where I was born—in the human realm—but you said I might never go back. So, how do those two things fit together? How do I reach this Priestess?"

Maggie's brow creased; she picked up the black mirror again.

Dead silence.

The witch blinked a few times and muttered something. I felt like screaming. Maggie's hand dropped and rested against the table. "The Priestess isn't in the Gauntlet."

My stomach plunged into icy depths. Mouth agape, I asked, "She's in Aldar?"

Just a nod. And my world collapsed. My thoughts tied up in messy knots, I rambled. "So, this Priestess crossed the divide? I thought only the Wild Hunt could do that."

But Maggie just said, "I can't answer that question."

Whathowwhen?

Frazer reached out and gripped my shoulder. As if he could keep me from falling apart that way.

No chance.

My head rolled forward, slumping into my open palms. A weight pressed down on my shoulders.

"There's something else." Maggie rubbed her eyes.

Adrianna huffed irritably.

I wanted to snap and bite and cry and rage. Enough with the life-altering revelations already.

Maggie's gaze pinned each of us in turn. "The gods—and their courts—brought your pack together for a reason."

She left us with that for a moment.

The thread vibrated, quivering. Frazer's hand jerked from my shoulder. He was dazed. Spooked even.

Adrianna's wings quivered a little. "What does that mean?"

Maggie continued, gesturing around the table. "You've all sensed it. Your pack is bonding. Becoming a unit. A family. So I can't say it any plainer—work together. Guard each other's backs. It's how you'll survive the coming years."

Adrianna blinked. And again. At least she didn't seem angry, just baffled.

Liora folded her arms atop the table, staring down into a cup of untouched tea. "You don't mean as Iko soldiers, do you?"

She looked vulnerable. As if bracing herself.

Maggie gave her a look. Almost pitying. "The trials are important, but what comes afterward ... Becoming a soldier in someone else's war is not Serena's future. Since you are all joined by fate, I doubt that it is any of yours, either." She splayed a hand over the bones. "My visions have been growing bloodier, more violent, for a while now. Change is coming. A war to end all wars. And going off this reading—it looks like your pack will be right at the center of those battles."

Cai held up his palm, cutting her off. "Wait, wait. Who the fuck are we going to war with?"

"D'you really not know?" Maggie's eyebrow rose in disbelief.

Adrianna was the first to mumble, "Morgan?"

Maggie shuddered a touch. "This is bigger than her. But yes, she's certainly part of it."

"Why haven't you told the Rivers Court all this?" Adrianna leaned in, demanding.

Maggie's amber eye glowed, and her silver eye spun as she retorted, "I told them months ago."

A muscle tweaked in Adrianna's cheek as she sagged back into her chair. Like she was diminishing, fading.

Frazer gave me an alarmed sidelong glance. "What's Serena's role in all that?"

Maggie sighed. It was heavy, resigned. "There are limits, even to my sight—"

"Not good enough," Frazer snapped and jerked his chin at the mirror. "Try."

Rude. Abrupt. But I couldn't help agreeing with him, so I stayed silent.

The witch hesitated and then looked again at the black glass. A waterfall of onyx braids fell to shadow her face as she squinted. As if trying to see something from a distance.

An angry humming started under my skin. It was desperate to be freed. To run away. A cool, loving hand reached out, sweeping through my mind, calming the surging and swelling of emotion. *You can handle this, darling. You were born to it.*

Auntie, I—

Feel like you're shattering into a thousand pieces? That will pass.

The weight crushing my chest eased, just a little.

Maggie's voice cracked and changed. Growing hoarser, deeper. "You are Light. The Darkness will be an ally and an enemy. You'll travel far— farther than anyone before you. The burden of what you are, what you will become, won't be easy. The cost will be high ..."

A blade waited over my head, ready to fall.

"But your kin, your pack, and your mate will help you bear this burden."

I couldn't stop myself. "Mate?"

"That's possible—with a human?" Frazer asked, his voice sharp, cutting.

Maggie blinked. And smiled. It was weak; she looked haggard. "If it wasn't, you wouldn't have become kin."

"The mating bond is different. It's more." Adrianna ended abruptly.

A useless explanation.

Frazer snarled, showing his teeth.

Adrianna just raised an imperious eyebrow. "Don't start. You know it's different." She faced me. "You only get one mate. One. You don't choose it—you don't say words. It just happens. And the bond is rare: unique. A fae can go millennia without meeting their intended."

"Sounds nice." Cai grinned across at her.

Adrianna clucked her tongue. "You don't get it. Our kind treasure that bond above all others because it nearly always produces faelings. For a fae to find that connection with a human ... Well, you know Morgan's policies on marriage and inter-breeding. What d'you think she'd do to a mated pair?"

Yep. My heart just stopped.

Cai shrugged. "I still think it sounds nice."

Liora groaned a little. And Frazer had become a statue. But somehow it cracked the ice encasing me. I could've kissed Cai. A whisper of a laugh rumbled in my chest. "Agreed."

Adrianna shook her head in annoyance but didn't say a word.

Summoning my courage, I addressed Maggie. "D'you know who he is? Who my mate is?"

That word—*mate*—encased my heart in an iron grip and squeezed.

Maggie groaned as she pressed her palms into her eyes, massaging. "Your future's difficult. Tangled and blurred, and something—or someone—doesn't want me looking into it." She lowered her hands, her attention fixing on my chest, on the necklace, on *Auntie*. "But the mating bond has a soft spot in all fae hearts. Take my hand."

Maggie put her palm out flat across the table toward me.

I didn't hesitate; I reached out for her. Maggie's warm hand enveloped mine, and she stared into the mirror's depths, breathing deep. One, two, three heartbeats was all it took before she was rasping, "He is far from you. His heart and soul are dying. Shrouded in dark. You are the eye, the center, while he is the storm that rages."

Maggie jerked her hand from mine and dropped the black mirror. Slumping back, her eyes fluttered. Then, her nose started to bleed. Violent curses were heard all around the table as Cai rushed to her, placing his hand on her forearm.

"I'm fine. Don't fuss." Maggie pulled away from him.

Liora's voice was soothing. "Let him help you. We're trained by the healing coven."

"I'm aware," she said, wiping the trickle of red away with a sleeve. "But your training wasn't completed, was it?"

Cai straightened, hands stiff by his sides.

"No," Liora answered for him. She sounded sad.

I made a note. Perhaps, when my world stopped spinning, I'd ask about it. But right now, my hands were trembling.

Storms and dark and death.

Having a mate wasn't so romantic after all.

Maggie stood, bracing her hands against the table with a breath and a pause. Her back ramrod straight, she did a sweep of our faces. "I have one last task to perform before we can be done with this day. To scry for this witch and give you her location. But to do that—Serena, I'll need a drop of your blood to make it work."

Everyone talked at once.

Liora said, "Are you strong enough for that? We could wait until morning."

Frazer growled. "Why d'you need her blood?"

Cai added, "I've never heard of a scrying needing someone's blood before."

Maggie sighed as if biting down on a retort. She turned to Adrianna, avoiding the questions. "The tea will be stone cold, and I find myself in need of a restorative brew. Could you boil more water?"

Adrianna just nodded, uncharacteristically silent. She set to work clearing the cups and teapot from the table.

Frazer cracked and demanded, "Why blood?"

There was nothing reproachful or calculated in the look Maggie gave him, just cold fatigue. "Because this Priestess isn't a normal witch. Her wards are so potent that I can't find her the traditional way. But stripping Serena's magic would've left a connection, an open channel between them. I can use that to locate her."

No one argued.

Maggie swept the bones back into the pouch. A tremor gripped one of her hands. I stood, intending to help, but Liora got there first and gathered up the cards.

I needed *air*.

Spinning on my heel, I headed to the door and opened it an inch. The firelights lit up the night, dancing above the water amidst the spectral fog. I sucked in one breath. Then another. I'd always imagined a swamp would stink, but other than a faint musky note, it was pleasant, even comforting.

A hand gripped my shoulder. I turned, expecting Frazer.

"Stupid question, but how are you?" Liora asked with worried eyes.

I closed the door and slumped back against it. "No idea. Terrified, exhilarated, tired. You?"

She looked lost. "I'm not sure either. It'll take a while to sink in." Her throat bobbed as she went on. "The most annoying thing is we don't have a timeline. The things she told us—this war: it could start in a month or a year." She blinked. "Or it could already have begun."

I pushed myself away from the door and crossed my arms. "When they told us the trials would be difficult, I don't think they had this in mind."

"It could've been worse." Liora managed a half-smile.

I gave her an incredulous look.

"We could've gone to another witch and been cursed," she finished.

That sobered me up. "I don't know about that. All this feels a bit like a curse to me."

Liora moved in to hug me. I was slow and stiff returning it.

"You're not alone," Liora whispered in my ear and pulled away.

"At least I got a nice cup of tea."

Empty, stupid words that caused Liora to huff a sad laugh.

Maggie muttered something about needing scrying tools and disappeared into the back room again. The kettle started to whistle, and Liora wandered over to help Adrianna. I walked back to the table, and Frazer and Cai moved to stand either side of me.

Liora brought clean cups over, and Adrianna followed with the teapot.

Cai took a sniff as they poured, screwing up his face in disgust. "I can't stand herbal tea. Our relatives always brewed it and forced their foul-smelling concoctions down our throats."

Adrianna picked up a full cup across from us, blowing on the surface. "Fine. But we should at least refill our canteens before we leave. The fewer stops we make on the way back, the better. Once we get the hair, I won't feel safe until we place it in Goldwyn's hands."

Cai frowned over at her. "You're worried about Tysion."

Her shoulders went up to her ears. An attempt at a careless shrug. "He won't have given up."

"They might've already nabbed someone," Liora reasoned. "We don't know they'll come after us."

Adrianna's mouth twisted. "You don't know him. He'll want revenge for what Cai did. My guess is he'll set a trap in the one place he knows we'll be—near the camp."

Cai hooted appreciatively. "Damn. Maybe you should've been the leader."

Adrianna bared her teeth. "Definitely."

"We'll discuss this later. One thing at a time." Liora handed me a steaming cup from over the table.

I gave her a thin-lipped smile and set the tea down. My belly was already churning, and no amount of herbal tea could soothe those nerves.

Maggie returned with a silver knife, a rolled-up map, and a quartz necklace. She dumped the items on the table and took her place at the head of it. Spotting the teapot, she immediately poured herself a cup. She downed the whole mug in one. I winced. It had to be scalding.

Maggie put the cup down, smacking her lips. "Serena, come join me."

She beckoned but didn't look up. Her focus was on the map she was rolling out.

I joined her left side as she offered me the knife hilt. "D'you want to do it?" Maggie asked.

Reluctant to take the blade, I bought time by asking, "What do I do after I've cut myself?"

Maggie pointed to the quartz. "Place a drop of your blood onto the crystal."

Frazer cut in. "First, a lock of your hair."

Maggie *tsk*ed and brought the knife up. Mercilessly, she sliced through a chunk and shoved it into Frazer's open palm. He went to put it into his bag by the door. Once he'd returned to us, Maggie offered me the blade again.

Bracing, gritting my teeth, I swept its cool edge across one of the red puckered lines Frazer had given me only yesterday. The biting sting made me hiss a little as I swapped the knife for the quartz, holding it against the welling blood.

Maggie snatched the crystal away the moment it touched a drop of red. Dangling it over the map, she began to swing it in wide circles. The quartz soon slowed.

The witch sucked in a raggedy breath. "There."

The crystal dropped onto the map.

Everyone leaned in. It was southwest of here and rested on the border between the Riverlands and the Solar Court.

Maggie confirmed the location. "Sapor village. That's where you'll find the Priestess."

A telltale crease formed on her forehead. Shit.

I had to ask. "What is it?"

"There's a witch by the name of Hazel Greysand who dwells in those parts, but she's not meant to be anything more than a peddler of healing brews and the odd charm."

"You think she's the one we're looking for?" Cai asked.

We. That tiny word was a gift and a balm to the fear twisting my guts up.

A muscle twitched underneath Maggie's silver eye. "I don't believe in coincidences. Even if she's not this Priestess, she might point you in the right direction. And here—you may as well take the map."

She rolled up the parchment and passed it to me. I walked over to my bag by the door and shoved it down to the very bottom.

Maggie's voice rang out loud and clear. "I'm sure you're eager to be going, but the swamp's no place for land-lovers, especially at night. So, you'll all be resting here until daybreak. Understood?"

"That's generous. We'd be grateful for the shelter," Liora said politely.

As I turned back around, I noticed a look pass between Adrianna and Frazer, but neither objected.

"Good. You're welcome to share my meal of wimpet fish, as humble as it is."

"Sounds delicious," Cai said. All grace and charm.

We didn't have to wait long before a few fish had fried over the fire; something my stomach was exceedingly pleased about. Maggie ate her portion straight out of the pan. The rest of us made do with wooden bowls and fingers. We all sat on the floor on our sleeping bags while Maggie had the stool by the fire. She seemed determined that there would be no more discussion of prophecies. Instead, she told us stories of her life in the swamp.

Straight after the food, Maggie dumped our bowls in the sink, blew out the lanterns, and left for the back room, mumbling "goodnight" on the way.

My eyes shut as soon as I climbed into my bedroll. The crackle and the spit of the fire immediately lulled me into a silent, sleepy haze …

Maggie's silver eye was there, spinning in its socket, peering out at me from a dream.

Her words echoing, *mate.*

Mate.

CHAPTER 19
FOLLOWING BREADCRUMBS

Gods, Adrianna *definitely* had a built-in alarm, because she was rousing us at dawn when the cabin had turned cold and nothing but embers flickered in the hearth. Cai wanted to slip out quickly and quietly without waking Maggie. I debated arguing; the witch was the only one with any answers, after all. So much had changed last night. So much had been said.

I had light magic in my veins. Meant to be impossible.

I had to find the Priestess. Or die.

War was imminent.

Somewhere out there was my *mate*.

But, in the end, I didn't fight going. Maggie had come close to a burn-out, trying to see my future. Even if she'd do another reading, it might damage her permanently.

Adrianna left a note, thanking her, and then we were gone.

A dense fog bank hovering over still waters greeted us outside, along with a peach and rose-tinted sky, just visible through the limbs of cypress trees. We took a moment to grab our weapons and harness them. I buckled everything tight; who knew what we'd face on the journey back. But pulling my rucksack's straps tighter only caused shooting pains to sear through my shoulders and back, like a branding. Humid weather and walking for hours didn't mix; the skin had been rubbed raw.

Damn. What I really needed was a bath. A swim—anything. Frazer and Adrianna must've been sick to their stomachs with so many unwashed bodies floating about.

Once ready, our pack traced the same path as yesterday. Past the old willow and across the swamp, through the veil of mist, we made it back onto dry land again and fell into a familiar line. Cai in the lead, Liora and I in the middle, Frazer guarding our backs, and Adrianna as our eyes in the sky. But something had changed between us. Something that went bone-deep—an affinity that wasn't there before. Maggie was right. We were bonding.

THE SAME TEDIOUS trek followed for three days. Hours of walking, broken up by the odd five-minute rest and a few cloudbursts. Our conversations went around in circles. From the possibility that Tysion's pack might be setting an ambush for us, to Maggie's revelations. The hunger gnawing at my belly all day until the evening meal didn't help, either. It made me cranky. Hell, it pissed me off.

But what came next was much worse.

The fourth day of our march began with a brittle tension brewing. As we moved out into the forest, it was becoming harder and harder to ignore the twisting knot in my stomach.

Around midday, Cai called us to a stop. We'd agreed ahead of time that Adrianna would fly on ahead and scout the area for ambushes. It wasn't a guarantee, but still, better than nothing. We watched her navy-blue blur vanish.

Cai continued to stare up into the canopy, even after she'd disappeared. His expression was unreadable.

Liora moved closer to her brother's side. "They won't find her. Adi's too good for that."

A completely unnecessary comment.

Liora's expression tightened as Cai looked down to flash a quick smile. It was painfully obvious that he was acting his ass off. "I know. I'm just annoyed we're stuck here until she gets back."

He'd been actively shielding our scents, our sounds, and now we needed to stay put for Adrianna to find us or risk discovery by those vexing fae senses.

Cai ran his hands through his hair, which over the past few days had become an unruly mess with frizzy tufts sticking out at all ends. "I've been thinking. If Tysion's pack is lying in wait, it seems reasonable to assume it'll be by the tree line."

He met Frazer's eyes, and a line of understanding passed between them. Their camaraderie seemed to be flowering. Into maybe even friendship.

Cai began, "He's most likely to hit us when our pack breaks cover. But if Adrianna's right, and he's held off from completing the trial just because of some rutting grudge, then he might not stop at taking one of us hostage. Even if it's against the rules."

"You think he'll try to stop us from finishing the quest," Liora said, looking stricken.

Cai sucked on his teeth thoughtfully. "We don't know how much information Tysion was given. His pack could know what our quest object is, and if he finds the hair, he might destroy it. It's an outcome we need to prepare for, anyway."

"It definitely sounds like something he'd do," I muttered.

"What's your strategy?" Frazer asked Cai. A soldier to his leader.

A hesitant heartbeat. Cai seemed to be building up to say something. Something told me I wouldn't like what came next. "None of us wants to become Tysion's hostage, but we won't get kicked out if we do. And getting the hair to Goldwyn and passing the trial is our end goal. So, we split up. They won't know who to go after."

Liora crossed her arms, frowning thoughtfully. "But what if the person carrying the hair gets caught with it?"

Cai replied with a lazy, lilting grin. "They could hide it up their ass."

A sharp snort of laughter burst from me as Liora rolled her eyes in reply.

"Go hang," Frazer snarled. "Although ..."

"Great. You're coming around to the idea," Cai played.

Frazer gave him a haughty look. "D'you ever tire of hearing yourself speak?" Cai opened his mouth, but Frazer quickly added, "Never mind. Just listen. We'll divide the hair into three sections, and split up into pairs. That way it'll give us more shots of getting through, but we'll still have someone watching our backs."

He gave me a not-so-subtle sidelong look, so I finished his thought. "For those who need it—like me."

His jaw clenched. Frazer started, a warning implicit, "Yes. Because given your history with them, we can't be sure they won't hurt you." He surged on, scowling. "I might've refused to protect you in the beginning, but I'll be damned if I'll fail you now."

That was guilt in his eyes. My heart shifted a little. Less anger, more love.

Liora's back straightened and her hands hung loose at her sides. "As long as you give some to me."

Cai stiffened, but Liora just continued, louder, steadier than before. "I haven't had as many issues with them, and they won't expect that you've given it to one of your weaker warriors. It only makes sense."

Indeed. Cai was still slow to nod his approval.

At the sound of humming wingbeats from above we went for our weapons, but it was just Adrianna. As soon as she hit the ground, she said, "I didn't spot an ambush, but I had to stay high to use the cloud cover."

Frazer filled in the blanks. "Then, there's a chance you missed something?"

A curt nod.

"Well, I think we've got a solid plan if it all turns to shit." Cai relaxed his grip on his sword.

Adrianna listened to our idea. "Fine. Although, if you gave it all to me, I'm sure I could out-fly the bastards."

Cai's eyes danced. "Now, now, don't get cocky."

Her expression turned lethal. "Don't underestimate me."

"No danger of that," Cai replied with a flirting smirk.

Adrianna looked away first. Huffing.

Cai added more seriously this time, "Adi, how far is camp?"

"On foot, maybe fifteen minutes."

"No point delaying then. Frazer?" Cai gave him a little nod.

My kin shrugged off his quiver and bow to get to his rucksack. He pulled the hair from deep inside and gave a third to Liora, and divided the rest between himself and Adrianna.

They all found different places to hide the lock of hair—no one chose up the ass, unsurprisingly.

Cai gave his commands—a general in the making. "Liora stays with me. Frazer with Serena. But we stay in sight of one another. Adrianna, obviously the same rules don't apply. You'll have to go it alone."

A slight rigidity entered Adrianna's body posture. As if daring him to ask whether she minded. But Cai just continued, oblivious. "Then, when the camp comes into view, Liora, Serena—I want you to run out first. I'll signal when with a birdcall. We'll follow, and surprise them from behind."

"What?" Frazer growled, his features clouding over.

"The sound barrier will break, and they'll be in plain sight. It might draw Tysion and his minions out."

Adrianna cut in, doubt coloring her voice. "They're not that stupid."

"You're biased," Cai argued. Albeit calmly. "When a fae's blood is up, they can lose all sense and reason. I've seen it again and again. It's a weakness; one we can exploit."

So true. I tried to hide a smile.

Cai looked skyward. "Adi, d'you want to lead us out?"

Adrianna didn't bother saying farewell or good luck. Her wings flared, and she soared, circling above. We split into our pairs with Cai and Liora walking thirty paces to our left, staying within sight and reach of the sound barrier. The forest thinned soon enough, and then we saw it. Kasi.

I'll be right behind you, Frazer whispered.

I nodded and waited for Cai's signal.

A hoot sounded. My insides churned.

Frazer gave me a push in the small of my back. *Go.*

I moved. Liora was out in front, sprinting. We were in the open now, racing down the hill, the open meadow all that stood between us and victory.

A high-pitched whistle sounded, and I *knew* it was them. Nipping at

Liora's heels, I risked a glimpse over my shoulder. Frazer was nowhere to be seen, but there were three fae flying, hurtling toward us. I veered right, away from Liora. If something had happened to the boys, it was up to me to distract the wild fae from going after her.

I became winded. I clutched my side, not giving the pain an inch. Refusing to let it slow me down, I kept on running.

A rustling sounded. I knew they were closing in. There was nothing else for it; I whipped around. And stopped.

The largest of the three fae was a giant with a mane of brown hair. He was stringing an arrow to his bow. The blood froze in my veins.

What the fuck? They weren't allowed to hurt us.

They'll try to pin you, Auntie hissed. *Wait until the last second. Then, dive out the way.*

She was right. The other two fae— fair-haired twins—hadn't drawn weapons. They were swooping down low, flying straight for me.

I crouched down, readying to roll away.

Cai finally appeared from out of the forest. He was sprinting toward us, his tattooed palm outstretched.

A sickening crunch sounded. The three males slammed straight into an invisible wall of hardened air. Their shared oomph's turned to panicked shouts, when a whirlwind blew them halfway across the meadow.

A hand suddenly gripped my elbow from behind. Instinct made me bring up my elbow.

"It's me!" Liora yelled, blocking.

"Shit. Sorry."

I twisted around, checking there was no damage. Nothing.

Cai reached us, waving at Liora. "Go! Keep running. Get the hair to Goldwyn. Serena—"

He glanced back to the forest. My heart stopped. Like a spear, I hurled my whole self down our thread, searching, searching.

Dead silence; only a distant echo. The bond must be weaker this far from each other. *Rutting hell.*

"Where is he?" I demanded.

A second of silence was a moment too long. I readied to hurtle past Cai, all reason gone.

He rushed out breathlessly, "He's gone to help Adrianna. As soon as the whistling started, Frazer heard Tysion yelling. The rest of the pack went straight for her ..." He faltered, his voice breaking.

His eyes creased over with pain. But there was no part of me caring, only panicking. "Where?" I shouted.

Cai's jaw set hard, but his voice was steady. "He's faster, he can get to her sooner. I told him to go help."

"Why didn't you go with him?" Liora asked. Anger brewed in her voice.

His Adam's apple bobbed. "He wouldn't have gone if I'd left Serena unprotected."

"What aren't you saying, Cai?" Liora pressed.

His face ticked. "Frazer heard Tysion order them to use weapons. He thought it might be a trap."

I bolted forward. Like an arrow from a bow.

Cai didn't try to stop me. He was too busy restraining Liora.

"For moons sakes, this is what they want!" Cai shouted at her. "They want us to fail! Go give Goldwyn the hair. Report them. That's an order!"

I didn't hear Liora's reply.

Lungs in a vise, my legs ate up the hill. I plunged into the forest, skidded to a halt and closed my eyes.

FRAZER!

Distant shouting. There was something, but not enough to get my bearings. He'd said the kin bond could be used to sense each other across distances. What was wrong with me? Gods damn it, why hadn't he shown me how to use this thing?

Thready breathing sounded behind me. I spun.

It was just Cai. "Liora?" I glanced behind him.

Red hair on the horizon, headed back to camp: I felt only relief.

He bent over, wheezing. It must've been the strain of using magic. Cai was fitter than me by a mile. "I convinced her to find Goldwyn. Using weapons is against the rules—she can stop them."

I nodded, distracted. Turning, my eyes swept the surrounding area. Praying ...

"Can you hear his thoughts?" Cai asked, straightening.

My reply came out forced and angry. "I've tried. He's too far."

"But the kin bond—"

"Nothing's working!"

My voice broke with a sob. Panic mounted, vast and staggering.

Cai gripped the tops of my arms and spun me around to face him. "You can do this, Serena," he breathed.

"I can't use the magic—you heard Maggie."

"You won't have to draw on your power." He shook his head, insistent. His strong fingers bit down deeper. "Bonds have their own source of magic. But it won't be like talking mind to mind. Fae connections are ancient, primal. They're accessed through emotion, through feeling. Not thought. So don't talk to him. Visualize Frazer; imagine the thread between you, and follow it to its source. Find his heart."

It sounded like babble.

"Serena."

"Can't you use a spell?"

"It would take too long. You can do this." He stepped back, and magic filled the air. Another sound barrier. "Breathe."

Listen. Auntie ordered.

I closed my eyes and breathed in deep, visualizing his raven hair, the fine features that could cut glass, and the ever-pale skin. Our bond sparked to life in my mind, a living, breathing line of gold light connecting us. It was there, just like always, only this time threaded with red. Pulsing.

Glimpses and echoes ... Tysion was bringing a sword down in a violent overhanded attack—

The images stopped. Reining in the blind panic that threatened to spill out into the world, I held the filament in my mind, and my eyes fluttered open. Beneath my feet a ribbon appeared. A trail to follow.

I was already running. "This way."

Cai's footsteps sounded heavy behind me, whereas mine were light, fast. Almost like racing the wind itself across the earth. And now that ribbon of light was in my center, my core, pulling me onward. Instinct guided me, molding my movements into a fluid dance. I leaped over rocks and fallen logs, and dodged trees. Sure, my breathing was shallow, but it didn't stop me from pumping my arms and legs even harder, until the sounds of clashing steel and shouts caught my ear. I halted, unsheathing my Utemä.

Cai arrived beside me, panting. He pulled his sword free and gave a little nod. I didn't need the bond to find Frazer now. Flying through the forest, heading toward the sounds of the fight, I rounded a bend and got a quick picture of the scene.

Adrianna faced Cole and a fae with white wings and features seemingly dusted with snow. I knew his name to be Lucian.

She fought on the ground. Her wings looked crumpled, her bag's straps had frayed, and a spent quiver and an abandoned bow lay on the ground. It all spelled one thing—someone had been at her back. She rolled, picking up arrows embedded in the ground. Holding them crossed over her body, she slashed out as Cole and Lucian closed in. They'd both drawn their swords, but angled them low. She was to be the hostage.

Another bend revealed Tysion swinging a sword, locked in combat with my brother, who had a swollen jaw and a bleeding bite mark on his neck. My kin had nothing to defend himself; his bow was broken and scattered in pieces over the loamy earth.

A breath, forced out by contracting lungs, died on my lips, but the sight electrified my blood. I felt the sound barrier break at the exact moment my whole being just reacted. *Exploded* with a burst of singular speed and a howl to the gods.

Frazer's eyes found me and widened in horror. I flipped my Utemä and threw it to him, hilt-first, screaming *catch* down the bond.

Tysion turned at the sound. I had seconds. Leaping onto his back, my legs snapped together, knees pressing deep into his spine. I seized those mighty, fierce wings and *tugged*.

Frazer caught my Utemä as Tysion let out a wild, throat-tearing scream. It didn't sway me. I had no mercy left in me.

Tysion panicked, dropping his sword to reach over his shoulders and grab for me. I leaned back, putting all my weight—all the strain—on the wing joints. Wilder had helped me perfect the move. But Tysion wasn't half the warrior he was. He didn't even try falling onto his back. Instead, the fae frantically spun and flapped his wings, snarling and screaming, "Get this bitch off me!"

Pathetic.

Adrianna yelled to Cai, "No! Cole's mine. Take the other one."

Cai answered with a laugh that was rough and abrupt, crashing to a halt.

"Your friends can't help you now," I hissed in Tysion's ear.

He snarled savagely and began rocking, trying to buck me off.

Serena, let go now! An image shuddered down the bond. A vignette that showed Frazer's bent knees, growing canines, and a sword primed for action.

I released his wings. Jumping off, I backed away. Tysion didn't get a chance to turn his ire on me; Frazer barreled forward and pinned him to the ground with a hand to his throat and a sword aimed at his eye. His teeth extended, and he snapped, "Call off your dogs."

Tysion didn't look surprised to hear Frazer talk. They must've already shared words—or insults. "You wouldn't," Tysion spat out, his eyes giving off sparks. "You don't have the balls, you wingless freak."

Frazer responded with a terrifying grin that had my blood freezing over. "You're right, I won't kill you. But if you think that's the limit of my imagination ..." He moved his arm up to dangle the Utemä over Tysion's right wing. A scythe ready to fall, and a deadly warning.

Tysion bucked, wriggling like a hooked fish. Without pause, my kin stabbed down, piercing the bat-like membrane.

I flinched as Tysion gasped and choked on the pain.

"Enough," my brother barked, his face paling.

Frazer's revulsion of what he'd done sung down the bond and spiked my heart. I stepped closer to him.

My kin leaned in, his voice a sweet, threatening whisper. "Attack my pack again, and I'll make you like me. A wingless ghost. A wretched thing."

That had emotion swelling, closing my throat.

Tysion stilled, real fear etched into his face.

An undignified spluttering noise made me look up. Cai was standing at the roots of a tree, his inked hand raised in a fist so tight I could see the bones in his hand. Lucian stood in front of him, clawing at his own throat, struggling to breathe.

"Cai, should I be worried?" I tried for a light tone.

"Not at all," he said. As cocky as ever. "Just waiting for this snowflake to pass out."

I didn't believe a single word. The strain of the magic was showing in every quiver of his body.

Lucian slumped to the floor, unconscious.

Frazer wrenched the sword out of Tysion's wing only to growl down at him, "Call Cole off!"

Tysion refused to give the order. His eyes were alive with hate.

Cai had fallen to his knees, obviously spent, but he'd started crawling toward Adrianna, adamant about helping. Because Cole would not quit; like a cornered wolf, he circled Adrianna. It was still only arrows against sword.

I strode forward, intending to rush the bastard.

A hand clutched my shoulder, stopping and spinning me.

I shared a breath with Wilder.

"Leave it to Goldwyn," he said, low and rough.

The hum of wings sounded behind me. I didn't turn. Rooted to the spot, my heart skipped and pounded.

His grip on my shoulder grew tighter for just one heartbeat. Then he let his arm fall, and he side-stepped around me. I turned with him, watching as he gripped Frazer around the midriff and tossed him aside. Goldwyn landed with Liora in her arms. And while she helped her brother stand, our mentor viciously yanked Cole's hair back and bit him. He didn't struggle.

Save me from the world of the fae ...

Wilder pulled Tysion up. I should've said something in Frazer's defense, but the cloud of shock hadn't shifted; neither had the sudden and demanding desire that crashed into my body upon seeing Wilder, so unexpectedly. How the hell did he do that to me?

Tysion was speaking, lying his ass off. "Master, I don't know what the human told you, but they attacked first." He jabbed his finger at Frazer, who was now standing. "He stabbed my wing—"

The sound of a loud smack rang in my ears as Wilder's fist crashed into Tysion's face. "Save the sniveling for Dimitri. The rest of your pack is with him now. He isn't best pleased that you failed your trial."

Tysion grimaced as he held the side of his face. "Please," he began hoarsely, "we have time."

Wilder was a statue. "We gave you clear instructions: no using weapons on the hostage, no sabotaging the pack's quest."

"They attacked first. It was self-defense."

"Liar," I growled.

Tysion's teeth snapped down as he turned on me. "Mad bitch. You'll be gone by sundown. You nearly ripped my wings off—"

Wilder's reply was instant. Faster than a blink, he grabbed one of Tysion's elongated canines and pulled him in, nose to nose. He whispered something outside my hearing, but whatever it was made Tysion blanch. He was almost trembling.

Shoving him away, Wilder raised his voice. "You'll be given an opportunity to explain your actions to Dimitri, but as far as your trial goes, that ends now. Pray that another group fails too, or else you're gone. For now, you can walk back to camp."

The last of Tysion's fury and spite drained away, leaving behind a nauseated-looking ghost. Wilder turned his back, dismissing him in the same heartbeat. A fae custom.

Tysion's injured wing twitched and crumpled to his side. He whirled around and stomped back to camp. Goldwyn ordered Cole to follow in the footsteps of his disgraced leader. And after a slap to wake him and a bloodless bite to the neck, Lucian was sent packing too.

Wilder faced Frazer, staring him down. "You were stupid for marking his wing. Dimitri will use it as an excuse to let them off and demand your dismissal. Goldwyn and I will stand for you this time, but don't expect us to be so lenient in the future." Wilder's eyes held pure dominance.

I opened my mouth, ready to argue.

Leave it be, siska.

My brother dipped his head. "I won't be so stupid again. You have my word."

Wilder frowned, crossing his arms. "You're speaking. After all this time ... What changed?"

Frazer's gaze flickered to me. Only for a second, but it was enough. Wilder tracked his line of sight and found me. He blinked. Just the tiniest sign of shock. Then, his nostrils flared delicately. Something dark and unnameable distorted his features. The scars on his face deepened, making them somehow more menacing than before. Stars, was he taking in our merged—our bonded—scents?

Goldwyn called out, "I'm taking Cai back. He's still too weak to walk. Adrianna's flying Liora, are you—"

Wilder blurred, lifting me into his arms in one fluid movement.

Goldwyn smirked over at him. "Don't take too long. We need to get to Hilda before Dimitri's had too long to whine in her ear."

Goldwyn promptly took to the skies with Cai in her arms. Adrianna followed with Liora. As Wilder's wings opened, he looked to Frazer. "You will walk."

A flat, cold command.

A mewl of protest escaped me as we shot upward. I glanced down, but barely caught a glimpse before my eyes had to close to avoid being scratched out by groping twigs. After we'd burst free from the canopy, however, I glared up at Wilder. "Take me back."

"No."

A face of granite. Fine. Rutting fantastic.

Neither of us talked on the flight back. Two iron wills at odds, embattled. What was he thinking? Frazer was alone; Tysion was near. My mind ticked, ticked, ticked. I peered over Wilder's shoulder to scan the now distant forest.

"Don't even think about it," Wilder growled in my ear.

"About what?"

"Going back for him."

My body tensed. "I wasn't." A lie.

His reply was a growl. "You keep looking back there."

Detecting strain in his voice, I wondered. More like hoped.

His cheeks carried a flush. Maybe it was a simple case of windburn. That didn't explain why he looked like a male at war with himself. His words came out clipped, slamming into me. "Frazer can scent Tysion's route and avoid it. You can't. Something you should think of before running headlong into the path of three fae who'd gladly rip you to shreds. You're not this stupid, so stop acting like it."

His words gutted me. He was right—I was stupid. Stupid to hope that his tone had held jealousy and not contempt.

An invisible wall went up between us, and a cold silence fell. The flight was annoyingly labored and slow. Adrianna and Goldwyn landed minutes before us.

Wilder finally touched hard earth in the shadow of a watchtower, just outside camp. He let me down.

Without looking him in the eye, I muttered, "Thanks."

"Are you going back there?" His voice was a nip warmer.

"No, but I'm waiting here until he gets back."

I risked a look, then. He wasn't smiling, but neither did he seem as dark and grim as before. "I expected nothing less. I'll wait with you."

"You told me that we weren't allowed to be seen together." I tried for casual and got snappy instead.

Wilder rubbed the back of his neck. Did he look *embarrassed*? "I've already made a fool out of myself. A few more minutes more won't make any difference."

"What are you talking about—"

I broke off upon seeing Wilder's head tilt to the side. Gone was the sheepish expression, and in its place was the predator. He growled so low, it reverberated inside my chest. I followed his eye line, but there was nothing.

Wilder explained in a whisper. "Dimitri's talking to a guard. He's close. He'll be coming to see if Tysion's back."

I whispered back, "You should go." I stepped aside and gestured toward camp.

All I got was a withering look. "I'm not leaving you alone after you just embarrassed his best fighter. Give me some credit."

Those words stupidly caused my head to spin and my heart to pound.

Wilder's hand slipped around my wrist, and without asking, his wings took us into the sky again and straight onto the walkway above. Then, he was pushing and jostling me through a door in the enclosed watch tower.

"Eyes front. Say nothing," Wilder muttered to the two armor-clad fae on duty.

The quiet command sent a thrill through my blood. I couldn't fathom why, but the power lining his voice made my very bones want to obey.

The guards turned away and went still as stone, surveying the area, as if nothing had happened. Not a question between them. The perfect soldiers.

Wilder pushed me down to the planked floor and sat beside me. I rested against the high railings that shielded us from view. His wing curled around me, tucking me in close. A hot breath coiled up the shell of my ear as he leaned in. "Not a word. Understood?"

I nodded, but Wilder wasn't paying attention to me. He'd plucked something from an inner pocket in his leathers. I caught sight of green crystal before his hand closed over it. His lips moved in a silent rhythm.

The seconds stretched by, and the guards didn't move or speak to us. They didn't give a single sign that a mentor was currently shielding a recruit under his wing. A hum, a tingle, shimmered through the air. My blood recognized magic. It felt weak, but ...

Wilder. Clearly, I knew nothing about this fae.

Dimitri's voice sounded from below. "You stupid, reckless idiot!"

I broke out in a nervous sweat when the reply came. "They attacked first," Tysion growled low. "Goldwyn and Wilder must be bedding one or more of them. They showed favoritism."

A tremor went through Wilder's wings. I dared to peek up at him from under my lashes. Shadows plagued his eyes, but he caught me looking and smiled.

Sure, it was small and crooked, but it still caused my pulse to sing.

"Oh, spare me the excuses," Dimitri said with flawless disdain.

"That wingless dick cut my wing, and they did nothing," Tysion protested.

Auntie clucked her tongue. *Aww, poor baby.*

A savage grin cracked my face in two. Wilder's eyes went there. To my mouth. My body came alive, bursting into flames.

"I don't hear any of the others complaining."

Dimitri's voice now sounded miles away. Like I'd slipped under the sea. More voices punctured the air. Lucian and Cole. But the words escaped me.

I didn't how long we stayed there like that, sharing each other's breath. It put me on the edge of something, tilting, staring down into a fathomless abyss.

A fall. I was falling.

Wilder's wings crumpled in on themselves, and the world opened back up. He pulled me out the door and straight into his arms.

We jumped and landed with a thud. But I didn't stop falling.

He released me, but his arm kept a light grip on my forearm. He stood, watching me. And I drowned in those eyes. Lost in the forest.

Words bubbled to the surface—words that I shouldn't say.

Wilder snatched his arm away like he'd been burned, and he took a very deliberate step back. "Frazer's coming."

My head whipped toward the tree line. The sight of that familiar tall figure shook a relieved laugh loose from my lips.

"I have to go."

That had my gaze snapping back to his.

"Dimitri will have gone to ooze excuses into Hilda's ear. And I need to be there to support Goldwyn and speak on your pack's behalf."

His wings twitched, flaring.

"Wait! You can't just ..."

"What?" he pushed out.

I thought fast. A delay. "Why didn't you tell me you had magic?"

"I don't owe you anything."

My chest collapsed. I didn't know what I'd been summoning the courage to say—maybe that this, us, might be worth a risk. I swallowed the words. It felt like hot ash slipping down my throat.

My body reacted and moved back as if instinctively protecting itself from an assault.

Wilder sighed a little and opened his palm to reveal the now clear crystal. "It was borrowed magic. A charm that allows me to blanket a small area and disrupt fae senses."

I went somewhere far, far away. "Right, well, thanks for helping me."

Again, my body knew what to do. It turned its back to him.

That was my goodbye. To all of it.

Slow and heavy wingbeats murmured alongside the faint and broken echoes of my heart. I didn't look back.

None of it mattered, not really. Maggie's words—the reaper at my back, the quest to find the Priestess—they needed to be the priority. Everything else paled in comparison. Or at least, it should.

I just needed to try harder to control myself. To shut him out. So I buried my feelings as deep as they'd go and watched the meadow, waiting for my kin to return.

CHAPTER 20
BY THE LAKE

After I reunited with Frazer, our pack came together in the barracks. This was followed by a visit to the baths and a short trip to the food hall to stuff our faces. We'd rushed in both places because we wanted to be alone with Goldwyn. She'd promised to give an update on Hilda's ruling, and I kept hoping and praying that there'd be no consequences for us—especially Frazer.

So, now we waited for the news. I'd told them all about my hiding from Dimitri with Wilder, and after that we talked, mostly idle words to distract ourselves. Only Frazer sensed what I wasn't saying. That my heart had frozen and was burning, all at once.

Through the barrack windows we were witness to a blanket of night falling over the world, coal-black and starless. The firelights flickered to life in the lanterns, and a pitter-patter became a hailstorm hammering against the window and roof. Finally Goldwyn appeared, ducking in the door, her leathers sticking to her. She greeted us, shaking her mane and sunshine-colored wings free from the raindrops.

We all stood at once.

"What happened?" Adrianna asked, bracing a hand against her hip. A curt manner, but I saw the nerves brewing beneath.

Goldwyn brushed the hail from the shoulders of her black and silver uniform. At least she didn't seem upset. Just annoyed. "Hilda's playing the middle. She's not punishing either side. Although, she's upheld Wilder's judgment that Dimitri's Boars have failed the trial. She'll allow them to fight for their place in the arena, *if* another pack fails."

Bleak expressions were exchanged.

Adrianna took the words right out of my mouth, "If they get that chance, they'll win."

Goldwyn didn't bother denying it. She nodded. "No doubt, but right now you have other, more pressing concerns."

My pulse sped up. Cai had lied to Goldwyn about how we'd "stolen" Maggie's hair. We'd agreed on our journey back to Kasi that the truth would only lead to difficult questions about the reading I'd offered in exchange. So what was she referring to?

"Dimitri won't forget this slight. You've made his pack of vicious vipers look weak," Goldwyn said, her eyes twinkling, her mouth quirking. "And if they stay, he'll have a group of angry male fae with which to lash out at you all."

Cai collapsed back on his bed and stretched luxuriously. "Gods, how did that dickless wonder become a mentor here, anyway?"

My eyes instinctively shifted to Adrianna, then to Frazer. They both looked uneasy. Goldwyn hadn't been our instructor long. We didn't know how she'd react, nor how casual or free we could be.

But she just regarded Cai in cool amusement. "As refreshing as your lack of propriety is, Caiden," she emphasized his full name with a smile, "I will not discuss the politics of this place. Not only do I find it *deathly* dull, but it also wouldn't help you." She stepped closer. All humor gone. "*However*, I will say that Dimitri is a vindictive male who's amassed a killer reputation for pettiness."

Cai barked a mocking laugh.

"Don't underestimate him." She snapped a little there. "You've embarrassed him, and now he'll use whatever influence he has to come after you. So, I have to ask, is there anything he can use against you?"

Where should we start? Everything could be used against us. Our secrets had secrets at this point. Not that we could tell her that.

Adrianna was the first to speak. "If he's determined to have us thrown out, it won't matter what's true or not. He could just make shit up or twist the truth."

Goldwyn's brow furrowed as she tilted her head. "True enough. He's already tried to get Serena kicked out."

"What?"

That came out more loudly than I'd anticipated.

Everyone stared at me.

Goldwyn's lips thinned. "During the meeting today, he accused you of seducing your mentor."

Anger—and maybe a bit of shame—flooded my cheeks.

"Hilda didn't care much," Goldwyn said. "*Technically*, it isn't even against the rules, especially since he passed your training off to me. Speaking of which, it's another three days until the next trial's announced. We should make use of the time and continue your lessons."

Gods damn it.

"You don't have to do that," Frazer said, cutting a sidelong glance to me. "Our pack will be training with one another from now on."

A fissure of surprise ran through me. Cai and Liora exchanged looks that said the same thing. But Adrianna nodded and flexed her fingers. "That's right."

Ho, ho. That was a change.

Goldwyn was all swagger and audacious smiles. "That's your decision, but Serena won't be rid of me so easily. Besides, Wilder's very noble and all that, but to survive here, she'll need someone to teach her to play rough. And that happens to be my specialty."

THREE DAYS PASSED, during which Goldwyn and Frazer took responsibility for my training. Their combative styles were fresh and different, so they gave me a whole host of new tricks and counterattacks. Adrianna stepped into the role of mentor for Liora and Cai, but only when she thought he was doing something wrong. So, all the time.

Every hour of our pack's time was carefully regimented and exhausting. But without saying a word to one another, we'd taken Maggie's words to heart. None of us trained alone. We were together every minute, which had its own frictions and challenges. One good thing came out of it though—my bond with Frazer strengthened. Now, whenever we were apart, which wasn't often, I could track him easily and vice versa. I cherished the thought that one day, no matter the distance or the ocean separating us, we'd find our way back to each other.

Thanks to the full days and dreamless nights, I didn't have time to dwell on certain unpleasant truths. One, however, was difficult to avoid; it breathed down my neck daily. Wilder's pack had failed the trial. They'd battled it out in the ring with Tysion and his thugs. Except it wasn't a battle—more like a three-minute slaughter. It culminated in the Bats being dismissed from camp with a few broken bones for their trouble, while Tysion and his gang remained. Goldwyn's warning about Dimitri's possible wrath was just one more reason we stuck together. On the evening of the third day, however, as the instructors—and oddly, Bert —gathered the remaining four packs in the ring, it proved impossible to avoid certain feelings. Specifically, a gut-wrenching pain triggered by a set of green eyes and wings.

As always, Liora saw through the cracks in my pathetic attempt at an unfeeling mask. She moved an inch closer, her shoulder brushing mine in solidarity. Adrianna mimicked her, standing closer on my right side. I didn't know if it was for the same reasons, but it warmed my heart, nonetheless.

Mikael was the first mentor to speak, his voice deep and rumbling, with little feeling. "Tomorrow, the next trial begins, and it'll be a hunt for sprites."

A hiss of whispers broke out among the recruits.

"Silence," Dimitri drawled.

The whispering ceased immediately. Mikael continued without missing a beat. "You must bring down two sprites per pack. You may choose any sprite as long as they're classified as a threat to fae and humankind."

Dimitri interrupted with a flick of his wrist. "Of course, if you really want to impress, you could bring back a devos sprite." He said it with a nasty smirk in our direction.

Cecile said in her quiet tones, "Those sprites have been classified as first-class killers. Do not attempt to slay one unless you are confident."

Cecile clasped her hands behind her back and went on. "If you fail to bring back evidence of the kill, you will be automatically expelled. No second chances in the ring. If you succeed, however, you are to present your proof to Bert."

Cecile's eyes slid to Goldwyn, who picked up the conversation. "We're recommending that the packs split into teams of two or three, to improve your chances of success. You'll only have six days this time, so be smart about how you approach this one."

Frazer caught my eye. *Together?*

A tendril of his dry humor reached me.

Of course, brata.

His lip quivered.

My stomach dropped at the sound of Wilder's voice. "And we're also allowing magic again, for those among you who can use it."

"So, just Cai then," Dimitri barked, glaring over at our pack. "A clear bias, which we must squash."

"Well, if we're going to quibble over fairness, perhaps we should discuss allowing the fae to fly to their destinations while the humans walk?" Goldwyn sounded lightly.

Wow. She really liked poking the monster.

Dimitri looked like he'd swallowed poison as spontaneous murmurs broke out among the recruits.

Wilder cut across the noise by teasing in a droll voice, "Goldwyn, that's not very helpful."

"Apologies," Goldwyn purred.

Wilder shot her a smile that had my guts boiling with a *very* unwelcome emotion. He faced the recruits. "You may leave at any time tomorrow. We won't be seeing you off again."

Dimitri had to have the last say, barking, "And if any of you *are* brave enough to go after the devos sprites, rest assured that when the time comes, the instructors will be happy to recommend those individuals for the best placements."

From Dimitri, it didn't seem like a helpful tip. More like a push to do something stupid and get ourselves killed.

Mikael confirmed my suspicions by drawling, "But if you hunt a devos, be prepared to lose a limb."

"On that happy note, we're leaving you with Bert," Goldwyn sang. "He'll provide you with the details of the fourth trial."

I blinked. *Fourth?*

Every recruit seemed to be holding their breath.

Goldwyn swept the recruits with an amused eye. "That particular trial is unique because it starts now. You have until just before the final trial to complete it. It's also singular in that the instructors are not aware of the nature of the quest, and are forbidden from asking their packs anything about it, or helping them in any way."

She paused. I almost rolled my eyes. Goldwyn reminded me of Cai —theatrical.

"Good luck."

With that, all five mentors took to the skies. Bert—today, sporting a multicolored smock—observed their flight paths from behind his spectacles. Once they were out of sight, he began speaking. "The fourth task requires each recruit to steal an object from one of yah instructors."

Gasps, laughs, and titters spread through the crowd.

The ogre waited for a few heartbeats, and that's where his patience ended. He stomped the ground with his dark-green feet, snorting heavily. Almost like a bull readying to charge.

The chatter ceased immediately.

He put his hands behind his back and continued. "The object must belong to, or be in the possession of, the instructor yah've chosen to steal from. And yah should each have an object to present by the final trial— like Goldie said." He cleared his throat with a mighty *hem, hem*. "None of the instructors know anything about this quest, and yah'll are forbidden from simply asking them for an object. Because they're not stupid, and they'll figure out what the trial is." He puffed up a bit and peered down his spectacles at us. "Once you've got yah item, bring it to me in me cottage. Fail, and yah gone. Anyone caught cheating, and yah gone. That said, I wish yah all the best. Dismissed." He ended with a proud nod of his head and clomped off.

Cai spun, addressing us—his pack. "We need to talk. Barracks or lake?"

"Lake," Adrianna replied at once.

No one argued, and we moved off.

Almost immediately, Liora linked arms with me. Slowing us to a crawl, she whispered, "I know things didn't work out between you and Wilder, but maybe now you could use what happened to your advantage."

I frowned down at her. "What d'you mean?"

She grinned impishly. "Fourth trial."

A raven's caw slipped my lips. "What, you think stealing from him will change his mind about us?"

Liora responded with a soft, contrite laugh. "No, but isn't that all the more reason to steal from him?"

That got me laughing.

A short stroll had us settling down in a circle on the pebble-covered lakeshore, where a gentle breeze wrinkled the usually glassy surface of the lake, and birdsong filled the air. Protected within our usual sound-proof bubble, Cai grinned from his position opposite me and said, "Well, I didn't see the fourth trial coming, did you?"

He scanned each of us, but his eyes rested on Adrianna the longest. It was heartwarming and exasperating. His affection wasn't going away, no matter how many times she refused to flirt back.

Remind you of anyone? Auntie mused, chuckling.

Ouch. That stung.

But Adrianna took the bait this time. "The staff quarters aren't far from us. Taking something from their rooms might be easier, or at least safer, than trying to pick their pockets or grab their weapons."

Liora tucked a strawberry curl behind her ear, frowning. "Agreed. And it shouldn't be too hard getting into Goldwyn's rooms."

"How come?" I asked, bemused.

An impish smile tugged her lip up. "It was before our pack was formed, but Goldwyn's said time and time again that we're welcome to go ask her advice on anything, at any time."

Cai reacted with a lion's smile. All teeth and swaggering arrogance. "True, but I'm more tempted to steal from Dimitri. Breaking into his rooms seems more entertaining, somehow."

Adrianna remarked, "Dimitri will probably be easier to steal from than Goldwyn."

I wasn't the only one looking at her as if she'd gone mad.

She explained in the next breath. "This trial has loopholes within loopholes. Tysion just has to knock on his door and hint at what the trial involves. Dimitri won't give a shit that it's cheating. His recruits are still living with the disgrace of losing one trial, which means he is. I wouldn't put it past him to start leaving his damned door wide open." A pure, feline smile lit her azure eyes. "But the day you steal from the Ghost Cat or the Snake—that's the day people whisper about your potential. That's the day you've really earned something."

Her uncharacteristic wistfulness got me to smile freely. "I'll stick to Goldwyn and leave the impossible to you."

"Not Wilder?"

A shrug. Acting at being casual.

Sweet, wonderful Cai changed the subject. "Shall we agree to steal our own items, but if any of us are running out of time, we'll pitch in and help one another?"

Adrianna showed her disapproval in a frown, but even she mumbled her agreement.

Cai stretched and rolled his broad shoulders. "That leaves us with the third trial." He peered over at Adrianna. Concern lined his voice as he asked, "I'm guessing you'll be hunting one of the devos?"

To my surprise, Adrianna nodded toward me. "That depends on Serena. Because I've been thinking about what Maggie said. Actually, I haven't been able to stop."

A dry-bordering-on-fatigued tone slipped from me. "Neither have I."

"Nor me," Frazer added under his breath.

Liora met Adrianna's eyes. "You want to use this trial to find her, don't you?"

Confusion roiled in.

"What are you talking about?" Frazer grew stiff.

That instantly put me on edge.

Adrianna breathed through it. "We all heard Maggie's words. The trials and the quest to find the Priestess walk hand in hand. This task provides us with freedom of movement and a unique opportunity to visit Hazel Greysand. I can fly us out to Sapor and be back within six days. And we can hunt either on the way there or back. I know the terrain we'll be traveling over—it shouldn't be too difficult to find a sprite."

Even though Frazer had asked the question, she'd directed her answer toward me. Something I appreciated. My voice came out as a whisper. "You'd do that for me?"

"It's not just for you."

Oh.

"We're bound together now," Adrianna said with an elegant twist of her wrist, sweeping her hand in a circle. "This is for all of us."

"I'm her kin," Frazer said. He didn't sound combative—more like defeated. "I should be the one to go with her."

Sympathy rang clear in Liora's expression and in her voice. "Not this time. Adi's the only one who can do this. You know that."

She didn't need to say why. The pain it caused Frazer was too much to bear. It was enough to make me wish, for one fleeting second, that we weren't becoming so finely attuned to each other's emotions.

Adrianna tucked her wings in tighter to her body. As if conscious they were the source of his grief. "I know what the bond's screaming at you to do, but no harm will come to her."

I felt a stab of annoyance.

"Swear it." Frazer's voice snapped like a whip.

Adrianna took a particularly pointy-looking pebble and slashed it across her hand.

A noise halfway between shock and anger punched out of me.

Adrianna tossed the stone aside and raised her hand, showing him the welt. Frazer's nostrils widened, and he nodded, satisfied.

Gods-damned fae.

"All right," Cai said testily. He hurled Frazer a particularly reproachful look as he added, "Enough cutting ourselves with rocks. We still need to decide where the rest of us will go."

Adrianna cradled her wounded hand on her lap and drew a tissue from her jacket pocket. Dabbing at the welling blood, she said, "A lot of the lower-grade sprites have migrated north to the mountains for the spring hunts. You won't be able to travel that distance in six days."

Cai muttered under his breath, "How helpful."

Frazer said quietly, "I've heard of kelpies inhabiting sea caves on the coast. That's within walking distance."

"Where did you hear that?" Adrianna's brows nudged together.

Frazer answered, "Fae hearing. Plus, for weeks people didn't bother to lower their voices around me. It's like they assumed because I didn't speak, I must be deaf, too."

A small smile hit his mouth, a veil to cover the sadness that the bond sang to me. I could feel him trying to smother it, but that didn't really work. He might have been able to keep certain thoughts from me, but this bond between us, forged out of loneliness and strengthened by blood, was a direct line to his soul.

I burned for him. I wasn't so naïve as to think I could heal the wounds of his past. I certainly had no desire to pick over scars and reopen old wounds, but I couldn't help wishing he'd let me in more.

Cai disturbed my reverie. "You think we'd be able to catch one?"

Frazer replied with a little shrug. "I know the theory."

That's not very reassuring, I told him.

Silence.

"Well, I can use magic," Cai said, a little too breezily. "So maybe we'll actually survive the encounter."

No one laughed.

A quick look around our circle revealed worry and doubt written on each face. To me, it wasn't just battling a monster or meeting Hazel that twisted my heart. It was that we'd be going our separate ways. I itched to lean into Frazer, to take comfort and give it in return. But physical contact was something he only tolerated. That much I did know about him.

"We've talked enough." Adrianna's voice broke through the gloom that had descended. "We need to head to the armory and the food hall. They're likely already swamped with recruits. And I don't want all the decent weapons signed out before we get there."

"Holy shit!" Cai exclaimed, jumping up. "Never mind that—all the good food's being plundered." He sprinted for the hall. In a blink, I was up and running like the Dark Lord Archon himself, was after me.

CHAPTER 21
HAZEL

"Come on, you lazy slugs! Up!"

My eyes flew open; I was instantly awake.

"Adi, for gods' sakes," Cai groaned into his pillow. "We don't have to leave this early. Go back to bed."

It made no difference to me. I'd barely caught a wink. Too many nerves, too many chaotic thoughts sending me spinning into what ifs, hows, and whys.

Hazel Greysand. Priestess.

What answers would she have for me? If any ...

No more brooding. I couldn't stand it.

I pulled my bedsheets around my shoulders and rocked up onto my feet. The bare floorboards sent a shiver barreling up my spine.

No one else was moving, though.

Adrianna spoke loudly. "I'm not going back to bed, Caiden, and you shouldn't either."

"Don't call me that," he grumbled.

Oh, he definitely wasn't a morning person.

Adrianna kept on. "While you were wasting time sleeping, I completed the fourth trial and stole from Goldwyn."

A pause. Followed by Cai chuckling, tossing his covers aside, rolling out of bed, and standing in nothing but his underpants.

Mother have mercy. I still hadn't gotten used to my pack's complete disregard for modesty. It made me feel like a fool for dressing under a sheet every morning.

"Already?" Liora said, sitting up, slack-jawed.

"I only went to scope out the staff quarters—I hadn't planned on actually taking anything yet." Adrianna watched as I struggled under my sheet to force two pairs of black leggings on. That had been her suggestion; we'd be flying across mountains. It would get *cold,* even in Aldar springtime.

Frazer was pulling clothes on fast. He snapped out, "What can you tell us?"

"Getting in is easy. They don't even lock the outside door," Adrianna answered. "The only issue is that once you get inside, they've got a dampener—"

"Dampener? As in magic?" Liora asked as she dressed in a whirl.

A short nod in reply. "It was like being smothered. I couldn't scent which room was which, so I chanced it and knocked on a random door." Adrianna braced a fist on her hip and watched me again, waiting.

"Risky," Cai commented, flashing her a toothy grin. "You could've come nose to nose with Dimitri and been speared for trespassing."

That elicited a tiny smile from Adrianna. "I was lucky. Wilder answered. His is the first door on the right, by the way. For anyone interested in that information."

I straightened up from cramming my feet into boots, and said, "Subtle," adding a sarcastic smile.

Adrianna puckered her lips, blowing me a kiss.

I snorted in mock disgust and threw on the layers: jacket, cloak, and gloves. But the temptation quickly proved too great. I had to ask. "What did you tell him about why you were there?"

"I lied," she admitted baldly. "I said I needed to see Goldwyn. He pointed me opposite and warned me that she might bite me for waking her."

Now fully clothed, Cai swept his hands through his hair—his version of brushing—and asked, "And did she?"

Adrianna rolled her shoulders carelessly and huffed. "She was a bit blurry-eyed, but this is Goldwyn we're talking about. She invited me in, and even offered me a glass of braka. I lied and said I'd come to ask whether she'd heard of kelpies at the coast. Then, when her back was turned, I took this."

She unveiled a teaspoon from her cloak pocket.

My pack's soft laughter answered back. I was still smiling when I buckled my Utemä to my waist and slipped my bag over my shoulders.

Cai's mouth formed a devilish smile. "Congrats. Fourth trial down."

Adrianna's brow knotted, causing the tattoos lining her forehead to contort. "I still want to try to steal from Mikael or Cecile."

"You're insatiable," Cai said, mirth sparkling in his eyes.

I could almost hear him crying out, Go on—flirt back.

All he got for his efforts was a scowl. "One of you should take it."

She held the spoon out, waiting. No one took her up on her offer.

"Come on." Adrianna thrust it toward us again. "Someone should have it."

Liora stepped into her boots and said, "Keep it for now. If we get to the last trial and one of us needs it, we can use it then."

Adrianna wavered, then moved to grab her quiver, bow, and bag from the foot of her bed. Strapping everything tight, she closed the distance between us and offered me the spoon. "Put it in my bag, will you?"

She spun. I tucked it in and in the next heartbeat, Adrianna was facing me. "Time to go."

I gave her a tiny nod. A flutter—no, more like a rutting storm—of anxiety roiled, knotting my guts up.

"We'll walk you out," Liora offered.

My stomach dropped an inch. Adrianna led the way, and Frazer, Cai, and Liora went with us. Outside, a springtime chill, and the sun's first light greeted us, brightening the sapphire sky.

Adrianna tilted her chin up and spread her wings, basking them in the warmth.

I felt a tiny ping of jealousy.

Be careful. Frazer's mental voice was hushed.

A lump rose in my throat as I faced the people we were leaving behind. Frazer refused to hug or even touch me. He left that to Liora. "We'll see you soon," she said, pulling me into a tight embrace.

I squeezed back, hard.

She released me and moved away. There was no window into each other's souls—no kin bond—but we didn't need it. Liora had everything she wanted to say written on her face. *I'll miss you. Come back safe.*

I hoped she saw how much it meant to me. How much *she* meant to me.

She gave me a knowing smile.

Cai tackled me into a one-armed hug. "Don't die."

I winced a bit at the forced playfulness in his voice and ducked out from under his brotherly hug.

"You either," he shot over my shoulder toward Adrianna.

Adrianna made a low noise in her throat; something between a growl and a laugh. "Just don't get cocky with the kelpies, and we'll all see each other again."

I moved in close to Adrianna so she could pick me up. Her arm went under my knees and the other braced my back. "I'll try not to fly too high, but I won't have a choice once we hit the—"

"The mountains. I know."

"Bring back something hideous," Cai called out to us.

I looked over at them, the emotions sticking in my throat. "Be safe." My voice was a croak.

"Don't worry, we'll take care of Frazer for you." Liora grinned.

Frazer chuffed, indignant. And a smile touched my lips.

Adrianna didn't say goodbye. She whirled and ran, letting her wings sing with the wind. Once we were up, she hovered and slowly spun so we were facing the rest of our pack. We continued to climb like that. I didn't know if it was for me or if it was her way of saying goodbye.

Liora and Cai waved, but not Frazer.

I'll miss you.

A flicker of sadness, quickly smothered. *I know, siska.*

His words were distant now. Soon we'd lose the ability to speak, but thank the gods, the kin bond would hold strong.

Eventually, Adrianna had soared far above the camp and our friends were blurs. At least to me. She spun in mid-air and we started west, to the home of Hazel Greysand.

～

"I DON'T KNOW if it's Sapor, but there's definitely a village down there." Adrianna nodded to a spot on the horizon, too distant for human eyes.

I squinted. "All I see are trees ahead and mountains behind."

Adrianna grunted as if unsurprised. "Well, it's in the right spot, so it's worth checking out."

She wasn't wrong. Over the past two days we'd stared at the map and the tiny dot that was Sapor so many times, it felt like the image had become burned into my eyelids.

As we drew closer, the outline of the village took shape for me: russet-timbered buildings splattered with greenery, thin chains of smoke rising from chimney stacks, and the vein of a river—the pulse of the community—that rushed on by. No building dominated the others in size or grandeur. There was also nothing in the way of defensive fortification. I guessed fae villages didn't need them. And although smaller than Tunnock, it still brought back memories and forced a gut-ache. Not for the first time, I wondered what John and Viola were doing.

"I'm going to start my descent now," Adrianna warned, a glimmer of tiredness undercutting her words. Hardly surprising. Two days of almost non-stop flying had to take its toll. Especially with a passenger and supplies thrown on top.

Adrianna shifted into a glide and did a final circle of the village. I tried to ignore the unpleasant lurch of my stomach as her body readied for descent by tilting back, and her wingbeats grew heavier and more labored.

A familiar and welcome thump shuddered through me as Adrianna's feet hit the ground. She put me down. Finding my legs felt stiff and numb, I stretched and shook them out to get the blood flowing.

Once recovered, I did a sweep of the immediate area. We'd landed on a dirt path. On the right was the forest, home for towering evergreen trees and a musky, earthbound scent. To the left was a house with a mossy roof and a tiny garden jammed on the side.

"Should we knock on doors?" My heart beat just that bit faster.

Adrianna met my eyes with a frown. "Let's walk around first. Witches often advertise their services. There might be a sign up somewhere."

She started down the trail in a loping stride. I tried to keep up, but she outpaced me with every step. Rounding the side of the building, we came upon a row of cottages on the right. All had blooming gardens filled to bursting; poppies, lilacs, daffodils, and sunflowers smiled back at me. A female with blue wings stepped out of a house near the end of the row. Her red hair caught the sun, reminding me of Liora, forcing me to question what the rest of my pack might be up to right now. Were they safe?

My anxiety ticked up a notch.

We made straight for the strange female. By the time we'd reached her, she was shutting the gate in the ivy-strewn wall enclosing a garden. Adrianna greeted her.

"Excuse me, I was wondering if you'd know where we could find Hazel Greysand?"

The redhead's grip on the gate tightened; she turned slowly, her square jaw lifting an inch. "Can't you just leave her alone? Haven't you lot harassed her enough?"

Adrianna and I exchanged fleeting looks. Huh?

"You must have us confused with someone else," Adrianna started. "We've never been here before—"

The fae's face became even colder, harsher. "Maybe not, but your *cohorts* have."

Adrianna's eyes tapered to points. Spotting the warning signs that a barbed comment was imminent, I interceded. "Like my friend said, you're mistaken. It was another witch who sent us here. She thought Hazel might be able to help me."

The female's eyebrows rose in surprise, but the lines around her mouth didn't soften. "Which witch was that?"

Adrianna was now glaring at the fae in open contempt. "Maggie OneEye."

The female was shorter than us. Maybe that's why her posture shifted as she stretched up to her full height and said, "I know the name, but I still don't see why I should help you."

A faint growl ripped free from Adrianna. Before teeth could start snapping, I stared right into the redhead's eyes. "Please. It's life or death."

The fae's head crooked to the side. She gave me a blank look that made my chest tighten.

After a tense moment, the stranger jerked her chin to a standalone cottage directly ahead.

Its structure was made from similar chestnut-colored timber, but it had white and purple starflowers growing up its walls, lending a speckled appearance. Its herb-covered front garden wrapped around to the back and overlooked the forest beyond.

"You'll find her there." Without another word, the female marched off in the direction we'd just come from.

Adrianna stepped back and gestured up the row. "You first."

My toes curled.

"I'll be right behind you."

I nodded distantly.

Go on. Nothing to fear.

Auntie's words settled in, loosening, unleashing. I straightened, shaking my shoulders. And with curled fists, I strode up the path and through the gate. I knocked. No answer.

"Try again?" Adrianna suggested from behind me.

I tried again, this time a little louder.

Still no answer. An itch to bang on the door erupted. Where was she? Adrianna grasped my elbow and pulled me around gently. "We can come back."

"No." That got me a disapproving look, but I continued. "I'm staying, but you should go. We didn't find anything on the way here, and we can't afford to hold off on the hunt anymore."

She didn't say no, but she released my arm, her lips scrunching up at the sides. The same look Viola got whenever she was contemplating saying no.

"I can look after myself." My chin went up a touch.

Stars bless her, Adrianna said, "I know that, but what are you going to do? Stand here and wait?"

"Yes."

Her lip quirked at that.

"You go—find us something to hunt."

I waved my hand and smiled, hoping she bought the fake confidence.

Adrianna nodded, lips pursed. "All right. I'll be back in about two hours, but that redhead seemed wary of us, and we don't know why. So don't go wandering."

Not likely. "Okay."

Her long braid swung as she whirled around. A few bounds and she was up into the dove-colored sky. Watching her soar over the labyrinth of trees, my stomach clenched. Instinct pushed me to reach for the bond. There was the faintest spark of a life at the other end. No emotion; more like an echoing whisper or an ember in the fire. I held on, anyway. It calmed me, at least for the first few minutes. Soon, however, my impatience swelled, and my feet needed to move. I circled the house, checking each paneled window. No luck—Hazel had her curtains drawn. Once I'd completed a loop, I went to knock again.

"She's not there," a voice said from behind me.

I spun around. It was the female we'd seen earlier.

"Where is she then?"

The redhead gestured toward the forest. "She headed out this morning."

Damn.

"If you knew that, why didn't you tell me?"

"Because I don't want you hassling her," she said coldly. A hand on her hip, she paced toward the gate. "The work she does for the village is too important. My son would've died if not for her."

With the tether on my temper fraying, I retorted, "I told you, we're not here to bother her. I just need her help."

The female looked away, her mouth shaping a grim line.

Distrustful much?

"Marcy, what's going on?"

The silvery voice belonged to a female. She appeared from around the side of Hazel's house; she must've come from the woods behind. I scanned her features greedily. She had long ebony hair with generous streaks of silver, and a lined face that still carried the remnants of great beauty. The wings at her back were a dark purple—almost black. She carried a wicker basket filled with fungi and clippings from herbs. The clothes she'd chosen were simple and practical; beige trousers, a floaty white top, and worn leather boots. Nothing like Maggie, who'd embraced more elegant fashions with heavy robes.

I put two and two together. "You're Hazel?"

I was buzzing with excitement ... and fear.

The lithe female gave me an appraising look. "Perhaps. Who are you?"

A haughty tone. Yet, I thought I detected real curiosity.

I glanced over at Marcy, hoping she'd get the hint. She crossed her arms in a silent challenge.

Marcy was becoming a real pain in the ass.

Suppressing my irritation, I looked again to the elder female. Her delicate lips coiled in what appeared to be droll amusement. Deciding to drop the pretense, I asked, "Can we talk alone?"

The female looked me up and down, and with the smallest of smiles, pulled her basket a little higher, and said, "To answer your previous question, yes. I am Hazel Greysand."

My heart thudded painfully. "You are?"

She walked around to her gate and gestured to the green door behind me. "You may go in."

Marcy gave me another disapproving look. Ugh.

"It's not locked," Hazel informed me. "I'll follow in a moment."

Not wanting to give her an excuse to change her mind, I spun and walked straight into her cottage. I didn't bother closing the door behind me.

I was standing in a fire-warmed living room with a kitchen in the top-right corner. Pale wood furniture and sage-colored walls gave the space a welcoming feel—almost homely.

Biting my lip, I looked over my shoulder and glimpsed Hazel and Marcy talking in hurried, hushed tones before an errant wind pushed the door closed. I went to pull on the doorknob—it wouldn't open.

Panic punched into my chest.

I swept the room, looking for another exit.

Opposite wall.

I was halfway across the room when Hazel walked in. She snapped the door shut behind her, saying, "Sorry about that."

I gestured wildly at the door, and my voice wobbled. "Why did you just lock me in?"

Hazel let out a caw. "I didn't: the house did. It can be very rude when it wants to be."

Wait ... what?

"The house has its own reasons for doing things. It might not trust you yet."

"Yeah, well, the feeling's mutual."

I flinched and leaped about a foot as a waterfall of soot fell down the chimney.

"Well, if you'd rather leave, feel free," she drawled and angled her head back to the door.

"No," I replied instantly. "I want to stay."

She shrugged, nonchalant. "As you will."

She moved to her right where a kitchen had been fitted. Placing her hamper on the counter, she started to pull out various fungi and offshoots.

What now? How did I begin this conversation? Would she even welcome my seeking her out? What if she—or the house—took offense and locked me in again? Because protector or not, if she was the Priestess, she'd be dangerous. Not someone to mess with.

"Why don't you sit down?" Hazel said as she continued puttering around the kitchen, putting various herbs in jars.

An armchair and a sandy-colored couch sat in front of the hearth, both moth-eaten and tattered. I chose the couch. I dropped my bag to the floor, unbuckled my sword, and went to sit. Springs squeaked and groaned, and now, with my knees up to my ears, a wheezing cough sounded. I could've sworn it came from beneath me.

I tried to stand. And failed.

Hazel's eyes found mine for a brief second. "Don't worry, it's just the couch. He's very old; he gets a bit wheezy when someone sits on him."

My breath caught, and my spine prickled; she didn't seem to be joking.

It provoked another careful scan of the room; five bookcases were lined up next to one another behind me, all outfitted with more books than I could count. Every spare bit of wall space had been taken with paintings and illustrations, mostly murals. A collection of memories amassed over centuries of living, presumably. There were also three other doors at each wall, a strangely ornate hat rack, and the kitchen held six cupboards, an icebox, a lit woodstove, and a large array of brightly colored teapots.

There was nowhere for a prankster to hide.

I looked down at the couch again and frowned.

Hazel left the kitchen space and walked over to the armchair. It wasn't backless, which surprised me, given her wings. She settled down and dipped so low, it appeared the seat was eating her. Casting a lazy gesture toward me, she said, "Relax. You've nothing to fear from Salazar —he's just a sprite who, for some reason, decided that my couch was the perfect place to rest his weary soul. Also, if you hear the hat rack or the hearth playing up, just ignore them too."

That did *not* make me feel better. I knew little enough about the different sprite species, but what beings lived in couches, hat racks, and hearths?

Hazel must've guessed my next thought, because she said, "Don't get up. He likes the company. You'll offend him."

I stared open-mouthed as Hazel extended a hand to a glass dish atop the low table in front of us. "Help yourself to some candied almonds."

"I'm fine, thank you."

It was difficult to shake the wariness. Thankfully, she didn't insist; instead she moved to perch on the fringe of the chair. Her back as straight as a rod of iron, her clear gaze settled on me, piercing me like a thousand shards of glass. "Perhaps you'd care to explain why you and a female fae sought me out? Marcy seemed convinced you were more spiders sent by Morgan to harass me, but—"

My nails punched down into the couch. "Morgan's assassins come here?"

Salazar let out a little groan. Hazel's brow creased. "Be careful, you'll ruin his upholstery."

My nails retracted a little. "Sorry."

Hazel cocked an eyebrow. "From your reaction, it would seem that Morgan did not, in fact, send you."

"I'd die before I worked for her."

An unreadable expression crept over her face. Maybe grief and rage combined? "A treasonous statement—you want to be more careful."

I tensed. *Rutting hell*, what had possessed me to send Adrianna away?

A long-suffering sigh escaped her as if she knew I was questioning her loyalties. "It is not, however, a crime in this house. The spiders have never stepped foot in my home. They never will." A whisper that promised violence.

Still, best to get this conversation over with. I braced myself, and asked, "Can you make sure no one's listening?"

Hazel didn't seem surprised at my request. "You've obviously had dealings with witches before, so let me assure you that this house has long been warded against fae hearing and sensory spells. I'd never attract any clients if it wasn't—particularly females of your age."

"My age?"

She gave me her first warm smile. "Yes, it's usually birth control or a love potion. Is that why you're here?"

Gods. *Birth control.* This woman was likely responsible for changing my entire life. That was what she thought?

That idea alone was enough to spur my blood, lending me the courage to drag the necklace out from under my cloak. "Do you remember me now?"

Confusion. Then ... A horrible recognition pressed in as she stared at the droplet, transfixed. Hazel's hand came to rest on her throat and she blinked, wide-eyed. A ghost had taken her place. She croaked, "Did Sati send you?"

I eyed her narrowly. "Who's Sati?"

Hazel pulled a face. As if I were mad. "Your mother."

My heart was beating so fast: too fast. "Her name was Sarah."

Hazel snorted and sprang up; the armchair released an audible sigh. Gods, was everything alive in this house? She placed a hand on the fireplace and stared into the hearth for a second, looking distant.

Dead. Silence.

Finally, something clicked under her features and she met my gaze, sadness etched into her face. "Are you here alone because your mother's gone?"

A nod. That was all it took for a tidal wave of grief to barrel into me—

unexpected and unwanted. My vision blurred and lowered to the floor. I sucked a steadying breath in, out, in, out.

"Serena?"

My chin lifted. "How do you know my name?"

Hazel continued. "Your mother told me that's what she was going to call you ... I'm so sorry for your loss. I only wish I could've been there."

"It's fine. She passed when I was six. I barely remember her."

Liar. Now I'd done it. A deluge of fat, salty tears ran down my cheeks; my chest shuddered as I tried in vain to keep the sobs locked inside.

"Would a song cheer up the mistress?" I heard from behind.

A mousy squeak passed my lips.

"Not right now, Hatty. Don't mind the hat rack. She's got a terrible sense of timing."

Salazar's springs groaned as Hazel's weight settled on the couch. She wrapped her strong arms around me. A motherly hug. I cried harder, hiccuping, "So—so—sorry."

Hazel clucked. "Don't be silly. Here ..." Releasing me, she dipped into her linen pants pocket and handed over a hanky.

Aside from the occasional sympathetic clucking sound from Salazar, I mopped my face up in silence. Once the honking and sobbing had receded on my part, Hazel returned to her seat. "I'd like to hear your story ... Serena." She said my name with a smile.

I shook my head and bit my lip. "I came here for answers."

Hazel was quiet but forceful. "You shall have them, but I must hear how you came to be here. What you already know."

A harsh, weak laugh broke free. "I don't even know where to start."

Hazel gave me a thin smile. "From the beginning."

My story—warts and all—poured out. I didn't expect it to be so hard. Showing Frazer had been easy, in a way. No need for explanations.

A decorative clock above the fireplace marked the time; my sorry tale took twenty minutes to relay. When Hunter and Kesha finally came up, Hazel interrupted with a mighty huff. "Wild Hunt, indeed. A fancy word for slavers. Morgan always did have a flair for narrative."

I felt awkward telling her the next part. About how Hunter had helped me and become a friend—sort of. I needn't have worried. She hardly reacted. Neither did she so much as blink at my revelations regarding Auntie or the trials. The only sign of alarm came upon hearing about the eerie and the magic now in my system. I finished with our trip to Maggie OneEye, and that we'd used this quest as an excuse to seek out the Priestess—her.

Now finished, Hazel's face had grown pinched and lined. "You must hate me."

What could I say? "I guess it depends."

She cawed, "An honest answer. Before we continue, d'you wish to wait for your friend—this Adrianna—to be with you? Because I must warn you that what I have to say will be difficult to hear."

My belly crawled with nerves. "Just ... tell me."

She closed her eyes. As if in pain. "I suppose I should start with why I'd strip a babe still in the womb."

She reeked of guilt. No wonder: in the *womb?* My mother *must've* known then, and lied about everything, even her name. To me. To her husband. The world got kicked out from under me. Off-kilter, spinning, I clutched my stomach and collapsed farther back into the couch—into Salazar.

Hazel continued. "First, it was your mother's decision to remove her magic, and through her, yours."

I blurted out, "So, my mother had her own magic?"

A quick nod had a shudder climbing my spine. I'd tangled with the thought of her as a witch, but to have it confirmed ... That was something else.

The Priestess went on. "The only reason she tracked me down here was because I was more well-versed in such spells. I only agreed to perform it to protect you both from Morgan."

My stomach flipped over again and again. That meant ... "My mother was here—in Aldar?"

Hazel let out a small, sad sigh. "Sati was born here."

My screaming pulse pounded in my ears as I dared to ask, "And stripping my magic was the only way to protect us from Morgan?"

Hazel tipped her head, assessing. "Think of it like this: all magic leaves a footprint—something that can be tracked by a skilled witch-hunter, or the right scrying spell. And Morgan was not only a prodigy, she was utterly dogged in her pursuits. My strongest wards and protections wouldn't have lasted forever, so we needed to do something extreme. Something that obliterated all magical trace and exiled you to land that, at least back then, was out of Morgan's reach."

Hazel paused, rallying. One heartbeat in time was about all I could manage before urging her on. "How did you meet my mother?"

The Priestess's brown eyes cut through me. That *look* told me this was would be difficult to hear. Shit, shit, shit.

"I met her through your father, who I'd been married to for a time. Thankfully we'd gone our separate ways when they found each other, and we were able to remain friends." A sad tilt of the mouth.

Well. That was unexpected. "What ..."

Nope. I couldn't even finish a sentence. Breathe in, out, in, out.

Had Maggie sent me to a madwoman? An imposter?

My father *couldn't* have been born in Aldar. The whole village had known him since he was a babe. A Tunnock man, born and bred. I needed to clarify. "You went to the Gauntlet? You risked marriage to a *human?* To a blacksmith?"

Hazel was a picture of compassion. "My husband was no blacksmith. And I've never set a wing in the Gauntlet."

So what, now my father had a secret life, too? I was dizzy, nauseous.

"Your father's name was Dain Raynar. At the time of your conception, he was both seer and leader of the Crescent; otherwise known as the Witch King."

A physical blow to my core, pushing me down, down, down.

I shook my head with vigor. "No. His name was Halvard."

Hazel's voice was gentle. "Halvard wasn't your father, Serena. Sati was already pregnant when she fled Aldar. He cannot be your sire."

Some distant fragment of my soul resonated, ringing with that truth. A dread, heated and fierce, rose from belly to heart to throat as I opened my mouth. "My mother—*Sati*—left this Dain and then married another man ... What was my father—what was Halvard to her? Just a convenience? Someone who could be tricked into raising another man's child?"

My lips trembled; I clamped them together. Over the years, my mother's memory had been a source of comfort. Now, that had been blown to smithereens, and the loss was more than I could bear.

Hazel didn't seem all that sure of herself as she went on. "I can't speak for your mother or what she felt for Halvard. But she couldn't have tricked him. Your mother was two months pregnant when she met with me to perform the spell. She would've been showing by the time she reached your village. No man, unless he were a simpleton, would fail to realize the child wasn't his."

I wasn't sure whether to laugh or cry. "He knew ..."

"Yes. He raised you and married your mother, anyway."

An upsurge of love and pride flooded me. "He kept us safe."

I got a nod in response. "And as for abandoning Dain, he was the one desperate for your mother to strip your magic and flee."

My mood took another fierce nosedive. "Why didn't he go with her?"

"You were conceived at a very volatile time. Morgan was still only a witch in the Crescent, but she was quickly gaining in power and control by stirring up the fae with half-truths and promises of more freedoms— in particular, breaking the barrier between our realms and re-establishing our so-called rights to seize human slaves. Dain was opposed to that, so he stayed—to keep fighting."

I wasn't sure what to feel, or what to think. "Dain was a seer. Couldn't he predict that she'd win?"

"The sight doesn't work like that. Visions are notoriously fragmented and difficult to read." Looking gloomy, Hazel braced her chin against a propped hand. "Although saying that, he foresaw what would've happened if Morgan discovered your mother was pregnant. It's what finally convinced Sati. It's the only reason she left his side."

She broke off. As if waiting for me to prompt her. As if unclear whether she should continue.

"Tell me all of it. Tell me everything."

Those words sounded distant, even to my ears.

Hazel sucked in air through clenched teeth. "Morgan would've tortured Sati with you inside her to break your father to her will. And once she'd given birth, Morgan would've separated you from your mother to raise you as her own, all to see what your parents' bloodlines had gifted you with. Dain was strong: some might say unyielding." Her face showed the faintest trace of a smile. "But the sight of that would've destroyed him. He would've surrendered; given her anything. Then, she'd have got what she really wanted."

Anger and a burning hatred leeched into my bones, filling every pore. Morgan was a monster. As if I'd needed more proof. "Which was?"

Hazel's eyes glazed over. Bitter memories? "For Dain to name her as his successor to the High Witch throne. Then, tell her how the barrier between realms worked."

Something clicked. "Dain discovered how to breach the barrier before Morgan. That's how my mother made it to the Gauntlet all those years ago, wasn't it?"

Hazel smiled briefly. "Not quite. Dain was the one who erected the barrier to prevent fae *and* humans massacring one another. That sneaky bastard designed the gate with a loophole and entrusted the secret to Sati. She never told me what it was, only that he wanted her to use it if he lost to Morgan." She heaved a sigh weighted with sorrow, a true heartache. "Which, of course, he did."

Whoa. My hands went up, palms flat. A signal for her to stop. "What are you talking about? The High Priests in the Gauntlet created the barrier."

"Is that what they've been telling you all these years?" Hazel *tsk*ed and added, "Then, you've been lied to. Dain told those human *priests* and the royal family of Undover what he intended, but they never lifted a finger to help him."

My mind fumbled with this new information. "Even if that's true, Dain would've had to be alive centuries ago."

"Four, to be exact," Hazel corrected. The corners of her mouth tightened as she held my wide-eyed gaze. "Serena, your sire was a fae. So was your mother. You are a full-bloodied faeling from two ancient bloodlines. The Aldarian light magic now in your veins comes from them. From your ancestors. That's why your human body can hold it without disintegrating. Because the necklace not only held your magic, but a drop of your fae blood. Both now flow in your veins, thanks to this Auntie."

Such silence in my mind. Blankness. A hollowed-out bit of air punched out of me. "That's impossible. Look at me." I bared my teeth and tapped my shoulder. "No fangs. No wings."

Hazel had an explanation for that, too. "Both yours and your mother's bodies were altered during the spell to strip you both. Just another way to avoid detection and protect your true natures in the Gauntlet."

My mouth was a desert of burning sand. "This isn't …"

I couldn't form thoughts. Let alone words.

Fear fired in my gut as another thought came to pass. "What happened to Dain? Did he crack and tell Morgan how to cross? He must've done, right?"

Hazel suddenly looked as ancient as she undoubtedly was. Her expression flat and dead, she went on. "No, Dain died on the battlefield soon after your mother left the Crescent. I was with her when … we received the news. Her—*our* only solace was that Morgan failed to capture and question him."

My chest swelled with emotion. "But Morgan *still* found a way to send fae through to the Gauntlet."

With a tiny nod, Hazel added, "Yes, but not until years after your father's death."

My father … "He's truly dead?"

Hazel's voice cracked. "We were told Dain faced Morgan on the battlefield and won, but he showed mercy and hesitated for a second too long … Morgan seized upon that weakness and murdered him."

Thoughts scattering to the four winds, I scanned the room. Maybe for an escape route. Maybe for a distraction. This was too much. It didn't help that Salazar had started cooing, making the whirlpool of confusion and rage and sorrow feel somewhat absurd.

A croaky clearing of the throat had my gaze swiveling back to Hazel. "There's something else," she began. "It doesn't make up for losing your parents, but it's something you might be happy to learn."

I doubted that, but I said, "Go on."

"Your mother was a widow when she met Dain. She'd been married previously, to a male named Lycon II, King of the Solar Court."

A part-whimper, part-groan escaped me. "My mother was a queen?"

"For a time. And—"

A murmur of hysterical laughter escaped me. "*And?*"

Hazel's eyes shone. "They had a daughter. Sefra, the former queen—"

"I know who that is." I sounded sharp and brittle, even to my ears.

Hazel seemed to be waiting for my true reaction. I didn't have one. Numb and exhausted—that was all I could manage. A sister. I had a half-sister.

A memory—a distant echo from my time with Hunter—made me say, "Didn't she flee her court to avoid fighting Morgan?"

Hazel's lips thinned. "Most fae believe that, yes."

A lie. This was just another truth that came to me, whispering to my blood. "That's not right though, is it." My voice went up at the end, but it wasn't a question. Not really.

Hazel gave me a wan smile. "No. But Sati never told me where Sefra went. Only that your sister was searching for a way to defeat Morgan, so that you'd be safe. So that we all would."

My heart was in my mouth. A sister I'd never met—maybe would never meet—had done that for me. A tear slid down my cheek, leaving an icy trail in its wake. My mother hadn't even told me she existed. My voice was faint as I said, "Couldn't she have told me something? *Anything?*"

I didn't need to clarify who "she" was.

Hazel's face slackened with sympathy. "You were only six when Sati passed. She would've explained everything once you got older and it came time to return."

My voice became even weaker, wobblier. "Return?"

Hazel crossed her legs, clasping her hands. Like this was what the conversation had been building up to this whole time. "Sati never intended for the exile to be permanent. She never wanted to take your magic or birthright—that's why she sought to preserve it. And she *always* planned on coming back to Aldar once you reached adulthood. I can only imagine your mother's torment, not knowing what had happened to Sefra or her people in the meantime."

And would she have just left Halvard—my father—behind? I suppose I'd never know, so I asked a question she could answer. "Wasn't that risky? I mean, did she look so different as a fae that no one would recognize her if we came back?"

Hazel looked over to her right and stood. She spoke while walking over to the opposite wall. "No, but perception's a powerful thing. And many aren't even aware that appearing, or *becoming* human is possible. Unless you're a skin changer and few, if any, of those still survive."

She stopped and reached up to a painting—one of the few portraits. My heart slammed against my chest and a fizzing sensation claimed my stomach. Hazel pulled the canvas down and strode over with it clenched in hand.

She offered me the painting. I took it with trembling hands, scanning greedily. There wasn't that much difference: the same brassy brunette with green eyes and angular features. Obviously the amethyst wings were new, but it was still her—still my mother, the woman who'd died all those years ago. My fingers traced the outline of her features without thinking.

Hazel spoke. "You remind me of her a lot, you know?"

I glanced up to find her eyes moving between me and the portrait, smiling.

"I look nothing like her," I said. My mother had been beautiful, for one thing.

She wore a sad smile. "Oh, no. You're the spitting image of Dain. He had hair the color of a raven's feathers and a brooding brow, too. All the females were mad for him. But how you carry yourself ... your expressions; they're pure Sati."

I was only half-listening because my very soul had caught fire at her words. I reluctantly put the painting aside and picked up a short strand of hair hanging by my temple, examining it. "My mother loved this color. She used to call it a raven's black."

My gaze lifted to Hazel's. She was blinking. A lot. "I'm sure she saw Dain every time she looked at you. I only wish you could take her portrait with you."

So did I. But it would never fit in my bag. A blossoming ache in my heart spread through my body like an ink blot atop a piece of parchment. A weighty grief settled upon my shoulders, and my hand lowered to the droplet. "Why didn't she use the power in here to save herself?"

Hazel went to sit back in her armchair. "I'm afraid your mother lied to her friend, Viola, because the necklace was never an heirloom. A colony of undines—water sprites—gifted it to Sati at Lake Ewa. That's where the spell was performed on you and your mother. It was there that the undines told us the droplet could only hold so much power, so we chose to protect the essence of *your* gifts and fae blood. Whereas, your mother had to live with losing those parts of herself to the void forever. She couldn't have used the magic within if she'd tried. We never even understood if the necklace had power on its own or if it was simply a receptacle for yours." She continued, gesturing to me. "For instance, I don't know who this Auntie character is of yours."

My mind felt on the brink of spilling over into madness. I rested my elbow against the armrest, cupping chin in palm. With the other hand, I twirled the droplet between my fingers. Panic pushed me to say, "Maggie said I couldn't channel my magic." Her warning sounded in my head as I added, "But that you could help—you could stop it from destroying me?" I risked a glimpse then.

Hazel was slow to react, but she nodded, thank the gods.

"It won't be easy though," she said, her brow lines creasing deeply.

I almost laughed. Of course not. Why would it be?

Hazel's wings rustled as she sat a tad straight. As if preparing herself.

"I'm sorry to say this, but I don't know why you can't access your magic."

My mouth popped open.

Hazel raised a hand and said, "*However,* my guesses are usually better than most when it comes to magic. And I sense this has more to do with the necklace than the fact you're human. It may be blocking you intentionally. Perhaps, if you don't use your gifts, then the strain on your human body is lessened. Could you ask this Auntie if I'm correct?"

I blinked stupidly. *Auntie—*

Heed the Priestess's words.

As vague as ever. Nevertheless, I repeated them to Hazel who simply nodded.

"Good. Then, there's a way to save your life."

Baffled, I said, "There is?"

"We'll have to switch you back. To make you a fae again. Sati and I had always intended that for you. This only makes changing you all the more urgent."

The bottom dropped out of my stomach. "You can do that?"

"Fortunately, yes," Hazel finished with a dull-edged smile.

A feeble huff escaped. "It doesn't really feel like a good thing."

To become a fae—to grow wings—wouldn't that be extraordinarily painful?

Holy shit. *Wings.*

Hazel's lips puckered. Disapproval. "It's better than dying." She continued bluntly. "Because that drop of fae blood in your veins isn't enough to keep the likes of bound light magic at bay forever. Your human body *will* crack under the weight of it. It's just a matter of when. To be frank, I'm surprised you haven't already started to feel the strain. The necklace's protective magic might be in part to thank for that, too."

Frustration made me force out, "All right, so what do we do? How do I switch back?"

"We must return to the lake, with the necklace." Hazel's eyes darted to the door. "We're about to have company."

"What? Who?"

I went to jump up, but the damned couch foiled me again.

"Don't bother. I'll go."

Hazel stood and crossed the room. She got to the entrance just as a furious knocking began. I pitched forward to get a clear view as she opened the door.

"Adi?"

Adrianna caught sight of me, and a panicked expression melted away into relief.

Hazel stepped aside. "You'd better come in," she said, sounding like she had a head cold.

Not very welcoming; I couldn't fathom why.

Adrianna moved over the threshold in a slow, careful movement. The two females eyed each other for a moment too long.

Predator on predator.

Adrianna broke the tension first by blurring across the room to me. "Are you all right?" she asked, kneeling, looking me over as if searching for injury.

"Yes ... Sort of." I sighed and tried changing the subject. "Did you find anything to hunt?"

"No—what's wrong? Your scent reeks of grief and fear." Her voice was urgent, adamant.

There'd be no hiding from this; she wasn't Liora, who would've waited for me to be ready. Adrianna had a zero-bullshit policy.

How did I explain this? Should I even tell her?

Of course, Auntie butted into my thoughts.

Adrianna seized my chin to where it had drifted—to my knees—and dragged my eyes to her.

I couldn't face the explanation. "Hazel will have to tell you."

I yanked my chin away and collapsed backward into the sighing sofa.

Adrianna's eyes went wide and flitted about the room. "What was that?"

"There's a sprite in the couch."

My voice sounded small, defeated.

Adrianna stood and turned to Hazel. "What's happened? What have you told her? Tell me."

The Priestess watched us from the kitchen, leaning against a countertop, wearing a grave look. "Serena, if you want me to explain, then I will. But I'd be careful about placing your trust in this one."

Adrianna's spine stiffened in response: a defensive maneuver. There was pride in her voice as she said, "We're pack—she can trust me with her life."

That empty, cold hole in my chest warmed just a little.

Hazel's reply was a little too calm given that her eyes were glowing with ire. "Does she know who you are? Does she know your kin name?"

I sat up straight and blinked. "What's she talking about?"

Adrianna's fists curled into tight, tight balls. "It's not relevant."

Hazel's chin went up a jot. "I disagree."

"What's going on?" I asked.

Hazel's blazing eyes met mine as she said, "Her full name is Adrianna Andromeda Lakeshie. Her mother is Diana Lakeshie, who has been Queen of the Riverlands for centuries. A queen with a tarnished crown, without honor or respect since she turned her back on Sefra," she said, her voice bitter and harsh. Almost unrecognizable.

My mind was racing, skipping from thought to thought. There was one in particular that I kept returning to time and time again. *Why* hadn't she told me?

Adrianna's shoulders drooped a little, but she sounded steady, calm. "Diana is no kin of mine."

"Don't try to deceive me, *faeling!*"

Adrianna growled at that and Salazar let out a whimper.

Hazel continued. "I'd know Diana's blood anywhere. You're the twin image of her."

Hazel stared down Adrianna with a domineering glower. Some stupid fae standoff was taking place. After a strained silence, Adrianna's head lowered. A concession.

Hazel turned her back in response. Gods, was that my future? Adopting this strange, animalistic culture?

The Priestess busied herself around the kitchen, washing and slicing up the fungi she'd collected earlier, wielding the knife with such force that I had to suppress flinching. I turned away, looking up to Adrianna; her chest fluttered with shallow breath, and her eyes were glazed. All I managed was, "Is it true?"

"Yes."

A whisper that felt like a physical assault.

Adrianna sighed in frustration and twisted to face me fully. "I never said anything because I didn't want the recruits to start treating me differently. No better, no worse. Can you understand that?"

I studied her, catching a flicker—just a flicker—of the creature beneath the hard mask. To the fae so terrified of rejection that she'd hidden the greatest part of herself. To the female who looked like she was waiting in line for the gallows. There was no space in my heart for anything but honesty. "I wish you'd told us."

Something like guilt made her striking features crumple. "I would have, eventually. I just needed time."

My back steeled; my gut churned. I had to decide. "Hazel, I want you to tell her."

The angry *chop, chop, chop* sound ceased as she lowered the knife. Hazel swiveled around, regarding me for a heartbeat. "All right." No judgment. No attempt at scolding. Just cool acceptance.

Adrianna slumped down next to me, casting a suspicious glance to the couch behind, while Hazel walked over and reclaimed her armchair. Locking her spine and rustling her wings, Hazel began talking.

I tried to tune it out for one very awkward reason: my mind had put the pieces together. Adrianna was about to learn that her mother, Diana, had refused to help my sister, and had left the Solar Court to fall to Morgan. What it would do to us, I'd no idea.

Hazel continued for far longer than I would've liked. I struggled to watch Adrianna: I only peeked over once or twice. She'd settled in to a deathly stillness. My heart plummeted, my mind spun, and I thought I might be sick all over poor Salazar.

Hazel finished, and there was a painful pause. Then, Adrianna was kneeling in front of me.

A squirm of displeasure hit me at the sight. "What are you doing?"

In a broken voice, she said, "I've never forgiven my makena for the choice she made and the dishonor she brought to our name. But discovering that our greatest shame was responsible, at least in part, for what happened to you; it's too much. Can you forgive me?"

Her head bowed.

Emotion rose to the back of my throat, choking me. "You didn't make your makena do anything. You have nothing to feel ashamed about. Don't carry it, Adi. It's not your burden to bear."

She looked sadder than ever. Damn it. This was so unlike her that I could barely stand it.

A tremble caused her voice to go down an octave. "You know, I admired Sefra—hero-worshiped her, really. I chose to train as an Iko in honor of her."

Hazel sounded almost curious. "Diana couldn't have liked that."

A hollow cackle sounded. "No. She wanted me to command the armies, but after her betrayal, no one would've respected me. Many Riverlanders think our bloodline's rotten now." She paused as if waiting for Hazel to agree, but thankfully, she remained silent. Adrianna went on, her stricken gaze shifting to mine. "I've been desperate to prove to my people that our line isn't lost—that we're worthy of their respect again."

"And you will."

She shook her head. "Serving as an Iko was supposed to be a penance. My kin's punishment. Yet, it was a fool's quest; I knew that. Accepted it." Her eyes shone a little brighter. "But us being in the same pack can't be a mistake. I'm meant to help you."

Alarm and gratitude swept through me, carrying any reply far away. Adrianna stood back up and faced Hazel. "Can you really change her back?"

She nodded, a tad disgruntled.

"Is it dangerous?" Adrianna demanded.

Hazel *harrumph*ed. "Of course it's rutting dangerous, but we don't have a choice."

Adrianna wasn't done. "Obviously. But she needs to know what happens after the change."

That had every muscle tensing.

Hazel's expression became hooded and dark as she drummed her fingers on the rolled armrest. Contemplating.

My hands twisted in my lap as the silence stretched. My patience snapped quickly. "What happens?" I demanded.

Adrianna looked down at me, her expression softening. "You've got light magic. So unless you go into hiding for the rest of your life, you won't be able to stop word from getting out about you. And you see what that choice did for Liora."

Hazel's features turned sharp, inquisitive. I just felt nauseous.

Adrianna wasn't finished. "The alternative is that you use your gifts, which will draw Morgan to you like a bee to honey. She'll be desperate to capture you. All so she can try to bend you to her will."

I wished she'd shut up. My head was pounding, and it felt like Salazar was trying to give my ass a hug. All too much. Too absurd.

Adrianna was still going. This time, speaking to Hazel. "Sati's gift was sunlight. What was Dain's?"

I blinked. *Sunlight?*

Hazel was frowning up at Adrianna from her armchair, but it wasn't out of irritation. "He was blessed with moonlight *and* waterlight."

Adrianna sucked in a little gasp. "That kurpä still defeated him?"

She sounded disbelieving: horrified.

Hazel's voice rang with pure sorrow. "Morgan's power didn't just lie in abilities, but in her cunning. And she had help." A smoldering look.

The shock vanished from Adrianna's expression. The hard, commandeering mask slipped back in place. "I know. That's why our pack will protect Serena. It's why we'll go to Ewa with her."

I felt all at once touched and terrified and stunned.

The faint wrinkles around Hazel's mouth tightened. "I question the wisdom of you going. Your movements will be watched. I'm guessing your instructors, for instance, know who you are?"

Adrianna gave me a sideways look before answering, "Yes, but I'm still going with her." She continued with fervor. "And good luck stopping the other members of our pack from coming along. We stick together. Maggie told us we were destined to watch each other's backs."

She raised her chin an inch as if daring Hazel to argue. All she got was a cocked eyebrow. "Very well. Then, once you've completed the trials, you must escape and meet me at Ewa."

I showed her my palm, cutting her off. "Wait. What if I burn up before the end of these trials?"

Hazel's throat bobbed slightly. It didn't give me confidence. "We'll have to risk it and hope the necklace's power holds. After the last trial, recruits wait about a month for a posting. That'll be your window. It's usually when the fae see their families. And the humans ... say goodbye to theirs. Any sooner, and your absence will be obvious and noted. You'll be considered deserters, and you do *not* want trackers on your tail. Besides, if we're smart, we can use the sixth trial to our advantage."

A pause.

Adrianna soon filled it by huffing out a noise of irritation. "Care to explain?"

Hazel looked down and picked at her fingernails. "D'you know what the rest of the trials are?"

Adrianna beat me to it. "Of course not. Each camp guards their secrets jealously. The armies clip wings and pull nails if an instructor or recruit talks about them."

Hazel tossed her head, snorting. "Only if you're stupid enough to get caught. I'll tell you right now that Kasi's fourth trial is the only one decided by someone other than your instructors."

Adrianna and I exchanged a fleeting glance.

Hazel smiled knowingly. "I see you've already found that out. The fifth trial takes place in the arena, where you'll each battle it out with another recruit."

Shit.

Adrianna was the one to ask the obvious. "How d'you know these things?"

A sly smile lit Hazel's eyes. "I might live on the outskirts, but I've got ears and eyes everywhere. Those instructors of yours, the army brats; they all talk. Despite your faith in their discretion," she said to Adrianna. "In this case, their loose lips are a good thing because I know what the sixth challenge is, and how your pack can use it to our benefit." Her heavy gaze met mine as she continued. "If we're to return you to your natural form, we'll need spell ingredients. To be specific: the feather of a phoenix, the golden claw of a white tiger, the fire of a dragon, and the sap from a nightshade thorn. That trial's the perfect opportunity to retrieve all four items, as you're given two weeks to choose and retrieve an object or creature of power. The only snag is that you're meant to carry out the quest alone, and splitting up might be dangerous. Unavoidable ... but dangerous."

Words failed me at this point. Adrianna, thankfully, picked up the slack. "Those items won't be easy to find. Let alone ..."

My stomach knotted. If Adrianna had been rendered speechless, what chance did we have?

Hazel, however, remained stoic. "D'you honestly think I've been idle all these years?" Her shining eyes bored into mine. "Sati always wanted you to have your magic and fae body back. She told me to be ready. While I haven't dared to seek the items myself—not with Morgan sniffing about—I have pinpointed locations for all the ingredients. But this won't work unless each member of your pack contributes."

Adrianna straightened. "I can speak for our pack. We'll each go after an item."

I wasn't sure how Liora, Cai, or Frazer would feel about her speaking for them. Still, I had to appreciate the gesture.

"Very well." Hazel bolted upright and said, "Hand over the map Maggie gave you."

Adrianna dumped her bag and dragged out the bit of parchment. Hazel snatched it and crossed the room. Sandwiched in between two bookcases was a writing desk. She placed the map atop it and opened its tiny drawer to pull out a fountain pen and brush the tip. Ink bulged, and she bent over to mark the map and make notes on the back. Adrianna sat next to me while we waited. The clock showed a good five minutes passed before she called to us. Salazar bumped us off his cushions, and we walked over.

"First, in the matter of your third trial, you'll find a korgan nearby." Hazel pointed to a section of the map close to Sapor, and added, "He moved in last week. I've been planning to get some villagers together to try to oust him, but no one's been willing to go with me to face a devos."

A devos sprite. Holy fire.

Hazel's mouth turned down. "At least if your trial demands a kill, it'll be a sprite with real malice in its heart."

Adrianna shifted. As if she was uncomfortable.

"The rest of the sections circled are for each of the items we need. On the back is where I've written the information you need to find them." Hazel dragged a finger to four separate sections of the map: the Wisinder Cliffs, the Azar Forest, the Barsul Mountains, and the Attia Forest.

They were all in the Riverlands, thank the stars.

Adrianna arched an eyebrow and looked at Hazel with something resembling respect. "You really found them all?"

She got a thin smile in return. "A life's work," Hazel confirmed. "As for what happens after you've collected the ingredients—go back to Kasi. Reunite, but don't let the objects out of your sight. And complete the last trial."

"What is it?" Adrianna asked, folding her arms.

"It's another battle in the arena ..." Hazel spun to face her front door. Adrianna's eyes followed, and she did a familiar head tilt.

"What is it—"

Adrianna shushed me frantically.

Hazel cut in. "They can't hear us. But you both need to leave now. Go through the back door." She waved to our left. Looking to Adrianna, she added intensely, "Carry Serena, and keep going until you reach the korgan hollow."

Nodding and rolling the map up, Adrianna asked, "What about our scents? Will they track us?"

"They're only here to harass me," Hazel reassured. "They'll assume you're clients because that's what I'll tell them."

Adrianna made for her bag by the couch and stuffed the map back in. I was still clueless. I looked to Hazel. "What's going on?"

"Morgan's spiders are outside."

A shiver blasted up my spine.

"Don't be scared. I'm only asking you to leave to be extra cautious," she said, trying for a reassuring smile.

I didn't feel any better.

Adrianna appeared at my side with both our bags in one hand and my sword in the other. "Why is Morgan interested in you?"

Hazel regarded her coldly. "Because I refused to join her court, so she sends the vermin along to harass me."

Adrianna's brow furrowed but said nothing.

I strapped my Utemä to my hip. Both of us shouldered our bags and set toward the back door. Adrianna picked me up in one swift movement and said, "Remember, once we're out of this house, don't speak until we're out of range."

I nodded, showing just how silent I could be.

Hazel rushed forward and put her hand on the door knob. "Follow the instructions—collect the items and stick together. And once you reach Ewa, find me."

As if it were all that easy.

"If I'm not there, show the undines the necklace. Ask for their help," she ordered.

My gut seized with a sickening turn. So many words, so many responses to *that*. None of which we had time for, so I dipped my head in thanks. "We'll see you there."

Hazel flashed me a tight-lipped smile and opened the door. Adrianna gave her a respectful nod and then ran a few steps before unleashing her wings. She jumped into the air, and keeping low to the ground, headed for the tree line.

CHAPTER 22
THE MONSTER IN THE WOODS

Adrianna tore through the wildwood, though maneuvering past cloud-busting trees with no supportive wind streams wasn't an easy task. Her wings pulsed harder than ever, sending out a ripple so strong, it set boughs and thickets aquiver as we passed. I quickly succumbed to dizziness.

A steadying breath, in and out. And once again.

With my gut churning and niggling away at me, it was difficult to focus on anything else. Still, I caught glimpses over Adrianna's shoulder in between the thrumming wings; there was nothing and no one behind us, just the rousing of leaves and the song of the wind whipped up in our wake.

Eventually, we slowed and landed. I slipped from Adrianna's arms with a palatable sense of relief and immediately doubled over, sucking in the heady scent of sharp pine and rich earth: quintessential woodland.

"Are you all right?" Adrianna sounded a touch breathless.

Palms on knees, I looked up. "We can talk now?"

Wiping away the thin sheen of sweat coating her face, she said, "We're well out of range."

I straightened up. "No one followed us?"

Adrianna looked back and angled her head, listening. "I can't hear anything. But the spiders are a twisted version of the Sami—they're experts in remaining undetected. Still, there's no reason for them to come after us, other than curiosity. Let's hope our luck holds."

Adrianna gazed out into the aged forest and jerked her chin to a spot ahead. "The korgan lies that way."

I dreaded asking. "How d'you know?"

"I can smell blood. A lot of it."

It felt like I was swallowing syrup.

Adrianna's eyes darted to me. A new expression rested on her face: doubt. "D'you want to stay here? I could fly you into the treetops."

My mouth twisted into a frown. "Since when are you all right with me hiding behind you?"

Silence was my answer, so I went on. "That's not happening."

She considered me for a moment. "Fine. Then you should know that korgans are stone sprites and can kill in a single blow. So if it comes at you, don't let it land a hit. Dodge or run. In the meantime, I'll try to tackle it from the air."

My brows knotted together. "How are we even supposed to kill something like that?"

"Their eyes and ear sockets are their weakest points," she said, tapping the side of her head. "Don't bother drawing your Utemä. You'll just dull the edge or shatter the blade."

So, the sword at my waist was now utterly useless. I was useless.

"Take these." Adrianna pulled two arrows from her quiver, handing them over. "If you get the chance, stick them in its eyes or its ear holes. Worst-case scenario, find somewhere to hide and stay quiet. Korgans can't see very well."

I nodded, not trusting myself to speak.

Adrianna struck out for the hollow. I followed her long strides, roving over moss spattered earth that cushioned and silenced each step. All the while, I clutched the only weapon that might work against a stone sprite—two sticks with bits of metal stuck on the end. My bowels quickened just thinking about it.

Soon there was evidence of the korgan in the air. Adrianna had mentioned blood, but what wafted toward me on a stale breeze was far,

far worse. Grease, decay, shit, and something akin to rotten cheese suffused my nostrils.

I clapped a hand over my mouth but couldn't stop my stomach from convulsing. A sudden rush of bile left a burning sensation at the back of my throat. I couldn't be sick. Not here, not now. So I gulped and dragged my woolen cloak over my nose.

Adrianna mimicked my action, the only sign that the stench bothered her.

We continued to creep forward, and my hearing seemed to pick up on everything. From our soft footfalls, to our muffled breath, and the sighing wind.

My hands grew clammy as the smell only got stronger.

Finally, we stumbled upon a small clearing, and Adrianna raised her hand, signaling me to stop. I took in the scene and rolled away, unable to breathe. Bracing against a nearby tree's limb, my eyes burned with gruesome images of splayed ribs. It brought me right back to that night in the cage. Only that paled in comparison to the korgan hollow.

There were stretches of skin spread out carefully, and organs piled high into mounds. Deep tracks from a huge, lumbering beast marked the craggy earth, and gruesome patches of a vivid red stained the grass.

The hollow was a monument to death. The insides of creatures were sprayed everywhere. Is this all we were? Meat for the crows. Bits of flesh and bone sewn together? Pints of blood waiting to be spilled?

A hand on my shoulder.

I wheeled around, disoriented, ready to strike.

Just Adrianna. "The korgan's scent is only a few hours old, so we'll hold out in the tree tops until it gets back."

She didn't wait for my response. I wouldn't have been able to give one, anyway. Catapulting upward, Adrianna settled on a thick branch with a decent view of the clearing below. She hadn't taken any chances: at least thirty feet now lay between us and the carnage below. I was doubly grateful because the smell had abated.

Adrianna placed me down. I straddled the bough, my bag resting against the trunk, and looked back in the direction we'd just come. Anything to avoid seeing the guts and fluids spilled below.

Coward.

I shoved that spitting voice into a box and locked it tight.

Of course, Adrianna was standing and even walking along the branch, using her wings as counterweights and displaying perfect balance.

Would that be what it was like for me as a fae? No longer bound to quite so much fear, because I could always just fly away? Frazer's memory had shown me how glorious it could be to ride the skies. But to do it myself? It didn't seem real. And then there were the canines. I scraped my tongue over my teeth, imagining another set erupting there. I couldn't help it—I pushed against the pointy ends of my teeth with the pad of my thumb, testing, feeling.

Adrianna snorted delicately; it wasn't hard to guess what she'd been so amused by. I met her stare just as her head cocked and whipped to the side. She was staring down at the ground.

I gripped my arrows tighter.

It started with a few snaps, then a low rumble filled the hollow. Huffing, grunting, and a *crack.* I tried to identify the sounds without looking down. Please, *please,* let it be twigs underfoot—not bones. Please, not bones.

Not able to stand it any longer, I glanced to the forest floor.

I wished that I hadn't.

The devos sprite had shuffled in to view. It was munching on a leg; going by the enormous size, it had to be an animal. Not human. That brief twinge of relief was swallowed by the sight of what was holding the leg. A giant, misshapen boulder: the korgan.

My limbs turned to jelly as it came to a moss-bearded rock in the clearing and perched on the end. It finished the leg and shifted. The noise was horrendous—rocks grating against rocks.

I squinted and tried to hone in on its eyes. But its large, nodular head obscured them. It was obvious why Adrianna hadn't tried to shoot it down with her bow.

The korgan soon stilled, and we waited, watching.

Adrianna eventually gestured to the ground. I nodded and shifted forward. She gave me a pained look, unfurled her scaled wings, and jumped. Leaving me behind.

Shock, relief, anger—it all rushed through in one heartbeat. Did she think I wouldn't be able to help? Or was this some instinct born from guilt over our kin's shared history? Adrianna was such a gods-damned hypocrite. After the way she'd berated Frazer and Cai for being overprotective ...

Adrianna neared the korgan, and the swell of resentment drained away as quickly as it came. She landed behind the sprite's rocky mass and silently drew an arrow from her quiver. She pitched forward ever so slightly to peer around the side of its head. She raised the arrow, angling her arm up, preparing to strike.

A roar shattered the hollow.

I lurched forward instinctively as the korgan swung around with his arm outstretched. Adrianna's wings were spreading, flapping—

She wasn't quick enough to stop the sprite's gnarled stump from grasping her jacket. Adrianna brought the arrow up again, but the korgan bellowed and whipped around. It twisted in a loop and sent Adrianna flying into a pine tree. Her side got the full impact; her body crumpled to the ground.

I whimpered. The korgan roared again and beat a stone fist against its chest. It started toward her fallen body lying only a dozen paces away. She hadn't moved. It would pummel her to death and chomp on her bones.

I didn't think. "OI! YOU UGLY PILE OF SHIT! IF YOU TOUCH HER, I SWEAR BY THE DARK COURTS, THE LIGHT COURTS, AND EVERY GOD THAT EVER LIVED, I WILL SMASH YOU INTO A THOUSAND PIECES!"

The sprite stopped and slowly raised its head. I couldn't find its eyes, but I'd no doubt it was staring right at me.

"I'm right here! Come and get me!"

My voice cracked in fear as the korgan made a noise like falling rocks.

Gods. It was laughing. That couldn't be good.

I almost pissed myself as it lumbered toward my tree. Could it climb? Surely not. It reached the base, pulled back its grotesque fist, and *boom!*

A second before its punch connected with the bark, my arms wrapped around the bough beneath me. I narrowly avoided impaling myself on the arrows in my hand.

The whole tree shook as it took another pounding.

Suddenly, the sticks in my hand looked useless.

Climb down, Auntie shrieked at me.

"What?"

My mind blanked, disoriented and stunned by the pounding it was getting inside my skull.

Get down there and stab it in the ear!

I groaned as the next tremor hit the trunk.

It would soon splinter in two; I was going to die in a tree, hiding like a coward.

Not if you climb down! Auntie screamed.

My attention went to the branch below mine. Too far down. It wouldn't be a simple drop. I'd have to fall.

Better to fall a few feet than thirty, Auntie said in a rush.

I held out for the next blow.

Boom! A second lost, waiting for the worst vibrations to fade. I lifted my leg up and over. My body dangled for one precarious heartbeat. I looked down, aimed, and dropped. I landed heavily and threw my weight forward; both arrows snapped like twigs. I tried not to die inside at the sight of the shortened sticks, and kept ahold of the arrowheads while letting the fletchings fall.

The korgan's fist pounded into the trunk again. I could hear the splintering of wood. It wouldn't be long now.

The next branch down was too far to the right. My body froze, locking to the bough beneath me. I looked down to see the sprite had begun to push, shoulder-first, into the bark. I closed my eyes and clung on with every bit of strength, waiting for the inevitable fall.

The next blow hit true, and when the splintering and breaking came, it rang in my ears. As if a sentient life was being lost; a creature screaming in pain.

The tree snapped at the bottom and tipped backward. My stomach dropped away, and my breath held fast as the pine tree collided with the earth behind me: splintering, cracking.

I'd escaped being flattened or impaled. Yet, my limbs remained frozen to the branch. Shock. That's what this was.

Move!

Kinetic fire flooded my body. I slid off the massive trunk and scrambled away. Keeping low, hiding among the branches, clinging to the arrow heads, I crawled past the korgan until his back was to me. I looked down at the tiny pieces of metal.

I had a choice: attack the sprite or run over to Adrianna. The second option appealed the most. She had more arrows, and I might be able to wake her ... if she wasn't dead.

No. She'd be okay. She had to be. I batted away the parts of me that wanted to kneel, crying in the dirt.

What should I do? *Auntie?*

Listen to your instincts.

What instincts?

Silence.

Damn it. Think.

I couldn't see her body from this position. That alone almost made me sprint over. But some wild impulse urged me to abandon the easier path and look instead to the impossible one.

I spun on my knees and inched forward. Ragged stones and riven branches pierced and scraped the skin on my hands and legs. Biting back a curse, I stopped and chanced a look over the trunk.

There, the korgan; bending down, tearing apart the tree, sniffing. A shiver electrified my spine. It was searching, and when it found me, I'd be just another pile of organs for his heap.

I didn't have to attack. I could stay still and hope. That *thing* had terrible eyesight. It might lose interest. But what would it do to Adrianna once it got bored? I peered over my shoulder. I saw nothing but mangled animals and splintered boughs. Nothing but dead things. No sign of my friend.

I sucked in a deep breath and turned back around. Now or never. Adrenaline splintered my heart and flooded veins. I hurtled over the trunk and ran for five heartbeats.

Adrianna dropped from the sky, straight onto the sprite's shoulders, roaring a challenge. It barely had time to buck and rear before she was twisting, contorting her body, avoiding those massive stone fists.

Labored humming from wings, ragged breaths, and roars pitched the air.

I was still running, holding up the arrowheads, aiming.

Adrianna corkscrewed in mid-air and landed in front of the korgan. In a perfect stop-thrust, she plunged two arrows into its puny, moss-colored eyes. With a bone-shaking bellow, it fell to its knees. I skidded to a halt as the forest floor quaked.

Adrianna backed away quickly. The korgan raised a hand to its pierced eye sockets, but it didn't get halfway before pitching sideways into dirt.

I let the last shudder sing through the earth, then I moved to flank my friend.

Her face was sweaty and screwed up in pain; her hand cradled her left side.

Fine. I'd wait to shout at her for leaving me in that tree.

I stared down at the creature that had nearly killed us both. Taking in his heavy hide, I said, "Any ideas for how we get that back to camp?"

Adrianna sunk to her knees. I kneeled next to her.

She slipped her rucksack off with a wince. "You'll have to bandage my ribs. There's some gauze in there."

Opening her bag and rifling through, I asked, "What happened to your quiver and bow?"

"In pieces," she rasped out. "Colt's going to bite me."

Not a joke. "If he does, I'll set our pack on him. Cai'd be there in a heartbeat. Anything to defend your honor."

She cocked an eyebrow and regarded me in cool amusement. I'd injected it with humor, but she'd obviously heard the questioning tone.

Surprisingly, Adrianna said nothing and shucked off her cloak, jacket, and top to reveal—

"Rutting hell," I gasped.

A blossoming reddish bruise covered her entire left side.

"Be quick." She sounded breathless.

We lapsed into silence. I did my best to wrap the gauze around her ribs and over and under her shoulder. I tied the dressing, and Adrianna stayed still, staring down at the sprite for one long minute. Then she reached forward, grabbed the fletchings, and plucked out its eyes.

I suppressed a groan of disgust and was glad there hadn't been a chance to look away. I didn't want another reason for her to think she needed to protect me.

Adrianna packed away the eyes inside her bag and stood, shouldering it. Hysteria beckoned as adrenaline crashed inside me. The whole thing had taken on a surreal feel, so when Adrianna suggested we move to get away from the stench, I followed blindly.

Despite her fae blood, I wondered how Adrianna was standing or walking, given her injury. As we moved, I piped up once or twice to suggest we stop. She refused until we'd gone far enough away that the korgan's smell no longer infected the air. We took a break and ate and drank from our rations. It can't have been more than an hour or two before her breathing evened and no longer sounded like a death rattle.

Adrianna soon grew impatient. She wanted to try flying. When I objected, she said, "It's afternoon light already. I want to put some miles between us and the spiders, and the kill sight."

The stormy gray sky didn't appeal to me and neither did hurting Adrianna, but she insisted.

My heart sputtered as she grimaced upon lifting me, but we got airborne. I didn't know whether we stayed aloft because of her training or just plain stubbornness, but either way, she didn't falter. Bursting through the treetops, my eyes traveled down, watching the canopy melt away.

We'd survived, but it didn't feel like a release. Part of me remained in the hollow; fear still coated my tongue.

Dragging my gaze away, I looked toward the mountainous region we'd be passing over again. A single thought brought me back with a sickening jolt; my life had irrevocably changed, my entire world turned on its axis in a single afternoon. Soon, I'd be facing my friends—my pack. Reliving everything, asking for their help, planning a trip to Ewa.

The scale of the task ahead settled on my shoulders, a great weight pushing and dragging me down. Failing to form another coherent thought, I blanked and watched the white-capped peaks grow ever closer.

CHAPTER 23
THE THIEF

A largely silent and wholly uneventful journey back to Kasi took two and a half days. We arrived in the afternoon and reported to Bert, who took one look at the korgan's eyeballs and threw them in his fire. He waved us out, and the burning desire to see them—to be with my kin—consumed me. I bolted, sprinting for our barracks. The bond was pulling me, *tugging* me all the while. Adrianna followed and shouted something about fresh scents.

Faster. Faster.

I wrenched the door back and rushed through with Adrianna just behind me. Cai and Liora sat on one bed, facing each other. Clearly, they'd been talking; now they beamed up at us.

I didn't return the smile. Because my eyes were scanning for Frazer.

He rose from his bed. *Slowly.* Pillow creases in his hair, he stood perfectly still. An eerie fae statue.

His visage paralyzed me and simultaneously woke me up. The deadening stupor—the void my mind had collapsed under—suddenly vanished. With our gazes still locked, something cracked inside me. A fissure in some mental barrier I hadn't known existed until that moment. It let the world back in, and with it came my brother.

Serena ... Palpable relief shuddered through me.

I didn't answer as inertia continued to hold me.

A frown, concern flickering. *It's okay. Whatever's happened.*

He took a careful step in my direction. Adrianna moved to my shoulder. Frazer saw, and something unreadable crossed his face. He fidgeted, and in a guttural voice just said, "Siska."

That made me fly into his arms. A restorative balm. No hug back, but he didn't fidget or push me away. Progress then.

"What are you doing?" Adrianna's voice made me pull away from Frazer. I tried not to be hurt by the obvious relief in his expression.

I turned to see Cai's arms outstretched toward Adrianna, but her deep-set frown had them going limp at his sides. He huffed a little too loudly and ran a hand through his hair. "Just thought you might want a welcoming hug too."

"I don't do hugs," she answered flatly.

Cai cleared his throat. "Oh." His gaze caught mine, and a smile erupted. "Are you going to reject me too?"

He held out his arms again. My heart twanged at the sight and we met midway in an embrace. Liora's unique scent of roses and grass tickled my nose as she joined us.

I pulled back, asking them both, "So, how was the trial for you?"

"Oh, we passed," Liora replied mildly.

"No need to be humble, sis," Cai said, clapping her on the back.

Liora shot her brother an impish grin. "That's not something anyone could excuse you of."

"What happened?" I asked.

Cai cut in. "We captured a kelpie. Liora sang to it and acted as tasty bait while Frazer and I trapped it."

"Really?" Frazer sounded in mock surprise. "I don't remember you doing much except throwing a net over it."

Cai clicked his tongue. "A vital role it was, too."

Liora reflected my own smile back at me.

"It was close to being boring," Frazer drawled. "So ... Are you going to leave us in suspense? What happened with Hazel? Did you find her?"

My brief elation crashed and burned. I sighed through my nose. There was no hiding from this. The air grew leaden with unspoken words, and our bond strained. Silence, waiting and expectant, was on the other end.

"You smell strange." A prompt.

"Five days without a bath will do that." A vain attempt to make a joke.

Frazer folded his arms and settled into an immortal stillness that carried a warning. He wouldn't move until I'd said what was needed. I cast a sideways glance to Adrianna. I didn't even have time to open my mouth before she showed me her palms. "This is your tale to tell, Minun Katun."

Whatever she said made Frazer's face slacken. As if stunned.

I nodded bleakly. "I know."

"In your own time," Liora's gentle voice sounded.

I gave her a feeble smile and looked to Cai. "No one can hear this."

"Spell's already up," Cai said, moving to his bed. "I think I'll sit. This feels like one of those conversations."

"It is."

I perched on the bed opposite his. Liora joined my side in a show of solidarity. Adrianna and Frazer stayed standing but moved in closer. My eyes went down to my clasped hands. I started in barely more than a whisper. "Hazel *was* the Priestess."

From there I recited everything Hazel had told us as best as memory allowed. Liora gasped a few times, and Cai swore a lot. Frazer, however, remained silent. I was worried about his reaction the most. A glassy, vacant expression and bloodless cheeks rarely amounted to anything good.

I finished by telling them about the korgan. There was only one thing I'd kept quiet about—Adrianna's identity. But our pack had a right to know. So once my explanation was done, my eyes lifted to hers.

"D'you want to tell them ... your bit?" I asked.

Her blue eyes turned glacial. "Not really."

"I didn't look at you any differently," I reassured quietly.

"That's because you didn't grow up here," she muttered.

Liora made an "Oh," sound beside me. "Is this when you tell us what you've been hiding?"

Adrianna gave her a barbed look. "What is it you think you know?"

"You go quiet or deflect when any of us mention our pasts or our families. So, what's the big secret? Are you Sati's daughter too?" Liora quipped.

Adrianna snorted. "I wish. No, my kin aren't nearly so worthy." A tense pause was followed by, "Diana Lakeshie is my mother."

Liora blinked. Cai burst out, "Are you serious?"

"I'm not likely to joke about it, am I?" Adrianna used a sharp tongue.

Cai went somewhere else, his expression freezing over. Adrianna seemed more interested in Frazer's reaction though. I followed her line of sight and saw why. My brother was baring his teeth in disgust. "Then your makena's a coward and a traitor."

A nasty silence followed; I gulped down the nerves sparking in my belly.

Adrianna looked to me and angled her head toward my brother. "Now you see why I've kept it a secret."

Frazer's vicious growl rattled my bones.

Adrianna faced him and jerked her chin upward in defiance. "I don't blame you for hating her, but given your history—"

I felt the tether on his temper snap, but I wasn't fast enough to stop it. Frazer pounced. Adrianna moved half a second later. They flew at each other, snapping and biting.

Several things happened at once.

Cai threw out his inked hand, and a wind battered into the two fae but failed to break them apart. Liora started dragging me from the room while I struggled against her, yelling, "We have to stop them!"

She didn't stop pulling me toward the exit. "No, we don't. They're fae."

Hardly an explanation, but Liora was rarely so obstinate. My resistance weakened, and I let her lead me from the barracks. She didn't release me until we'd stepped outside. I turned on her, frowning. "Why did you do that? We could've helped."

Liora took a brief scan around in the afternoon glow and stepped in closer, whispering, "Trust me, you can't stop two fae fighting when their blood is raging like that. They need to get whatever that was," she gestured behind her, "out of their systems."

We stayed silent for a moment, locked in eye contact. I broke the tension first by freeing a held breath and dropping my gaze.

"Let's go for a walk," Liora suggested with a sigh. "You seem like you could use the space."

I nodded distantly and remarked, "I don't even know why he got so angry."

Liora waved for us to turn toward the arena, and we set off at a gentle pace. She was quiet as she went on. "I've lived among the fae my whole life. I still find it difficult to understand their behavior. All I can say is that many fae despise Diana. Maybe more so than Morgan."

I slowed to a snail's pace, and a confused mutter rolled out of me. "Why?"

"True friendship is almost sacred among the fae. And Diana and Sefra were close. Diana's refusal to help was a betrayal of that connection. I imagine Frazer probably feels that even more keenly. You're his kin," she added simply. "That makes Sati and Sefra his family too."

I glanced sidelong at her. She wouldn't judge. "If I'd have known how complicated our bond would make things ..."

Liora flashed me a smile as sweet as honey in summer. "You'd still have done it."

"Mm." My not-convinced sound.

Liora continued. "Because, you know he'll always guard your back. Just like Cai, and just like me. That's why you don't even have to ask ..." She looked around, checking for earwigging fae. A whisper followed. "We'll get the ingredients. We'll go to Ewa, together."

My heart expanded so rapidly and thoroughly, I could only mumble, "Are you sure?"

"Yes."

Absolute confidence resonated, warming me.

Liora halted to watch the horizon.

"What is it?" I asked, coming to a standstill.

Eyes twinkling, she pointed with her chin.

My head cut to one of the larger buildings in the camp. It stood above the row of barracks, next to the arena. All the recruits knew it housed the staff quarters. I threw her a questioning glance; she held up four fingers.

Four ... *Fourth quest.*

"We should do it now," Liora murmured. "While the camp doesn't have as many people around."

"But we haven't planned anything."

She shrugged, causing her curls to bounce. "We'll do what Adi did. Think of an excuse to visit them in their rooms and take something when they're not looking."

I looked toward the staff building again and considered how to play it. "I guess if Goldwyn isn't bothered by us going to her with questions, that's what I'll do."

Liora began carefully. "Actually, I was thinking it might be an idea for you to try with Wilder."

"Why?" Cold infused my voice with a snap. I instantly regretted it.

Liora's head tilted slightly at the tone; however, her voice was even as she replied. "Because they might not even be in. And if they haven't locked their internal doors, then you're the only recruit who could be found in his rooms and not be bitten to death."

My body went rigid. "I wouldn't be so sure."

Liora said nothing, but the words played across her face. *You know it's true.*

My mind was whirring with thoughts that all had one thing in common: *Wilder, Wilder, Wilder.*

Silently, we moved toward the staff building side by side. Upon arriving at the door, Liora gave me a look. *Ready?* she seemed to say.

I nodded reluctantly, and she opened the door oh-so-quietly. I barely heard the click as she shut it behind us.

A corridor with six doors, three on each side, greeted us. Liora went straight to the first room on the left, which, thanks to Adrianna, we knew belonged to Goldwyn. She peeked over her shoulder, her eyes traveling from me to Wilder's door and back to me, as if to say, *You know you want to.*

Liora flashed me a bracing smile and spun to tap on Goldwyn's door. Six anxious heartbeats passed before an answer came from within. "Come in." Liora tried the handle. It clicked open, and she walked through. My heart raced, watching her disappear into Goldwyn's quarters.

Jittery sparks set my gut fizzing. Not wanting to be found loitering, I took the three paces to Wilder's rooms and dithered.

Did I really want to steal from Wilder?

Yes and no.

Did I want to see him?

Maybe ... definitely.

Should I knock?

I copied Liora and tapped at the door. My nerves meant that I held out for a mere second before letting myself in. I realized a moment too late that I hadn't thought of an excuse.

I was going to need one.

Shit.

I'd walked straight into his living room: a large space with bare wooden floors and few embellishments or furnishings. A divan and three armchairs faced a brick hearth. On the opposite wall, a bay window looked out onto the gate and the rolling hills in the distance. Six or seven bookcases filled the space, but the actual books were scattered around the room in columns and piles. There were also four separate stands that held weapons. Like Utemäs, broadswords, daggers, and gods, was that a mace?

In the next blink, everything melted away. There was Wilder, standing next to the mantlepiece, a glass of amber liquid in one hand and a book in the other. He was now staring at me, open-mouthed.

"Serena?"

He snapped the book closed, and I shut the door behind me.

"Is everything okay?" he asked with a furrowed brow.

He seemed more concerned than angry.

Right. *Think!*

You really should've thought of an excuse before you barged in, Auntie said, clearly amused.

I leaned against the door, murmuring, "You're not helping."

Wilder cocked his head. Great, now he'll think I'm rude *and* crazy.

"Sorry." My voice came out calm, even. A surprise, given how my body was reacting. "Adi told me that this was Goldwyn's room."

Auntie groaned.

Wilder didn't look convinced. He chucked the book onto the divan, set his glass above the hearth, and faced me again. "So barging into Goldwyn's rooms would've been acceptable?"

"I knocked."

"Yes, I heard a tiny tap. I assumed it was a mouse scratching in the walls."

A flush of embarrassment flooded my cheeks. "I wasn't thinking."

"Clearly. Is something wrong?"

He sounded impatient, eager to be rid of me. It hurt, and maybe that's why words just spilled from my tongue. Words that ought not to be said. "I needed to talk to someone about the third trial."

Heat pricked my eyes; my voice broke. Oh, crap.

I hated myself for coming undone. And Liora for suggesting this.

But I couldn't find it in myself to leave. Then, his blurry outline moved, and his hand slipped around my wrist. Tears rolled from relief *and* real grief.

Wilder led me to an armchair. His touch was firm but not unkind as he pressed his hands on both shoulders and pushed me into a seated position. He vanished from my side.

I wiped the water from my eyes and looked around.

A door to the right of the fireplace was open. I heard clinking, and before a thought could form to steal, he reappeared, a glass of water in one hand and a handkerchief in the other, presumably for my face.

I took both from him and stared down at the white linen. Carefully stitched into the corner in red thread were the initials "WT". I wondered what the "T" stood for and whether this would count as stealing.

Wilder sat in the chair angled toward mine, his legs crossed. "So, what's this about?"

There was nothing calculated, but also little gentleness.

I had the handkerchief. There was no reason to stay and say something I'd regret. "It's not your problem. I'll go find Goldwyn."

I brazenly tucked the linen up my sleeve and put the glass down on the floor in preparation to leave.

Wilder spoke. "You're here now ... I'd like to hear what's wrong."

Interesting.

"You would?" I asked, straightening up.

Wilder's jaw tightened. "Well, I certainly can't send you on your way when you've just broken down in my living quarters."

It felt like being squashed underfoot. "I didn't plan on it."

Wilder's voice melted. "I know."

That warmed me a little.

He continued. "Are you upset about the korgan you killed?"

I blinked. "How did you hear about that?"

"Bert has to inform the instructors the minute their recruits return, and Goldwyn told me. She couldn't resist gloating about the fact you'd taken on a devos. She always was a talker," he said as his mouth quirked.

I almost laughed in relief at the sight.

He went on, more seriously. "I, on the other hand, am not. You can trust whatever you have to say will never go beyond these walls."

"Another fae won't hear us?"

I glanced toward the door and back again. A crooked mouth greeted me. "Our private quarters are warded; otherwise, we'd all have to listen to each other's nocturnal activities."

Adrianna was right then. A dampener cloaked the whole place. I strived not to think about whether he'd ever used that to his advantage.

"So?" He let that hang.

What could I say? Could I trust him? I knew next to nothing about his past. In the end, I settled for a half-truth. "I found out something about my kin when we were hunting."

His cheek scars tightened a bit, the only shock he showed. "Go on."

My mouth drained of all moisture. "It was kind of ... earth-shattering. And then, Morgan's spiders landed on the outskirts of the village we were visiting. The whole thing just shook me up a bit."

Gods. That was an understatement.

Wilder moved to the edge of his seat to stare at me unblinkingly. "You found out this information from them?"

"No, we never actually met them face-to-face."

Something flared in his eyes. Doubt, maybe. "Yet it shook you up?"

I dismissed that with a soft chuckle, weak even to my ears. "Yeah. I know it's stupid."

His gaze glued me to the back of my chair. "You're not one for empty words."

My pulse quickened.

Something horribly like recognition dawned on his face. "Serena, are you trying to tell me that your kin are tied up with the spiders ... with Morgan?" He whispered her name. Not in reverence, but fear.

My mouth popped open.

Wilder didn't even need me to answer; his voice cracked like a whip. "This earth-shattering realization wouldn't be that your kin are on the run from her, would it?"

My insides hollowed out into an icy, barren space. "No. Most of my kin are dead."

His face showed little sympathy. Instead, those piercing green eyes shifted to my throat. To the necklace.

They stayed there for five full heartbeats.

Sound crashed into my ears; it took a moment to realize it was my pulse. Then, just like that, he collapsed back into his chair. As if to create more distance between us.

He didn't seem to want to look at me as he said, "Perhaps you should keep the rest to yourself. Something tells me you're not ready to share the rest, anyway. But, I want you to know that if you were in any kind of trouble, I would help you."

"What about not being allowed to be friends?" A careful question.

Wilder stood in one quick movement, snatching the glass with the amber liquid and downing it in one gulp. Then, he turned his back on me and stared into the fire that burned low, murmuring, "We don't have to be friends for me to help you."

"I've got my pack. I'll be fine." To *not* sound like a spoiled brat, I added, "Thank you ... for offering."

"Yes—I noticed Frazer's appointed himself as your new protector."

He was so quiet.

I shouldn't have said it, but something was pushing me, driving me. "Jealous?" I asked lightly. As if I could fool him.

He set the glass down on the mantelpiece in a *slow* movement and placed both hands there, gripping the wood it was made from. He was white-knuckling it, his shoulders knotted and rigid. I waited for the denial. For the put down.

"Maybe I am," he breathed. "His scent's all over you. Did you know that?"

He remained with his wings to me, wood cracking beneath his fingers. I didn't know what made me confess; maybe it was my utter shock that he'd admitted that much. "It's not like that."

Wilder released the groaning mantle, squared his shoulders, and turned to me with a dead expression. "I'd like to believe that."

My heart was in my mouth.

"But your scents are too entangled for it to be anything else."

"We're kin," I blurted out.

His gaze slipped from mine with a stunted chuckle. "That's not possible."

I remained quiet, not moving, not backing down.

I waited … He turned to me again, scanning up and down, searching for signs of a lie. A growing unease clouded his face.

I almost denied it then. Laughed it off.

Then, his expression flipped; eyes gone wild, he rambled, "How? Are you … You look alike … are you siblings? Is Frazer a demi-fae?"

Before he could keep on losing his shit, I corrected him. "You've got the wrong idea. We weren't born kin."

That only made things worse; his face drained to a grisly white. "Then … No, please, *please,* by all the fucking gods, tell me you didn't. Tell me that you didn't make that bond with him!"

I shifted ever so slightly to the back of my chair. "We did, but—"

"Are you insane?" he hissed, his face crumpling in incredulity—in rage. "D'you have any idea what you've done? Who suggested it?" he demanded. He didn't wait for an answer before spitting out, "It was him, wasn't it? I'll rip his heart out!"

My blood roared. I reared up in an instant. "You won't *touch* him."

Seeing me glowering seemed to temper something in him. The lines of anger vanished from his face, and his mouth jerked upward in an involuntary spasm. His arm looked like it was reaching for me, but at the last second, he swept it upward and clenched the back of his neck. He looked so lost, the murderous rage drained away. That didn't stop me from saying, "Don't threaten my brother again."

And just like that Wilder slipped back into smooth, neutral tones. "He's put you in danger."

Yet despite my words to Liora, I didn't regret it. "I know other fae might not like it, but it's done now. Let the world think we're just lovers. That's not forbidden," I said, sourness coloring my voice.

Wilder didn't seem to notice. He collapsed back into the armchair. His elbows bracing against his knees, he began rubbing his forehead.

An awkward silence stretched. I sat back down again and scanned the room. Anything to stop myself watching him. It was then my attention snagged on something. Of the many books scattered around the divan and chairs, there was one in particular that pulled my focus. It was small, with a black leather cover and a gold-embossed title: *The Darkest Song.*

I tilted slightly toward it, unthinking; on pure instinct.

"I don't think you understand," Wilder said suddenly, lifting his gaze to mine.

I jerked back up.

Wilder went on in a raw, scratchy voice. "You are right, of course. Fae take human lovers. But your scents will stay merged for the rest of your lives. No matter the distance or time apart. So what happens when you become soldiers? What if you're in different encampments, sleeping in shared barracks? Other fae may wonder why a strange male's scent never fades from your body, even though you're never in the company of said fae?" He didn't wait for my response before continuing. "It's just a matter of time before someone asks questions you can't answer. Then there's Morgan ... Gods, Serena—if word ever reached her that a fae had made that vow to a human, she'd drag you both to the Solar capital—Alexandria —and interrogate you. And trust me, it won't be with words and bribes. It'll be with people and things that can snap bones, pluck out eyes, and much, much worse. She'd likely kill one of you just to break the bond."

I felt weak. Almost fever-like. I scrambled for something—anything —to make me feel less shit-scared. "But we're in the Riverlands ..."

Wilder's brows nudged together. Pity and contempt marked his face. "You think that makes you safe? Don't be deceived into thinking that the Riverlands is some kind of haven from Morgan's rule. Diana's spine bends every time that—" He clamped his lips together. Obviously biting back a curse. Finally, he spat out, "My point is, I can count on one hand the number of times she's openly gone against Morgan. And for those rare moments, the witch has spies and agents in every gods-damned corner of this court to push her agenda."

"You mean like Dimitri?" I shot at him.

Wilder choked out a dark laugh. "Guessed, did you?"

That pissed me off. "Adrianna told me about him ... and about who she is."

He huffed derisively. "Yet, you still made an unbreakable vow to a fae. Gods, Serena, I stayed away from you to prevent something like this from happening." He gestured between us. "So that dangerous fae, like the ones surrounding us at this very minute, don't take an interest in you."

My fists curled into balls. "Or maybe it's just because you're a legendary Sabu Warrior. Whereas I'm ..."

I tripped over the word "human" because that wasn't entirely true. Not anymore. Wilder just looked confused. "Anyway, there's nothing that can be done now. Frazer's scent is in your blood and vice versa, and the fae have long memories." He passed a hand over his eyes. As if to block out the sight of me as he spoke. "After you complete the trials, you should leave together. I'll cover your backs for as long as I can."

I looked away. Wilder misinterpreted my silence and snapped, "Serena, you can't become a soldier now, do you understand? Take your brother and *leave*. They'll hunt you when you don't show up for your posting, but you should have enough time to disappear. Run, hide— don't come back."

His tormented expression made me ask, "How d'you know so much about what she'd do to me and Frazer?"

Wilder threw me a look. I couldn't read it. "Because I used to serve her."

My eyes flickered to the door. Was I fast enough?

"I said *used* to," he emphasized.

I could still run. My traitorous body refused. Or maybe it was my morbid curiosity, because I gazed back into his bleak eyes and asked him, "What changed?"

A heavy brow and sad eyes met those words. "You know that I used to be a Sabu, but not that I served in Sefra's armies for over two centuries."

That had my chest tightening. My sister ... two *centuries?* Holy fire.

His throat bobbed before he continued. "And when Morgan came, she gave me a choice: kneel or die. Obviously, I chose the former. I'd like to tell you that it was because she threatened to kill the males and females in my charge—"

I couldn't keep the sharpness from my voice as I cut him short. "It wasn't?"

If he noticed my mood, he didn't react. "Yes and no. The 'no' part being that I didn't want to die. Not because I was afraid, exactly. I was still young, at least by Sabu standards, and I wanted *more*." He grimaced and sucked in a shaky inhale. "And after Morgan came to power, my company and I did ... terrible things—unforgivable things. I thought about running, but her retribution for such acts were monstrous."

My breathing snagged. "So, how did you get away?"

He chuckled, the sound cold and laced with self-disgust. "I didn't. She let me go."

I blinked. Stars ...

Wilder stood abruptly, making me nervous. He grabbed the glass from the mantelpiece, and a decanter from a hidden spot by his chair. He stayed standing and poured himself another drink. "I began to lose battles—to disgrace myself on purpose. I fell into whoring, gambling, and drinking." He raised his glass as if to emphasize, and sloshed the liquid around, peering inside ruefully. "She beat me, and when that didn't work, she set in on my fellow Warriors. I thought about giving in every damned day." He inhaled his drink, draining the glass dry in seconds. "But I just couldn't do it anymore. I couldn't look into the eyes of another innocent and end their life. All in the name of that power-hungry demon. So, I did what I could to take my Warriors' pain away. When I didn't stop, she threatened to force a blood oath on me—"

I couldn't stop myself. "Blood oath? As in a bond?"

His gaze shifted to mine; his eyes hollowed out as he clarified. "We only call them bonds when they're consensual. A blood oath to Morgan would've been a twisted play on the guardian bond. It most often takes place between a ruler and their subjects. But to swear it to Morgan would've meant eternal damnation. There would've been no honor in serving her. So I promised to kill myself if she tried. For a Sabu, there's no greater dishonor. Morgan was so disgusted, she exiled me from her court and sent me here. Told me to have as many females or males as I liked—to get it out of my system. It shows what she really thinks of these camps; of Diana's armies."

I winced. "How long have you been here?"

"Years," he replied curtly.

"And she could call you back at any moment?"

Wilder hesitated, his eyes growing stormy. "I'd risk crossing the sea and joining up with our eastern brethren before going back to her."

Gods, I wanted to believe that. But he'd served the very fae that had ripped apart my family, murdering my father, and forcing my sister and mother into exile.

He must have read something in my expression because he said with some force, "I'm still the same male, Serena."

Ah. That got me.

My arms crossed over my body. My shield. "I don't know if I ever knew that male in the first place."

Wilder kept quiet, kept staring. "It's true, we haven't known each other very long. Two months is a blink in the lifespan of a fae. Yet here I am, finding myself fucking terrified about what happens to you when they discover you're kin with a fae."

Those words seemed to build in my chest and stomach, a great, golden sun expanding, touching my skin, radiating outward. They compelled me to say, "We'll leave—me and Frazer. As soon as we've finished the trials."

"Something tells me you've already discussed this." He looked as if he didn't expect a real answer.

I stayed silent. I'd made a big enough mistake admitting to the kin bond. However, Lake Ewa, Maggie OneEye; all the secrets Hazel had revealed should remain with me.

"Fine," he said shortly. "Then, there's nothing more to say."

He set his glass aside and bent down to grab one of the books piled high on the floor. Wilder chucked it to me. I caught it and stared back, confused.

He gave me a shallow smile in return. "I saw you earlier. You were reaching for it. I don't know why, but you're welcome to take it."

My fingers traced the title, *The Darkest Song.* "You won't miss it?"

"Does it look like I'd miss it?" he asked, gesturing to the stacks of books surrounding us.

"I suppose not." I stood to tuck the book under my arm and added lightly, "What if Dimitri finds out you've been giving me books?"

The fire in Wilder's eyes died, and he turned to the flames burning bright in the fireplace, showing me his back. "We can only hope now that Frazer's scent is mixed up with your own, he'll stop believing we're in a physical relationship. Fae avoid having multiple partners for that very reason. Scenting other fae has a way of spoiling the romance."

I gulped, trying to dislodge the lump in my throat.

"You should go."

Before cracking and spilling everything pounding away inside my traitorous heart, I left. Quickly.

CHAPTER 24
BEGIN!

Four days. Four *long* days, our pack trained constantly, and every movement caused some odd ache or pain. Still, progress felt slow. At least for Liora and I, who had yet to win a bout with Cai. Let alone Adrianna or Frazer. So being matched in a fight against a fae like Cole or Tysion—who to my dismay passed the third trial—was the very thought that caused fear to hound me day and night, chasing me from nightmares only to wake to the pain of a battered body. The only bright spot in the grayness was handing over the linen pocket square to Bert, who'd accepted the item gladly.

On the dawn of the fifth trial our pack sheltered in the food hall, where the windows had misted over from the buttery baking scents and the delicious heat from the fire.

"Go on, have a little toast? A bit of sausage?"

Cai sat opposite me, floating his breakfast plate under my nose. I gave him my best scowl, to which he sighed heavily and dropped his plate. "Thanks, but I feel sick just looking at food right now," I added to be polite.

Frazer fidgeted. "You should eat."

Somehow, he made his suggestion sound like a demand. I bottled up the exasperated noise fighting to get out. In the end, it was Adrianna who said, "Frazer, you keep looking at Serena like you're about to fall on your sword for her."

Frazer replied with nothing but a glare cut in her direction.

I almost groaned aloud. There'd been a fragile peace between them in the wake of their fight. Today, just hours before the trial, the conflict looked ready to spark anew.

Of rutting course.

Adrianna shifted forward and kept on. "You can't afford to let your protective instincts take over. Not with witnesses around."

I interceded. "Adi, we *know*. He knows."

Frazer drank deeply from his glass and upon coming up for air, said, "You're not my princess, so stop bullying me."

A faint blush colored Adrianna's cheeks. I could almost see the struggle for self-control behind her eyes. Then, she leaned back, her spine stiffened and a preternatural stillness, a black frost, gripped her. "I just don't want to see either of you dragged before Morgan because of your recklessness."

Frazer's glass broke in his hands. No one heard the sound, thanks to Cai, but the noise barrier couldn't hide the juice spreading and dripping down the side of the oak table.

Speech abandoned me.

"All right, enough!" Cai slammed a palm down flat.

No one spoke as Liora mopped up the sticky liquid.

"Adrianna." Cai swiveled to his right to face her. "We know you're worried, but what's done is done."

She scowled but stayed silent.

Cai's wrath turned on Frazer who was placing shards of glass onto his plate. "And if you can't control your temper, you'll start drawing attention to us. A bit like you're doing right now."

He wasn't wrong.

Individuals among the other packs were shooting curious glances our way. The only group to ignore us was Tysion's, which seemed more suspicious somehow. Their whispered conversations had become a regular occurrence that set my teeth on edge. Although I couldn't explain exactly why. In my scrutiny, I missed Goldwyn striding over to us.

I felt the release of the sound barrier, and then, "Oh dear."

I swiveled around to see her halt, flank me, and stare down at the broken glass. "An accident? Or a bout of nerves?"

"Both," Frazer grumbled.

"Not surprising. Now, if you could all follow me outside?"

Goldwyn whirled and strode out. A mighty brisk attitude.

We all scrambled along behind, but she didn't slow once we'd left the hall; she sped up. My knees went weak upon realizing we were headed for the arena.

I matched her stride, saying, "I thought the trial didn't start until 9."

The hint of panic was all too clear in my voice. *Damn.*

"Correct. But I want you to have the time to get familiar with the space."

Her words were edged; not as sunny and carefree as usual. I shared a surprised look with Liora.

Goldwyn had always been by far the most relaxed instructor. The idea that she might be competitive, or a strategic thinker hadn't really occurred to me. My mistake.

The towering, roofless construct of limestone and sand loomed large, etched against a perfectly clear, blue sky. It was glorious *and* terrifying.

I'd been inside once before to watch the match between Wilder's and Dimitri's packs. Now it was my turn. I'd done everything to prepare for this, but it still didn't feel like enough. It would never be enough.

I wiped sweaty palms down my jacket and looked around. My pack was quiet. Everyone seemed trapped in their own little pockets of fear. We couldn't help one another this time. On this day, we stood alone.

Goldwyn veered right. I'd expected to enter via the main gate, but instead she led us toward a heavy wooden door. Goldwyn used a hidden key from around her neck to click the lock open. She ushered us through the low archway, into a long, narrow tunnel with burning torches set into brackets on the wall. Goldwyn grabbed one and held it out in front, illuminating the cold stone passage. I fell into line behind the others, walking along the sloping corridor, listening to the eerie echoes of our boots hitting the flagstones. *Clack-tap. Clack-tap. Clack-tap.*

At the end was a square room with benches set against the walls.

Opposite was an annex with mounted weaponry. To the left, a ramp led to the ring. This must be the fighter's entrance.

Goldwyn slipped the torch back into an empty bracket and beckoned us out onto the sands. A huge circular ring awaited us. Tiered benches ran all around the outside. Thousands of seats rose to the open sky. I spun in a circle, taking it all in, anxiety burning a hole in my gut.

"Can tell us who we're fighting?" I asked, attempting to sound innocent.

A knowing smile touched Goldwyn's face. "Sorry. The instructors don't choose your opponents."

"Then, who does?" Adrianna said sharply.

"Hilda," Goldwyn answered.

"She's going to be here?" Adrianna asked, intrigued.

I let their voices fade away and concentrated on taking everything in. From how well my boots gripped the sand, to the position of the sun. Frazer stuck close but didn't seem interested in surveying his surroundings. Maybe he'd done it the instant we'd walked through the gate.

Sight of Goldwyn's wings spreading punched through my haze of thought, and I turned to her again. Listening.

"I'll be back later. And if you have the first pick of weapons and armor, then so be it." She winked. As if we needed the hint.

"Are you allowed to leave us here?" Adrianna asked.

"I'm not entirely sure. I suppose we'll find out."

She shot us a fox-like grin and soared into the sky.

During the next hour, Cai complained that his breakfast had been interrupted ... many, *many* times. We also kitted ourselves out in basic armor: leather tunics, and gloves reinforced with chain mail. Then, we picked blunted weapons from the armory. There were no bows or shields; otherwise, there was a wide variety.

I chose my beloved Utemä, long and slender with its protective hilt. Perfect for my slight build. Frazer was the only one among us to not chose a sword. He went for a spear instead. The very image was enough for fear to sink into my belly like quicksand. I wasn't exactly afraid for him. No—I'd seen him with a spear. A striking asp, a violent tempest in action, and that was the problem; if I was matched against someone even half as good—or stars forbid, Frazer himself—then I'd be kicked out. It wasn't clear where homeless humans went, either. Back to the slave markets?

After we'd picked our weapons, our pack moved on, testing the blunt edges in some warm-up bouts in the ring.

Eventually, the other recruits started to arrive. Dimitri was the first with his brutish pack treading along in his wake. When he spotted us training, he scowled but surprisingly said nothing. Next came Mikael and Cecile's groups, and then Goldwyn returned via the main gate.

Those of us with swords sheathed them and greeted her in the middle of the sand pit. She gave us a fleeting smile, but the tightness around her eyes and jaw showed she was nervous for us.

"What are we waiting for?" Adrianna asked her briskly.

"Hilda. And the guests, of course." She nodded to the stands.

My heart died inside my chest. "Guests?" I croaked.

"We've sent out invitations to the recruits' kin and opened the grounds to paying customers." Was that distaste in her voice? Goldwyn added, "It's the first time we've ever let outsiders watch. It ruins the secrecy element. Hilda *definitely* wasn't keen. But someone higher up in the court thought an audience would test your ability to focus. Or some such bullshit."

She rolled her eyes. I didn't smile. There would be nobody in the stands cheering for me. Yet, I *still* had to endure a bunch of strangers watching me.

I noticed Adrianna's nails punch upwards and scrape beneath her palms. She folded her arms quickly, perhaps to hide the evidence. "You haven't invited my mother, have you?"

Goldwyn's face softened in sympathy and understanding. "Hilda felt she had to. I don't know if she accepted or not."

Adrianna's expression clouded over as she scanned the sky.

Liora was already voicing comfort from her side. "Block it out. We're fighting for one another now. That's all that matters."

The fury lining Adrianna's body went nowhere, but she did manage a curt nod.

Soon, the guests began to appear. Since nearly all the fae were flying in, I found myself sky gazing. Minutes ticked by, and a cyclone of nerves continued to spin within. All the wrong sensations claimed my body.

Thirsty. Sweaty. Shaky.

Then I saw someone fly into the stands who made my insides petrify. Hunter.

He sat somewhere in the middle tier, and I lost him in the crowd.

I wobbled precariously.

"Careful." Frazer gripped my elbow, steadying me.

"Sorry." It was a ghost of a whisper that passed my lips.

"Are you all right, Serena?" Goldwyn asked from beside us.

I looked over to find my pack and instructor staring. "I've just seen someone I know."

"Oh," Goldwyn said, sounding a touch surprised.

The pressure on my arm increased as Frazer squeezed. *Who?*

Hunter.

"It wouldn't be that male fae waving at you, would it?" Goldwyn queried, squinting up at the seats.

My gaze flew back to the stands. Oh gods, he *was* waving at me. I raised my hand and *forced* it into a small jerking motion.

Adrianna snorted, mostly scornful and a touch amused. "Some member of the Wild Hunt. Aren't they meant to be terrifying?"

Goldwyn moved to my side and offered me a quirky smile. "You do seem to have rather a lot of fae admirers, don't you?"

"He's just a friend," I replied too quickly.

Goldwyn's eyes flickered to Frazer's grip on my arm. He let go immediately.

"I see," Goldwyn answered pointedly.

"So, she came," Adrianna murmured.

Distracted from my Hunter drama, I tracked Adrianna's line of sight. Even without the sharp eyesight of the fae, Diana Lakeshie wasn't hard to spot with her copper skin and giant pale-blue wings. She flew in to the stands with four male fae at her side.

Adrianna was radiating pain and rage. "Why now? She hasn't bothered with me in years."

I hadn't missed the vulnerability—the tremor in her voice.

I searched for the right words, for something to comfort her with, when the bond shook; my attention got pulled to Frazer like a piece of iron to a lodestone. His eyes burned with a dark fire, and his jaw had glued together in a sign of aggression. I grabbed his wrist reflexively. *Keep it together.*

He wavered. Then gave me a nod, albeit reluctantly. I released his arm, but not before Dimitri saw. I didn't know where he'd come from. He'd been behind our pack and now he was parallel, staring right at us. The look on his face made me queasy, but I blinked, and he was gone, trailing back to his pack. I wasn't sure what to make of it.

Beside me, Goldwyn announced, "I can hear Hilda by the gate, so this is where I leave you. She'll give you your sparring partner and explain the rules." Looking us each in the eye, she added, "Don't pull your punches. Be savage and win."

She left for the stands, swiftly followed by Cecile, Mikael, and Dimitri.

Time to find out if all that training had been worth it.

I whirled toward the huge double doors to the arena.

Wilder walked through with Hilda. He was wearing his usual sidearms and instructor's garb. All leather armor and rough cloth. The only new addition was a full-length black cloak tied around his throat that made his shoulders look impressively wide—foreboding even. Hilda held her own beside him with that striking height and tawny coloring, complemented by brown leathers, a gray fur cloak, and a wicked assortment of blades. She looked every bit the huntress and warrior.

Intimidating as fuck.

"Here we go," Adrianna breathed next to me.

Wilder and Hilda neared. My brother's thoughts rushed through our bond, low and hurried. *Remember, you might not be strong, but you* are *fast and tall. Your reach is better than most. Try to keep the bout as short as possible. Avoid getting locked into parrying, but when you cross swords, use the blow's momentum and sweep it away from your body. Don't let them close in on you.*

I'd heard that advice a hundred thousand times before, but I still nodded and repeated his points over and over in a panicked mantra, hoping they'd seep into my muscles and become second nature.

Hilda reeled off a speech that sounded tried and old. She welcomed the packs and congratulated us on getting this far. It was all just empty noise until she began explaining the rules. "As you've all no doubt heard from your instructors, you are to fight another recruit. Although, you might be pleased to hear that we're sparing you from being teamed with a member of your own pack."

Relief, swift and sublime, found me then.

Hilda continued. "Now, once your match starts, it won't end until someone lands three blows to their opponent. Your weapons have been dulled, but they can still break bones if used with enough force. Any fae matched with a human would do well to remember that." She swept the crowd with a grim expression, adding, "We're not going to be impressed by berserkers aiming to cause undue pain. Also, please note that magic is forbidden during this trial. As is flight."

Her warning hung in the air. So did the mounting tension.

I felt my hands tremble.

"We've split the class in to two groups, so you won't all be fighting at once. But, before we do this, we must make a cut." Hilda went on grimly. "Unfortunately, we've got an odd number of recruits. At this point in the trials, we must let someone go. After much discussion, we've reached a decision."

Loaded whispers swept through the arena. Like a hive buzzing. Fear gripped my heart and squeezed. I couldn't breathe properly.

It was me. It had to be.

My mouth went bone-dry as my eyes roamed the stands, frantically, wildly. Was that why Hunter was here? He'd come back to reclaim a slave?

Hilda kept on rambling as I was losing my mind. Something about how the person had showed promise, blah, blah, blah. Then, the 'but' came. "Even though this person is being asked to leave, you won't be destitute. There's a member of the Wild Hunt in the stands who'll help you find a new position."

Liar. I hated her in that moment. I hated Hunter.

And many of the fae recruits visibly relaxed, laughing it off. The outcast was clearly human; what did they care who left? I even noticed a few curious and cruel eyes sweeping, finding possible targets. Quite a few stares settled on me.

Of course they thought it was me.

Over my dead body, Frazer growled down the bond.

Alarm and terror peeled through me. If Hilda called my name …

I'll rip her wings off for suggesting it. And then kill that faithless worm you called a friend.

He wasn't exaggerating, and if he did that, they'd execute him.

No. *No.*

I'd do anything to stop that. Begging, bargaining, fighting; I was preparing to do all three, but Hilda stopped me by saying, "Cassandra Hart, can you come here?"

A girl detached herself from Cecile's group. She looked terrified. It was the expression that I should be wearing right now. But it wasn't me.

It *wasn't* me.

I hadn't paid much attention to the other recruits in our sparring sessions. At first, because of a certain distracting fae. Then, our pack had become totally engrossed in each other and our mission. From the brief glimpses I'd seen of her, she was a decent fighter—better than me, anyway.

Frazer grunted softly beside me. *No, she wasn't, siska.*

Oh.

Hilda was muttering to Cassandra now, gesturing back toward the waiting room. The arena was deathly quiet as she walked out of the ring, her head held high despite her shaking shoulders. She was sobbing.

I wanted to scream with bloodthirsty rage. To run over and promise that one day things would be different. That we'd make Morgan and the Hunt pay for putting us in chains. That we'd prove we didn't deserve to be thrown away just because the world saw us as weaker.

Then, she disappeared from view. And I was still here.

Somehow, I had to make that count. To do that, I had to get past this damned trial. My stomach calmed, and my pulse stopped its frantic hammering.

That's right, Auntie whispered. *Time to put aside the trembling girl and become the female you need to be.*

Who do I need to be, precisely?

The fae who can do more than make empty promises to the damned.

She left me, her words ringing in my ears.

Hilda yelled, "When I call out your name, you're to go stand by your opponent. Everyone named now will be in the first group to fight. The second team will go stand by the outskirts in readiness." She ended by gesturing to the edge of the arena.

Wilder pulled out a scrap of parchment from an inner pocket. He handed it over to Hilda. A hush fell over the stands as she unrolled it and stared.

I counted the seconds. One. Two. Three ...

She bellowed, "The first name, Andaline Beatrice. You will face Roan Kerstal."

Andaline was a female fae and more than a match for Roan. Maybe this damned list would be fair.

Hilda powered through the names. It was only when she called out Frazer's name that my heart quickened again. "Frazer, your battle will be against Cole Vysan."

"Good." Frazer flashed me a feral grin. I knew it was for my benefit.

He sought Cole's face in the crowd and moved off. Pain lanced through my chest.

You don't have to worry. Just focus on yourself. His confidence carried through the link. I let myself feel cheered by it.

Then, the next blow came. "Adrianna Lakeshi, you will face Tysion Kato."

Her identity revealed, the silence shattered, and whispers broke out everywhere. A tiny scattering of applause started and died quickly. Meanwhile, Adrianna showed no emotion as hundreds of eyes followed her every move toward Tysion who, I was surprised to notice, didn't seem his usual smirking, sneering self.

Ha. I hoped he was shitting himself.

Hilda called out four more names before asking everyone else to stand aside. I guessed that made me Team B, along with Cai and Liora.

I spun and aimed for the stands while sneaking glances at my competition. With a few exceptions, like Cai, the best in our class were fighting in the first group. I didn't bother celebrating.

Reaching the barricade, I turned and searched the battlefield for Frazer and Adrianna. Cai and Liora did the same.

Wilder moved to the edge of the arena and boomed, "If your weapons are sheathed, draw them!"

A sharp slide of steel punctured the air.

Hilda joined Wilder ringside, and then she whirled around, yelling, "Be advised. If we call your name out that is our official ruling that you've lost the battle. You will come to stand behind us, and you will *not* continue the bout."

Watching Frazer take a position opposite Cole's enormous bulk made blind panic set in. I reached down our bond, but his thoughts and emotions felt fuzzy. I suspected he'd become too focused on the task at hand to notice me lurking. It made me feel closer to him, at any rate.

"Get ready! Begin!"

Steel met steel in a violent dance.

I couldn't bear to watch.

The second I felt alarm in the bond, I *had* to look.

Frazer was on the ground, rolling away from an overhanded strike.

My arms crossed over my stomach, a reflex born from wanting to protect myself from the sight.

Now, he was back on his feet, deflecting Cole's monstrous blade.

As the fight progressed, I relaxed a bit. Frazer got a touch within the first five minutes. Watching him move through the blows was like seeing a virtuoso at work.

I craned my neck, moving between Frazer and Adrianna.

The next hit to land was Frazer's again; a blow to the belly this time. Cole stared down in disbelief. For one heartbeat he was distracted. Frazer seized the advantage, and with a flick of the wrist, levered the spear upward. Cole retreated quickly, but he was still too slow. The blunted end smashed against his granite jaw.

Liora and I seized each other's hands, waiting, hoping.

Hilda called it. "Cole. Over by the wall."

"Thank the moons," Cai whispered to my left.

Frazer made for us, not bothering to stay and watch Cole slink away, cursing as he went. I let my relief shine through our bond, and then my amusement, after spotting a slight strut that had entered his gait. *Cocky bastard.*

Frazer's eyes met mine. *Don't know what you mean.*

A vague smile tugged at the corner of his mouth as he joined my side, making Cai move up the line. I let myself bathe in my kin's victory for a moment more, then turned back to Adrianna, who was still fighting Tysion.

While other recruits got pulled out and our ranks swelled, they remained locked in their battle of steel and will. Truthfully, I hadn't imagined Adrianna would have such a hard time landing blows. There were a few more nail-biting, tongue-chewing minutes before she slipped past his guard, landing a tap to his ribs. But in the next heartbeat, Tysion swung around and clipped her on the head with his hilt. And in another devastating blow, he tapped her right arm.

Two to one in Tysion's favor.

A nasty jolt hit my midriff. She wouldn't lose. She couldn't. We needed her with us.

Adrianna snarled and attacked outward with an explosive force. She ducked, performing a vicious sweeping kick, which had Tysion on his ass. She pounced, pinning him, bringing her sword to his throat.

Two hits apiece.

Adrianna let Tysion throw her off. She was attacking again within seconds. Tysion was back on his feet, but even to my unpracticed eye, it was obvious he'd lost balance. Adrianna gained ground. She had the advantage. As they crossed blades once more, Adrianna swept a blow aside, thrusting directly toward his upper thigh, landing a light hit.

I found myself disappointed that she hadn't aimed for the groin.

"Tysion, you're out," Wilder yelled. "The bout goes to Adrianna."

The stands erupted in polite applause. A few recruits joined in, but not many. Obviously, our pack cheered loudest. Cai even whistled.

Adrianna kept her features stiff, almost lifeless, as she walked over to us. But I thought I detected a faint smile slip past her guard when Cai patted her on the back.

Wilder's shout had my heart doing a wild drumbeat against my ribs. "Second set of recruits—you're up!"

I blanked and moved forward in a kind of trance. Ten recruits shadowed me, including Cai and Liora. We came to a natural stop, crowded together. Hilda had that damned parchment out again.

The earth swayed beneath me.

"Caiden Verona, you're paired with Moso Yumi."

The leader of Mikael's pack against the leader of Goldwyn's. A good match.

Hilda got through another set of names before bellowing, "Liora Verona, your partner is Reese Miller."

Reese was a brunette human with a dour expression. She also happened to be middle-ranked. Liora would have a chance then.

Only four recruits left. Two fae and another human. Surely, they wouldn't pair me against a fae?

The other human went by the name of Annie Dara. The only thing I knew about her was that she had a hopeless infatuation with Cai. I desperately tried to remember how she ranked. Something told me it was low down.

Her name was called out. I waited for mine, bracing myself.

"You're with Maria Claren." The female fae.

My mouth popped open.

That meant ... my opponent was a male fae, and he definitely wasn't bottom-ranked.

"Jace Skarsden, you're with Serena Smith."

He was one of Mikael's. Tall, blonde, handsome. And by the smirk playing about his mouth, arrogant as all hell.

He strutted over, taking his time.

Auntie was there, speaking more than she had in weeks. *Pride and vanity—those are weaknesses you can exploit. You'll need to be quicker and smarter because he's going to hammer you with strength. Just remember, darling, you have fae blood now. Not as much as him, but the instincts are there. Let them guide you.*

Jace took his position opposite. Wilder shouted for us to take our stances. I angled one foot in front of the other and prayed that my training would get me through this.

"Same rules as before. Prepare your weapons!" Hilda bellowed.

I drew my Utemä. The steel hummed as it came loose; something about the sound comforted me.

I waited for it.

"Begin!"

Auntie had been right; Jace attacked with full force.

I flitted out of reach. Thank the stars he hadn't chosen a longsword.

He was charging again, pursuing the most aggressive line of combat. I planted my feet and moved. Fighting, dancing, running away—I couldn't tell.

I heard rumblings in the crowd. Laughter. Maybe it was because of me, but it didn't matter. I had a plan. Sort of.

He threw his weight behind each attack. With each swing, savage and heavy, he left himself open to a nimble counterattack. He was too eager for the win. Too sure of himself. He swung again.

I dodged and twirled away from a blow that could've easily broken my neck.

"Jace!" Wilder bellowed. "You're trying to make contact, not kill!"

My opponent didn't hesitate, didn't slow. Instead, he brought his sword out in a torso-level sweeping strike. I stood my ground this time.

Duck. Thrust. Straight to his ribs.

One hit for me. Wilder called it.

Then Jace crashed into me; his hand was on my neck, his weight pushing me onto my back, flattening me. I felt steel at my throat. Wilder confirmed the blow, but Jace stayed crouched over me, exposing his fangs.

I'd released my sword on impact, but the hilt stayed within reach. I scratched at the sand with my fingertips; Jace pressed his blade deeper. A warning not to move. The cold steel bit, but no part had been left sharp, thank the gods.

Cursing inwardly, I waited. He would not move, and no one ordered him to back down. My temper cracked. That fire—that glittering *rage*—built and crested like a wave. This time it crashed, and it appeared, brushing my thoughts, tickling my skin: my magic.

It wouldn't answer my will, not yet. But I knew ... I just knew that one day soon it would. That thought made me bare my teeth in a feral smile.

Mocking amusement answered back in Jace's eyes.

That was before I snaked my leg up and rammed it into his groin.

A heartbeat—that's all I had to act as he groaned and his sword lifted from my throat by an inch.

My forearm jerked up, connecting with his wrist, knocking his blade hand wide. I locked him into an arm hold. He'd be out in a second, but I used that precious moment to snatch my right hand out for what I needed.

His chest was exposed; my Utemä went there. Another tap.

Jace tried breaking my grip by pulling away, so I let his momentum carry me up and I released him. He quickly backed away, snarling like an injured wolf, a wrathful intent in his eyes. And that's exactly what I wanted. I smiled, goading him.

He ran at me, roaring, swinging his sword down from overhead. I waited, then dodged. His body turned with me, but not fast enough to stop my hand striking, seizing his unprotected wing joint and squeezing viciously. Frazer had shown me the right spot.

Jace howled, his side collapsing, his knees buckling. And I pressed that wicked steel to his neck. It seemed to gleam and sing, *I'm light and quick just like you. If they blunt my fire, I'll burn with ice instead.*

Jace hissed as the blade touched his skin. As if the sword truly did burn.

"Jace. You're out," Wilder shouted.

I freed Jace's wing and stepped away. He stood and turned *slowly*. I hadn't sheathed my Utemä, just in case. Our eyes met, and the hatred emanating from him sent a shudder rushing up my spine and creeping over my skin. I refused to show fear or break our staring match.

He bared his pointed teeth. I gripped my hilt a little harder.

Then, Jace stalked off. The tension drained from my body, and my locked, taut muscles eased a tad.

A bad instinct, but an instinct nonetheless, overrode my good sense. My eyes found Wilder, and for once he was staring at me openly in public.

There was a glimmer of something. Wilder looked triumphant.

The strings around my heart—the ones he controlled—twanged. I wanted to go to him then, but that wasn't an option. So, I sheathed my blade and looked up and out. A sea of interested faces stared back, some outright stunned. My cheeks heated, but the Utemä sang its warrior song to me again. *That's right. The fae aren't so superior after all.*

My gaze traveled to the recruits by the barrier. Frazer and Adrianna waited. I closed the distance, but about halfway, the fog of adrenaline cleared. Cai and Liora weren't among rest of the recruits.

I stopped and spun, searching for them among the fighting couples. They were there, but something was off. I did a head count. Four groups remained—I'd been the first to beat my opponent. Blinking in shock, I whirled back around and joined Frazer and Adrianna by the barrier.

"That was incredible." What was more incredible was that Adrianna had praised me for something

I mumbled, "Thanks."

A strangled noise erupted from Frazer. I met his blistering blue eyes. He looked damn near tormented. *I'm still here.*

Frazer blinked, once, twice. *Yes, you are.*

"Just don't let this go to your head," Adrianna said to my left.

I was about to snap, but stopped upon seeing the humor and real relief marking her face. "Next time, your opponent won't underestimate you."

A low, rough laughter rumbled out of Frazer. "No, they won't."

"Moso Yumi. You're out."

My gaze returned to the playing field. Cai was victorious and already walking over to us, his toothy grin on display. The only time it faltered was when he saw his sister still fighting for her place. Since watching Liora dodge Reese's thrusts tied my gut in nasty knots, I could only imagine what it was doing to him.

Cai settled in between Adrianna and me. We didn't greet each other; an unspoken agreement. There'd be no celebrating until we'd all come through this. I knew it was close. Liora and Reese had landed two blows apiece.

Two more names got called out. Then, they were the only pair left standing. Liora was on the defensive. I wanted to close my eyes, block out the image. Instead, the nerves made me reach for Frazer's hand and as an afterthought, Cai's. He looked painfully neutral. Although even he couldn't stop his hand trembling as Liora winded Reese with a kick to the chest.

Liora advanced as if sensing weakness; she twisted underneath an overhead strike, taking out Reese's knees with a well-timed blow, then raising her sword to her throat. Hilda called it.

Cai whooped as Liora jogged over to us.

Somehow, we'd all made it. We caught her in a hug.

Hilda and Wilder muttered words to the losing recruits before dismissing them and moving over toward our group. I couldn't believe it. Tysion, Cole: gone.

Hilda boomed for the audience's benefit, "Congratulations to our surviving ten."

A brief scattering of applause filled the stands.

Hilda continued. "However, despite the new restrictions, we're able to extend a second chance to one lucky recruit later on in the trials. So, if you've just seen your favorite lose, there is hope." With a slightly forced smile, she dipped her head and lowered her voice for our sakes. "Return the weapons to the armory. Then, you are to proceed to your barracks. Your instructor will meet you there to discuss the nature of the next trial. Dismissed."

Hilda moved aside, and our now much smaller group streamed toward the side room and down the ramp. I marched straight into the armory along with everyone else. I was glad to be free of the gloves and tunic, but not the Utemä. That was tough to leave behind.

As a pack, we moved out, heading for the exit. No one else stopped to look at the rejected recruit, Cassandra Hart.

I hadn't noticed her until now, sitting on a stone bench in a corner, tears staining her round cheeks. Her short blonde hair stuck up at odd angles as if she'd been running her fingers through it repeatedly.

I wavered. Frazer instantly halted. "What is it?" he asked me.

Ignoring the question, I went to sit by Cassandra. "Is there anything I can do?"

The rest of my pack stopped and gathered together. They kept a respectable distance away. All apart from Liora, who joined us on the bench. Cassandra wouldn't look at any of us. She just croaked, "Make that fae waiting in the stands take you instead of me."

Frazer hissed; Cassandra flinched. "I wasn't being serious," she muttered.

Liora asked, "Why are you waiting in here?"

Cassandra bit down on her lip so viciously that the soft flesh bled in spots. "Hilda told me to wait until the end and then head to the main arena entrance. That fae, the one taking me—he'll be waiting."

"D'you want us to go meet him with you?" Liora inquired gently
—kindly.

Cassandra shrugged and sniffed a bit. I tried another tactic. "The fae
you're meeting—I know him. He's the one who brought me here. Maybe
I could persuade him to help you somehow."

She looked at me then. A challenging frown. "Why would a fae from
the Wild Hunt listen to someone who used to be its prey?"

A fair question.

Liora had an answer though. "Don't underestimate her. The fae
considers her a friend."

Cassandra spoke with venom. "You can't be friends with a fae. Are
you sure it wasn't something else?"

Her eyes narrowed in suspicion and my back went up. It wasn't just
me though. Frazer stilled, Adrianna's lip puckered; even Liora was
leaning away, doubt worming its way into her face.

I took a breath and continued. "We were friends. Nothing more."

I stood alongside Liora and said, "D'you want my help or not?"

Cassandra wavered, staring down at her boots, scowling.

"Bye then."

I was turning when she stopped me.

"Wait!" Cassandra jumped up and rubbed the wetness from her
cheeks. "If you can do something ... anything, I'd be grateful."

A nod was my response.

No one said a word as we walked back along the stone tunnel and
out the other end, into daylight. I didn't even need to search for Hunter.
Liora immediately pointed and said, "Over there."

He stood stock-still next to the arena's huge gate. The perfect picture
of a mindless minion. As soon as he saw me, however, his face lit with a
sweet smile.

It awoke such joy and disgust and sadness in me.

Adrianna moved to my side, her head tilted, questioning. "That's the
slaver?"

Hunter's smile faltered. He'd heard. Of course he had.

Adrianna said, "Hilda wanted us to go back to the barracks ... You
might get in trouble if you talk with him."

"I know."

Adrianna nodded once. No censure or disapproval. Just acceptance.

I looked around at my pack. "Don't risk trouble for my sake. Go. I'll meet you back there."

"I'm not going anywhere," Frazer said, glowering at Hunter.

Liora clucked her tongue and took him by the elbow. "Don't fuss."

He blinked and frowned down at the touch, but amazingly, he let her steer him away. Bound or not, Liora had her own brand of magic. Frazer peered over his shoulder. *Send something down the bond if he gives you trouble.*

Yes, brata.

He flashed me a dry look at the obvious exasperation in my thoughts and spun back around. Cai gave me a quick grin goodbye, and Adrianna just left.

Alone with Cassandra, I asked, "Ready?"

She said nothing in response; she only stared dead ahead with a locked spine. I took it to mean "yes," and led the way.

My heart jumped into my stomach as we closed the distance. Green cloth, brown leathers, daggers at his hip, just like I remembered him. The only changes being that he didn't carry a bow, and he had no over-coat, presumably because of the fast approaching summer season.

"Hi," I said. Gods, that sounded lame.

"How have you been?" He seemed genuinely interested. Concerned, even.

The softness around his mouth caused a flowering ache in my chest. His brown eyes never left mine, which meant he'd yet to acknowledge the human he was about to take into chains. I gestured to my left. "I'm guessing you know who this is?"

The words punched out of me. Hunter noticed and frowned. "Of course. I've got orders to escort Cassandra to her new position."

I came close to spitting the words at him. "And can you tell us where she's going?"

Hunter's wings rustled. The only sign of discomfort. "The Solar Market."

Cassandra blurted out, "Where I'll be sold, *again*."

Hunter's eyes cut to Cassandra's, finally. "Yes."

My palm tingled; I wanted to slap him. But those violent urges would do no good. Reining myself in and schooling my voice into even tones, I said, "Is there nothing you can do to help her?" No answer. I persisted. "You know what Solar is, Hunter."

He stepped closer. Barely a foot separated us. "The law is clear: a human without magic or position is eligible to become fae property."

I blinked. *Property.* That word echoed in my mind long afterward.

Hunter continued, gesticulating, clearly agitated. As if desperate to explain. "She didn't make it as a soldier. The only occupation left is a domestic. It's that, or the brothel. And I'm guessing she doesn't want to go there."

"*She* is standing right here," Cassandra burst out.

Hunter's focus shifted to her. Backing up a touch, he asked, "You want to be a whore?"

Forget slapping him, I wanted to pummel every inch of him.

"No." Cassandra raised her chin and tried valiantly to stare down her nose at her captor. "But what I want doesn't matter to your lot, does it? So I'll stick with what I can live with. If I'm going to be owned and abused," her voice cracked and so did my heart as she said, "I'd rather it be out in the open with other women around me who know how to survive."

I felt a huge surge of respect for her. Hunter, on the other hand, merely frowned. "Not every household is alike. And not every fae is cruel. It sounds like you've listened to a couple of horror stories and assumed we're all the same."

I snapped then. "If there's no danger, why did you fight to bring me here?"

His focus whipped to me. "Serena."

It was a groan and a plea.

He knew. That rutting coward *knew* how dangerous Solar was for humans.

My thoughts must've shown. He dipped his head, murmuring, "I haven't got a choice."

The storm swelling in my heart's blood turned me wild and cold and distant. "Yes. You have. So, please, for me, take Cassandra to a brothel. One of the better ones, if such a thing exists."

Hunter's clay-colored eyes found mine. There was a pain there. One that I didn't understand. Finally, he sighed through his nose and looked away, but he also nodded.

"Thank you," Cassandra muttered to me softly.

That just made me feel guiltier. Guilty that I'd once called this fae a friend. I hoped that showed when I stared into her round, fearful eyes and said, "I'm sorry it wasn't more."

She tried to hide the tight misery gripping her body with a shrug. "I'd never have made it as a soldier. At least in a brothel I'll have a chance at life." She continued in a terribly bright voice, "Maybe I'll get lucky and some wealthy fae will take a liking to me. I hear they sometimes pamper their whores."

There were no words in me. Just a cold, sick feeling. Hunter suddenly grabbed my elbow and ordered Cassandra to stay put. He pulled me a good distance away, only stopping once we reached the fence around the training ring. Rounding on me, he breathed, "How are you, really?"

I blinked. Totally speechless.

Spooling myself back in, I hissed, "How ... *how* can you ask me that right now?"

He didn't even flinch. "I'm not talking about this exact second. How are you finding the trials?"

My lips parted in surprise. "Well, apart from the constant fear of failing and being ripped away from my friends, fantastic. How are you?"

Pure sarcasm.

"You have friends now?" he asked with a sad smile. "That's good."

I shook my head in disbelief. "*That's* what you decide to focus on?" Something in his slumped posture made me hesitate and soften. "What is this about? What's wrong?"

He stepped into my shadow. With a quick glance over my shoulder, he whispered in my ear, "Just get through the trials, Serena. Please. I can't protect you anymore."

Fear and desperation broke his voice.

"What are you talking about?" I muttered.

His hot breath tickled my ear. "D'you remember what Hilda said on your first day? That other camps wouldn't take you on, and it was a new policy?"

He leaned back slightly so he could look me in the eye. An intense stare endured.

"Of course ..."

Hunter didn't wait for me to finish. "Well, there have been a lot of changes in Diana's policies regarding humans lately. That was just one in a long list. D'you remember what I said about Morgan's fears of conflict with the east?"

I was already nodding. "Yes. Hunter, what—"

"The rumors among the Hunt suggest something's triggered Morgan into speeding up preparations for war. That's why she's started interfering more with the Riverlands Court. First, by getting Diana to break her laws on buying and training slaves—"

I'd heard this last bit before. I stopped him with a wave of my hand. "What's this got to do with you thinking you need to protect me?"

Hunter wet his lips. A hoarse whisper followed. "In the past, the recruits that fail the trials more than once were re-sold in the Riverlands, and often went on to be domestics in high born houses or the court."

A cold spike barreled down my spine at the thought.

He went on quickly, *quietly*, "But Diana's changed her laws again. All to accommodate Morgan's war efforts. So now, the Hunt is getting called in to escort the failures to the Solar Court, where we hand them over to the spiders."

I swayed, and the earth moved with me. I fought to calm my thoughts, to clear my mind. "What would Morgan want with Diana's castoffs?"

His reply was barely audible. "Officially, the Wild Hunt doesn't ask questions. We take orders."

A pause, during which my skin crawled. "What about unofficially?" I prompted.

Hunter went impossibly stiff. "Morgan thinks Diana's camps create soft soldiers, and she's grown impatient. It's why she pushed for no second chances and for the weaker recruits to be brought to Solar. From there, Morgan plans to transform the humans into *real* warriors and re-conscript them for the Solar armies. Hilda only handed out an opportunity to come back today because Diana ordered her to. My guess is she wanted to make sure her daughter got through to the end."

My core tightened in response. *Stars,* Adrianna wouldn't like that.

Hunter looked away. Shit. He seemed ... shifty. *Guilty.*

"There's more?" I urged.

Hunter's pained eyes drifted to mine again. "The Solar camps aren't kind to humans. They're segregated from fae recruits so that friendships, like the ones you've developed, don't happen. Then, they're forced into harsh training cycles. Harsher than at Kasi, anyway."

I blinked. *Harsher.*

Suddenly he gripped my elbow, pinning me with a wide-eyed stare that had the look of a cornered animal. I'd seen such fear before in the game my father would trap, in the rabbits that would spot the knife intended for their throats. The sight had always made me nauseous, and now that same horror claimed my gut.

Hunter began, "Morgan's decreed that it's too wasteful for humans to become domestics now that the east is stirring again. It won't be long before she declares all humans to be the property of the army. All except the witches, who'll form their own units. D'you understand what I'm saying? The Riverland's camps—their armies—they're the only safe place left for you. And I pulled in every favor, every string, to be the one to come here on escort duty. All so I could warn you. If you lose a trial, run."

It took a few stunned blinks before something finally clicked. "What about Cassandra?"

His wings twitched. Although, it could've been a tremor. "There's nothing to be done. I can't do what she wants. We'll both be killed."

That resigned tone. He'd lied.

Disgust made me break away and push him back. I was about to turn, to scream at Cassandra to run, but he pulled me in again, his grip biting down. Hissing under his breath, he said, "Don't you understand? I'm risking everything just by telling you. All I've thought about over the past couple of months is trying to find out what I can. I've lied. I've—" He cut himself off, his face crumpling.

Enough. I was *done.* "No more excuses."

A low growl reverberated. A one-word warning. Flame and shadow guttered in his eyes, his grip tightened, and I realized he'd never let me see this side before. This was his other face—the one with no mercy. Where had my friend gone? Had he ever existed?

"Aren't you even going to warn her?" My voice was soft, so soft.

That's when the darkness in him snuffed out. He released me, and his arms fell to his sides. A haunting emptiness echoed in his voice. "A good hunter knows that it's better if the prey doesn't see the knife coming."

I blinked and blurted out, "You're sick."

Hunter looked like he'd been speared through the gut. "I'm trying, Serena. I want to be worthy ..."

"Try harder."

I whirled around to tell Cassandra. She deserved a rutting *chance*.

My blood crystallized in my veins. Dimitri was there, speaking to her. Then his malevolent eyes shifted to us. He made straight for us.

"What's this?" he drawled as he stopped. "Surely not another one of your fae lovers?"

His voice was mocking and oily. I resisted the urge to hit him square in his smirking mouth, and tried to sound light and pleasant in my reply. "Sorry—I don't know what you're talking about."

"No?" he crooned. "What about poor Wilder? Or have you finally spurned him? I suppose now that you no longer get any perks as his student, whoring yourself out to him isn't worth the effort."

He's goading you. Keep calm, Auntie warned.

My chin went up a jot. "There was never anything between us."

His lazy smile had my eyes narrowing. *Bastard.*

He prowled close; I didn't budge an inch. He studied me for a moment, pure disdain written into every line of his face. Then he spat on the ground next to me. "What about your wingless protector?" he snarled. "You're clearly lovers, given your scents, but his reaction to you in the arena wasn't right or normal."

"Normal?" I voiced delicately.

A mistake to tease the snake; he bit back. "He cares for you too much."

I smothered the abuse I so longed to hurl at him. And managed a polite response—barely. "We're lovers and allies. It's not against the law."

He bared his teeth and loosened a breath, which made an odd rattling noise as it hit the gap in his front teeth. And yet, he said nothing.

Hunter silently moved to my side. I could only guess what was going through his head right now. I wasn't sure that I cared. Let him think I was a whore. He obviously didn't mind throwing the word around.

Dimitri's eyes darted between Hunter and me as if seeking revelation. He twisted the knife deeper by saying, "You have some very interesting friends for a perfectly *normal* human. You've not only won the affections of a seasoned and previously celibate Warrior ..."

I nearly choked. *Celibate?*

"... but you've also bedded a wingless deviant who can't seem to stop himself running to your rescue. And by the hurt looks this one's been shooting you during our conversation," Dimitri gestured to Hunter, "I suppose you're somehow involved too?"

Silence. I didn't dare glance sideways for his reaction.

Dimitri turned to Hunter and tutted. "You want to be more careful. You serve the Solar Court—you serve Queen Morgan. We can't have your judgment compromised, can we?"

Hunter blurted out, cold and defiant. "We're friends. That's all."

Dimitri looked triumphant. Oh. You stupid, stupid—

"A member of the Hunt friends with a human. I wonder how that came about?"

I'd had enough. "Is there a point to this? Or can we go?"

I took a step. Just one. And Dimitri closed the gap, blocking me with an arm, settling in close to my ear. "My point is that to entice so many notoriously difficult fae to stick their cocks into you, means you must have hidden talents," he said, little spittles hitting the side of my face. "And if you've gained their loyalty, or gods forbid, their love, then that's a source of *great* concern to me. There are many others who share my beliefs. You would be advised to stick to your own kind. I won't do you the courtesy of warning you again."

His soft tones sent my skin into spasms of disgust. "Consider me warned."

He drew away, his dark eyes glinting maliciously. "Be under no delusions; our kind can fuck and enjoy yours. But love, respect, loyalty? Those things cannot exist."

I wanted to bite and claw and shred him to pieces. "Why not?" I challenged.

His eyes bulged, livid. "Because, you are *not* our equals. We cannot mate with you, nor marry you, nor make children. The monsters of such unions are well-known for being unstable. Do you understand *now*?" he asked with fervor.

My lips parted; to say what, I didn't know.

"I think she gets it, Dimitri."

Dimitri whirled. Wilder was striding toward us, a grim look on his face.

"Here was me thinking you'd grown bored with her," Dimitri cawed, cruel laughter ringing in every note. "But you're still willing to play her rescuer. Wasn't the time in the woods enough?"

Wilder came to rest by Dimitri's shoulder. He peered *down* his nose and replied, "I wasn't aware she needed rescuing. I came here to get you, not her. Goldwyn's looking for you," he said, pointing with his chin.

Goldwyn had landed behind us and was now chatting to Cassandra. She caught sight of us staring and waved Dimitri over. With a face like soured milk, he threw me a curled lip and stalked off.

"I believe you're also needed," Wilder said, looking to Hunter.

He looked baffled. "I am?"

Wilder was stone. "Don't you have a prisoner to transport?"

I risked a glance over at Hunter; his shoulders were stiffening, and his wings were tightening against his back. "We don't call them 'prisoners.'"

That. That was the breaking point. One stupid, defiant expression. I couldn't bear to look at him.

Wilder barked, "It doesn't matter what you call her. That's what she is. Now, leave."

"Serena?"

Oh, Hunter. There was such a plea in his voice. A plea to *look* at him, to say goodbye. I wasn't going to give in, but then ...

My eyes snagged on Cassandra. So I tossed my pride aside and spun, moving in to hug him. He responded more eagerly than he should have, considering Dimitri's watchful gaze would still be on us. I squeezed him; a vicious, ruthless part of me wanted to hurt him. Instead, I whispered so very, very low, "Try, Hunter—for me. Don't lie to her. She deserves more. Humans deserve more."

I felt his chest expand, swelling with emotion. I was about to step away, but he held on. "You should know, I didn't forget my promise. I got word to them in the Gauntlet."

Oh, stars. John and Viola.

My heart was breaking.

That's when he let me go. The smile I gave wasn't fake. It was my way of thanking him. "Goodbye, then."

He gave me a nod. As if to say we'll see each other again. I watched as he walked over to Cassandra's side; Dimitri and Goldwyn had already disappeared.

Hunter was talking to Cassandra in hurried whispers, then, *slap*.

Cassandra hit Hunter across the face. He said and did nothing in retaliation, just hoisted her into his arms. She didn't struggle. Why didn't she? Had he told her the truth? Did she think it was hopeless to fight back?

Hunter shot into the sky. This time I refused to feel his loss as before. A child had felt those things. A child who had believed we could be friends. No more.

CHAPTER 25
TEA AND WHISKEY

I watched until Hunter and Cassandra had become a speck, and the mist had drifted down from the hills. The clear cerulean sky, now masked by ash-gilded clouds and rainy showers, matched my feelings exactly.

That could've so easily been me in his arms.

But it isn't, Auntie said gently.

I loosened a savage breath, breathing his name. Hunter. You stupid, sweet, cruel headache. How could you?

Wilder hadn't moved a muscle; he'd stayed by my side. Eventually, with my heart still heavy, my head lowered to discover him watching me. There was a slight incline of his head to the left, and then he was striding away. I followed a little way behind, my heart skipping as he led me to his living quarters. He shut the door behind us and swiveled around, asking, "Are you all right?"

"Define 'all right.'"

Wilder didn't bat an eyelash. "Sit. I'll make us some tea."

Something in me softened and warmed at that. "Actually, that stuff you were drinking the other day looked like it did the trick.'"

A terse nod. "I'll bring both."

He departed for an annex room, presumably the kitchen. I walked over to the cold fireplace, choosing to sit on the frayed rug. Strangely, it now steadied me to be here, close to him, among the scents of wood and the parchment within his books. Those tomes were spread about me, surrounding me. Some large and bound in leather, others palm-sized in covers of leaf; a few were written in the elegant Kaeli script, but most were in the common tongue, shared by fae and human alike. I wondered whether he'd noticed or even cared that I hadn't returned the book he'd lent me: *The Darkest Song*. I'd taken just one peek through its pages and become engrossed. The content had been familiar and disturbing—legends from the gods and the three mythical courts.

There was the famed light court among the stars, where good souls feasted on light and music and art. And of course, the dark court that was nestled beneath the unnamed volcano. Evil doers, demons, and all manner of twisted creatures found their home there. The third realm was the moon, or "mirror" court, where fate herself resided.

Every child in the Gauntlet knew the descriptions of the gods and their courts. We grew up hearing about them through song and story. That's where it ended in Tunnock; fervent worship had fallen from favor. Viola had told me that most of the population were too busy surviving to pray for help that never came.

But a fae had written *The Darkest Song* as if the gods and courts were real. It was a written history, not a religious tome. None of my studies with Viola had revealed half as much. Of course, humans in the Gauntlet had always known that our lingering religious beliefs had been shared by the fae. If the book was to be believed, then humans had lost so much. Our spirituality was ash and vagaries compared to the rich tapestry presented in *The Darkest Song*.

Curiosity got the better of me. Perhaps there were similar books among the heaps. I picked one with a gold-embossed cover and rifled through its pages, running my fingertips over dry parchment and ink, drinking in the tactile sensation. I even raised the book up to my nose to breathe in that comforting, musty smell.

My eyes scanned the page. It was exactly the type of book I expected Wilder to own: battle strategies and tactics.

Discarding it, I grabbed another that turned out to be a little more interesting. A hero with a quest. A beautiful maiden. Nothing original, but I imagined still quite thrilling.

The next one surprised me; poetry, dedicated to the fae's love for the natural world. I got lost somewhere in meadows and rolling hills.

It gave me an urge to see the real thing. I stared out his window to the right. Rain clouds now covered the mountains, but the path to the wall was still clear. It hadn't occurred to me last time just how exposed we were. There weren't even any curtains. Dimitri could walk right by here and see me lounging around.

Wilder walked back into the living room carrying a tray with two mugs and two glasses. "D'you like poetry?"

"Yes." I closed the book with a snap and set it aside.

He crouched and placed the tray in front of me. "Sorry it's not more. I'm not really set up for having company."

The china cups were brimming with a ruby-colored tea, whereas the glasses held the same dark liquid he'd downed the last time I'd been in his quarters. Curiosity struck me. "What's the amber stuff called?"

"Braka. The closest thing humans have to it would be whiskey." Wilder swept away books on the rug to give himself more space to kneel opposite me. He'd removed the thick boots he usually wore and was now bare-foot in my presence. He sat and crossed his legs, rubbing the back of his neck.

There was something so *casual*, so human in his actions, his expression. That thought forced me to smother a smile. I continued to peer at him from under my lashes as he picked up his mug. Determined not to be caught staring, I did the same and stuck my nose in my cup, breathing in raspberry and honey tea. *Bliss.*

The perfume helped clear my mind. I took a breath and said on the exhale, "Wilder, why am I here? Didn't you hear what Dimitri said?"

"Actually, no," he said, frowning. "Goldwyn spotted him talking to you and came to get me as backup. I only caught the tail end of your conversation."

He gave me nothing else. "Oh."

Taking a slow sip of his tea and watching me, he said, "What else did he say?"

"I'm sure you can guess." I cringed at the bitterness laced in my words. Trying to temper my voice, I said, "He doesn't want me anywhere near you or *any* other male fae."

Wilder's hands tightened around his mug. "He threatened you."

A statement. Not a question. "Yes."

He stared at the floor for a good minute, not saying anything. I sipped the fruity-scented goodness, and taking advantage of his attention elsewhere, my traitorous eyes fixated on the sun-streaked strands of hair falling around his face, on the delicate crease between his brows.

Finally, those green eyes found mine again. "What about the fae from the Wild Hunt?"

Startled out of my reverie, I blurted out, "Hunter? What about him?"

"Do we need to be worried about him?"

I couldn't help it. "*We?*"

Wilder's face contorted; his concentration slipped, and his mug crashed down on the tray, spraying tea everywhere. "*Damn.*"

He was dripping. Laughter came out of my nose.

Wiping his face with the back his sleeve, he muttered, "Yes, *we*. Because I'm worried for you."

My laughter died.

Not bothering to mop down his fitted leather tunic, he continued, oh-so-seriously. "When you fought Jace, Frazer failed to keep his instincts in check. That's the way it is with bonds when they are first created. And Frazer already seems damaged." I almost erupted, but he hurried to explain himself. "I mean, he's overprotective, even for a male fae. I don't blame him—how could he not be? He's suffered the worst fate imaginable for a fae, and spent years in silence. The loneliness and isolation must've been crushing."

Those words were an arrow to my heart. *Oh*, Frazer.

"The problem is that such intense feelings for a human will be noticed—they *were* noticed. When Jace pinned you, Adrianna had to stop Frazer from running to you. People saw that. It's why Hilda didn't order Jace off you: she was too distracted."

"Why didn't you stop Jace?" I asked innocently.

"Because I was busy, watching for anyone who was showing an interest in your connection, which they have. Dimitri knew about us, he saw Frazer's reaction, and straight afterward he found you talking privately with a male from the Hunt." His eyes shuttered as if in pain. "The ice is melting beneath your feet, Serena. Monsters lie in wait. So yes, *we* need to be ready."

Goosebumps prickled my skin. I didn't know what I'd expected him to say next, but it definitely wasn't what he did. "And one way to do that is for me to accompany you during the sixth trial."

"You can't," I said, louder than I'd intended. "We're meant to do it alone."

Auntie snorted a bit. I knew why. I was already cheating, because Frazer had insisted on accompanying me.

Wilder eyed me narrowly. He leaned in. "Who told you that?"

Avoiding his gaze, swallowing hard, I replied, "I can't say."

"Serena!"

I cringed. He *knew* I hated to be barked at like that. "What?"

He looked strained to breaking point. I expected him to yell, but his eyes just smoldered. "You're really not going to tell me?"

I relented, just enough to confess a little. "It's the same person who told me more about my kin."

Wilder rubbed his stubble, his expression a full-on grimace. He continued. "Fine. I can live without knowing your mystery source. But cheating or not, I can't let you go alone when your life might be in danger. Dimitri could easily use this trial as an opportunity to capture you and take you before Morgan."

My sip of tea went down the wrong way. Spluttering, I said, "I haven't done anything wrong!"

His face turned grave. "Dimitri doesn't see it like that. You're a human. You've gotten too close to certain fae. Like me, for instance."

It was my turn to bang my cup down on the tray. "That's it? That's my crime?"

Wilder's gaze simmered with some deep, dark emotion. "It's my crime. Not yours. Because I was wrong. From what you've said, Frazer's scent hasn't convinced him that there's nothing between us. That, and his incessant jabs at me lately make me think he's planning something."

"Jabs?" I asked weakly, bracing my hands against my knees.

I got a sad little smile in return. "Dimitri keeps insinuating that my time in exile needs to come to an end; otherwise, I'll *forget* what it is to be fae. Basically, he thinks I'm going soft."

It took a second to put two and two together. A little gasp escaped when it came to me. "Morgan? He wants you to go back to her?"

A sourness marked Wilder's rough laugh. He picked up his glass of braka and started to swirl its contents. I almost lost my patience, but then he said, "*Morgan* wants me back. She's never been able to control me. Not fully. It intrigues *and* infuriates her—always has. And Dimitri's her faithful dog. Anything she desires, he wants to get her. And I've tried," he huffed. "Gods, I've *tried* to convince him. To stop him from thinking he'd found leverage on me through you. Because if he thought he'd found the right leash to drag me back to her, he'd do anything to get it."

The revulsion in his voice sent a line of hot anger slicing through my senses.

He snorted, disgusted, and took a slug off his drink. Shaken, I followed suit and brought the glass to my lips. Flavors exploded in my mouth: coffee, caramel, coconut, and something like leather. I coughed and cringed. Blinking back the strong taste, I found Wilder staring. His face was ... intense, searching. It made me giddy. Or maybe that was the drink.

He gulped down another swig of the foul concoction. So did I.

Wilder's cheek feathered as he sucked in air to clear his senses. "Look, Dimitri's not stupid. He won't make a move in Kasi. Too many eyes on you, too many fae asking questions if something were to happen. Diana's daughter being one of them."

I cut him off. "But in the wilderness, I'm vulnerable?"

A curt nod and an edged smile answered. "Yes, so I'm going with you."

The line of his jaw was granite. Absolute. Unyielding.

I spoke just as sharply. "Look, the truth is, Frazer wants to go with me. So you don't have to take this on. I'm not your responsibility."

His expression hardened to seem primal and ferocious. "Yes. You. Are."

I blinked at the intensity there. He looked sick—morose, as he stared down into his nearly empty glass. My heart dropped with a mighty whoosh. *Of course.* I probably reminded him of those he'd failed to protect under Morgan. I said the only thing I could think of. "You didn't make me attracted to you." I sounded sad. Quiet.

"True," he began, so softly worded. "But if you travel on foot, you'll be trackable and open to attack. And I understand why he wants to go with you, but you'd be safer in the air, with me."

I bit back a retort. Because he was right. That didn't make it easier to swallow. This wasn't what I wanted: for him to view me as some onerous duty. "So, how does that work? Do we just stroll out of camp together?"

"No," he said blandly. "We'll meet somewhere outside of Kasi. How much *exactly* d'you know about the trial?"

My tongue flicked over my lips, wetting them. Wilder followed the action, making me even more nervous. "We have to bring back an object or a creature of power, something worthy of a quest."

An incredulous laugh reverberated in his chest. He set his glass on the tray that rested between us. "Yes, that's right. And it lasts for fourteen days. Have you chosen something?"

I nodded.

Our pack had already deliberated which item we'd each retrieve, making the decisions based on distance and individual strengths. Cai had chosen the golden claw of the tiger, Liora had claimed the dragon's fire, which turned out to be far less terrifying than expected; remnants of the dragon's magic could be found in glass cliffs they'd melted and molded eons ago. Adrianna had gone for the phoenix feather, and Frazer had insisted on helping me retrieve the deadly nightshade, while also completing his own quest. He'd planned on bringing back the hide of a navvi sprite: a rare, shape-shifting creature.

He'd chosen that sprite because its hunting grounds lay in the Barsul Pass, near to where the nightshade grew. But if Wilder took Frazer's place, I'd no idea what his reaction would be. I tried to see the upside—at least it'd give him more time to hunt. He'd be safer. But this was Frazer; he wouldn't accept those reasons.

Ugh. I was screwed.

"Serena?" Wilder prompted.

My reply was flat. "I'm bringing back the sap of the nightshade plant."

Wilder looked taken aback, but his voice remained neutral. "D'you know where it grows?"

"North, in the Attia Forest, near the Barsul Pass."

I thought he might ask more questions, but he just said, "Okay. In three days, at dawn, head out the back gate and into the forest. Don't go far, and don't go alone. Walk with someone from your pack. I'll meet you out there and fly us north."

"How long to get there and back?"

"That all depends on how much time it takes to get the nightshade. What I really want to know is what you plan on doing after the seventh trial." Such a careful question.

My mouth went bone-dry at the sight of him pushing the tray aside in one smooth movement. Nothing was between us now. Every muscle locked. I didn't know what to do with my face, my body, my hands. "What d'you mean?"

A slight crease etched his brow, and his scars tightened as he answered. "There's a chance that because of me, you won't just have Riverland trackers who deal with deserters on your tail; you'll have spiders. If that happens, you'll need more protection."

I shouldn't tell him, but I was speaking before I could stop myself. "I'll have my pack."

Wilder was suddenly there on his knees, pulling my chin gently toward him so our eyes met. His stare was blistering, demanding, and my chest caught fire. "Are you saying they're all going with you? Even Adrianna?"

I kept my mouth closed. I'd already said too much.

He dropped my chin and rocked back onto his heels. Wilder went on, using dry, amused tones. "I see. Since your whole pack's going into hiding with you, can I assume you've got a plan and a destination in mind? Because I'd like to know where I'm fleeing to. *Before* I arrive."

I blinked. Wait ... What?

"Didn't you realize that I'd included myself in your escape plan?"

There, a twitch of his lips that had my heart expanding until it was too big for my chest. Until it hurt and ached with all the right emotions. "*Why?* Why would you do that?"

"I can't stay here. Not anymore. Dimitri might be a bloated ball sack, but it'd be stupid to underestimate him. It won't be long before he moves against me."

A simple enough explanation, and not what I'd hoped.

His eyes tracked my every movement as I brought the half-filled glass to my lips and took two long gulps, draining it dry. Warmth coated my tongue and throat, setting a fire in my chest and belly. It was kindling to my soul, giving me courage. I put the glass down next to me, suddenly in a daring mood. "You don't have to come with us in order to leave."

His brows knitted together. "No, but—"

My voice was hoarse. "You could leave after you've flown me back from the sixth trial. You'd certainly be safer without us slowing you down."

Wilder interrupted my rambling. "Maybe, but there's strength in numbers."

And that was it. He just watched me. I tried for a joke. "Are you sure this isn't just an excuse for you to run away with me?"

Deathly. Painful. Silence.

I shut my eyes, shielding myself from his grim face, praying for the world to swallow me whole. It hadn't been funny, but come on ...

The silence went on and on. I opened my eyes to say, "I've already told you that this isn't your fault. I don't want you to see me as some rutting burden."

A muscle feathered in his cheek. "How many times do I have to say it? I only left you alone to protect you from fae like Morgan and Dimitri. And I failed. So there's no reason for me to keep up the fucking pretense anymore, is there? And maybe I wasn't clear." Stars, he looked pissed. "Let me be now—I'm not just going because this is partially my fault. I *want* to go so that we're *not* separated."

That, there, liquified my insides. I floated up to my knees so that we were at eye level, and let my hand drift to the line of his jaw. Just a fingertip. His body tensed at my touch, but he didn't move away. So I let my other flattened palm rise to his chest, to settle against him: a warm, solid male.

I waited for the inevitable squirm of embarrassment, but it never came.

"Wilder ..."

Suddenly, I felt something snap and give way within him. Frustration drained from his body and face; his light eyes glazed over. Dipping his head, moving his mouth to my fingertip, he rumbled a throaty purr, "Serena."

My thoughts scattered. Like being hit over the head with a rock. He moved a little closer. Wisps of hot breath caressed my cheek; he smelled like the braka, and I breathed in coconut and caramel and wanted to taste it—to taste him.

His hands, large and rough, braced my hips. Pinning me in place. Such a careful move. As if not sure whether to pull me in or push me away. Then, *finally*, he leaned forward, and the length of his nose slid down mine until we were touching foreheads.

I was about to combust. My hand on his chest curled into a fist, grasping his leathers, while the other roamed, slipping into his hair. The wanting—the longing—pounded against my insides, thrummed against my core.

A breathless, jagged sound punched out of him. "We have to take this slow. I'm fae, and you're human. I—We need to come to terms with what that means. We're destined to lose each other."

The catch in his throat made me breathe him in. I wanted to confess to my heritage, but my body sang, *Not yet, not yet, not yet.*

"I'm serious." He looked out from a lowered brow.

No doubt.

I let my gaze flutter to his lips and feast there. "Excuses, excuses," I murmured and taunted.

Something sparked in his eyes. Like lightning glimpsed through an evergreen canopy. That beautiful mouth curved, transforming into a smile. Pure. *Playful.* Both his hands left my hips to graze my ribs, and then went down, down to my ass. Two palms flattened, and in a deliberate and slow move, he pulled me in another an inch so that our bodies pressed against each other. That mouth went to the nape of my neck.

I waited, spine tingling.

A kiss, moth-like and soft, had a thrill rushing through my veins. My chest froze, and my guts boiled as his lips moved up the curve of my throat. Another kiss and another and another until Wilder had left a trail of burning spots across my skin. Then, with nowhere else to go, his teeth snagged on my earlobe. Just a tiny sharp pressure, joined by a lick of pleasure that made me melt and mold my body against his. Arching just *slightly* ...

My breath caught as he stood in one fluid action and held out his hand. "Come on, temptress. You're leaving before my control slips completely."

Whatever charge had been building in my blood went stone dead. "You're kidding."

I gave him my best brooding scowl. A quiet rasping laugh was his only response.

Bastard.

He caught my wrist and smoothly pulled me up. There was nothing of desire left on his face. I searched and searched. How the rats did he just switch it off like that?

Wilder gestured toward the window with our hands now entwined. "It might be safer if you go out this way. Even Goldwyn can't have kept Dimitri busy all this time."

I let him lead me over to the bay window. "You know, for someone so cautious, you should really think about buying some curtains."

Wilder stopped to tap a knuckle against the glass.

"All the mentors' windows are made of spelled glass, so if you're looking in from the outside, all you'll see is timber."

"Of course its enchanted," I muttered.

He disentangled our hands and stepped back. "I'll see you in three days at dawn. Don't try going without me. I can track better than any fae from the Wild Hunt. Especially that one you were hugging."

I almost glowered at that last comment, but his quirky smile stopped me. Before I lost all control over my limbs and became rooted to the spot, I moved to release the window catch. Not bothering to say goodbye, I cracked it open and climbed through. After a glance in both directions, I ran toward my barracks.

CHAPTER 26
A QUEST BEGINNING

I arrived at the barracks feeling lighter than air, replaying every touch. Then I got hit in the face by a hard truth. Goldwyn had been and gone, only stopping long enough to disclose details of the sixth trial. It wasn't anything we didn't know, thanks to Hazel, but my pack still discussed and picked at every thread. Now, I had to add to their worries: Dimitri's threats, Hunter's warning, and Wilder's proposition. Or should that be demand?

Their reactions weren't unexpected. Shock, and more shock.

Adrianna paced. "So, this Hunter of yours—"

"He's not mine."

That low snap made Adrianna pause and switch her tack. "Okay, but do you trust him? I mean, enough to believe what he said about the Riverlands?"

She was trying so hard not to sound like the idea pained her.

My temper slipped, and I softened. "Hunter's complicated. He has so many parts, I could never trust him completely. But on this ... I don't think he was lying."

A quiet hush.

Liora's whisper fractured the silence. "Poor Cassandra."

The two men—males—in our group sat on the bed opposite us,

wearing matching grim expressions. Cai was the one to add, "So is this what we've come to? Morgan rounding up all the domestics and stray humans, and throwing them into her war machine? A war we don't even really know is coming?"

Clearly rhetorical questions. Yet, when no one answered, he muttered, "Fuck," and cradled his head in his hands.

A straight-backed Frazer looked over to Adrianna. "Can you get word to your contacts in the Riverlands Court? Maybe they can clarify, or at least confirm what Hunter's said."

Adrianna, who'd continued pacing the boards, halted and turned to us. There was a jolt around my midriff as I realized her expression had smoothed into a vacant stare. As if her inner most being had fled to some deep, private place within.

"If something this big has happened without them contacting me, then I don't have any friends left in that court."

A neutral response. She almost fooled me, but I caught the tremor in her wings. With that, we all sank into our own muddle of thoughts.

Minutes passed before Liora muttered to me, "Wilder used to work for Morgan, and he's one of the mentors. He might know more about her plans. Maybe you could ask him?"

I nodded, distracted. Suddenly a red-hot pulse in the thread got me to meet Frazer's insistent stare.

What is it?

He answered aloud. "You know that you can't travel alone with him, right? No matter what he says."

I'd been dreading this part. But I felt sure that Wilder hadn't exaggerated the threat Dimitri posed. And Wilder had wings. Frazer did not.

An inconvenient truth; one that Frazer was now grappling with, if the seething grief shimmering in our bond was anything to go by.

I *truly* despised the fact he was going to make me say it. "Frazer, I trust you more than anyone, but—"

Of course, he got there before me. "There is no 'but.'"

I stood with a steel spine. "Don't you dare go all dark and twisty on me."

Frazer's head lowered, his expression clouding over as he traced the lines in his palms. Thinking. Brooding.

My voice thawed. "You're my kin—a part of me. But that doesn't give you the right to order me around like that."

"You mean like Wilder does?" he said quietly—lightly.

A blow that knocked the wind out of me. I collapsed back onto the bed.

He still hadn't lifted his gaze to mine. My voice grew cold and distant. "I didn't fight him on it because if he's right about the threats being real, then flying to Attia makes things easier."

A sticky silence fell for eight fast heartbeats, during which his eyes traveled up to bore into me with those midnight blues smoldering like molten ore. "Then go with Adrianna."

I looked over to where she stood at the head of our pack; her jaw muscles bunched together, her tattooed brow heavy with lines, she argued, "I've got the longest journey, and the feather's the hardest object to find."

"It's on your way. Drop her off," Frazer said, his eyes never leaving mine.

Adrianna's mouth parted, but Liora cut across her. "Listen to yourself, Frazer. If Dimitri's planning something, she needs someone to guard her back the entire time."

A reasonable, calm tone that failed to soothe the beast. Frazer continued, speaking directly to me. "Have you considered that if Dimitri finds out that Wilder's accompanied you, it might push him to take things even farther? It might be all it takes to confirm his suspicions about you two."

I blinked. Shit. That *hadn't* occurred to me.

Cai drew a deep breath and eyeballed my kin. "This still sounds like the best play we've got."

Frazer didn't even acknowledge him. He just stared at me. "You'd really rather have Wilder watching your back?"

That quiet, unsure sound made my heart melt and plummet at the same time. "Never. It's just this once, brata, I promise."

I got a snort in response and tried not to wince. "At least you won't have to do two quests now." My voice was a mousy murmur.

He looked away with a grim turn of his lip.

Adrianna addressed me then, arms folding as she frowned. "Are you *sure* about this? About Wilder?" Gods. I felt like screaming. It must've shown because she showed me her palms and said, "I know you care about him, but he did work for Morgan."

I was ice and fire. "I'm aware."

Cai coughed awkwardly. "His decision to come with us to the lake places you in a difficult position." He nodded to me, adding, "You'd have to tell him about your magic and your fae heritage. Are you ready for that?"

I shrugged. "I'm more upset about putting someone else in danger. Especially when I know he'll be safer on his own than with us."

"Soon to become Morgan's most wanted," Cai said with a muted chuckle.

Not missing a beat, Liora quipped, "How thrilling."

They shared identical grins. An unaffected connection, as easy as breathing, and born from years growing up together.

I envied it. Looking over at Frazer's veiled gaze made my chest splinter. We'd yet to learn how to navigate all the bumps and kinks. Then, he was there, projecting. *We have lifetimes to figure it out.*

A dark mood blanketed me. *We hope.*

Adrianna took a step forward, pulling all our focus to her as she pressed me. "You get why I'd be suspicious? Because even putting aside his history, he was willing to take you back to his private quarters today."

My silence was my answer.

Liora was there, speaking for me. "What's that got to do with anything?"

Despite their recent tension, Frazer answered for Adrianna. "Dimitri had just finished warning Serena away from him. What would he have done if he'd caught her leaving his place?"

A heavy listlessness settled into my soul. To think, not long ago I'd been floating on air.

But my pack deserved whatever reassurance I could give. "He knew Dimitri might be a problem. That's why he made me leave through his window."

"The window?" Adrianna cocked an eyebrow.

I faced her. "Apparently it's enchanted glass, so you can't see their quarters from the outside."

Adrianna and Frazer stiffened at this.

Adrianna muttered, "And I'm guessing they've used that trick on the other instructors' rooms too?"

"I suppose so ..." She lit up with a telling smirk, and something clicked into place. "You want to use that to break in and steal something else?"

She replied with a little nod of acknowledgement.

Cai braced his elbows on his thighs and placed his hands in the steeple position, adding, "Good idea. I think I might try to steal from Mikael. He's just as tough as Cecile, but not half as nice."

Adrianna looked down at him with a bemused expression. "What does it matter how nice they are? It's not like we keep the items."

Cai grinned like a cat that's had cream for its supper. "Cecile told me to apply to train as a Sabu Warrior in a few years. They hardly ever take humans on, but she seemed to think I had a chance. I doubt I'll ever be able to apply, but I'd feel like I was being disloyal if I stole from her now."

I could've sworn Adrianna looked impressed.

Liora chirped, "Well, whoever you decide on, you three better hurry up. Because right now, you're choking on our dust." She gave me a playful nudge with her knee.

Cai was already there with a comeback. "Thanks for the reminder, sis. Apologies if we're not satisfied with an instructor *literally* handing us the trial."

That got my blood heating, but Liora just flashed her teeth. "Don't you think we've got more important things going on? *Pride* shouldn't come into it."

Cai response was to lean back on the bed and stretch his legs. As cocky and careless as ever.

Frazer straightened and twisted toward Adrianna. "On that note, can I have the teaspoon you took?"

Her eyebrows rose. "You don't want to take something yourself?" she asked, incredulous.

A nonchalant shrug was his answer. "Not particularly. I take no pleasure in sneaking and thieving."

That was that. Cai frowned a little, but Adrianna barely reacted.

Instead, she went to the pack on her bed, pulled out the teeny spoon, and tossed it over. Frazer twirled it between fingers, his eyes drifting to mine. "Are you going to be seeing him before you both leave?"

I shook my head, waiting for it.

"Good. Because I don't trust him."

There it was.

Adrianna cut in. "Me neither. At least not yet."

"Moons," Cai muttered under his breath, staring up at the ceiling. "This'll make for a cheery journey to Ewa."

Liora turned to me, her eyes shining. "Well, I'm glad a Warrior fae with centuries of experience is looking out for Serena—for all of us."

I felt sure it'd been said for my benefit, so I mouthed, "thanks," at the precise moment Cai clapped his hands. No one saw her smile back at me and nod in acknowledgment.

Cai stood. "All right! Enough suspicion for one day. Time for food."

"Do you ever think of anything else?" Adrianna asked, somewhere between amusement and contempt.

"Wouldn't you like to know?"

Cai beamed with his best roguish grin. Adrianna dismissed him with a mock groan of anguish and turned on her heel, leading the way to the food hall. I was the only one to catch the blip of disappointment crossing his face.

My hand reached out for him as the others moved away. "I always get the best sweet buns with you next to me."

Cai's grin returned. "What can I say? I'm irresistible."

But the joke sounded hollow to my ears.

We clasped hands, and as we moved outside, he squeezed mine ever so slightly. Maybe he knew I'd seen through his mask, or perhaps it meant nothing. I still squeezed back.

We were the same: both lusting after fae that seemed so far above and beyond that they were as cold and as distant as the stars. Sometimes, you just needed a hand to hold through the dark. I got that.

∾

I STEPPED outside three days later to be greeted by a coral-tinted sky, billowing clouds, and a crisp breeze that chilled my cheeks and made me glad I'd taken steps to guard against the cold, despite the season. Wrapped up in a cloak and gloves, I breathed in deep, filling my lungs with the first whiff of a fragrant summer.

I hitched my rucksack higher and checked my belt and blade. The instructors had given permission for the recruits to sharpen their weapons, so my Utemä's fire could burn bright again. We'd had consent during other trials, but this felt different. We were all going our separate ways, and that keen edge felt like a turning point; a new and more dangerous era.

Adrianna moved to my shoulder. "Ready?"

Frazer had insisted she be the one to deliver me to Wilder, given that she had wings.

Of course, I'd wanted him to take me. A brief and bitter argument had ensued. Frazer had won.

My heart squeezed.

I sought out the bond, purely for comfort. I'd already said goodbye. Although, since Cai, Liora, and Frazer were setting out later, our farewell had been naught but two sleepy "Good lucks," and a "Be careful."

Stamping down on rising sadness, I gave Adrianna the all clear. She hoisted me up and ran forward into what now was a familiar pattern. We soared, banking and circling the camp. As I stared down at the building that contained our sleeping friends, my stomach tumbled. "D'you think they'll be okay?"

Adrianna was silent as she set a direction for the forest ahead. Then she said, "I doubt any of us will have it easy. Phoenixes, nightshade, and white tigers. Navvi sprites—even the dragon's fire. Liora only has to chip some rock off a cliff face, but there's still the journey there and back to consider."

She released a little sigh.

I *really* should've known better than to ask. My throat stuck, thinking about the friends—the kin—that'd be putting themselves in danger. All for a spell to save me.

Adrianna looked down. She must've noted my silence because, unusually for her, she spoke gently. "The trials weren't designed to be easy, but we've faced down a korgan and an eerie. We'll get through this too."

I returned her weak smile and looked toward the looming forest. She'd meant well, but her words hadn't stopped the guilt from churning. We kept the silence until Adrianna landed just inside the tree line. She let me down and asked, "What now?"

I scanned the canopy and sky above. "I suppose we wait."

Adrianna invaded my space by leaning in close. "Serena, do me a favor?"

Wariness stole over me, but I nodded anyway.

She whispered, "Don't let your attraction to him cloud your judgment."

I sighed through my nose, exasperated. "Adi, I got this."

She continued regardless. "I just want you to keep your eyes and ears open. This quest won't be easy."

You think? Smothering that sarcasm, I said, "Just worry about your phoenix feather. I've gone through worse in the last couple of months than picking a poisonous plant."

Her navy wings rustled, and she rolled her weight to her other hip. Crap. I sensed a lecture coming. Sure enough ... "Don't underestimate the Attia Forest. All manner of horrors call it home."

Mother give me strength. "Adi, I said it to make you feel better. I'm petrified," I said flatly.

She mouthed, "oh." The next second, she was tilting her head upward, her braid swinging at her back. She'd heard something.

"Is it Wilder?"

"There are wingbeats."

Adrianna plucked an arrow from her quiver and strung it to her bow. I melted to her side, pulling my sword out a hair. Seconds clunked by. The only sound was birdsong coming in lulls and bursts and improvised melodies.

Adrianna jerked her chin to the right. "There."

She stowed her bow and arrow as my head craned up to the tangled canopy.

Wilder.

Wilder.

Something eased in my chest. Instead of floating down, he froze and perched atop a thick bough. A watchful eagle.

His head lifted, nose in the air. All the saliva in my mouth dried at the sight; that movement usually meant a fae was tracking a scent. After a minute of this, he floated to a lower branch, and then another, and another, until he took one giant leap and landed in a crouched position. He rolled up in one sleek move. I had to resist the urge to stare.

He still wore his black leathers and knee-high boots, but there were several new additions. Two silver vambraces, and lightweight pauldrons that were molded to resemble bird feathers, which now covered his shoulders. Straps crossed his chest; a bag designed for a fae nestled between his wings, I assumed. The belt at his waist held a dagger and a long, wicked blade. He also wore an ankle-length cloak with wing grooves, which he now untied at the clasp and tugged off.

Adrianna paced forward, talking fast. "I could come with you. I'd only need to grab my things, and—"

"I'm faster than you, faeling. You'd never keep up."

I always forgot how his voice shifted among his own kind. Deeper, stronger. Wilder's fir-colored wings unfurled again.

Adrianna shot me a desperate glance. There was nothing to be done now but say, "I'll be okay. Take care of yourself, Adi."

She actually looked worried. Wilder didn't stop to reassure her. He made straight for me and wrapped me in the inky pool that'd been his cloak.

With a slight bend in his knees, I blinked, and we exploded upward. Quickly, I shouted a startled and breathless, "Bye," to the ground. There was no response, but my human ears might not have picked it up. We'd already burst through the canopy. He was so rutting fast that my knees clenched together instinctively. The muscles in my arms had started to spasm from holding on so tight. A rough laugh rumbled in Wilder's chest. "What's wrong? You've flown before."

"Not like this. I just left my stomach on the ground." I struggled to hear myself above the roaring wind currents streamlining us, but figured Wilder wouldn't have any problems.

A sudden tremor in his chest made me squint up at him. His expression ... "Are you purring?" I shouted a bit.

A fierce grin. "I'd call it more of a humming." He kept his eyes on our flight path, but dipped his mouth to my ear to explain. "When a fae is truly happy, their chest vibrates."

On my first night in Aldar, Hunter had hummed. I'd assumed he'd done it to help me sleep. He'd just been happy. *Very* happy. Still, it changed nothing. I couldn't feel pity or forgive him; not when Cassandra's face still haunted me.

Wilder nuzzled my ear slightly. Distracting and toe-curling. "What is it?"

Not wanting to talk about Hunter, I dared to point something out instead. "We're about to go extract a poison that could kill us instantly. And you're happy?"

His head pulled back, enough for me to see the wide smile there. "I'm flying, which I don't get to do as often as I'd like. And I have you in my arms. I think I'm entitled to purr."

The wind provided a cooling blanket to my flushed face. Adrianna's warning resonated once but not again. Because our bodies were close. Much too close. There was no running from the strong arms that held me, nor the intimacy that came with sharing breath. It didn't help that with every mighty flap of his wings, his body was producing more and more heat. Any lingering reservations melted away as that delicious warmth seeped into my muscles, my core, igniting me. I grasped for something, someone, who could pull me back from losing myself in him —to him. *Auntie?*

Silence answered. So my mind stilled and my body took charge. My head dropped onto his shoulder, and I buried myself in his neck and shut my eyes. I couldn't bear to look at the ground; I might've been used to flying by now, but I was having trouble adjusting to his speed. My stomach dove and rolled again as we dipped. As if reading my mind, Wilder lowered his chin to the top of my head and asked, "Want me to go slower?"

I considered. "How long will it take for you to get there at this rate?"

"We'll get there tomorrow, but it won't hurt to slow a little."

His speed eased a touch, but I hardly noticed. "You're that fast?" My head lifted to find shining amusement. "Adi said it'd take her two to three days."

He nodded distantly. "Well, I'm older than Adrianna. It takes time to build wing strength and endurance; they only stop developing after our hundredth year."

No arrogance, just confidence. Spoken with the gravity of a fae who'd seen countless seasons and changes. It was intimidating as all hell.

"Exactly how old are you?"

I heard an amused rumble in Wilder's throat. "I stopped counting after the second—"

He was interrupted by a sudden headwind. Wilder tilted and dove; I opened my mouth to scream but the wind killed it. With the air stolen from my lungs, I struggled to breathe. Seconds of heart-racing, breakfast-losing free fall followed. That only ended when Wilder's wings opened with a mighty *whoosh*. Mercifully, we leveled out quickly, but as we skimmed across the forest canopy, I blinked rapidly through the shock, staring up at him like a doe blinded by the sun.

He caught me staring and gave me the once over. "Don't worry. You'll adjust." Laughter in his eyes, he told me, "Before faelings can fly, we take them up and introduce them to the sky by doing complex maneuvers. Spins and flips. You might get used to the speed if I recreated—"

"Don't you dare, Wilder ... Wait, what's your kin's name?"

His brows came together. "Why?"

A wary question. I couldn't imagine why. It was such a small thing to ask. "Because when my friend Viola used to scold me, she'd always use my full name to do it. That way, I knew she meant business."

A strange, sweet smile smoothed out his matching cheek scars. "She sounds like my makena."

As my thoughts whirled around Viola, I tried to ignore the flowering ache in my chest. I just added quietly, "Then, your mother must be wonderful."

Wilder's eyes lightened at that. "Her kin name is Thorn, as is mine."

"You took your mother's name?" I voiced, interested.

"My father wasn't worthy." A flat, frozen voice; his expression hardened to slate. Clearly not inviting more questions.

I let the silence stretch. Lost. Not confident in my abilities to pull a centuries-old fae from his brooding session. Instead, I scanned the horizon.

Forest blanketed the ground beneath, but in the distance, a dark, hazy smudge shimmered, beckoning. The ridge of a mountain range, perhaps. The only other landmarks happened to be two wide rivers on each side of us. One foamy ribbon twisting away to the west, the other flowing east.

Wilder broke the hush. "You've mentioned this Viola before. She was the one to pass on the necklace?"

I hesitated for a heartbeat, then gave a nod. He continued. "She sounds more like a maternal figure than a friend."

A questioning tone that he didn't push. I figured he might be like Frazer and open up once I'd made that initial step. So, I offered up slices of my past. Viola, John, Tunnock, Elain, and Gus. I even gave him snippets of my parents.

Occasionally he'd interrupt to ask things, and we spent a while in that pattern. I finished by telling him about being caught by the Wild Hunt. About Billy and Brandon and Isabel. It was tempting to edit my failed friendship with Hunter out, but it felt wrong, somehow.

Wilder peered down and said, "This Hunter's the one who tasted you, isn't he?"

I flushed and blinked. *Tasted?*

A wolfish grin stretched across his face. "I was referring to your blood."

Embarrassment warmed my face. "Right ... Yes, he was."

His smile slipped, and an eyebrow rose. "Of course, if he's feasted on any of your other exquisite parts, we're going to need to have a conversation."

A cough mixed with an indignant splutter burst out of me. "We haven't ... It wasn't like that. We're not even friends anymore."

"Oh?"

An innocent sounding plea for information. One that had my eyes narrowing. "I can't forgive him for Cassandra."

That drained all amusement from his features. "You asked him to help her, didn't you? Like he helped you?"

Resentment and anger simmered in my blood. "He wouldn't do it though."

Wilder's response was cold. Almost vitriolic. "I'm not surprised. From what you've said, his affection for humans begins and ends with you."

A darker emotion showed in his voice. It made me want to deny any feeling had ever existed between us; it made me confess. "He said he couldn't, because spiders are taking the recruits that fail in Diana's camps. Did you ... D'you know anything about that?"

The only sign of alarm was his fingers flexing and tightening against my body. "Hilda told us about a new order; one that had us handing over those recruits to the Hunt. But I assumed they'd be taken back to the Solar Markets, to be sold on. Morgan despises weakness in all forms. Why would she ever buy failed soldiers? Did this Hunter give you his suspicions?"

I nodded and shared the rumors. His reaction was slow in coming. "I guess I shouldn't be surprised. The only things stronger than Morgan's contempt for human weakness are her arrogance and paranoia. And she's been banging on that war drum for a while now."

A hoarfrost claimed my very bones as he pulled a face. "What is it?"

Wilder didn't shy away from my gaze. "The Solar camps are notoriously cruel."

A memory tickled the back of my mind. Hunter had something similar. "What exactly do they do to them?" I asked.

It was a form of self-harm, but it felt cowardly not to ask.

"Well ... One of the more infamous training exercises is called the Kula where the fae hunt the human recruits. It's meant to teach the humans how to hide from enemy forces, but if they're caught—and they nearly always are—the fae who tracked them down are given leave to torture them for days on end."

His voice and expression resonated with my own feelings. Horror and disgust, and finally, black, toxic rage.

"Morgan deserves to burn for eternity in the dark court."

Wilder swallowed hard, but he said nothing. I was left with grief and guilt thundering through my veins as my thoughts dwelled on Cassandra's fate.

Wilder muttered, "What worries me is why now? What's made her so twitchy?"

"Dimitri's her informant, right? Maybe we should capture *him,* and make him talk."

The venom in my voice had Wilder's lip half-curling. "As much as I'm tempted to watch you hold his feet to the coals, my love, we don't want to piss Morgan off any more than we have to."

My body heated. Everything after "my love" was a blur. Thankfully, Wilder didn't seem to notice as he descended into a thoughtful silence. My mind drifted.

Wilder's delicious purr had ceased, but the steady hum of wings, and the warmth from the two cloaks and his body set me into a kind of stupor for the rest of the morning.

When the sun climbed to its zenith, we returned to the ground to eat some dried biscuits and apple. I'd barely tossed the core away before he picked me up and took flight again.

Time seemed to slow to a trickle in the afternoon. After a few failed attempts to start a conversation, the lulling effect of being in his arms soon sent me into another stupor. I was meant to be testing my limits during this trial. I should've felt guilty. And yet ...

Wilder finally fell into a glide as the sky deepened to a velvety twilit blue. He landed on a branch high up in the canopy, and with feline poise, moved to the trunk, lowering me to nestle in its crook. It was so wide, I could sit cross-legged, resting my back against the ash bark.

"Give me your rucksack," he said, holding out an arm.

Pitching forward, I slipped my bag from my shoulders and handed it over. He placed it in the tongs of two nearby branches.

"Wilder?"

"Mm?"

He was distracted, unbuckling the straps at his chest, pulling his own rucksack around to the front.

"What are we doing up here?"

"We can't camp on the ground at night. The animals and sprites roaming these parts can be dangerous."

He crouched and dug through his rucksack until he found preserved meat and mixed nuts. Our dinner for the night. I watched on, bemused. "I can't sleep up here. At least not without falling out at some point."

His eyes found mine then. Laughter lines crinkled at the corners.

"You'll sleep in my arms. I won't move an inch: promise."

My heart stuttered. Then pounded faster and faster. "So, to clarify, I'll be sleeping in your arms for the rest of the night?"

A flush of heat coursed through my body, causing my palms to go slick with sweat. His prior amusement had vanished. "That's exactly what's going to happen."

He sounded raw, almost carnal. As if he knew what it'd do to me.

Damn.

A flare at his nostrils had my mouth drying. What was my scent telling him? Wilder stared a moment longer, only to unleash a self-satisfied smirk. A lion's smile. I folded my arms and scowled—a mask to cover the fire in my belly. He didn't seem all that convinced.

We soon began our poor substitute for an evening meal. As I washed down squashed nuts and dried meat with water from a skin, my eyes slid to the darkening forest floor. "I don't suppose there's anything nearby we could hunt that would make for a better dinner?"

He frowned over at me from his position opposite. "Making snares and traps would take too long. Especially now that the light's fading."

"You should've brought a bow and impressed me with your epic hunting skills," I teased.

An eyebrow jumped up. "Without doubt. But I don't like to take one on long flights. Gets in the way too much. Besides, hunting's not really worth the risk in these parts. Not if you've got supplies."

With a violent surge of anxiety, I said, "What kind of things are down there then?"

"Well, excluding the usual wildcats, bears, wolves, and navvi, occasionally you'll get a korgan wandering through, or a few zepefras."

Fear for Frazer made me ask, "Have you ever seen a navvi?"

He grumbled, and my stomach dropped. "Yes. They're disgusting. At least their natural form is. Their skin's blue and clammy, and their legs are inverted like a goat's. Unfortunately for us, they're twice as tall as fae, just as strong, and love drinking our blood."

My skin crawled at the thought of Frazer meeting *that* in battle. "Have you ever fought one?"

Wilder signaled for me to pass over his skin. "I've fought two. Why d'you ask?"

I turned over the flask and replied, "Frazer. He chose to hunt one for the trial."

His eyes widened a touch, but he offered a slice of comfort. "He's the best recruit we've had for a long time. He'll be fine."

Still, my stomach churned with hot shame. Frazer was alone because of me. Because I'd agreed to let Wilder escort me. I hadn't even asked him how dangerous the navvi were. And I was a selfish shit for it.

While guilt was eating me alive, Wilder packed the skin and what was left of the food away. Finally, he walked to me, reaching out his hand. "We may as well try to bed down now."

Wilder lifted me and spread his wings wide. Spinning on the branch, he sat, resting his immense bulk against the trunk. Then he prompted me to shuffle around so that my back was to him. Now, slumped against his front, those muscular arms and wings wrapped around me and tucked me in. It felt a little like spooning.

Any flicker of desire was quickly cooled as my mind wrestled with images of Frazer fighting off some nightmarish goat-thing.

I looked up at the thousands of stars that watched us, coldly winking through the canopy. Sleep began to feel like a remote possibility. Especially as howls and snuffles accompanied the rising moon. My body grew as taut as a bow string. Wilder's purr started up again, deep in his chest, vibrating outward into my body. The sound soothed the knotted tangles in my muscles. Like slipping into a hot bath. A small and failing part of me tried to stay tense and alert. Somehow, it felt disloyal to relax in Wilder's arms while my kin wandered the wilds alone. Auntie's voice entered my thoughts. *He's more than capable of taking care of himself, and you won't help him by worrying.*

That shifted something in me. Enough for me to close my eyes and whisper, "I thought you only did this when you're super happy."

I knew he'd sensed my teasing because a chuckle rasped from him. He moved his chin so that it was resting atop my head, and said, "That's right."

It was less playful than I'd expected. More earnest. The corners of my mouth tilted as he traced lines down my arms. I sent out one last desperate plea for Frazer's safety before finally submitting and sinking into oblivion.

CHAPTER 27
THE HEART OF THE FOREST

The pale light kissed the lush grass underfoot and painted the sky in strokes of pumpkin, lavender, and rose. To the right, in the north, a swollen storm cloud threatened. It hung over the Pass; the valley and doorway to the Barsul Mountains, whose jagged peaks were broken teeth dominating the landscape, lurking over us. And yet, I would've happily endured rain and ominous stone giants to avoid descending into the black cavern that awaited me.

Attia. A web of twisted black trees that stank of rot and damp and death. Home of nightshade. Hazel's map placed the sap in the center of its sinister, gnarled heart. Wilder had already circled the area from above, trying to spot a discernible path. But even fae eyes couldn't see past its impregnable mass of thorns and tangles. Only one option remained: to land and hope where fae sight failed, his keener sense of smell might save the day. For nightshade had a distinctive scent: decay.

Wilder's touch at my arm meant it was time. "Do you want me to go first?"

I fought the impulse to weep tears of joy. "Well, you're the one with the tracker's nose."

A lofty eyebrow and a curling smile answered back. "Was that a yes?"

"Yes."

With a subtle nod, he walked on a few paces, his wings flaring a bit, rustling against the folds of the cloak he now wore. I filled my lungs with a calming breath and forced my chin up to face the forest. Shoulders back, spine locked, I joined him, striding into that hostile shadow. The cold light of the morn quickly got cut off, strangled by the latticework above. I halted in the twilight and said, "This is going to get a lot more dangerous if I can't see properly."

In the gloom, I spotted a sidelong smirk. My mouth parted in a question, then immediately closed as he pulled something from his pants pocket. A whisper passed his lips as he revealed a glowing gemstone in his palm. A living ember that spawned dozens of firelights and chased away the darkness.

I blinked in wonder. "Are you going to tell me how you did that?"

"I told you when we hid from Dimitri that it's not my magic. I just know a good supplier of spelled stones. And firelights don't often dwell in dark places like these. I wanted to be prepared."

He didn't get a response. I was too busy tracking the firelights' swarming patterns, mesmerized by their bee-like movements as they danced and swayed in sync with a silent melody.

Wilder moved closer, brushing a hair from my face. My head twisted up toward him as he tucked the offending strand behind my ear. His head tilted. As if to say, *We need to get going.*

My pulse skipped. I hid it with a steely jaw and nodded, determined to keep my wits intact. He turned and led us into the forest's depths. I stuck close, keeping a firm hand on my sword's hilt.

The ground gradually changed underfoot. The earth turned damp and soft as moss and lichen replaced grass. I almost slipped a few times, even with the grips on my regimented boots. After long minutes spent wandering, watching Wilder track, it came to me that without him, I would've been hopelessly lost by now. For Hazel's written instructions gave a general northwesterly direction and a starting point—to the left of the Barsul Pass—but there was no sun with which to orient myself, and so little in the way of landmarks. Only a sea of tree skeletons with twisted trunks and branches formed like fractured bones, their life being sapped away by parasites: fungi, thorns, and creeping vines.

To find the nightshade alone in this twisted maze would've been tantamount to searching for a favorite star among a sky's worth. Impossible.

We continued at a brisk pace, but it still felt like over an hour before we neared Attia's heart. It was obvious when we did, because the trees became denser and the air thickened. That disgustingly sweet tang of rotten fruit now saturated everything. And no wind streams moved through to lift the heaviness. So a vicious cycle began: inhaling more to compensate for the stuffiness, and having the rot stick in my throat, which only caused me to breathe more deeply.

To make the situation worse, Wilder had to intervene more than once to stop our path from crossing with murderous sprites. Once for a korgan—Wilder flew us into the rafters and waited for its moss-stained hide to amble away—and the second and third times he saved me from grasping trees that contained benors. They were new to me. Apparently they lived in the root systems, snacking on the odd passerby.

These near misses had my heart pounding-pounding-pounding in my veins and feeling more useless than usual, but when the firelights suddenly hung back as if scared, my very bones quailed.

Attia's core loomed large. No birdsong reached us. No sigh of the wind. Just our ragged breath as we moved forward *slowly*.

Wilder caught my arm, halting me. "Be careful where you step. The nightshade's close."

"You're sure?" I breathed.

The firelights' distance meant we moved in semi-darkness, and I had to squint to see him wince. "The smell of the sweet rot gets stronger."

Stronger?

I whimpered. The forest was already too hot and cloying. Panic rose in my chest, drowning me.

"Wilder ... I can't breathe." I choked as the forest stole the air from my lungs.

He pulled me in close, one hand resting on the small of my spine while his other went to cradle the back of my head. "You're okay. I've got you."

Sticky mouth. Sweaty palms. Erratic heartbeats. It felt like dying. I was dying.

"You're not going to suffocate," he said firmly.

The command had his voice deepening, but it didn't stop my anxiety from ticking up another notch. Faintness circled.

Wilder released my cloak's throat clasp with one hand. It cascaded down over my bag and hit the floor in a puddle. He moved to my wrist, peeling my glove off, throwing it aside. He let his thumb trace the inside of my palm, stroking, teasing in concentric circles. Then, he slowly lifted my arm up and over his shoulder.

A rustle made me gasp. Fingertips met wing membrane. I'd touched one before, but never with permission.

Wilder released my arm, letting me at his wing. Such trust in that one move. It made my heart ache with joy. His hands settling again on my lower back, he said, "You're not going to pass out. Because if you do, I'll have to break through the canopy to get into the open. And you'll be responsible for ripping these beautiful things to shreds."

I detected a hint of laughter, but also sincerity. He'd meant it; Wilder would endure that—the agony and the risk of permanent damage. The beat of my heart changed. It was still fast—too fast—but it shifted from panic to something far more intense. That feeling expanded in my chest, giving me wings *and* throwing me in chains. Because what if it didn't work out? What if he rejected me? What if he found another reason for us to be apart?

Auntie's voice was a whisper, urging me on. *You'll only find out if you try, darling.*

I trailed lines across the membrane of his wing. Stroking gently. He shuddered and groaned a little. Emboldened, I moved onto the balls of my feet and encircled my free arm around his neck.

The twilight turned from oppressive to freeing, because his face was obscured in shadow, as was mine; I wouldn't have to stare into the face of a winged immortal—a beautiful male—and see the scrawny human reflected there.

The girl with a thousand scars collected from years of abuse and neglect. The woman who'd endured absolute and ceaseless rejection from her neighbors. So that when the sentence for exile had been carried out, there'd been a tiny part of her—of me—that believed it'd been justified. And I'd survived, only to be thrown into slavery. To suffer the complete and utter destruction of self.

Because I wasn't human.

I wasn't even Serena Smith.

I was something more.

Maybe, whatever was between us would become another scar on my heart.

But ... I *had* survived.

Now, I wanted to live.

I pulled my hand back from his wing and grazed my thumb down his jawline of stubble. His touch tightened at my back. "Serena."

A whisper that caused our hot breath to intermingle.

The beats of his quickening heart reverberated inside my chest. It was an effort to remember how to breathe, to blink, to focus on anything but that rough, warm skin beneath mine. He dipped his head. I arched into his touch, waiting. Expecting ...

Instead of ducking to meet my tingling lips, he moved so that our foreheads touched. "Not now."

Not disapproving. In fact, his voice had gone as soft as butter. A slow purr. Gods, I was *so* ready to argue. Only, I never got the chance.

"I don't want our first kiss to be in darkness. I promise that when we're far away, when you're safe, we can start."

Wilder drew away, breaking my grip, then crouched to pick up my glove and cloak and handed them over. Once I'd slipped my glove back on and stuffed my cloak in my bag, he encircled his fingers with mine and pulled me forward. "Come on, you've got a trial to complete."

I almost laughed. So much for being an instructor. He was actually leading me toward the nightshade now. Although it might've been for the best. Because stringing two thoughts together had become challenging, and a throbbing frustration prowled inside, scratching and tearing at the walls of my chest.

We walked in shadow for a minute more, then he came to a halt. I stayed close to him, blinking into the gloom.

"Through here," he breathed.

Wilder took me through a particularly dense weave of hanging vines and grasping branches. I threw my arm up to shield my eyes from spikes and scratches. Finally, illumination. A cold sunlight spilled in, slicing through my vision, blinding me, momentarily.

I lowered my arm slowly, allowing my eyesight to adjust.

A glade of moss and fungi and toughened grass greeted me. For no trees grew near the thorn bushes, nor close to the inky pool that lay in the center.

I took a timid step forward, maintaining a safe distance. Surveying.

The brambles' black thorns oozed nightshade poison, and with every breath, cloying decay stung my nostrils. The water was equally blood-curdling: a hot spring that leaked filth with each bursting bubble, like pus from an infected wound.

"Gods," I breathed.

Wilder squeezed my hand. "I don't think they'll hear you in a place like this."

No ... A forsaken place.

"Then let's get out of here."

Mouth tightening to the side, he said, "You should take this."

Breaking our handhold, Wilder cast his rucksack onto the ground. He reached in and pulled out a leather pouch. Standing, he offered it to me. "It'll be safer to store the thorns in there."

Not wanting the extra weight while I retrieved the sap, I dumped my bag next to his and took the pouch by its strings. I drew my Utemä, picked a spot to the left of the pool, and closed the short distance to the brambles.

Wilder's deep rumble of a voice came from behind. "Focus on a small area and cut slowly. You don't want the blowback hitting your skin."

"Thanks. That's only the hundredth time today that we've cheated. Some instructor you are," I joked lightly.

"My priorities always were skewed when it came to you." An amused tone.

Always? A smile broke free, even when faced with handling a deadly plant. I dropped the leather purse to the forest floor and scanned for a stem that looked safe to hold. There were none. Every inch was thick with thorns.

There was nothing for it. I chose a spot and with both hands on the hilt, brought the blade up and started to saw *carefully*.

One drop of nightshade was poisonous. More than that meant instant death. And there was no antidote.

My instincts screamed to shut my eyes as fat droplets of sap splattered the ground like blood. But I kept my focus on the slicing motion.

A few stems fell away from the main beast.

Wilder moved to my side. "That's enough."

Relieved, I wiped the blade on the stunted grass and sheathed it before I bent to pick up the purse. Now to get the thorns in.

I loosened the pouch's strings. Ever so gently, I tried scooping the prickly stems into the bag without touching them. That failed. So with a writhing gut, I prepared to grasp a stem with my thumb and forefinger. I'd taken leather gloves from the supply closet. Surely they'd be enough to protect me from the thorns?

Wilder blurred, his hand shooting out to grip my wrist. "No." His stare locked on mine and stayed there as he unsheathed his dagger. "Together."

A clammy sweat broke out on my body. "Okay."

I opened the strings of the pouch as far as they'd go and placed it next to the brambles. Wilder used the edge of his dagger and a flick of the wrist to maneuver the stem. The thorns snagged on the sides of the bag. My heart thudded once and stopped.

Then, *success.*

Wilder sheathed his dagger and jumped up. I tied and double knotted the purse strings. As an extra precaution, I encased the pouch in a spare jacket and pushed it to the very bottom of my rucksack. My hands now sweaty, I shed the gloves and stuffed them alongside.

I straightened and shouldered my rucksack. Wilder moved to my side. He was putting on his own bag when his head tilted.

I heard a hiss.

Wilder crashed into me, pushing me to the ground, body and wings arcing over me, creating a shield for what came next.

A sharp whistle pierced the air.

A jarring motion and a growl.

Wilder's body slumped. Almost crushing me beneath him, his breathing labored, he whispered into my ear. "Keep behind me. When I say run, *run* and don't look back."

He released me. It gave me the chance to turn onto my side and look up at Wilder standing.

I choked on a scream. A dirty great arrow had gone through his right wing, leaving a tear. An ugly wound.

My belly writhed, and I almost heaved my guts up, because he'd chosen to stand in front of me, wings stretched out, his body acting as a barrier between me and whatever was out there.

He drew his sword and cocked his head, listening.

Where had the attackers gone? Why had they stopped? How had they sneaked up on him?

The world blurred as red rain trickled down his wing. *Drip. Drip. Drip.*

His wing ... his beautiful wing. Torn and brutalized.

We should be running. He needed help.

I braced my weight with my palms and pushed up to a seated position. That's as far as I got.

I was shaking, trembling like a loose leaf in a stray breeze.

"Stay behind me. Don't give them a clear shot at you," Wilder hissed from the corner of his mouth.

I tried to stand—my legs wouldn't hold my weight.

Shit.

Auntie groaned. *Don't go to pieces on me now, girl.*

Right.

I engaged my core, rolled up, and stood at his back. Through a fog of terror-fueled adrenaline, I stared around for an escape route. We couldn't fly, so ...

He was deathly quiet. "You need to run. I'll cover you. Go—go now."

Hysteria edged into my voice. "Let me help."

"No! You'll be exposed. Serena, *please* just go." An order and a desperate plea.

Heart in mouth, I gripped my hilt and pulled the Utemä free by a couple of inches. There was the faintest murmur of sliding metal, which Wilder still heard. "Damn your stubborn hide," he growled and sheathed his blade.

I released my sword with a snap as he closed his wings and spun to me.

Another hiss. An arrow sliced straight through his bicep, taking blood and muscle with it. Red droplets splattered my face. Bile rose.

Wilder grunted through gritted teeth, but despite his wounds, he lifted me into his arms. His whole body shook as he sprinted back into the forest. How was he still upright?

Twilight fell over our eyes. Wilder whistled into the darkness—I had no time to wonder why, because he threw me from him.

I flew, landing heavily, inhaling dirt. I groaned and rolled onto my side to stop my bag from digging into my back. Searching the shadows, I saw something flash in the darkness.

I blinked. Once. Twice. Panic sluiced through my veins as I recognized light reflecting off a blade edge.

A firelight swarm abruptly appeared, blinding me. Wilder's whistle had brought them. They'd braved the shadows on his command. Now, the scene took shape.

Tysion, still in his camp uniform, stood with his sword to Wilder's throat.

I gaped.

The Sabu Warrior was on his knees. I blinked back tears. How had that happened? Had his injuries caught up with him? His breathing ragged and shallow, he looked over to me and groaned, "Serena, run."

Those green eyes shuttered, and he toppled onto his front. Still and lifeless.

Gods, no. Please, *please.*

"What have you done?" I whispered.

Tysion kicked Wilder. No movement. His smirking face turned to me. "Captured a traitor."

Captured? Did that mean he was still alive?

Tysion yelled, "Hunter! Come and get the girl!"

For a split second I thought it must be a coincidence. Then I spotted familiar green and brown clothes, short black hair, and stormy wings. An iron fist seized my heart and lungs, and squeezed and squeezed. My heart's blood poured out as his eyes met mine. "*Why?*" was all I could manage.

Hunter said nothing as he grasped my elbow and dragged me to my feet. I flopped against him, all my training useless. Frozen and staring into that face. Those eyes that refused to meet mine.

He'd betrayed me. Lied to me.

Traitorous, lying bastard.

I shoved and punched out. I caught Hunter's chin and he twisted away, taking the hit. Somehow that just made me more furious. I rained blows down. Sobbing, screaming, "Rutting coward! You *coward!*"

"What are you waiting for? Restrain her," Tysion snapped.

Hunter moved on me. Sobs become splutters and gasps as he whipped my wrists behind my back in a muscle-wrenching hold. He held them there with one hand as he coiled his other arm around my chest, squeezing me into his front while my bag was crushed between us.

Tysion rolled an unconscious Wilder onto his side. Blistering anger turned to cold sickness in my belly. Because this had to be Dimitri's doing. Was it on Morgan's orders? What would she do with Wilder? What would she do with me? Torture me? Cage me? All to make him bow before her?

Don't think about that. Don't think about anything but escaping, Auntie whispered to me.

How could I not? My deepest fears were about to be fulfilled.

Not death.

Imprisonment. Being locked up in another cage. Freedom forever denied.

For me that was the worst fate. Hunter had known. He'd seen it in me when he'd suggested training. For me to live under the whip and used as rutting leverage—to be sealed away—would be a living death. Madness assured. Oblivion was preferable.

Auntie began, *Don't you dare!*

If I have to die to spare myself from that fate ... to spare Wilder, I will.

I meant every word. But my resolve, my iron will, shattered like fragile glass the second Tysion traced Wilder's cheek scars with his cold steel. This was a game to him. Like a cat playing with a mouse, he pressed down and made a slow, taunting swipe ...

"Don't! *Please.* I'll do anything—just don't hurt him."

Wilder's wound was shallow, but it nearly had me on my knees, crawling, pleading.

A serpentine smile twisted Tysion's mouth as he said, "Whatever I want?" His eyes roamed, sweeping over my body, stripping me naked. "What could you possibly do for me that I couldn't get elsewhere?

Although, you must be good, to have snared a Sabu." A pause and a curious head tilt followed. "How about you get on your knees?" He pointed his sword to the ground in front of him and said, "If you're good enough, I'll refrain from telling your lover what you did for him."

My reply was slow in coming. "You'd let him go?"

Hunter's bear grip contracted slightly. As if in warning.

Tysion's voracious grin got bigger. "Maybe."

Not a promise. Probably just an act to get me to humiliate myself. And if it wasn't?

Tysion laughed, the sound mocking and shrill. "That's what I thought. You can rest easy—we won't kill the bastard. We're just going on a little trip. If things had gone to plan, you'd be slumped on the ground alongside him with sedatives rushing through your blood. Completely ignorant and having a nice nap. Alas, your lover saved you from that kindness."

And with that, Tysion turned to Hunter. "I thought you were the best bowman in the Hunt."

Gods. *Really?*

"I am." Hunter was calm. Too calm.

Tysion's eyes narrowed and became demonic shadows in the fire-lights' glow. "You had a shot at her, and you missed."

Hunter replied, "Everyone has a bad day."

His relaxed manner woke the magic in my blood. It thundered against the inside of my skull and thrashed inside my chest, desperate to be set free. I willed my magic to spill out into the world, to obliterate Hunter and Tysion. But nothing happened. *Auntie? Auntie, please. Help me. There has to be a way to use the magic safely.*

No, Serena. Not yet.

I wanted to scream at her and tear down the entire world in frustration. Auntie's voice was clipped. *Stall. Tysion loves to talk, loves to gloat—keep his mind occupied.*

Then what?

Just do it, Auntie hissed.

"What d'you even want with us?" I blurted out. As if I couldn't already guess.

Tysion's leering gaze moved from Hunter to me. Hate and disgust fueled his words. "*We* don't want you. But there is someone who wants to restore Wilder to the fae he used to be. The male that used to fell armies before breakfast and cut males down like stalks of wheat." Angling his sword back to Wilder, he added, "Not this pathetic husk that allows himself to mope over a bitch who's so desperate for advantage, she fucks a debased fae. You're not even good enough to scrape the mud off his boots. Once he's come to his senses, he'll see it too."

My fury broke free from its reins. Hunter's arm tightened as if he'd heard the snap of the leash. My voice was a taunting whisper. "It sounds like you're in love with Wilder. Or maybe, you just have a problem with females? I wouldn't be surprised if you were feeling bitter."

Such reckless words.

Wrath contorted his face at the implication. "What are you talking about?"

"Adrianna," I sang lightly. "A female fae beat and humiliated you in front of hundreds of people. So if anyone's the bitch here, it's you."

Stupid, stupid, stupid.

Tysion closed the distance between us in two bounds, his fangs going for my throat.

Then I was eating dirt—literally. Hunter had shoved me aside. Coughing, spitting out earth, I looked up to see Hunter had strung his bow. His arrowhead marked for Tysion's chest. "Enough," he commanded. "You've had your fun. No one ordered you to damage the hostages or stand around gloating."

Tysion snarled in his face, but he didn't go for me again. "She'd have healed by the time we got to court. Besides, what's one more bruise? She'll have far worse once *she* realizes how deep his attachment goes."

She? Shit. Of course, Morgan.

Hunter was quiet, thoughtful. "I know. That's why you're going to take Wilder and leave us behind. He's the prize, not her."

I scrambled to a kneeling position, my mind racing, trying to order his actions into a chain of events that made sense.

Tysion's shock mirrored my own. "She's the key to controlling him."

Hunter lifted his chin a touch, but otherwise, he was unmoved. "Perhaps. You're still going to leave her behind."

A wicked snarl came from Tysion as he dipped his head, his eyes darkening. It was an all too familiar fae stance. A threat, plain and simple. "Why would I do that?"

Hunter looked down the length of the arrow. Almost exasperated. "Isn't the arrow pointed at your chest a good enough motivator? If you want to keep pushing me, take another step."

"You'll shoot me?" Tysion asked, his words a lethal embrace.

Hunter cocked his head. "Obviously. But I won't shoot to kill. I'll leave you to bleed. I'm sure one of the sprites haunting this place would be very happy to eat you alive."

My gut spurred with dread. I'd never seen true cruelty in him before. Just infamous fae arrogance.

Tysion's hooded eyes focused in on the arrow's tip, and suddenly widened in stark realization. "You missed your shot at her on purpose, didn't you?"

Hunter's huffed in polite incredulity. "Finally got there, did you?"

Tysion just scowled. "You're a fucking idiot. D'you have any idea what she'll do to you?"

Hunter's shoulders jerked up in an attempt at a casual shrug, but he couldn't hide the despair that shadowed his face. "Force a blood oath? Make me into a spider? Torture me for years? Who can really say with her?"

"You're risking damnation for *that?*" Tysion jabbed a finger down at me. "For a human—for a *woman?* What use is she? She'll grow old. You'll be stuck with sagging teats and a graying bush."

I almost snorted aloud, but things were already on a knife edge.

Hunter sounded soft and deadly as he responded. "That doesn't matter to me. Now, take him and go."

I stopped breathing.

Tysion hissed through an adder's tongue, "You're making a mistake—"

"*Go!*" Hunter roared.

The sound made my knees wobble as I stood. Tysion tossed me one final filthy look before slinking back to Wilder and lifting him. I let out an agonized groan as he fled with his prize. The firelights seemed agitated and confused, but they didn't follow Tysion. They stayed with me, circling above.

Hunter released a held breath and relaxed the bow string. He stowed the arrow in the quiver at his back. Finally, his tortured eyes found mine. Before he could speak or make excuses, the black wrath that had been building now fixated on him. I drew my Utemä and advanced. Two paces. My blade went to his neck. Hunter made no move to defend himself. It didn't matter; I was one step from opening his throat onto the ground. "Go after him. Get him back."

No movement. Not even a blink.

I screamed so savagely, so wildly, it was as if my throat had been torn asunder. "DO IT! DO IT NOW! Or I *swear,* I'll kill you."

My voice broke. *Damn.*

"No, you won't," he said quietly. So assured. So rutting confident.

My sword-arm twitched, but I didn't strike. I needed him. "I can't track them, and I can't beat Tysion. But you can."

"Probably. But I won't go after them," Hunter whispered.

"Fine."

I lowered the blade to my side. I'd had my chance. He was right: I didn't want his blood on my hands.

I made a move to pass him, to go after Wilder. Hunter blocked me, spreading his gray wings wide. I made another move that he also stopped. My fists curling, nails biting into palms, I spat, "Get out of the way!"

Hunter shook his head. Just once. "Tysion would only capture you, and then both our lives would be over."

I swallowed the rage roiling beneath my skin with monumental effort. "Explain."

Hunter hurried on. "After Dimitri saw us together, Morgan sent me a summons. And she got inside, Serena." He tapped the side of his head; a grimace of remembered pain flashed across his face. "She saw you through my eyes."

"What d'you mean she got inside? Got inside how?"

Eyes shuttering, he answered. "Morgan can break minds, hear thoughts. She extracted my memories of you. The cage. Your attacker. The knowledge I'd shared ... My feelings. Our friendship."

I tried to hide my disgust, my contempt. As if I could feel anything for him. All I could think was *Wilder, Wilder, Wilder.*

"Serena?" Hunter whispered my name. Like it meant a damned thing. Like we were still friends. As though he *cared* for me.

A creeping suspicion bloomed into a question. "Why would she send you? If she saw that you had feelings for me, why trust you to capture me?"

Hunter shook his head; a slow, sad movement. "She doesn't trust me. She doesn't trust anyone. Picking me to capture you was a test *and* a punishment. If I proved disloyal, she promised to make me into one of her spiders. Enslaved to her for all eternity." A tremor had made its way into his voice.

Emotion swelled and closed my throat. I pushed it down to where it belonged. I needed answers, not excuses. "Why risk that to save me then? You're more than willing to sacrifice Wilder."

His wings collapsed a little. As if some great weight settled on his shoulders. "I can't hand you over knowing what she'd do. You're the only friend I've got."

I blinked. Anger met grief in a violent outburst. "Well, then, you've got nobody!"

"Serena ..."

"No—no excuses! You betrayed me! You've lied to me! You never told me how bad things were in the Solar camps. And you sold Cassandra out because it was easier than fighting back. And you're doing the same thing now!" A sob got caught in my throat as the truth of what he'd done really sunk in. I kept on. "You sacrificed Wilder! You shot at him. At his wings—his *wings*!"

Hunter's eyes twitched in a wince. "I had to."

I clenched my jaw so hard it hurt. *Treacherous, lying ...*

Hunter suddenly crossed the gap between us, snapping his wings in with a thud. I barely had time to react, to bring my sword up.

He got in close and broke my grip on the hilt, disarming me. I went to grab it from him, but he angled the blade behind his back and put his palm out flat, saying, "You're going to listen to me. If you still want to kill me afterward, I'll give you this back."

He raised my Utemä. A promise and a peace offering.

My palms itched. I could *strangle* him. But he didn't wait for me to reply; he was already rambling. "Morgan didn't execute Wilder or force the blood oath on him because she wants him to be her general. Even enslaved to her, she'd find it difficult to control someone like him every minute of the day. Worst of all, she desires him." He croaked out a bleak laugh. "My point is that she won't hurt him. She's never seemed capable. You, on the other hand ..."

In a brittle tone, I snapped, "She'd torture me to get him. I know. That doesn't mean you should save me and let him be taken."

"She wouldn't torture you. Not like that."

That shut me up.

He rushed on in one breath. "Morgan might be jealous. She might desire Wilder. But she's no fool, and she's got a gift for spotting potential. And when she saw my memories, she was *intrigued*, Serena." He winced. As if this was the worst thing that could've happened. "She thinks you'll make an excellent addition to her *collection*. To her armies."

Shock pulsed through me, setting my mind adrift. Rudderless in a stormy sea. "For gods' sakes, *why?* There are better fighters. I'm not even fae."

Not yet, anyway.

Hunter frowned. "Making you her creature's the best way to destroy Wilder's affections. And then she saw how you defeated Jace, that you had a friend in the Hunt. Even your wingless lover." His teeth clamped together in a silent rebuke. "Can you really not understand why she wants you?"

The world spiraled; I was unraveling.

Hunter's voice was barely more than a murmur now. "I'm sorry, Serena. For everything. But if he's back at court with her, it might be the only way she leaves you alone."

He had the audacity to look to me beseechingly. He wanted forgiveness. White-knuckling, fighting the urge to skewer him, I fired, "Why would she do that when she wants me so badly?"

There was a hollow truth in his words. "He shielded you with his body. Trust me, he'll make a deal to spare you."

I wanted to hurl my guts up. To scream and scream and scream.

He must have seen something in my expression because he moved toward me. I backed up, glaring. "Don't *touch* me."

Hunter showed me an open hand. A sign for peace. "I swear that I'll make this right. I've got a plan."

The *absurdity* of that promise struck me so forcibly, I sniped. "What plan?"

His Adam's apple quivered. "After Morgan heard Wilder was coming here—"

I stopped him with a wild flap of my hand. "How did she know about that? No one knew."

Hunter angled his head toward me. "Dimitri must've found out, because he's the one who told Morgan where to send us, and he ordered Tysion along to act as my second."

I couldn't stop myself from barking, "Why him?"

A pause. "I think ... I think Tysion might be Dimitri's son."

My jaw went slack. I shook myself inwardly. "Fine. Get to the point."

Hunter's brow creased as he looked down and thumbed the hilt of my sword. "Morgan didn't want either of you permanently damaged in the capture. It's why she gave us a sleeping potion to tip the arrows in and ordered me to take the shot, because I'm the better bowman."

The *best,* if Tysion was to be believed.

Hunter met my angry eyes again to say, "But I thought Tysion might try to snatch the bow from me if he sensed any hesitation on my part. I wasn't trusting him to shoot anything anywhere near you, so before we set out, I went looking for a weapon that couldn't be used against you. Something that might help you—us—survive."

Despite my wrathful thoughts, my eyes still darted to the maple recurve bow strung over his shoulder. "The bow?" I asked to confirm.

Hunter nodded vaguely and ran a finger along the silver string. He looked pensive. "It's called a kaskan. Once enchanted, it can't be used to harm its owner. It's yours now, and it won't ever miss, as long as your target's in sight and you've got the focus and the heart to shoot someone. They're practically impossible to get. So I went to the only witch who still makes them. Luckily, he'd taken up residence in the Solar Court to trade his other weapons, but he wouldn't even let me in the front door, so—"

"You stole it?"

He shook his head and a smile flickered into existence. "Oh, no—that was Isabel. After Kesha sold her, she became the one and only apprentice to the kaskan crafter."

I was stunned. "Is she okay?"

He nodded again. "She wanted to help you, so she spelled a bow to recognize you. You're the only one who can make this thing work now."

I couldn't think what to say as I stared at the bow. *I'm yours*, it seemed to whisper.

"Isabel gave me something else—something that will help us." His free hand dug into his brown leathers to pull out a chunk of quartz crystal that appeared to be giving off light waves. "It holds a powerful concealment charm at its core. It stopped Wilder from sensing us, but now it can do the same for you and me." He pocketed it and went on in a brighter, more hopeful tone. "Come away with me, Serena. With the stone, I can get us across the sea to Asitar or Makara. We might be safe there. We'd have a chance at a life outside Morgan's control—"

"*Are you crazy?*" I screamed, and Hunter recoiled. "D'you honestly think I'd run away with you while Wilder gets dragged back to that *monster*?" Breathing heavily, anger licking at my insides, I ranted on. "What makes you think we'd even make it? She saw into your mind—she must've seen this stupid plan of yours?"

Hunter just stared, glassy-eyed. When he spoke, his voice was broken. A mere rasp. "I hadn't thought of it yet. Morgan isn't all powerful, and the mind isn't some book to be flipped through at will."

I didn't know what to make of it. And I didn't care. "Fine. You've had your say. Now, give me my sword." I held out my hand, waiting and expectant. "Because I'm leaving. I'm going after him, and you'll have to kill me to stop me."

He hesitated. "I'd never hurt you."

"You already have."

He blinked, pain crushing his features. Then, his nostrils flared, and his head whipped around. "Serena, we have to leave. Someone's coming."

He threw my sword aside and came to me. As if to pick me up.

Probably just some ploy to get me to go with him. Not happening. I let him get in close then brought my knee screaming up into his balls. He grunted. I didn't stop to congratulate myself. I ran.

But I hadn't gotten ten paces before running headlong into another male's body. I stepped away, disoriented. Tysion?

Then, the firelights illuminated another male.

I let out a giant sob and threw my arms around Frazer. He didn't reciprocate. I released him and moved back a step to see his eyes fixed over my shoulder. The intensity and loathing scared even me. He flew past me, not even bothering to draw his Utemä, and crashed into Hunter like a hurricane, flooring him, landing heavy blows to his face and abdomen and ribs.

I felt numb. Adrift.

Hunter tried to kick him off. When that didn't work, he closed in on his attacker's neck, canines free and snapping down. Frazer responded by landing a hit to his jaw, and then he went for the wings. I winced as Frazer dragged Hunter off the ground by those beautiful things that were storm and cloud made flesh.

Hunter's nails scraped into the dirt. He was clawing, desperate, and sobbing my name.

My stomach clenched and twisted. I wasn't made of stone after all. A sickening crunch followed. Frazer had thrown him against a tree and now pressed his thumbs firmly down on two spots either side of Hunter's neck.

He would pass out soon; Frazer's application of pressure points was flawless. I had to speak quickly. "I'm sorry, but I'm not your possession. You don't get to decide what's best for me."

Hunter's eyes found mine. His hand stretched out for me. Help me, *help me,* he seemed to say.

I noted the seconds and held his pain-riddled gaze. Anything less would've made me a coward. Hunter's clay-eyes slid back into his head on the count of four.

A sigh mingled with guilt and relief rushed out of me.

Frazer pushed him back with a look of deep disgust and paced over to me. Without saying a word, without making eye contact, he scanned me carefully. He even turned me around in a rough spin to stare at my back.

Bewildered and annoyed, I asked, "What are you doing?"

"Checking."

I clucked my tongue and batted his hands away. "I'm fine. Now I need you to go on a hunt."

A tiny smirk and a raise of the eyebrow. "What am I hunting?"

"Wilder, and the fae bastard who took him: Tysion."

Frazer let out a belly growl.

"Go after them! Before it's too late," I pleaded.

He was unyielding. "Not without you. Grab your sword and we'll go."

I made an impatient noise and went to sheath my sword. Then, my eyes snagged on Hunter, and the bow. My hand itched to take it. But it was the weapon that had ripped through Wilder's wings like they were gossamer silk. A second of wavering.

It's meant for you, Auntie whispered.

No doubt.

Hunter's body was slumped against a tree and I felt nothing. Well, okay, a little sadness. And a lot of anger. So I wasn't gentle as I pulled the bow and quiver loose from his shoulders. I made one last snap decision and set the kaskan and quiver on the ground to root through the pockets of his leathers for the quartz crystal. He hadn't said if it would work for anyone who possessed it, but I hoped it would. It could go a long way to helping us on the road ahead.

"What's that?" Frazer appeared at my side.

"Concealment charm," I said, shoving it into my bag.

"Good."

No interrogation. I could've kissed him.

Frazer's eyes went to the kaskan. "Why take the bow? It's just extra weight."

I paused. "It's been enchanted to never miss. And it's mine."

Frazer picked up the quiver and bow from the forest floor, shouldering them. "I'll carry them. We don't want it to get damaged while you're in my arms."

I began, "But you just said—"

"We can't leave a kaskan behind."

He lifted me and *finally,* we were sprinting, chasing after Tysion.

Dreading the answer, I asked, "Can you track them?"

Frazer looked strained, but he gave me a curt nod. "Just, but their scent's disappearing."

Shit. "Already?"

"This forest muffles everything. I lost yours halfway in and had to rely on our bond to find you."

After a minute of being jostled around and furiously wiping Wilder's blood off my cheek, I choked out, "D'you really think we can catch up?"

I was prepared to hear a no.

"Adi's waiting at the edge of the forest. She might be able to stop him."

A spring of hope welled up, and my curiosity finally trumped my fear. "Why is she here? Why are *you* here?"

Frazer chuffed. "Did you really think I wouldn't follow when I thought Wilder might be a traitor?"

I wanted to smile, but the muscles in my face had frozen. "How did you catch up to us?"

Something, a memory, shone through the bond. It was difficult not to gasp aloud. *You let Adi carry you?*

His lips thinned and the pressure on my legs and back intensified. *To my humiliation, yes.*

My mind reeled. I knew his character. To have submitted to that would've been excruciating for him. I loved him even more for it.

Frazer continued aloud. "We didn't even need to track you, since we knew where you were going. It nearly killed Adi though, trying to keep up with Wilder. She was frothing at the mouth when we arrived."

My stomach flipped over. "Why didn't she come into the forest with you?"

Frazer's laugh was wheezy and thin. "I'm faster on the ground, and she didn't want to run into Wilder. Ever the obedient student," he said with a sarcastic lilt. "But she volunteered to watch from above and keep an eye out for signs of an ambush in the surrounding area. Although if she'd picked up Tysion's scent, nothing would've kept her away."

Silence fell between us after that, and the minutes ticked by until the first ribbon of sun trickled down to bathe the earth. Scanning the gaps now appearing in the canopy, I couldn't bear to voice the question that was tearing me up inside. So I whispered down the bond instead. *If Tysion's already flown off with Wilder, will we be able to track him?*

Frazer's reply was soft; so soft. *You already know the answer to that question.*

Heat prickled my eyes, and my head slumped against his shoulder. I went utterly limp and despondent while memories of Wilder shielding himself with his wings, his body, floated to the surface of my mind. Unbidden and unwanted.

My heart was aching, bleeding. Gods, it hurt so much.

It's my fault.

Frazer's words were a gentle murmur. Almost a lullaby. *No, sweet one. Morgan is to blame for this. No one else. We shouldn't be punished for those we love. It's as much in our control as the turning of the tide, or the rising of the sun.*

I nodded, vacant. Lost to a waking nightmare.

CHAPTER 28
BECAUSE OF YOU

S igns that we'd soon be free of the forest emerged. More watery
shafts of sunlight filtered through and a breeze, fresh and glorious,
broke Attia's spell. The brightness lifted the lifeless, oppressive mood,
waking me up, helping me breathe again.

"Can you still smell them?"

Frazer's nostrils widened. "Yes."

No inflection in his voice.

"They've gone, haven't they?"

Frazer remained silent, but he picked up speed. There was my
answer. All hope and pretense shattered and a heart-rending grief
unfolded, a pain that threatened to flood and wash me away in its mighty
force.

The trees thinned, and as we reached the last of their skeletons, the
firelights left us, and my head went up, scanning the open skies. Nothing.

A sob got twisted in my throat, becoming more of a whimper on the
exhale.

Frazer set me down, cupped my chin, and moved my head to the left.

There was Adrianna, crouching over Tysion's unconscious body.
Examining him. Wilder lay next to him. Still unconscious.

But he *was* there. Not being dragged to Morgan.

There weren't words ...

Adrianna saw us and stood, beckoning. We jogged over, and I went straight to Wilder's side, gently checking his wounds. The fraying skin and torn muscle at his bicep had begun to knit together, thanks to the healing abilities of the fae. But his wings—they weren't faring so well. The delicate membrane had clotted, yet the hole was still visible. The sight felt like a shard of glass piercing my gut.

Adrianna spoke first. "I hope you don't mind." She booted Tysion's leg. "As soon as this bastard came hauling ass out of the forest with Wilder slumped over his shoulder, I dropped out of the sky and smashed him over the head. Thankfully, his skull isn't as thick as you'd think."

I looked up to find Adrianna patting a weighty and wicked-looking crossbow. The harsh lines of her face were fierce and unforgiving. A warrior's mask.

A harsh cackle—part relief, part hysteria—croaked out of me. I clapped my hand over my mouth as Frazer touched my shoulder, in comfort and solidarity.

"So, what d'you want to do with this worthless worm?" Adrianna crinkled her nose and bared her teeth at Tysion's still form.

My voice was hardly human as I uttered hoarsely, "Let him rot. If Hunter doesn't track him down and silence him, then his father's reaction to his failure will be punishment enough."

"Father?" Frazer echoed.

Adrianna asked, "What's Hunter got to do with any of this?"

My tongue had gone thick and heavy, and a headache battered against my skull. I was so very, very tired. Not trusting my legs, I stayed kneeling with a hand flattened on Wilder's chest and let everything spill out. The gaping wound in my heart bled upon recounting the ambush and Hunter's story. His excuses and his so-called plan. I ended by explaining the kaskan and the stone.

Adrianna hissed like a tea kettle once I'd finished. "I can't believe that that besotted idiot thought you'd leave with him. After what he'd done." She pointed a loaded crossbow down at Tysion, and growled, "And this *thing* is Dimitri's offshoot. Ugh, no wonder he's so vile."

"We should go," Frazer said abruptly. "I don't trust Hunter not to come after her; even if the stone works for us, it doesn't make us invisible."

Adrianna slipped the crossbow's strap over her shoulder and adjusted the quiver and bag at her back, fidgeting. "Well, I can't fly very far. Not yet."

Her magnificent head drooped a bit. I recognized the look and the cause. It was the face of someone disappointed by their own limitations.

Frazer jerked his chin toward the gully. "I've heard the Pass is riddled with caves, all the way up into the mountains. There might be a few that'd be safe to bed down in for the night."

Adrianna was nodding. "Okay. I'll take Wilder and come back for you both."

Frazer stole a look at me. "We're not staying here. I'll carry Serena to the Pass. You can pick us up there."

Adrianna nodded again and prepared for flight by tucking her long braid into her jacket. She moved to pick up a bag off the ground and threw it over to Frazer. "You can carry your own rucksack now. Wilder's heavy enough as it is."

Frazer answered by clipping his bag on, maneuvering it around the quiver and kaskan.

I watched, concerned, as she gingerly lifted Wilder. His head rolled. Like a lifeless doll.

From my seated position, I said, "I could take his bag, or the blades. It might help."

She lifted a haughty brow. "I'll manage."

Auntie tutted in my head. *Prideful faeling.*

My gut tumbled as Adrianna turned to run, her scaled wings straining with the effort. For a moment it looked like she might not make it, but finally, her feet cleared the ground. That's when I moved to stand on shaky legs. Frazer was there, lifting, supporting me. We didn't speak as he veered north and ran over the grassy plain, our weapons and bags rattling as he moved.

I stared into nothingness.

"What is it?" he murmured, his breathing even despite his pace. "We got Wilder back—why do I feel you falling deeper into despair?"

The words rolled around, coating my tongue. The heavy *emptiness* in my chest stopped me from speaking my truth. A heartbeat later, something changed all that. A downy cloud got wiped away by a stray wind, and the sun appeared, beaming down.

I'd never been a sun-lizard, but now that light illuminated my world. It made the shadowed mountains glow anew in copper hues as the bracken clinging there was exposed. Then, as the valley stirred to life under my awed gaze, I watched the meadow move, singing in tune with the summer breeze. Dandelion fluff floated on lazily by and wild flowers swayed, waving and glistening with dewy residue. I drew in a deep breath, catching the whiff of recent rainfall. The canopy had been so thick in Attia, it wasn't surprising I'd missed a cloudburst.

The now glorious brightness threatened to dazzle me. I closed my eyes but still *felt* the magic warming my skin. It whispered, shifting and banishing the burden eclipsing me.

My eyes flew open and I burst out, "Wilder protected me. He stood in front of me and took two arrows. And then, Hunter ..."

Frazer's fingers stiffened against my body. "... betrayed you."

In a quiet tongue, I continued. "Yes—*and* he saved me. Again. He's good at that. Being a treacherous worm, and then acting the savior."

"I wouldn't have let Tysion take you," Frazer assured.

"You would've been too late, Fraze."

His chest vibrated with a silent growl of displeasure, but it was true. And he knew it.

"Then, Adrianna was the one who rescued Wilder."

Frazer made a chuffing noise. "I know what you're getting at, but—"

I rambled on. "I was useless. More of a liability than anything. And I haven't really known how to feel about becoming a fae. But right now, if it were possible, I'd march straight to Ewa and demand Hazel change me on the spot. As long as it meant no one would shield me like that again."

Frazer eyes settled on mine, his brows bunching together.

"You disapprove?" I challenged.

"People make their own choices. Besides, given your background, you might have to get used to people guarding you. Once people know the truth, there are many who will consider you their rightful princess— maybe even their queen."

Princess. Queen. Not likely.

He just didn't understand. That was a first. "D'you know what'd happen if I got you killed? If I got Wilder, or Adi, or Cai, or Liora hurt?" My voice cracked under the strain of saying their names, but a storm of fear and guilt made me grit my teeth and continue. "I'd want to die."

"*Stop.* Never think that. Never say that."

"But—"

"No!" he snarled.

A brittle silence fell, whereupon we entered the valley's mouth. A pause, and then he was softly spoken, but fierce as he confessed. "I wanted to die too. To take my life and leave this sorry, rutting world for good."

Oh. I blinked back tears and asked, "When?"

"After she enslaved Lynx. After I failed him."

"What stopped you?" I croaked.

His voice was grim as he said, "The male I knew might be gone, but that doesn't burn away my memories. And Lynx would've told me to be brave. To live—even if every day was a struggle."

My heart died. One tear rolled.

Frazer clutched me tighter. His version of an embrace, I supposed. He went on, murmuring, "Because as long as you keep breathing, there's a chance that things will get better. That you can make them better. If you're blessed with the long life of the fae, it's almost inevitable."

Despite myself, I bit my lip and asked, "And that's enough?"

He gave me a pained smile. "Those words and thoughts aren't mine. They belong to Lynx. I'd never have come up with something like that on my own. Way too optimistic."

I laughed a bit at that.

Frazer went on, his voice stronger now. "Those memories and echoes of a life lost kept me alive, but to be honest, for the longest time they were just words to whisper to myself in the dark. I didn't believe them until I met you. So you might not have taken arrows for me, siska. But you saved me from myself—from letting the grief swallow me whole. Because I think if I'd been left alone in that silence much longer, I'd have cracked."

That, there, stole my breath, my voice.

Frazer slowed, surveying the area. Obviously satisfied there were no threats, he put me down and I stood, allowing his eyes to hold me. I didn't try to hide the track of salty water staining my cheek.

My throat closed as we kept staring at each other. His blue-silver stare stripped me bare. Eventually, I dared to utter, "Can I hug you?"

I felt a flash of black humor in the bond. It was so Frazer. "If you must."

Not exactly an invitation, but it still made me hurl myself at him. I felt a slight pressure at my back. He was actually reciprocating. I made a surprised noise, half-whimper, half-hiccup.

"You idiot," he whispered into my hair.

I nodded. "I love you too."

A cawing laugh was his response. He gripped the tops of my arms and pushed me away in a gentle but firm move. Nodding over to a nearby granite slab, he said, "We can wait for Adi over there."

He made a beeline for the slab's smooth surface upon which he sat. Frazer removed the kaskan from his shoulder, placed it on his lap, and brushed his fingers along the curved limb, testing, flexing. I unbuckled my sword before settling down next to him.

A few minutes passed while we listened to the hollow silence stretching through the gully. High, steep walls pressed in on all sides, and every whisper echoed. It definitely wasn't a place I wished to linger in.

So it was with a relieved sigh that I heard humming wingbeats. Adrianna landed next to us. Before I got a chance to ask, she said, "It's done. He's safe. I'll take you there now and fly back for Frazer."

Normally I'd have protested, but the urge to check on Wilder was too strong. I stood and murmured a quick goodbye to Frazer. He watched on silently as Adrianna took me in her arms, and soared up, up, up.

The moment Adrianna leveled off, I asked, "Is he awake yet?"

"No. D'you know what they dosed him with?"

Her frown had my belly churning. "Sedatives. At least that's what they said."

I watched her carefully. No flickers of concern. A small comfort.

Adrianna added, "We'll have to wait for him to wake up, but I've cleaned his wounds and done a patching thread on his wing. It's the best I could do with the shitty medical kit they gave us."

"It's better than anything I could've done," I said gratefully.

We landed outside a cave on an overhanging rock face. Nowhere near the jagged peaks, but high enough that the wind wrestled with Adrianna as she locked her wings in. She didn't lower me until we'd ducked into the small cavern.

There was Wilder. Adrianna had set him on top of a bedroll. His armor had been removed along with his boots, blades, and rucksack, and placed against the cave wall. There were even firelights flickering above him.

He looked peaceful: fussed over. Something about that had my heart plummeting into a hollow space. I tried to distract myself by asking, "Where did you get the lights?"

"I called them. Firelights love the mountains." Adrianna suddenly grasped my shoulder. "We got him back. You can relax now."

"*You* got him back," I murmured.

Adrianna eyeballed me as her fingers squeezed my collarbone. A commander on the battlefield giving heart to a soldier. That's what it felt like. "I'll give you some time alone with him."

She spun, ran, and leaped from the lip of the cave. She hadn't opened her wings. My mortal instincts screamed as I watched her dive into thin air. Then she appeared, buffeted by scaled wings. Adrianna circled, banked, and glided out of view.

I felt another sting. Envious of the freedom that came with flight. Maybe I'd welcome the transformation more than I'd realized.

I placed my sword alongside Wilder's things. My boots and the bag, too. Such a joy to be free of all that weight.

I hurried over to his side. He painted a peaceful portrait.

My knees buckled. I shuffled, coming to rest next to his shoulders. Just as Viola had done for me whenever I'd complained of sickness, I felt his brow to check for fever. There was nothing, so I pushed aside the cloak that was draped over him to examine his arm and wings. Adrianna had done a good job. Apart from a couple of angry, puckered scars and some stitching, there was little evidence of the arrows' impact.

Dropping my head to his chest, I rested there, listening to the rhythm of his heart's blood. Tears trickled down my nose. "Why did you do it?" I whispered.

The hiss of the arrows, and the growls as they tore through his wing. Blood splattering my cheek. The sounds and images tumbled around like water around a wheel.

A whisper of, "Serena," had my whole body clenching. I sat up and looked down. He was shifting, head rolling, eyelids fluttering.

I breathed, "I'm here. Tysion tried to take you."

His mouth parted a little. No sound came out. He wet his lips and tried again.

"I'll get you some water."

I moved to get a skin, but he grasped ahold of my forearm. "Don't. Just ... stay," he croaked.

His eyes opened fully then. Two fingers reached up, tracing the curve of my lower lip.

My heart cracked. A broken sob erupted; I knocked his arm aside, bent over, and covered his mouth with my own.

It wasn't the smoothest move, but I didn't care—not after what we'd been through. Not after what I'd almost lost.

No more waiting.

Wilder's eyes widened. He stilled. For a moment, it was like kissing rock. Then, his nostrils flared as he caught my scent. He groaned softly, and the sound sluiced through my veins, making my heart race. His fingers worked their way through my hair, grasping.

My eyes shuttered as he moved with me. A gentle kiss that was more than a little hesitant, intensified as our tongues met, caressing, exploring. I thought my heart might fail from running so fast.

Total sensory overload. I pulled back. I needed to breathe, to think, free of his scent and power.

Wilder didn't let me go far. Stopping me an inch from his lips, he let out a ragged whisper that teased my mouth. "That wasn't fair. I was barely awake."

"Sorry."

A lie. And he knew it. "No, you're not," he said.

I gave him my best playful smirk. "I hope I didn't take advantage."

Wilder's eyes burned, shifting to my mouth, heating my blood. "I'm glad you did," he said, slowly rising to a seated position. Once he was at eye level, he scanned the area and asked, "Where are we?"

"A cave in the Barsul Pass."

His stare settled on the fissure in the rock and the blue sky outside. A frown creased his brows. "How did you get us up here?"

I rocked back onto my heels, saying, "I didn't. Frazer and Adrianna showed up and saved us. Adi's gone to get Frazer now."

Wilder's eyes found mine. A twinkle of mirth. "They followed us because they didn't trust me, right?"

I nodded, nervous of his reaction. There was no annoyance or anger. He seemed more impressed than anything. He continued to peer around the small cave. Probably sizing up our territory.

"Do you need anything?" I inquired.

He went to brush a chin-length strand of hair from my face. Those fingers leaving behind a flaming trail in their wake, he answered. "Some water."

The weariness etched around his eyes made me move quickly. I got to my pack and yanked out the half-empty flask. Glancing over my shoulder, I asked, "Are you hungry?"

An instant reply. "Yes. Check my bag. I still have some dried meat slices."

"Yum," I mumbled.

A grumble of amusement sounded from Wilder as I fished out his rations. Gods, they looked even more unappetizing in daylight.

I hurried back to his side as he was inspecting his injured wing. I watched, fascinated, as he ran a fingertip over the membrane around his stitches. He didn't show any signs of discomfort. A relief. Then, he moved on to prodding and sniffing the inflamed area, presumably testing for infection. Once his wings had settled against his back, I asked, "Is it okay?"

"I've had worse," he said.

His matter-of-fact attitude made me cringe. I'd no reason to doubt his word. The amount of injuries he must have sustained over centuries of fighting didn't bear thinking about.

I silently handed over the rations and watched him gulp water and tear into the meat. His movements were slow and stiff. That just brought to mind what could've happened, and suddenly my words bubbled up and spilled over. "I owe you the truth."

Wilder blinked, shocked. In between mouthfuls, he replied, "You owe me nothing."

My body strained and tightened. A bowstring ready to snap. "You risked your life for me. You deserve to know."

His brows came together, but he didn't argue. Instead, he finished the dried meat off in one bite.

I continued. "I won't tell you now because I don't want the others around. They've already heard the story."

He set the flask aside. "Understood."

I wondered if he'd guessed that I didn't want my friends to advise me against it—something told me he knew.

"Speaking of." Wilder cast his chin toward the fissure in the rock.

Adrianna ducked into the cave and propped her archery equipment and bag against the rock wall. I felt a slight tug on the kin bond as if Frazer was checking. I stayed kneeling, but projected, *I'm fine. Safe.*

Frazer still gave me a once over as soon as he entered. Then he started to sniff the cave out.

Adrianna clucked her tongue. "It's just bat shit. Relax."

Frazer ignored her and paced over to the wall to drop his bag, sword and my kaskan.

Wilder piped up, "Serena tells me that you both saved us. I can only say I'm very glad you suspected me of being a traitor."

Frazer's expression remained neutral, but Adrianna had the good grace to look sheepish. "Well, I'm relieved we were wrong—I don't think Serena would've forgiven me for killing you."

Wilder lifted a brow. "*I'm* relieved you didn't feel the need to try."

Adrianna suddenly flushed. I smothered a grin.

Wilder turned to me. "Now that we're all here, we need to decide our next move. D'you want to tell me what happened in Attia first?"

I gnawed on my lower lip as the image that'd lodged itself in my heart now flared to life. Wilder acting as my shield, my protector. A savior. A sacrifice. The very thought made me sick with fear. Smothering the visage, I recounted the events he'd missed.

Wilder's eyes stayed glued on me as I talked, while Adrianna and Frazer rolled out bedrolls to sit on.

When I was done, Wilder curled his fingers into the folds of his cloak. His hands balled into tight fists, he said, "I hope for this Hunter's sake we never come face-to-face. I might rip his throat out on sheer principle."

"He sounds delusional," Adrianna remarked coldly.

There was still a tiny part of me that wanted to speak up for him. Frazer's voice cut into me. "I've met fae like him before. He wants you for his pet, Serena. Not his equal."

I glared back. "Stop snooping."

I'd forgotten about Wilder. He growled. "Am I missing something?"

I found him glancing between the two of us, wary-eyed.

"That's a tale for another time," Adrianna said, bailing us out. "So, what are we thinking?" She stared over at me. "Should we go back to Kasi?"

Frazer spoke first. "Morgan will want blood when she learns the ambush failed, and Dimitri will hate you both for humiliating his son. You won't be safe if you go back."

An emotion flitted through our thread on gentle wings. His fear for me urged me to say, "We're not abandoning Cai and Liora. You know how spiteful Dimitri is—"

Adrianna interrupted. "I could go back alone and try to protect them …"

I shook my head, but Wilder was the one to say, "Dimitri's noticed how close your pack is. All the instructors have. If two of your group suddenly disappear along with your former instructor, even Hilda will start asking questions. And when Tysion dares to show his face to his father, he'll find out that you're the reason he failed. At the very least, he'll petition Morgan to have you watched more closely. And then, good luck trying to get away when the time comes."

Her mouth set hard with doubt, but she said nothing.

There was also the thorny matter of the ingredients, but until I told Wilder everything, it was best to stay silent on that. One thing I would never say—that I buried so deep inside my soul, even Frazer couldn't find it—was that I couldn't bear to hide away, to cower, while someone else took my place, while someone else stood in front of me.

Frazer nodded to me. Maybe he'd seen my thoughts anyway. "Then we'll need a plan to shield you from them taking their revenge."

Wilder interceded. "I don't think Morgan will be the problem. She set the ambush to happen away from camp. Nice and quiet—no witnesses. There are reasons she didn't want to take us publicly. Those are still valid. And whatever else she is, she's not impulsive like Dimitri. She knows how to play the long game. My guess is she'll wait until we're vulnerable again."

Frazer's lips paled as his jaw worked furiously. I recognized that look —he was biting down on frustration. "And what about you? From everything Hunter told Serena, it sounds like Morgan won't wait any longer. It *sounds* like she's in love with you. If you come back with us, what's stopping her from taking you and forcing her way into your mind? She could see our pack's plans to desert." His eyes found mine and he added, "And anything else you tell him."

My chest seized. I'd never thought ...

Wilder's reply was steady, calm. "I'll write to tell her that she's made her point. That I'll go back to being her commander once the training cycle's over, as long as she leaves Serena alone. In short, I'll lie."

The hard lines of his face made my heart ache and stutter.

Frazer's voice was low. Almost a growl. "D'you expect her to agree to that? Gods, it'll probably have the opposite effect once she realizes how strongly you feel."

My cheeks burned. I resisted peeking over at Wilder. Afraid of his response. He let out a small sigh that broke my will; I turned to find a troubled, thoughtful expression. Wilder replied, "I'll tell her my feelings ended when I discovered she'd been with you."

Adrianna picked up the conversation, saying, "Doesn't that contradict what you did for her in the forest?"

My fingernails bit into my palms as the memories resurfaced.

Wilder shrugged and crossed his legs. "Morgan expects shit like that from me. She's always thought I've been soft on humans. She'll believe me if I say I did it to avoid spilling their blood."

No one spoke, but everyone wore similar expressions: thoughtfulness mixed with doubt.

I found one question circling, plaguing my mind. "Is Morgan really in love with you?" I blurted out.

Wilder blinked, then pushed out a weak laugh. "Morgan doesn't love.

She likes powerful males and wants to be adored in return. And when she isn't, she becomes obsessed and even crueler than usual. That didn't start with me. I've seen her become so jealous that one of her favorites had found his mate, that she ordered the male to bed her the same night."

Adrianna made a noise of pure disgust. An echo of my own feelings.

Frazer was the one to ask, "Did the male betray his mate?"

Wilder answered with a grimace. "Yes. But from what I heard, it was the mate who convinced him to submit. She thought Morgan would kill him if he didn't."

A cold fury, fierce and consuming, rattled my bones.

Adrianna *harrumph*ed. "That sounds like a female you can really rely on to restrain herself."

Her sarcasm prompted Wilder to say, "I still think the main danger will come from Dimitri's need for vengeance rather than Morgan's. And apart from maybe the fae in his pack, he doesn't have any allies."

"That you know of," Frazer put in darkly.

Wilder frowned. "It's true, I might have miscalculated. But we'll still have allies to help curb his wrath. Hilda and Goldwyn and Cecile all hate him." He trailed off and turned to face me. "Either way, I won't stay behind."

Those words punched a hole through my chest. I managed a weak smile. A part of me wished he'd fly away and abandon us. To spare him from me and all the arrows in the world that one day would be aimed at my head. That is if Morgan had her way.

My eyes sought Frazer's. Then Adrianna's. And finally, Wilder's.

I should've tried to persuade him to go, to leave us, but instead selfish, *selfish* words poured out. "Are you all right to fly back?"

A smile twitched at the corner of that full mouth. "If I can rest my wing tonight, I should be ready to fly by tomorrow."

Adrianna stood, shouldered her archery gear, and briskly said, "Good. Frazer and I will leave once we've completed our trials. Since Serena's already finished hers, I've got some catching up to do." She flashed me a teasing smirk and went on. "Which means, I need to be making the most of this light."

Concerned, I dared to ask, "Shouldn't you rest or something first?"

One word punched out of her. "No." And that was that.

Adrianna turned on her heel.

Frazer straightened up. "Can you take me down there?"

She paused. "What if I don't return before you?"

Frazer didn't growl or snap. Just whirled and stalked over to grab his Utemä. He answered only when he'd strapped the blade to his waist. "Then, I'll make the climb."

Adrianna stared for a moment. "Don't be stupid. Shout my name when you're at the bottom of the mountain. If I don't respond, do the smart thing and wait."

Shadows and flames kindled in his stare, but he was quiet as he followed her to lip of the cave. Without hesitation, Adrianna lifted him as if he weighed no more than a babe and took to the skies in a single leap.

Wilder and I were alone again.

My breathing snagged as I caught him giving me a sideways look.

In one smooth motion, he'd hauled me onto his lap. I felt breathless, and *daring* as I shifted to straddle him. His wings splayed out a bit, but he didn't move to kiss me. Wilder's hands instead traveled to the top button on my jacket. I watched him undo it, *slowly*, purposefully, and move to the next one down.

Close to forgetting my own name, I spoke quickly. "I should tell you who I am. You might not feel the same ... You might not want me afterward."

Fingers paused on that last button. Those green eyes flickered, lifting. His focus locked onto my mouth. Wilder's lip curled lazily. "Not possible."

A promise and an answer.

A tight, near-panting answer rushed from me. "You don't know that."

My thoughts scattered as he continued unbuttoning. He tugged away my jacket, peeling it from my skin gently. My shoulders were left feeling impossibly light. A shiver played its tune down my spine as he slipped his hands beneath my shirt to press his knuckles into the small of my back, kneading out the kinks. I sighed softly and moved into the soothing motions that quickly became featherlight strokes. He drew whorls and lines there until at last those beautiful, teasing fingers left my top to travel up, up. Aware of every inch between us and every move he made, I watched with bated breath as he plunged his thumb and forefinger down my neckline and plucked out the droplet. He let the blue gem rest in his palm and whispered, "I know this has magic. I know you've got something big to tell me. But Frazer wasn't wrong when he advised caution. Trusting me with your story *is* dangerous, and if Morgan ever got in ..."

Raw, rasping words. He released the necklace and both his hands lowered to brace my hips. Wilder sagged against me; his forehead touched close to where my raging, thunderous heart pounded. I chewed my lower lip, weighing the risks. He wasn't wrong. I shouldn't take Morgan's obsession with Wilder lightly. And yet ...

My arms floated up to wrap around his neck. I spoke quietly. "Are you still wanting to come with us—with me?"

He pulled back from my breast to look up and say, "Of course." As if I were mad for even asking.

"Well, then ..."

With a deep breath to prepare, I began from hearing Auntie's voice and talking to Frazer mind to mind. And finished with meeting Maggie, Hazel, and the purpose behind the items we were collecting.

Wilder sat in silence for the entire tale. The only sign of his true feelings being the grip on my hips tightening.

With no more words left to say, I waited for his reaction.

All I got was a vacant expression.

I bowed into his shoulder, whispering, "Say something."

His chest expanded rapidly. On the exhale, he breathed, "It's hard to know what to say. I'm shocked, terrified, relieved—"

I leaned back to consider those pained eyes. "Relieved?"

His gaze deepened. "If becoming fae—if shifting back means you'll live longer—then I'd welcome it."

One of his hands flattened against my back, the other reached up to play with my hair. I moved into the touch, cherishing it, and got a crooked smile in return. One that made me want to kiss that tiny spot where his lip curved.

Wilder began, "And as a fae with light magic, you won't be as breakable. Maybe, then, I won't worry every time you leave my side."

Desire, hot and heavy, shattered me in a pulse. A frown touched my brow. My lips drew apart to say something ... anything.

His hands stopped their roaming. "What's wrong? Did I—"

Wilder didn't get another word in. I covered my mouth with his, devouring the sound.

This time, he didn't hesitate. He tore into my mouth with a fervor that stole the will from my limbs. A kiss. Possessive and wild and frantic. His hand pulled at my short hair. Not hard, but enough to show how much he wanted me.

I'd been so lonely for so long. Rejected, exiled, scorned. Others had helped fill that cold, barren place in my chest. But this—*this*—set the whole damned place ablaze. Burning up the darkness until there was nothing but light. And *life.*

He sunk backwards with me astride him. I felt like I'd been winded as he deftly flipped us, rolling me onto the bedroll, his body covering mine. A mighty wall of muscle settled between my legs. Enough that something hard pushed against me, nudging me.

Heat flooded my body, the flames pooling at the apex of my thighs. A pulse started up, insistent and loud.

His hand slipped down my thigh to cradle the underside of my knee as the other hand traveled up to entwine our fingers; he pinned my arm above my head.

His mouth left mine with a small nip at my lip that made me inhale sharply.

A glassy gaze met mine and roamed, scanning every bit of me. The way he was looking at me with such rawness brought a boldness crashing into my chest. I relaxed, softening so that his full weight hit that oh-so-needy spot. My body cried out, *more, more, more.*

Wilder's canines snapped down. "Look at you—beautiful." A hoarse whisper. Animalistic and sincere.

He lowered his head and paused at my nape. My free hand rushed to twine my fingers into that golden mane as the sharpened points of his teeth awaited. I was breathless, anticipating.

His canines scraped up against soft, soft skin in a perfect duet of strength and tenderness.

Sweet, exquisite torture. That's was this was. Every sense narrowing to that single point of contact where my heart's blood pounded and his needles waited. I moaned a little as his ass clenched and he grated into my hips.

I was overwhelmed by him—his scent, his weight—

My male's body.

Molten flames liquified my insides as that *claim* sent a thrill through my blood. I groaned, and at that precise moment, Wilder flicked his hot tongue against my flesh, licking up to my earlobe.

I trembled beneath him.

He moved back a touch and released my hand. The perfect opportunity for me to reach up and start to tug his top off.

Wilder gripped my wrists and brought them up over my head, pinning me. *Again.* He took one look at my pout and loosened a beautiful laugh that snaked up the groove of my spine, setting my scalp tingling.

"Darling, you can't think I'm going to take you right here? We need time to explore; not rush because I think your kin's about to arrive and slaughter me to defend your honor."

I opened my mouth to say that I didn't give a damn, but Wilder was already saying, "Forgive me, but you've never been with a male before, have you?"

I turned my head to the side, cheeks flaming.

Of course. Stupid. *Stupid.*

I *was* inexperienced. Maybe he didn't want to be with a virgin. Or maybe he just thought I was a harlot for rushing things. But today, he'd almost been taken from me. Just like so many others. I was *sick* of it. I wanted for something to be in my control, to forge something good and permanent and lasting.

"Look at me, valo." A growl and an order.

I struggled to meet that hardened voice. He released a hand to grab my nose between thumb and forefinger. It didn't hurt, but he wasn't gentle as he dragged my eyes to his. "Don't shut me out." He freed my nose and continued. "I'd be honored to be your first, but I don't want it to be in a cave, that's all."

I gave him my best growl.

He beamed beatifically. "You'll make a magnificent fae, darling."

I jostled him. "Who cares if we're in a cave. I think it's romantic."

Wilder chuckled lightly. "On a bedroll, when your friends could come back at any moment. That's romantic to you?" he asked. His laughter died, leaving him with a relaxed smile.

I reached up and traced the outer corners of his mouth. "Yes."

Wilder eyed me in wicked amusement. Contemplating.

I waited ... In one swift, heart-stopping move, he pulled my top and bra over my head and tossed them aside. He knelt above me and stared and stared. A heat wave swamped me, causing sweat to prickle all over my body.

I almost moved to cover myself when a strange sound had me pausing ... Then, blushing. He was purring again. My body relaxed into the bedroll, loosening, melting, a newborn confidence awakening.

Next, he ripped off his leather tunic and black undershirt, being careful to maneuver around those beautiful, fragile wings. Revealing himself.

My breath came in a shudder as he wavered long enough for me to take in the broad shoulders above muscled arms. A sculpted, but scarred torso. Tanned, gleaming; rutting gorgeous. A portrait of a Warrior's strength. A damned work of art.

Lowering himself over me, his body covering mine, his hand traveled up to find the underside of my breast. A slow, taunting circle around, followed by a thumb pressing against my peaked nipple.

The movement wrung a moan from my parted mouth.

My fingers ran through his hair. "Wilder, *please*."

He drew back, looking amused and a touch wicked. Poised over my breast, he asked, "What is it that you want, exactly?"

As if he needed to hear me say it. My tongue stuck to the roof of my mouth. This was so not my territory. *Don't be a coward, don't be a coward, don't be a coward.*

"I want you to touch me." I whispered.

A low, velvety purr responded. "I am touching you ..."

As if to emphasize the point, he flicked the tip of his tongue against my nipple. That grazing motion made words tumble out before I had time to be embarrassed. "I want *more* ... more of you."

His body stilled. "Shall I tell you what I want, Serena?" He pulled back so that he could stare, his eyes like two burning stars, drawing me in and drowning me. "I want our first time to be away from everyone, where you'll be most comfortable. Where I can make love to you."

The stark intensity there fired my blood, and at the same time, a tiny tremor racked his body. "But, I'm not so cruel as to leave you without release."

I almost mewled. He moved to lie by my side, dragging the cloak next to us up and over me. Bracing himself on his elbow, he gripped my hand and guided it down, down ... "I won't touch you until you've felt for yourself."

We plunged under my waistband together. And found that sensitive spot. He got me to pause for a heartbeat, brushing, stroking ... before continuing down.

Something about that broke the tether on his control. He ripped our hands from my pants and grabbed my chin, yanking me to his mouth. Unleashing himself on me. I couldn't think past his burning lips and the way his tongue slipped inside, dancing with my own. A mad passion made me bite his lip. He moaned into my mouth and went to grasp my hand, the one that had circled that bundle of nerves. Wilder dragged my fingers to his parted mouth and paused there. He gave me a taunting smirk that had my knees snapping together, clenching hard.

Then I nearly ignited at the sight of him sucking on my fingers. On me. My insides were a molten puddle. It was unbearable. "Stop teasing," I barked at him.

His eyes flashed for a moment. *Shit.* He pushed himself up. A tight movement; his back and wings tensed. Staring at me as if ... As if he wanted to feast on every inch. He brazenly yanked my leggings, under-pants, and socks down and mounted himself between my legs.

Gods. He gripped each knee, spread my legs and lowered himself. I burst from my seams at the first touch of his tongue. My hips bucked, and his hands went to my waist. Pushing down, pinning me to the floor and growling. His tongue swept up and down, circling that burning need. Never letting me fall over the edge—never enough to release me. I moved my hips in time with his movements, begging him silently, *fasterfasterfaster.*

A long, slow stroke down ended with me arching up. A plea and an offering.

Then, he paused.

I panted softly, gulping in air. "Don't stop."

He came to rest back beside me, his head braced against his elbow. "Don't worry. I just wanted to watch this."

A lazy, sly smile lit his face as his hand traveled straight down to my core. My patience frayed. I grasped the back of his head and pulled him toward me. Our mouths met in a savage clash. I tasted myself at the exact moment as he pushed *up*.

I broke our kiss with a moan at the tender soreness. The strokes were gentle, exploratory. I lost all sense of time and space and self as he moved. Once, twice, slow, slow—*fast*. I bayed as pain and pleasure fought for dominance.

"You're glorious. You know that?" he whispered.

Moremoremore.

My eyes fluttered, and he ducked his head next to my nape, snarling. Nipping. Loving.

I turned my head toward him, half out of my mind. "Wilder ..."

He unleashed a soft snarl that heated the side of my face. "Come home to me, my love."

My hand drifted to his mouth. To his beautiful, filthy mouth and traced the curve. He caught my forefinger with his canines. The restraint with which his teeth held me combined with the fast, certain sweeps to my core ... It was almost too much. My hips bucked as that fire and friction built and built into skin-tingling, fire-breathing pleasure.

His thumb moved up and flicked, *pressed*—

Seeing stars, flushing with pleasure, I exploded around him. My release charged down my spine. He freed my finger from his fang and bent down, raining light kisses over my face.

Moans turned to whimpers as he gently withdrew from me.

He pulled back a bit to stare. "I'd consider myself a lucky male if I could watch you do that for the rest of my days."

"Wilder," I gasped his name.

"Darling," he purred.

That got me burning again.

Maybe he sensed this because he rolled away. I scowled as he pulled his undershirt back on. He saw and smirked, but his only response was to grab my top and say, "Up."

I sighed through my nose and rolled my eyes. He just grinned and crooked a finger. "Come on."

I sat up and let him pull my shirt over my head. At least he hadn't bothered with the bra. Maybe ...

Any thoughts that he'd give in were demolished when he reached out for my pants and leggings. He slid them on one foot at a time and jerked his chin up. An order to buck my hips. I growled, but submitted. When I was fully clothed again, he gently flipped me onto my side and moved behind me.

The sensible part of me knew it was better to take it slow. Frustration still boiled over when he covered us with his cloak and tucked me into the crook of his arm. I let out a little grumble to show my feelings. A rumbling laugh answered back. "Trust me, my love, I'm not happy about this either."

He landed a quick kiss on my neck and then ran his hand up and down my spine until my frustration left me and a peace descended.

We stayed like that, occasionally breaking the silence with the odd teasing string of words, until the light outside dimmed. As shades of apricot, ruby, and amethyst illuminated the cave, my eyes grew heavy, and I drifted, perfectly content.

CHAPTER 29
FLYING, FALLING

Muffled sounds and an *absence* woke me. I blinked rapidly, adjusting to a weak light flickering against gray rock. I was still buried in the cloak, but that comforting warmth was gone. Wilder stood at the cave opening and fell over the edge. I sat up, my lips parting in a tiny gasp.

"Don't worry," Adrianna mumbled behind me.

I twisted to see her dressed in uniform and kneeling on a bedroll which she'd placed at the back of the cave. Frazer looked fast asleep beside her.

"He's testing his wings," she murmured.

"By throwing himself off a mountain?" I said, faintly.

"Easiest way to check, I suppose." She collapsed back on her heels, straightened, and went on. "And if he doesn't plummet to his death, he'll want to leave soon."

I resisted the urge to throw something at her and set about finding my jacket, socks, and bra instead. As I moved around, collecting things, the tenderness in my core made me wince more than once. A reminder of last night.

As if I needed one.

Lost in daydreams, I didn't bother to hide under anything when lifting my top to don my bra.

"That's different," Adrianna commented.

I waited until I'd wriggled back into my shirt to ask, "What is?"

Footsteps bounced off the cave walls as Adrianna came up next to me. "You used to hate people seeing you naked."

I looked up and shrugged. "I guess waking up to all your bare asses every day has changed me."

Adrianna responded with a lifted eyebrow. "Right."

She turned her head as if to hide a smile. Heat flooded my cheeks. She must assume it had something to do with Wilder. Maybe it did.

My jacket and socks went on last. I jumped up and moved over to where Adrianna stood frowning down at the kaskan. "What is it?" I asked, forcing my feet into boots.

"I've never even seen one of these bows," Adrianna noted.

I thought I detected a hungry glint in her eyes. Of course, she was a warrior. A bow that never missed would be like candy to her.

Adrianna continued. "The witch who gave it to Hunter might be a powerful ally."

I tied my boot laces and uncurled to say, "Maybe we should go find Isabel in the Crescent. She might make bows for all of us."

Adrianna frowned at the joke and folded her arms. Oh dear.

"I'm more interested in the charm she created. Hunter obviously thought she had enough power to hide him from Morgan. And a crafter on our side could be vital in the war to come."

My head spun. I couldn't bring myself to plan that far ahead. At least not this early in the day.

"One thing at a time, Adi," Frazer croaked.

That support brought a smile to my lips, as did the sight of his ruffled hair and bleary eyes as he crawled out of his sleeping bag.

I searched for a less volatile topic. "So, how did the hunts for your items go?"

Adrianna's expression turned sour. "Badly."

Frazer stood, quickly smoothing out the wrinkles in his rumpled uniform. "Mine went a little better. I managed to find a few promising caves. I'm going to go back and scout out the locations tonight."

My heart twanged at the thought of him fighting the monsters Wilder had described. "Why at night?"

Frazer stifled a yawn. "Navvi sleep during the day and given their speed, trying to slay one in a confined space is a bad idea. So I'll wait for them to come out to me."

Adrianna's wings rustled, adjusting, as she leaned against the cave wall. "Then why didn't you stay out all night?"

"I didn't want Serena to worry," he said coolly.

Adrianna pulled a face: one of annoying smugness. "Well, you needn't have bothered. She didn't even notice us come back."

I flushed down to my boots. Adopting a demure attitude, I kept myself occupied by strapping my sword to my hip. My fingers stilled on the buckle as last night sang back into my memory. I'd told Wilder the truth, despite Frazer's warnings. Would he hate me for it? Think I was an idiot for trusting? But keeping secrets from my kin wasn't an option. I caught his eye and confessed. "Wilder knows everything now."

He gave me a prim nod. My heart lightened immediately.

Adrianna surveyed me baldly. "Was he pleased about you becoming fae?"

"Yes," I said softly.

"Good," Adrianna snapped briskly.

Confused, I asked, "Why good?"

Adrianna moved away from the wall, taking a wider stance. "It says a lot."

I gave her my best scowl. "You're being uncharacteristically vague."

A haughty brow. "I'm allowed to have layers."

My laughter came out as a snort. I didn't have time to think of a retort, because both fae froze, ears cocked. I whirled toward the cave opening. A telltale hum was my only warning. Wilder landed on the rock face and turned outward, tilting his head to the sky, and spreading his fir-green wings. He was basking, and looked even more striking as the summer sun struck his wings and lit up a thin tapestry of veins akin to the branches of a tree. My pulse quickened at the thoughts and images that stirred.

Wilder ducked into the cave, already kitted out in his armor and carrying his bag and blades. His eyes flitted to me, assessing, then sidled straight past, to Adrianna and Frazer.

Feeling deflated, I dipped my head so he wouldn't read the disappointment marked on my face. An inner voice sniped, *What were you expecting?*

"Has your strength returned?" Adrianna asked Wilder.

"Yes." A curt response.

Doing my best to ignore the sinking feeling in my stomach, I spun around and shouldered my bag, kaskan, and quiver. An awkward silence pervaded until I turned back around to Adrianna and Frazer. "I'll see you both soon."

It was more of a plea than anything.

Adrianna produced a tiny smile and a sharp nod. "You will," she confirmed.

Frazer's next words weren't for me. He rounded on Wilder, who was currently picking his cloak up off the cave floor. "Take care of her." The shadows dancing in his eyes seemed to add, *or else.* A clear warning. As if he'd meant far more than the obvious.

Wilder went rigid as his eyes locked onto Frazer's. Nothing friendly or kind in either face, they stared each other down. The lion and the panther. I'd no idea who'd win in an actual fight.

I kept waiting for Adrianna to step in. She could usually be relied upon to call bullshit when she saw it, but she remained silent.

I felt like rolling my eyes. How typically fae.

Auntie mused, *And to think, you've got all that to look forward to.*

Any thoughts of a witty retort vanished as Wilder's wings twitched and spread. I recognized it for what it was—a display of dominance. I cursed in my mind and turned to Frazer. His face had locked in a painful grimace. That had something ancient and powerful roaring, coursing through my blood. I could almost taste it ... I knew *it* was my magic.

For now, any real power remained tantalizingly out of reach. A good thing, perhaps; otherwise, I might've blasted Wilder out of the rutting cave for pulling that shit.

I didn't bother with words, just strode out and broke their gaze by standing directly between them. My stare was for Wilder.

His eyes flared in surprise at the message written all over my face:

stand down. But the stubborn bastard didn't so much as bat an eyelash. His jaw hardened, and the lines of his scars tightened.

Fine.

I dropped into a prowling swagger, hips rolling with each slow measured step. His gaze darkened, turning positively carnivorous. Maybe he was pissed off. Maybe he thought I'd taken Frazer's side—I guess I had.

When there was only a sliver of space separating us, my eyes snagged on the slight bob at his throat. My lips curved at the sight. Because it wasn't fear emanating from him—no, never that. This male had refused to yield to a queen. He wouldn't bow to me. It was hunger in that flat, glossy expression. A promise that hit me square in the gut. He must've seen his own desire reflected on my face, because he grinned, baring his teeth. Another predatory display. I huffed a dismissal and brushed past, our shoulders touching, his low growl coiling around my ear. I suppressed a shudder, and walked out into the open air, where a slight wind and some cloud cover waited.

Perfect flying conditions.

A shadow fell at my back. I knew what was coming. Quickly, sending love down our kin bond, I projected, *Hurry back to me.*

Frazer made no such promise. *Stay safe. I don't fancy flying to Alexandria and slaughtering their entire court to find you.*

A movement behind made me brace myself.

Wilder was there, sweeping me into his cloak, lifting me up and catapulting off the mountainside. His wings locked in tight, we dove for the gully below.

I screamed.

Wilder hissed a laugh. He was enjoying this way too much.

Suspended in falling motion, the wind resistance battered my face, but my eyes wouldn't close. They were fixed on the ground. The ground that was careening up toward us.

"YOU BAST—ARGH!"

My howl got cut off as his wings snapped out, slowing us, causing my stomach to vault into my mouth; the jarring motion set my teeth on edge.

We smoothed out into a glide, allowing me to swallow the dryness blasted into my mouth by the roaring wind current.

Wilder uncurled a wolfish grin. "That serves you right for going all fae on me."

I bristled. "Well, if you'd acted like the aged, run-down heap of bones you're supposed to be and not tried to intimidate my brother, I wouldn't have needed to."

Wilder gained height with a few powerful blasts of his wings. He was smirking.

Ass.

"Fae society doesn't work like that."

"Fae society can go hang," I retorted, scowling.

"Mm." An insufferable response when added to that faint smile. "Well, I promise that when *you* are a fae, maneuvers like that will make you feel incredible."

I snorted softly, ruefully, because he might have a point.

Wilder began pushing us up, up, up until we were soaring higher than I'd ever dreamed of going. Something clicked as we stopped and hovered above a cloud. As if he was waiting for something.

"Not again," I groaned.

We plummeted. I clamped my mouth closed, refusing to give him the satisfaction of hearing me squeal.

Auntie grunted. *I think he heard enough of that last night.*

We leveled out, my blush deepening as Auntie's laughter sounded inside my mind.

Wilder appeared not to have noticed. He was shining with the rush, the exhilaration. Even the scars on his cheeks were gone, creased and folded into the lines of his face. Those smiling eyes moved to me. "Lie back for a moment," he said, painting images of legs entangled, of breathless gasps. "I've got you."

The heat on my cheeks still stinging, I glanced down and saw we'd come to rest atop a mighty cloud, the color of white marble with a subtle hint of rose-colored morning. All whipped cream and candy floss. Hidden from the world below, I let that boldness he always incited ignite. "You want to watch me?"

There was something a little too strained in the smile he gave me. "Of course. But that's nothing new. I've always had a hard time looking anywhere else with you nearby."

Always. "Even before I pinned you?"

He let out a reluctant laugh. "Darling, as much as I'd like to tell you differently, you're not the first person to do that."

A wall slammed up. My reply was stiff, "I wasn't saying—"

Wilder cut across me. "But you are the first person to make me submit."

Words utterly failed me. I could only gape and say, "Oh."

He murmured, "And you will be the last."

His expression carried a weight that had me reeling. Something locked and tightened in my chest. It felt like a prophecy *and* a promise.

"Relax, Serena."

A gentle purr started up again and made me soften. I released my hold on his neck and let go, trusting my body to his arms. Wilder dipped a bit and I twisted slightly, looking down to see us skimming over the cloud surface. It was akin to skating on the ice that the villagers back home had enjoyed whenever in winter's grip.

Wilder slowed, and as we floated, his wings whipped up puffs of pearly-gray. He pulled me in, and in an even tighter embrace we dove straight through mist and drizzle, and out on the other side of the cloud. Heart palpating, blood singing, I looked up and gasped. Wilder's golden hair had become laced with thousands of raindrops, each one glistening in the sun's rays and filled with a melting pot of color.

A crown for a king.

Curious, I reached up with my fingertips. A well of emotion that couldn't be denied made me open my mouth and say, "Wilder, I ..."

I trailed off because to finish that sentence felt too dangerous— maybe even destructive.

Thoughts in turmoil, I was completely blindsided when he ducked down to kiss me lightly. Then he *licked* up my face.

I jerked back. A reflex. But I couldn't exactly go anywhere as he did it again. And again. Caught between disgust and amusement, I waited for him to stop to ask, "What was that for?"

A sheepish grin. Something I'd never thought to see on such a hard face. "You looked tasty."

I clamped my lips together, but they couldn't shackle the laughter from spilling out. A breathless but pure sound.

"Was it that bad? Serena?"

My name sounded like a laugh and a prayer on his lips. That thought caught me in its grasp, making me want to burst into light and glow like a star in the heavens. And I forgot.

I forgot that I was young and he was old—at least by human standards.

I forgot how terrified I was of rejection.

And I spoke three words. "I love you."

I stayed fixed on his eyes, a hole burning in my gut, waiting for his reaction.

And *something* slipped. And I saw my mistake.

Wide eyes, inflamed nostrils, furrowed brow. Shock and fear and wariness.

Gods, that hurt.

His expression soon evened out ... to something worse. A sad smile which was damningly close to pity. "Valo—those words shouldn't be said lightly to a fae."

Lightly.

That alone was enough to hollow me out.

Wilder continued. "After marriage or the mating bond, claiming love is the most powerful and significant binding that we recognize."

Incensed, I didn't wait for him to finish. "You don't think it's the same for humans?"

A muscle tweaked near his lip; he looked stressed. "I think that with their shorter lifespans, they're more likely to rush feelings. They're also far more prone to wanting reassurance and permanence in love. And as strange as it sounds, once you've lived for centuries, and know that barring disease or injury you'll live for many more, you realize that nothing is forever. Not unless you're lucky enough to find your mate."

That's when he broke off; he couldn't look me in the eye.

Where was this coming from?

"So, what are you saying? Don't you want ..."

Me? Us? Small words that I couldn't seem to utter.

Kind eyes held me as he replied. "I want us to be sure of each other before we say and do things that change us permanently."

That drove the breath from my lungs, rendering me silent. Because I was sure. Clearly, he wasn't.

Wilder dove again, not waiting for my null response.

A sticky silence settled, and my courage to push for clarity evaporated. I surrendered to it, consciously unknotting the pockets of tension claiming my body. But without conversation, other thoughts—other fears—circled and preyed again. Sometime later, I crumpled and gave them a voice. "D'you think Tysion will have gone back to Dimitri?"

"I don't know," he answered quietly. "But I'll keep you safe, no matter what."

My muscles froze and my gut boiled. "No. I don't want people shielding me. You are *never* to give yourself up to her. Understood?"

"I will do what I must, valo," he murmured.

His gaze locked onto the horizon and stayed there. He wouldn't even look at me. It felt useless to argue, but I wondered if he knew what it would've done to me if those arrows had found his heart.

THE DAY BLAZED by on swift wings and few words spoken. I hoped the lull on his part was simply because we were headed toward danger. But that night, curled up in the canopy after dinner, his newfound reserve became obvious. Wilder held me—gingerly, and despite my attempts to nuzzle his neck, he remained stiff and unresponsive.

I sensed a barrier had gone up, and worse, it was obvious my declaration had caused the distance.

Too much of a coward to bring it up, I unleashed another string of questions, all on what his plan was for tomorrow. Anything to get him to talk to me.

He told me that he wanted to consult with his allies in camp and expose Dimitri and Tysion's loyalties. Not that anyone would be surprised.

Spotting a flaw in this scheme, I asked, "If you tell them what happened, won't they disqualify me? Dimitri will have the perfect excuse for calling in the Hunt."

Wilder's brow puckered. "They won't do that. Not when they understand why. I'll tell them you led the hunt for the nightshade, and leave out how you discovered its location."

"You won't tell them who I am?" I asked flatly.

He pulled back a bit to stare. "You have to ask?" Guarded words that pushed me to scan his face; there, pain and ire showed.

The frost around my heart cracked. "Sorry. I ..."

As I fumbled for the right things to say, he moved to kiss each of my eyelids shut. "Sleep, Serena."

My mouth parted, but he closed it with a soft kiss. I leaned into that touch, but he drew back almost immediately. Whatever was going on with him, I sensed that tonight this had to be enough. So I settled against his chest, listening to the beats.

Tomorrow we'd fly back to chaos and scheming, but right now, our canopy acted as our cave. Safe, hidden from the world amidst swaying branches. The stars as our only witnesses.

UNDER SILVER CLOUDS and sprinkling showers, the camp came into view the following morn. Wilder paused and hovered. "Ready for this?"

My mood slipped, blackening. The breach between us hadn't healed, and he'd been detached and brooding ever since we'd woken. It seemed whatever world had opened for us—whatever we'd grown into—had been put on hold. I could only hope it hadn't been obliterated. I sighed, suddenly bone-weary, and answered, "No, but let's get it over with."

He nodded and fell into a nosedive.

Exhilaration—one free from fear—caught in my throat. I didn't breathe properly until we'd landed outside the back gate. Wilder set me down, and we scanned the area. Apart from two winged sentries saluting him atop the watchtower, Kasi seemed deserted.

"What now?" I mumbled.

Wilder's nostrils flared, breathing in the scents. "I'm taking you to my rooms." Surprise rocked me as he continued. "Your friends won't be back yet, and you can't be left alone."

"Won't that look bad?"

Wilder pressed into my elbow, steering me toward the staff quarters.

"There's no point pretending; our scents are entwined. Along with Frazer's."

My cheeks warmed a touch. *Stars.*

We made it to his living room without incident. Wilder closed the door, dumped his bag and cloak on the floor, and turned to me. "I can't stay. The sooner I've sent word to Morgan and met with the others, the better off we'll be."

I gave a tight nod, anxiety surging.

Wilder held out a splayed hand. "Give me the nightshade, and I'll take it with me. You're meant to present your item to Goldwyn, but I'm sure she won't mind me doing it."

I dropped my bag next to his stuff and dove in, dragging out the leather pouch. I handed it over and as I pulled away, our fingertips and eyes met. Breathing become difficult. All too soon, he stepped back. "Stay here. I'm locking you in. Don't open the door for anyone," he said roughly.

There was no sign of a key.

"How are you locking it?"

He paused, long enough to explain. "There's a phrase that activates a warding spell around the room. It only prevents people from getting in, so if there's an emergency, you can leave."

Wilder left quickly. I propped my weapons up against the wall, shucked off my cloak, kicked off my boots, and stood, hovering.

What now?

Not wanting to think on what Wilder would be facing, I searched for something to do. Exploring seemed like a good place to start. Veering left, I crossed the room and ventured through a door. The book piles and the ruffled sheets on the bed confirmed this was Wilder's room.

And it was a double bed. I hadn't thought ... hadn't considered what staying with him might mean. Suppressing a pulse of knee-wobbling emotion, I studied the details. There was a bedside table with a firelight lamp, a pine trunk shoved into the corner, another door leading to an annexed bathroom, and a window with a light splattering of rain coating the glass.

Feeling drained, I sat on the bed and let my feet dangle off the edge.

Utter silence. Alone with my thoughts. Not a good place to be.

Collapsing back onto the bed, watching motes of dust float through the still air, I slipped into blessed numbness.

I awoke to find the room cloaked in darkness. Disoriented, I sat up and fumbled in the gloom. As soon as my hand brushed the firelight's crystal shell, it flared to life.

Stunned by the sudden brightness, I picked the lamp up with narrowed eyes and stood. I moved into the living space, hopeful. Light flooded the room in a flickering glow. My stomach fell. No Wilder.

A knock on the door made me nearly drop the lamp. I regained my composure, only to have the tapping sound grow more insistent.

I froze. Unsure.

Wilder's instructions had been clear: don't open the door. But he'd been gone all day. What if something had happened? Could the person knocking have information I needed?

The tapping subsided just as my recklessness and desperation almost won out. Feeling jellylike, I walked to an armchair by the cold hearth and sunk down. Placing the lamp by my side, I grabbed a blanket to pull over my lap and chose a book to flip through. The words blurred together, and I reread the same line at least a dozen times.

Every hour that lagged had my impatience ticking up a notch, until I felt like screaming and kicking down walls. I considered just leaving but decided to at least wait out the night. My stomach had long been protesting, so I moved over to my bag by the door and seized leftover food parcels. I swallowed tasteless mulch and almost gagged as the door opened. Backing up, I stumbled to a halt.

Wilder.

A half-stifled gasp shuddered out of me. He'd only just got in the door when I ran over and collided into that hard male body, throwing my arms around his neck. Wilder caught me and for a moment, his defenses crashed down. One arm wrapped around my waist and lifted me so that my feet trailed along the floor. Then we lingered in an embrace. Relief choked me to the point where the questions I'd wanted to ask died in my throat.

"Are you okay?" he mumbled.

"No," I said, my voice muffled.

Wilder released me and stared. "What's wrong?"

"It's been hours. I thought—well, I don't know what I thought."

He clasped my hand and guided me to an armchair. "I'm sorry. I've been stuck with Hilda and the others."

"Dimitri too?" I asked.

"Unfortunately, yes," he said, freeing his hand from mine. "I'll build a fire; you're far too cold."

I tried to smother the frustration, but the caged animal inside my chest still felt like it was growling, pacing. "Please, just tell me what happened. I've hated sitting here, not knowing."

Wilder hesitated for a wingbeat, then crouched and started to stack firewood in the grate. "I know. But I'm glad you weren't there. I'm not sure I could've kept my temper if you had been. Dimitri's insults were even more vile than usual." A quiet, wrathful response that sapped the strength from my limbs.

I slumped back into the cushiony lining of the chair as he grabbed a box of matches from atop the hearth. Lighting one, he threw its spark amidst the wood. Garnet and gold flames came alive, crackling and dancing. I watched and waited for him to explain.

He didn't.

"And?" I urged impatiently. "Am I getting kicked out? Is Morgan coming for you?"

Wilder rounded on me. "Tysion and Hunter haven't returned. And since both sides are just hearsay, Hilda's reserving judgment."

A frown knotted my brows together. "What does that mean?" I asked, tucking my legs up on the chair.

"It means she's not punishing anyone. But since I admitted to helping you, and Dimitri's claiming innocence, she's really siding with us."

Given what had happened, that still didn't seem fair. "Didn't you show Hilda the stitches on your wing?"

He rubbed his neck, grimacing. "Of course. She thought about sending trackers after Tysion to get some answers. But so many of them are spies for Morgan, it'd be pointless."

Resigning myself to that fact, I said, "So, what now?"

He unbuckled his weapon's belt, dropped it to the floor, and slipped into the chair next to me. "We watch our backs and get you through the seventh trial."

If only it was that easy.

A nagging worry got me to add, "Someone came by here earlier, knocking. D'you think it was Dimitri?"

Wilder's back straightened. "What time was this?"

"No idea—it was already dark outside."

"The only instructor that left Hilda's early was Cecile," Wilder said, stroking his stubble. "But she would've known that I wasn't here." He sucked on his teeth and continued. "She's an excellent tracker, so she might've caught your scent from outside. I can't think why she'd need to talk though—"

I jumped in, hopeful. "Maybe she wanted to tell me that Cai and Liora are back."

Wilder shook his head distantly. "They're not—I checked." My disappointment might've shown because he said, "They'll be fine. They've still got plenty of time to return."

A sour tone colored my next words. "What do I do until then? Stay locked up here?"

The muscles in his back and shoulders steeled further, and a grating sound filled the air as his wings shifted against fabric. Slipping into that Sabu Warrior skin, Wilder's voice deepened. "I'm trying to keep you safe, Serena."

Maybe. But it felt like another cage. And I'd had enough of those.

Gloom burrowed in.

Wilder offered me a flattened palm. I stared at it, resentful and sullen.

Don't play the child, Auntie grumbled.

I relented and let him pull me onto his lap. He entwined his fingers with mine and I brushed against the hard callouses on his palm with my thumb. Meanwhile, his other hand made great sweeping lines on my back. Massaging, comforting.

"Help me take my armor off?"

He gestured to his vambraces and shoulder guards with our encircled hands.

Silently, I found the loops holding the metal together. Wilder wouldn't stop staring at me as I removed piece after piece of armor and put it aside on the rug. Once the last section hit the floor, he said, "I don't want you sleeping alone; is that so wrong?"

My heart and lungs stopped working as I watched his expression in the sand and sanguine light. "When you say, you don't want me sleeping alone ..."

A flush of warmth traveled down my spine, hitting my core.

Wilder smiled ruefully. "I didn't mean we should sleep in the same bed."

There was no dismissiveness there. Just uncertainty. My stomach rolled and clenched as I summoned the strength to say, "I wouldn't mind sharing a bed with you."

He sucked in air with a tiny gasp. Some primal part of me glowed at that. Then, his muscles tensed. "Serena."

Oh, shit.

"I know I've been distant with you."

No kidding.

Wilder's hands slipped to brace my hips. "That was wrong of me, but I needed to sort things through. And the truth is that I meant what I said about us taking our time to be sure of each other." He continued with a lowered gaze and a grimace. "Back in that cave it was easy to forget what was facing us, and who you are. Partially, because I was so relieved that you were going to become a fae."

I balked at that. Almost unleashing on him.

"I've lived long enough to see many of the humans I've cared for die. Wanting you, wanting this, meant having to accept and endure your death. Not to mention the danger I'd be putting you in. I was ready to take that on. By the time we'd set out for Attia, I was ready. And I'm a selfish bastard for it."

I slumped against him to stop from swaying.

"So when you told me about your heritage and being fae, it felt like the solution to all the obstacles facing us."

My thoughts raced. "But now?" I asked in an off-handed sort of way.

Dark green eyes bored into mine, intense and grim. "Now, there's a whole new set of obstacles."

We stayed frozen in each other's arms. I caved first. Although, every word cost me dearly. "It seems like you only started having these doubts when I told you how I feel."

I felt sick waiting for the reply to form on that sculpted mouth of his.

Wilder pushed the hair from his eyes. An exasperated gesture. "Look, you're still human. We don't know what things will be like when you're fae, or if you'll even still feel the same way—"

Oh gods, enough.

I wrenched myself from his grasp and stood. Anything to get some space, some distance from that black pit yawning wide beneath my feet. Wilder was at its center. But the stubborn bastard was up and blocking me before I got two paces. "Don't show your back to me."

An inner shield slammed up and instinct took over. I slipped into a cool, detached skin. A woman who didn't care, who didn't feel the sting of rejection. "I'm showing my back because I have nothing to say to you."

And just like that I whipped past him. I'd no idea how, I just moved. Like ice cascading down a mountain. Of course, I didn't get far before he'd wrapped me in an embrace and pulled my back against his front. He held me hard and fast, his grip chaining me to the earth. "Listen," he hissed, his words hot upon my neck. "If war is coming, then admitting and *claiming* love for each other makes us both vulnerable. It could destroy us—" He broke off with a sigh and slumped against me slightly.

I almost saw myself turning, pulling him to me, kissing that beautiful full mouth. I resisted. Because this time ... This time I knew he'd stop me.

He murmured into my nape. "Serena, if *she* gets her hands on you or me, she'll use whatever emotions she can to manipulate us. And even if we defeat Morgan, then you'll be the heir to a court, or at the very least a princess. You can't be with a disgraced Warrior who killed sprites and fae in that evil bitch's name. We can be friends and lovers and much else besides, but to love ... that's different."

I jerked away, but he kept ahold of my forearm. As if he couldn't let go. I faced him. Anger along with desire smoldered low in my gut. "You do *not* get to decide that for both of us, Wilder. For gods' sakes, everything you're talking about is probably years away, and a hundred things can happen between then and now to—"

"My soul isn't dying."

I blinked. *What?*

"Maggie's prophecy," he forced out. "You told me about it, remember? Your mate's soul is dying, in darkness—that's not me, Serena."

"So?" I couldn't think what else to say.

His hand dropped. Almost recoiling from me. "*So*, you have someone else out there, waiting for you. There's already a claim on your heart. And even if there is love here ..." He swallowed hard, clenching his jaw. "You'd choose him. Everyone does. The mating bond is too strong. And until you understand that, and understand what loving me really means, and what sacrifices and compromises it might force you to make, we shouldn't be together."

Finally, he'd said the words. Maybe he'd been desperate to say them ever since my confession. Perhaps I'd just imagined something deeper, something ... *more.*

I huffed a cold, flat laugh. I was beyond caring at this point. "Let me be clear on this. You're fine with us being friends and having sex, but we can't love each other because of a male I've never met? A fae that might not even be alive? Or because Morgan *might* capture us? You're a coward."

The color leeched from his skin as he hissed through his teeth. "What did you just say?"

A festering wound had been ripped open before my eyes. I'd bitten too deep, gone too far. I should apologize. Instead, I snapped, "You're a coward. You don't even know for sure that we're not mates. Things could change or click into place later, and you're not giving it a chance. You're just using a prophecy that makes no sense to put distance between us."

"Why would I do that?" he asked, his teeth flashing.

He looked like he wanted to spit fire. But in his eyes, there was something so familiar, that words came tumbling out. "Because if there is someone else out there for me, then there's a chance I'd reject you. You're scared."

Given the shock and hurt riding his face, I knew I was right. Guilt washed through me. "Wilder ..." I began.

I choked up as he turned vicious and snarled, "I'll take the sofa. You can have the bed. Just get out of my sight."

A ringing started in my ears. An alarm—a fall was imminent. Spinning, I somehow found my way into the bedroom. Closing the door, shutting out the light, I felt for the bed and slid in between icy sheets. How had this happened? Last night we'd been curled up in a canopy, and the day before that, his fingers and tongue had been between my legs. Now, I slept alone.

Grief broke down the dam inside my mind. Ripping, clawing, sweeping me away. I grabbed a pillow and pressed my face into its folds, desperately trying to smother the tears and rasping sobs. I wanted to go to him, to apologize, but—

Get out of my sight.

Exhaustion soon stopped the salty water from spilling. And the tide pulled back, the emotional weight breaking me and leaving behind a husk.

I HOPED the rift between us might mend once the heat from our words had faded. Sadly, I was mistaken. Time crawled by and a frostiness stuck, separating us, poisoning the air. I berated myself over and over again; I should've learned by now that the heart rarely healed as quickly or as easily as the body.

Ignored and confined, I sought distraction—chiefly training and reading. Obvious choices, given the plethora of weapons and books surrounding me. Neither activity held my attention, and I'd always abandon it halfway through. Even my sessions with Goldwyn had been cancelled. All to *protect* me.

Finally, after a five-day wait, a sentry came with news that Adrianna and Frazer had been spotted returning.

Despite desperate pleas to go see them, Wilder convinced me to stay put while he went to greet them. I was left alone to pound the lounge floorboards, waiting.

The door lock clicked. I ran to embrace whoever appeared first.

It was Frazer.

He caught me in a crushing hug, and the festering ache in my chest eased a tad. *Good to see you, siska.*

He pulled away quickly, but the bond echoed palpable relief; something far more valuable to me than any words.

Adrianna stepped out from behind him, and I pounced. She stiffened at the embrace and patted my back awkwardly.

Hm. I'd forgotten that I'd never seen her hug anyone. I drew back and scanned them both. They must've just got back—their bags and weapons were still strapped to them. "Did everything go okay?"

Adrianna closed the door and turned to me to say, "Of course."

I smiled for the first time in days.

Frazer dropped his bag and said, "Wilder caught us as we were landing. He's told us to stay here with you."

Seething quietly, I said, "Well, at least I'll have company in my new prison."

Adrianna's eyes sharpened. "Prison? Haven't you had fun locked up here with—"

She halted mid-sentence, studying my face. The rush of energy that'd sparked to life at their arrival had dulled, flickered, and died. Clearly, I didn't wear the bitterness or rage lightly. It made me spiky. "He hasn't touched me."

Frazer walked past me and I noticed a faint pinkness coloring his hollow cheeks. He started snooping, scouting the area.

Something told me he didn't want to hear about his sister's sexual frustrations.

A grumbling rang back through the thread. *You're not wrong.*

Adrianna waited until Frazer had disappeared into the bedroom to ask, "What happened between you two?"

My eyes reluctantly shifted to hers. "*He* decided that we shouldn't be together."

"Ah." Adrianna's lips thinned, and she asked, "Did he say why?"

"He reckons it'll make us more vulnerable, but I think it's just because he doesn't believe he's my mate—thanks to Maggie's prophecy. So he wants to wait until I understand what it means to love him."

I almost spat out the last part.

"Well, it all sounds very sensible," she said mildly.

A sad chuckle whispered out of me. "Yes. Very sensible."

Adrianna's face lit with a sage smile. "But you don't want that, and you hate that he's the one who decided, and that he's shut you down so quickly."

My brows lifted. "Where did that come from?"

A little careless shrug. "I'm only thirty, and there aren't many faelings in our society. The males that *are* young tend to only be interested in fucking and fighting. Sadly, more is expected of me."

A rasping laugh tickled the back of my throat.

Adrianna continued. "So every fae I've liked has been an elder. The older the fae, the more cautious they are. It's why I've never had sex," she admitted baldly.

I tried to smother a wink of surprise. "And you haven't considered being with a human?"

Adrianna angled her head in a careful, guarded move. "Actually, no, I haven't," she said, frowning. "I didn't want the complications that came with taking a human lover. Why, did you have someone in mind?"

I spoke much too quickly. "No. Just interested."

Adrianna made an *uh-hu* noise. Poor Cai.

A distraction came in the form of Frazer, who'd returned from scouting and was now staring out the bay window. "What are you doing?" I called to him.

"Just checking."

Adrianna left my side to walk over to him. "So, this is the enchanted glass?" she asked, brushing a fingertip along the window pane.

"Mm."

Adrianna looked over her shoulder. "Wilder mentioned that Hilda's summoned the instructors. They should be gone most of the day."

I smiled faintly and walked over to rest by their sides. "Who d'you want to steal from?"

"Cecile," Adrianna answered. "I've already tried the doors in the hall, but only Goldwyn's was open."

"Wilder told me that the doors are warded with a phrase. I couldn't hear what it was though."

Nodding distantly, she propped her bag and archery gear against the wall.

Frazer was the one to question her. "If you can't see the rooms from the outside, how d'you propose to find her window?"

Adrianna moved to sit on the windowsill. "Cecile's room will probably be next to Goldwyn's. As far as the spell goes, I'm hoping because I've seen these windows, I'll be able to visualize them. That's sometimes enough to break through glamours."

"The key word being sometimes," Frazer said with a raised brow.

Adrianna fumbled with the latch. "Won't know until I try. Just look after my bag—it has the feather in it." Glancing up and down the path outside, she pushed the window open and climbed through. Once outside, she waited just long enough to say, "Don't go anywhere—I'll need you to let me back in."

"I won't," I said and closed the window.

I watched her disappear, but Frazer's stare pulled my focus. "What's wrong?" he asked.

My reply was short, distant. "It's nothing. I just feel ... drained."

"Because?" Frazer pressed, steel ringing in his voice.

He wouldn't let this go.

I mustered a shrug and tried to divert the conversation. "Why don't you tell me how you killed the navvi? Or how Adi got the phoenix feather?"

He scowled, obviously seeing right through me. "There's nothing to tell. I chopped off its head and took its shape-shifting hide for proof, and Adrianna flew around for days looking for a nest. Telling stories doesn't interest me. What does concern me is why our bond feels so weak." He landed a swift poke to my chest—the place our thread connected. "You were bursting with energy a few days ago, and now you feel like a ghost. Why?"

That last word rang with a silent demand.

I leaned against the windowsill, resting my head against the cool glass. My words were a whisper. "I can't handle this."

"Which part?" he asked, moving in close. Not a touch, but still meant to be comforting. "Your new identity? Morgan? Wilder?"

"All of it," I rasped. "It's too much. Too fast. The bigger and more complicated this all gets, the smaller I feel."

Frazer stared. "Is this coming from you or him?"

I eyeballed him. "Who? Wilder?"

He didn't say anything. He didn't even blink. Instead, something passed through our bond. A fragment of a dark emotion that made me utter, "You still don't trust him? Fraze, he stepped in front of arrows for me."

My kin's stare cut me to the bone. "I trust him to protect your body, but your heart's a different story."

I braced my hand on the ledge. For some reason my core was shaking, fraying. "What are you saying?"

Frazer's arm went to grip my elbow, as if he thought I'd need the support. "Wilder was right—he's not your mate."

My limbs weakened. Frazer pushed me back to a seated position on the ledge. His hands stayed on my upper arms, and when I didn't collapse, he let go and stood, staring.

I gaped. "How could you possibly know that?"

"Well, apart from him not fitting Maggie's prophecy, I've seen the bond in action, and I've seen your memories. And deep down you crave adventure and danger. An open horizon. You come alive in those moments. And a mate would know that instinctively."

Sadness swept in. "You don't think he sees that?"

Frazer replied coolly. "Actually, I think it's one of the reasons he's so attracted to you. But he still pushed you to stay confined to his rooms for days."

A feeble protest passed my lips. "He said it was to protect me."

A quick flash of pity thawed his face. "Yes, he's acting like a male guarding someone he cares for. But he'd rather sacrifice his life for yours than risk having you work alongside him. And I'd probably have done the same thing, but Maggie said your mate's meant to help you, not shield you from danger."

I opened my mouth, but I didn't know whether to agree or argue. Adrianna's sudden arrival spared me from having to choose. I flung open the window, and she dove back in, panting heavily, looking stricken.

Frazer joined her side but didn't move to touch her. "What's wrong?" he demanded.

Adrianna sagged against the ledge. "Cecile's dead. Murdered."

Her broken words had the world slipping out from under my feet. My hand instinctively fluttered up and gripped her shoulder. "*Whathowwhen*?" I reeled.

Unblinking, Adrianna began. "I got the glamour to fail and climbed in through her bedroom window. I grabbed these." She pulled out a shell and a pearl comb from her pocket and set them on the ledge. "I was leaving when I smelled the blood."

Adrianna exhaled a heavy breath and wrinkled her nose, as if to clear her nostrils of the scent.

"How was she killed?" Frazer expelled.

Adrianna did blink then, grimacing. "I found her in the lounge with a knife embedded in her back."

My eyes misted over. "What do we do?"

Frazer and Adrianna shared guarded looks.

"Did you scent anyone else in the room?" Frazer's voice was cold. All ruthless efficiency.

An act. The grief and disgust shimmering in our bond was all too real.

Adrianna straightened up, but her eyes were glazed. "No. There was so much blood ... I couldn't smell anything else."

My arms went slack at my sides. "Should we go to Hilda?" I asked.

"No," Adrianna retorted. Seeing my flinch, she relented. "Cecile used to be a spy for my mother. I need to be the one to go to court and explain what's happened. If we tell anyone else now, it'll mean asking for permission to go see her. Something that might not be granted."

"Why not just send a message to Diana?" Frazer asked.

Adrianna didn't reply as she ducked down to where her bag rested. Rummaging through, she pulled out a large ruby feather and handed it to Frazer. Only then did she speak. "Because I want to look her in the eye when I ask if she knows who'd want Cecile dead. *And,* I've wanted to have it out with her ever since I learned she was sacrificing the recruits under her charge to that evil crow, Morgan."

Frazer nodded, satisfied.

Grabbing her crossbow from beside the window and securing it between her wings, she added, "Wilder's earned our trust. Tell him what's happened, but hide the shell and the comb until Cai and I can hand them over to Bert." She jerked her chin to the ledge where the items lay and went on. "I'll be back soon."

Before we could raise any objections, she'd shouldered her bag and quiver and was out the window, running into the sky.

I locked the window and mumbled, "This whole thing is spinning out of control."

Frazer stared down at the feather, twirling it around. "We don't know what happened. This might not have any connection to us."

I didn't believe that for a second. Feeling slightly sick, I pocketed the comb and shell and moved for what had become my go-to-spot by the hearth. Dragging my legs up, I wrapped my arms around them and rested my forehead against the tops of my knees.

My heart felt a little twinge. I hadn't known Cecile that well, but she'd seemed honorable and in her own way, kind. And she'd been a spy ... had someone found out? Had Dimitri? A knife in the back certainly seemed like something he'd do. A cowardly, evil act.

Frazer appeared by my side. He used quiet tones. "I need to stash the feather. Where did you put the nightshade?"

Without looking up, I said, "There's a spelled trunk in Wilder's bedroom. After he showed it to Goldwyn, he locked it away."

Frazer sounded strained as he asked, "He told you how to open it though, right?"

I nodded against my knees. "Put your hand on it and say valo."

He stalked away, returning a moment later to build a fire. Frazer seemed content to remain in silence. Something I was infinitely grateful for; there were no words left in me, anyway. As he moved around, making tea and then sitting down next to me to read, I stayed still, somewhere between sadness and exhaustion. I dozed off around noon, only to be jerked awake by the creak of a door.

Wilder walked in and took a quick scan of the area. "Where's Adrianna?"

Frazer got there before me. "Gone."

A scream erupted from out in the hallway. Wilder whirled and bolted out the door.

I peered over at Frazer who was staring at the door, frozen and unresponsive. "What do we do?" I breathed.

"Nothing," he whispered through pale lips.

I tried to will my pulse to calm while we waited, but to no avail.

A dirty growl came from the doorway. "I knew you'd be somewhere close by."

Dimitri was there, wings flaring.

Frazer stood, and with one *casual* move, sat on the edge of my armrest.

Dimitri's dark eyes glittered at the protectiveness in that single motion. "Cecile gets murdered, and you and your wingless demon just happen to be the only ones around?"

He flashed his teeth. I felt his thirst for biting—it made me shiver. Thankfully, he didn't see that vulnerability because his attention was drawn by something in the hallway. Wilder pushed past him into the lounge. Acting as our buffer, he said in an icy calm, "Leave now."

Dimitri got right up into Wilder's face. My throat constricted at the sight of his teeth so close to my male's—

To *Wilder's* throat.

"Good idea," Dimitri drawled. "I'll go and inform everyone that your pet and her *friend* were the only ones around at the time of Cecile's murder."

Frazer went rigid beside me. I looked up to see him wearing a death mask. "Adrianna Lakeshi was with us," he said in a murderous growl. "She's already gone to tell her makena what's happened."

Wilder's shoulders bunched together, but he didn't comment. Dimitri, on the other hand, hissed with his adder's tongue. "That just proves my point. If you lot didn't commit the crime, how did you know what had happened? How did you get into her rooms?"

Contempt echoing in every word, Frazer retorted, "You'll have to ask Bert."

Dimitri's mouth curled into a gloating smile. Like a squat spider. "I suppose you're referring to something for the fourth trial ... but whatever you're required to do, breaking into her rooms isn't possible. She locks her door; only those with the pass phrase can open it. D'you really expect me to believe—"

That had my patience snapping. "We're not asking you to believe anything. Adrianna discovered that the glass was enchanted. She was the one to find Cecile. So, unless you want to accuse the Princess of the Riverlands of murder ..."

I let the threat hang, hoping I hadn't played this wrong.

Wilder unleashed a breathy bark. "No, he won't do that. Will you?"

Dimitri showed his teeth in a bitter twist of his lip, but it looked more churlish than threatening.

Wilder moved to close the door. "Leave. Or the next person accused of murder will be you."

Dimitri snarled once and slithered away.

The door slammed shut and Wilder spun to face us. "Were you telling the truth about Adrianna?" he demanded.

"Yes," Frazer and I said at the same time.

"She didn't smell or see anything unusual in Cecile's room?"

"No," I answered from my seated position. "Frazer asked her about other scents, but she said there was too much blood."

I pushed down the gruesome images that threatened. And Wilder paced over to the window. He looked restless, caged, like a winged lion unable to fly. "The warding means that either Cecile let her attacker in, or they knew about the windows and got in that way. I'd think this was Dimitri, but Cecile hasn't been dead long. And he's been oozing lies in Hilda's ears for hours."

"What about Hunter?" Frazer glanced down at me. "D'you think he would've done it? Maybe he had another one of those concealment charms."

I lifted my weary gaze to his fierce one. "He made it sound like he only had one, but it's not as if I can trust him."

"Tysion then?" Frazer suggested.

"Why though?" Wilder muttered.

"D'you know that she used to be a spy?" I said to Wilder's back.

He turned slowly. "Adrianna told you?"

That answered that question.

I nodded, and he gave a little sigh. "Cecile gave me the impression she'd quit," he admitted. "I suppose living and breathing secrets is a hard habit to break."

Silence fell. I went over and over all my interactions with Cecile. Had she been acting strange? When did I last see her? Like a blow to the head, inspiration struck. "You said Cecile might've been the one who knocked on the door that day we got back. D'you think she found something out?"

Wilder's brow crinkled. "Why would she approach you and not me?"

I had no answer. No one said anything as we got lost in our thoughts. Minutes dragged by with Wilder treading the floorboards and Frazer stoking the fire.

I shivered and pulled my limbs in, conserving heat. For some reason, the warmth in the room wasn't sticking. Then, a black frost spread, growing and biting deep into my bones. What was *wrong* with me?

Auntie's voice came in a deathly whisper. *Serena? The clock's started ticking. I can't shield you from the magic in your blood much longer.*

An icy spear barreled down my spine. My pulse slowed, as did the ambient noise. I stared into the flames, watching amber and sapphire dance together. The magic in my blood—my fae inheritance—had begun its destructive course.

A hand grasped my shoulder. I looked up to see a face wild with fear. Frazer. "What is it?" he whispered, peering into my soul.

"I'm dying."

CHAPTER 30
THE BOND

Death was slow to claim me.

In the days that followed it waited on the periphery, lurking in my nightmares, haunting my waking moments.

Frazer became my constant companion, never leaving my side for long. He even slept next to me, but on the floor. I'd tried convincing him otherwise. He was kin; I saw nothing wrong with him sleeping on the mattress. But there were mutterings and vague references to fae customs. I didn't have the energy to argue because my time was measured by severe mood swings. One second I'd be filled with sparks and lightning, ready to take on the world. The next, I'd crash and want to sleep for years.

Adrianna returned to us three days after Cecile's murder, arriving in a wrathful storm. I'd never seen her so unhinged. After discarding her archery gear and hurling her bag in the corner, she spat out that the trip had been pointless. "She wouldn't answer any of my questions! Then, she ordered me to leave it to Hilda. At least we'll be spared her company at the final trial—she's promised not to come, so that's a bonus," she said, bitterness poisoning her voice.

Wilder regarded her coolly from the kitchen doorway. "If you'd consulted me before you left, I could've told you that. Diana won't interfere in internal camp politics. Especially when the kill could've been ordered by Morgan."

Adrianna looked like she was swallowing a lemon as she bit back a retort. She changed tack, and asked, "Has anything happened in my absence?"

A pause. Frazer met my heavy, drifting gaze from our seated positions by the hearth. I was currently swaddled in blankets and had been freezing for hours, despite the blaze licking up the chimney. Unable to think past the ice that held me, or the headache pounding behind my eyes, I gave Frazer a nod. *You tell her.*

He obliged. Adrianna waited a whole second before erupting. "What the rutting *courts* are we still doing here then? We need to be headed for Ewa, now!"

Frazer spoke for me ... How things had changed. "Hilda's doubled the guard since Cecile's death, and we still can't leave without Cai and Liora. Without their ingredients, it won't matter if we're at Ewa. The spell won't work."

Adrianna stopped pacing and twisted to Wilder. "What d'you have to say about this?"

My chest hollowed out. It made me rasp, "He doesn't say anything. He hardly speaks to us."

Adrianna blinked, gaping. I dropped her gaze and didn't bother to acknowledge the soft snarl coming from near the kitchen. Frazer sprang to guard me as Wilder closed the space between us. "You're not touching her," my kin said, blocking his path.

Wilder stopped a few feet away. "D'you honestly think I'd hurt her?" he asked quietly.

Frazer's hackles rose. "A stupid question, given how you've been treating her."

Adrianna grasped my shoulder and pressed me into the back of the armchair. A protective gesture, and the only sign that the aggression worried her.

Wilder called my name. I was determined not to respond. But my traitorous, useless body responded. Gaunt eyes greeted me. "I know I haven't been here for you."

Frazer snarled with such loathing, I was surprised he hadn't moved to kill him. "You haven't even acknowledged what's happening to her. You've just been ignoring us and disappearing for hours at a time."

Wilder moved into Frazer's space; imminent violence coated the air. "Yes," he said in a whisper. He felt more dangerous for it. "Forgive me, but I'm not capable of sitting here, watching her waste away. I've been keeping busy, tracking and spying on Dimitri instead."

A stunned silence followed.

"Why didn't you tell us that?" Frazer ground out.

"I thought you might feel like you needed to help and your place is here, with her."

Insufferable. Just when I was set on hating him.

After Wilder's confession, Frazer thawed a bit and even offered to help. Adrianna claimed that job and insisted that my kin stay with me. So I had to watch them take on all the responsibility while I wasted away, utterly helpless.

The following day, I was sitting in my favorite chair with two blankets covering me and a book on my lap, as Frazer stoked the fire. No doubt for my benefit. Because despite the blaze licking up the chimney, my fingertips were like icicles as they caressed the pages of *The Darkest Song*. I'd had a hard time putting it down lately. For some reason, it comforted me. Frazer was just talking about making lunch when the door clicked open. I didn't bother looking up. Wilder had told us the pass phrase days ago and we'd kept it locked. I knew it could only be one of two people.

The sound of a throat being cleared dragged my attention toward Adrianna. She was in the doorway, smiling.

"What is it?" I asked.

She moved aside. Cai and Liora walked through; they'd returned with only one day to spare.

Rallying, I scrambled to stand. Frazer's arm was instantly at my elbow, supporting, lifting. My book fell to the floor as Liora walked straight over. I held out my arms and we collided in a fierce hug. Cai wasn't far behind. He enveloped us both.

"We're sorry it took so long," Liora breathed into my ear.

"Quests are a lot longer and a far sight more boring when you don't have wings," Cai said cheerfully, rubbing my back.

I pulled away to stare at them both, and their smiles warmed the very bones of me. For the first time in days, I wasn't numb.

"I take it you got the items?" Frazer asked.

Cai hitched his bag higher. "They're in our bags. But we'd only just returned our weapons when Adi found us, so we haven't had time to show them to Goldwyn yet."

I stilled and exchanged brief glances with Adrianna and Frazer.

Cai continued, oblivious. "We should probably go see her now—"

"Goldwyn's not seeing anyone," Adrianna said, sadness inflecting her voice. "Show them to Wilder instead."

Liora took her in. Then Frazer, and finally, me. "You need to tell us something?"

Adrianna laughed weakly. "Where do we start?"

Liora's bright eyes found mine. A plea for information.

"Wait." Cai showed us his palms. "Before we learn things that will undoubtedly make our lives more complicated and horrible, can we have something to drink and a whole ton of food? Because I've had enough stale buns and dried meat to last a fae lifetime."

He stuck his tongue out in disgust.

Liora clucked her tongue. "Such hardship."

A little smile nudged my cheeks. It felt forced.

Adrianna stalked over to the kitchen and without looking back, said, "Kitchen is through here. I'll make us some coffee—we'll need it."

"How reassuring," Cai joked sarcastically. He still dumped his bag on the rug and trailed after her.

Liora looked around. "Adi says you've been keeping the feather and nightshade in a safe? Where is it?"

"It's the trunk in the bedroom," Frazer said, pointing the way. "Pass phrase is valo."

"Okay. I should go put our stuff in the safe, but just know that whatever's going on, we'll fix it—together." Liora's hand squeezed my wrist in a quiet promise. She didn't seem to need a response as she disappeared into the bedroom with their bags.

Her words lifted my spirits, but not enough to sustain my strength. I fell backward into squeaking springs and reached for the blankets that now scattered the floor.

Frazer was already there, covering me, tucking me in. "Fussy," I mumbled.

"Just doing my brotherly duty," he said with a one-sided smile.

I suspected he did it to make me relax. Because underneath that mask, the bond rang clear with echoes of a pulse-pounding terror. I wanted to tell him how sorry I was, but the apology got lodged in my throat.

Recognition flickered on his side of the thread as my emotions leaked through. Frazer's eyes burned brighter in response. Throat bobbing, he leaned down and swiftly kissed me on the top of my head.

Stunned into submission, I didn't move or speak until everyone had gathered around, minutes later. Liora slumped on the floor in front of me, leaning against my legs. She must've been desperate for answers, but restrained herself with typical calm and poise. To keep my mind still, I lazily braided her red-gold curls.

Cai and Adrianna brought through multiple slices of date cake, muffins, and ginger biscuits. All sweet, fattening, and *necessary*. They'd also found a coffee service set, one that seemed oddly formal for a male like Wilder. A space was cleared on the rug, the tray set down, and my pack settled in a circle below me.

Adrianna poured coffee into cups and balanced them atop plates, each set with goodies. No one spoke as she handed out nourishment.

Cai's patience broke first. "So, before we start with the tale of inevitable woe, am I right in assuming Wilder's hiding the spell thinga-majigs because you've told him what we're doing and who you are?"

All eyes on me. "He knows everything."

Cai said rather bluntly, "All right. Who wants to start?"

Frazer's eyes lifted to mine. I nodded. No words necessary.

He began recounting the drama of the last thirteen days. I curled my feet up and carried on plaiting Liora's locks—it kept my hands busy and distracted me from their reactions. But it soon became hard to ignore the color draining from Cai's face, or the shaky rise and fall of Liora's shoulders as she fought back tears.

Frazer finished and Liora spoke thickly. "Poor Cecile."

Cai bobbed his head in a stupor. "I can't believe it."

The weight of sorrow and fear caused a stiff pause, one in which

Liora set her plate down and swiveled around on her knees to look at me. Her expression intent and blazing, she said, "We might've been too late to save Cecile, but I know how we can help you."

That got everyone's attention. Adrianna seemed interested; Frazer, desperate; and Cai looked oddly guarded.

"Well, what is it?" Frazer urged, bowing forward.

"There's a spell that can sustain you," Liora began, not breaking eye contact with me. "It won't last forever, but it gives us time."

"A spell that's incredibly dangerous," Cai whipped out.

Liora turned to meet her brother's stare, and said sharply, "It isn't dangerous for the caster."

Cai looked like he'd been force-fed poison; he slammed his plate down so that coffee and crumbs flew this way and that. "That's not what I meant, and you know it."

It must be bad.

Liora drew herself up and went on calmly. "She deserves to hear her options. You can't deny her that choice."

"I'd be the one rutting casting it," he said angrily.

Frazer confronted Cai. "Don't you want to save Serena?" His whisper sounded dangerous.

Exhausted, despairing, my head wilted and fell into my palms.

"Don't. You. Dare." Cai's magic rumbled overhead, a storm brewing.

Blood whirring, some ember of my magic crackled in response. Lightning to join thunder.

Heads twisted in my direction.

Adrianna grasped Cai's arm in warning. "Before this room is obliterated into teeny tiny splinters, d'you want to explain what you're referring to, Liora?"

"It's called twining," she answered.

Cai groaned, and his magic blew out. Mine with it.

Liora continued. "It was discovered when a fae-witch was watching her mate die. She got so desperate, she bound their life forces together to give them time to reach a healer."

My body went cold then hot in the space of a breath.

"I've thought it might come to this," Liora added in a murmur. "I've told Cai that I want to be the one to help you."

Cai burst out, "Li! Your energy's already too fractured by the binding—"

"You don't know that," she retorted. "What's the alternative? We let our best friend die on us?"

My heart twisted and glowed at the same time. "Li, I can't let you …"

"Let me. *Let me.*" Liora confronted me, eyes wild.

I leaned back, alarmed.

That instantly broke something in her and with a shaky breath she said, "You need help. And we need you. There's nothing more to be said. I can do this," she added oh-so-quietly.

Oh, Li. My chest expanded and my eyes blurred.

"No," Frazer said, stiff-necked.

Liora's head spun to meet his challenge.

His voice was firm. "You might have magic, but you still have the physical limitations of a human. If anyone is tying their life to Serena's, it should be someone who's already done it once, and with the physical abilities to bear the burden."

Liora opened her mouth, scowling.

Frazer cut across her with ruthless words. "I don't doubt your heart, but it's obvious you're offering your life to prove a point to yourself. And you're not the best choice, so don't let whatever's going on with you damage Serena's chances of survival."

Liora's wrath vanished; she diminished.

It broke my heart. "This argument is pointless. No one's tying themselves to me."

"Yes, they are. And it'll be me," Frazer said coolly.

Arrogant, presuming ass.

Adrianna waded in, asking Cai, "What would happen if she didn't get to Ewa in time? Would the spell kill her *and* Frazer?"

The question was brutal and to the point. My gut roiled.

Cai's silence was more than enough confirmation.

More cogent than I'd been in days, I said, "That's settled then. I won't be responsible for killing any of you."

Frazer regarded me with a pained look. "If you die, I die. I've lost someone once before, and it nearly destroyed me. If it happened to my kin, and I could've stopped it, I'd either lose my mind or cut my throat so I could go into death and bring you back."

I stared, horrified. How could I argue with that?

Frazer must've sensed my resolve slip because he turned his attention to Cai. "What do I do?"

Cai's eyes flickered with a wince and he left a pause that Liora filled. "You hold hands while he casts the spell. Then, you'll need to repeat the words: 'I offer my life unto you. I share my soul with you. If you die, so shall I.'"

A nauseating tremor ran through my hands. "So, Frazer and I would die on the same day?"

Liora pushed herself up. "This isn't like a bond—Cai can break the twining when he needs to."

Frazer wore only grim acceptance as he stood. Adrianna straightened next to him and murmured, "You don't have to bear this burden. I can do it."

He didn't acknowledge her. Just stepped with purpose toward me and held out a hand.

"Cai," Liora said in a silent order to stand.

His movements were rigid and reluctant, but he still got up.

I was the only one left resisting. I stared again at Frazer's open palm. At the offer. I couldn't accept it. I wouldn't kill my brother.

"Siska."

His voice called to me to join him. The tug on our bond was unyielding, growing ever more insistent. That braided light wound up, making my core tighter and tighter.

A battle of wills. And I was weak.

It's all right, child. He needs you to live; we all do. Now stand.

Auntie's reassurance was the final blow. My resistance shattering, I held back tears as I took his hand. He pulled me up and entwined our fingers.

All I could think was how I was a damned coward, and sick with guilt, I watched Cai chant in a foreign tongue. Then, Frazer repeated the phrase that would damn him.

Our souls connected, bonding for a second time. A braid that was two strands now become three as another uncoiled and fixed into place.

Cedar, snow and citrus hit my nostrils. A rush began in my ears, quick-ening to a roar, and wave after wave of energy flooded my veins. I doubled over, choking on it. Intoxicating, nauseating, and a complete rush.

Auntie sighed deeply. She sounded relieved.

Liora's arms encompassed me, supporting me as I leaned on her and met Frazer's eyes. He was pale but steady. Cai, on the other hand, collapsed into a chair, shaking and sweating. Adrianna moved to his side but didn't touch him. In clipped tones, she asked, "Are you okay?"

Cai's drawn face lifted to hers. I thought I saw something pass between them. An understanding, perhaps.

The creak of a door had us all turning; Wilder slipped into the room and stopped, taking in the scene. He loosened a growl. "What have you done?"

~

DESPITE FIRST IMPRESSIONS, Wilder turned out to be glad about the twin-ing. He'd sat on the divan to my right during Liora's explanation, and when she was done, he'd nodded, and said, "Good. If it keeps Serena alive, I'm happy."

Anger, sharp and sour, crashed in—everything I'd failed to feel in the numbness. No matter his reasons, he'd left me to face confinement and death alone.

I felt his eyes on me then. "As Goldwyn still refuses to see anyone, Hilda's appointed me as your instructor," he said quietly.

I didn't know what I might say if I opened my mouth, so I kept it firmly closed.

Adrianna did the decent thing and gave him a response. "Are you wanting us to continue to stay here?"

A swift nod. "It's for the best. You should be close to the quest items in case we need to leave quickly." His wrist flicked between Liora and Cai. "Did you two get the last ingredients?"

Liora replied, "They're in the safe."

"Good. Now that Serena's better, you should all get back in training for the arena battle."

Frazer was sharp. "We're still doing that?"

Wilder's lip tucked up at the side, those twin scars creasing. "I suppose that depends. We shouldn't take the changes Hilda's made to the guard lightly. If the twining can withstand the delay, then it's worth waiting."

All eyes went to Cai, but Liora was the one to answer. "It depends on Frazer's strength, but the origin story had the twining lasting months—"

Cai cut across her. "Neither of the fae in that story had to sustain light magic. That'll shorten their time. Maybe by a lot."

Frazer's arms folded. "My strength can hold out an extra four days."

"Sure?" Wilder asked, glancing to Frazer.

His eyes narrowed at the question. "Yes," he punched out.

Wilder's gaze pulled at me then. I resisted. The pull didn't vanish, though, even as he said, "Have you all completed the fourth quest?"

Cai shifted, visibly uncomfortable.

"Yes," Adrianna answered quickly. "Cai and I just need to check in with Bert before the final trial."

My eyes traveled to Cai. He didn't look annoyed or triumphant. In fact, he was staring at Adrianna. His expression seemed to say, *Look at me. Look.*

Wilder was talking, distracting me from their non-courtship. "After you finish the last trial, I'll escort you all back here. It'll go easier on us if you all win your bouts. We don't want the wrong kind of eyes on us as we prepare to leave."

He didn't look my way, but I knew his words were aimed at me. I was the only one who could draw the Wild Hunt's attention to us.

Wilder continued. "We'll wait for cover of darkness and then set out. In the meantime, you should gather together everything you'll need for the trip to Ewa. We have to be ready to leave at a moment's notice. And we need a plan in case we get split up. Or get attacked."

Tension—*anticipation*—coiled tight in my gut like a spring. I couldn't swallow. My mouth had gone too dry. No one said anything or moved an inch.

Wilder scanned our faces. He waited a beat before planning for us. "Those of you unfamiliar with the terrain, start learning. Don't mark any maps with the destination. If we're attacked *and* outnumbered, we'll split up and meet at the lake later."

He went along in this vein, planning with such ruthless efficiency that even Frazer seemed to respect him for it.

As impressed and anxious as it made me, my feelings didn't lose their brittle edge. That is, until his green eyes finally caught me unawares. "You'll need to fill your bags with rations," he barked out, keeping his gaze locked on me. "All of you go to the hall. Tell them I gave you permission to bring back as much food as you can carry as a reward for completing the trial."

I prepared to stand with the others.

"Not you, Serena."

My pack stilled, watching us.

"Why not?" I asked quietly.

"It'd be safer for you to remain here."

I felt the argument spark on my tongue. Before I could say anything, he'd added, "I would speak with you."

A fissure of shock cleaved my heart. "Oh."

Adrianna was the first to follow orders. Cai followed quickly, muttering something about a bath. Liora and Frazer hesitated, waiting for my say-so. "It's fine," I told them.

Liora's mouth quivered in a hidden smile. Then, she dragged a very reluctant Frazer away.

Wilder was moving the second the door closed, crossing over to where I sat. Not to kiss or touch, but to kneel. *Kneel* before me. This proud, strong male was humbling himself. And I had no clue why.

I gaped. "What are you *doing*?"

"I swore that you'd be the last person I submitted to, and I meant it."

I leaned into the back of the chair as he unsheathed a dagger from his hip.

He placed the curved blade across my thighs. An offering. "I need you to do something for me. Or rather, I need you to let me do something for you."

Wilder held out his hands and put them on either side of my body. Complete surrender.

Emotion, hot and heady, stuck in my throat as the moment stretched, and he didn't budge an inch. A tear slipped through my control. And then, another, and another. I hated every single one of them.

My hurt pride prevented me from speaking first.

He stared into me as if he'd guessed my thoughts. He wet his lips nervously and spoke in a rasp. "I've acted shamefully by ignoring you. My only excuse is that I mistook my age for wisdom. I thought by distancing myself, I'd save us both. You were right. I was a coward."

He dipped his head a little, and added, "I didn't lie to you though. *When* you resume your rightful place in court, no one will want us to be close. And things may change when you become fae, and if you meet your mate, he'll fight for you. And maybe, he'll win ..."

The vulnerability in the line of his shoulders and jaw, in those low, rasping tones, almost made me reach for him. Almost.

A bolt, a *thrill*, passed through me as he continued. "The thing I *know*, right now, is that I don't need a mating bond to tell me how I feel. And it won't stop me from wanting to be near you—or from fighting by your side. So, no matter what happens to us, I want—no, I *need* to know that I have a place in your court. One so powerful that others can't force or manipulate me into leaving."

"What are you saying?" I forced out in a whisper.

"I want to fight for you, Serena ... Smith? ... Raynar?" he said, a smile playing on his mouth.

That beautiful, stupid mouth.

His expression slipped. More serious. More sincere. "So let me swear the guardian vow to you. It's the only bond I can offer. The only service I can provide. I know I don't deserve this, but if you'll let me, if you'll have me, I'll pledge my sword and honor to your cause. Now and forever."

The *weight* of those words left me scrambling and breathless. "You can't. I can't."

He cut me short. "This isn't a hasty choice on my part. I've thought about this. A lot. It's the right thing to do. I know it is—*trust* me."

There was nothing to say. I'd made one bond before without understanding the consequences, how could I do so again?

"Please, valo."

It was so quiet, so soft. A plea that *tugged*.

Damn him.

Auntie? Any advice?

Trust your heart.

Double damn.

He looked so hopeful.

I'd surely burn in the dark court for agreeing. "I'll only do it if you tell me what valo means."

His eyes flared in surprise. Then his face split into a grin, broad and with a hint of mischief. Not breaking my stare, he took his dagger from my thighs and brought it sweeping across his wrist.

A little gasp escaped me as the blood beaded there.

He reached up slowly. My whole being narrowed to the point on my lips where he pressed his wrist. The metallic scent assaulted my nostrils, but I didn't dare move.

A murmur. "It means light of the heavenly stars. The only thing that all fae kneel before."

Then, a string of whispered Kaeli words bound us together. To honor, to protect, to cherish. Now and forever.

CHAPTER 31
THE BLOODY BATTLE

"Serena Smith, your opponent in this trial is Myla Peron," Hilda announced.

The former leader of Cecile's pack.

I didn't need to scan the sand pit. Not with only nine of us left.

The crowd in the arena clapped politely as I walked over to join the female's side. I kept a firm grip on my Utemä; anything to keep my hands steady.

Now, shoulder to shoulder with Myla, she gave me a little nod and a smile.

Damn.

I'd always liked Myla. It would've been so much easier to fight a hateful person.

Who cares how nice she is? Auntie spoke. *You fight for your pack.*

My pack. I searched for their faces.

Frazer and Cai had already been matched. Cai was standing, hand on longsword, next to Lucian, that spineless worm who'd ambushed Adrianna. Cai's thunderous expression made it clear he remembered their last encounter well. By the wrath in Lucian's red-eyed glower, it seemed he hadn't forgotten either. He looked like a bitter frost. Like winter made flesh. My mind conjured up images mixed with fable from

The Darkest Song, of a battle long ago, between the God of Ice and the God of Wind. In the legend, the latter had won. I prayed for the same outcome.

My eyes traveled to Frazer. Hot guilt seared my gut at the sight of the hulking body beside him. Another member from Tysion's defunct pack. Who knew how much the twining had weakened my kin? Maybe I'd made him vulnerable to the likes of the giant winged fae, currently cracking his knuckles.

"Liora, you're with Emilie Gretson."

Hilda's voice carried across the ring and my head immediately shifted to Liora. She was the closest to me. And even though she stood tall, her face paled underneath her freckles, and her fire-kissed features dimmed.

Adrianna was the last candidate to be paired off.

I felt Frazer hovering at the edge of my mind. *There's no one left.*

One of the instructors? I suggested.

Hilda walked among us, shouting, "Due to our numbers, we're left a recruit short. Adrianna Lakeshi cannot progress without facing an opponent; therefore, we've enacted the fifth trial clause. Cole Vysan has been granted a second chance."

He stomped in via the portcullis. Unable to look at those monstrous, armored arms wielding steel, I roamed the stands searching for Wilder. He'd taken a seat near the barrier and was flanked by Dimitri and Mikael. It was too far to see his expression, but I no longer doubted him; I knew he'd be nervous for us—for me. Although we hadn't rekindled our intimacy from the cave, our new bond had gone a long way to healing the fissure between us, and to melting my kin's built-up resentment toward him.

Hilda bellowed, "Be aware, the same rules apply as in the fifth trial: land three hits and you win. No magic. No berserkers. The victor will stand by the ring edge until all other matches are concluded." She paused as she walked to the outskirts of the ring to oversee. "Face your opponent, draw your weapons."

My sword sighed as it came free.

"Prepare to engage!"

I dropped into a fighting stance, studying Myla's movements. She looked calm, her pink wings tucked in tight. I guessed she'd seen my match against Jace and decided to play it safe.

Good. Fae suffered without proper wing mobility. She'd be slower and clumsier.

"Begin!"

Myla prowled, circling me, forcing me to mirror her. She moved carefully, her whole body adjusting to the tiniest movement on my part.

You're letting her dictate the terms. Do something, Auntie urged.

"Like what?" I mumbled aloud.

Myla's head angled; she must think me mad.

SUN! Auntie yelled.

I had a panic-stricken second to realize my mistake, to raise my defenses. Manipulated into the sun's path and blinded, my only warning to where her attack was coming from was sand crunching underfoot. I moved, lurching back, whirling left.

Every action felt disjointed, separate from my will.

Clashing steel met and danced in the bloody song of battle.

Myla was smart; she dodged more attacks than she bothered to match. A strategy similar to Jace's. Only he'd relied on aggression and strength to exhaust me. Myla used patience and restraint.

I knew which one was more dangerous. Warning bells chimed deep inside. If I didn't do something soon, she'd win. That wasn't an option.

I changed strategy, attacking with full force. Myla adjusted easily. Frustration urged me to kick out, hitting her gut. A sharp gasp was my cue. I'd winded her. I struck with my sword, aiming for her chest.

A hit.

Don't stop.

I'd barely moved the sword from her chest before push-kicking into her knee. She stumbled. I performed a thrust straight to her shoulder blade, stopping short of causing real harm.

Two hits.

Myla didn't panic, annoyingly. She recovered quickly enough that my move for her wing failed. Instead, she lashed out with her sword, forcing me to engage and parry.

Get her off balance again.

Our swords met, angled away from our bodies. I took a risk and crashed into her side, steel edges grating as my blade scraped along hers. She hardly moved; I'd miscalculated.

Before she could push back or bear down, I did the stupidest thing imaginable; I freed one hand from my sword.

In that single heartbeat where she failed to crush my resistance, my hand grabbed her shoulder. My leg snapped between hers and performed a scissor lock. We tumbled to the ground on our backs. If it were a real battle, we'd both have been dead; we raised our swords to land blows at the same time. My blade against her ribs, Myla's sword at my throat.

Victory.

"Myla Peron, you're out!" Hilda called.

We stared at each other, panting slightly. Myla's whiskey-colored eyes met mine. There was no surprise or anger. More like weary resignation. Her sword left my throat, and she flipped up to standing in a graceful maneuver. Myla's ebony skin gleamed with sweat as she extended a hand. I clasped it, grateful, and pulled myself up. We stayed, staring at each other for a moment. Then, she inclined her head. A gesture of respect, maybe. The moment gone, she broke contact and left for the ring's edge to join Lucian.

A smile tugged at my lips at the sight of the male. I sheathed my blade and walked to ringside, to the winner's area. Cai was the only one there. I ran and caught him in a fierce hug. "We did it," I whispered.

"Of course," he said, his breath tickling my ear.

I drew back and searched the crowd for Wilder's face.

I stared and stared. The instructors had gone.

A twinge of unease sparked bright. But Liora, Frazer, and Adrianna were still fighting for their places, so I twisted back around to watch the battles unfold.

Adrianna and Frazer were struggling. Liora, on the other hand ...

"Emile Gretson, you're out!"

Cai muttered something that I thought might be, "Thank the sisters," as Liora sprinted over. We collided in a three-way hug, our heads touching. I whispered over to Cai, "Can you shield our conversation?"

His eyes flared in surprise, but he nodded a fraction. A warm pulse shuddered through me. We pulled free from each other and Liora spoke. "What's wrong?"

"The instructors have gone. Wilder too."

"You think something's happened?" Cai asked in a hushed voice.

I deferred to Liora. "Your senses are sharper than most—what d'you think?"

Brow crinkled, she did a sweep of the arena. "Wilder wouldn't leave without good reason."

That's what I was afraid of.

My hand drifted to the necklace. A nervous habit.

Liora linked arms with me. "We'll find him."

Cai mumbled in agreement. I plastered a watery smile on my face and turned my attention back to the pit.

Frazer was engrossed in holding off his opponent's bulk, while Adrianna danced around Cole, baiting the beast into snapping his jaws.

A good strategy; however, I groaned aloud when it backfired. Predicting a feint, Cole clipped her arm. A hit in his favor. Adrianna's wings splayed wide in shock and she stumbled—actually stumbled backward.

My heart jumped. Cai took a step toward her, as if he couldn't stop himself. "What's wrong with her? Why does she look like that?"

Liora released me to place a calming hand on his arm, stopping him, reminding him where we were. "She probably just didn't expect it, that's all."

"Icarus Bale, you're out!"

I was the first to recognize Frazer's win. His familiar loping stride kicked the air from my lungs. I greeted him with a rattling sigh and a wan smile. He took his place at my side.

"Four down," Cai muttered, his eyes fixed on Adrianna.

"Cai cast the sound bubble," I explained to Frazer in a breath.

Frazer's head bowed, angling toward me. *Why?*

"I noticed the instructors had left, and I needed to tell the others."

Alarm marked him in quick, tiny movements—darting eyes and flaring nostrils. He masked it by rounding on me with a lofty, *amused* brow. "Right, and were you the first to win your bout?"

I smiled despite myself. "No. That was Cai."

A deft nod. "You still beat your opponent before me. I'm struggling to forgive you for that."

"You'll find a way."

He chuffed; a breathy bark of a laugh.

My attention shifted again, moving to Adrianna. After another nail-biting minute, she landed a hit as she bludgeoned Cole in the ribs.

In retaliation, he punched Adrianna in the tit. Winded, hand clutching her chest, she staggered back. Then Cole brought the full force of his broadsword down on one of her slightly splayed wings.

Adrianna dodged but wasn't quick enough to avoid contact. Except her wing didn't crumple from the impact of a blunt weapon—the sword sliced clean through a section of fragile membrane. She was bleeding, spraying red over the arena's sand.

Such a deafening silence in my head.

Cai was the first of us to sprint forward, howling. I chased after Frazer and Liora.

Hilda bolted forward, winging her way toward Adrianna as she fell to her knees and Cole raised his sword up in a deathblow. This had suddenly become a very public execution.

Cai threw his inked hand out, shouting something.

Cole dropped his blade, his hands going to his chest, seeking to stem the flow of the blood that spurted forth. His mouth stretched in a silent scream and he collapsed sideways, spread out on the sand. Motionless. Dead.

Hilda slowed for a fraction too long. That was when a spear skewered her through the gut. An impossible throw seemingly from across the arena.

I stumbled; the world stilled as Frazer doubled back and lifted me into his arms.

Cai reached Adrianna first. She was conscious and struggling to stand. Cai grasped her arm, pulled it around his shoulders and ran, leading the way.

Screams blasted my eardrums as the noises that had dulled in those explosive moments poured in. Fellow recruits and people in the stands were fleeing, pushing one another out of the way.

A second later, Frazer bellowed, *"Cai! Arrows!"*

Whistling sounds made me close my eyes and brace for impact. Only it never came. I dared a look. Close to the portcullis, Adrianna was being half-dragged, half-carried into the annex room beyond by Liora, while Cai faced us with both palms outstretched. I looked over Frazer's shoulder in time to see three arrows hovering in mid-air; they were swept aside by a magical wind.

Frazer reached Cai and shouted, "Move!"

My mind lagged, taking in Cai's drawn face, his pale lips, and glassy eyes. Had he used too much power? But his movements were steady as he twisted and followed.

As we ran into the stone room, I heard someone cry, "Don't!"

Eyes blinking, adjusting to the darkness, I captured shadowed fragments.

Jace was lying in wait with a strung bow, an arrow pointed at my chest, marking me for death.

Roaring, "*Bitch*," he let the fletching fly.

Frazer spun, covering his body with mine.

No, no, no, no, no.

Fear for my brother's life made me thrash and scream and throw my arms around his back. As if I could catch the arrow.

A sickening thud. Fire and ice consumed me, then stopped dead in my veins. Because Frazer was spinning around, unharmed.

Cai had blown Jace back into the stone wall opposite. He was bleeding from a head wound. Dead or unconscious, I didn't care which.

I hit Frazer's chest. "Never do that again! D'you hear me?"

Sounds of Cai's vomit splattering against flagstones traveled over the top of my shouting.

Adrianna silenced me by croaking out, "We need to get to Wilder's. Now."

I didn't like the look of her, her features stretched thin in pain, slumped against Liora who was struggling to support her weight.

"Right, you." I poked Frazer in the chest. "Let me down, now!"

No objections. He lowered me and went to lift a groaning Cai. I ducked under Adrianna's arm, propping her up, sharing her weight with Liora. We all lurched forward, running as best we could down the tunnel to the oak door.

Outside was chaos. The human guests were fleeing through the arena gate on foot. They screamed and trampled one another in an effort to escape arrows and the bodies of fallen fae raining down from above.

So much for doubling the sentries. There seemed to be few guards actually fighting back. And those striving to reach the archers atop the walls faced swarms of fae—panicked, stupid fae that didn't huddle together, but flew off in every direction, making themselves easy targets for arrows.

A veritable bloodbath.

Bile stung my throat as we moved again, sticking close to walls, avoiding open spaces whenever possible. Frazer led us, glancing back every other second to check on me. Cai's eyes scanned the skies. Probably searching for arrows to stop.

Somehow, we made it to the staff quarters without being impaled. Through one door and then the another.

With the lounge door slammed and locked behind us, Adrianna staggered to a chair, gasping. Frazer set Cai onto his feet; apart from swaying slightly, he remained upright.

A blessed relief.

Mind racing, world askew, I ran into the bedroom.

It was empty. Wilder wasn't there. A feeble hope, but its loss still burned and ached. I walked back into the lounge, half in a stupor, and found Adrianna struggling to stand. "We should get the bags and go."

Cai kneeled in front of her. He examined her wing and scowled. "We're not going anywhere with you like this," he argued.

"Don't have a choice," she pushed out in a rasp.

"Bullshit!" He staggered back up.

Something about the sight had Adrianna collapsing into the cushion.

Cai reeled off orders. "Li, Serena, take her to the kitchen. Wash her wound, get her something to eat and drink. Frazer, gather the quest items and anything we might've forgotten. I'll grab the bags and a medical kit."

He stopped. A heartbeat passed. Then, everyone did as commanded. Liora and I hauled Adrianna into the fawn-colored kitchen. I scanned the room: four rickety cabinets that held food, and a stone sink for water.

Adrianna pushed us away and slumped to the floor. I moved to keep her upright, but she waved me away. "I just need a moment," she said, breathless.

Liora set the tap running and filled a bowl. The bloody glove-prints on the wall; the long, bleeding cut in her wing; and that metallic smell staining the air caused a cold sickness to churn in my belly. *Keep moving. Don't think*, Auntie's voice sounded, calling me back from the oblivion that beckoned.

Liora set down a basin, a towel soaking within.

"I'll wash the wound myself," Adrianna said while peeling off her soiled gloves.

Liora paced over to the sink, murmuring, "I'll get you something to drink, then."

Adrianna forced out, "Not water. Something stronger, to dull the pain."

"Braka's second cabinet from the right," I said, naturally, all too familiar with Wilder's quarters.

Adrianna hissed through her teeth as she put the soaking towel against the tattered edge of her wing. It made me add, "Liora, grab enough glasses for everyone."

She didn't bother to ask why. The reason was obvious. What had just happened—what we'd seen—was too horrible for words.

Frazer appeared with the medical kit while Cai waited in his shadow.

Adrianna looked up and frowned. "*You're* going to do it?"

Frazer kneeled beside her. "I've got more experience tending to wings. I'll stitch, and Cai will heal what he can with magic."

"Cai isn't using his magic on me," Adrianna said flatly.

"Don't be stupid. Of course, I am," he insisted.

Adrianna and Cai stared each other down while Frazer prepared a curved needle and thread.

"No, you're not," Adrianna spoke heavily. "You'll need every bit of your magic when we flee, and my wing will heal itself in the next few hours anyway, so don't waste your resources."

Cai opened his mouth, furious, and she cut him across. "It's what's best for all of us."

That stopped him. Adam's apple bobbing, he passed a hand over his smarting eyes and rubbed, as if to hide the watery evidence. When his hand dipped, his gaze was clear and *pissed*. "You are a serious headache, you know that?"

Adrianna answered with a grunt as Frazer dabbed a cleansing paste on her wing. Cole had almost cut clean through the side.

"Adi, down it." Liora shoved a knuckle's width of braka into her trembling hands. She then offered one to Frazer, who refused. Liora offered me the braka instead. I downed it in one gulp and my chest caught fire. A bit of life returned to my bones.

The needle met delicate flesh, slipping in and out, binding the wing together. Frazer worked quickly, but I still couldn't stand to watch. So I maneuvered carefully through the cramped kitchen and set to looking for food.

I pulled out some apples and handed two over to Liora and Cai, who were both nursing their glasses, taking measured sips. "Don't drink that stuff without filling your belly with something."

They both reached out to take one with vacant expressions, mumbling their thanks. Adrianna refused to eat anything. Not surprising —she looked ready to throw up. I started in on some crackers. After a minute of silence, Cai muttered, "What now?"

"We run," Liora answered. She looked more present now, her eyes blazing as she watched Frazer slowly stitch Adrianna back together.

I put the crackers aside. I'd lost my appetite. "What about Wilder?"

No one spoke because no one wanted to suggest it. But their thoughts were clear. "We can't just leave him," I said hotly.

Frazer was the one to point out the obvious. "Without Hilda's and Wilder's protection, this place has become a giant sprite trap. There's no one left to help us, and we can't mount a rescue with no information."

I wasn't ready to give up, but I couldn't think what to do. I was lost.

All was quiet while Frazer tied off Adrianna's stitches. Then he stood, confronting me. "Serena, Wilder planned for this. He knows where to meet us."

Ewa.

"He wouldn't leave me behind," I rasped.

I knew it with every fiber. He'd hunt me for however long it took— follow me to whatever end. He'd proven that, the second he'd bound his service and life to mine.

"Exactly," Adrianna said as she lurched to her feet. "He's strong and devoted, which means he'll find you. Wherever you go."

I sounded like a ghost, mumbling, "What if he can't find me because he's dead?"

I blinked back tears as Frazer came up beside me to dump the bloody water and wash his hands. "We still have to change over our weapons. Let's take a minute."

Any time was a gift. He knew that.

"D'you think we should take our armor?" Cai asked, fiddling with the sleeve of his leather tunic.

Frazer turned to him. "It's up to you, but the tunics won't stop sharpened blades, and they'll feel hot and heavy on the road."

Cai nodded curtly.

With that settled, Liora left the kitchen. After a beat of hesitation, Cai held out his arm for Adrianna. A subtle offer of support.

"I'll be fine," she said stiffly.

"Right." Cai's eyes creased, the only sign of pain he showed before walking through to the lounge. Adrianna hobbled through afterward. Would she ever let him in?

Frazer didn't move from my side. Instead, he leaned against the cabinets and stared at the floor where drops of blood lingered. I felt him preparing to say something. I had a sense I knew what. "If you're going to try to make me feel better about abandoning him, don't bother," I said.

A grave, mournful look was my answer before he tugged me roughly into his arms. Shock was my initial reaction. As he continued to hold me, my pain spread through my body, pushing me to *feel*. My throat closed, but there were no tears to be spilled. No words to be said. So I pulled away, and we stared at each other—our mirror opposites. There, I saw my own fear and grief and determination reflected in every line and curve and shadow of my brother's face.

The strings on my heart grew taut as I plucked one. *Wilder.*

"I am going to find him."

"I know," Frazer said instantly.

"But today—today we should run," I said, hating every vile word that spilled over my tongue.

"Yes, siska," he whispered.

That almost wrecked me. "Come on. Let's grab our stuff before I lose it."

We walked into the lounge together and turned our attention to the weapon racks. Surprisingly, Adrianna was the only one not seeking to swap her blade. She'd slumped in a chair by the hearth, wearing a fuzzy, vacant expression.

Frazer and I joined the others by the rack beside the window. I exchanged my blunt sword for another Utemä. Only this one had a black sheath with green engravings that reminded me of Wilder. That felt right —I wouldn't forget my promise. Finding the balance and weight satisfactory, I slipped it into my belt and tightened the buckle.

Liora had chosen a slender, straight blade. Cai had gone with a longsword. After stowing the medical kit, Frazer picked out a dagger and Utemä. Adrianna was the last to the racks, selecting a long, thin double-edged blade; one side sharp, the other serrated. When she moved toward the bows, Frazer blocked her.

Adrianna hesitated. "We might need a second bow."

"Yes, but bows are awkward to fly with and you're not even fully healed. So I'll be the one to carry it," Frazer said, grabbing a quiver.

Adrianna backed off. A minor miracle.

With all this talk of bows, I marched into Wilder's bedroom and snatched up the kaskan, clipping it to the full quiver and slinging it over my shoulder. I was about to turn, but a tether to the room—to him— prevented me. Leaving felt like a statement. Like a goodbye.

"Have we got everything?" I heard Adrianna say from the lounge.

Frazer answered. "I packed the quest items, but everything else we did days ago. We don't even need to refill the water."

We'd done that this morning. Wilder had thought of everything. Heaving a sigh that carried my guilt with it, I left the room and joined my pack.

All the bags were piled on the rug in front of the fireplace. There were six. Frazer had hoped ...

I stared, rooted to the spot. "Should we leave Wilder's rucksack here?"

A hush. "It's up to you," replied Frazer. "But he could end up back here and need his supplies. We don't want to leave him with nothing."

I nodded distantly and stole another minute by removing my gloves, and my tunic. The leather was already sticking to my undershirt, and would only slow me down. To my surprise, my pack followed my example. Adrianna had trouble maneuvering around her injured wing, but with Liora's help, she managed it on the third try.

Every single loving instinct made me want to linger, but we were ready. No reason to delay, except—

A soft knocking on the door.

I bolted forward, but Frazer barred my way. "It might be Dimitri."

I tried to push past. "Or it could be him."

"Why would he knock?" he reasoned.

I deflated instantly. Of course, Wilder would've just walked in.

The knock on the door quickened to a pounding sound. "If you're there, let me in!" It was Goldwyn.

Cai got to the door first and beckoned her in. It'd been a while since I'd seen her; the change in her appearance was striking. Cecile's death had ravaged her—purple bruises stained her lower lids, her tanned skin had become sallow, and that golden halo of hair looked greasy. The only parts of her that stayed true to her warrior status were the black armor plates she wore, and the curved blade at her hip.

"What—" Liora began.

Goldwyn silenced her with a look. "I can see by the bags you're planning on making a run for it. Considering what's just happened, I don't blame you. But if you want the chance to get Wilder back, I'm here to help."

There was no trace of the gregarious female I'd come to know. Her face looked stern and utterly joyless.

"What d'you mean *back*?" Adrianna asked, her eyes tightening.

"Dimitri's taken Wilder," she said grimly.

My pulse screamed. Frazer grasped my elbow, supporting me, throwing waves of calm down our bond.

Goldwyn said in a rush, "If we hurry, we might be able to intervene. I'm not as good a tracker as Cecile ... But she taught me enough. Obviously, I'd prefer it if I had backup. Dimitri's a vicious bitch when he wants to be. I'll go on my own, if necessary."

I became a squalling sea breaking against jagged rocks. Leaning on Frazer, latching onto his strength, I made him my anchor.

"Won't we lose them as soon as they've taken flight?" Cai asked.

Goldwyn replied as she swept up her hair and secured it with a band from her wrist. "My source says that Dimitri's handing him over to a spider in the forest. After that, his orders are to come back here and take control of things. Apparently he's obsessed with capturing you," she finished, staring at me, her lips puckering.

"What source are you talking about?" Adrianna interrogated.

"Mikael," Goldwyn said, cold disgust lining her voice. "He's a traitor; one who just tried to kill me. But more about that later, unless you've decided not to come with me?"

I tried to be rational, but my heart was yelling my answer. I waited for someone to take the lead, to reply, but my pack just looked to me. They were giving me the choice. Surely that was a mistake.

I naturally gravitated to Frazer. His night-blue eyes swallowed me whole. "We'll be okay," he said.

He knew me too well. The only thing that had stopped me running out the door was a concern for him—for my friends. My eyes traveled to Cai. He may not have been the only natural-born leader in our pack, but he was the one I turned to.

Understanding and recognition crossed his face. He opened his mouth to pass judgment, but then his gaze flickered to Liora. In that one action, I knew he was torn.

Liora, straight-backed and resolute, said, "We're going after Wilder."

Decision made.

Cai started passing out bags. "Then we should hurry."

Taking my rucksack from him, shifting my kaskan and quiver around, I secured it to my back. No one spoke as Goldwyn led us out.

A dead silence had descended over the camp. As Goldwyn sniffed out invisible signs and studied the grass underfoot, I caught glimpses of Bert and the surviving guards moving bodies from the arena. My only solace was that the murderous worms who'd killed so many, appeared to have been defeated.

We moved away from this sickening sight and left via the back gate. Goldwyn guided us up into the sun-drenched hills, skirting the silvery river at a jog. Now in the midst of summer, the water had lost its icy depths. We crossed where it ran ankle-deep.

Up and over the riverbank, we entered the forest's wild expanse, leaving the bright blue sky behind. Goldwyn immediately ducked down to study the ground, breathing in deeply, but whatever she saw or smelled was lost on me.

Frazer used the pause in pace to ask, "How are you tracking them so easily? Their movements are barely traceable."

He wasn't wrong. There'd been no trampled grass underfoot or signs of a struggle. I'd assumed the famous fae senses were being used to track them—obviously not.

Goldwyn uncoiled to look him in the eye. "I got a general location from Mikael when I tortured him to death." A cold-blooded response.

Liora and I shared the same expression: shock.

Frazer's expression darkened. "Was that necessary?"

"He tried to stab me in the back. Just like he did with Cecile," she answered, her voice raw and bleeding.

"He killed her?" Adrianna asked harshly.

"I missed your trial this morning due to my seclusion." Goldwyn blanched—she didn't need to add that it'd been because she was in mourning. "That bastard turned up at my door just before everything went to shit. Spun me some crap about how a messenger arrived and lured them from the stands. I knew it was a filthy lie the minute he said he'd escaped from Dimitri but Wilder hadn't been able to," she said, her face twisting in loathing.

None of us knew what to say. Mikael had always been quiet, foreboding even. It was still hard to imagine him murdering Cecile.

Goldwyn whirled back to scope the tree labyrinth ahead. Stalking forward, she brushed her fingers over a broken branch and waved us onward. "We keep going this way."

There was no time for a discussion. The only hesitation came from Frazer when he frowned a second too long at the ground. *What's up?* I projected silently, jogging to keep up with the group.

His shoulder brushed mine as he ran alongside. *This feels too easy. Dimitri might be arrogant as all hell, but he's not stupid. The trail's thin, but traceable. And there's no sign of a struggle which makes me think Wilder's unconscious. So, then why isn't Dimitri flying on ahead to the meet point? Why stay on the ground where he can be followed?*

Sidelong, I met his troubled gaze. *You think this is a trap?*

Dimitri knows you've got trackers in your pack. Maybe he's hoping you'll follow and attempt a rescue.

Fear lashed at my insides. *Should we warn the others?*

He was silent for a time. My anxiety ticked up in the pause. I tried distracting myself by navigating the loose earth and dense tree cloud.

Finally, *Signal Liora. Just be discreet.*

Meaning? I said down the bond.

Meaning if this is a trap, we might be being watched. Spiders can move undetected, even by fae. We don't want them thinking we're suspicious.

We could just stop and explain to them—get Cai to use his magic?

After what happened at the arena? I think he needs to save himself for whatever we find waiting for us.

Of course …

I dropped back a bit to flank Liora and meet her curious expression. I motioned to my kaskan and nodded to her sword. Trying to signal with my face and body, *Be ready.*

Those discerning eyes lit with understanding. She moved off to pass on the message to her brother.

Our race through the forest must've continued for almost an hour. A couple of months ago, the pace would've killed me. Now, I dug deep and kept going, even if the brutal pounding on my knees turned my thoughts to mush. I welcomed it—it stopped the mental tailspin that beckoned.

One among our pack was suffering far worse: Adrianna. She didn't complain, but her skin had sickened to a deathly gray, and her gait had become more of a hurried shuffle.

Goldwyn eventually slowed and rounded on us, whispering, "Their scent's grown fresh. Now, we'll need to move quickly if we're to catch him. Because at the first sign of trouble, Dimitri'll take to the skies, and right now I'm the only person that could give chase." Her amber eyes darted to Adrianna's haggard appearance.

A memory shook loose and laid itself bare before me. I murmured, "I'm carrying a concealment charm. We might not be detectable."

Goldwyn's brows shot up. "Have you charged it recently?"

What in the burning courts did that mean?

My confusion must've shown because she went on. "If you don't know, we can't rely on it to work. Charms like that need to be charged every month at the full moon. But just because we can't trust the charm to work, doesn't mean we can't use magic." She glanced over to Cai expectantly. "Can you cast the spell that stops others overhearing us?"

A pulse in his neck throbbed, but a second later a familiar tingle brushed the air. "I'll try to contain our scents too."

Goldwyn smiled tightly. "Good. Then, we go in hard and fast. Any objections?"

We stayed quiet. Although I felt Frazer's doubts in the kin bond. His face, however, was as stone. Cold and impassive.

Goldwyn was generous and gave us another breath to protest. No one did, so she turned to Adrianna. "You'll have to stay behind."

Her bright blue eyes became savage. "Absolutely not," she said somewhere between a hiss and a gasp. "My wing's patched. It's just the blood loss."

"Which has slowed your reflexes," Goldwyn finished, toneless. "Are you going to risk your life—your friend's lives—because of your pride?"

Beneath Adrianna's cold rage, a glimmer of pain shone through. I almost cracked and insisted she come along.

Just when I thought she was preparing an epic argument, Adrianna's closed fists slackened, and she looked away, muttering, "Fine."

Nothing was fine, that much was clear. Goldwyn still nodded. Not in approval. But bleak understanding. "As for the rest of you, your priority should be to get Wilder out. I'll deal with Dimitri."

She didn't wait for our agreement before prowling forth on silent feet. Each of us gave Adrianna a commiserating look or touch before going. I followed last, rolling my shoulders, trying to loosen the tightness caused by the rucksack, quiver strap, and kaskan. Once we'd traversed a fair distance, I looked back to check on Adrianna, but she'd already dropped out of sight. My thoughts blackened. What were we getting ourselves into?

CHAPTER 32
UNMASKED

Goldwyn slowed after a few minutes. She'd led us to the base of a leaf-strewn hillock. Up ahead, a small gap in the trees appeared, and the whisper of a woodland stream sounded nearby.

We climbed, inching forward. All of us with hands on weapons, prepared to draw at the slightest provocation, but not daring to speak, despite the spell. That was until Goldwyn crested the slope and halted, transfixed. "There." She nodded ahead.

I almost rammed into her in my eagerness to see.

My heart twanged.

Across the glade, Wilder sat with his eyes closed, obviously unconscious. He was bound to a tree. That caramel hair had come loose from the knot he usually kept it in, and he had an ugly cut on his lip. Other than that, he looked to be in one piece.

My stomach did cartwheels. Dimitri was nowhere to be seen.

Goldwyn broke our stalemate, rushing headlong into the glade while tearing her sword free. Our pack gave chase, but before the ring of trees could thin, Frazer caught my arm, yanking me back. "Stop!"

Cai and Liora staggered to a halt, looking back as if Frazer had lost his mind. Goldwyn had reached Wilder and was trying to hack the knots apart. Through whitened nostrils and darting eyes,

Frazer hissed, "There's something *wrong* with this place. Cai—is it magic?"

Cai's brow crinkled, and he twisted back to the glade. He stilled for a moment, head cocked as if listening.

Then he recoiled, and his face collapsed in horror. "It's the opposite. My spell's fraying. We have to get out of here."

Cai hauled Liora away.

Frazer went to pick me up.

A whistle blasted through the air.

Tysion dropped out of the sky.

I moved at the same time as Frazer—too late.

Tysion knocked Cai aside and seized Liora. Wheeling around and around in a tight ring, he released her. Cai bellowed like a wounded animal and staggered after his sister as she flew, crashing against a tree across the glade. The image of him bending over, shaking her limp body, had frost coating my bones, chilling my blood. A screaming started in my mind. I tried to sprint over to help, but Frazer caught me up in a tight grip. *Don't go into that glade. No matter what. We fight from here.*

My mind in turmoil, I could only obey.

Frazer released me and reached for his bow. So did Tysion.

Two arrows nocked.

Two bows raised.

Frazer aimed for the heart, and Tysion responded in kind. Only the death he sought was mine; his arrow was for my throat.

Neither male moved. A stalemate.

Serena! Draw your weapon! Auntie yelled.

How had it gone so wrong?

SERENA!

Auntie's deafening shout pulled me back from the brink of cracking. As this was close-quarter combat, my instincts urged me to go for my Utemä. It slid from its sheath in an icy breath.

No, not the—

Auntie got drowned out by the cluck of a tongue and a strangely cold female's voice. "Play nicely, children."

My head whipped to my right. What I saw stole the strength from my limbs: Cai was kneeling, guarding Liora with nothing but his bare hands, for his sword was still sheathed. Goldwyn—*Goldwyn*—had her curved blade pressed against his chest; that kind, courageous female had vanished. As if she'd just slipped a skin, in her place stood a coldhearted bitch with a cruel face.

My heart stopped working, but my mind was running on lightning. What? *Why?*

A rustle of wings disturbed the air. Dimitri dropped from above, landing by her side, sword at the ready. We were surrounded, three weapons against two.

Goldwyn's voice was blunt, crisp. "I wouldn't loosen any arrows, Frazer dear. Not unless you want me to disembowel your friend."

Frazer answered by moving to block me from any arrows that Tysion might fire, so his lifeblood would spill instead of mine. My sword shook in my hands.

"Enough, Goldwyn." I groaned aloud as I recognized Hunter's voice.

Four swords against two. We were so very, very dead.

Hunter landed in the glade; I doubted he was here to save me again. That easy smile of his seemed long gone, and those spring-green linens and brown leathers had been replaced by ungodly pitch-black armor studded with spikes.

Never once catching my gaze, he pulled a curved dagger loose from his belt and said, "Now that I've helped set up your trap, I'm taking the captive."

"You'll miss all the fun," Dimitri said in mock cheeriness.

"I've no wish to be part of this," Hunter replied, hacking at Wilder's ropes.

Goldwyn went as stiff as the blade in her hand. She positioned herself so she had eyes on Cai *and* Hunter. "You won't go anywhere until I give you permission."

Hunter ignored her as he snapped apart the last of the ropes. When a growl slipped from Dimitri, Hunter straightened and flipped the dagger in an impressive move. Instead of threatening them, he sheathed it and spoke in cool, sharp tones. "You have no power over me. I'm a spider now."

I moaned loudly. "Hunter, *no*."

He looked to me then, his eyes glacial. "I risked everything, *everything* for you. In return you stole my only hope of escaping." I had a guilty flash, remembering the charm I'd taken. "Now, I'm her slave—forever ... And I wish I hated you, but mostly I'm just sorry. So fucking sorry. For everything."

Goldwyn looked disgusted by his misery. "Are you so weak as to try to help her again?"

Dimitri's sword hand twitched in response.

Hunter heaved a soft, dead laugh. "I couldn't, even if I wanted to."

A knife twisted in my heart. No hope there, then.

"I'd be careful with that one by the way." Hunter jerked his chin to Frazer and continued, each word quieter than the last. "He might be wingless, but he's slipperier and faster than a navvi. And he'd die for her."

I saw Frazer's hackles rise, but he kept focus on Tysion.

Good. Someone had to watch that conniving bastard.

Goldwyn's mouth cut an ugly line. "You're blood sworn to Morgan. You'll do as you're told."

"Exactly," Hunter said grimly. "I'm hers to command—not yours. She told me to capture Wilder, and I've done that."

Wilder was free; Hunter was lifting him.

I wanted to scream, to charge, to fight.

Don't move, Frazer warned.

Hunter was spreading his wings and something snapped. I bolted forward. Frazer did the unthinkable and let his arrow fly. Tysion ducked just as Frazer dropped his bow to snatch out and grab me. He wrapped one arm around my middle, shackling me, while the other hand drew his sword. He leveled it sidelong at Tysion, who was regaining his footing and looking murderous. Frazer's thoughts touched mine. *If they capture you, you're dooming Wilder, too.*

That felt like a cold slap, freezing my body.

Half-feral with rage, Tysion raised his bow to meet Frazer's throat again.

"Enough!" Goldwyn snapped. "Stay your hand, Tysion."

"We don't need him."

"Stand down. I won't ask again."

Tysion snarled and crashed his foot down on Frazer's bow. A

crunching sound made him smirk, but he didn't let an arrow fly. A stay of execution. I peered back at the glade and released a tight breath.

Hunter hadn't left. His wretched eyes still held mine. I had to do something. *Anything.* But Frazer's words acted like a paralytic. Sensing my doubt, my brother pounced with more cold logic. *You're no match for Goldwyn and Dimitri. Let Hunter go—he'll be one less fae to fight. Then we'll stand a chance of saving Cai and Liora.*

All true.

The sight of Wilder's harsh features softened by sleep had common sense flying out the door. A begging sound rode my voice as I said, "Hunter, please, *don't.*"

A cruel laugh snaked out of Dimitri.

Hunter looked close to possessed as he forced out his words. "I don't have a choice."

"There's always a choice," I said, near tears.

"Aren't you listening?" he snarled. "I serve her until death."

That's when one of his hands discreetly tapped his bow and his head bobbed an inch.

Auntie rushed out. *He wants you to kill him. Drop that bloody sword and draw the kaskan!*

I haven't been able to use it properly, I despaired.

Hunter braced for takeoff, his wings beating like the panicked echoes of my heart. I got one last tortured look as he muttered, "Goodbye, Serena."

I wanted to strangle him with my bare hands, *and* I felt desperately sorry for him.

Do it now! Auntie cried.

I sheathed my blade and struggled with Frazer's grip. *Let go!*

It's too late, Serena. He was right, of course. The two males were breaking through the canopy. A sob caught in my throat.

Wilder ... Would I ever see him again?

Dimitri spat on the forest floor. "Good riddance."

Goldwyn peered up at the two fae fading from view. "Time to move things along."

So, this was it—we were about to be captured or killed.

Seizing the single wingbeat in which Goldwyn's eyes were elsewhere, Cai rolled away and pulled his sword out.

She beat him in three moves. Dimitri hadn't even bothered stepping in.

"Stupid boy!" Goldwyn drove Cai back to his knees and made him drop his sword. Scowling, she pressed her blade against his chest again. "Any more moves like that, and your sister will be weeping over your gutted corpse."

Anger and a burning hate marked Cai's expression. "Why are we even still alive? You've got what you wanted."

"Isn't it obvious? You're valuable. Well, not you." She brandished her sword a little and croaked out a laugh. "Although, you might prove useful in controlling your sister."

My stomach plunged to my boots—to the dark court itself.

All the color drained from Cai's face. "Liora isn't powerful—take me instead."

The lie only made Goldwyn snort and drawl, "You know, her binding almost fooled me. If you'd been man enough to do the same to yourself, I might never have guessed what she was. It's rare, you see, for one sibling witch to be strong and the other so weak. Still, I had to bide my time and make sure. Morgan doesn't suffer fools gladly, does she, Dimitri?"

Dimitri grumbled and dipped his head, humiliated. Morgan must truly be terrifying to bring a monster like him so low.

All the fight seemed to leave Cai as he murmured, "You're a spider?"

Goldwyn cricked her neck slightly. Like the label didn't sit well. "I like to think of myself as more of a chameleon." And then, as if speaking to a child, she bent down a touch, adding, "I'm many things you see—an assassin, a spy … but my passion is trapping witches for Morgan. It's what you sensed, isn't it? That this glade is a magical void." She straightened, nodding to the earth, saying, "Lines of salt and iron and that accursed stone run under this glade."

Auntie groaned. Before I could ask why, Goldwyn continued. "Although, I'm not ashamed to say I needed guidance. Voids can be tricky beasts. Luckily, I had a certain witch in chains who was most helpful. I think you know her, Serena? Isabel Montagar?"

A groan of despair slipped out.

"Morgan was very *amused* that Hunter thought a charm was all it took to protect him from her. Still, it brought the witch to our attention."

"What did you do to her?" I spoke through clenched teeth.

"Oh, she's alive," Goldwyn said with a spider's smile. "A bit beaten up, but nothing she won't heal from."

The control on my temper strained.

She's trying to bait you into attacking, Frazer warned.

I thought we were supposed to fight now Hunter's gone?

Snatches of a dozen thoughts or more hit me all at once. As if they'd broken through the dam in Frazer's mind. As if he'd lost control. His inner monologue was fast but focused. He followed every action through to its conclusion, anticipating the outcome, weighing the cost. He was playing chess. Finally, I felt him tip over into a decision. *We can't move. Cai needs to get free first.*

His words didn't stop the bloodlust almost boiling over, but it was Cai who said, "It's hard to tell who's more of a crazy bitch—you or Dimitri."

Dimitri lunged for him, sword swinging. Goldwyn snarled a command and just like that, the dog was leashed. Cai responded with a mocking laugh that would make most males show their teeth.

Goldwyn resumed in one icy-calm breath. "You know *nothing*. I do what I do to keep Morgan's empire strong—to protect its people from something worse. You think I've liked wasting away my years in that godsforsaken camp, spying on Wilder? That we've liked it?" She twitched her head to Dimitri. "But Morgan wanted her pet male, her *Sabu*. Oh, when you came along, Serena, it was a blessing from the light court. Dimitri had to try very, very hard to hide his glee. Still, I was the one with the hardest job; I spent weeks listening to Wilder's dreary monologues. He couldn't be with you, but he hadn't felt this way before, blah, blah, blah."

A tear found my cheek.

Goldwyn's voice bored into my skull. "Then Cecile told me he was going with you for the sixth trial—"

"How did she know that?" I blurted out.

An involuntary tremor shook Goldwyn's sword arm. "Cecile's always kept a close watch on him. Diana's orders."

Cai spat out, "Why would Diana care about Wilder?"

Goldwyn made a disgusted sound. "He used to work for Morgan, you fool. Does she need another reason?"

"Did you kill her?"

My soul sang in relief as Liora sat up.

"Woken up already?" Dimitri sneered, twirling his sword to show his feelings.

Liora, the reader of souls, ignored Dimitri and stared into Goldwyn. "It was you, wasn't it? You killed Cecile. She realized that you were the only one who could've set up the ambush. That you were a traitor."

Goldwyn's head tilted in quiet study. "You'd make a fine spy."

"Tell me," Liora demanded.

A scowl answered back. "It's as you say. She had to die because she grew suspicious after Dimitri's *failed* ambush," Goldwyn said coldly.

Dimitri's flinch had a wink of smug satisfaction flaring in my chest.

Liora said, "Mikael never tried to stab you."

Goldwyn laughed; a harsh and bitter sound, like glass smashing. "That stupid kurpä tried to stop us taking Wilder, so ..." She mimed slicing her throat with a delicate sweep of her finger.

"Why?" Liora asked. "You must see what Morgan is."

For the first time, Goldwyn looked totally unhinged, and an explosive charge rippled through the glade. One move, one wrong word, and we'd all ignite.

"None of you know what's going on in this kingdom or abroad!" Goldwyn snarled, her body quivering in suppressed rage. "You're so quick to condemn, but Morgan is the only fae strong enough to stand up to Abraxus and his legions."

"Abraxus?" Liora said, hushed. "He's real?"

"Of course he's real!" Goldwyn yelled. "He's the one you should be shitting yourselves over! He hates us. Wants to bleed us out into the earth just so he can drink the magic lingering in our veins! His army of fae hybrid *stains* are planning to invade—"

A yell pitched the air. A match struck, and we erupted. As if we'd been waiting for this all along. Frazer pushed me to the earth, dodged a whistling projectile and charged Tysion. I jumped up; instinct made me seek to protect my brother. I strung an arrow to my kaskan and sought my target.

Frazer's quiver, Tysion's bow, both had been reduced to splinters. The two males were locked in a lethal embrace, all fangs and bone-snapping blows. Then, their blades crossed, and a furious, dirty battle for dominance began.

It was too risky to loosen an arrow—I could easily hit Frazer. I'd failed to make the kaskan work previously, why would now be any different? In practice, the target had always been in sight, but the focus and the heart remained elusive.

My nerve wavering, I swiveled toward the glade, searching for easier targets.

Holy fire ... Adrianna was there. She'd flown in and landed on Goldwyn's back. Their swords had fallen to the wayside during the struggle. And now, they were a blur of twisting limbs and flapping wings. Adrianna held fast.

A few paces away, Cai suddenly roared and barreled into Dimitri. Liora drew her sword, advancing, her legs shaking underneath her. I had to do something.

Use the bow, Auntie whispered. *Trust yourself*.

I breathed, and my heart echoed a name. I knew the target.

I spun, aimed, and fired. It found its mark in Tysion's shoulder, pinning his wing, causing him to drop his weapon. His wild roar tore through me, but Frazer didn't miss a beat. He grasped Tysion by the hair, dragged him to the edge of the glade, and pressed his sword against his neck. "*Dimitri*—stand down! Or I kill your son!"

I drew closer to his side, nocking another arrow in one smooth motion. I swept the glade for the best mark. Adrianna still tangled with Goldwyn, neither stopping for breath. Cai and Liora had joined to fight Dimitri. Sword to sword. But now, the male fae was backing off, glowering at Frazer, his black eyes a whirling death pool. As if he were plotting exactly how he would murder us all. Dimitri hissed, "You'd kill an unarmed fae?"

Frazer answered by pressing steel into Tysion's neck until it pricked the skin. A bead of blood appeared.

Cai and Liora turned to help Adrianna. I kept my arrow trained on Dimitri. Who knew how deep his kin bond went? As it turned out, not very far. "Kill him then!" Dimitri jeered. "He's failed me too many times to count. A total disappointment, just like his whore makena."

"Isä? *Please.*"

Tysion's rasping plea tugged on my heart. I didn't have time to wonder at that blip of insanity. Dimitri charged at us.

Frazer bared his teeth, stepped back, and in one clean swipe, severed Tysion's left wing. Drops of ruby red sprayed forth, splattering the forest floor.

Dimitri faltered. A flicker of shock crossed his face. In one breath, I saw it die and shift to disgust.

We all seemed powerless to watch as Frazer threw Tysion, bleeding and screaming, to the opposite end of the glade. Frazer bared his teeth again, spinning his sword, beckoning our enemy forward. Dimitri's black wings fanned and he flew at my brother. He got close enough for me to see the whites of his eyes. Life—no—love thrummed through my veins. *Protect. Protect. Protect.*

"Dimitri." I whispered his destruction and let the arrow fly.

He ducked, but the arrow still lodged itself in his chest. He floundered, and Frazer moved. In one brutal motion, he opened Dimitri's throat out onto the ground. The male slumped and fell, dead. I wanted to retch, but Liora's sudden scream kept me going, seeking my last mark.

Goldwyn was a whirlwind, kicking Adrianna into the dirt and sending Cai flying toward us.

Thank stars for Frazer. He caught Cai before he could barrel into us and set him on his feet.

I drew another arrow, but it was too late. Liora and Goldwyn's swords had been lost in the fighting, but that two-faced bitch had a hidden dagger and was currently pressing it to Liora's throat.

My bow finger twitched. From the corner of my eye, I saw Frazer holding Cai back, whispering something in his ear.

"Take one step, make one move, and I'll start poking holes," Goldwyn said in an ungodly purr.

I could loosen the arrow, but it would be the ultimate test of faith. Goldwyn had Liora pinned against her. There was nothing to hit except my friend.

No, Frazer projected.

My eyes shifted to his, seeking explanation.

The glade's a void; the bow's magic could fail.

Of course, the fletching's path might falter. I could kill Liora.

Goldwyn snarled over at Adrianna, who'd begun to inch toward them. "Unless you want dear sweet Liora's blood on your hands, go stand by your friends. Now!"

Liora's wide eyes found Adrianna's. *It's okay*, they seemed to say.

A noise between a groan and a growl came from Adrianna and she conceded. With a gigantic effort, she moved to join us, picking up her sword on the way.

Panic and frustration pounded through my veins, pushing my heart to race. Goldwyn stood alone. I had one last mark, but I couldn't fire. Gods, help me.

Goldwyn peered down at Tysion. He was bleeding out, crawling closer to her. She barked, "Get up, you shit!"

A whisper of a choked laugh escaped Liora. "You *should* be worried."

At that taunt Goldwyn's mask slipped, hatred burned, and her knife dug a little deeper. Liora winced and Cai's hand rose.

Laughter echoed. "Try if you like, magic can't enter," Goldwyn mocked.

Cai tried anyway, summoning and unleashing a blast of air. It caused a cyclone, whipping leaves and debris asunder, but the destruction didn't disturb us or the heart of the glade. It only ravaged the outskirts upon which we stood. Those currents kept moving, pushing, testing the void until Cai fell to his knees. The windstorm vanished, and he was left looking exhausted—burned out—while Goldwyn and Liora remained untouched.

"How pointless," Goldwyn said lightly. Her sharp eyes darted to mine. "Now, I'm not leaving here without the key to Wilder's obedience. Come." A clear command. Her voice deepened to a guttural rasp. "*Or*, I'll make your witch friend suffer agonies you couldn't imagine."

"You can't carry us both," Liora muttered up at her.

That made Goldwyn place her free hand at the side of Liora's cheek and dig her nails in, dragging them down, marking her. Liora's eyes filled with tears, her lips pressed tight. She didn't cry out. My heart swelled with love and pride.

"I won't need to," Goldwyn said, dipping her lips to Liora's ear. "I have friends, loyal spiders who will come when called. Until then, Serena's going to walk beside us like a good little pet, aren't you my dear? Unless she wants to watch as I break you?"

I relaxed my bowstring slowly and let the kaskan and arrow drop to the ground. Before I could walk over, Frazer and Adrianna restrained me. "No," they snarled together.

Cai groaned somewhere to my left, but he didn't object.

I kept my stare fixed on Liora's. *Don't, Serena,* she begged me with her eyes.

"Keep your idle threats," Adrianna snapped at Goldwyn. "You need Liora. I'm guessing you want to lick Morgan up the ass? That's why you're bound and determined to bring her presents."

"Have it your way then."

Goldwyn pulled Liora's head back and brought the dagger up.

"*Stop!*"

"Why should I?" Goldwyn crooned.

"Serena, don't," Liora gasped out, squirming.

There wasn't a choice. The dagger's tip was poised, ready to take her life. "Take me instead of her. She's bound. You need me more."

Goldwyn sneered at that. "We can always break the chains binding her. Now, come! No more games, or else Liora bleeds."

As if to prove her point, she lowered the dagger and swept it across Liora's collarbone. A necklace of ruby drops gleamed so very, very bright against her soft skin.

A resistance within finally crumbled, and this time I didn't ask. I demanded that my magic come forth. A gigantic wave of cold, glittering rage crested and paused for a moment as Auntie's voice thundered in my ears. *Child, no! You'll rip yourself apart!*

I was beyond reason, beyond doubt. *You're just a voice in my head.*

I'm much more than that.

It didn't matter—not now. Yet, I hesitated for Frazer's sake.

My eyes snagged on Tysion as he looked up at Goldwyn. Shock and pain—such endless agonies—haunted his eyes. I didn't care, but I heard myself say, "What'll happen to Tysion?"

Goldwyn's eyes narrowed to slits. "What business is it of mine?"

"So you'd leave him to die?"

She cawed harshly as if to say, of course. Meanwhile, Tysion crept along on his belly and reached for her.

In one smooth move, Frazer wrenched me aside, out of Adrianna's grasp; eyes burning, he hurled words down the bond. *Whatever you need to do, do it. We'll survive. I won't let you die. I'll be your anchor.*

And so with only a thought and my steel will, I threw open all the doors and let the power and the light take over. *Just let me save her*, I whispered to the magic.

If you're doing this, wait one more minute and let me help, Auntie said, her voice pleading.

How?

I was only vaguely aware of Tysion grabbing Goldwyn's ankle, murmuring something while Auntie rattled on. *The necklace's power sustains leylines of salt, iron, and obsidian in your blood. It smothers the magic now in your system, so fae can't sense it, and it's what prevented your power from destroying you instantly. But the leylines are incompatible—they act as a void and put a dampener on your magic. I've been slowly erasing them so you can access more of your power, but I've held back from cleansing you, hoping to preserve their protection.*

If it'll save her, burn it away.

It'll drain me. I won't be able to speak to you again. Just promise me you'll get to Ewa as soon as possible. You'll be relying solely on Frazer's strength—on the twining—to stop the magic from burning you up, so don't delay. Once there, give the necklace to the undines. They'll be able to release me.

I didn't bother considering the strangeness of her request. *I promise.*

This will hurt, she warned.

The droplet warmed. I clenched my jaw and fists in expectation.

"Get away!" Goldwyn abruptly kicked Tysion in the head. He groaned and rolled away.

"I'm waiting, Serena!" she barked. "Or do I need to slice Liora's ear off before you'll listen?"

She clasped Liora's earlobe and Cai darted forward. Adrianna dropped her sword to lunge for him.

Then, the necklace—Auntie—roused a blazing inferno. My hands stopped working, my back arched, and my spine stretched. I was powerless as the droplet set a fire to my flesh. I was being torn apart. Ripped, shredded, and burned. Someone screamed in the distance. No, not someone. Me.

Hands gripped the sides of my face as I bowed to my knees. Frazer fell with me and kept me upright as his thoughts battered against my own. The pain acted as a barrier. Nothing could pass.

The screaming stopped; my voice had collapsed. The force inside carried on raging and plundering. Blood roared in my ears and spurted out my nose and mouth. I gagged on it.

Shouting filtered in and out. The world flickered, becoming dark, but on the periphery, I saw Frazer kneeling with me, blood dripping from his nose. My mirror; we were dying. *Just let it mean something. Save her. Save someone.*

Then let go, Serena. Let it out. You're free now, Auntie whispered.

I asked and ordered and begged the blinding light searing my vision and scorching my veins to go: for that wave of ice and fire to roll out and wreak destruction on Goldwyn and her gods-damned void.

The wave heeded my call. Firebolts, moon-bright lakes, and a night sky filled my vision. Somewhere far off, thunder rolled and rumbled in response. And a pure white light tinged with silver and ruby flame exploded outward, carried on the back of a star-studded shadow.

I was light; I was dark. Order and chaos entwined.

Auntie quickly channeled my magic's fury, directing it into a stream that looked like liquid threads dancing in the wind. It had a job to do. Plunging deep into the earth, seeking lines of salt, iron, and stone it devoured them, flooding the glade until everyone else disappeared. Only Frazer and I existed. His cool forehead touched mine. Blue eyes ringed with molten silver held me steady as the world blazed on.

I felt something snap and burn. My bones? No—the salt, the iron, the stone. A blazing, mad laugh full of agony and joy rushed from me.

Then, I was falling. Drifting away on a cold current until arms caught me, pulling me up, up, up and into a dark-tinted world lined with a glorious sea of sun-sand. A desert at night. My mother's face smiled back at me, but not the one I'd known as a child. It was her true face— sharper, stronger, and more ethereal than the one I'd known. Amethyst wings flared.

I'm dead ...

A faint smile creased those warm eyes—the eyes of a woman I'd grieved for most my life. "No, my darling, your heart still beats, but it won't for long if you don't reach Ewa."

I had to check. I whispered, "Are you Auntie?"

"No, I am not the guardian of the necklace. I wish I could explain about that and so many other things, but speaking like this is forbidden and there's so little time, so you must listen. After Ewa, seek your sister, for you *will* need her. She waits for you across the sea, in the east where the sun shines brightest. To save these lands, and the many more that await, you must also find your mate. It is not in my power to know his location. I can only warn you not to shy away from the darkness he is wreathed in. You were born to light it up. Tell Sefra I'm sorry; that I didn't want to lie. Remember, Ena, I love you to the moon and the stars and the shining sea."

Her hand reached for my face. I closed my eyes, expecting and needing to feel her touch, but instead there was a massive force, pushing me back to the waking world. My mother's face faded. *No ...*

"Stay with me. Please," I breathed, heartbreak sticking in my throat.

"I never left. And I never will," she whispered.

This still felt like another goodbye. And as she disappeared, fresh pain cut me clean through as my body stirred. The magical storm flowing through my veins had died, leaving behind ash and smoke, and a memory.

Light filtered in. Frazer was there. "Siska?" he croaked.

I blinked. We were still touching foreheads. "Hi," I rasped back.

Frazer's face cracked in two. He rarely smiled, let alone *beamed*. It gave me the strength to ask, "Did it work? Is she safe?"

That beautiful smile dropped, and he rolled away.

A ring of scorched earth surrounding the glade was the only sign of what had happened. Goldwyn and Tysion were both gone. And Cai was helping a stunned Liora off the ground. Knee-wobbling relief struck, fierce and fast.

Adrianna walked over to me and held out a hand. I used her strength to stand. Mercifully, she didn't let go.

Frazer stood without help and sheathed his fallen sword. He was a complete mess. His coloring was pasty and gray, clashing horribly with the blood staining his nostrils and upper lip. I'd no doubt I was an echo of this.

"Where's Goldwyn and Tysion?" I said throatily.

"Gone," Adrianna murmured. "Goldwyn got distracted. First by Tysion clawing at her leg, and then by your screams. Liora broke free when your magic …"

An awkward pause. Obviously, she wanted an explanation. I just wasn't sure what to say; how to explain. Because to do that, I'd have to understand. And I didn't. Never one to wait for the truth, Adrianna pressed me with a hard stare and asked, "D'you know how you finally accessed it?"

Liora spared me from answering by hobbling over. I scanned her. The blood was still ruby-bright on her collarbone and she had a small scratch on her cheek, but otherwise, she seemed fine. We moved at the same time and met in a hug. Over her shoulder, I watched as Cai collected their scattered blades.

"How are you?" I mumbled into her strawberry locks.

"Alive," Liora breathed. "My rucksack took most of the impact from slamming into the tree."

I broke away from Liora's embrace when Cai moved to join us. He returned his own weapon to his hip and offered Liora her rapier, which she carefully stowed. Then he dipped down and grasped Adrianna's blade. The one she'd dropped when lunging for him. Cai offered it back with an expression I couldn't quite place. Adrianna took the blade with a grateful nod and slid it into her sheath.

All eyes were now on me. They wanted an explanation. I repressed a sigh and bought time by going to grab my kaskan from the ground. As I clipped it back onto my quiver strap, I relayed Auntie's words to them—her warning. The vision of my mother, however, I kept to myself.

A stunned silence followed my explanation.

Liora spoke first. "I didn't know it was even possible to use leylines in a person."

In a weak attempt at a joke, Cai added, "Just one more mystery, eh?"

Ugh. How true.

Cai couldn't resist turning to Adrianna to ask, "How did you know to come after us? Did you guess about Goldwyn?"

"No. I'm just not the type to be left behind."

Her accompanying coy smile eased something in my chest. The violent shock left over from the battle faded. Although, Dimitri's slitted corpse and the sickening smell of blood ensured I couldn't forget completely. "So, what now?" I glanced skyward, aching for Wilder.

"Well, Goldwyn's seen your power," Adrianna remarked. As blunt as ever. "And what she saw is enough for her to be pissing her pants in joy. She'll squeal to Morgan the first chance she gets, so we need to be gone long before then. I guess our march to Ewa begins now."

Reading my guilt and grief, Liora said, *"Then,* we'll get Wilder back."

I grimaced as everyone else mumbled their agreement. They hadn't heard my mother's words, and now the potential implications were tormenting me.

Seek Sefra. Before everything else? Before we could save my ... lover? Companion? I hated the idea, but my mother had broken the rules of death itself to warn me. How could I ignore her advice?

My kin's thoughts broke through my confusion and heartache. *No matter what path we take first; all of them will eventually lead us to Morgan. And to Wilder.*

You heard what she said? A tiny part of me had wondered if I'd imagined her.

A pulse-pounding fear filtered through. *Your pain was overwhelming. It's not surprising that your mind was completely open to me.*

My heart stumbled.

Adrianna interrupted our silent conversation by snapping her teeth. "I'll never get used to you two talking like that."

"Sorry," I lied.

Adrianna's lip turned as if she suspected the truth. "Just tell me—is whatever you were talking about something we should know?"

Cai and Liora looked curious, expectant.

I wanted to keep the memory buried deep, deep in my soul. But they were all willing to flee and face the wolves with me ... I owed them the truth.

"My mother came to me in a vision when the magic poured out. She told me to go east and find my sister."

Jaws dropped, and eyes widened in surprise. All except Frazer's.

Adrianna cast off the shock first. "How in courts name d'you expect to find one female on a continent five times the size of ours?"

That had me stumped. My mother hadn't exactly given me a place-name.

"We'll figure it out," Liora said, soothingly. "Besides, we should be far, *far* away from Morgan when Serena's learning to use her magic, and adapting to her fae body. And it'll give us an opportunity to find out if Goldwyn was lying about Abraxus."

Frazer and Adrianna grew very, very still. My back prickled in response. Something told me I'd regret asking, but I had to know. "Who is he?"

My eyes instinctively focused on the two fae in our group, but they seemed stricken. In the end, it was Liora who answered. "I always thought he was just a fae legend."

"Oh, he's real enough," Adrianna said, sounding hollow. "But our history can wait. We need to get moving. Goldwyn will be sending every tracker and spider in the Riverlands after us." Her gaze flickered behind me to Dimitri as she finished. "There's blood everywhere."

Frazer ignored Adrianna completely, and said, "Our elders say Abraxus almost single-handedly chased the Aldarian fae from the east. He was a leader, undefeated on the field of battle. And yet, he had no magic of his own."

My mouth popped open.

Frazer continued with the horror. "He's said to have hated our kind for our wealth and power, particularly our light-magic casters, who were unique to our race."

Dread uncurled in my belly.

Fear haunted my kin's eyes, and I felt his protective instincts roar to the surface. He added in low, harsh tones, "So, he mounted an army against us—one so feared the world over, our people agreed to exile ourselves."

"What are we saying then?" Cai tugged his hand through his straw-colored hair, looking lost. "Abraxus is a godlike warrior who had no magic but somehow made the only light-casters in the realms flee?"

His expression went slightly wild.

Liora picked up the conversation's thread. "And he might be coming for us all."

"That about sums it up," Adrianna said grimly.

"Well, fuck me," Cai said, unleashing a cracked laugh.

My stomach turned again as things clicked. "Morgan's been building her armies with human slaves to face *that*. We'll—They'll be massacred."

"Absolute carnage," Cai said harshly.

Liora winced.

Adrianna snapped her teeth. "Enough. We need to get going, not stand here discussing future dooms." Her wrist then flicked to me. "Goldwyn saw what Serena did. And she doesn't have the leylines to protect her from detection. All we've got is a concealment charm that may or may not work."

"It'll work," Cai interrupted. "Making those charms might be beyond my abilities, but I can charge one easily enough." He peered up into the noon sky. "I just have to wait until the moon shows its face."

Adrianna followed his gaze upward. "Then we still have hours where we could be traced magically. I'll fly above us and keep a watch."

Cai's head lowered and cocked to one-side. "What about your wing?"

Adrianna's eyes drifted to his. "This isn't time to coddle one another. If my stitches rip, you'll just have to patch me up."

She'd made a valiant effort at acting nonchalant. The twitch in her injured wing gave her away.

Cai stared for a moment too long. Adrianna raised her chin. A silent standoff.

Cai broke first. "Fine. If you think you can handle the pain, you best get up there and start guiding us. I'll use my magic to hide our tracks and our scents as we go. I won't be able to keep it up indefinitely, but my strength should last until we're clear of this mess."

Adrianna's face was grim as she tightened her equipment in preparation for flight. Once done, she said, "I'll call out directions if you need them." With that, she soared upward.

Cai pushed out an exasperated sigh, hitched his bag higher and turned on his heel to march across the glade.

I had difficulty following; my eyes had locked onto Dimitri's body. "What about him?"

Liora slipped her hand around my wrist. "There's nothing we can do for him now."

Of course, she was right, but I couldn't seem to move. I'd avoided looking, *really* looking, before now. His eyes were still open, glassy and lifeless. The arrow I'd sent through his chest stuck out at an absurd angle, while his son's wretched wing lay in a pool of blood beside him.

"It doesn't get any easier," Frazer murmured. As if he, too, had experienced that cold, writhing shame.

Tears burned up my eyesight. I blinked rapidly and whirled away. "Let's go."

Liora released my wrist and we walked side by side. Frazer padded along next to us on panther-soft feet. As I moved under the forest's latticework, I tried to reason with my ghosts: the feelings of disgust at taking another life, and the guilt for not going after Wilder. They simply settled atop of my mind's surface like oil on water. Head and heart locked in battle, I was only partially aware of Frazer sending me something through our bond.

Then it struck: love, unconditional and fierce. He'd never said the words. He'd never shown it through the bond. Not that he'd needed to. I'd known.

Yes, I'd known deep down. But sensing it, *feeling* it was different.

Because he'd seen everything: the vile thoughts, the good deeds; every memory. Through it all, despite everything, he still loved me. No limits, no requirements, no end.

I studied the harsh lines of his face, the parts of his back where his indigo wings once rested, and those blue eyes shot with silver where shadows still dwelled. Maybe, those nightmares would always haunt his face, even if love shone in tandem. *That*, there, was what made us kin. Because he understood what it was to be a lost soul in the world. A fallen star, exiled from home.

A grim sort of recognition flowed from him.

It didn't wash my hands clean or bring back loved ones. And that *emptiness* born from my parents' deaths that now ached for Wilder; it was still there. But our affinity and his absolute acceptance sustained me. Frazer's thoughts brushed mine. They had a tentative feel. *If the night sky doesn't want us, we'll build our home together.*

Another emotion shuddered down the bond. I recognized the light that flowed and warmed us both.

Hope. Frazer hoped.

I let that carry me north, to Ewa.

"ONLY THROUGH THE darkness of night can we be guided by the light." - Meera Garland, Advisor to the Draken Queen.

AUTHOR'S NOTE

If you'd like to be told about new releases, special offers, bonus content and giveaways, visit sbnova.com to be a part of my mailing list.

DID YOU ENJOY THIS BOOK? Please consider leaving a review on the site you purchased it from, or the AKOE's Goodreads page. Reviews can make all the difference to an author. Thank you!

ALSO AVAILABLE BY NOVA

A Kingdom of Exiles and *Draken* are linked ... even across worlds. It is my intention to join these two storylines with just one more in *Merlin Rises*. Pick up Draken today to discover *The Southern Fire* series!

ACKNOWLEDGMENTS

AKOE was crafted with the support of three very talented women.

Linda, editor extraordinaire, thank you so much for lending your eagle eye to this story.

Rachel, what can I say? Your cover art is a dream.

Melissa, the map is amazing. You captured Aldar perfectly.

This book owes a great debt to R.L.P. You keep me sane. You keep me laughing. And most of all, you keep me believing.

To my mother, sister, brother, I love you all.

Roo, you're a wizard cat, and the sweetest fluff ball imaginable. You keep me company when I'm struggling with the words. Although, your unfortunate habit of sitting on my lap while I'm writing, makes you quite literally a pain in my ass.

Lastly, to you, the reader. If you've taken Serena and this merry (and not so merry) band of outcasts into your heart then thank you, thank you and thank you again.

Made in the USA
San Bernardino, CA
23 November 2018